A DIFFERENT SKY

Meira Chand

A Different Sky

Harvill Secker
LONDON

Published by Harvill Secker 2010

2 4 6 8 10 9 7 5 3 1

First published in Great Britain in 2010 by
HARVILL SECKER
Random House 20 Vauxhall Bridge Road
London SW1V 2SA

www.rbooks.co.uk

Addresses for companies within The Random House Group Limited
can be found at: www.randomhouse.co.uk/offices.htm

The Random House Group Limited Reg. No. 954009

A CIP catalogue record for this book is available from the British Library

ISBN 9781846553431

The Random House Group Limited supports The Forest Stewardship
Council (FSC), the leading international forest certification organisation.
All our titles that are printed on Greenpeace approved FSC certified
paper carry the FSC logo. Our paper procurement policy
can be found at www.rbooks.co.uk/environment

Mixed Sources
Product group from well-managed
forests and other controlled sources
www.fsc.org Cert no. TT-COC-2139
© 1996 Forest Stewardship Council
FSC

Typeset in Sabon by Palimpsest Book Production Limited,
Grangemouth, Stirlingshire

Printed and bound in Great Britain by
Clays Ltd, St Ives plc

Especially for Mia, who was not here the last time.
And also for Zubin, Natasha and Adi once again.

PROLOGUE

ON THE JOURNEY THEY spoke about the island, a pinprick on the great body of Asia. Some now wondered why they journeyed towards it, thought that perhaps they had made a mistake. On the open deck of the ship the travellers sat pressed together, voices low, as if to contain their hopes. By day they watched the horizon and rushed en masse to the rail of the ship at the sight of a passing islet or even the fin of a whale, disappointed that days of sail still remained. They covered their heads against the sun, limbs roasting beneath their rags. Some journeyed from the west across the Indian Ocean, others from the east over the China Sea but, east or west, all remembered impoverished villages, a muddy bullock, an empty stomach, dung-strewn fields. Some said Singapore, the name of the island, was derived from the Malay for lion. There was talk that these creatures roamed the jungle along with tribes of ghosts. It was said the island was a haunted place of ancient executions.

In the silence of night each man, huddled unbearably close upon the open deck yet each separate in his own circle of thought, listened to the ship cutting through the waves, licked the brine from his lips and trembled. A light on the bridge swung loosely above while beneath them the ocean rolled, a great creature upon whose back they rode. Dark thoughts rose up then to shape the future, to clothe it in both terror and hope.

Singapore rested beneath the tongue of Malaya, fabled treasure of crystal seas, the Golden Chersonese. The island was diamond shaped, and its geographical placing at a point pinning down two oceans made it forever a transit stop for travellers and merchants alike. Stamford Raffles had seen the wealth convergent in these things when he took possession of the swampy region. Trade not territory, he famously declared, but these two words could not be parted. The island fulfilled its promise, never faltering in the flowering of prosperity. It became a place of dreams, holding the souls of men to ransom.

PART ONE

1927–1937

FOR SOME MINUTES NOW the trolley had been stationary at the Kreta Ayer crossroads, the breeze of movement gone. The heat lay thick inside the vehicle and Rose Burns dabbed her neck with a handkerchief. The driver gesticulated angrily, leaning out of a window. Rose wondered if someone had tried to commit suicide by throwing himself before the trolley, or if a rickshaw was in the way. Then she heard shouting and the beating of drums; the sudden crackle of firecrackers sounded although Chinese New Year was long gone.

'I'm hot,' Howard complained, kicking the empty seat in front of him and leaving a dusty footprint.

Rose turned distractedly to her son; if the trolley did not move forward soon she would be late returning to Belvedere. The houseboy Hamzah would supervise the laying of tables for dinner and in the kitchen the cook, Ah Fong, would have the meal under way but her lodgers might wonder what kept their Eurasian landlady. As she did each week, she had been to visit her Aunty May in Queen Street and sent a servant for Kolade Powders to calm the old woman's stomach. Then, Rose had gone into Chinatown, to one of the traditional medicine shops for some roots and herbs to boil with black chicken to improve her own stamina. It had all taken much longer than expected. She thought now of Cynthia, left at home with the *amah*; the child would be fretful and waiting for them.

Howard slouched in his seat. The heat in the bus aggravated the prickly heat under his collar and he stretched his neck in distress. He had not wanted to accompany his mother on her visit to Aunty May. The old woman's home reeked of garlic and drains, and she of sweat and lavender water and something unsavoury besides. Her dark skin was wrinkled as a walnut, and her short white hair grew up from her head like the bristles of a brush. He was afraid he would dream about her. The return to Belvedere weighed upon him; he thought of impenetrable corners, the movement of shadows and the cold terror of waking at night.

'Why is the trolley not moving?' Rose demanded of the conductor, raising her voice, fanning herself and Howard with the limp folded square of her handkerchief. She spoke to the man in a manner that brooked no nonsense. It was already March, the rains were long gone and the heat had built up full blast. In the stationary trolley the passengers fretted, feet roasting on hot wooden floorboards, arms branded on molten window frames.

'Chinese demonstration.' The conductor shrugged, engrossed in picking his nose with an extra-long fingernail grown especially for this purpose. He made no effort to help the Chinese woman and child who now clambered aboard, taking advantage of the unscheduled stop. They settled into the empty seats in front of Rose with breathless giggles. Howard kicked out again in anger and the girl turned around with a scowl. Rose smiled at the child, giving Howard a light slap on the hand. Sweat gathered uncomfortably in the small of her back, her blouse was stuck to her skin. Passengers were now leaning out of the windows to see what was wrong.

In the street the shouting grew louder and a metallic screech announced the arrival of another trolley drawing to a halt behind them. Rose too now stood up and leaned out of the window for a better view, and saw a crowd of unruly Chinese thick in the road before her. Men were converging on the trolley in a threatening manner waving banners on bamboo poles, craning their necks to peer in at the passengers in a belligerent manner. Heart pounding, Rose drew back in fear but noticed the trolley had stopped near the Kreta Ayer police station. Just the sight of that colonial building topped by a cupola and a weathercock filled Rose with relief. On its veranda Malay constables were already gathering to appraise the crowd, rifles at the ready. Rose knew that inside the building there would be an English police inspector who would soon put an end to the chaos. She placed an arm about Howard and although he resisted, drew him close. In front of her the Chinese woman had also gathered the young girl protectively to her breast. The woman was an *amah*, dressed in the white top and loose black trousers that all the nursemaids wore. Her charge, in a pink dress of drawn thread work with matching hair ribbons, turned her face for comfort into the woman's flat breast. The *amah* looked

anxiously out of the window while the girl ι
shoulder, regarding Howard with curiosity. Ι
small but unfortunate birthmark stained the cl

Outside, the shouting increased as demonstra
against the side of the trolley; the thwack of stic
Rose's knees. At the Kreta Ayer crossroads traffic ha
cars, rickshaws and bicycles all piled up together. A ι
in turban, shorts and long black socks gestured fran   the
trapped vehicles. His hands were encased in large white ga   ιlets and
white basket traffic wings were strapped to his back. Standing in the
middle of the crowded road he resembled an incongruous angel, but
his efforts at order were futile.

'What's happening?' Rose shouted in panic as the beating of sticks
on the trolley intensified; all about her frightened passengers echoed
her terror. Across the aisle an elderly Chinese in a boater hat, beige
linen suit and a pair of spats over old scuffed shoes nervously stroked
his watch chain.

'Madame, I fear it is a communist demonstration. Today is the
second anniversary of Sun Yat-sen's death,' the man explained in a
courtly manner. Although he spoke in well-enunciated English the
words appeared to be squeezed from a pair of bellows, so bad was his
asthmatic wheezing. Overhearing his explanation, a nun at the back
of the trolley escorting two schoolgirls from the Convent of the Holy
Infant Jesus, began to say a loud Hail Mary.

'What they are wanting? What is this Sun Yat-sen?' an old Indian
woman queried, clutching a cloth bag of rice on her lap.

'Sun Yat-sen is Founding Father of Chinese Republic,' a young
Indian, dressed in a limp *dhoti,* spoke up. He sounded pleased with
himself for offering this information but Rose regarded him disapprovingly. His mouth was stained red with betel nut juice and she
hoped he was not going to spit the stuff at her feet. She judged him
to be a clerk or a shopkeeper, and as such found his manner too
forward. The Chinese in the boater hat nodded confirmation.

'They are coming from a celebratory gathering nearby and want
the trolleybuses to stop until the procession has passed. Such behaviour does not make them popular, but they will lose face if the trolley
proceeds before them.'

'What are communists? What do they want?' Howard pulled at his eeve. His anger had turned to excitement as he sensed the ...er of the situation. Someone might get shot, blood would be shed and he could tell about it at school.

'They are hooligans and gangsters, that's what they are. They want to destroy our way of life,' Rose answered angrily. She feared they could be stuck here for hours and looked anxiously across at the police station where the weathercock gleamed in the sun. Sikh constables with long rifles had now joined the Malay policemen on the steps.

'What are they shouting?' Howard asked fractiously.

'They are shouting, *Down with Imperialism*,' the man in the boater hat told him.

'What is imperialism?' Howard observed the protruding mole on the man's chin from which sprouted several long hairs.

'Colonial rule; the rule of the White Man over Asiatics,' the Chinese explained in a matter-of-fact way, smiling all the while.

Rose was about to give a tart reply when an Englishman on the stalled trolley behind them decided to exert some authority. Leaving the safety of the vehicle he attempted to force his way through the angry crowd, furiously shouting directions. As he reached Rose's trolley the demonstrators pushed him against the side, shaking clenched fists in his face. Pinned against the hot and dusty metal, the man stood his ground, still barking out orders in the manner of an army commander.

'He will see that the bus moves soon. He is an Englishman; everything we are proud of in Malaya is because of British rule.' Rose looked defiantly at the dapper Chinese who appeared nonplussed by her sudden outburst.

'Madame, I am not a communist. I too am an admirer of the British and happy to live peacefully under their excellent rule. I have spent some time in England. I am a Christian like yourself; my name is Joseph Ho.' The man smiled although his tone was defensive and his wheezing deepened as he observed the angry Rose. She was an attractive Eurasian woman, he thought, there was a regal quality about her although, when looked at feature by feature, her nose was too wide, her brow too prominent and her eyes too deeply set. A knot of hair was coiled low on her neck in a matronly fashion; she was one of those women, Mr Ho thought, who from puberty appeared middle aged.

Outside, the Englishman's voice could be heard rising in a hoarse crescendo. He repeatedly demanded a clearing of the road with sweeping gestures of his arms. The demonstrators, who were mostly hot-blooded Hailams, refused to do as they were asked. Neither side could comprehend the other's language but all understood the gist of the argument. A further procession from the Sun Yat-sen gathering was now arriving at the Kreta Ayer crossroads to join the excited crowd.

In new terror Rose saw that the infuriated mob had no intention of obeying British rule. She kept her eyes on the Englishman, whose face was now purple with anger at the insolence of people who were expected to obey him. The demonstrators continued to press dangerously about him as he edged his way forward along the side of Rose's trolley. Still shouting orders, the man reached the footplate and jumped up to tumble inside. Righting himself, he at once urged the driver to start the bus and force a way through the crowd.

There was a hiss and some clicks as the electric wires connected above the vehicle. Incensed by this show of defiance, the communists threw themselves anew at the trolley. Stones were hurled, one hitting the driver on the cheek. With a yelp of pain he abandoned the levers and the engine fell silent again. The demonstrators gave a roar of triumph and began to rock the bus to the accompaniment of rhythmic chanting. The trolley swayed violently from side to side. Rose gave a sob and began to pray, clinging tightly to Howard as she was tossed about upon her seat. Men around her shouted; women began to scream. Within a few moments the trolley steadied as the demonstrators tired of the effort to overturn it.

'Hooligans!' Rose glared accusingly at the asthmatic Mr Ho who now wheezed like a clogged up pipe. Then, taking in the full extent of his distress, she leaned forward to speak more kindly.

'Lean back. Loosen your tie,' she advised, alarmed by the man's ashen colour and his struggle to breathe.

The demonstrators were now attempting to board the trolley. A pole was pushed inside, catching the Englishman on his chest as he stood beside the conductor. Losing his balance, he keeled backwards to land in the driver's lap. Demonstrators swarmed forward to board the bus, but the driver and conductor parried their moves with the umbrellas carried on the trolley in case of rain. After much diligent thrusting and flailing, the assailants were prised off the vehicle.

A siege mentality had now overtaken the trolley; passengers huddled together in the centre isle. Rose looked across at the Kreta Ayer police station and saw that the Chief Inspector, a tall blustery-faced Englishman with a ginger moustache, straight-backed beneath a sun helmet, was coming down the steps and making his way towards the bus. Behind him Malay constables with raised rifles stood ready for trouble. Rose was dripping with sweat; outside the shouting grew louder. She marvelled how a day begun so blandly could sink abruptly into nightmare. At Belvedere now the cook, Ah Fong, would be dancing about in a pre-dinner ballet of anxiety, the lodgers would be pacing up and down near the dining room and complaining in low voices. Her mind filled with thoughts of her daughter. The *amah* would see to Cynthia's dinner and put the child to bed, but what if she and Howard were stuck all night in the bus, what if the rioters turned upon them? No one knew where she was.

'I'm hot, Mummy. I'm thirsty. Will the policemen kill the communists?' Howard asked. Rose drew him to her breast again but he pushed her away, fractious at the touch of her hot, damp flesh, avid to see what was happening.

'They will listen to the power of a gun,' Mr Ho wheezed from across the aisle; he had loosened his necktie and taken off his jacket, revealing braces and an open waistcoat.

'Soon now the trolley will move,' the young Indian, Raj Sherma, predicted with a red-lipped smile; his eyes were bright and his manner more ebullient than fearful.

Howard kicked the seat in front of him again and the Chinese girl turned to frown at him. He stared at the birthmark on her jaw, at the delicate tracery of red lines and small blotches, and decided it resembled a gecko.

'Children thirsty,' the *amah* worried, speaking anxiously to Rose in broken Malay.

Rose suddenly remembered that in the bottom of her handbag there were a few boiled sweets a stallholder had given her in the Beach Road market the day before. She opened the bag and extracted the sweets, giving one to the girl and another to Howard. The children cheered up immediately.

'This is Howard. What is your name?' Rose asked the girl.

'Name, Mei Lan,' the *amah* answered for the child. Sucking silently on her sweet, Mei Lan stared at Howard while he crunched noisily upon the hard sugar. Although he returned her gaze, his eyes kept slipping to the mottling on her jaw. Aware of his interest the girl obligingly stuck out her chin, moving her lips to make the mark dance for him. Impressed but disappointed he could not compete, Howard scowled thunderously.

Outside, the Chief Inspector appeared to be making no progress. A new burst of shouting began and the bamboo poles were raised angrily once more. The demonstrators poked savagely at the inspector's chest as if they were sticking a pig. Throwing up his hands in surrender, the Chief Inspector backed away in the careful manner of a man retreating from a snarling animal. To the sudden shout of *pah pah* the bamboo poles came down upon him in a rain of heavy blows. One thick staff smashed through the crown of his sun helmet; the hat fell off and rolled away, blood poured down his face. Two Malay constables ran forward. Supporting the injured man between them, they dragged him up the steps of the Kreta Ayer police station and into the building, pursued by the angry rioters. Then, the crack of rifles filled the air as policemen fired shots in quick succession over the heads of the demonstrators.

'Get down, son. Do you want to be shot?' Rose tugged frantically at Howard as he leant out of the trolley to follow events, pulling him down on the floor beside her.

Looking around, Howard saw that all the passengers were similarly positioned away from ill-directed shots. Mei Lan had begun to sob in fear against the *amah*'s shoulder. The suffering Mr Ho had collapsed on the floor, his legs stuck out in front of him. Rose surveyed him anxiously as she took hold of the excited Howard. Imprisoned against his mother's breast, her heart beating wildly in his ear, Howard watched the man weakly roll up his sleeves.

'Don't give me trouble now, son,' Rose hissed as Howard freed himself from her arms.

Crouched down between the seats, Howard found himself beside a louvred ventilation panel in the side of the bus through which a narrow slice of the world was revealed. Outside, there was renewed activity after the first shots. The agitators were now surging about the police station, attempting to enter the building, all interest in the trolleybus gone. The firing of guns had succeeded only in inflaming them.

From an upper window of the station a grey-haired Englishman leaned out and shouted an order. The constables levelled their guns once more and released their second volley of shots directly into the rioting crowd. Amongst the demonstrators Howard then observed the sort of implosion that occurred when his sister, Cynthia, maliciously moved a wooden brick in one of his elaborate architectural constructions. The mob disintegrated, backing away from the police station. Several bodies pooling blood could be seen lying in the road, limbs flung out at odd angles. Torn banners and bamboo poles littered the street as the demonstrators melted away. Rose turned from the scene with a sob of relief, aware once again of Mr Ho's struggle to breathe. Looking up, she saw that the young Indian with the red lips was also observing Mr Ho in concern.

'The uncle is needing only air,' Raj Sherma informed her, making his way towards Rose and the sick Chinese.

He gave a wide smile and Rose smelled the aniseed on his breath. She nodded, anxious to be rid of the invalid and the responsibility she would feel if he died. As the traumatised passengers hesitantly returned to their seats, Raj helped Mr Ho to his feet and steered him down the trolley to a vacant place. Outside, the shooting was over, the shouting had ceased and the demonstrators were already disappearing into alleys and side roads.

As the trolley began to move again Mei Lan knelt up on her seat and stared at Howard. Although her heart was racing with shock, Rose smiled at the child and reached into her bag to find a further sweet. She gave one to the child and another to Howard and also found sweets for herself and the *amah*.

'Where are you going?' she asked the girl, still unable to believe she was safely free of peril.

'I am going to Ah Siew's *kongsi fong*,' the child announced in perfect English.

Rose swallowed the boiled sweet in surprise. She was shocked that a well brought up child should go to a servant's *fong*; she would never let Cynthia or Howard experience the misery of such a place. By the way she was dressed the child appeared to be from the Chinese upper class, and must go to an English mission school to speak so naturally in English. Why was she not riding in a car or even a private rickshaw instead of a common trolleybus? She was a pretty child, Rose observed, but for the birthmark on her jaw and must be about seven or eight years old, a little younger than Howard. The *amah* continued to smile at Rose, sucking noisily on the sweet. Although she had a pleasant expression, her weathered skin was pitted from smallpox and her teeth protruded.

At the back of the trolley the dapper Mr Ho appeared somewhat revived. He had rolled down his shirtsleeves and re-knotted his tie and, although he still wheezed, his smile returned. The young Indian helped him on with his jacket as his stop approached.

'Uncle, I will accompany you home,' he offered, seeing how the exertion of even standing up caused the man's laboured breathing to return. Mr Ho turned to him gratefully.

'You are a fine young man. What is your name?' the Chinese wheezed, lurching forward on trembling legs and tipping his boater to Rose.

'My name is Raj Sherma,' the young Indian replied as he steered Mr Ho down the bus.

Rose watched them alight with a pang of regret. To have survived together such an ordeal made the men in some way her compatriots, and now they were gone from her life. The moment passed as the trolley travelled on towards Rose's own destination. Soon, she tucked Howard's shirt into his shorts, slicked down the damp curly hair that would never lie flat and, taking his hand, stood up and smiled at the Chinese girl and her *amah*.

'Say goodbye,' she instructed her son, but Howard stuck out his tongue instead. In reply Mei Lan pulled down the corners of her eyes, pushed two fingers into her mouth and stretched her lips open grotesquely; on her jaw the birthmark leapt about. As Howard began an answer of some further inelegance, Rose pulled him down from the trolley. She watched the vehicle continue its journey, like a nightmare receding as she opened her eyes to the day.

2

LOATH TO BOARD A further trolley, Rose had taken a rickshaw back across town. Soon the peaceful environs of Bukit Timah and then the gentle slope of Mount Rosie was before her again. When at last they entered Belvedere, the subdued clatter of cutlery and conversation could be heard in the dining room. Ah Fong had already served dinner and Rose was relieved to find they had not been missed. She hurried to take her place at the table before the window, where they always sat for meals. Howard followed his mother as she crossed the room, nodding apologies to her lodgers whenever she caught an eye. Cynthia was already eating, with the *amah* crouched attentively on her haunches beside the chair. At the sight of Rose the child jumped up, a whirl-wind of tawny hair and milky skin, and threw her arms around her. Her face, pressed against Rose's dusky cheek, could not easily be prised away.

With no more than a glance at his sister, Howard took his place at the table and stared about the dim and flickering room full of moving shadows. The glow of the candles that were lit each evening saved electricity and, said his mother, created a gracious ambience, but nothing for Howard could eradicate Belvedere's intrinsic sadness. Whatever efforts were expended upon the house it remained to him cavernous, gloomy and secretive. The long windows were open to the evening, the perfume of night flowers and damp earth mixing with the odour of poached fish and the melting wax of candles. The lodgers, who sat two or three to a table, were exclusively young European men in Singapore on a first tour of duty.

Howard hated the way he must sit before them, subject to scrutiny and comment, evaluated over a sea of tables. He already understood it was his sister who held the lodgers' attention; any cursory glances that came his way were solely of a curious nature. Sooner or later everyone remarked on the difference between the siblings, comparing

Howard's darker cast of skin to Cynthia's creamy appearance and her startling green eyes. That a mother could produce at one time a swarthy son but at another a daughter of such delectable properties was, he already realised, one of nature's foibles. Once, he had overheard a loud-mouthed man from Cardiff remark that Landlady Burns must have had it off with one of her lodgers nine months before Cynthia appeared in the world. Snorts of laughter greeted this remark. Howard had turned and run, his heart pounding. Although he had not understood the comment, he understood the besmirching of his mother and for some time afterwards he had secretly believed that he and Cynthia had different fathers. Later, he realised this could not be, for Cynthia had been born in Upper Serangoon before their father died, before they came to Belvedere and the world of lodgers.

After the happenings of the day, Howard's knees still trembled and his stomach closed at the prospect of food. He pushed a fish fillet listlessly about his plate, remembering again the crack of bullets at Kreta Ayer. Looking up, Howard caught his mother's eye and saw that she too could not eat her dinner. In the candlelight her face appeared unfamiliar, her eyes cratered in shadow beneath her brow. He hated the old house at this time of day. The lurking presence he sensed in the dark cavity of Belvedere was already actively stalking about. The only thing tolerable in his new home was its overgrown orchard. The gnarled branches of the mangosteen trees, hung with dark fruit the colour of burgundy, encircled a secret world of twisting vines and foliage. Sometimes, thickly smeared with a home-made insect repellent, he climbed up a tree to pick the hard globes of fruit, peeling off the thick skin, sucking on the white flesh within. Only the slither of snakes, the movement of lizards or the buzz of insects reached him in this place of hot rotting smells.

All he wanted was to return to their old home in Upper Serangoon with its green-latticed shutters and orderly garden and the cricket he played with his friends. There, the neighbourhood boys were Eurasian like Howard and rode with him to school in a mosquito bus, squashing into the vehicle together. The conductor balanced on the back step, clinging to a rail, and swung dangerously around corners. There were orchards about the houses in Upper Serangoon from which they stole rambutan, durian and mangosteen. The Eurasian boys made up two cricket teams and Howard's father had coached them. Then, when his father died, they moved away and Howard found himself far from his friends and the small local school he had attended. Now, he went to St Joseph's Institution, a school of Catholic Brothers who used the cane, and where he had no friends. He hated the new house, Belvedere, with its dilapidated façade and the European lodgers his mother was so happy to serve; it could in no way be called a home. He reached into his pocket and pulled out his father's compass and, opening the lid of the flat wooden box, stared down at the red-tipped needle. Rose had found the compass while clearing out Charlie's desk after his death and given it to Howard. When they moved to Belvedere he had set the compass to point in the direction of Upper Serangoon, so that he could find his way back there if needed.

That night sleep pulled him under quickly, the weight of his dreams heavy upon him. Howard heard again the shouts of the communists as they rocked the trolley and remembered the Inspector's battered sun helmet upturned in the road, stained with the blood of its owner. He awoke with a start to his dark room, listening to the pipes in the belly of Belvedere grumbling with elderly flatulence. Outside the heavy splatter of rain could be heard. Lightning flashed and thunder froze him where he lay. He found he was bathed in sweat but dared not move or reach for the glass of water that stood on the table beside his bed.

Although, when the shots were fired, Howard understood his mother's fear as the wounded Chief Inspector was dragged into the police station, he was disappointed that the man was not dead. He did not know who the communists were, but already he felt allegiance; they had demonstrated a daring that excited him. His heart pumped with outrage on behalf of the rioters whose courage before authority had met with such brutality. Now, in the darkness of Belvedere, he pondered what it was about the Chief Inspector that seemed to him so familiar. As a gecko clucked loudly from the wall, he realised with a start that the inspector resembled a man at Great World Amusement Park who Howard would never forget.

Not long before his father died, they had gone together to Great World. Howard loved these outings to the amusement park with its shooting galleries, eating stalls, theatres, musicians and the excitement of the boxing ring. In the cavernous dance hall the taxi girls with red lips and high heels danced for money with men, the moving bodies of the swaying couples were pressed together as one. Some women had skirts slit high up their thigh; others wore gowns exposing their cleavage. Howard's hands became clammy and the muscles of his legs grew tight as he stared into this tawdry world. A band played in a dark corner and the music ran wildly through him. The strong odour of beer and cigarettes accompanied a licentiousness he recognised but could not frame in words.

'I'll bring you here when you're older. We'll find a real beauty for you to dance with,' his father laughed that day.

Howard had been allowed to have two rounds at the shooting gallery and to buy a stick of candyfloss in an unhealthy shade of pink. His father drank a couple of beers and Howard an orange squash, and eventually they had made their way to the lavatories. These were situated to one side of Great World and were modern and clean with the novelty of a chain to pull that released a flush of water. In Upper Serangoon they were still visited each morning by the honey-cart with its odorous buckets. When Howard went out with his mother he was still young enough to go with her into the Ladies' lavatories of public places. That day at Great World he was proud to be out alone with his father and enter the door marked Gentlemen.

Inside the lavatory Howard followed his father to the row of urinals. A tall Englishman stood with his back to them and Charlie Burns took a place beside him. From a skylight, sunlight fell on the Englishman's greying head and his father's chestnut hair, and burnished the fountain released from the Englishman to an arch of liquid gold. The remaining urinal lay in shadow, and Howard positioned himself before it. He noticed with pride that his father's skin, in spite of some cricket under the sun, was paler in shade than the bronzed and leathery skin of the other man; he looked more English than the Englishman. At last the man buttoned up his fly and nodded to Charlie in a friendly manner. Then, as he turned away, his gaze settled on Howard who was still struggling to undo his shorts and he stopped abruptly. Stepping forward with a frown and grasping Howard by the scruff of the neck, he began to shout.

'You are not allowed in here, you dark-skinned rascal. If you were older I'd call the police.'

Shocked by the sudden attack, Howard cowered in terror, sure the man was going to hit him. Instead, dragging Howard roughly forward, he frogmarched him to the door. Before being ejected into the noisy clamour of Great World, Howard turned in mute appeal to his father. Charlie Burns stood rigid at the urinal, his face turned away, his eyes on the wall before him and uttered not a word. Outside, the Englishman wagged a threatening finger at Howard as he strode away. Howard stared after him in confusion; his bladder was full and his shorts open to expose him. More than the shock of expulsion was his father's refusal to acknowledge him. His throat constricted and he thought he might cry before the closed face of the door.

'Sorry, son,' his father whispered when, at last, he emerged from the lavatory. He pointed to the door next to the one he now shut behind him.

'That's the door for you, and me too of course if that man really knew. He thought I was a whitey, like him,' Charlie chuckled, delighted. Directing Howard's attention to a higher level, he pointed out the word EUROPEANS above the door from which he had just emerged, and the sign OTHERS over the door to which he now pushed Howard. He did not accompany his son inside this alternative toilet but waited outside, lighting up a cigarette, leaning back against a wall.

Now, in the darkness of his home Howard heard the gecko cluck once more, and he knew the dark presence of Belvedere had settled in the shadows thickening the corners of his room. In his mind the face of the Chief Inspector and that of the man in the lavatory of Great World had already fused into one. So it was that he had wished for the blood of the Chief Inspector, although he had no knowledge of why he wished this. He had just wanted the man to die. He knew these memories were part of him now and would live within him for ever. Something inside him seemed changed, as if he had grown several inches in just those few minutes at Kreta Ayer. Already he felt an old man.

Rose Burns tossed and turned and could not sleep. She stared at the parchment shade of the lamp hanging above her bed. The long electric wire was lost in the darkness of the high vaulted ceiling. Caught by moonlight the shade hovered luminously, disembodied as a ghost. The thunder had become more distant as the storm abated. Now, the low rhythmic boom of bullfrogs and the shrilling of crickets returned again from the garden. The scent of the sea and the faint stench of sardines drying on a faraway beach drifted through the open window. The night seemed full of strange perfumes, unsettling thoughts and the violent residue of the day. The shouts of the mob at Kreta Ayer still echoed in her ears, as did the terror she had felt when the trolley was rocked about. With each crack of thunder she remembered the sound of gunfire spitting through the air. She saw again the Chief Inspector's sun helmet abandoned in the road, the empty cup a dark and bloodied hole, and knew in sudden terror the fragility of life.

A flash of lightning caught the silver frames of photographs arranged on the chest of drawers, the familiar faces frozen in time like the flies in lumps of amber she had seen once in a museum. Before her Charlie smiled, debonair and handsome, holding Cynthia and Howard as babies. There was fifteen months between the two children and in the photograph Charlie's head was turned towards the green-eyed Cynthia, as if to disown his dark son.

With his ginger hair and quiet demeanour, the Chief Inspector at Kreta Ayer had reminded her of Charlie. Although as Eurasian as Rose, Charlie wore his fair skin like a badge of honour. For Rose, the sight of her dusky limbs against his pale body had always filled her with humility. Yet suddenly now, the thought of Charlie brought an angry lump to her throat. He had left her stranded in the middle of life to face alone situations as precarious as that at Kreta Ayer. The unexpected heat of these emotions took Rose by surprise. For a time after Charlie died she had felt she was drowning. Although he'd had a good job at the Asiatic Petroleum Company, he had made little provision for his family and she saw now that a great resentment had accumulated within her.

Charlie had not chosen to marry her but had 'done the right thing' when she found she was pregnant with Howard. After a dance at the house of a mutual friend in Katong they had gone for a walk on the beach, where he had forced himself upon her. Although, as was right, she had put up a fight, some part of her was flattered by his attentions and had not found the outrage to resist. Turning her thoughts away from Charlie, she thought again of Mr Ho and his laboured breathing. Then lightning illuminated Charlie's face once more, and behind him the bank of silver frames holding further images of the dead. Just as the Chinese revered their ancestors, finding their future in their past, Rose too felt the same.

Her ancestors carried the names of disparate European cultures: Pereira, Martens, Rodrigues, de Souza, O'Patrick, Thomas, McIntyre, van der Ven. Washed up upon the shores of Malaya these men married local women, and their children then intermarried again and again until a hybrid people was formed. There was Cousin Ella with round owlish glasses who might be mistaken for a plump English matron but for the narrow tilt of her eyes. There was Agnes Martins, wife of Thomas O'Patrick, first generation Eurasian son of a tavern keeper in Penang. Thomas's dark face had the boning of a European while beside him Agnes, thin as a bird in her European clothes, had features and colouring more Indian than Dutch. Seated in her garden Matriach Thora, stern in a black dress with lace collar was surrounded by six daughters and their husbands. On these faces the patterning of genes shifted even as Rose looked at them. The darkness of hair and eyes, the depth of a feature, the angle of an eye or a cheekbone, each traced a unique heritage. We are a people of shadows, Rose thought looking up into the darkness above her. A further weak flash of lightning revealed the worn paintwork of the ceiling and the damp stains of mould on the walls.

The chance to acquire Belvedere had arisen unexpectedly for Rose soon after Charlie's death. The place had once been the residence of a British government official but had later been converted into a boarding house. It had never taken flight as an enterprise and was eventually abandoned lying derelict until Rose, looking for accommodation and the means to support her family, was shown it by a house agent full of apologies for its state. With the sale of the house in Upper Serangoon and the little Charlie had left her, she had enough to consider buying it, provided she made careful plans. The house crowned a low rise, and stood in beleaguered dignity like an ageing dowager reluctant to admit infirmity. Whatever its faults and state of decay, the charm of the place overwhelmed her. Rose was taken by its black and white timbered gables and elegant whimsy that seamlessly combined Tudor, Gothic and colonial elements in a graceful symmetry. Built of brick below and whitewashed wood above, the red-roofed house was longer than it was wide. Verandas running along both floors were a distinctive feature but the double portico, originally built to shelter a horse and carriage, appeared like a generous afterthought in an otherwise compact plan. The neglected orchard bore little fruit, and mosquito and snakes had laid claim to the place. The crumbling kitchens were the haunt of vagrants and stray dogs, the tennis court was invisible beneath a waist-high field and the dining room ceiling had partially collapsed; but the price was a bargain and Rose had seen possibilities at once. She also liked its location at the base of Mount Rosie. Long ago, the road had been named after a Rosie de Souza, pretty Eurasian wife of a German, and Rose was drawn to this strange connection. I shall be Rose of Mount Rosie she had told the house agent and, even as she spoke, she knew she was destined to live there. After the purchase she had set about Belvedere's restoration with enthusiasm.

Although Rose had bought Belvedere two years before she was still surprised to find herself living in this part of town. Bukit Timah was largely an enclave of wealthy Europeans. Only the odd Chinese family, such as her neighbour, the business tycoon Lim Hock An, dared venture beyond Chinatown on the wheels of their new money. In her old home in Upper Serangoon she had been surrounded by other Eurasian families but here there was no sense of community; few people knew their neighbours. Each large house was an island in a sea of manicured lawns, people kept rigidly to their own social stratum and the races never mixed. In Upper Serangoon, a place where everyone knew everyone, locals chatted over garden walls, borrowed flour and sugar from each other and attended church and musical evenings together. If she had not been so busy, first renovating Belvedere and then attending to the young men who were her lodgers, it would all have been unbearable, she thought.

Rose was an orphan and when she married she had hoped Charlie's family would become her own. This had not happened. The family's European ancestor was no more than a generation removed and this showed in their fair skin, especially in Charlie who, much to everyone's delight, could easily pass for a European. The desire of the Burns family to distinguish themselves from other Eurasians and associate with Europeans, even if those Europeans would have little to do with them, proved a stumbling block for Rose. She was not what the Burns family needed. They considered she had trapped handsome Charlie into marriage by the age-old ploy of pregnancy. It was feared his promising career at the Asiatic Petroleum Company would be stunted by the presence of Rose. She had also been born in Malacca of a confusing line of swarthy intermarriage, and could not trace her Portuguese ancestry to any white-skinned individual. At every turn her Asian roots showed through, from a love of salt fish pickle and *belachan* shrimp paste, to an enjoyment of eating with her fingers. She had no sense at the beginning of her marriage of what was 'done' or 'not done' in the Burnses' code of behaviour. Although she worked hard to eradicate her faults, the family never accepted her. In spite of marriage to Rose, Charlie did well at the Asiatic Petroleum Company, but merit had its ceiling for all the local communities and this inevitability had had a profound effect upon him. He grew depressed, and finally suffered a fatal heart attack. Even at the funeral Charlie's family offered Rose little comfort, already blaming his early demise upon the frustrations of his marriage. His death was an opportunity to cut all contact with her.

Rose was a taciturn woman, often called withdrawn. Full busted, small waisted and ample hipped she had worn, even as a young woman, dresses with high necks and demure collars. It was her sister, Heather, who had been ever anxious to reveal her creamy décolletage and her shapely arms. Rose was the elder of the sisters, watchful and responsible. Their parents' deaths, one after the other, had placed responsibility upon her early in life. The girls were taken in by a childless aunt and uncle; Rose had been fourteen and Heather eleven. Aunty May and Uncle Reg looked to Rose to keep her young sister in order. Yet, even at that tender age men's eyes rested on Heather; Uncle Reg was no exception. Whenever Heather sat beside him, his hand sought out her bare knee. Later, Heather learned the full power of her attraction and as a consequence many cruel things had been said about her. Fate extracted its comeuppance when she died after a crude abortion. Rose thought now of Cynthia, of her auburn hair and wide green eyes, so like Heather's, with a pang of fear. And Howard, once he became a man, would be no less vulnerable to accident through a careless spreading of his seed. Had Charlie not been so moral and God-fearing a man, her own fate might have been no different to that of her sister. Instead Charlie married her and gave her a good home, allowing her to send bits of money to May and Reg, even though he advised it was best not to see them.

Whatever her feelings about the part of town she now lived in, Rose had been surprised at her relief on returning to the area after the events of Kreta Ayer. Bukit Timah Road, shaded by rain trees, with huge epiphyte ferns nesting like plump roosting birds on their branches, was now comfortingly familiar. The calls of cicada and birds filled the lush profusion and a sweet fragrance of blossom pervaded the air. Sometimes, the European residents of nearby bungalows could be seen on a veranda, languid in basket chairs, glasses of refreshment beside them while from tennis courts the soft thud of balls was heard. Rose was even glad to see the turrets of Lim Villa before she turned into Chancery Lane and the approach to Mount Rosie. The back of Lim Villa's estate adjoined the end of Belvedere's garden and was the extravagant whim of the enormously wealthy Lim Hock An. Part French château and part Norman castle, Lim Villa could be glimpsed from Belvedere, which was at a higher elevation, across a dividing storm canal behind a fringe of trees.

Lightning no longer flashed and the roll of thunder was gone. Rose turned in her bed to look again in the direction of Charlie in his silver frame. Frozen in time, these photographs were like the flowers she pressed between the pages of books, devoid in the end of the very life she wished to retain. In the dark room the only sound now was the grumbling of Belvedere's ancient water pipes.

3

SOME TIME AFTER ROSE and Howard returned to Belvedere, Mei Lan and her *amah* rode in a rickshaw up the shady avenue of Bukit Timah. Lanterns burned before the wrought-iron gates of Lim Villa, and Sikh watchmen stood to attention. The gates swang open and the rickshaw proceeded up the long drive to the turrets and towers of Lim Hock An's great mansion. Already, shadows were dense amongst the trees, although a streak of pink still clung to the darkening sky. Marble statuary gleamed dimly on great swathes of lawn. The day's experiences settled uncomfortably in Mei Lan like an over-rich meal. She rested her head against Ah Siew's flat breast, glad to return to Lim Villa where she slept in a bed of soft down pillows and not upon a wooden shelf in a dark smelly room, like Ah Siew's sisters in their *kongsi fong*. Her mind was so full of the *fong* and the exciting things she had seen and learned that she had almost forgotten the shouting men and police with guns that had delayed them at Kreta Ayer.

It was Mei Lan who had requested the treat of a trolley ride; a chauffeured car usually ferried her about. The day before, her parents had sailed for Hong Kong, and Second Grandmother had been glad to agree to the outing as long as she was with Ah Siew. Once the trolley was free of Kreta Ayer and had begun to move again, they soon reached their stop. Mei Lan had been hungry and so they walked towards People's Park for a bowl of steaming noodles. Mei Lan sat on a stool at a small table beside a stall and watched the *mee* stirred and tossed in a huge pan, pork, noodles and vegetables all jumping around together. At the other tables half-naked coolies and rickshaw pullers played cards and rattled dice; as she ate, an acrobat turned cartwheels beside her. Mealtimes at Lim Villa were nothing like this. Mei Lan must eat decorously and keep silent, sitting at a separate table from the adults with her brother, JJ.

After the noodles they walked past the house in Chinatown where

Ah Siew said Mei Lan had been born; she stared at it in amazement. They had moved to Lim Villa when she was a baby and she remembered nothing of it. After the soaring façade and endless lawns of Lim Villa, it seemed a poky place with a confusing number of courtyards and gates. In the road before the house two watchmen sat on upright chairs just as they had when the family of Lim Hock An lived there. They allowed Mei Lan to peer through the gate into the house where she had been born.

'First Mistress was still alive when we lived here,' Ah Siew murmured. Mei Lan looked up in surprise; no one ever spoke of First Grandmother. Mei Lan knew only Second Grandmother who lived with Grandfather in Lim Villa and had feet as small as a doll.

'Did Second Grandmother also live here with First Grandmother?' Mei Lan asked and Ah Siew nodded.

'First Mistress died in this house; it was before your grandfather, Ancient Master, built Lim Villa,' Ah Siew said softly and her face grew sad. Mei Lan was eager to hear more about First Grandmother but Ah Siew fell silent.

Ah Siew's *kongsi fong* was not far from People's Park and she took the short cut through Sago Lane to the room she had once shared with the friends she called her *sisters*. Sago Lane bustled with the business of death and the discordant clamour of funeral parlours. Cymbals and gongs accompanied the droning chant of priests; percussion bands led wailing mourners seeing off the dead. Shops selling candles, joss sticks, coffins and wreaths lined the road and above these the dying awaited their time in Sago Lane's many Death Houses. Next to the coffin maker, whose deep boxes were stacked to the ceiling of his shop, were paper effigies of worldly things the dead would need in the afterlife. Sleek limousines, many-windowed mansions, beautiful women, a boat, servants, a bicycle, a mah-jong set and stacks of paper money would be consigned to the flames for transition to the afterlife. Mei Lan ran ahead along the narrow street towards the big Death House that Ah Siew had earlier pointed out.

It was not easy to run in Sago Lane so thick was the traffic of the bereaved, vagrants, lepers, hawkers of food, stray dogs, beggars and keening women singing the Song of Mourning. Food stalls and confectioners catered to the road's never-ending wake and smells of sugar and roasting pork floated on the perfume of incense. At the rickshaw station the big-wheeled carts were clustered closely together, hoods erect like an army of spiny insects. The runners smoked and chatted, washed their vehicles or sucked on bowls of noodles. The odours of food and sewage and joss sticks filled Mei Lan's nose; she had never been to Ah Siew's *fong* before.

'Slow down,' Ah Siew panted but Mei Lan ran on.

The mouldering buildings, infested with cockroaches and human suffering and festooned with laundry on bamboo poles throbbed with a pulse that excited Mei Lan. Hardened undertakers and red-eyed mourners turned to stare at this manifestation of starched pink linen, complete with black patent pumps, clean white socks and shining well-brushed hair.

When at last Mei Lan drew to a halt before the big Death House its grim façade, devoid of colourful laundry, appeared suddenly daunting. A grey-haired coolie slept on a bench outside and through the open door a yellow-robed priest could be seen moving about. The dark interior was filled with rows of wooden bunks upon which lay the sick and dying. As Mei Lan wondered if the departed spirits who roamed the house were visible to those inside, Ah Siew came running up to take her hand.

'Not here, little goose. We have not brought sister Ah Pat here yet,' Ah Siew said and pulled Mei Lan into a narrow alley leading off Sago Lane.

They entered a slim opening in a dank wall, and climbed the steep stairs to Ah Siew's *fong* above, Mei Lan clinging tightly to her *amah*'s hand. The stench of garlic, urine, fermenting rice and all manner of vile effluvia enfolded her in a greasy blanket of odours. Eventually, they reached the top of the stairs and in the half-light filtering through a broken shutter, Mei Lan saw a long, grimy corridor with cubicles lining each side. A rat moved in the shadows and she stepped closer to Ah Siew who now walked briskly ahead, the pleasure of home-coming filling her step. She turned suddenly into one of the grimy cubicles, ducking under a ragged strip of curtain to a chorus of greeting. The sisters were seated in a group about the dying Ah Pat who lay upon a sleeping shelf in the dark and tiny room. A narrow rack stacked with boxes and jars ran along one wall; light filtered through from the corridor. Baskets of foodstuffs hung on long strings from the ceiling beyond the reach of rats. Ah Siew thrust Mei Lan forward and began the introductions.

'This is Ah Thye, Ah Ooi, Yong Gui and Ah Tim. And that is Ah Pat,' Ah Siew smiled at the invalid.

Ah Pat's face was as yellow as old parchment and her hair unravelled from its knot. A pillow of rolled up clothes supported her head, a swelling deformed one side of her neck. The shelf was shorter than her legs and her bare feet protruded over the end. Mei Lan observed the sisters apprehensively. She knew they were not real sisters, yet they all bore a resemblance to Ah Siew. Each had hair pulled into a neat bun and wore identical black trousers and high-necked white blouses. The sisters were from the Pearl River Delta where the women were useful and did not bind their feet. They had met in the *nui yan uk,* the Girls' Home near their village. Such homes were found only in the Pearl River Delta, a region of China where women refused to be slaves, Ah Siew boasted. They came one by one to Singapore, meeting each other off the boat, living together in their rented *fong* until employment was found.

The sisters rushed to make Mei Lan comfortable, chattering excitedly. A box was found for her to sit on; a cake filled with bean paste and a small tangerine were given her to eat. They stroked her hair and examined her hands; there was debate about her birthmark. Mei Lan hung her head, ashamed, trying to hide the hated mark of which she was always conscious. She had once overheard her mother discussing it with her mah-jong friends; it was a sign of ill luck and because of it few men would want her for a bride. Already, it seemed her fate was sealed. Yet Yong Gui, who the sisters said knew about these things, was not of this opinion. She lifted Mei Lan's chin with a finger to observe the birthmark better.

'A little nearer the mouth and it would denote greed, a little further away and it would bring ill luck. Instead, it is aligned exactly beneath the eye. This means it is a lucky mark; a mark of protection,' Yong Gui decided.

The sisters laughed, and began to prepare some tea. Mei Lan returned her attention to the tangerine, filled with relief to hear her birthmark might not be a stain on her life. She began to eat the cake, holding it carefully in her palm while the sisters sipped tea, exchanging memories of their homes in China.

'Each month we ate different vegetables. In March long beans, in August taro, sweet potatoes in September. Onions were all year round,' Ah Ooi remembered.

'Our house had mud and reed walls and a patched roof that disintegrated whenever it rained. We froze in winter; every year someone died,' Yong Gui recalled.

'Father bought silkworm eggs.' Ah Siew spoke suddenly with a smile. 'They hatched into worms as thin as a hair, I picked mulberry leaves for them. Once the cocoons were sold in the market, the worms were fried, dipped in batter as a treat.'

'My sisters and I all wished for bound feet and the good marriages this brings, but we were needed for work in the fields. Now I am glad; our ugly feet have given us independence. Where would we be without them?' Yong Gui joked

'Kwantung and Kwangsi were always at war. The soldiers came and killed our pigs and chickens. They took our men away as pack-bearers and raped the women. We had no means to resist,' Ah Ooi remembered.

'There were fifteen of us,' Ah Pat croaked hoarsely; because of the swelling she could only swallow liquids. 'Each New Year my father would line us up to count how many of us were still alive. The numbers in the family were always changing. However bad times were, my parents resisted selling us girls.' Ah Pat gave a sigh and fell back exhausted upon her pillow.

For a moment the women were silent. Memories washed through them as water passes over rough pebbles. Mei Lan returned her attention to the last of the bean cake; some crumbs still lay in her palm. Transferring them to her mouth upon a wet finger, she followed the progress of a cockroach negotiating the string of a hanging basket. From the road the call of hawkers, the trundle of carts, the barking of a dog and the screams of a baby rose up to her. A rat scuttled past the door of the cubicle. Such sounds were not heard in Lim Villa where there was only the silence of the garden filled with the whirr of cicada and the swish of the gardener's scythe.

'They say it is better to raise geese than girls.' Ah Siew began to speak. 'In our village there were always floods and famines. My father sold two of my sisters to agents scouting for brothels in Nanyang; he got three silver pieces for each girl. Another year when we were all starving, he sold another two as *mui sai* to passing rich families and got a few *kati* of rice for each. They did not want to go and screamed and clung to me, for I was the eldest. The brothel woman slapped their faces and Mother told them if they wanted to eat and to stay alive, they must go. After that, each new baby that was a girl Mother drowned in the river as it took its first breaths. Where my sisters are now, whether they are dead or alive, I will never know. I still hear their cries in my dreams.'

Mei Lan's heart gave a lurch. Ah Siew had never spoken like this before. That girls could be sold for a *kati* of rice or three pieces of silver turned her blood to ice. Mei Lan stared at Ah Siew, imagining the tunnel in her mind leading back to a past of dark images. She wanted to ask what a brothel was but thought the sisters might not approve; it must be a place even worse than the Death House or they would not look so aggrieved. Second Grandmother owned three *mui sai* that Grandfather had bought for her on a visit to China. Had he paid for each girl in silver or rice, just as Ah Siew's sisters were bought as slaves?

'Why didn't any of you get married?' Mei Lan asked. The sisters looked at her in surprise and then began to laugh. They laughed until the tears ran down their faces. Mei Lan scowled and bit her lip, it was all she could do not to cry. Finally the sisters wiped their eyes.

'I'm too ugly to find a husband. Even brothel keepers took one look at me and turned away.' Ah Siew pointed to her face, pitted like old bark. A flange of crooked teeth protruded and her eyes, almost lost beneath the fold of her lids, were slightly at odds with each other. Only the humour in Ah Siew's broad face saved it from complete disaster.

'The truth is, Little Goose, we did not want to accept the Second Obeying. That's why we all took the vows of *Sor Hei* before the Goddess Kwan Yin,' Ah Siew said and the sisters nodded in agreement.

'The First Obeying is to a father, the Second Obeying to a husband and the Third Obeying is to a son after the death of a husband.' Ah Tim leaned forward to explain.

'I was afraid of childbirth, I'd seen what my mother went through,' Yong Gui announced.

'Who wants to be a servant to parents-in-law and brothers-in-law?' Ah Thye said.

'My sister was carried to her husband's village in a red sedan chair. Her bridegroom was away at the time working in a tin mine at Ipoh, so a cockerel took his place at the marriage ceremony, as was the custom in our parts if the husband was absent. Her husband died in the mine before he could even see her. After that my sister always said she was married to a cockerel. I didn't want the same thing to happen to me.' Yong Gui shook her head.

'A missionary sent me to the *nui yan uk*, the Girls' Home. I learned how to cook and sew there. The other girls told me I could work in Nanyang, all those places beyond China, and be independent,' Ah Tim said and the sisters nodded agreement again.

Eventually, Ah Siew looked at the pocket watch she kept in a pouch about her waist, and saw it was time to go. The sisters accompanied them down the dark stairs of the *fong* and into the busy road where a rickshaw was summoned to take them back to Lim Villa. Mei Lan waved until the sisters vanished from sight, filled with a sense of loss. However dark and smelly the *fong* had been, the sisters' warmth had dispelled dreariness, and their talk was a revelation.

'How did you become "sisters"?' Mei Lan asked, wanting to prolong the Sago Lane interlude.

'We were all determined to leave the village and earn our own money. We had arranged for a sisterhood ceremony at the local temple,' Ah Siew explained as the rickshaw rattled along.

'We had to promise before Kwan Yin, the Goddess of Mercy, that we would have nothing to do with men and that the bond with our "sisters" would be stronger than with our own blood sisters. After we lit joss sticks a nun passed a comb through our hair and tied it up into a bun. This is *sor-hei,* the "comb up" ceremony. It meant we were not alone when we left our village to find work in the world, our sisters would be with us,' Ah Siew explained.

'*Sor-hei.*' Mei Lan giggled at the strange word.

'There is nothing to laugh at. Unmarried girls wear their hair in a plait. Married women tie it up in a bun. *Sor-hei* is like a marriage ceremony: we sisters are married to each other and our work. If women are not married nobody knows what to do with them. They don't fit in anywhere, they are without a use or a place.' Ah Siew was so serious that Mei Lan fell silent.

'We were saved in this way from the nunnery or the brothel, which is where we would have to go if we refused to marry,' Ah Siew added in a low voice.

Mei Lan stared at her in confusion. If what her mother's friends said about her birthmark were true, she too might never marry. Then, people would not know what to do with *her*, she would be of no use to anyone and could not escape the nunnery or the brothel like Ah Siew.

'What is a brothel?' Mei Lan demanded, but Ah Siew was disinclined to answer and turned her gaze to the road.

4

WHEN RAJ SHERMA RETURNED to Serangoon Road and Manikam's Cloth Shop where he worked, his employer was waiting impatiently for him. It would be useless to try and explain to Mr Manikam the extraordinary events of the afternoon and how he had seen not one riot but two.

'Good for nothing; only knowing how to waste time,' Manikam shouted as Raj entered. He pushed a bale of white cotton shirting angrily back on to a shelf.

'Big riot in Chinatown,' Raj explained, placing the money he had received from a maker of mosquito nets in Pagoda Street on the counter top. Manikam's specialised in muslim for curtains and netting, and was known to have the best *dhotis* on Serangoon Road. It was also a place to buy shirting material. There were no peacock-coloured silks or bright woven cottons in Manikam's. The monochrome tone of the stock, although unexciting, gave the cramped premises an air of spacious calm. It was a place in which to sit and think without distraction, and Raj was happy to do this for hours at a time.

'Riot, riot, what is this riot? How many hours are you taking for riot?' Manikam raged, his heavy black spectacles sliding down his bulbous nose as he spoke. He wiped his sweating face on a small towel that hung over one shoulder.

'Trolley and rickshaw not moving,' Raj explained.

'Legs are there,' Manikam insisted, picking up the money Raj had placed upon the counter.

'Rioters were communists,' Raj informed Manikam.

'What is that?' Manikam asked, rubbing his hands on his vest.

'Communists are killers,' Raj elaborated, remembering the old Chinese man he had escorted home and the bloody events that had punctuated his afternoon.

'We are all killers in our way,' Manikam replied.

'People were getting killed,' Raj insisted, and Manikam turned in sudden concern.

'You all right? Not getting hurt?' he asked, the edge sliding out of his roar. Reaching under the counter, he fished out a dented metal cash box to stow away the money.

'Old Chinese man on trolleybus ill with asthma, I had to help him home. This also was taking time, and then at his house another riot happened. Everywhere today there is rioting,' Raj explained. Manikam nodded, his anger abating as he counted the cash into the box. Raj would have elaborated further on the afternoon, but Manikam had lost interest now that the cash was in the box.

'It is good to help those in need. Good things come back to us, as do the bad,' Manikam counselled. Since the death of his wife the year before, his thoughts had turned religious.

'Pagoda Street man wanting more muslin to make mosquito nets. Two hundred metres or more maybe,' Raj said, knowing this was the news that was wanted. Manikam looked up with a smile.

'He has liked our muslin, now he will give regular order; he is making nets for Europeans. So many nets those people are needing. Because their skin is white and sweet all mosquito are wanting to eat them,' Manikam chuckled.

After the death of Mrs Manikam things had not gone well for Manikam. His marriage had been fruitless and he now mourned not so much a wife as the lack of a son. Ill health, the state of widower and a fall in business had brought him low. When he could no longer pay their salaries, Manikam's other two employees left. Only Raj had remained to work for three meals a day. This show of loyalty decided Manikam to treat Raj as a surrogate son. From the beginning Mrs Manikam had taken a liking to him, and had always fussed about him while she lived in a manner that annoyed her husband.

'Tomorrow I will do our accounts for this week,' Raj promised as Manikam turned the key of the cash box. Under Manikam's instruction Raj had learned how to add and subtract and balance neat columns in a large ledger. He soon found irregularities in Manikam's account books, careless mistakes that created unnecessary and sometimes shocking deficiencies. Soon, Raj's disciplined management of the business had produced small profits in a pleasing way, and almost imperceptibly control of the shop had passed from employer to employee. Manikam was happy most of the day to read a newspaper and drink tea. In the beginning Raj had slept in the shop on the counter top but recently, after Manikam had raised his salary by a small amount, he had rented one of the dark tenement cubicles upstairs. Manikam himself rented the entire ground floor of the shophouse for his business premises and living space.

Soon Manikam disappeared into a back room. Raj sat down on the chair behind the counter and, turning the tap in the earthenware water jar, filled a metal glass and drank thirstily. Now the violence of the afternoon was over and he was safely home he felt suddenly weak, as if he had been pummelled all over. In the quiet of the shop with the familiar sights and sounds of the street beyond, the alarming events of the last few hours filled his mind, and his thoughts returned to Mr Ho.

He had helped the Chinese alight from the trolley, increasingly alarmed by the man's huffing and puffing. 'Uncle, if your house far then we take a rickshaw,' Raj had suggested as the tram drew away.

The man's colour was not good and his breath continued to rattle in his chest like a bag of marbles. Demonstrators still straggled along the road murmuring angrily; outside the Kreta Ayer police station the dead bodies were being dragged to one side and covered with straw mats.

Raj hailed a rickshaw and they climbed in, squashed together on the seat. The Chinese had pushed his boater hat to the back of his head at a rakish angle, and the long hairs sprouting from the raised mole on his chin lifted as they bowled along. Both his wheezing and his courtly manner gave him the appearance of age, yet Raj judged him to be no more than forty-five.

'I have a biscuit factory near here,' Mr Ho told him, extracting a gold watch from his waistcoat pocket. The sun flashed on the long chain across his chest as he noted the time. Raj stared at the watch, at its smooth pebble-like shape, the intricacy of its fine workmanship, and vowed that one day he too would own a similar timepiece. Beneath them the runner flexed stringy muscles and suddenly picked up his pace, throwing them back in the seat.

Soon they reached Pearl's Hill and the demonstrators were left behind. Mr Ho directed the runner towards a dusty compound with a broken gate standing open upon one hinge. Above the gate was a sign that read HO PROSPERITY BISCUIT COMPANY. The rickshaw stopped before a dilapidated house behind which corrugated factory sheds were visible. Tiles were missing from the roof of Mr Ho's bungalow, and the shutters like the gate hung crookedly. A sweet smell of baking pressed about them as the rickshaw drew to a halt. Raj jumped out and helped Mr Ho down.

'You have been very kind. Have some refreshment before you go. Taste my biscuits,' Mr Ho smiled.

Raj hesitated but the vanilla-edged scent was overwhelming and after the happenings of the afternoon he was both hungry and thirsty. He followed Mr Ho up some steps and on to a veranda stacked with old chairs and wooden crates. Mrs Ho, plump and grey haired, hurried out of the house followed by her pregnant daughter-in-law, Yoshiko. As both women fussed about the breathless Mr Ho, the noise of shouting came to them from the direction of the biscuit factory behind the house. Mr Ho turned in alarm with a wheeze of distress and, ignoring Mrs Ho's pleas, hurried back down the steps and disappeared around the side of the bungalow. Mrs Ho gave a small moan and followed, her daughter-in-law and Raj trailing behind.

'What is happening?' Raj asked the young woman, from whom he caught the scent of crushed flowers. The loose shift she wore already pulled tightly across her thickening body and he realised her baby must soon be due.

'Again the workers are troubling us. The communists encourage them to strike,' the daughter-in-law explained as they hurried towards the factory, her eyes fixed on Mr and Mrs Ho a distance ahead.

Raj observed the luxuriance of her hair pulled back into a soft bun and the creamy quality of her skin, like the petals of a magnolia. Another roar from the factory made Yoshiko Ho exclaim in alarm. She broke into an awkward run, her hands supporting her heavy belly, Raj keeping pace beside her. Ragged palms fringed the two factory sheds before which a group of workers were gathered. They shouted, punching the air with a loud chant that was now all too familiar. More men were spilling out of the building to join the agitated assembly.

'They are turning today's Sun Yat-sen anniversary into a communist demonstration wherever they see an opportunity,' Mr Ho gasped as Raj and Yoshiko reached him.

'What are they saying?' Raj asked.

'Workers of the World Unite. Stand up to the Imperialist traitor Ho. Down with Ho Biscuits. Down with Imperialism,' Mr Ho replied, passing a hand wearily over his brow. With Mrs Ho hanging on to his arm, trying unsuccessfully to hold him back, he began to walk towards the unruly crowd. Yoshiko gave a groan and crossed her hands protectively over her swollen belly. Raj hurried forward beside Mr Ho who was wheezing alarmingly again.

'Send Yoshiko back inside – who knows where this may lead!' Mr Ho shouted to his wife before turning an anxious face to Raj.

'Feelings are high and our daughter-in-law is Japanese. There are always mixed feelings about the Japanese. We have had many boycotts of Japanese goods in the last few years,' Mr Ho explained, squeezing out words between asthmatic rasps.

Work in the factory sheds with their boiling vats of syrup and baking ovens was hot and sweaty labour. The men now facing Mr Ho were stripped to the waist, but the powerful sight of so many gleaming muscular bodies massed together, alert and waiting, did not deter him. He walked forward, hatted and spatted and wheezing, the watch chain across his linen waistcoat gleaming in the sun. From the factory sheds the mouth-watering smell of Ho Biscuits continued to float above the angry men with their loud cries of *Imperialist Ho*.

'Listen to me,' Mr Ho shouted, but his voice quickly sank beneath the din. The workers moved restively, the blood high in their faces, determined to be free of the dark hot shacks where they toiled all day long. A banner of crudely daubed characters was suddenly waved in Mr Ho's face, forcing him to retreat a short distance. Raj watched in alarm as Mr Ho gasped and clutched at his chest, and in sudden concern stepped forward to face the angry men.

'Listen to him,' Raj roared, and his unfamiliar presence had an instant effect. The workers stopped to stare at his short, burly frame, and the shouting died down. Mr Ho took advantage of the lull to put his case to the men.

'I am no different from you. We are all Chinese brothers. I am not an Imperialist. This is not the way to improve our lot,' Mr Ho wheezed with as much force as he could muster, but even as he spoke a loud heckling began, drummed up by the two most prominent agitators.

'Freedom is found in working hard and taking opportunities,' Mr Ho implored, but the shouting continued.

'Down with Imperialist exploitation! Demand better wages from the dog Ho. He eats pork and duck while we have no money for rice,' a young man shouted. Mr Ho gasped in shock at this new accusation and the cheers that it released.

'I am not a rich man. You have seen the mansions of rich men. You know I do not live like that. If you have complaints come and talk to me. Let us stop this nonsense and get back to work. The biscuits will burn.' Mr Ho panted, anxious now to get inside the factory for he knew only too well the smell of an over-baked biscuit. At this appeal the men hesitated, allowing Mr Ho to enter the shed. Raj hurried after him.

A fiery, vanilla-scented world enfolded them as they entered the darkness of the sweltering factory. Bare light bulbs dangling on long wires from the corrugated metal roof could not alleviate the gloom. After the brightness outside Raj was momentarily blinded, even as his head reeled with the intoxicating aromas. As sight returned he saw large cauldrons of boiling pineapple jam perched precariously over flaming burners. The syrup bubbled with soft sucking sounds; the scent of scalding sugar ran hotly through him. Long tables of rolled dough cut to the shape of hearts or rabbits were visible, as were battalions of chocolate fingers waiting their turn in the oven. Ancient conveyor belts that appeared to be fashioned from bicycle chains chugged and clanked incessantly around the shed. The angry men now encircled their employer shaking their fists and kicking up dust from the earthen floor that then fell upon the biscuits.

'Biscuits are burning,' Mr Ho cried in a trembling voice, stepping towards the ovens from which a charred smell was emerging. In desperation he pushed his way into the crowd before him, hitting out to right and left. His watch was knocked from his pocket and flailed about on its long chain, the straw hat was tipped forward and he reached to hold it in place. As he neared the ovens the agitators crowded closer chanting slogans again. A man brandishing a bamboo pole moved forward and, with a loud cry, brought the cane down on Mr Ho's head. The boater fell apart as neatly as a cut sponge cake and blood spurted up from Mr Ho's skull. At the sight of this blood the crowd abruptly fell silent and drew back. Mr Ho staggered and lurched, finally collapsing in the hot space before the oven.

Mrs Ho, who was hovering nervously about the factory door, gave a shriek and ran forward and dropped to her knees, cushioning her husband's head in her lap. Mr Ho's crushed and battered boater lay a short distance away and Raj stared at the hat in shock, remembering the Chief Inspector's sun helmet in the road at Kreta Ayer. For the second time that day he had watched a man swatted like a fly by an angry mob.

The communist agitators began shouting again but Mr Ho's workers, observing their injured employer, appeared confused. There was a sudden move towards the ovens and the doors were pulled open. Immediately, a cloud of black smoke billowed out like fire from a belching dragon. Mr Ho's nose twitched, he opened his eyes and groaned. Seeing that all momentum was gone, the two main agitators, professional men sent to work up the crowd, disappeared as innocuously as they had come. At their departure Mr Ho's employees carried him out of the shed and back into the house.

He was placed upon a rattan couch and cushions were stacked behind him. A servant brought water and first aid, and Mrs Ho bandaged her husband's head with enough wadding to make a turban. Yoshiko poured jasmine tea into a tall mug and Mr Ho was persuaded to take a sip. Slowly, he revived and turned to Raj who sat nervously on the edge of a chair.

'My son Luke went to Ipoh yesterday. If he had been here he would have stood up to those ruffians. It is a sign of the times we now live in that such a thing could happen. I came to this place on the deck of a ship, just like my workers. In my village in China I tilled the land with my father, just as they did. At ten I left school to help my illiterate parents. I became a hawker selling vegetables my father grew and the oysters and crabs I collected each day.' Mr Ho's eyes grew moist and Mrs Ho begged him to put a stop to remembering.

Yoshiko refilled the cups and offered Raj a plate of Ho biscuits. As she stood before him he caught her light flowery scent again and glanced up into her face. She nodded her head and gave a slight smile; he looked away quickly, disturbed by the fullness of her lips. Staring down at the assortment of crisply baked shapes, he chose one with a bright red centre. As he picked it up he remembered a packet of similar biscuits his father had bought from a salesman who came to his stall on the road into Naganagar, near Raj's village in India. The stall sold rice and wheat, betel nut and gram, chillies, sherbet powder, nails and soap, tin buckets, brooms and sugar; everyday things needed in the village. His father had done some favour for the salesman and in return was given the biscuits. The packet was wrapped in pink waxy paper and the biscuits inside were encrusted with ants. Raj and his sister Leila had brushed the insects from the pastry, savouring the sweet taste, chewing slowly. He saw again the crumbs about his sister's lips and the red stain of the jam on her tongue.

'Everyone has come to this place with hope in his heart.' Mr Ho sighed and sipped his tea.

'I too came here to Singapore on the deck of a ship, sun on my head all day. I was twelve years old,' Raj remembered.

'We dreamed of a better place and followed that dream, and many have found it,' Mr Ho nodded agreement.

'But you are such an educated man, a rich man.' Raj was surprised when Mr Ho shook his head.

'When I arrived here I found a job in a biscuit factory. That is how I came to know about biscuits. One day I got into a fight and was left for dead. An English missionary, Reverend Luke Bartholomew, found me and nursed me back to health. He was a great man and took a liking to me and paid for me to go to a mission school here in Singapore. I studied hard and passed all the exams, and I converted also to Christianity for it was this faith that changed my life. Reverend Bartholomew gave me the name of Joseph when I was baptised. He persuaded his mission to send me to England for further study. I stayed there three years and learned many things.' Mr Ho leaned back against the cushions, exhausted.

'He needs to sleep now,' Mrs Ho said; she bustled forward, impatient for Raj to be gone.

'Come back and see me again. You are a good boy,' Mr Ho mumbled sleepily as Raj stood up.

His thirst quenched, Raj placed the tall metal glass on the counter in Manikam's shop and wiped his mouth on the back of his hand. In his mind the smell of burning biscuits lingered as he puzzled over Mr Ho and the many events of the afternoon. That a man who came from such frugal beginnings could now own a biscuit factory and be called an Imperialist seemed a strange achievement. Raj thought with trepidation about his own life and what the future might hold. Although so much was already behind him, the way ahead lay uncharted. The events of the afternoon reminded him that life was precarious. He knew then that he must always keep small goals before him, like stepping stones stretching into the distance to whatever destination awaited him.

Raj began tidying the newspapers and old bags kept on the counter for wrapping purchases, and stared out of the open front of Manikam's shop on to Serangoon Road. The light was fading fast and the clunk of milk churns being washed was heard from a nearby dairy; dogs barked, cows mooed, goats bleated and babies cried. Stewed all day beneath the sun, the stench of animal excrement, rotting vegetables and fish bones enveloped the road as always. As evening approached the aroma of frying onions and spices thickened the air. When Raj first arrived on this road the proximity of these familiar smells had comforted him, as did the dark skins of people like himself.

Across the road from Manikam's, Subramanium the parrot astrologer still sat at his stall beneath the shady colonnade called the five-foot way, chopping chillies for his birds. As Raj watched he opened a rusted tobacco tin to retrieve a few swatted flies for his parrots, adding them to the chillies he fed the birds to improve their intelligence. He was a tall man with a thin neck and a stained white *dhoti*, strands of grey hair pushed through the holes in his vest. In the cages his parrots scratched for seeds and grumbled.

'These are good parrots. Not all parrots are good for fortune telling,' Subramanium always said. When a customer stopped, Subrimanium at once picked up a pack of dog-eared cards depicting Indian deities and opened the cage for a parrot to emerge. Strutting about in an ungainly dance the creature cocked its head flirtatiously whenever a fortune had to be told. Subramanium fanned out the cards on the tabletop and the bird dipped its head to choose one, picking it up in its beak.

Subramanium had been the first person Raj met on Serangoon Road and he still retained the aura of a mentor. When the long sea journey from India was over and Raj set foot again on firm land, the enormity of what lay ahead had come down upon him for the first time. Not only his village but also the whole great land of India was lost to him over the momentous swell of the sea. He had lived his life in a village, a group of mud-walled huts about a well; a few hundred yards this way or that and the place ended. There was nothing then but the land, stretching dry and brown and endless to the horizon. Everything had been all right until the fever came and killed his mother and his brother. Within a year the fever returned to take his father, leaving Raj, his seven-year-old sister Leila, and their grandmother. A neighbour bought his father's dry goods stall. Raj accepted the money he was given, knowing no way to bargain for more.

He was old enough to work but there was nothing for him in the village. The scouts who sometimes came to recruit labour for the faraway places said he was too young for their kind of work. They came on a decorated cart beating a drum as if on their way to a festival. They gave a fistful of silver to the families of men who went with them. One of the scouts, sympathetic to Raj's plight, explained how he could go to the faraway places by himself, and return to his village a rich man. He described the large towns of Penang and Ipoh and Singapore, and how men had only to arrive there for wealth to fall into their hands; they returned to their villages with enough money to build a temple and acquire a bride.

The man helped Raj buy a ticket to Calcutta with the money from the sale of his father's stall and also a passage on a boat. Raj had never seen a train before. So great was his excitement on the long journey to Calcutta that he hardly noticed the discomfort of the crowded carriage, or the engine soot that blew in through the window to blacken his face. He struggled to comprehend the great vistas of land continuously sucked away behind him, and then to understand the conglomeration of humanity and buildings that was Calcutta, the first large town he had ever seen.

As with the train ride, the ocean journey was lightened for Raj by the wonders that surrounded him. The way was strewn with miracles; the size of the ocean and its moods, one moment reflective as glass, the next seething with rage. He stared for hours into the foamy wake of the ship; sometimes, a fish leapt from the depths or dolphins appeared and kept pace with the vessel. And always the sunset came down in a magnificent way, dissolving him, just as the world was dissolved on that strange cusp of the day. It was only the night he dreaded, for in the dark the ship heaved and shuddered. He was twelve years old and fear of the future lay like a stone in his belly.

He remembered a man called Dinesh, recruited to work on rubber or pineapple plantations in Malaya, who had taken him under his wing when he boarded the ship. He told Raj to spread his mat alongside his own and when the urine of a nearby baby trickled over the deck, Dinesh shouted at the mother to cover its bottom or hold it out over a rag. He and his friends shared their food with him, and Raj carried drinking and shaving water to the men. Raj learned to play cards and learned about women as he sat listening to them on the burning deck each day. But at last they arrived, and the island that had existed for so long in his mind was beneath his feet.

On the quay he had sat upon his bundle of belongings and tried to stifle his panic, not knowing where to go. At last, a kindly Tamil had given him a ride on a bullock cart filled with bales of cotton. When their ways diverged Raj tried not to show his apprehension as he clambered off the cart.

'Go to Serangoon Road, all Indians live there. Find Subramanium, the parrot astrologer,' the driver advised.

Raj had picked up his bundle and taken his first steps in the direction the man pointed out. Ramshackle buildings lined narrow roads overflowing with people, carts and rickshaws. At last he had come into wider streets where imposing buildings of graceful architecture dwarfed a man. For the first time Raj had seen large wheeled motor cars and trams. These sights had taken his breath away.

On that first day Subramanium received him brusquely. 'I have no work for you. I am not a charity. Ask around for work like everyone else. Nowadays young people are lazy,' he barked. His stall was pushed up against the wall of a shophouse under the shade of the five-foot way.

Already dusk was descending. It had been a long walk from where the bullock cart dropped him. Raj had stopped only once to rest beneath a banyan tree, eating the remains of some rice rolled in a piece of paper. He looked up at the darkening sky; his legs ached, his head ached and his stomach was empty. Thoughts of his grandmother and his sister Leila, so far away from him now, overwhelmed him. On Serangoon Road oil lamps were lit as the dusk tumbled into night. Raj lay down, exhausted, stretching out on the pavement. He awoke the next morning to Subramanium's bare toe in a filthy sandal prodding his ribs. The man had bought him some breakfast wrapped in a banana leaf and when, after days of trying, no proper work materialised, had persuaded Manikam of Manikam's Cloth Shop to employ Raj as an assistant.

Later that evening, Raj made his way along Serangoon Road towards Sri Perumal temple to make a delivery of several muslin *dhoti* to the chief priest there. There were no communists on Serangoon Road and the place, like Manikam himself, had little interest in the riots at Kreta Ayer and indeed had not heard of Sun Yat-sen. Raj knew the name only because his friend Krishna, the letter writer, was interested in revolutionaries and had once briefly and dangerously lived such a life himself.

Once he had made the delivery, Raj did not immediately return to Manikam's but walked towards the premises of a garland maker beside the temple. Most evenings Krishna was to be found here beneath the temple's colourful pagoda of gods, taking dictation from the illiterate, writing letters to their families in India. Sitting as he did outside the garland maker's shop with flowers heaped around him, the sweet perfume of jasmine filling the air and the gods looking down upon him, Krishna had acquired the reputation of unworldly status. His work as a schoolmaster at the Ramakrishna Mission further added to his aura as did his tall, lean frame and deep faraway eyes. People came to him not only for the writing of letters but to consult about marriages, horoscopes and ailments, or for mediation in family quarrels.

When Manikam had finally realised his dependence upon Raj, he had agreed to him taking English and Mathematics lessons from Krishna for a nominal fee. Manikam himself was a literate man, and he viewed the education of Raj as a business investment from which he expected to reap a good profit. Raj had proved an avid pupil, quickly building on the rudimentary education he had received in his village schoolroom. He carried his books with him throughout the day, poring over them at every opportunity behind the counter of Manikam's Cloth Shop and by an oil lamp late into the night. Krishna could not resist such a willing pupil and soon would take nothing for these lessons, much to Manikam's satisfaction.

'My reward will be to see him thrive,' Krishna told Raj and Manikam. A friendship developed between them, Krishna treating Raj like a younger brother, and even when Raj no longer had need of Krishna's lessons, they continued to meet.

Now, as Krishna was still busy Raj waited, sitting on a low wall beside a trinket stall piled with gaudy glass bangles. Watching Krishna scratch away with his pen, head bent to his board, listening to the dictation of the men crouched at his feet, Raj remembered the days when he too had waited for Krishna to write a letter for him to his sister Leila. In the darkness the booths and small shops of Serangoon Road were lit by a blaze of oil lamps. The fake diamonds and gaudy gold chains of the trinket stall gleamed seductively. Once, this had been largely a road of men who left their families in India, but times were changing and people had prospered. Those who could afford it were now bringing their wives from India to live on the road, and jewellery appeared to be the first thing they needed. Beside the rows of new shophouses that had sprung up, attap-roofed dwellings, dairies or wheat-grinding sheds still stood next to enclosures for animals servicing the dairies and the slaughterhouse near the mosque. Behind Serangoon Road lay the racecourse, and horses were kept in the road's many stables; bleating goats and wandering cows continually obstructed the thoroughfare. Eventually Krishna was free of his clients and Raj hurried towards him to blurt out his news.

'Communist demonstration at Kreta Ayer. Police shooting guns and some Chinese killed.' Raj beamed, proud to be the bearer of news he knew would be of importance to Krishna.

'Communists? A demonstration?' Krishna stopped, a bottle of ink in his hand, and stared excitedly at Raj over wire-rimmed spectacles. Only those who knew him closely were aware that Krishna, in spite of his scholarly reputation, was a secret revolutionary. He was well schooled in the writings of Marx and Lenin, and while still in India had been deeply influenced by the fiery rhetoric of the young revolutionary Subhas Chandra Bose. Bose had spoken at a student conference and his words had so inspired Krishna that he had turned to anti-British activities with a local revolutionary cell.

'Demonstration was big, many hundreds of men, all shouting and ready to kill. These communists are dangerous people,' Raj replied. Krishna shook his head dismissively as he thrust a cork into the bottle of ink and placed it in a basket along with his pens.

'Just like us Indians, the communists also struggle for freedom from colonial rule,' Krishna answered; his hair stood up in a curly halo about his head and he had an intense, owlish appearance. Picking up his stool and writing board, he strode forward in the direction of the garland maker's shop where he rented storage space amongst dripping buckets of flowers. He had been forced to leave India when a plot he was involved in, to blow up a British government official, was foiled. Krishna's family were educated people and had found the means to smuggle him out of India as the police came after him.

'Communists are killers,' Raj decided. He tried to understand Krishna's view of the communists but found he could not agree. Watching the garland maker's goat nibble some crumpled paper at Krishna's feet, he recalled the unbridled violence of the day, the bloodied hats that had punctuated his afternoon and their wounded owners, the Chief Inspector and Mr Ho, and knew he was not wrong.

5

THE MEMORY OF HER visit to Ah Siew's *kongsi fong* continued to absorb Mei Lan. On their return to Lim Villa, Ah Siew put her straight to bed after a light meal of rice porridge. The next morning Mei Lan struggled to surface from sleep. Frightening dreams had buffeted her about all night and she awoke still tired and fractious. As she opened her eyes to the day the strange and jumbled images of her dreams dissolved, and she saw with relief that Ah Siew had already drawn the curtains at the window and the sun streamed in. A pair of golden orioles perched in the branches of the tree outside; a blue dragonfly hovered against a blue sky.

Mei Lan pushed back the covers and stretched. Ah Siew was already laying out her clothes and directing her to the bathroom. It was Tuesday, Ah Siew reminded her, and they would spend the afternoon with Second Grandmother. Tuesday was Second Grandmother's foot day. She liked Ah Siew to bathe her feet and bind them up in fresh bandages. This was not Ah Siew's work for she was exclusively Mei Lan's *amah*. Mei Lan's mother, Ei Ling, grumbled at the hijacking of her servant but Second Grandmother's word was law. Second Grandmother owned three slave girls who were at her service day and night, but she said only Ah Siew's gentle hands could soothe the pain of unbinding her broken feet. Mei Lan accompanied Ah Siew to Second Grandmother's quarters on Tuesday if her mother was out dancing or dining or playing mah-jong; now she was in Hong Kong and her protest could not be heard.

After lunch Ah Siew took hold of Mei Lan's hand for the journey through Lim Villa to Second Grandmother's quarters. Stairs must be climbed, corridors travelled and the great ballroom crossed. The large reception rooms lived in permanent gloom, curtains drawn against a sun that faded upholstery from Paris and carpets from China. On rainy days Mei Lan played in these dim rooms with her elder brother JJ, their rubber ball bouncing amongst Ming porcelain, bronze ornaments and nude nymphets of Italian marble. The place filled Mei Lan with melancholy. She hated the fusty smell of damp upholstery and the rotting wheat and onion pellets strewn about to deter the cockroaches.

Beyond the ballroom was the door to Grandfather's jade museum, housed in a part of Lim Villa that had been built especially for this purpose. Glass cases lined the room displaying the precious stone carvings. Sometimes, Mei Lan crept unseen into the museum to gaze at its extraordinary contents. In the shuttered half-light the smooth green stone exuded a strange opalescence. Mei Lan's mother wore a small jade pendant as a protective amulet; it had been taken from amongst the bones of her grandmother during the cleaning of her grave, long after her flesh was rotted and gone. Jade was a stone of magical properties prized above all else, Grandfather Lim Hock An had told Mei Lan. He had bought his first piece decades before with the initial profit he earned from his tin mine.

Lim Hock An had been a tall, muscular man when he arrived in Malaya from China at the turn of the century, to work as a coolie in a tin mine near Ipoh. His intelligence was apparent to everyone; he rose quickly to the position of coolie supervisor and eventually began to prospect for tin on his own. As he hacked his way through the jungle with little relief from heat or the throttling vegetation, his slender resources were soon exhausted; he was ready to give up when he struck his first deposit. After that he had the luck to strike it again and again. Soon he was the owner of several large tin mines and employed coolies of his own. When his parents died he brought his wife Chwee Gek from China to join him. She handled the money, paid the coolies and did the accounts for she had some slender education. An American missionary couple in her home village had opened a school for girls; Chwee Gek had been allowed to go for a while to learn about numbers and letters. In later years, Lim Hock An got himself teachers and more education than his wife. He had a zeal for education that only the uneducated know. Although he never learned to read or write fluently, he sent his son to study in England and built schools that bore his name in China. He belonged to a generation that left their homeland in order to survive, but wherever they landed and lived, always looked back to China. Singapore was never more than a temporary place to acquire wealth before returning home. Now, trailing after Ah Siew,

Mei Lan passed the closed door of the Jade Museum and thought of the green magic pulsating within.

Lim Villa appeared pinned to the ground by its four octagonal turrets. In the upper rooms of these towers the Lim family had their separate quarters. Lim Hock An occupied one tower and Second Grandmother another; Mei Lan with her family lived in a third. Although the fourth turret lay empty for the use of guests, it was said that Lim Hock An was merely biding his time and soon this area would house a new wife. Such gossip was not mentioned before Second Grandmother – any thought of an additional wife in the house drove her to shout dementedly and claw at her slave girls until their blood ran.

Second Grandmother's rooms exuded a powerful smell of heady French perfume, the medicated lineament rubbed on to her arthritic limbs and the opium she regularly smoked. One by one Mei Lan liked each of these smells, but together they combined to make her head ache. When at last Mei Lan and Ah Siew entered her quarters, Second Grandmother was waiting for them seated on a black lacquer chair, regal in embroidered silk. At the sight of Mei Lan her face creased in a smile, revealing her many gold teeth. Mei Lan approached for the kiss Second Grandmother expected, and was forced to examine her at close range. Tobacco discoloured her remaining teeth and her breath was soured by opium. Mei Lan concentrated on the smell of the perfume that was always strongest about her ears. As Second Grandmother held her close and whispered words of affection, Mei Lan tried to remember the impossible name of her perfume. *Schiaparelli*. Sometimes she managed to remember the whole name, and sometimes there was no more in her head than a *Schia* . . . and nothing could get her beyond it. A forest of embroidered pink peonies covered Grandmother's long *sam* and matching trousers; jade earrings green as spinach and lit with diamonds hung from her ears. Jade covered her wrists and more diamonds her fingers; pins of silver fili-gree speared her upswept hair. Second Grandmother appeared encrusted all over by workmanship. Even the black lacquer chair she sat upon was thickly inlaid with mother-of-pearl.

'So late. *Aiiyah*, my feet are aching. Waiting so long.' While she embraced Mei Lan, Second Grandmother rebuked Ah Siew.

At once Ah Siew hurried to check that the towels and bandages, the water boiled with monkey bones and the soft red sleeping slippers placed side by side, were ready. Then, two of Second Grandmother's young *mui sai* gently levered her up from the chair to begin the journey across the room, their mistress swaying painfully between them upon her tiny feet. Sometimes, Second Grandmother's feet were too painful to bear her weight and she demanded to be carried. At these times she mounted a slave girl's back to be taken to the garden or the dining room; she rarely went out of the house. Only women with big feet went out of the house, she always said in disapproval. Once she was installed again in a chair Second Grandmother called for Mei Lan to sit near her. Mei Lan noticed that tonight only the *mui sai,* Gold and Silver, attended Second Grandmother and that Little Sparrow was absent.

'Where is Little Sparrow?' Mei Lan asked. Little Sparrow was Second Grandmother's prettiest slave girl. Behind her Gold and Silver giggled, Ah Siew turned to look sharply at the girls, who bit their lips and fell silent. Ah Siew tested the temperature of the water, adding spoonfuls of ground almonds, mulberry root, frankincense and white balsam; her hand disappeared into the milky water, mixing in the oil and herbs.

'Little Sparrow has gone to the nunnery; she was getting too fat. When she is thin she can come back,' Second Grandmother answered tartly. At the mention of the word 'nunnery', Mei Lan's interest was alerted.

'I never heard of going to a nunnery for being fat,' Mei Lan replied in surprise. She had thought a nunnery was a place of praying women, a refuge for the sick or homeless or unmarried girls like Ah Siew's sisters.

'Ssh, Little Goose. It is rude to ask questions,' Ah Siew whispered.

'A nunnery serves many purposes,' Second Grandmother added more kindly. Behind her Gold and Silver smothered another giggle and Grandmother turned to glare at them.

The girls were dressed identically in floral *samfoo*. Their hair, plaited in pigtails, hung over their breasts and a thick fringe covered most of their brow. Little Sparrow had always been similarly attired and Mei Lan had not noticed that she was fat, only that her eyes were bright, her lips a soft red and that when she smiled dimples pricked her cheeks. Now, with the knowledge she had gained from Ah Siew and her friends, Mei Lan appraised the girls anew. Gold and Silver and Little Sparrow must all have been sold by their parents for a bag of rice or a few coins when they were seven or eight years old, just like Ah Siew's sisters. Now, Little Sparrow was already fifteen and Gold and Silver thirteen years old. Sorrow for the girls and horror at their plight blew hot and cold inside Mei Lan. What would *she* feel, what would *she* do if her parents decided to sell her? Worse than this was the realisation that it was her own grandfather who had bought the girls as a present for Second Grandmother. That one person could be bought as a gift for another filled her anew with distress.

Mei Lan looked down at the opaque broth of long-boiled monkey bones awaiting the immersion of Second Grandmother's feet. Whenever she was given chicken soup she remembered this bowl of perfumed broth, and was unable to eat. Ah Siew stirred more scented oil into the water and an astringent smell drifted up. Second Grandmother's feet were the ideal three inches in length that society had once demanded, and were small enough to rest in Ah Siew's palm. The *amah* slipped off the tiny embroidered shoe and began to unwind the bandages. Second Grandmother groaned and stared grimly at the unbound feet of her slave girls.

'How lucky you modern girls are; no need to bind your feet. In my day a man looked only at your feet. If you had a tiny foot and an ugly face you could make a better marriage than if you had a big foot and a beautiful face. Nowadays, men judge beauty only from a face. Everyone has gone mad.' She spoke through clenched teeth and then roared at Ah Siew.

'*Aiiyah*, don't tear at the bindings like that.'

The bandages criss-crossed Grandmother's feet in a figure of eight, pulling her heel towards her toes, pushing up the arch, which had finally snapped allowing both ends of a foot to meet. Mei Lan took a deep breath and held it for, as the bandages were unwound, an unbearable stench was released. Ah Siew unravelled the bindings, until the tiny hoof-like protuberances that were Grandmother's feet were at last revealed. Second Grandmother was now breathing hard for the pain of release seemed almost to equal the pain of confinement.

'My feet were bound at the age of five. *Aiiyah*, I remember it still. Nowadays Government has stopped foot binding, but I have heard there are men who still want women with lotus feet,' Second Grandmother announced, proudly surveying the crushed stumps as the final bandage was removed.

'Didn't your mother know how much it hurt you?' Mei Lan asked. She could not imagine her own mother putting her through such torture.

'My mother was far away, but had she been there she too would have done what every mother did for a daughter to find a good husband.' Second Grandmother's silk trousers were pushed up high and she scratched her bare knee with a long painted nail. The soft calves of her legs were wasted, but her thighs were muscular beneath the silk from the peculiar gait she was forced to adopt to walk on her tiny feet.

'The Master married me for my feet. Feet as small as mine can drive a man crazy. Look at my beautiful little red dumplings, my golden lilies, my lotus buds.' Second Grandmother stuck out her legs and crooned to her mangled feet.

'If your mother was so far away, who bound your feet and took care of you?' Mei Lan insisted.

'Oh, an aunty.' Second Grandmother always swept aside questions about her family. She had no stories to tell of her village in China like Ah Siew, and never mentioned brothers or sisters. Everyone, even Gold and Silver and Little Sparrow, had memories of a former life to root them in the world. Only Second Grandmother's past appeared hermetically sealed. It was as if she had sprung from nowhere into marriage with Lim Hock An. The only thing that Mei Lan knew was that, before she became Second Grandmother, her name had been Lustrous Pearl.

'Why an aunty? Was your mother dead? Did you live in the aunty's house, in the aunty's village?' Mei Lan was full of questions.

'Ssh, Little Goose. Learn some manners, it is rude to question an elder,' Ah Siew said, turning sternly upon Mei Lan.

'Where did you meet Grandfather?' Mei Lan ignored the *amah*'s admonishment and tried another line of attack.

'I was just fourteen when the Master saw me. He said he had never seen feet like my little lotuses. Once he drank wine from my shoe.' Second Grandmother smiled a secret smile as Ah Siew steered her 'red dumplings' into the bowl of scented water, then sighed in relief as the *amah* massaged almond oil into her callused skin and the crevice between heel and toes.

'You married Grandfather when you were fourteen?' Mei Lan asked, wondering how anyone could drink wine from a shoe, let alone a shoe that held such a stinking mutilated foot.

'The Master preferred me above all the others,' Second Grandmother replied softly.

'What others?' Mei Lan frowned, petulant with frustration. 'If you were fourteen then you were younger than Little Sparrow is now.'

Second Grandmother's expression was suddenly so fierce that Mei Lan retreated into silence. Grandmother's past was shrouded in silence and not even Ah Siew would explain it to her. It seemed all of life's real knowledge must be gathered piecemeal from adults, like parts of a jigsaw that she must later assemble. The knowledge about the sale of girls, picked up so inadvertently in the *kongsi fong*, she had already slipped into its rightful place to illuminate many new things.

Gold cleared away the dirty bandages and Second Grandmother gave a sigh of contentment as the warmth of the oily water relieved her aching feet. Silver sprayed a little of Second Grandmother's precious *Schiaparelli* perfume into the room to freshen the air, holding up the crystal bottle and pressing the rubber bulb held in a tasselled yellow net. It must be dreadful, Mei Lan thought, taking her first deep breath of the evening, not to be able to wriggle your toes but to have them lying in five flat strips almost under your heel.

On these Tuesday afternoons it was Mei Lan's duty to help prepare Second Grandmother's pipe. Grandfather's opium was of the very best quality, and was kept buried in the garden beneath a tall tree where it aged in the earth as wine aged in a dark cellar. Mei Lan ran to where Silver crouched over a small bowl of muddy opiate, preparing to heat the *chandu* on a long needle over a flame.

Mei Lan took the needle from her, rolling a pellet of the sticky black tar between her fingers and fixing it expertly on to the needle. She knew just what to do, and was already as deft as Gold or Silver at roasting the needle's precious cargo until it smoked and spluttered. Soon, bubbles covered the pellet and a pungency dense as velvet, cloying as molasses, filled Mei Lan's nose and lit the very centre of her. Afterwards, Mei Lan scrubbed her hands so that no clue remained of her work in Second Grandmother's quarters. Her mother did not approve of the opium habit and knew nothing of her daughter's willing assistance.

Soon Grandmother, now changed into her pale silk nightclothes, was carried to the smoking couch upon Gold's back, her freshly bandaged feet in red satin bed slippers sticking out each side of the *mui sai*'s hips.

Second Grandmother was considerably larger than tiny Gold and the slave girl bent low beneath her weight. Silver hurried forward and together they lowered their mistress on to the bed of cushions.

'My pipe, my pipe,' Grandmother groaned, holding out her hand. Mei Lan held the needle steady; the drug was now bubbling hard and she carefully placed the hot pellet of *chandu* in the jade bowl of the pipe while Second Grandmother sucked hungrily at the ivory tip. Refilling the pipe was a laborious process and Gold soon took over the duty. Already, Second Grandmother's eyes had grown glassy as her dreams expanded.

Mei Lan looked around for Ah Siew but she had left the room on an errand. She made her way to Grandmother's great red lacquer bed and scrambled up to stretch out upon its soft pillows. Usually, a small stepping box was pushed up against the bed to enable Second Grandmother to climb in more easily. Now, the box stood to one side and Mei Lan pulled herself up as best she could. Settling upon the cool silk covers, she looked up at the carved bower of leaves and flowers on the wooden canopy above, a long-throated phoenix nesting at its centre. Only a single phoenix was allowed to exist in the world at any one time, Ah Siew had told her, and it never lived less than five hundred years. When death approached the phoenix built a nest, settled upon it and set it on fire. When the flames had almost consumed the poor creature, a new phoenix sprang to life from the smouldering pyre. Ah Siew said the phoenix was a creature for women to emulate and when things got really bad in your life, it should be remembered. Women were like phoenixes, always rising anew from the ashes of their lives, Ah Siew said. Mei Lan stared up at the phoenix, at the great wings and strong beak and fabulous tail and was stirred by its strange, wild soul, its power to transform death into life. She wished she had a phoenix to look down upon her each night, like Second Grandmother in her bed. Her mother had given her a fan with a delicate painting of the creature. The fan had belonged to First Grandmother, who had been Mei Lan's father's mother and who had died when he was ten. The subject of First Grandmother was rather like the subject of Second Grandmother's past. Nobody spoke about her.

While Second Grandmother dozed, Gold and Silver cleared the room chatting softly with each other. Mei Lan listened and her attention, drawn away from the phoenix, fell upon the Second Grandmother's footstool. She saw it had a drawer in its side that was usually hidden against the bed. She knelt down beside it, curious to know what the drawer contained. Pulling it open she found a folded square of soft muslin wrapped about another set of sleeping slippers. The red silk was embroidered like all of Grandmother's shoes, but the lining of these secret slippers was equally adorned, painted with tiny scenes of an extraordinary nature. Mei Lan had to turn the shoes almost inside out to get a proper perspective. In the pictures men and women were coupled together in unbelievable postures. The same images were repeated in much larger detail in the book that lay at the back of the drawer. Here, within ricepaper covers were revealed paintings of a strange violence. People sat pressed together half clothed, an arm or a thigh flung out of a curtain of draperies. In other pictures their robes lay discarded and, divested of their colourful attire, naked bodies were white and vulnerable as larvae. In these pictures bare limbs were strangely entwined, bent almost double, spreadeagled apart or wrapped acrobatically about each other. The women wore the elaborate hairstyles and intricate robes of Chinese history and their expressions were always decorous. Yet they displayed the most secret parts of themselves with such flamboyance it caused Mei Lan's heart to beat and her cheeks to flame. All the men had the same long barb protruding from them and the women offered themselves up to be impaled upon it.

Absorbed in the book, Mei Lan did not hear Silver unexpectedly approaching until it was too late. Silver laughed, kneeling down beside Mei Lan.

'That was Mistress's pillow book. It must have served her well in the brothel and also with Ancient Master,' Silver giggled, wrapping the muslin neatly about the slippers once more.

'What is a brothel?' Mei Lan frowned in confusion. It was the second time in two days the word had been mentioned, she was determined to know where it was that Ah Siew's sisters had been sent.

'It's a place where men go and pay money to do all these bad things to women.' Silver leaned forward so that her mouth was near Mei Lan's ear and pointed to the book Mei Lan had thrust back into the drawer.

'It's where Ancient Mistress lived before she came to the House of Lim. She was sold to the brothel before she was five. In the brothel they called her Lustrous Pearl. When she came of age it is said Ancient

Master paid a great price for her because of her tiny feet. Even though it's illegal now, I've heard some girls in brothels still have their feet bound to please old men who want such things. They say Ancient Master paid also to be your grandmother's first man.'

'Why is Little Sparrow fat and in a nunnery?' Mei Lan asked, swallowing hard, sensing this was the moment to secure the elusive replies to those questions no one would answer.

'Because soon she will have a baby. Ancient Mistress is so angry she will not have her in the house.' Silver pushed the drawer shut and stood up.

'Why can't she stay in the house?' Mei Lan was excited at the thought of Little Sparrow's baby.

'Because it is Ancient Master's baby. If the baby is a boy Little Sparrow will become Ancient Master's concubine or maybe even his wife. Then Little Sparrow would be your Third Grandmother and her baby would be your uncle. If this happens then Little Sparrow too will wear jade earrings and an embroidered *sam* and eat bird's-nest soup like Ancient Mistress. Sometimes Ancient Master looks at me now in the way he used to look at Little Sparrow. One day, if I have a baby boy by Ancient Master, then maybe I will become your Fourth Grandmother.'

'How do you get a baby?' Mei Lan's voice sank lower with each question she asked, for she was dreading now to hear the answers. Silver looked at her in some surprise.

'Why, by doing what they are doing in those pictures of course, silly. Didn't you know that already?' Silver laughed out loud.

It was too horrible. Silver's laughing mouth grew wider. Mei Lan stared at the soft wet tongue, and the dark hollow of her throat leading down deep into her body, to secret places and secret processes. It was more than she could bear. Leaving Silver staring after her in surprise, Mei Lan ran from the room. On her opium bed Second Grandmother did not stir, her eyes wide but seeing nothing. Gold still sat before the lamp roasting the *chandu* over the flame, refilling the pipe that Grandmother grasped with her long red nails. The door stood open, but as she turned out into the dark corridor Mei Lan collided with Ah Siew, returning to the room.

'What's the matter, Little Goose?' Ah Siew opened her arms, enfolding the child.

Against the familiar warmth of the *amah*'s breast Mei Lan could at last unravel the tangled threads knotted up within her. The words came out in no order and made no sense, although the thoughts were clear in her head. People could be sold like onions or fish or a length of cloth. Her own grandfather had paid money for children and then filled Little Sparrow's body with a baby. And Second Grandmother too had been sold at five and sold again at thirteen to Grandfather. Behind all these things were the pictures in Second Grandmother's pillow book, which could not now be erased from her mind. Grandmother knew about the things that must be done with men, even her feet had been broken to please them. Suddenly, Mei Lan remembered the trolleybus ride and the communists, heard again the crack of guns and saw the bleeding bodies in the street. Under the weight of other things she had almost forgotten that death as much as life had been included in these terrible two days. A weight of knowledge was settled within her for ever and she could never return to a time before it.

Ah Siew held her close, stroking her head, not minding the tears that wet her shoulder. 'Too much growing up too quick,' she sighed.

6

THE SUN PUSHED IN through the shutters to illuminate the glass cases in Lim Hock An's jade museum. The mysterious light came not from the sun but from the aqueous reflection of jade. Even as a child Mei Lan had entered this silent world in awe; it was no different now that she was sixteen. From the mountain of packing cases in the room came the raw smell of new wood, its astringency a relief after the fetid smells of the sickroom upstairs. There, the sight of her mother with her distraught face and unkempt hair lank from illness and fevered tossing alarmed her. Mei Lan had been happy to leave the room with JJ when the doctor arrived.

The floorboards creaked as she and her brother stepped into the jade museum. As children they had not been allowed into the room, but JJ had always known where the key was kept. Known too how to open that one special cabinet of frosted glass that held Lim Hock An's collection of erotic jade carvings. The things inside are not for girls to see, JJ always told her with a superior smile, locking the cabinet and pocketing the key almost before she had looked within. Now, Lim Hock An's secret collection was gone, the doors to the cabinet stood ajar, shelves empty of the miniature people in contorted postures and the men who sported giant phalluses. The family were soon to move out of Lim Villa, and the crating of valuables had already begun.

'They've gone already,' Mei Lan said staring at the empty shelves that had once housed the lewd carvings. Only one showcase remained to be packed and Mei Lan stared sorrowfully at the remaining jade cabbage, translucent Ming goblets, and a pink jade mother and child. Soon these familiar things would join the mountain of wooden crates stacked at one end of the room.

'I'm glad I'll have sailed for England before we move out,' JJ said in a low voice. Behind wide-set eyes, his expression was suddenly uncertain and he looked at his sister for encouragement. In preparation for the travel ahead the barber had cut JJ's thick hair in a pudding-bowl shape, leaving his ears looking vulnerable. He ran his hand over his head in distress, trying to flatten a disobedient tuft of hair on his crown.

'It will grow,' Mei Lan reassured him. She was tempted to take his hand as she had done when they were much younger and he was unhappy, but she knew he would push her away. There were just two years between them but the gap appeared more for he spoke to her now condescendingly, as if already he had entered the world of men. Their father had introduced him into his own clubs and she suspected might have arranged for JJ to visit a prostitute. This thought filled her with angry revulsion; she had been left far behind. Soon he would leave for university in England, sailing out of her life. Too many things were changing too quickly.

Lim Hock An had been forced to sell his grand mansion, Lim Villa; it was soon to become a Methodist girls' school. His fortune had been one of many that had not survived the recent years of severe economic depression. The price of rubber and tin, in which Lim Hock An had invested the bulk of his fortune, had dipped to unbearable lows. As he slashed and sold off to save his name, Lim Hock An was unaware to what extent the extravagant gambling of his son, Boon Eng, had already undermined him. When eventually the day of reckoning came, the great House of Lim collapsed like a fragile pack of cards around Boon Eng's monstrous debts.

Through the windows of the jade museum, Mei Lan could see Bougainvillaea House, the small home Lim Hock An had built for Little Sparrow on the edge of the Lim Villa grounds, when he had made her Third Wife. Now, Little Sparrow was being sent to a cottage on the East Coast, and within days Mei Lan and her parents, with Lim Hock An and Second Grandmother, would move into Little Sparrow's house. How would they fit into the tiny place? Mei Lan wondered. How could they stare from its windows at Lim Villa, never to enter it again? Mei Lan sat down on a hard wooden bench beside JJ. The raw smell of the packing cases was a painful reminder that change was already upon them.

'All men gamble,' JJ said as if picking up a conversation, referring in a low, fierce voice to their father. Side by side on the wooden bench they stared at the empty glass cases before them.

'But Father knew the situation, why couldn't he control himself?' Mei Lan's voice was full of resentment; her father's gambling had ruined their lives and made their mother sick. Lim Hock An's old friend Tan Kah Kee, who himself had troubles because of the Depression, had generously offered to arrange JJ's fees at Oxford, much to everyone's relief and embarrassment. The shame of it all was in Lim Hock An's face, and it shocked Mei Lan to see such vulnerability in her grandfather.

All her childhood her grandfather had been a distant figure, but when she entered her teens an unexpected bond had developed between them. She was not afraid to speak her mind; she did not swallow her words in fear before him like JJ or their father, Boon Eng. Even when small, Mei Lan had looked directly into his face, querying his commands. When she grew older he seemed to seek her company; he spoke to her of his early years and once took her with him to the Chinese Opera, leaving Second Grandmother behind much to her displeasure. Once, he told her he wished she were a boy. Once, on an outing, as they passed the docks Lim Hock An had ordered the car to stop and from the window observed the great ships berthed along the quay.

'Once, I was like those men,' Lim Hock An said, pointing to lines of coolies carrying coal to a lighter, bent low beneath the weight on their backs. He spoke softly near Mei Lan's ear and she had the feeling he had admitted this to no one before.

'You look like *her*,' he told her another time, staring at Mei Lan so hard that she felt uncomfortable. She knew he referred to First Grandmother whose name had been Chwee Gek, but Mei Lan could not tell if the resemblance to her grandmother was a positive or negative attribute, for nobody ever spoke of her.

'It's shameful. We've lost face before everyone,' Mei Lan said to JJ, kicking the dusty floor, seeing again the weary expression on her grandfather's face, and repeating words her mother had spoken. Her parents, between whom there was always a frosty space, were now no longer talking.

'Even if I have to earn the money myself, I'll follow you to Oxford. I want to be a lawyer too, then we can practise together,' Mei Lan vowed, but to her surprise JJ gave a snort of laughter.

'There are no Chinese women at Oxford, and not many English ones either. Women don't become lawyers. Besides, you're still a child.'

He turned to stare at her as she sat beside him in her school uniform of starched white cotton. His dismissal brought tears to her eyes and she turned upon him furiously; he was just like her teacher at the Chinese Girls' High School who said ambition in a woman was outlandish. She was a good student, top of the class, yet the confines of the school closed about her while JJ, at the Anglo-Chinese School, was encouraged like all boys to look out at the world, take scholarships and enter university.

'Then I will be the first,' she insisted, pigtails swinging as she angrily tossed her head. JJ looked at her sharply, sensing danger; her round eyes were aflame. She was tall like their mother, with the same natural elegance and a gaze that thrust straight to the centre of him; she always seemed to know his thoughts, uncovering every subterfuge, her cool scrutiny unsettling.

'What will happen to Little Sparrow now that Grandfather has sent her so far away?' Mei Lan asked, seeking to change the subject.

She felt sorry for Little Sparrow. Whatever she gained in life she seemed destined to lose. Mei Lan remembered how Little Sparrow had returned from the nunnery with a baby boy, to the wrath of Second Grandmother. No longer a slave girl now, but elevated through the birth of a son to the position of Lim Hock An's concubine, she soon became pregnant again. Although Little Sparrow's second child was disappointingly a girl, whom she called Ching Ling, Lim Hock An still insisted on marrying her, further raising her status to that of Third Wife. Second Grandmother had nearly gone mad, refusing to allow her former slave girl to be ensconced beside her in Lim Villa. Lim Hock An then built a small home for his Third Wife in the garden of his great mansion. Bougainvillaea House had all the charm Lim Villa lacked, and was surrounded by a profusion of flowering magenta shrubs. Second Grandmother watched its construction in cold fury. In retaliation she demanded that Little Sparrow hand over her son to be reared in the main house under the eye of his father. Second Grandmother had produced no children, but as Senior Wife she had the right to claim a junior wife's child as her own. Little Sparrow had no recourse to protest, and was forced to bow to tradition. She became thin and sad and afflicted by migraine and, on those rare visits she made to her old home, her eyes remained fixed on her son. Things did not improve; Lim Hock An eventually lost interest in her for, as

Second Grandmother pointed out, his fortune began to diminish from the day he made Little Sparrow Third Wife. It hurt no one now to evict her from Bougainvillaea House and banish her to the distant East Coast. Although still young her face was drawn, life's inadequacies now surfacing in her vacant eyes and a nervous fluttering of hands.

At last the doctor left, and Mei Lan and JJ were summoned back upstairs to the sickroom with its trapped heat and sour odours. The room was stifling, the shutters closed at the windows to lessen the glare of sunlight. Even the draught of the fan was too much for Ei Ling who had suddenly fallen sick the week before with a high fever that refused to respond to conventional treatment. Mei Lan was filled with fear; the sallow-faced woman, thin as a bird, tossing and groaning beneath the sheets, was but a reflection of her vivacious mother. The nurses who tended her waited, white and still as ghosts in a corner. All that could be heard was the ticking of a clock and the screech of cockatoos settling for the night in the garden. As they entered the room their father, Boon Eng, followed them in, dressed for the evening in a black bow tie and a white dinner jacket, an ivory cigarette holder clenched as always between his teeth.

'They may take her into hospital tonight.' He looked down at his wife dispassionately. Mei Lan watched a strand of smoke twisting up from the cigarette and a rush of terror filled her.

'I will not. *I will not.*' Ei Ling stirred and began a delirious babbling, the words pulled up from deep within her. Boon Eng continued to look down upon her without expression.

'The fever has risen. They now think it's dengue fever,' he told his children. Until that morning he had dismissed Ei Ling's indisposition as an insignificant bout of flu and had not interrupted his social life to sit beside his wife. Although nothing was said openly, everyone knew other women existed for him beyond the company of his wife. He kept no official concubine, had not installed a Second Wife in the house as his father had done, but the quarrels Mei Lan had listened to as a child and the memory of her mother's tear-stained face held new meaning for her as an adult. She understood too something of her mother's difficulties in the House of Lim.

Ei Ling was a Straits Chinese, the daughter of an established and educated family that, unlike Lim Hock An who had arrived in Singapore as an illiterate coolie, had left their country generations before to settle in Malaya. Although proudly Chinese in beliefs and ritual, the Peranakan Straits Chinese did not look back to China as a home-land as Lim Hock An did, nor did they oppose colonial rule; instead they adapted to its ways, educating their children in English missionary schools, adopting westernised ideas and habits. To Lim Hock An, Ei Ling had been a good choice of wife for his son, adding culture to his own raw wealth. The spoilt and dilettante Lim Boon Eng had reluctantly acquiesced to the match, meeting Ei Ling only twice before the marriage.

'Why are you going out?' Mei Lan demanded, trying not to shout at her father. Boon Eng frowned, pursing his lips, glancing again at his wife.

'Because there is nothing I can do here. The doctor has given her an injection; it should work soon and she will sleep,' Boon Eng said impatiently, as if he had acquitted himself of his duty.

Even as he spoke he was stepping towards the door, the scent of tobacco and cologne drifting behind him. As her father retreated into the shadows Mei Lan gazed at her mother's dry lips and waxen skin, turning in appeal to JJ. They both knew where their father was going. There was the sound of the shutting door and then his footsteps fading away down the corridor. Soon, he would move lightly over the dance floor, smiling down into his mistress's upturned face.

'Let her sleep now,' Ah Siew said, coming forward to stand beside the children. The doctor's injection had already taken effect, for Ei Ling appeared calmer, her breathing easier as sleep drew her in. Mei Lan turned as JJ took her hand and led her out of the door.

As they walked together up the corridor towards JJ's room, Little Sparrow's son, Bertie, ran towards them from the direction of Second Grandmother's quarters. Even before the child came into view they could hear his small grunts of anxiety and the heavy padding of his feet.

'Get rid of him,' JJ hissed at Mei Lan, but Bertie was already upon them.

'Want to play,' he said, following them through the door.

Mei Lan greeted him resignedly but JJ cursed under his breath. Little Sparrow's son, who was now Second Grandmother's son, had at birth been given the name of Koo Chai. Soon after she claimed the baby, Second Grandmother had seen a popular American film at the

Alhambra Cinema in which a handsome actor played a character named Bertie. As it was fashionable to have a Western name to run beside the Chinese name, Second Grandmother at once announced that her new child would be known as Bertie Lim Koo Chai. Bertie was now a rotund child of ten, but as he grew it became apparent that his brain was as soft as a lightly boiled egg and his thoughts ran this way and that. When Bertie's handicap became clear everyone expected Second Grandmother to return the child to Little Sparrow, but instead, surprisingly, he inspired her devotion. In contrast, Lim Hock An ignored the child, refusing to be associated with any infirmity.

In JJ's bedroom two large cabin trunks had been in residence since the previous week, in preparation for his departure to Oxford. They stood open and half packed and Bertie at once ran up to them to examine the contents, pulling out a belt, a sock and a couple of books.

'Get away,' JJ pushed Bertie roughly aside.

'Leave him be,' Mei Lan said, stepping up to shield the child.

'Leave him be. Leave him be,' Bertie echoed Mei Lan, yelling angrily at JJ as he cowered behind her. In an effort to calm him, Mei Lan drew up a chair and seated the agitated Bertie upon it. Opening a jar of pineapple cookies that stood on the chest of drawers, she gave one to Bertie. He at once stopped sobbing and began to munch contentedly, swinging his short legs about, knocking his heels in their brightly polished brogues against the rungs of the chair. Nothing placated Bertie like food. Second Grandmother doted on her half-witted child, always ordering the choicest food for him, dressing him in the latest fashions, even giving him a puff of her opium pipe to calm him down whenever he had a rage.

After dinner, when Bertie returned to Second Grandmother's rooms, JJ and Mei Lan went back to the business of packing the trunk. Ah Fat the houseboy had already folded and stacked the many shirts and trousers, items of underwear and tweed suits that JJ would need in the miserable climate of England. At their mother's insistence pots of Tiger Balm for headaches and bags of dried ginseng that JJ must chew each day for stamina, had been added to the trunk. They were sorting through the books and photographs when Ah Siew came running, demanding they return to the sickroom.

Although it was late, their father had not yet returned to the house. Ei Ling lay upon her bed thrashing about in an alarming manner. The sweat stood in beads on her brow, the whites of her eyes were yellow. She seemed unaware of where she was and strange cracked moans escaped her.

'The doctor is coming,' the nurse said, holding down Ei Ling's flailing arms while another nurse applied a cold compress to her brow. Mei Lan was filled with panic; her mother appeared to be wrestling with something ferocious against which she could not win.

The room was lit by a single lamp on the dressing table, and the mirror above it reflected only shadowy shapes; outside a sudden downpour had begun. Mei Lan sat on a stool hugging her knees, listening to the sound of rain splattering on foliage outside and gushing off the eaves; in the distance thunder threatened. It was some time before Boon Eng returned, flinging open the door of the sickroom, bringing with him the fresh scent of the night and the rain. The bite of his cologne filled the air and his voice, loud in the silence, demanded impatiently to know why Ei Ling had not improved.

'What am I paying you for?' he admonished the nurses. He had returned unwillingly after a call from the house and his anxiety and displeasure, even though he held it in place, was a liquid thing lashing about them all. He breathed hard through his nostrils, staring down at the semi-conscious Ei Ling. Mei Lan sensed that her mother was in some way disobeying her husband, pulling him back to her side, forcing him to recognise her, perhaps for the first and last time.

'I will stay with her,' Mei Lan insisted, but Boon Eng began shouting and JJ took her arm and drew her away. As they left the room Ah Siew hurried behind them down the long corridors of Lim Villa, like an old bent rabbit, scuttling along.

'Call the doctor again! Why is he not here?' Boon Eng could be heard asking as the door closed.

7

MEI LAN LAY IN her bed and could not sleep. Outside the rain continued, cascading from guttering, running off leaves, silencing the bullfrogs in the garden; water was everywhere, while her eyes were dry. In the darkness she heard the occasional voice, a running of feet, the creaking of pipes. Ah Siew slept as always on a pallet at the foot of her bed and Mei Lan listened to her light, intermittent snoring.

There was the sound at last of the doctor's car drawing up on the gravel outside. Careful not to wake Ah Siew, Mei Lan left her bed and crept to the great staircase of Lim Villa, peering over the banisters into the darkness below. A servant opened the front door and Mei Lan drew back into the shadows as the doctor passed, climbing the stairs with laboured breathing; a light caught his pocket watch and a saucer of baldness in his thick greying hair. A nurse appeared and he followed her to the sickroom. As the door shut upon him a wave of fear swept over Mei Lan, her breath caught in her chest and her hands became clammy. At the bottom of the dark and empty stairwell the marble flagging and Blackwood chairs of Lim Villa's great entrance hall, illuminated faintly by a single lamp, appeared part of a spectral world.

Returning to bed she dozed intermittently but at 4.30, in the black light of early morning, Mei Lan was awoken by JJ, his eyes wide and frightened, hair tousled, the stubborn tuft waving about like a weed in water. Ah Siew was not to be seen. Mei Lan ran behind JJ up the corridor to their mother's room. There, Boon Eng now stood beside the bed, head sunk despairingly upon his chest; Mei Lan let out a cry and rushed to her mother. Ei Ling gave a low groan as Mei Lan pulled on her arm. Then Ah Siew was at her side, steering her away to where JJ stood miserably in a corner. Mei Lan saw then that chairs were arranged along the wall and Second Grandmother and Lim Hock An were already in the room, sitting on special Blackwood seats with marble insets, composed and silent as Ancestor Portraits. She met her grandfather's eye and he nodded, his face creased in distress. Mei Lan bit her lip and held his eye, finding some strength from his presence. With further despair she saw that Second Grandmother had already changed into an appropriately dark *samfoo* with an embroidered collar, ready for any eventuality; there was an expectant look in her eye. Beside her Lim Hock An sat glumly on his chair wrapped in a purple silk dressing gown bought in Paris many years before, his body slack, hands folded, contemplating the bill for a funeral he knew he could ill afford. Mei Lan was surprised to see that Little Sparrow was also present, sniffing into a lace-edged handkerchief. Second Grandmother flashed her rival a steely glance that Little Sparrow took care to avoid.

'We could not risk moving her to hospital. The dengue must run its course. We can only hope now,' Boon Eng told his children in an unexpectedly contrite voice.

Mei Lan stared bitterly at her father; anger churned inside her, but when she opened her mouth to speak only a sob of pain emerged. In equal distress JJ turned and strode to the door, unable to stand any more, but his father called to him.

'What kind of a filial son are you? It is your duty to sit by her side, to wait with her.'

'You did not wait,' JJ burst out, tears in his eyes.

'Earlier the doctor expected improvement,' Boon Eng answered in a low voice, accepting his son's admonition.

They waited in the meagre light from a pink satin lampshade, silent but for a clearing of the throat, the odd whispered order or exchange. Mei Lan stared at a framed photograph on a bedside table of herself as a two-year-old: in it she sat beside Ei Ling, arms about her mother's neck. Ei Ling wore a *sarong* and embroidered *kebaya,* her round eyes and the lift of her nose indicating a mix of origin as a Peranakan Straits Chinese. Her hair was fashionably coiled, pearls hung from her ears, diamonds encircled her fingers but her beautiful face wore a wistful expression, as if life held back its true harvest. In distress Mei Lan returned her gaze to her mother; the hollow-cheeked invalid labouring to breathe bore little likeness now to the real Ei Ling. Mei Lan found she was breathing in time with her mother, willing her own energy to her, willing the breath through her body. She had no words to shape the knowledge that had surfaced in her recently: that her mother had made a poor bargain in life. Mei Lan pushed the thought away, concentrating on her breath, her eyes focused on her mother's exhausted body. At last, through the window she saw the first streak of pink crack open the sky. In that moment Second Grandmother stirred and let out a piercing wail. Little Sparrow followed with a loud cry of her own and Mei Lan knew the waiting was over.

Later, from her window Mei Lan looked down on the broad gravel drive and saw that already the servants had hung a white banner over the door, announcing the death; they must have had it ready, Mei Lan thought in horror. Now that it had happened she was numb, no tears came and her mother's delirious words of the night before echoed insistently in her head: *I will not. I will not*, the broken sounds wrenched up from deep within her. Mei Lan could not understand why the words stayed with her, or sounded so familiar.

The door opened and Ah Siew appeared with the new white mourning clothes the tailor had made in just a few hours, and the *xiao*, the mourning pin she must wear now for one hundred days; already the rituals of death had overtaken them. It was then that she remembered standing once outside her parents' bedroom door and listening with dread to the quarrel within. Her mother's voice came back to her, *I will not. I will not put up with it any longer.* At last the sentence completed itself. Mei Lan realised in new distress that Ei Ling had screamed out the words to Boon Eng as he strode away from her, dressed as always for a promiscuous evening, slamming the door behind him. He had not seen Mei Lan, who hurriedly flattened herself behind a tall cupboard beside the door. At this memory her tears welled up again and Ah Siew stepped forward. Mei Lan bent to sob on the *amah*'s birdlike shoulder.

Within a week of the funeral JJ was gone. Second Grandmother had protested that he must fulfil his filial duty and stay for the required mourning period of one hundred days, but the boat was sailing and at Oxford the term would start. In the end Lim Hock An decided JJ should go as long as he observed some required rituals.

A week after JJ's departure the family moved from Lim Villa into Bougainvillaea House, squeezing into a home that seemed the size of a box after their previous palatial residence. A dividing fence was immediately put up along one side of Bougainvillaea House, cutting it off from Lim Villa's grounds. Soon, in the distance, across manicured lawns, workmen were seen divesting the mansion of its ostentation and turning it into a school.

In a strange room, in a strange house, bereft at one blow of her mother and brother and also her home, Mei Lan woke often at night. Sometimes, hearing the crack of thunder or the splash of rain, she knew she would never again listen to these everyday sounds without remembering that night of waiting beside her mother's bed. Life was now full of missing parts: her mother, Lim Villa, JJ – all familiarity was gone. The solitariness she felt was not new to her, but was compounded by the suddenness of the change in her life. At school other girls talked about family outings and shared emotions but Mei Lan could only recount the formality of her home, each person locked into a life of their own, each separate from the others. She was never part of the giggling knots of girls who invariably fell silent when she appeared; teachers spoke of her as self-contained and possessing an exceptional brain. Each year on Mei Lan's birthday her mother had arranged a party, and all her class was invited. The great ballroom of Lim Villa had been festooned with decorations, while magicians and jugglers and dancers were called to entertain the children. Mei Lan had hated the fuss and tried to fall ill, but was always forced to attend her own party. It was useless to tell her mother that although everyone waited for the event, it only helped distance her further from her class-mates. In the end she immersed herself in the solitary world of study, placing herself amongst the elite in a more effective way.

The school holidays had begun as Ei Ling fell ill, and without her mother the time lay heavy upon Mei Lan. Although usually unavailable, during school holidays Ei Ling had always taken care to arrange a special treat for Mei Lan and herself. They sometimes went to the cinema, shopped at Robinsons or visited the Botanic Gardens where concerts were performed on the bandstand; sometimes they visited an aunt in Penang. Mei Lan found herself missing these holiday treats almost more than she missed her mother, yet, she thought guiltily, if it had been Ah Siew who had died she would have been inconsolable.

Now, it shocked her to find that already, within days of her death, she could not clearly remember her mother's face, could only sense her in fragments of memory. She recalled the intoxicating smell of her perfume and the strains of the dance music that Ei Ling played on a gramophone with a great brass ear. There were the flounces of gauzy Western clothes, and the silks of her form-fitting *sarong*, *kebaya* or *cheongsam*. Her mother had flitted in and out of the day always unreachable in those moments when Mei Lan needed her most. Through an open crack of door or through the banisters on the stairs, Mei Lan observed her mother from a distance as Ei Ling turned before a mirror at the fitting of a dress, span on her toes in the arms of her dance instructor in the ballroom of Lim Villa, or laughed with her friends at the mah-jong table with its constant clack of ivory counters.

Her father was now rarely seen. As a residence, Boon Eng considered Bougainvillaea House shamefully mean, and he preferred to stay away, living at his club, pursuing his usual diversions with ever more reckless vigour. Lim Hock An and Second Grandmother could be heard quarrelling continuously, for they found the close proximity in which they must now live distasteful. Both knew it was in these very rooms that Lim Hock An had lain with Little Sparrow to the pique of his Senior Wife. His huge Blackwood bed with its mother-of-pearl inlay and Second Grandmother's red and gold phoenix bed were fitted with much difficulty into the tiny rooms.

Without direction to the day, Mei Lan felt by turn anger, abandonment and grief as much for herself as for her mother. Rules of mourning forbade her to leave the house and, restless, she looked for diversion. Bougainvillaea House was not a place Mei Lan had ever explored, and its terrain was different from the cultivated dignity of Lim Villa with its army of gardeners forever pruning trees and weeding lawns. Bougainvillaea House had been left half wild with papaya trees, mango, wild orchid, spider lilies and an abundance of the bougainvillaea after which the house was named. At the back was a wide storm canal that channelled torrential rain and prevented flooding. The canal also harvested a nearby underground stream and was usually half filled by a sluggish flow of water. Its grassy banks ended in coarse *lallang* upon which monitor lizards sometimes sunned themselves. A metal service ladder descended into the water to one side of the house. Mei Lan had seen minnows, and crabs and crayfish stalking about amongst the weeds.

Sometimes, on those first days in Bougainvillaea House, Mei Lan heard a saxophone playing down by the canal; a volley of scales, a sad wail of sound or a fragment of melody floated to her. The notes echoed through her, capturing the sense of solitariness that deepened in her day by day. Leaning out of her second-storey window, she tried to discover who played the music. Across the canal she saw only the overgrown garden and orchard of mangosteen trees that belonged to the rambling house, its shutters closed against the sun, which sat at the top of the slope beyond the water. In the evening shouts of laughter and the soft thud of balls from a tennis court could be heard. Ah Siew said it was a boarding house for European men run by a Eurasian woman, and added sternly that Mei Lan should not look in its direction as curious male eyes might rest upon her.

Each afternoon Mei Lan took a walk or sat beside the canal, which she now regarded as her own private stream. One day she found an old wooden chair by the kitchen door and pulled it up to the edge of the canal. The fusty odour of the water came to her, golden orioles flitted between the trees and their sweet song in the dying afternoon filled her with emotion. A kingfisher flashed by, paused on a branch and was gone, disturbed by a sudden splashing. Mei Lan looked up in annoyance to see a man, his face hidden beneath a wide straw hat, wading about with a long-handled net. She wondered if he was one of the lodgers in the boarding house Ah Siew had warned her about. All at once, the man gave a cry and began hopping comically around on one foot.

'I've been bitten by a crayfish!' he shouted in annoyance when Mei Lan began to laugh, hobbling towards her through the water. Scrambling up the bank, he sat down on the grass near her chair to examine the bite. He wore a white shirt and old patched shorts and his long narrow feet gleamed wetly, a few drops of blood smudging the wounded toe. Mei Lan saw that in spite of his height he was no more than eighteen or nineteen, no older than JJ.

'I'll bring some Mercurochrome,' Mei Lan said in apology, standing up abruptly, embarrassed. She turned her cheek away from him in an effort to hide the birthmark.

He raised his head and smiled, his face open to her as if they already knew each other. Beneath thick and untidy brows his dark eyes regarded her quizzically. When she returned from the house with the antiseptic he was lying stretched out with the hat over his face to shade himself from the sun, but sat up as he heard her approach.

'We haven't introduced ourselves; I'm Howard Burns. I live over

there, in Belvedere. We're neighbours,' he said and pointed to the dilapidated house across the canal.

'We used to live over there in Lim Villa, but now we've moved into
Bougainvillaea House,' Mei Lan explained pointing to the distant
shape of Lim Hock An's mansion and then to the small house behind
her. Howard looked gravely from one residence to the other with an
expression of query; Mei Lan felt bound to reply.

'Changed circumstances; Grandfather crashed in the Depression.'
She was surprised at how easily she could admit this to him.

Howard nodded sympathetically. When he had moved to Belvedere
after his father died, Lim Villa had just been built. He knew something about the wealthy family with its two wives, and its numerous
cars and rickshaws parked in a garage that he could see from a window
of Belvedere. His mother was always commenting on the careless
wealth of their neighbours and the ugliness of their great home. She
had pointed scornfully to Bougainvillaea House, 'the Second Wife's
house', and described its polygamous use as wilfully immoral. Howard
had regularly watched the children of Lim Villa being taken to school
in a private rickshaw or one of the many cars in the garage. He did
not tell Mei Lan now of the absorbing hours spent studying her home
and its comings and goings, or the way he had kept her in view. One
birthday, he remembered, he had asked for a pair of binoculars with
which to see her better.

He stared at the girl before him, and marvelled at the reality of her:
the feathering of her brows, the fullness of her upper lip and the birthmark on her jaw that she was trying to hide. Seeing his eyes settle
upon the hated mark, Mei Lan was sure he would be repulsed.

'It's my lucky mark, my protection,' she told him, pushing up her
chin defiantly, remembering Ah Siew's *fong* and Yong Gui's pronounce-
ment so many years before.

'You shouldn't worry about it,' he shrugged, brushing the flaw aside
with such certainty that she suddenly felt no need to hide it. Her hair
was thick and straight and burnished by the sun that emptied down
upon them. She held the small bottle of Mercurochrome forgotten in
her hand. Howard remembered a recent funeral hearse.

'My mother died a few weeks ago,' she replied quietly when he
asked about it. Her face saddened, and he was distressed that he should
have been so blunt.

'I don't mind telling you,' she said and looked down at the grass, preferring not to see the sympathy in his eyes. The death of his father and the painful move to Belvedere was imprinted for ever on his memory. How much worse it was for her, he thought, left almost bereft of everything familiar.

'It makes you feel ill,' he said, hoping she would know he understood and was rewarded by the emotion that shadowed her face. Hurriedly, to cover the awkward moment he began to explain about his life and how they came to Belvedere. As he spoke he glanced across the canal, hoping his mother was not at one of Belvedere's windows to see him.

'Must have been horrible for you,' she said, handing him some wadding at last and the bottle of Mercurochrome.

'No more than for you,' he answered, as he knelt to dab the crimson antiseptic on his wounded toe. She looked down on the bent head of dark hair that curled with a life of its own, and felt that something was sealed between them.

'Don't you have a brother?' he asked, remembering a boy who had darted about Lim Villa's tennis court with his friends.

'He sailed for England last week, to go to university, to Oxford,' Mei Lan replied.

Howard listened, feeling a pang of envy at the mention of Oxford. He had hoped to go there himself or to Cambridge for further study; Rose dreamed of her son becoming a doctor or a lawyer. At St Joseph's Institution he was near the top of the class, and had been encouraged to try for the Queen's Scholarship which allowed a handful of bright local boys to continue their education in England at the government's expense. When the scholarship had gone to someone else, Howard felt wounded by the disappointment, felt he had failed his mother. Without a Queen's Scholarship he had no hope of paying for higher studies, even locally at Raffles College, let alone a university abroad. Although they lacked nothing, they lived on Rose's careful accounting, and luxuries were few.

'When you finish school you will just have to work like everyone else,' Rose told him firmly, struggling with her blighted hope.

His mother's sorrow weighed upon him, for his success would have proved her sacrifices worthwhile. Observing the European lodgers who passed through Belvedere, Howard did not miss the condescension shown his mother. He saw her swallowing her pride, ignoring the endless daily humiliations that must be braved as a landlady. She was a woman alone in the world and he knew it could not be easy for her. Mei Lan's brother had no need of a scholarship, Howard thought bitterly, his fees at university would be easily paid by his wealthy family.

'After all that has happened, we can't afford the fees at Oxford. A friend of Grandfather's is helping us.' She felt as if she read his mind, seeing herself as he must see her, and to her own surprise preferring to denigrate the House of Lim rather than risk his disapproval. He smiled again and his presence swept through her, filling her with amazement that, although for so many years he had been so near, she had had no knowledge of his existence.

From then on, each afternoon during the school holidays, Mei Lan stole out to the canal to meet Howard. They found they could squeeze through a gap in the new fence that now divided Bougainvillaea House from the Lim Villa estate. Mei Lan led him to a clearing amongst a copse of trees, to the cast-iron gazebo that Lim Hock An had once imported from Glasgow. She saw that although gardeners visited the place to trim the grass and keep down snakes, the gazebo was forgotten, with vines twisting thickly around its supporting columns above a wrought-iron bench. However, nothing could ever be hidden from Ah Siew, no matter how careful Mei Lan was. As she prepared to make her way to the canal one afternoon, Ah Siew barred her way.

'I know,' Ah Siew screamed. 'I know!' The *amah* shook a finger, incensed in a way Mei Lan had never seen before. 'Girls of good family do not behave like this, running out to meet boys. Remember who you are.' Mei Lan tried to protest but Ah Siew was not yet finished.

'He is not of your race; you are Chinese and he is Eurasian. If the elders find out I cannot protect you,' she warned.

'You are not to tell anyone,' Mei Lan instructed her angrily and for a moment Ah Siew hesitated, used, however grumblingly, to obeying Mei Lan's orders.

'You are my servant,' Mai Lan shouted. Reminded so forcefully of her position, Ah Siew drew back, lips pursed to contain her fury.

'You will do as I say,' Mei Lan demanded imperiously, the thought of Howard waiting for her overriding every other emotion. One way or another, she would see him; she would have her way.

'You are a wilful girl. The world will not be kind to you,' Ah Siew replied bitterly before turning away, slamming the door behind her.

'What do you know, you're only a servant,' Mei Lan shouted after her, tears filling her eyes.

Sometimes, he brought his saxophone with him and played for her, modern music of the kind her mother had danced to in the ballroom of Lim Villa. The music, although sometimes broken by a lack of breath or a squawking trail of notes, curled through them both. He told her interesting, irrelevant things such as how the rain tree had come to Singapore from South America or that a jellyfish was not really a fish and was without a brain. He always carried a book, was always reading. Sometimes he brought fishing nets with him and they kicked off their shoes, scrambling down into the shallow water of the canal. Tucking her dress into her knickers, unashamed, Mei Lan stalked crayfish with him amongst the weeds and slippery lichen. They always took care to keep to that part of the canal that was hidden from Bougainvillaea House by overhanging trees. Peering into the green and aqueous world at her feet Mei Lan watched minnows brush her ankles. He stood close, showing her how to net the shelly, long-legged crayfish and tip them into the lidded basket he carried; she felt his breath on her cheek. Later, they drank the soft drinks and ate the biscuits she had stolen from the kitchen of Bougainvillaea House. He added mangosteen from the gnarled Belvedere trees and thick slices of his mother's *sugee* cake. In the gazebo on the bench she sat close to him, their bare legs touching while he told her about himself.

'I wanted to go to university in England but I did not get a scholarship. Now, if I am lucky I'll probably get a job at the Harbour Board,' he informed her resignedly.

'I want to be a lawyer,' she admitted.

'Women don't become lawyers,' he replied, disapproval filling his voice. Mei Lan fell silent, unable to explain about Ah Siew, Second Grandmother, her own mother and Little Sparrow and how she did not want to be like them but free in the world, like her brother JJ.

One day Howard came with a gift wrapped in brown paper and secured with old string. She struggled with the complicated knots and at last lifted from the paper a small wooden box. Opening the lid, she saw a compass nestled within.

'It's to help you follow your dream. It belonged to my father,' he said.

Impulsively, she put her arms around him and for the first time felt the moist softness of his lips against her own, smelled the musky odour of him.

'When I first moved to Belvedere I set the needle in the direction of my old home, so that I would always be able to find my way back there,' Howard told her as he drew away, embarrassed and aroused. The taste and the feel of her filled him so powerfully that he felt dizzy.

'How does it work?' she asked, to cover her own embarrassment.

'You set the red needle to the Direction of Travel and it's never wrong.' As he showed her how to set the compass he noticed the trembling of his hands.

The hours together were filled with a strange expansion she knew he also felt. In the secret clearing under the gazebo with the rustle of insects in the vines above them, she stretched out on the wide iron bench. He lay beside her, pushing her hair out of her eyes and off her damp forehead to kiss her, exploring the hollow of her neck, the slope of her cheek, the soft place between her breasts. She felt the hardness of his arousal against her and understood the control it took to pull away as their emotions grew. Anything more would break the spell, the fragility of what they had; both were conscious of something held back, something that must wait its time. Only when she was away from him did she know that this was happiness. At night she remembered his face and slept.

The school holidays were almost finished when Second Grandmother saw her from a window of Bougainvillaea House, hauling up a large grey crayfish that struggled stiffly in the net. He had his arms about her, helping her hold on to the long-handled net so that she would not drop the creature and she laughed, her cheek against his neck. Then, in a moment Ah Siew came running and through the open windows of Bougainvillaea House Mei Lan heard the sound of Second Grandmother's voice screeching high alarm.

The next day Lim Hock An had a tall bamboo fence erected along the canal. The view of green water and kingfishers was gone. All Mei Lan could see now above the fence were the distant windows of Belvedere turning gold with the afternoon sun.

'I warned you,' Ah Siew told her tartly.

Mei Lan waited to see Howard's face at a Belvedere window, but he did not appear. Sometimes, in the evening she heard the notes of his saxophone beside the canal and knew he was playing for her, but could see nothing. The fence soared above her, pushing her back, cutting her off from herself. Only the compass remained with her, hidden in a drawer. She held it in her hand and just as he promised the red needle held steadfast, pointing always to Belvedere, her Direction of Travel.

Some days later, through the servants, Rose came to know the reason for the construction of the bamboo fence before Bougainvillaea House and confronted Howard angrily. Tall as he was, he cowered before her.

'Making a spectacle of yourself, shaming us with your behaviour,' Rose screamed, her face aflame. Howard hung his head, his heart cracking open as his mother continued to fly at him.

'If you were smaller I'd give you a caning. Don't I have enough trouble? It takes years to build a reputation and only moments to break it. Watch yourself, son. Eurasians mix with Eurasians, Chinese with Chinese, Malays with Malays, Indians with Indians; the races keep to their own.' Rose turned away, speaking to him only when necessary for the next few days.

PART TWO

1940-1941

8

ROSE BURNS SAT AS always at the long table before the window. The white shutters were folded back and the afternoon light blazed behind her. In the half-wild garden beyond the window the sun was caught in the mangosteen trees. The fruit hung heavily, the colour of burgundy and resembled a mass of hard cricket balls. From where she sat Rose had seen the new lodger arrive. Hamzah had helped him in with his luggage but, sitting in the alcove at the end of the room, she would not immediately be in his view. She continued with an account of the week's expenditure, one list for the wet market, another for Cold Storage where the greatest expense was the meat; it was her policy to put the best before her lodgers. Local mutton was no more than goat meat and the local fowl so tough it drew complaints; only Cold Storage with its imported produce, its Scotch beef and New Zealand lamb, could be relied upon.

She looked again at the new arrival who was just as young as she expected and saw he wore a woollen suit and that his face was wet with perspiration. Two large suitcases, an umbrella, a tennis racquet and a bulging attaché case stood on the floor beside him as he looked anxiously about Belvedere's dim vestibule. In his hand was a spotless white pith helmet of an expensive English brand Rose recognised. She wondered how much longer she could keep him waiting. It was her habit to hold back until the last moment from personal encounters or demands.

Already, Rose noted, even in the cool of the vestibule the man had wiped his face and neck several times with a large red and white spotted handkerchief; most of her lodgers used pale monogrammed handkerchiefs of fine Egyptian cotton. The man was growing restless now, taking small steps to the right and the left of his luggage, clearing his throat and coughing politely in the hope of attracting attention. She pushed a stray hair into place and straightened her skirt as she stood up, preparing to make herself visible.

'Mr Patterson?' Rose queried as she walked towards him. 'Welcome to Belvedere.'

'You must be Mrs Burns,' Wilfred Patterson answered in relief, stepping forward to hold out his hand, observing the short, thickset woman before him, hair pulled back severely into a coil on her neck. Her pale powdered face contrasted with the darker, moist skin of her neck.

'Did you have a hot journey?' Rose asked as he mopped his damp face once again. He had needed two rickshaws to bring him from the dock, one for himself and another for his luggage. Rose had heard the sharp crunch of metal wheels on the drive and knew he must have had an uncomfortable ride. As a new arrival he would not have known that for a few extra cents he could have taken a rickshaw with rubber tyres for a less bone-shattering ride.

'Did no one from your company meet you at the dock? You would have been more comfortable in a motor taxi than an old rickshaw,' she suggested as she led him inside.

'Someone was supposed to meet me. I waited about but no one came. On the ship I was advised that taxi fares were exorbitant, and rickshaws were just as good,' he explained as he followed her into Belvedere's cool and cavernous interior.

His nose was crooked, Rose noticed, as if it had once suffered a break and his open, pleasant face with a narrow moustache above a generous mouth was lit by eyes the colour of stagnant water. It was not an attractive comparison, but she thought of the lichen-covered pond in the garden and knew the colour a perfect match. Cynthia too had eyes that colour, although they appeared the more startling against her olive skin.

'I'll show you to your room. Hamzah will bring up your bags,' Rose said, surprised at how she had warmed to the young man.

'It's a beautiful house,' Wilfred remarked as he followed Rose up the stairs. Over the banisters he looked down upon the open space below, the red Malacca tiles of the floor swimming away beneath him. Belvedere's high ceilings and white latticed woodwork gave the place an airy, stately feel. Both downstairs and on the landing before him, large bowls of bright tropical flowers he could not name brought a graceful vibrancy.

'The ground floor rooms are more expensive. They are larger and cooler, but are usually shared by two gentlemen. They have their own bathrooms and a private veranda,' Rose informed him.

'I'm not fussy, a small room upstairs is fine,' Wilfred replied but rethought his remark as they reached the upper floor.

Climbing the stairs he had been aware of a rise in temperature, and already wondered how he would cope with the humidity and heat. As the rickshaw had turned off Bukit Timah into Chancery Lane on its way to Mount Rosie, he had been delighted to find that the shady, equatorial street, so far from its staid London namesake, was a road of lush jungle foliage, thick twisting vines and tall rainforest trees. Beneath the constant whirr of crickets and cicada, he sensed the drowsy silence at the heart of each tropical day.

Rose walked ahead of him to unlock the double doors of his room and he followed her inside, looking apprehensively about. The window shutters were closed against the afternoon sun and the small room vibrated with trapped heat. Looking up at the ceiling he saw, from the abrupt end to a line of wooden beading, that it appeared to be partitioned off from a larger area. Yet, the whitewashed room had the same fresh feel as the rest of the house, the rattan chairs with their chintz cushions looked new, the bed linen crisp with starch and on a carved desk was a small bowl of yet more flaming flowers. He was pleased with what he saw.

'You have a nice view,' Rose announced, walking over to the window to open the shutters and filling the room with light. The garden was lush with tall clumps of red-stemmed lacquer palms, white spider lilies, ginger flowers and orange heliconia that he thought resembled lobster claws. A frangipani tree laden with pale, fragant blossom stood outside the window.

'Everyone leaves their room doors open; it gives some through breeze. You'll still have your privacy with the swing doors closed.' Rose pointed to a set of short louvred flaps filling the middle of the door frame. She turned again to the window to adjust the slats of the shutters. None of the windows in the house had glass, Wilfred noticed, just these heavy louvred shutters.

'This time of year we have the monsoon. The rain comes down suddenly and if it's at night you'll have to let down the *chiks* yourself, otherwise the room will be drenched,' Rose said, touching the rolled up bamboo blinds before the window.

'The room rate includes your meals but not a Boy to clean, wait at table and attend to valet duties.' Rose mentioned this fact as casually as she could and saw the expected consternation in his face; she knew he would be earning the meagre starting salary of all young European men on a first tour of duty in the Straits Settlement.

'Usually, most of the gentlemen here are glad to share a Boy. I will speak to your neighbour, Mr Boffort. However, I'm afraid there is no way around the cost of the dhobi,' Rose added.

At the door she hesitated and then turned back to face him. 'It is not my business, Mr Patterson, but I would advise an outlay on some white cotton suits. It is what all the gentlemen wear here.'

Wilfred looked down at his woollen clothes and the colour deepened in his face. 'I had not expected quite this degree of heat, Mrs Burns,' he replied stiffly, but then asked in a lower voice, 'How many suits do you think I will need?'

'At least twelve or fourteen, that would be my advice,' Rose replied evenly.

'Fourteen.' Wilfred's face dropped in dismay. He sat down on the bed and looked up at the mosquito net gathered above him on a tall frame.

'A fresh suit must be worn every day, Mr Patterson. They go to the *dhobi* for laundering only once a week, so you need a week's supply in hand,' Rose explained as gently as she could.

'You will not have to pay the tailor immediately,' she added, hoping to relieve his despondency. 'In this country you sign a chit that can be paid off with a minimum sum every month, or later.'

'I don't want to get into debt. Do you sign chits?' Wilfred regarded her in a worried way, seeking reassurance.

She gave a slight smile, knowing he meant no insult. 'As a local person I have to pay my bills promptly each month. Come, let me show you the bathroom.' She walked along the corridor towards the back of the house.

'We have a flush system now for the toilets, not like the old days,' she assured him proudly. The bathrooms had been built out over a veranda with their own flight of stairs to allow coolies to carry up bathwater and, before the flush system had been installed, collect the buckets of waste from the toilet. A strong smell of disinfectant hung about the tiled bathroom but could not quite cover the odour of drains.

In a corner stood a huge Shanghai jar of water with a metal dipper. Rose turned to him apologetically.

'Water pressure is low and sometimes stops altogether. You have to sluice yourself down from the Shanghai jar for your bath, but you will get used to it, just like the heat,' she smiled, shutting the door. 'Dinner is at eight.'

Leaving Wilfred Patterson, Rose made her way downstairs, returning to her place at the table and old chintz sofa near the window, to put away the week's accounts. Ah Fong brought her a cup of tea and she drank it gratefully. The new lodger had filled her last vacancy, and she was surprised to hear him say that he found Belvedere beautiful. All she saw was a worn expanse of red Malacca tile, the dusty wooden fretwork below the high ceilings and the innumerable small dining tables that she had bought from a bankrupt restaurant owner. Still, it pleased her that Belvedere had established a good reputation; all the big firms recommended it to young men coming out to Singapore on a first tour of duty. She felt she had more than proved herself, but to whom she was not sure.

With the main doors and windows of his room open, Wilfred found there was some cross-ventilation as Rose had promised. He was intrigued by the novel arrangement of short swing doors spanning the entrance to his room; his head could be seen above them and his legs below. He remembered a book he had liked as a child, where each page with a picture of an animal had been cut into three. Flipping over the separate sections created beasts of fantastical design, the head of a dragon joining the belly of a bear and the feet of a duck. He thought he must appear just such a creature to anyone looking in from outside – head and lower portions visible, the middle part still blank. Inwardly, he felt no less cut about and abstracted, his battered emotions left at sixes and sevens by his sudden entry into this tropical world.

When he lay down upon the bed he was relieved to see that, at the horizontal, the swing doors assured his privacy; no one could see him from the corridor. He lay there for some time, the pith helmet sitting where he had deposited it on the bed, a resting place for his ankle. He had paid far more than he had wanted for the thing, which had come from Heath's in Bond Street. Although he had been offered a cheaper variety made from cloth-covered cork, he had liked the importance of the bolder shape, representative of the adventure ahead. At last he was back in Malaya, at the very centre of his memories, back where he had been born on a rubber estate near Johore. Already, Wilfred was beginning to see his life as a series of ever widening circles. Above him the mosquito net was bunched up in a gauzy cloud, bringing back to him memories of his childhood, of hot nights when he slept wet with perspiration, the enraged whine of a mosquito near his ear beyond the white shroud of netting. And always, in his memories, there was the distant sound of his mother's voice, shrill or broken by sobbing.

He remembered his mother's excited smile as they sailed back from England to Malaya to join his father after a long spell of home leave during which his father had remained behind. When at last they arrived back at the rubber estate, his father had shown him a new swing hanging from the mango tree, and happiness had exploded within him. His mother too had laughed, happy to be back. Yet, within days her expression changed to one of anger; she began to complain of the heat and humidity, of dust and untrustworthy servants. The bungalow was whipped into a frenzy of polishing and scrubbing, but whatever it was his mother wished to erase, it would not go away. He had run each day to the mango tree, the tree he now called 'his tree', with the sun-warmed swing. He had pushed his body backwards and forwards, looking up at the sun through the dark pattern of leaves, moving higher and higher until at last he flew with the clouds, the vast jungle sweeping away on all sides beneath him.

Wilfred stood up and went to the window, throwing off his unbearable woollen suit, stripping off his shirt as he pushed back the louvred green shutters. At once the hot sun poured over his flesh and he closed his eyes in pleasure. This was how he remembered it, running barechested and barefoot as a child in the compound of his home on the rubber estate with the servants' children. Although this was Singapore and not upcountry Malaya, a familiar smell drifted to him, of hot damp undergrowth and frangipani, of spice and carbolic and excrement. Already, some part of him had come home.

Cynthia Burns, walking along the drive of Belvedere after leaving her rickshaw, looked up at the house to see a naked man in the frame of a window. She was well used to the presence of young bachelors in Belvedere, and over the years had grown adept at deflecting unwanted attentions, so she quickly lowered her eyes before this unexpected sight. But when she looked up from under the rim of her straw hat, the man was still at the window. She saw then that he was oblivious to her presence; his head was thrown back and his eyes were closed. He had blond hair and muscular shoulders, and resembled the narrow-hipped plaster cast of a Greek god she had once had to draw in school. She put up a hand to secure her hat as she tilted her head for a better view, but lost her grip on the books she carried. Her hat slipped from her head as the books fell about her, and bending to retrieve them she cursed loudly in annoyance. As she straightened up she saw that the man at the window was now staring directly down at her. An expression of embarrassment filled his face and he closed the shutters quickly. Cynthia was left with an abrupt sense of loss.

At eight o'clock after a rest and a bath, Wilfred made his way downstairs to the sound of a melodious gong. As Mrs Burns had said, water pressure was low, and he had sluiced cool water over himself from the Shanghai jar in the bathroom. Although he could see there was a constant attempt to scrub it away, traces of green algae clung to parts of the tiled bathroom wall and floor. A high window filled by wire mesh let in filtered light. He recalled that childhood house in Malaya where spiders as large as a man's hand had stalked a similar window above a similar Shanghai jar. Now, as he walked down the stairs for his first dinner at Belvedere, he was surprised to find himself descending into a world of candlelight; everything appeared charmingly unreal and he looked about with pleasure. From across the room Rose saw him and came hurrying up. She had wound her long hair high on her head for the evening and crimson lipstick brightened her face above the lace collar of a dark silk dress. Although not beautiful, Wilfred decided, she was what was called a handsome woman and carried herself with dignity.

'I've arranged for you to sit with Mr Boffort since he is your neighbour and you'll be sharing a Boy,' Rose said as she showed Wilfred to one of the small tables, her smile almost motherly.

The glow of so many flickering candles gave the large dining room unworldly appeal. Doors and windows were thrown open to the warm tropical night and the powerful scent of the garden. Light from the kitchen outhouses illuminated part of an orchard of mangosteen trees, their branches knitted together in impenetrable darkness. A dog barked. For the first time that day Wilfred felt there was no need for a fan. Looking up he saw the extraordinary height of the ceiling, far higher than those of the second floor rooms. A single old-fashioned punkah of yellow cloth had been electrified and hung above the long table where Rose sat with her children at each mealtime.

A fleshy-faced man a few years older than Wilfred now came hurrying up to the table, his hand already extended in greeting from a distance away. Even before he was seated, Arthur Boffort began to explain that he was coming to the end of his first tour of duty and would soon be returning to England.

'Getting married. Valerie has been waiting five years. No firm will allow you to marry on a first tour of duty here.' He spoke forcefully, projecting spittle across the table from beneath a ginger moustache.

'When we return as a married couple, Mrs Burns will be giving us one of her big, cool ground floor rooms. I should be able to afford it on a second tour; promotion and salary raise and all that.' Boffort worked for Stewart and Lloyd, a British firm dealing in pipes and fittings.

'Gas, water or steam. Large stocks always on hand. Sole agents too for United Engineers.' Boffort stretched across the table to a pile of bread and began to butter a slice industriously. He asked no questions of Wilfred, speaking, even as he chewed, of his home in Manchester and his mother's battle with asthma. He absorbed without comment the information that Wilfred was a journalist and had come out to work for *The Straits Times*. Yet, on hearing that Wilfred had been born in Malaya on a rubber plantation his father had managed, Boffort paused in the midst of his buttering and looked up.

'I suppose that makes you half native; better be careful of going all the way. It's not done for the races to mix here, you know,' he murmured, returning to the bread.

'I have only the most shadowy memories of Malaya. I was seven years old when I returned to England, to go to boarding school. I never came out here again until now.' Wilfred was irritated but broke off as a Chinese man in a high-necked white uniform appeared beside their table. Boffort turned upon him impatiently.

'Food at last. Took you long enough. Need to learn to hurry your-self,' Boffort admonished before turning to Wilfred and gesturing in the direction of the man. 'By the way, this is our Boy.'

Wilfred nodded to the middle-aged Chinese, who placed a bowl of thin soup before him. 'What's his name?' Wilfred asked Boffort, unsure if the Chinese spoke any English.

'No idea. Just call him "Boy". They all come to the call of Boy whatever their age, no need to bother with names. They all look alike as well, you'll find it difficult at first to tell them apart.' Boffort sucked hungrily at a spoonful of soup. Wilfred glanced at their Boy and found his features distinctly different from the Boy serving at the next table.

'How long has he been your Boy?' he asked.

'Five years, ever since I arrived,' Boffort replied between mouthfuls. 'All these houseboys and cooks are Hainanese and come from the same place in China. They're probably all related; one big happy clan.' Some soup dripped on to his chin and he put down his spoon to dab at it with his napkin.

'Do you understand English? What's your name?' Wilfred turned directly to the Chinese.

'Name Wang, *Tuan Besar*.' The man gave a grin, revealing a mouth of nicotine-stained teeth.

'His English doesn't stretch to much more than that,' Boffort observed, finishing the last of his soup.

'I thought we'd get curry.' Wilfred stared down at the thin gruel before him in disappointment.

'*Tiffin* is on Sunday, and you need the afternoon to recover from it. You'll find Mrs Burns does a slap-up *tiffin*,' Boffort replied.

Wang appeared with a course of fish. This was followed by braised lamb and boiled vegetables, a dessert of sponge pudding and some cheese. The food was plentiful and well cooked but Boffort was critical.

'Chinese cooks never get the hang of anything other than their own food. Mrs Burns probably breathes down their necks to produce our Sunday tiffin. Now, that's *her* kind of food. Shouldn't think *she* was brought up on food like this. People like her want their spice and chilli.' Boffort laughed, blowing spittle over the dessert Wang had just placed before him.

'But her name is Burns. Was her husband English?' Wilfred had been wondering about his dark-skinned landlady. In spite of her name she was not European, but neither did she appear completely Indian or Malay.

'Lord, no. You really are wet behind the ears. Mrs Burns is *Eurasian*. Our Rose of Mount Rosie,' Boffort laughed. 'There was probably a long ago English ancestor who came out and married a local Malay woman, and whose name has been passed down the line. I believe she herself was born in Malacca, which means there would also be a large family tree of Portuguese or Dutch bits and pieces, all long ago married with Malay, Indian, Chinese or even Ceylonese women. Then local Malacca-Dutch marry Malacca-Portuguese, Malacca-Irish marry Malacca-Ceylonese, etcetera and hey presto, soon they're a community of their own. They're very particular about their white ancestors, however, even if they themselves are now as black as coal.

'They're a valuable community, don't get me wrong,' Boffort continued hurriedly, seeing the disapproval on Wilfred's face. 'They push our pens for us, so to speak; most are well educated and English speaking, so we give them all our clerical jobs. And of course they're also Christian like us, Catholic mostly. Couldn't run the Colony without them. You can't trust the Asiatics; most of the Malays are illiterate and, except for a minority of Straits Chinese who have been educated in English-medium schools, none of that lot can speak our language, and neither do the Indians, by and large. We depend upon the Eurasians to manage everything for us. They're a dependable lot.'

Wilfred looked across at Rose, who sat like a benevolent headmistress before a school dining room. He felt acute discomfort on behalf of his landlady as he listened to Boffort. 'Mrs Burns appears an admirable lady,' he protested.

'Yes indeed. A valuable community, just as I said.' Boffort stretched across the table to cut another chunk of cheese. Wilfred stared at the candlelight reflected on the balding crown of his head; the man filled him with shame for being an Englishman. Wilfred turned again to observe Rose, dignified and upright before the table. Beside her sat the girl who had cursed like a man below his window, and a boy of similar age.

'They are her children,' Boffort explained, following his gaze and swallowing in a single gulp the demitasse of coffee Wang had just served him. He called loudly for more, rattling his cup on the saucer.

'Howard and Cynthia. He's with the Harbour Board and she's doing nursing. Hot little chilli, isn't she? It's said Mrs Burns must have had it off with one of her lodgers before Cynthia appeared. Just look at those green eyes. We'd all like a piece of Cynthia, although of course not in any permanent way. I'm telling you right now at the beginning, stick to your own kind. You won't get better advice than that. Society here does not take kindly to intermarriage. A man's career is finished if he takes a dusky-skinned wife. It's just not done; you'll be cut dead by everyone who matters. She won't be accepted anywhere either or included on invitations, can't enter our clubs. And anyway, who wants children with a touch of the tar brush, eh? What kind of life can they hope for anywhere in the civilised world?' Boffort held out his cup as Wang approached with the coffee pot.

'I haven't even been introduced to the young lady.' Wilfred turned upon Boffort in exasperation.

'Steady on. Just trying to put you wise before you make a mistake. The races don't mix here, you see. Chinese keep to themselves in Chinatown, as do the Malays in Geylang, the Indians in Serangoon Road, the Eurasians in their Eurasian pockets and we of course, being the ruling race, can't afford to hobnob with any of them. Live apart, work apart, socialise apart. That old adage, familiarity breeds contempt, is more true than we know.' Boffort leaned forward, the candlelight carving up the fleshy crags of his face until he resembled a heavy-jawed gargoyle, and continued.

'It can get lonely here for a man; not many unattached young ladies of our own kind about. A man can easily fall prey to a local girl when he's lonely. It's not as if the Settlement has ever had a "fishing fleet", as in India. If you find yourself feeling low, let me know. You can get whatever you want in the right places: Chinese, Japanese, Malay even French or Russian girls too. And there are always the taxi dancers at any of the Great Worlds.' Boffort winked across the table.

Within a few minutes, to Wilfred's relief, Boffort stood up and announced that he had a letter to write to his fiancée, Valerie. The Boy, Wang, appeared with a pot of fresh coffee and Wilfred accepted another cup. It was strong, bitter stuff and he drank it gratefully, savouring the few moments without Boffort. He found himself staring at Cynthia. Her brother, Howard, was a good looking young man with his mother's dark colouring and hair, width of jaw and rounded brow.

Cynthia appeared something apart from these two, just as Boffort had indicated.

Cynthia's hair seemed lit from within by tawny light and framed a slim face of high cheekbones. Even from a distance he could see the hazel, slanting eyes, cat-like against her light olive skin. She appeared to Wilfred impossibly beautiful; unlike anyone he had seen before. Once, she looked across at him in a deliberate manner then turned abruptly to speak to her brother, taking no further notice of Wilfred. The directness of her glance surprised him, and her raw curse that afternoon below his window sounded again in his ears. At the end of the meal she disappeared through the door that led under a covered walkway to the kitchen buildings. Wilfred returned to his room and, as he climbed the stairs, he looked down on the dark candlelit space beneath him and knew he had entered the residue of his childhood memories. Nothing as yet felt real.

Later, as he lay in bed beneath the shroud of starched muslin Wilfred listened to the old house settle down for the night and wondered at the strangeness of the day. There was the low hum of voices and clink of glasses from the men who still sat in the coolness of the Lodgers' Lounge, an airy open-walled room above the downstairs portico. A mosquito whirred near his ear beyond the tent of netting that hung about him. The night was punctuated by the full-throated call of bull-frogs, the scent of night flowers mixed with the fetid odour of the manure spread upon the flower beds. Once he heard a clock strike, and then the heavy thud of the dining room shutters as the servants closed up for the night. From the other side of the thin partitioning wall came a rattle of glass as Boffort dragged out the crate of bottled drinks kept beneath each lodger's bed. He thought about the Boy, Wang, who to Boffort deserved no name, and the dignified Mrs Burns, so undeserving of Boffort's disparagement. Beneath every thought he was aware that Cynthia was constant in his mind. There was the sound of far off thunder, and he wondered if he would have to get up in the night to battle with the rain and the bamboo blinds. The last thing he remembered before sleep enclosed him was the naked, straining back of the rickshaw runner who had pulled him away from the docks. He heard again the man's rasp of breath, saw the bony protrusion of his ribs and the knotted blue veins in his neck. It had disturbed him that a man should be used like an animal for his own convenience.

He understood then that he had entered a world that was a distorted reflection of the one he had left, and knew already that he could not condone it. Then again he remembered Cynthia, a hand to her hat, books in her arms, staring up at him as he stood in the open window. At last he closed his eyes and slept.

9

IN MANIKAM'S CLOTH SHOP Raj rewound the bale of white muslin a customer had earlier inspected, and pushed it to one side. A pile of fresh garlands for the wedding was heaped on the counter, the sweet scent of jasmine filling the shop. Raj looked uneasily over the flowers to where his sister, Leila, sat on a chair, head bowed, waiting. The day was one of those turning points of which he had already seen so many; something was ending and something new was beginning. Leila had pulled her sari down over her face so all Raj could see was the gold hoop of her nose ring, a hanging pearl trembling as she breathed. Her hands twisted nervously in her lap, the nails bitten down to the quick.

'Krishna is a good man and my best friend,' Raj reassured her yet again, but Leila remained stubbornly silent. She had said little since her arrival a few days before, sitting with head covered and eyes downcast, answering his questions in monosyllables. It was natural for a bride to feel apprehensive, Leila knew nothing of Krishna and had not even seen him yet, but how many brides saw their husband before a wedding? Raj reasoned. He could not tell if her silence was one of anger or submission, and tried to control his impatience.

When Manikam died and he had inherited his business, Raj felt able at last to send for his sister. Within a short time of Manikam's death, Raj had also had an unexpected opportunity to diversify in business. Mr Ho, the biscuit maker, had introduced him to a man who was a ship chandler and wished to sell his company. After the trolleybus incident at Kreta Ayer, their friendship had grown over the years. Raj visited Mr Ho regularly, and the man had taken on the aura of a further mentor for him. It had been Mr Ho who encouraged him to think beyond the narrow confines of Manikam's Cloth Shop. If we do not risk we do not gain, Mr Ho told him. Mr Ho had also taken Raj to a Chinese bank and helped him to arrange a loan with which to buy the ship chandler's company. Next, Mr Ho had introduced him to his daughter-in-law's father, a Japanese shipping agent who lived on Middle Road. Mr Yamaguchi had contact with many Japanese ships, and it was through him that business had come to Raj. Now, Raj kept a desk at the back of Manikam's shop where he managed his new business, a far more profitable trade than the selling of *dhotis* and mosquito nets. He had been able to buy a gold necklace for Leila, and bangles to cover her wrists.

Leila wore this jewellery now, and Raj observed the gleaming ornaments against her smooth flesh with both possession and pride. Feeling his eyes upon her, Leila raised her head and met his gaze and he saw, with some surprise, resentment in her face. Then she quickly pulled the sari down over her head, showing him only the delicate fingers of her small hand clutching at the silk.

As her brother had done before her, Leila had sat huddled on the deck of the ship through endless days at sea, enduring the sickening pitch and roll, burned by the never-ending sun, queuing with men for use of a single stinking toilet. The last thing she had expected when she finally arrived in Singapore was to be married within days of reaching the place. All she had thought about on the long journey was seeing her brother again. Before the voyage she had gone no further than a kilometre from the village. The courage to leave India and travel to Malaya came from her brother, whose letters over the years she had waited for impatiently. She had been seven years old when Raj left India; now she was eighteen. After he left she had lived alone with her grandmother, in a crumbling mud hut that leaked when it rained. Eventually, the old woman died and after her death Leila had gone to live with an aunt in a neighbouring village who treated her like a servant, giving preference in everything to her own daughters. As soon as Leila was of marriageable age, the aunt began searching for an elderly widower who would overlook the absence of a dowry to acquire a young wife. It was at this time that Raj suggested she join him, and the aunt was only too happy to be rid of her.

At last she had disembarked from the ship to feel solid land beneath her feet once more. The noisy clamour of the quay and the alien Chinese faces made her realise how far she was from the village, how untraceable her journey; she might never go home again. What would she do if her brother were not there? How would she recognise him after all these years? Standing to one side of the gangplank, a bundle of belongings beside her, she anxiously scanned the crowded quay. As the wharf cleared Raj saw her and came forward, and the sight of him filled her in a rush.

It was Raj who suggested to Krishna the idea of marriage to his sister. The thought had suddenly appeared in his mind once he was certain Leila would join him in Singapore. Since the day, long before, when Krishna had written Raj's first letter to Leila, the schoolteacher's destiny and that of his sister had appeared to Raj to be linked together. At first Krishna had declined the offer, apologetically informing Raj that he intended marrying a literate woman, a schoolteacher like himself, and that, through a matchmaker, he was soon expecting to be engaged to just such a person. Yet, within days, Krishna learned that his prospective bride, far from being a schoolteacher as reported, was a deaf-mute and his trust in all matchmakers was shaken. Raj had quietly mentioned his sister's availability again, and had also set about convincing Krishna that her illiteracy was to his advantage.

'You will be able to educate her yourself to your own standard; no one's education will be there before you,' Raj suggested as he produced a faded photograph Leila had sent him some years before.

'She was a child then, now she is of marriageable age. You can see there are no defects – eyes are straight, colour not too dark, no harelip; you might call her beautiful,' Raj encouraged him and Krishna nodded, holding the photograph in his hand, observing the pleasant but unreadable face staring up at him.

'It will be proof of our friendship,' Krishna said slowly at last, unable to refuse his friend, and feeling it likely one woman might be just as good as another in the role of wife.

Later, Krishna had firmly refused the dowry Raj offered. 'I want nothing. I am not for these old ways of thinking; dowry should be abolished,' he said. His parents in India were long dead, and there was no one to protest his decision.

Against the advice of an astrologer the date for the wedding had been picked for no better reason than its convenience; Krishna was a schoolteacher and could not miss a day of work. Raj now wondered if it was right to conduct a wedding in so strange a manner with no family relatives, no musicians, no feasting or dancing, no gifts of sweet-meats to distribute. It was a wedding arranged by two bachelors without a need to prove their social status and with no women to question its form. Krishna insisted that besides the loathsome dowry system, traditional Indian weddings were a criminal waste of hard-earned cash. Raj had purchased garlands of flowers and the few sweetmeats necessary for the ceremony but, apart from the red sari and jewellery Leila wore and the new *dhoti* bought for himself and Krishna, there was no evidence of a wedding. The bride and the groom would walk together down Serangoon Road to the Sri Perumal temple and the waiting priest, in a manner against all convention.

Through the open front of Manikam's Cloth Shop, Raj had a good view of the road and soon saw Krishna approaching. He watched as his friend stopped before Subramaniam, who sat as always with his parrots at his stall under the five-foot way. Krishna helped the old man to his feet and guided him across the road between bullocks, carts and rickshaws. Manikam's was cramped and dark and smelled of the starch that impregnated the bales of muslin crowding the shelves. Krishna and Subramanium filled the recess as they entered, blocking out the light. Subramanium's two parakeets sat on his shoulder and gave occasional croaks.

Leila lowered her head, her hands twisting and trembling in her lap. She dared not raise her eyes but as the men entered the shop she had stolen a glance as she pulled the sari further forward over her face. At the sight of the unkempt old man with a beard of white stubble against his dark skin, and two parakeets sitting on his shoulder, she was filled with panic. Then she was vaguely aware of a younger man stepping forward, but did not dare lift her head to observe him. Instead, she shrank back into the chair, her heart beating violently, her eyes fixed upon Krishna's bare feet in worn leather sandals as he stood before her. Instinctively, she knew these were the feet of her future husband, but was unable to make a judgement of him from the limited view of his toes with their sprouting of dark hair.

The strong jasmine scent of the garlands was now tempered by the perfume of the sandalwood soap with which Krishna had scrubbed himself that morning. He wore the new clothes Raj had bought, the *dhoti* standing out stiffly around him. Raj stepped forward to welcome the wedding party but Krishna, his eyes fixed upon Leila, did no more than nod to him. Seeing Krishna's curiosity Raj turned to speak to his sister.

'Raise your head; look at him. There is nothing to fear. He is my friend and will be a good husband to you,' Raj ordered. In response Leila raised her head but pulled her sari further over her face so that she could see something of her bridegroom through the thin silk, but he could see nothing of her.

'Let us go,' Raj announced impatiently, picking up the garlands and a box of oily sweetmeats needed as an offering at the ceremony. Guiding Leila out of the shop behind Krishna and Subramanium, Raj began the short walk up Serangoon Road to Sri Perumal temple.

The road was crowded as always. A herd of bleating goats on their way to the nearby slaughterhouse filled the road with confusion. For a moment Raj saw his mute sister as similar to the confused animals, on her way to an irrevocable destiny. Leila took small quick steps to keep up with him, her thin shoulders hunched with tension. Krishna had overtaken them and was now some distance ahead, striding forward with his usual brisk determination. The frightened goats swarmed about them again and Raj drew Leila to the side of the road until the animals passed. They walked on past new rows of shophouses, goldsmiths, sari shops, vegetable sellers and the provision stores that had begun to appear on the road to meet the demands of a growing populace. The holding pens, slaughterhouses and dairies that had filled the road when Raj arrived were now all but gone.

At last they reached the temple, and Leila fell back apprehensively. The heavy silver doors stood open and the perfume of incense drifted out beneath the sculpted figures of brightly painted deities crowding the pagoda. Although she knew this was the home of the gods Leila hung back, understanding that to step across the threshold committed her to her future. Then Raj placed an impatient hand on her shoulder, guiding her forward towards the gate. As they entered the dim interior of the temple the scent of incense thickened. An ancient priest hobbled forward, his bare hairless chest and dark stringy limbs in stark contrast to his soft white *dhoti*. They followed him into the inner sanctum and sat together as he indicated; he showed little surprise at a wedding party whose only guests were a senile old man and two grumbling parakeets. His sparse grey hair was twisted into a knot and his old eyes watered as he mumbled prayers over a coconut decorated with flowers and leaves. Lighting more incense he began his incantations, the sounds humming through his nose and building rhythmically, beginning the rituals that would make Leila and Krishna man and wife. Next to Raj,

Subramanium flexed his arthritic legs. The birds shifted about on his shoulder and pecked at his ear for attention, their droppings splattering the cloth on his shoulder.

Krishna sat opposite his bride and observed her. Once or twice she accidentally caught his eye and at once pulled her sari down over her head in confusion. He was heartened to see a slim-faced woman with large eyes and a grave expression. Behind the overt modesty he sensed her alertness and knew already, approvingly, that she was a woman with a mind of her own. A feeling of relief washed through him and he realised how tense he had been since agreeing to Raj's proposal. His bride was not only passably attractive but appeared intelligent besides; he would teach her to be the modern woman he wanted as a wife.

The priest droned on and as the rituals proceeded, Leila began to feel numb. The scent of jasmine from the garland Krishna had placed upon her shoulders was overwhelming. As he had lowered the garland over her head she noticed his slim-fingered hands and looked up to meet his eyes. It was as if she had entered a dream. Within minutes she would stand again on Serangoon Road, a married woman, but when she tried to imagine what lay ahead no thoughts would form. Her mouth was dry and the garland's perfume so strong she had begun to feel sick. Once, as a child, she had seen a chicken carried to market with its wings broken and its feet tied together before its throat was slit. She did not know why this long ago image came suddenly to her in the middle of her wedding. The priest's nasal chanting continued, but everything within her had stopped.

At last it was over, and they emerged from the cool shadow of the temple on to Serangoon Road. Raj could not hide his pleasure at the thought that the lives of his sister and his best friend were now knotted together for eternity. Leila would return with Krishna to the room he had recently rented in a crowded shophouse around the corner from Manikam's Cloth Shop.

Raj did not think he had ever looked so deeply into himself as he did on Leila's wedding night. He kept waking, worried about all she must be experiencing. He realised there had been no older woman to explain how Krishna would act towards her now that she was his wife. In his anxiety to give Leila a life, everything had been done with undue haste and many important details had been overlooked.

As soon as he could the next morning Raj hurried to Krishna's room, pushing his way up the stairs against a stream of descending tenants. He found Leila crouched down on her haunches, sweeping the tenement room with a broom of soft twigs. He looked for some change in her face, but found none. Krishna had already left for the schoolroom. The remains of his breakfast stood on the floor beside the rolled up rush mat upon which they had slept the night before. The now withered garlands were heaped in a corner, their scent stale and lingering. Raj was overcome by embarrassment for all that must have taken place in this room the night before. He had brought some sweetmeats with him, and placed them beside Leila as she crouched silently before him, head bowed and covered as always.

'How will I cook him a meal? There is no pan. Until now he is buying his food outside, at the food stalls on the road.' She lifted her head, her eyes upon Raj, wide and anxious. The sari slipped and although she immediately pulled it back in place he saw in the tendrils of escaped hair and the line of her cheek the extent of her vulnerability.

'We will go shopping,' Raj laughed in relief. Already he sensed that Leila had given her trust to Krishna; everything would be all right.

She had had some notion of what might happen on her wedding night. Married women gossiped in the village, in the fields animals lived a randy life, but when it was done she found shame was the greatest trauma, even though it was quickly over. Much of the night she had lain awake, staring at her sleeping husband. A street light shone through the window and revealed not only the stealthy movement of cockroaches and the scurry of mice, but also the profile of Krishna's face. Afterwards, he had smiled down at her and had gently pushed the hair off her brow. You are now my wife, he told her. She said nothing, wet and sore between her legs. The only thought that came to her was that he had opened his life to include her, much as a fish opens its mouth to breathe in water, instinctively and without premeditation; she had begun to cry. Then, dawn was breaking and she knew she must rise and bathe and make her husband the cup of tea he would expect upon waking.

After taking Leila to purchase pulses and vegetables and then some pans to cook them in, Raj returned to open Manikam's Cloth Shop. It had been decided between them that Leila would cook a meal in the tenement's communal kitchen, and then bring some lunch for him to the shop. Later, as he ate and she squatted apprehensively before him waiting for an opinion on the quality of the food, he felt grateful that she was here. Life would be different from now on, not only for Krishna but also for himself.

'You are speaking and writing so many languages,' Leila spoke suddenly in a conversational tone, and he stared at her in surprise between mouthfuls of food.

'I am learning the Japanese language,' he boasted and was rewarded by a widening of Leila's eyes as he explained his new life as a ship chandler. 'I need this language for my work. I am mixing now with Japanese people.'

'What is this work?' Leila asked, looking up at him with the same admiration he remembered in her face as a child.

'Now, besides Manikam's Cloth Shop, I am selling things to Japanese ships when they arrive in port – fresh food, rice, cooking oil, rope, nails; many things. It is because of Krishna that I am doing all these things. Your husband will give you education, just as he gave education to me,' Raj informed his sister and Leila nodded, her face brightening.

'Already he has told me this,' Leila said in a low voice, her mind astir with excitement.

Later that evening Raj made his way once more to Krishna's room. As he climbed the stairs the smell of food came to him from the common kitchen in the tenement, and his mouth began to water. When he entered the room, Krishna was sitting cross-legged on the floor behind a low desk. He waved brightly as Raj entered, and lifted a loosely bound sheaf of papers in his hands.

'See, I have a copy at last of Subhas Chandra Bose's new book, written while he was in prison. It was smuggled here from India. This is a first draft, but already it is in circulation. This is a dangerous book to be seen with in India and many risks have been taken in getting it to us here. I will speak about it this evening,' Krishna said, returning to the papers on his desk, anxious to finish the notes for his lecture that evening at the Indian Youth League. Raj knew this talk would be like all Krishna's talks, a fiery and fanatical advocacy of the need for Home Rule in India.

With Leila bustling about the room, a plant in a tin can on a window ledge, a string bag of vegetables in a corner and Krishna's shirts hanging from a bamboo pole at the window, the place had already acquired the look of a home. Leila served a meal of rice and vegetables on banana leaves, and they ate with relish. When they were finished they rinsed their hands in the basin of water she offered. Then Krishna gathered up his papers and, with Raj behind him, made his way down the narrow staircase and out into the street for the short walk to Race Course Road.

They walked in companionable silence, Krishna taking long strides and Raj, who was a head shorter and of wider girth, hurrying to keep up. Soon they turned off Serangoon Road and walked towards the small bungalow that housed the Indian Youth League, a social club whose activities centred mostly on sport and the education of young Indians. It had a growing list of members and a comfortable lounge with an eclectic assortment of tables and chairs. There was also a library with biographies of Indian leaders, books on Hinduism and on other aspects of Indian life. Krishna's scholarship and commitment to Indian causes was valued at the League, as were the regular talks he gave on Indian history and culture. As they approached the club the young members smoking on the veranda outside straightened up with respect, stubbing out their cigarettes and greeting Krishna. Chairs had been arranged in the library and although there was a seat for the speaker, Krishna preferred to stand before his audience who were already settling expectantly.

The organisers of the Youth League, a committee of elders and wealthy businessmen from the Indian community, although dimly aware of Krishna's radical background, did not fully comprehend his true mission in life. They were grateful, for his regular talks on Indian history and politics were so well attended that extra chairs must often be hastily found. Yet, although the evening might be advertised as a lecture on Indian history, world history, Indian philosophy or any other of the topics Krishna spoke on, his slant on each subject was narrow. His mind was focused on the freeing of India from British rule. Of world history Krishna chose only to discuss the history of revolution. Similarly, in Indian history he picked out the tales of famous Indian revolutionary zealots, Velu Thampi, Tipu Sultan and the Rani of Jhansi, or he might talk about the Indian Mutiny or the unscrupulous doings of the rascal Robert Clive, hailed as a hero in his home country, but whose ruthless rape of India was impossible to catalogue. Philosophy for Krishna was always Marx and Lenin, Subhas Chandra Bose and Mahatma Gandhi.

'When an older generation of leaders have failed, youth have the responsibility of reconstructing society. We must prepare to defend India's pride and glory. We must end British rule. We must prepare to shed our blood, and sacrifice our lives if necessary for the independence of our motherland.' Krishna's voice began to rise, and the words flowed powerfully from him.

Raj was always fascinated to watch the transformation in the schoolteacher as he talked. Krishna appeared a self-effacing man and his lectures began in a mild enough manner, yet within minutes he was transformed into a fiery preacher. Men sat forward on their seats and sucked their lips in concentration whenever the schoolteacher spoke.

Raj looked about the room at the rapt and attentive faces and knew, with some sense of disappointment, that he could not share the enthusiasm around him. Listening to his new brother-in-law, Raj was aware all too clearly of the gulf between himself and the idealistic Krishna. He thought of the great men Krishna admired, Einstein, Bose, Marx and so many others, men of revolution and reinvention. Idealists though they were, Raj viewed these men not as dreamers like Krishna but as pragmatists. In their special worlds each had known that opportunity must be seized. So it was also with Raj. Through the schoolteacher he had entered a world in which men would lay down their lives for an idea. Yet commitment of this nature appeared insubstantial to Raj; practicality was the only realistic way forward in life. He knew already that money was what he wanted, and it was not of great consequence to him in what political circumstances he lived as long as he was able to acquire it.

HOWARD HAD NOW BEEN working more than a year at the Harbour Board, at an office in an old godown near Collyer Quay. Aunty May had a friend whose husband worked at the Harbour Board, and through him an opening there had been found for Howard.

'You'll have a good future at the Harbour Board,' Rose forecast. A job at the Harbour Board was not without status, and many Eurasian men aspired to such work. Once he finished his probationary period he was promised a rise in position to Assistant Traffic Supervisor, and this pleased her further.

'It always helps to see your way up the ladder. You'll do well, just like your father,' Rose told him.

Howard swallowed his disappointment. He was not happy at the prospect of a life at the Harbour Board but did not want to disappoint his mother.

'Many men would envy you such a job. You should be proud; the King trusts us Eurasians to run the colony above all the other races here,' Rose said, impatient with his lack of enthusiasm.

'There is the Public Service Examination. That would open the way to a higher level of employment,' Rose suggested at last, unable to watch her son's crumbling hope, knowing his dream of further education after finishing school.

From then on each evening Howard sat at the writing table before the open doors of the balcony adjoining his room, hunched over books on economics and accounting; determined. He slept briefly but woke most nights to his own restlessness and turmoil. The residue of strange dreams washed around within him and fragments of memory slid away before he could grasp them. Often, waking like this, he put on the light and went back to his books in the dark and silent house, focused on his hopes.

Much to his mother's amusement he began to read the The Straits Times, which was delivered to Belvedere each day for the benefit of the lodgers. It was not a newspaper for local people, being read almost exclusively by the European community, but Howard now absorbed the pages with concentration, hoping to glean new knowledge. For the last few weeks a debate had raged in its correspondence column on the rights of the local-born communities, and Howard had followed it with growing awareness. He noticed that none of the letter writers appeared to be local people. This omission, and the fact that the issues blithely discussed were written about by those who would never have to deal with them, filled him with anger. Until then, he realised, he had never considered that he might have rights under a colonial government, but had accepted his mother's reverence of all things British as the only valid perception.

At times, as he worked each night at his table, he wondered with trepidation if perhaps he was studying too hard, was too intent upon the future and all he felt bound to achieve. Everything was against him, and if he did not succeed, how would he cope? Nothing was more important to him now than breaking with the past. He did not want to be like his father who had grown tired of deferring to high-handed young Englishmen twenty years his junior whose expertise in matters of the Asiatic Petroleum Company was inferior to his own. Deep down Charlie Burns had always hoped that with his European colouring he could transcend the inflexible landscape of race that rooted him to his place. He could not accept that as a local person, merit meant little before colonial superiority. His death while at work had been unobtrusive. For some time after he died he had sat at his desk listing gradually to one side, before it was noticed that something was wrong. To Howard now it seemed the final dismissal that, even as the life seeped from his body, his father should sit on at his desk, ignored. He felt he understood the anger his father had lived with, and that now, more and more, seemed to sit upon his own shoulders.

Although part of his day at the Harbour Board was given to paper-work at a desk, Howard was also required to go on to the ships, to learn the work of the quay and the management of labour. His office was situated at the dock and was subject to the constant comings and goings of ships in the harbour. All vessels arriving and sailing must be listed along with their tonnage and details of cargo and crew. The unloading of cargo must also be checked and supervised, each ship examined and repairs arranged, sick crew must be dispatched to hospitals and ship chandlers summoned to replenish supplies. Timings must be confirmed and complaints investigated.

Howard was part of the boarding team that examined and counted cargo and stores and processed the crew of each vessel under a Senior Boarding Officer. The office was no different from any other in the colony where a regiment of Eurasian men, and a few educated Chinese or Indians with a good command of English, worked under the order of a European. John Calthrop accompanied his men to the ship, but always returned as soon as he could to the coolness of the office. His thinning hair revealed a patch of reddened skull that, like his face, became quickly inflamed in the sun. Howard soon came to welcome any time away from Mr Calthrop who sat sweating sullenly at his desk all day, barking out orders and delivering reprimands. His blue eyes, sad and cold as chips of ice, roved the room like a vindictive school-master seeking someone to thrash.

'Bloody heat,' he said many times a day, using the words like a curse, wiping his damp red neck with his handkerchief. Or, 'When I next go on home leave, God be praised, it will be the blessed winter.' From further comments it was clear that Calthrop was an unhappy man, whose father and grandfather before him had met early deaths in India.

'Do you lot ever think of the sacrifices Englishmen have made to bring you a civilised life, to make you part of the Empire? Bloody heat, insanitary conditions, dead children, dead wives, tuberculosis . . .' Calthrop never finished the list of inconveniences life in the tropics could bring. In different circumstances Howard might have sympathised with the man and his fate as an empire builder. As it was, he took care to avoid him.

From the beginning Calthrop's eye had settled upon Howard and he picked on him for one small thing or another. An elderly clerk, Teddy de Souza, whose desk was near Howard's, soon put his finger on the problem: Howard was the only one in the office studying for the Public Service Examination, and such ambition in a local man Calthrop found presumptuous.

'It irks him. You're too bright, boy,' Teddy de Souza told him with a nervous grin. He had worked all his life at the Harbour Board in a clerical capacity, struggling hard for each small promotion. 'Don't get stuck here like me. Do something with your life, but for the moment try not to anger Mr Calthrop. He has been overlooked for promotion and that I believe is his trouble,' Teddy warned.

The relationship with Calthrop was not helped when the following week *The Straits Times*, to Howard's shock and horror, printed a letter he had written on an impulse, entering the debate on the rights of the local-born in the correspondence column. One long letter, written he was sure by someone local like himself, had challenged all the previous letter writers and set Howard off on a trail of thought he had never pursued before.

The future of the peoples of Malaya depends upon the complete cohesion and co-operation between local-born communities ... there must be a Federation of Local-born Communities covering the whole of British Malaya. The aim of local administrators in bringing a decentralised scheme into being is to divide Malaya into different political compartments, preventing cohesion and co-operation between them, damning the hopes of the people for a government of the people for the people of Malaya. It remains to be seen if the administrators can get away with it. There are thousands of local-born men and women who will rise up to recognition if they can only have an outlet for their activities.

It was all put so succinctly that Howard wondered why he had never thought about such things before. Soon, his mind was charged with new ideas and he could not rest until he wrote them down. To his surprise the words had flowed easily. Old memories floated up, things he had all but forgotten: the Englishman in the lavatory of the Great World and the wounded Chief Inspector in the riot at Kreta Ayer, whom he had so fervently wished dead. He remembered the cracking of shots and the bleeding bodies under straw mats in the road. As he recalled these things, his anger grew; it surprised him to find that unknown to himself strange seeds of thought had germinated deep within him. He looked down at the letter in his hand and was amazed at what he had written.

The dream of the local British administrator is that of a Malaya where European British subjects can continue with their princely salaries, special allowances and great residences ...

Not all letter writers signed their own name but Howard had seen no reason not to do so, had given no thought to the consequences, just pushed the letter into an envelope and sent it off, never thinking it would be published. He had just needed to get the words out of himself and never thought of who might see them. It was Teddy de Souza who brought a copy of *The Straits Times* into the office and read the letter aloud during lunch break, the men crowding about him, peering over his shoulder: '. . . local-born races are denied the right of advancement to the highest posts and influential positions or equal remuneration with Europeans for the same work . . . condemned to economic and political stagnation'. Teddy broke off and the men about him murmured in embarrassment. Later Teddy took Howard aside, the newspaper folded neatly now in his hand, his thin face wrinkled with perplexity.

'What's the use of writing all this? You're asking for trouble, boy,' Teddy said in sad disapproval. Howard struggled to find an answer, wishing he had never put pen to paper, wondering where these complicated thoughts and outlandish words had come from.

'It needed to be said,' he mumbled sullenly, feeling both angry and contrite.

'Look, boy, we don't have politics here, with elections, political parties, people shouting out their crazy views on soapboxes and all that. We must count ourselves lucky; we've got British rule instead. We can just sit back and leave everything to *them*. Don't you have all you want? I can tell you, Mr Calthrop is very upset.' Teddy spoke patiently, as if to a child, shaking his head all the while.

'There are some people in this office who think they are too clever by half,' Calthrop announced frostily the following day looking straight at Howard but elaborating no more, his sad blue eyes promising further engagement.

Surprisingly, Belvedere's new lodger Mr Patterson commented positively on Howard's letter. 'It's a changing world and we Europeans must wake up to the fact.' It had been after dinner and they met near the stairs as Wilfred prepared to go up to the Lodgers' Lounge. The man had stopped Howard and held out his hand to congratulate him. The blood rushed to Howard's face as he mumbled embarrassed thanks and hurried away, acutely aware that Patterson was himself a journalist with *The Straits Times*. Wilfred looked after him, unable to reveal to Howard that the real reason his letter had been published was not to add fuel to the argument in the newspaper's correspondence column, but as an example of the upstart thoughts that nowadays filled local heads.

Rose too was full of shocked disapproval. 'I cannot believe it. Do you know where we'd be without the British? If you lose that job at the Harbour Board you'll have only yourself to blame. It's shameful – how can I face the young men in the dining room? What am I supposed to say to them?' Rose slapped the paper angrily down on the table, tears of distress in her eyes.

Each day in the office Howard felt Calthrop's eyes settled upon him and waited for the inevitable explosion. It came early one monsoon morning some days after the printing of Howard's letter.

'You *natives* can't get anything right,' Calthrop roared at Howard over a small mistake in paperwork listing the cargo of a ship. Howard stood chastised at Calthrop's desk, the man's face incandescent before him. Suddenly, the guilt and anxiety of the past week could not be contained.

'We're not *natives*, sir, most of us in the office are Eurasian or Chinese.' Howard spoke almost under his breath but was unable to stop the words that were spilling from him.

In the silence that followed his outburst, Howard heard the scratching of pens and the clack of typewriters cease abruptly. He turned his head, expecting support from those behind him, but saw only a room of shocked faces; the people he spoke for looked away. Calthrop pushed back his chair and stood up, his eyes dark as polished flint.

'We're not *natives*, we're *Eurasian*,' Calthrop mimicked the slight lilt in Howard's voice, his barrel chest and fleshy shoulders assuming Howard's nervous stance. A titter of embarrassed laughter rippled around the room as Calthrop continued speaking.

'I know you're Eurasian, Mr Burns, just as I know that I'm an Anglo-Saxon. Just because you're taking those exams don't get the idea you're a cut above everyone else. Your Eurasian blood is so mixed up your brains don't know how to function. You'll always be a bit of mixed up *chap cheng* born under a coconut tree.'

Calthrop sat down and after a moment the scratching of pens and the knock of the typewriters began again. No one raised their eyes as Howard returned to his seat. Only Wee Jack, a slight, bespectacled man with a ferrety face who was one of the three Chinese in the office, gave Howard a discreet thumbs-up as he passed. Howard looked across at Teddy de Souza but the man just shook his head sadly, as if admonishing a naughty schoolboy.

Back at his desk Howard found that his hands were trembling and to steady himself turned to look out of the window. The briny smell of the sea came to him mixed with the scent of coal and oil. The noise of the docks and the shouts of men rose up from the quay below. There was a hammering of metal and the loud bleating of goats that were being unloaded and finding their land legs after days at sea. Howard stared at the stooped and naked backs of coolies on the wharf, hauling sacks of coal like a line of ants. About them the bleating goats were running one against another under the raised stick of a labourer. Howard thought again of his father, thought of him sitting at just such a desk as he did now, ignored even as he died, and vowed his life would take a different curve.

Wilfred Patterson was getting used to everything but the heat. The humidity drained him of energy; he was never free of its insidious presence. On his first morning Mrs Burns had sent for a rickshaw and instructed the runner to take him to the office of *The Straits Times* in Cecil Street, bargaining a monthly price for this service. Wilfred had joined an army of rickshaws and cars, all going in the direction of the Singapore River, Cavenagh Bridge and the business district beyond. He had been pulled past a church set in a grassy compound that could have been part of an English village and seemed only to emphasise how far he had travelled. Then, rounding a corner he had passed the green expanse of the Padang and the steely waters of the harbour.

When he arrived at the office of *The Straits Times* he had been introduced to Patrick Collins, a junior reporter, who was to take Wilfred out and give him a taste of the town and the job. Collins had the pale, etiolated appearance of a plant kept away from the sun; from the back of his sun helmet a flap of white cotton hung down to shade his delicate neck.

Outside the office Collins summoned two rickshaws, giving instructions in rapid Malay. Since shipping was of such importance to the rhythm of the town, they went first to the Shipping Office at the mouth of the Singapore River to collect lists of the vessels arriving and sailing from port each day. From the Shipping Office they then proceeded to the Supreme Court. This early morning visit was to learn what cases were coming up in the day, and which were worth returning to report on later.

Mopping his perspiring face with a handkerchief, Wilfred stepped gratefully into the cool and echoing building. The place was crowded with people hurrying purposefully about clutching sheaves of paper. He pushed his way up a great flight of stairs behind Collins. European judges in gowns and wigs swept by, Tamil peons in white starched shirts and *dhoti*, Chinese and Eurasians with expressions of importance ascended or descended the main stairs. A bewigged Indian and then a Chinese lawyer passed them.

'Nowadays they're bringing in some local-born members of the Bar who have qualified at the Inns of Court or Oxford or Cambridge. However, as locals, they can never get appointed to the Bench.' Collins took off his gold-rimmed spectacles and applied a monogrammed handkerchief to them, polishing studiously as he spoke.

Eventually, when they returned to Cecil Street, Simmons the editor summoned Wilfred. He entered a room stacked to the ceiling with listing piles of yellowing newspapers and the sweet odour of Simmons's pipe. The editor was a stocky man with a quiet and determined manner, a man with his eye on the future.

'We live in a new age of journalism. There's no place any longer in this town for a ten-cent paper. We'll soon be dropping our price to five cents; we have to do this to survive. We need to increase circulation. *The Malaya Tribune* is a local English-language paper but it's winning the price war hands down. It's read by the growing middle class educated in English-medium schools that is suddenly emerging here in Malaya. They want news in English but they're not prepared to pay more than five cents.' Simmons's eyes were sharp behind his spectacles, assessing Wilfred before continuing.

'Now, I need a new crime reporter. Jenkins, who was handling crime has fallen ill and been shipped home. I intend to include more local reports to give a broader flavour to the paper. By crime I mean our local Singapore crime in Chinatown, the Triad wars, opium smoking, drug smuggling, gang shootings, etcetera. We need a series of investigative reports on these things, and I've a feeling you're the man for the job,' Simmons announced as Wilfred stared at him in surprise.

Later, Collins suggested they have a drink at the Cricket Club after work. *The Straits Times* had already put Wilfred's name up for membership of the Cricket Club and the Swimming Club. It appeared that membership of these organisations were essential to effect any form of social survival. Already, under Collins's tutelage Wilfred had learned he need not attend the King's Birthday Garden Party held each year in the grounds of Government House as all and sundry were invited. The event of the year was the King's Birthday Ball where invitations were restricted to an elite circle of Europeans. Listening to Collins's high voice already defining the shape of his life, Wilfred silently decided to attend neither event.

Collins led the way into the Cricket Club and climbed the stairs to the upper floor; Boys in white uniforms bowed as they passed. He pointed out a green baize noticeboard. 'You need to leave your visiting card on here so the *tuans*' wives know of your arrival in town. You'll be showered with dinner invitations; best way to get a good meal and fill up the evenings.'

The thought of leaving himself vulnerable to society matrons waving dinner invitations did not appeal to Wilfred, and he made no effort to extract the obligatory card from his pocket. Collins walked out on to a wide and shady veranda and they settled into basket chairs. Before them in the mellow light of the late afternoon the glossy green lake of the Padang stretched away. Collins called for beer and when it arrived gave a small sigh of contentment.

'You can almost forget where you are in here,' he chuckled.

A game of cricket was in progress on the Padang. To Wilfred, the hard crack of ball against bat and the shouts of 'well done' as a six was scored were redolent of familiarity. It was almost possible, as Collins suggested, to believe that an English village green on a hot summer afternoon had suddenly materialised before them. Wilfred saw now that two games of cricket were in progress, one before the spreading veranda of the Cricket Club, and another before a smaller construction at the far end of the Padang, one game seeming to mirror the other.

'What's that building?' he asked, squinting against the sun at what appeared to be a small but untidy replica of the Cricket Club. As he focused his eyes on the distant game and the moving figures in white flannels, Wilfred realised that the players were all dark skinned.

'That's the Singapore Recreation Club, the Eurasians' club. We play cricket with them regularly, although of course they can't enter our

Club. Eurasians are jolly good at sports, you know. Somewhere along the way they inherited something positive from us, although not the qualities that founded an empire.' Simmons laughed, lifting the beer glass to his lips.

Mrs Burns had mentioned her husband's love of cricket to him Wilfred now remembered, and he wondered if this was where the man had played. The thought of Mrs Burns led him immediately to the thought of Cynthia and the blood quickened in his veins. She had taken the initiative the evening before and sought him out, making the meeting appear accidental. In the dining room of Belvedere Wilfred stole surreptitious glances at her each evening, aware of Boffort's watchful face across the table, its plump undulations damp with perspiration, polished by the candlelight. He knew Boffort sensed his attraction to Cynthia. Each meal was now beset by strategy, with Wilfred waiting for Boffort to be involved with his food, concentrating on cutting up his dinner, before he would look across the room to Cynthia. Each time without fail Cynthia met his eyes; each time, for as long as Boffort was busy, Wilfred held her gaze. Usually, it was he who was obliged to look away to relieve the intensity of what passed between them.

The evening before, Wilfred had gone to sit in the Lodgers' Lounge after dinner; the pleasant airy terrace room due to its elevation caught each stray breeze. It was simply furnished with potted plants and climbing vines, comfortable rattan furniture with colourful chintz cushions, and a table on which were newspapers and periodicals. Cynthia had used the excuse of adding some extra magazines to those on the table to come up to the lounge. Absorbed in his book, he had not heard her come in.

'What are you reading?' Cynthia asked, after silently appearing beside Wilfred's chair.

Her voice was conspiratorial; it was as if they had agreed to this meeting. At the sound of her voice he looked up in shock, his pulse suddenly erratic. Closing the book, he held it up to show her the dust jacket with its sketch of Einstein and a spinning universe.

'Relativity. It's difficult to grasp, but amazing.' Wilfred marked his page and shut the book, trying not to reveal his confusion. The knowledge that she had known he was sitting here, had noticed that he had taken his book to dinner in order to read in the lounge after the meal, flooded through him.

'Mummy saw Einstein,' Cynthia announced unexpectedly. Wilfred could not hide his surprise; the thought of Rose and Einstein seemed incredible.

'Apparently Einstein stopped for a day or two in Singapore; he was travelling about trying to raise funds for a Jewish university. There was a reception for him in the house of a rich Jewish family here. Mummy was invited to help out with the organisation, provide some of the cakes,' Cynthia explained with a laugh, sitting down on the edge of the empty chair beside him.

Wilfred could not hide his agitation at her close proximity. The low lamp by which he had been trying to read illuminated her face. Her eyes locked on to him and words fell away between them so that they sat in an awkward silence for some moments. The sound of Howard practising his saxophone rose up from below, the notes sailing and spinning about them.

'What was Einstein like?' Wilfred asked at last, clearing his throat, pushing the words into the space between them. The sound of the saxophone rose gustily again, ending in a sudden shriek.

'She said he was nice, not like the other people at the reception. She said there were soup stains on his tie and a button was loose on his waistcoat. His hair stuck up in a frizzy mass.' A patchy vision of the scientist came back to her from a photograph her mother had kept of the event.

Wilfred laughed, breaking the tension between them. Downstairs the notes of Howard's saxophone collapsed one upon another, trailing off in a squawk of discord as if a bird were being throttled. Wilfred leaned forward, offering his book for inspection and felt the brush of her hand. At once everything was heightened and expanded within him: the dark lush green of the garden, the clink of glasses as the tables were cleared in the dining room, the sound of a buzzing fly. Howard ended his saxophone practice with another angry shriek of notes. In the unexpected silence the disconsolate croaking of bullfrogs in the garden filled the night. Wilfred watched a moth blunder against the globe of a lamp and knew his life had changed. Now, sitting with Collins on the veranda of the Cricket Club he knew he had already placed himself apart from society in the very way Boffort had warned him about only days before.

As Wilfred sat in the Lodgers' Lounge, talking of Einstein to Cynthia, Howard watched his sister from the garden. He often played his saxophone under the trees, savouring the peace of night settling about him. The distance from Belvedere removed him from the lodgers' inevitable complaints if he blew too loudly in the house. From the garden he watched the lighted square of the Lodgers' Lounge where he could just see Wilfred Patterson's head and the tawny hair of his sister. He had noticed the glances that passed between them each dinner-time and did not approve. Local women like Cynthia were prey to European men needing comfort during their stay in Singapore. Such liaisons were plentiful, but few became permanent as most men returned home to marry. Against his will a memory swam up to fill Howard's mind like sediment loosened from the floor of a well.

He had come home from school, and had run to seek out his mother, pushing open the door of her bed-sitting room. He heard first a soft mewling sound and then the rough whispering of a man. The door swung open and he saw that one of the lodgers, Mr Woodstock, was holding his mother down on the bed, a hand on her shoulder and a knee between her open legs. The man's face was hidden from him but the red neck, the pomaded hair and the patches of sweat on his shirt awoke Howard's worst fears. His mother's skirt was pushed up about her thighs and the buttons of her dress were open revealing the soft flesh of her breasts spilling out for all to see.

He stood in the doorway, terror spinning through him, sure his mother would soon be dead. In a rush he ran to pull frantically at the man, who turned his head with a look of fury and surprise. Howard still remembered the lax wet mouth, the unhinged expression on his face. He had pulled and pummelled, not caring what happened to him as long as his mother was released, and screamed for her to escape. The man had raised a hand and struck Howard hard in the face. Then, tucking his loosened shirt into his trousers, he strode from the room cursing loudly, slamming the door behind him. Howard flung himself sobbing upon his mother who had quickly buttoned up her dress and gathered him to her breast. He heard the rapid beating of her heart against his ear and remembered her words, soft as a sigh.

'It's all right. It won't happen again.'

'Tell him to go,' he had sobbed, his tears darkening the print of her dress.

And indeed, Mr Woodstock left Belvedere almost immediately. Yet, on the day the man departed his mother had cried as if her heart were broken. Suddenly, as he stood in the garden staring up at Cynthia and Wilfred together in the Lodgers' Lounge, he wondered for the first time if he had saved his mother from a fate she had desired. The thought was hot and overwhelming and he could bear it no more. He blew a powerful ripple of notes into the mouthpiece of the saxophone, repeating the same pounding sequence of sound until no breath was left in his body.

11

AT SIMMONS'S SUGGESTION WILFRED went into Chinatown for the first time. Get the feel of the place; write me something interesting, Simmons said. Wilfred's guide in Chinatown was Chen, a Chinese Eurasian who had lived many years in England and joined *The Straits Times* on his return to Singapore.

'There's to be a big raid on the opium dens tonight. Miller, the Chief Detective Officer, knows we're coming. They're looking for arms and drugs. Singapore can be a rough place,' Chen explained as they walked along Chinatown's dark crumbling alleys and Wilfred peered up at the filthy, peeling façades of houses festooned with poles of dripping washing. Stray dogs and ragged, skeletal men slipped in and out of the shadows. He thought of the unhurried world of the Cricket Club with its ubiquitous white-uniformed waiters, the beer and ceiling fans, and the vast green Padang floating always serenely before it. These images returned to him in a wave of unexpected nostalgia. Yet he knew that this visceral place was the true essence of the town, not the world he so easily inhabited. Everywhere here he sensed death, cunning and despair, bound together by the teeming tide of the living. He saw now that there were two towns on the island, as distinct from each other as summer and winter, each all but unknown to the other.

'That's Miller,' Chen said, recognising the Chef Detective Officer, a tall gaunt man who stood head and shoulders over his local detectives. Wilfred saw a group of men working on the door lock of a ramshackle house by the light of their torches.

As Chen and Wilfred joined them, the door swung open and they followed the men inside. Immediately, an overwhelming stench surrounded them, a stench that Wilfred now recognised as the odour of poverty-stricken Chinatown; a thick miasma of sewage and garlic, opium dross and the rancid fermentation of old cooked rice. The detectives quickly disappeared up an almost perpendicular stairway, Chen behind them; Wilfred climbed more cautiously, unused to the steep, shallow stairs. He found Chen with the detectives, who were shining their torches upon several men lying inert on the floor of a large unfurnished room. Chen nudged one of the addicts with his foot. The man looked up with a glazed expression.

'Everyone else has fled, they must have had word we were coming,' Miller said over his shoulder as he turned to search the house, emptying half-eaten bowls of rice, opening cupboards, raking through baskets of decaying vegetables, and probing the warm ashes of the kitchen fire. No drugs or arms were to be found in any of these locations and Miller's frustration was obvious.

As they emerged into the fresh air of the night, two figures ran off along the side of the house and up an alley. Miller gave a shout and with his men raced after them. At the corner the fleeing men turned and unexpectedly raised guns at the detectives. Before they could shoot, Miller fired his own revolver, the loud crack of the shots breaking open the night. Wilfred jumped in shock at the sound. One of the men was hit and collapsed in the road, the other took to his heels.

Even as he ran after Miller and Chen, Wilfred had the feeling that nothing he was experiencing could be real. Reaching the body, Miller bent to pick up the man's discarded gun then walked off without a word to a police car waiting at the top of the road. Wilfred stared down at the lifeless body. By the light of Chen's torch he saw a growing patch of blood spreading over the man's loose shirt; his eyes, still open in surprise, gazed up into Wilfred's face. Chen appeared unperturbed by the corpse.

'Gang members will come later to collect the body. We can go home now,' Chen announced unemotionally, walking ahead, looking for a rickshaw.

Soon Wilfred was on his way back to Belvedere, while Chen departed in the opposite direction. A cool breeze blew about him as the rickshaw gathered speed. The rasp of the runner's breath mixed with the sound of the wheels bowling unevenly over the road. A light rain had started to fall, Wilfred felt his shirt grow damp on his shoulders and found he was trembling. He had never seen a man killed before, shot like a hunted animal, and the scene returned again and again to his mind. When at last he reached Belvedere and lay in bed, his dreams throbbed with voices and faces. Rain beat against the window shutters and spat on the lowered bamboo *chiks*. A gecko clucked on the ceiling and he was conscious that the mosquito netting was entangled about his leg. Childhood memories welled up confusedly, pushing free of their hidden place.

He remembered the rubber estate where he had been born. He remembered a time when his mother had gone away, to stay with the wife of a neighbouring planter and he had been left alone with his father. She had departed with angry tears that frightened him, but it had been a companionable few days for him and his father. They had drunk the strong Indian tea his father liked, and he had been allowed to dip his finger in the evening *stengah* and suck the hard raw taste of whiskey. They had trekked together through the jungle and his father had examined the oozing wounds of the rubber trees and shown him the small cup of sticky white sap that would eventually make tyres for motor cars. Then, one day, the woman had arrived.

A little horse-drawn cart had stopped by the house and she had descended wearing a smile and a wide straw hat with blue ribbons. She sat with them on the veranda and spoke to his father as if he were a friend. She did not have the pale beauty of his mother; her skin was the colour of polished bronze, her mouth wide and red, and dark hair curled lavishly about her shoulders. He had thought her beautiful and, he remembered, the emotions had been thick in his father's face. Wilfred was sent to play and when he looked back to the house from the swing his father and the woman had vanished from the veranda, their drinks untouched upon the table. He thought something must have happened and ran back into the house. The door to his father's bedroom was locked; inside there was only silence and no one had answered his knocking. In the end a servant had pulled him away and he had returned to the swing, anxious and confused. Then, as abruptly as they had vanished, his father and the woman reappeared upon the veranda, as if they had never left. These shadowy images were all he remembered. His mother's death from a snake-bite a short while later he had all but blocked from his mind. After her death he had returned to England, to go to boarding school, sailing back in the charge of a missionary family, and was met at the dock by an uncle. He never saw his father again for he died of cholera one year later and the uncle adopted Wilfred.

Freeing his leg from the mosquito net, he flung it over the long thin bolster that Mrs Burns called a Dutch wife. He pulled it close and wished that instead of the kapok-stuffed case he could feel Cynthia's smooth body beneath him.

Howard made his way to the orchard. Already it was dark, the tennis court invisible in the shadows beneath the trees. There was a seat here near the shed where the gardener, Rama, sat in the day to smoke a *bedi*. Light from the kitchen outhouses, which were separate from the house and linked to it by a covered walkway, diffused the darkness so that he could make out the tangled branches of the mangosteen trees behind the shed. As the night descended Belvedere's windows brightened and the smell of frying fish came to him from the kitchen. There was no sign of the girl they called Nona. Part Malay, part Chinese, she was the least attractive of Belvedere's servants but raised no objection to assignations. Howard had only to appear at the kitchen door and within minutes she would make her way to where he always waited, by the shed that housed the heavy roller used on Belvedere's lawns and the gardener's scythe and shears.

The humid scent of the undergrowth, damp after a sudden shower, filled his head. In the distance the open doors of the candlelit dining room gave him a shadowy glimpse of the lodgers gathering for drinks before the evening meal. Beyond the mangosteen trees he could see the roof of Bougainvillaea House. As he did so often, he remembered Mei Lan, the taste of her lips, the smell of her hair, and the way she had made him feel, as if their lives ran together. Over the years he had only occasional glimpses of her in her small garden surrounded by bushes of bougainvillaea, the old nursemaid always beside her. In the beginning, after the fence was put up, he sometimes took his saxophone down to the canal and played in the hope that she might hear.

His mother's voice came to him ordering the servants about in the kitchen, and he was filled with shame for what he was doing. He came here despite his fear of scorpions and snakes, driven to risk such dangers by the heat of his need. There was still no sign of Nona and he paced about, his body full of anticipation. At last he heard the soft clack of her sandals coming towards him and saw her dark, squat shape emerge from the shadows about the shed.

He pushed open the door and Nona squeezed past him releasing an odour of cooking and perspiration. As soon as the door was closed he was ready and aching, but she held up a hand for patience, folding back her *sarong*. Unable to wait, he pulled roughly at the skirt as he forced her back against a pile of heavy sacks. He thrust into her but within a few moments pulled back from her warmth, spilling himself over her plump thigh. Teddy de Souza at the Harbour Board had told him to withdraw before the climactic moment, insisting that this one small sacrifice in a waterfall of pleasure would save him from disaster nine months later. Nona sat up and stared sourly at her wet thigh. He had come so quickly she had not even begun her usual heavy breathing and groaning.

'No having good time,' she hissed at him, small eyes glowering. Howard pulled a handkerchief from his pocket and she snatched it from him to wipe her thigh. Sometimes he closed his eyes and imagined it was not the sluttish Nona beneath him but Mei Lan, and afterwards was ashamed. Retying her sarong Nona departed angrily, slamming the creaking door behind her and taking the handkerchief to add to Belvedere's laundry. As the door shut and the blood no longer hammered through his body, the odour in the hut of manure, sacking and dry soil forced Howard to think again of scorpions and snakes. Hurriedly he left, letting himself out of the shed into the dark grounds of Belvedere.

This violent awakening to himself was all the fault of Teddy de Souza who, amazed at Howard's innocence, had seen it as his duty to instruct him in the ways of the world and had shown him some photographs besides. Teddy was married with a grown-up family, but although he was already a grandfather no moral restrictions appeared to pin down his life. Tales of his escapades with women raced around the office, and as his special protégé Howard was privy to the choicest of details.

In the office Calthrop made no further effort to hide his dislike of Howard. One morning he observed the rain sluicing down outside with the accompanying loud cracks of thunder, and fixed his eyes upon Howard; he ordered him to take some paperwork to a warehouse some distance away.

With the rain every rickshaw was suddenly in use, and roads flooded as drains overflowed. Cars and trams, bicycles, carts and rickshaws clogged up the streets, honking horns and ringing bells. In exasperation Howard removed his socks and shoes, rolled up his white cotton trousers and waded under his umbrella through the deluge. Soon, his trousers were sodden and muddied and his shirt stuck wetly to his back, but as the rain lessened he found a rickshaw at last and quickly delivered the damp bundle of papers. By the time he emerged from the godown the rain had stopped and the sun was already pushing open the sky. By the waterfront a Tamil tea vendor was removing the tarpaulin from his stall and washing thick china cups in a bucket of murky water.

'You'll have to wait a few minutes. I had to shut everything down because of the rain,' the man said as Howard approached, setting a kettle of water to boil on a small spirit stove.

The low sea wall was too wet to sit on and Howard stood staring at the island of sampans below him on the water, crowded together against the wall, rocking as one on the swell. Now that the rain had stopped, the first birds of prey had reappeared in the sky, gliding over the water on motionless wings searching for garbage riding the waves. Beyond the sampans the great arc of the horizon spread endlessly before Howard, filling him with its emptiness. There was nothing here to hem in his thoughts, nothing to impede ambition or will. His heart seemed to swell as if it would burst the confines of his body and he knew life waited only for him to fill it. Gazing again at the ocean, he realised he must focus on his own horizon, and the possibilities that lay beyond.

Remembering his tea he turned back to the stall but saw that another customer was being attended to. After waiting his turn he was served a cup of strong brew that he carried back to the wall. The other customer, an Indian in a mud-splattered *dhoti*, stood nearby, sipping loudly at his cup. While Howard watched, the man poured some tea from the cup into the saucer and as it cooled drank directly from it.

'This way tea is getting cold quickly and not burning the tongue. Try.' The man smiled, seeing Howard's interest.

Howard nodded but still sipped the scalding drink from the cup, burning his lips; drinking tea from a saucer was something his mother disapproved of. The man was looking curiously at Howard.

'Indian?' he asked, observing Howard's dark skin.

'Eurasian,' Howard answered and the man smiled, relieved to have Howard's indecipherable components explained.

'My name is Raj Sherma,' he offered.

'Working in one of these godowns?' Howard asked after intro-
ducing himself. Although he judged the man to be in his mid-
twenties, he had the beginnings of a paunch beneath his loose shirt
and a brash confidence that made him seem older. Howard wished
he had the same hard-bitten look about him, the look of a man who
knew the ways of the world. In spite of his smile, there was something guarded in the man's hooded eyes, as if he were constantly
appraising things and searching only for that which was of use to
him.

'I have my own business. I am a ship chandler,' Raj replied proudly.

Raj pointed to a ship anchored in the outer lanes of the harbour.
'That Japanese ship is one of my ships. I am supplying everything it
needs when it comes into port: meat, vegetables, rice, nails, beer, soap;
everything.'

'A Japanese ship?' Howard queried.

'I am only servicing Japanese ships. The Japanese are good people
to work for, they are a people who keep their word. British companies
are always finding some problem, making you feel like dog shit under
their shoe,' Raj replied.

'How are the Japanese so different?' Howard felt suddenly disad-
vantaged before a man he had immediately taken to be uneducated.

'The Japanese see Asia as a family of nations; they feel they are the
father of this family. They feel they must free their family from the
white man's rule. They want all Asia to have prosperity, free of colonial rule. This is their vision. The Japanese are also a powerful people
like the English people. Japan too is also conquering countries that
are bigger than themselves, just like the English. Now they have
conquered China, a nation that is like a giant beside their own small
island. The most important thing to remember is that, like us, the
Japanese are also Asiatics. It is a good feeling when you work for
another Asiatic, instead of for the English.'

Howard stared at the man in surprise, and for a moment was tempted
to tell him about his letter to *The Straits Times*. The tea had cooled
and he sipped it thirstily, the taste of condensed milk sweet on his
tongue. He was hungry, it was past tiffin time and Calthrop had sent
him out deliberately so that he would miss his lunch.

'We want them out of our country,' Raj said suddenly, draining his
saucer and refilling it.

'Who?' Howard asked, still absorbed in his anger with Calthrop, thinking of the phrases he had written in his letter.

'We want the British out of India. We want our Independence,' Raj answered, lifting the saucer of tea to his lips.

'How will you get them out? They are our rulers; we are their subjects,' Howard answered, puzzled yet excited by the audacious ideas coming from this unlikely source. Even when he had written his letter to *The Straits Times* he had never thought it possible to be rid of colonial rule, only hoped to expand his presence within it.

'My brother-in-law, who is a revolutionary, says that in India the time is coming soon; there is much agitation amongst Indians everywhere for Independence, even here in Singapore. India has the strength of millions, and the British are no more than a handful of people. Why should a handful of people rule so many millions?' Raj argued.

'Why should they?' Howard echoed, staring at the man in amazement. The words cut into him, opening a space in his mind into which already he felt something new shifting. In contrast to the radical thoughts just expressed, his letter, for which he had been so chastised, was a lame thing and he was glad he had not mentioned it to the man.

Unaware of his effect upon Howard, Raj tipped up the saucer and drank down the last of the tea. Wiping his mouth on the back of his hand he nodded then walked away, shoulders swinging, his step direct and sure. Howard stared after him, trying to absorb the unexpected things he had said.

Once he had finished his tea, Howard walked along the seafront, the Indian's unsettling words still racing through him; the sun was now hot on his head. This old part of the docks retained its tie to the days of sail, when ships were unloaded into the cavernous godowns that still lined the waterfront. Running above the open arches of the five-foot way before the warehouses, a long common veranda linked one upper floor office to another. In those faraway days of early sail every office was equipped with a telescope and from this veranda men would scan the horizon for sight of an arriving ship. At the same time each year a forest of sails descended upon the island as the indigenous tribe of Bugis from the Celebes came to trade in an armada of small boats. The town had then been a fishing village, a pirates' den, before Stamford Raffles disembarked, possibly on this very beach, Howard thought. The men who followed him from those cold countries across the sea had left their seed in local women, breeding a race of mimic men trained to serve the new colony. They had fashioned *him*, thought Howard, in clandestine meetings and filthy brothels, in marriages of convenience far from home.

He turned to look back at the tea stall but Raj Sherma was gone and he wished now that he had talked more to the man. The Indian was fighting to rid his country of men like Calthrop. Howard remembered again his humiliation in the office, the silence and embarrassed guffaws and Teddy de Souza shaking his head as if Howard were a naughty schoolboy. What had he to fight for, Howard wondered, if even those he would speak for disowned him?

As Howard climbed out of a rickshaw before the office the following day, Wee Jack was also arriving and called out a greeting. He waited for Howard to pay his runner and then walked with him towards the entrance of the building.

'Got time to meet after work?' Wee Jack asked.

He smiled in an unusually friendly manner. Other than a thumbs-up sign after the Calthrop incident, the man had not spoken to Howard before. He was a mystery to everyone, mixing with no one yet competent in his work and with a good command of English. He always departed the office with such haste that it was thought he might have a second job.

Later that day, they left the office together, Jack leading the way to a drinking place sandwiched between brothels in a crumbling shophouse outside the dock gates; beggars littered their path, dock coolies gambled and quarrelled. The sun was setting, dulling the metallic glitter of the sea to an oily beaten grey. Flies buzzed thickly over offal thrown out of a kitchen window and a couple of ageing prostitutes called to them as they passed. Howard always avoided this part of the docks, mindful of his mother's instructions.

A wall of tobacco smoke and alcohol fumes hit them as they entered the place. The narrow room was crammed with benches and tables at which sat Chinese tally clerks and the crews of ships in port. A couple of rough looking Europeans occupied a corner. Wee Jack had to raise his voice to be heard as he ordered beer.

'You're not like the others, happy to take whatever Calthrop doles out. Why should such people rule us?' Wee Jack hissed in a low voice.

An old Malay man in a worn sarong shuffled towards them with their beer and a tin plate with fried shrimp wafers.

'The world has had enough of colonial rule; native peoples everywhere now want to rule themselves.' Wee Jack leaned forward across the table, the light reflecting on his round metal-framed spectacles. Behind the thick glass his eyes were bright but deeply sunken; the ridge of his cheekbone high. There was a rodent-like quality about the man, Howard thought, something hidden and furtive of which he was immediately wary. Yet Howard leaned forward, excited in spite of himself to hear ideas of this nature expressed yet again. Just the thought of such things produced an effervescing inside him.

'The Indians want the British out of India,' Howard replied, recalling the man at the tea stall. Wee Jack clicked his tongue impatiently.

'They have their battle to fight in India; in China we have ours. They are different battles, even if there is the common motive of freeing Asia from Imperialist rule.'

'Are you a communist?' Howard asked in a low voice. The thought struck him for the first time. A distant memory of the riot of Kreta Ayer returned to him, and a shadow of fear flickered through him. He remembered the Chief Inspector's bloodied sun helmet rolling in the road and the bodies of young men covered with rush mats.

'Communists don't eat people. Have you read Lenin or Marx?' Refusing to commit himself, Jack took a gulp of beer. Howard had only a vague knowledge of these men.

'I can bring you some books to read,' Jack offered, assessing Howard over his spectacles. 'There is a new world taking shape where the workers will have power, not men like Calthrop. He's a clown.' He reached into his trouser pocket and took out a sheet of paper that he carefully unfolded and pushed over the table to Howard, looking about to see if anyone was observing them.

Workers of the World, Unite. Avenge the Martyrs of Japanese Tyranny. Beneath this heading were crude drawings of Japanese soldiers with bayonets killing Chinese women and children. The pictures were printed in red. A boycott of Japanese goods was demanded but British goods were not mentioned.

'You're not fighting the British, you're fighting the Japanese. This is nothing to do with Malaya. This killing is all in China,' Howard protested as he read the crudely printed page.

'The Japanese are also colonists. Their occupation of China is brutal. Chiang Kai-shek will never free us from the Japanese, but Mao Tse-tung has the people with him.' Wee Jack's eyes shone.

Everywhere he turned nowadays Howard saw posters urging people to give money to the China Relief Fund to support China in the war against the Japanese. On street corners Chinese students sold flags or paper flowers, urging everyone to donate to the war effort.

'If the Japanese ever come to Singapore perhaps they will treat us like equals; they're Asiatic like us after all,' Howard suggested, again thinking of the man at the tea stall. Wee Jack drew back on his stool with a frown.

'Do you know the things they're doing in China? The British are an arrogant race, but they're not animals.' He stared at Howard incredulously.

'Sorry, Wee Jack, I don't know much about the war in China,' Howard admitted hurriedly, seeing how much he had upset the man and wondering how soon he could escape him.

'I am neither Jack, nor *Wee Jack*,' the Chinese exploded, mimicking the false Scottish accent Calthrop adopted when he called Jack's name. 'My name is Wee Jiak Kim.' Howard began to apologise but Wee Jack cut him short.

'You're taking the Public Service Examination, aren't you?' Wee Jack leaned forward, his eyes focused intently on Howard.

'It will enable me to rise up the ladder,' Howard replied defensively, echoing his mother's words, staring at the tiny ghost of himself reflected in the polished spheres of Wee Jack's spectacles.

'That examination is just a plot by the British Imperialists to gain control of your life and enslave you further,' Wee Jack said angrily. Leaning over the table he began speaking in the cajoling tone he might use to a child.

'Calthrop and his kind are colonial stooges. Are you going to work under British running dogs or will you join the struggle to bring freedom to the masses? You should attend one of our meetings.'

The thick stale odours of tobacco smoke and liquor fumes pressed in upon Howard in the suffocating room; Wee Jack's words swam through his head. In spite of his misgivings, Howard's heart thumped unevenly with excitement. Once, on a trip to a nearby island he had climbed a headland and stood on the edge of a cliff looking down at the rocky shore far below and felt the same kind of excitement. A breeze had blown on his face and vibrated in his ears. Now, within the course of little more than a day, he had met two people who were convinced the world could be shaken. It shocked him to find that seditious thought and agitation grew underfoot like weeds, threatening to overthrow an immovable order, and until now he had known nothing about it. It was as if a skin had been peeled from his eyes.

The following day Teddy took Howard home for dinner; he had issued the invitation the week before. 'Olive, my missus, is determined to meet you. She has promised to cook her special coconut chicken if you'll honour us with a visit. That chicken is delicious, boy, as are her *sugee* cake and devil's curry; I'll be retiring soon, so you could call it a farewell dinner.'

Howard approached Teddy's small terraced house in trepidation. He had the feeling that the nimble libertine Teddy claimed to be might soon be threatened by reality. As they entered the house Olive's deep voice could be heard even before she was seen. She emerged from a back room to confront Howard, a large-busted woman with a dark florid face and penetrating eyes. Teddy shrank in her shadow, lapsing into uncustomary silence, his eyes apprehensively upon her.

'So, you are the young man Teddy feels is in need of some fatherly direction.' Olive's voice bounced about; her chin appeared to be lost in her neck. Under her scrutiny Howard understood that, to ensure his own survival, Teddy might well have described him as a reckless young man in need of guidance.

Already Howard realised, with a pang of loss, that Teddy's adventures were all in his mind. It was impossible to imagine his stringy limbs entwined with those of his fleshy wife, bending to perform the numerous contorted positions of penetration he had copiously described, his lips wet with vicarious desire.

'I am sixty next week,' Teddy told him proudly when they sat down at the table for dinner. 'As a retired man I will have more time for the ladies.' Teddy winked, his mournful eyes lighting up a narrow face. Olive was busy instructing a servant to add more *belachan* paste to the rice on the next preparation and did not hear Teddy's whispered comment.

'What will you do with yourself when you retire?' Howard enquired with a nervous smile. He did not like the hollow ring of the word 'retirement'.

'We're going home,' Teddy explained, his face full of pleasurable anticipation.

'But Malaya is your home, you were born in Malacca,' Howard answered in surprise.

'Singapore is nobody's home, boy,' Teddy chuckled. 'We're going home, to England. Our daughter lives there, as you know. We'll be with her for Christmas.'

'But you have never been to England, how can it be home?' Howard argued.

'A homeland is where your heart is, young Howard. England is our heartland,' Olive announced in her booming voice, returning to the conversation as the servant departed.

'The King, God bless him, has taken good care of me. It would not do to be ungrateful. I'm happy to sing the National Anthem until the day I die.' Teddy smiled, bulbous eyes earnest in his gaunt face. 'My great-grandad on my mummy's side was a Mr John Rogers from the town of Fleetwood near Blackpool. And on my daddy's side Great-Grandad was a Plymouth man, a Mr Prince, I believe. There has been a lot of intermarriage out here of course, which accounts for the name of de Souza that I now bear. And, although Olive was born a Remedios, her great-grandaddy actually hailed from Scotland. But through it all we have always looked homewards. Now the chance to return has come.' Teddy's deep-set eyes lit up as he spoke.

Howard looked at his thin dark face and the strands of grey hair that flopped over his brow and wondered at his future in the land of Calthrop.

12

THE MATTER OF MEI Lan's marriage began to obsess Second Grandmother. She would not let the matter rest until Lim Hock An and Boon Eng both took up the refrain. 'It's time you were married. You do not need more education. You're not a man; you've no need to earn a living.' Once the men of the household were of her own mind, Second Grandmother wasted no time in calling the matchmaker, who immediately suggested as a prospective bridegroom the eldest son of an abalone cannery millionaire. A bride viewing was suggested and Mei Lan's protest dismissed.

'Only seeing you, *lah*. Can do at distance in hotel tea lounge. You sit one end of the room and he sit another,' Second Grandmother suggested with an impatient wave of her blood-coloured nails, the scent of *Schiaparelli* and mothballs wafting about her.

It was unbearable. Mei Lan locked herself in her room and would not come out, anger and fear drumming through her. She threw herself down on her bed and listened to Second Grandmother beat her small fists on the door.

'Do you want to be an old maid?' Second Grandmother screamed.

'Yes!' Mei Lan screamed back. Outside the door she heard whispering and knew Ah Siew was also there.

It was unbearable. She was nineteen; it was almost four years since her mother died and her life was being squeezed into a box. After finishing at the Chinese Girls' High School she had expected to continue on to Raffles College where, she secretly hoped, she might win a Queen's Scholarship and go to England to study law. It was a shock to have her plans so brusquely thwarted. At last they left her alone and she heard the tiny shuffling steps of Second Grandmother, supported by Ah Siew, fade away down the corridor. After a while she got up and, opening the window shutters wide, observed the slender branches of the Mexican lilac pushing up beneath the sill, wondering if it would hold her weight.

It was not easy to reach the tree without falling from the window but at last she grasped a strong branch and swung herself forward, her feet scrabbling for a hold against the trunk. Almost at once she heard a loud crack, and fell with the branch the short distance to the ground. Her leg was scratched and her shoulder bruised but nothing more, and scrambling up she ran off through the gate of Bougainvillaea House to flag down a rickshaw on Bukit Timah.

She remembered a hairdresser near Robinsons that her mother had used, and directed the rickshaw to take her there. The bell rattled as she pushed open the door, just as it used to when her mother had entered. Inside Mode Elite, Madame Chan, who had always created the elaborate coifs Ei Ling demanded, greeted her in amazement, not having seen her since her mother's death.

'Cut it off,' Mei Lan ordered as the woman undid the long plait, weighing the thick hair in her hands.

'Really modern women nowadays not only cut but also perm their hair,' Madame Chan solicitously advised, pointing to a fearsome contraption of electrical wires. It reminded Mei Lan of a picture she had seen of a machine invented to milk cows.

'It's the latest thing from England,' the hairdresser informed her.

For several hours Mei Lan endured the torture of having her hair wound about the rods hanging from the monstrous machine. Rubber pads were placed upon her head, her hair was doused with vile-smelling liquids and then heated and steamed like a turnip, burning her scalp. At last it was done, and in the mirror Mei Lan saw an unrecognisable face framed by a frizzy halo of curls; it was just the reincarnation she wanted and she smiled in delight. Even the birthmark on her jaw seemed to gain authority. She wiggled her lips to make it move, pleased suddenly that it was there.

Bougainvillaea House was in an uproar when she returned. The open window and broken branch had been taken as an indication of dire events. Workmen had been summoned to force the locked bedroom door, and policemen were searching the neighbourhood for her. Ah Siew and Second Grandmother grew apoplectic at the sight of her as she came into the house. Boon Eng, who had been called home from the office, shouted and raised a hand as if he would hit her, although he did no such thing.

'*Aiyaah!* Look like someone pull her out of a bush. Who will marry her now?' Second Grandmother screamed, while Ah Siew scowled behind her. Mei Lan pushed her chin up determinedly; what was done could not be undone and this small triumph was pleasing. Only her grandfather, who had come into the room at the commotion, remained silent, staring at her enigmatically. The next day Lim Hock An made his decision known to the household: the question of Mei Lan's marriage could wait until she was of a more pliant state of mind.

Within weeks of Mei Lan's haircut, Lim Hock An suffered a stroke and lay in a coma for days, plunging everyone in Bougainvillaea House into foreboding and depression. Mei Lan wondered guiltily if her behaviour had added to his stress, as Second Grandmother angrily insisted. Yet, defying the doctor's worst predictions, Lim Hock An opened his eyes one morning as calmly as if awakening from sleep. Second Grandmother struggled from her chair with a gasp, startling Little Sparrow who had been allowed into the house to sit at her husband's bedside to await his death. At once Bougainvillaea House, sunk for days into a state of lowered voices and black reverie, regained its old momentum. The kitchen bustled with the preparation of elaborate dishes, gardeners were summoned to trim the trees, the barber was called to the sickroom, cars and rickshaws deposited a stream of visitors at the door, delivery boys from Robinsons and Cold Storage were forever begging entry with gifts. Lim Hock An was at a loss to understand the celebratory atmosphere in the house or the incredulous shaking of heads that afflicted whoever observed him. Little Sparrow rashly suggested they light firecrackers in celebration. Second Grandmother looked at her askance and soon withdrew permission for further visits to the house.

'While you were in your long sleep could you hear what we said?' Second Grandmother asked her husband, the smell of her decayed teeth covering his face.

'Did you say things I was not to hear?' he demanded, wanting at once to get up but finding his legs would not hold him. He could no longer bear the smell of his wife's rotting teeth.

'Get some more gold ones,' he told her as she threw aniseed into her mouth.

Mei Lan woke early. Ah Siew rubbed her ageing arthritic limbs and brought hot tea for them both. She drew the curtains and plumped up the pillows behind Mei Lan as the sun streamed in. Already, Ah Siew was opening the cupboard and asking what she would wear that day so that it could be ironed. Mei Lan gave directions from her bed as she stared out of the window at the distant turrets of Lim Villa and the shutters of her old bedroom; the loss of Lim Villa was still felt keenly by the family but no one spoke about it. Although his great fortune was lost, Lim Hock An had recovered enough for them not to have to live too frugally, but everyone understood they would never move out of Bougainvillaea House.

After a breakfast of rice porridge, Mei Lan made her way to her grandfather's room. As soon as he saw her Lim Hock An pulled himself up on his pillows; there was now no joy in his life like the joy of this granddaughter. Mei Lan, who from her own parents had received little more than a lukewarm love, subject always to their self-absorption, saw her world increasingly now in her grandfather. His love once of child brides and bound feet seemed part of another man. The most important thing about her grandfather, Mei Lan realised, the strength that accounted for his enormous success before the Depression, was his ability to embrace the new and leave the obsolete behind him.

Lim Hock An was hungry for news of the world and especially of China, afraid too much might have happened while he slept in his coma. His mind appeared to be working as usual but illness had shrunk him, his skin hung loosely upon his wide jaw, his eyes were clouded and rheumy. There was the smell of old age about him.

'What news of the China Relief Fund?' he asked.

After the haircut, which she had not regretted, Lim Hock An had suggested that Mei Lan become involved with the China Relief Fund to keep herself busy. The Japanese had pushed through China with unimaginable brutality to occupy most of the country. So great was the distress of the Chinese community in Malaya at these events in their homeland, that a relief fund was formed in Singapore to collect and send money to China; there was also a boycott of all Japanese goods. The China Relief Fund was the idea of Lim Hock An's old friend Tan Kah Kee, who was chairman of the Fund Committee. Contributions were demanded from all Chinese; even poor coolies and rickshaw runners were encouraged to give what they could.

Mei Lan had become a Youth Leader in the China Relief Fund, and helped to raise money by organising the selling of handmade paper flowers and flags. There was also the making of bandages to be sent to wounded soldiers in China, scarves and sweaters to be knitted for the troops, medicine and food to be collected. Dances, concerts, Chinese opera and patriotic plays, food fairs and boxing tournaments were organised; every Chinese in the colony was involved in the effort.

'Japanese goods are being boycotted everywhere,' Mei Lan reported as she sat beside her grandfather's bed.

'If we need to pledge more money to the fund, we can sell off some jade. Whatever it takes, we must give.' Lim Hock An closed his eyes, his voice unfamiliarly reedy. His famous jade collection, still packed away in stout wooden crates and stored in a shed behind Bougainvillaea House, remained unopened since the move from Lim Villa

Soon, the day nurse approached Lim Hock An brandishing a thermometer. Behind her Second Grandmother hobbled forward upon her two canes, her slave girls hovering at her side.

'Grandfather, open your mouth,' Mei Lan chided, and the old man obeyed with a sigh.

He looked up at the three women standing about his bed and knew himself reduced. He shut his eyes and his memories slid into a previous time when there had been no limit to what he could do. Thoughts came to him constantly now of Chwee Gek, his first wife, the mother of Mei Lan's father, his son Boon Eng.

'Chwee Gek.' He allowed himself to murmur her name.

Mei Lan looked at her grandfather in surprise; she had never heard him say First Grandmother's name. She glanced at Second Grandmother in trepidation and saw the shock on her face.

'Chwee Gek.' It was a low groan on the old man's lips. Second Grandmother turned upon her two sticks and hobbled hurriedly away.

The long days of coma had been dreamless but now whenever Lim Hock An shut his eyes the past rose up to claim him. Above all it was Chwee Gek's dead and reproachful face that he saw, the brandy beside her, the remains of his best opium clutched in her hand, her eyes staring at him. At other times there was his Second Wife, Lustrous Pearl, her feet so tiny in their red silk slippers that they fitted into his palm. Chwee Gek's large and unbound feet became hideous to him after they settled in fashionable Singapore and a new life claimed him. Then, the sight of them sticking out from beneath the quilt on their bed repulsed him; such feet proved her a peasant. In Singapore he now mixed with men of sophistication who frequented high-class brothels. There, to satisfy the nostalgic taste of a certain generation, women with bound feet could still be found. Now, he remembered Chwee Gek's long toes covered with mud at the time of rice planting when she had worked barefoot in the fields beside him. Love was not something Lim Hock An knew much about; lust was what he was familiar with and this was all he expected to feel. The warm ache that sometimes hollowed him out when he thought of his first wife, his dead wife, was something for which he had no explanation. Only now did he realise she was the only woman he had loved. And she had loved him more than life.

'Chwee Gek,' he murmured her name once again.

Propped up on his pillows he could see out of the window to the turreted mountain of Lim Villa. A tall fence shut him out of the great house he had built, schoolchildren now played on its lawns. Long ago he had lain in this very room in Bougainvillaea House with Little Sparrow, and delighted in his truancy from the bed of Lustrous Pearl and the manner in which he piqued her. Little Sparrow with dimpled cheeks and a body that so attentively serviced his needs had made him lose his head for a while. Now so much was changed, and regret washed through him. In the distance he listened to Lustrous Pearl's throaty voice asking if he had been given a laxative. Although she now encased her small feet in fashionable leather shoes, the smell of rotting flesh seemed always about her. She had taken him over entirely.

It showered through the morning, but later the sun returned and the drying earth steamed. After lunch Mei Lan took Lim Hock An's chauffeured car to the Chinese Chamber of Commerce on Hill Street. As the car entered Chinatown, the density of life closed about her; washing on bamboo poles protruded from windows and dripped upon the passing traffic, the cries of food hawkers, and the perfume of sewage and roasting pork assailed her. People and carts and rickshaws crowded the narrow streets. As she approached Hill Street she saw two small boys, smart in school uniforms, stop before a malt candy seller. The old woman, squatting by the roadside with her metal pot of sticky black molasses, was stretching the toffee back and forth between two sticks, chatting to the children. Mei Lan remembered her own delight as a child at buying a stick of malt candy. As she turned to watch the scene, a stone came hurtling passed her and struck the elder of the boys.

He jumped up in shock, his face stricken with fear. Almost immediately another stone landed on the younger boy who, with a cry, cowered behind his brother in terror, blood running off his thin arm and on to his clean white shorts. Mei Lan saw that a gang of rough youths were steadily closing in on the children. The malt candy seller put the lid on her pot and hurriedly backed away. The terrified children, hands clasped protectively over their heads, cringed beneath the hail of stones.

Stopping the car Mei Lan climbed out, recognising an overweight boy with a fleshy face known as Dumpling Pan. He was from one of the zealous groups connected with the China Relief Fund, whose work was the weeding out of pro-Japanese elements amongst the Chinese and those who flouted the Japanese boycott. In her duties as a Youth Leader she had come across Dumpling Pan before. The gangs assumed pretentious names such as the Singapore Assassin Corps or the Chinese National Emancipation Vanguard Corps; they sent death threats to people or vandalised property, and the more extreme had no difficulty in slicing off ears. Mei Lan shouted to Dumpling Pan, who turned to stare at her in surprise, a stone in his raised hand.

'They are Japanese children,' he told her, his podgy face creased in anger, his friends crowding menacingly behind him. Mei Lan moved to stand in front of the children and felt a small hand clutch her skirt as the younger child pressed close.

'Our father is Chinese. We live in our grandfather's house and he too is Chinese. Only our mother is Japanese,' the eldest boy explained in a trembling voice.

'Their mother is Japanese and their father buys soya flour for his biscuit factory from his wife's Japanese family in Middle Road. Let everyone know what traitors they are.' Although Dumpling Pan spoke threateningly, his hand had dropped to his side and he returned the stone to a cloth pouch still heavy with ammunition; he knew Mei Lan's position in the China Relief Fund, and knew he could not disregard her.

'I will take responsibility for them,' Mei Lan said, ignoring the angry shouts of Dumpling Pan's friends.

Once the gang turned away people began to come forward. The malt candy woman offered the children her toffee for free. From his pitch on the roadside a cobbler raised his eyes from repairing a clog.

'The children live around the corner. They are old Ho the biscuit maker's grandchildren. Already, that gang have thrown hot tar at his house and left a dead cat at his door.'

'It's not far,' the elder boy said, pointing out the way as Mei Lan helped the children into her waiting car; the sky was darkening again, threatening more rain.

Soon, they reached a tree-lined road of shabby houses. At the boy's direction they drew up before a larger but equally dilapidated bungalow. HO PROSPERITY BISCUIT COMPANY was written in faded letters above a rotted gate. The children scrambled out of the car and ran up the steps into the house. A powerful smell of baking enveloped the place and Mei Lan took a deep breath of the sweet vanilla-scented air. Soon, the children reappeared on the veranda with their mother who hurried down the steps towards Mei Lan, followed by an elderly man.

'They were so late returning, we were worried,' the children's mother said as the boys jumped about her, spilling out their news, showing off their wounds.

'I am Ho, the boys' grandfather. Who has done this? They are just children.' The man shook his head in distress while Mei Lan looked curiously at the children's mother.

'It is because of me, because I am Japanese, but I was born here in Singapore, I have never even been to Japan,' the woman protested, tears filling her eyes. She clasped her hands together below the sleeves of her white Japanese apron, pursing her lips to hold back emotion.

'They say you are baking biscuits with Japanese flour,' Mei Lan told them reluctantly, but old Mr Ho shook his head.

'We are using only what is left from our previous stock. Until now, Mr Yamaguchi, Yoshiko's father, has always supplied us with flour, so we are in a difficult situation. Now, at Mr Yamaguchi's own request, we are no longer buying flour from him as he knows the danger this would be for us,' Mr Ho replied.

'Won't you take some refreshment? Taste some of our biscuits, please,' Mr Ho offered as Mei Lan prepared to leave.

'I am already late for an appointment,' Mei Lan explained, climbing back into the car.

As the vehicle drew away, Mei Lan looked back to see the children waving to her and their mother wiping her eyes, and stared at them in confusion. The China Relief Fund had turned everyone against the

Japanese to such a degree that she had not opposed the punishment and intimidation of people who did not obey the boycott. The Japanese woman standing with her arms about her Chinese children was too complicated a matter to immediately decipher.

The sky had darkened again and the first drops of rain spat down as she reached the Chinese Chamber of Commerce, and saw a large crowd gathered before the building. With a sudden crack of thunder the rain began, emptying ferociously out of the sky. People pushed into the building or took shelter under ornate parapets and eaves. Banners dripped and sagged, food hawkers huddled beneath bits of tarpaulin, their charcoal fires stowed hurriedly away. Beggars and cripples, who had been vigorously demanding alms only moments before, now huddled together against the deluge.

Mei Lan was relieved that Tan Kah Kee had not yet arrived. Shaking the raindrops off her umbrella, she entered the building. The foyer was noisy and filled with people whose wet shoes and dripping umbrellas made the stone floor slippery. A ceiling fan sped around at a great rate but had little effect on the hot and stifling space. Leaving her umbrella with an attendant, Mei Lan looked about for faces she recognised and was surprised to see a tall Englishman standing self-consciously beside the stairs. As he observed the excited crowd, he was scribbling notes on a pad that he slipped into his pocket, only to take it out again. Looking up, he caught Mei Lan's eye and stepped forward with a smile, as if he was waiting for her.

'I'm Wilfred Patterson. I'm here from *The Straits Times* to write an article on the China Relief Fund.' He extended his hand in greeting, speaking in a direct and easy way. Still appraising Mei Lan, he launched into an earnest explanation of his reasons for attending the meeting.

'Is there any way I could meet Mr Tan Kah Kee for an interview?' Wilfred lowered his voice conspiratorially. The young woman had immediately caught his eye with her purposeful manner and natural elegance; her short, fashionable hair and chic clothes immediately set her apart. He noticed a small birthmark just above her jaw.

'Mr Tan is a family friend, but you'll have to sit through the meeting first.' Mei Lan found herself responding to his pleasantness; Europeans were so often condescending in their manner with local people, but Wilfred appeared to have genuine interest in the China Relief Fund.

Mei Lan pulled a small ivory fan from her bag and waved it

vigorously as she made her way towards the crowded auditorium, conscious of the curious glances the European man at her side drew to them both. Large electric standing fans were placed at intervals down the sides of the hall, but served only to ruffle hair and spread odours. Mei Lan burrowed through the crowd to a row of reserved chairs directly below a raised dais and Wilfred took a place beside her as she indicated.

Within moments there was a stir as Tan Kah Kee entered the hall. As he approached the stage people crowded about him. Wilfred knew the man was a mercurial figure who embodied the ideals of the Chinese community, yet his first sight of Tan Kah Kee was a surprise. Wilfred saw a small scholarly looking man in a creased suit and heavy spectacles who resembled a second-hand book dealer more than a legendary entrepreneur, social reformer and political activist. Although Tan came from poor beginnings and, with only a few years' education could not read a newspaper until late in his life, he was one of the few Chinese the colonial government trusted. At last Tan mounted the stage, made his way to the microphone, and prepared to speak.

Wilfred could understand nothing of what Tan said, but Mei Lan leaned towards him, translating in a low whisper. Wilfred stared curiously up at the man, noting the wide forehead and thin moustache, and the shrewd but restless eyes behind his thick-framed spectacles. He took out his notebook, writing whatever he could catch of Mei Lan's translations.

'The Overseas Chinese have always had the reputation of being the Fathers of the Chinese revolution . . . For any country at war the most important things are manpower and money. It is impossible to successfully fight a war if one of these two things is lacking . . .'

As Tan paused, taking the heavy spectacles off his nose, Wilfred whispered in Mei Lan's ear, 'He's known in the world as the Henry Ford of Malaya but I believe he doesn't live it up like his namesake.'

Putting back his spectacles, Tan continued. 'Since the Japanese invasion of our homeland we Overseas Chinese in South East Asia have spared no efforts in our fund-raising attempts . . . You may say you have fulfilled your moral obligation if you have given a few dollars to the fund but in terms of our sacred duty to our nation, it is not enough . . . You must give more.'

'He lives a very frugal life and expects everyone else to do so as well. His family have a hard time. It is said they're always in a state of near penury and on principle he allows no one to own gold jewellery,' Mei Lan informed Wilfred as Tan's voice flowed on above them.

'As long as the guns at the front continue firing, the supplies at the rear cannot stop . . . From now on all of us must exert ourselves more generously . . . We must wipe out the blood and humiliation brought by the Japanese upon our homeland.'

For as far back as Mei Lan could remember Tan Kah Kee had been in and out of her home, conferring with her grandfather. Lim Hock An was the elder by a decade, but their friendship persisted on the basis of the similarity of their frugal beginnings and the mutual regard of two shrewd minds. Once, she remembered sitting on his knee as he discussed with Lim Hock An selling a pineapple cannery both men had invested in. Both had suffered during the years of the Depression, forced to sell off their vast plantations, but Tan had survived the trauma whereas Lim Hock An had not.

As Tan finished his speech, cheering erupted. At both sides of the stage rally leaders began to recite the lines of the pledge that was taken at every meeting, shouting the words into their megaphones. The crowd joined in.

> We will not engage in trade with the enemy,
> We will not spread or read their propaganda . . .
> We will not communicate with the enemy or traitors,
> I will support the relief work with my savings . . .
> I am a Relief Fund worker and will do my best.

More cheering broke out as the pledge ended. A piano began to play the first bars of 'Selling Flowers', a popular song to boost the morale of the fund-raisers. Everybody knew the song and the hall filled with spirited singing. As Tan Kah Kee left the stage the rally leaders picked up their megaphones to read out the monthly list of Relief Fund donations.

'The Hawkers' Association raised $970 in the month of October. The Clog Makers of Tangjong Pagar raised . . .' As the list droned on Mei Lan and Wilfred made their way out of the hall.

'Do you have any booklets or pamphlets I could look at?' Wilfred asked as he pushed forward behind Mei Lan.

'I can get something to you and send it to the *Straits Times* office or your home,' Mei Lan replied as they came out into the fresh air of the foyer to see Tan Kah Kee surrounded by a crowd of people. Mei Lan moved towards him to request an interview for Wilfred.

'The office is fine. I live some distance away off Bukit Timah, in an old boarding house called Belvedere,' Wilfred replied as he followed her.

'I live next door to Belvedere.' Mei Lana stopped and turned to him, her heart jumping in shock. 'I know someone there – Howard Burns.'

'My landlady's son.' Wilfred smiled.

'I'll drop the pamphlets off at Belvedere on my way home,' Mei Lan decided, hoping she did not show eagerness.

13

WHEN THE RAIN STOPPED, Raj found a rickshaw. The runner wiped the handrail dry and spread newspaper upon the damp seat before heaving up the shafts as his passenger climbed in, muscles knotting in his shoulders under the sudden weight. Eventually Raj reached Middle Road and alighted outside the Japanese draper Echigaya where, within glass cabinets, rolls of bright silk and kimono fabric could be seen. Shoulders back, stomach pushed out, Raj swung his arms vigorously as he walked, eyes focused firmly ahead. He did not appear a man to hinder and people stepped aside to let him pass. Middle Road was home to many Japanese shops, mostly of the ten-cent variety selling toys, knick-knacks, buttons and thread, chinaware and household items such as graters and sieves. There were also Japanese photographers, dentists, barbers and brothels, whose expertise was always in high demand. The Japanese community in Singapore overflowed with shopkeepers; there were few rich men amongst them. It was this uniformity of status and lack of ambition that led to the rumour that they were all spies. It was said that through information gained from their citizens in Singapore, the Japanese government prepared for expansion into South East Asia

Soon, Raj reached the shipping agency, Nanyo Kaiun, sandwiched between Ono's Barber Shop and Dr Mori the Dentist. As he climbed the narrow stairs to the office above, the odour of fermented pickle drifted to him. In the beginning when he had first met Mr Yamaguchi, the acrid odour of this pickle had turned Raj's stomach. The Yamaguchis accompanied every meal with these sour pickled vegetables, which were stored in wooden tubs in a kitchen cupboard. The pungency permeated their home and conjured up for Raj the very essence of Japan.

As he pushed open the door Mr Yamaguchi looked up from his desk and gave a distracted smile. Raj saw with annoyance that the diplomat, Mr Shinozaki, was sitting with him again, and knew by the disapproval on Shinozaki's face that he had intruded. In spite of this Mr Yamaguchi smiled, pointing affably to a chair beside a standing fan.

'We will not be long,' he said.

Raj glanced nervously at Mr Shinozaki, who met his gaze with a deadpan stare of enigmatic appraisal. These days, Shinozaki was to be found with increasing frequency in Mr Yamaguchi's home. Both men were hunched over a map of Singapore spread out on the table between them. Raj settled down to wait, listening to the rapid exchange of Japanese and staring at Yamaguchi's bowed and shaven head shadowed with a four-day stubble. The sour odour of the mouldering pickles reached its peak in this room, and Raj moved close to the fan. His linen jacket was tight about the armpits and held the heat, and he thought constantly of that moment at the end of the day when he could change back into the comfort of an old *dhoti*.

Under Mr Yamaguchi's tutelage Raj had discarded his traditional loose attire of *dhoti* and *kurta* for Western-style suits of white cotton. He had also adopted the habit of wearing a gold watch-chain across his waistcoat, just like Mr Ho the biscuit maker. The Western clothes were constrictive after the soft flow of a *dhoti,* but to move successfully in his new world, Mr Yamaguchi advised, he must wear its uniform. Yamaguchi was an old seafaring man of earthy humour who, despite his counsel to Raj, was often found in a loose batik shirt. Raj noted that the intellectual Mr Shinozaki, press attaché at the Japanese Embassy, always dressed in a dark suit whatever the heat. It was a mystery to Raj what men from such different worlds could have in common, that they should meet so frequently.

'We have both roamed the world for too long. We no longer know exactly where we belong,' Yamaguchi said, laughing when Raj questioned him once. During the Russo-Japanese war Yamaguchi had been taken as a POW to Petrograd after his ship sank in action. When the war ended he was sent back to Japan, but on the way stopped in Malaya where he met and married Japanese Mrs Yamaguchi, and never returned to his country.

Yamaguchi's small office was an untidy affair with shelves of dusty files, and sheaves of browning paper that rustled as the breeze of the fan swept over them. The large map the men were huddled over lifted in its wake; Yamaguchi held it down with a fleshy hand on which was tattooed an anchor. On the wall above Yamaguchi's desk hung a painting of Mount Fuji in winter. The bare branches of trees and the gleaming white slopes of the snowy mountain fascinated Raj. He could not imagine cold such as Yamaguchi described, where water froze and fingers turned blue. Yamaguchi's talk of these strange things projected Raj into distant landscapes, so that he often left Middle Road in a state of expanded experience.

Raj, who had been learning Japanese for some months, strained his ears to understand what the men were discussing in lowered voices. The ships Raj replenished with supplies were exclusively Japanese vessels, and Yamaguchi had suggested that some knowledge of the language would give him an advantage over other local ship chandlers. Listening to the conversation, Raj found that although he understood words here or there he could not fit them into a meaningful context. As he watched, Shinozaki leaned across the desk to Yamaguchi, speaking in an earnest manner, his arms folded upon the map, his long face lined with anxiety. Before joining the Japanese Foreign Office Shinozaki had been a journalist and worked in China. Yamaguchi told Raj that, as a young diplomat, Shinozaki had been posted to the Japanese Embassy in Berlin. There he had fallen in love with a German woman and for such inappropriate behaviour had incurred the disapproval of the Ambassador.

Eventually, Shinozaki ceased speaking and drew back glumly in his chair. Yamaguchi folded up the map and replaced it in a drawer and then picked up a small blue teapot on his desk. Shinozaki put away his notebook and lifted his empty cup for Yamaguchi to refill with lukewarm tea. Yamaguchi poured a further cup of tea for Raj, and pushed it across the desk towards him.

'Hitler will soon invade England and win the war.' Yamaguchi grinned displaying his many gold teeth. Raj did not know how to reply to this statement and stood before Yamaguchi, teacup in hand. The year before in faraway Europe a war had started. Although Raj could not yet see what relevance such a distant event had for Singapore, Yamaguchi and Shinozaki discussed it often.

When the door finally shut behind Shinozaki, Yamaguchi walked over to the window and beckoned to Raj, pointing down into the road below. 'Watch that fat Malay in a checked sarong in front of Mr Nemoto's photograph shop. See what happens when Shinozaki-san appears.' With Yamaguchi Raj looked down at the peeling colonnade with its food hawkers, overflowing merchandise and mouldering shop signs. Within a moment Shinozaki emerged from beneath the office of Nanyo Kaiun and hailed a rickshaw. Immediately, the Malay stepped forward to follow Shinozaki in another rickshaw.

'The British authorities now think all Japanese are dangerous people. Shinozaki-san is a high-ranking diplomat and receives his orders directly from the Japanese government, so of course Special Branch detectives have their eye on him. A Chinese in a straw hat, who will be waiting somewhere in the shade, always follows me. I am just a nobody, but I have caught the authorities' interest because Shinozaki-san is my friend,' Yamaguchi admitted.

'Come, let us settle our accounts,' he continued briskly, turning to his desk.

Once the business of accounts was over Raj followed Yamaguchi into the living area behind the office. In these cramped rooms where the odour of pickles and dried seaweed was joined by that of honey buckets and disinfectant fluid, Mrs Yamaguchi ruled. She devoted much of her free time to the making of Japanese dolls with delicate white faces and elaborate hairstyles speared with ornate pins. They stood in glass cases about the room, one looking much like another and none bearing any resemblance to Mrs Yamaguchi with her wide jaw and a wart in the fold of her nose. Seeing Raj, she bustled forward to fuss about them. Soon, a Malay houseboy appeared with square lacquer boxes of cold noodles, bottles of beer and small plates of peanuts and pickles. Yamaguchi settled himself on a cushion before a low table and began to suck up the noodles with relish; Raj declined the meal but accepted the beer and peanuts. He had yet to acquire a taste for Yamaguchi's strange food with its odours of the sea and fermentation, but he had begun to enjoy the bitter taste of beer. The liquid washed through him, stretching him open inside and he had come to like these loosened sensations.

'I could not understand what Shinozaki-san was saying; it sounded as if he was asking about guns. Is that possible?' Raj asked. The beer gave him the courage to question Yamaguchi and he was rewarded by seeing his startled expression, before the man broke into a chuckle.

'Your grasp of our language is better than I thought. He did indeed mention guns, and also military installations. This is a British colony and, although the war in Europe is far away, Japan has just made a pact of friendship with Germany. Now, can you see how such a pact would reflect on us Japanese here, obligating us to Britain's enemy?' Yamaguchi sucked up a further mouthful of noodles with a loud appreciative slurp. The beer had weakened his usual discretion and he picked his teeth as he considered the situation, his small shrewd eyes resting on Raj as he continued.

'When the Japanese army reaches Singapore you Indians will have nothing to fear,' Yamaguchi said. Raj looked at him questioningly but Yamaguchi did not respond, looking down instead at his wristwatch.

'Nakamura-san is late today,' he commented, shaking his head.

Every Monday evening Raj came to Mr Yamaguchi's home for a Japanese lesson. Yamaguchi had arranged these lessons, but the fee was so nominal Raj suspected the old seaman might be subsidising the lessons in order to help him. He had come to regard Yamaguchi as a mentor, just as he had Mr Ho before him.

When Takeshi Nakamura at last arrived, Mrs Yamaguchi fussed about him in her usual motherly manner, pressing beer and cold *somen* noodles upon him. Takeshi responded with grateful delight, dipping up and down like a tall crane, in small obligatory bows. Takeshi was a mystery to Raj. At first, observing his slim frame, tall skull and ears prominent as wings, Raj had taken him to be a student, and was surprised to find he was thirty-four. He was a teacher at a Japanese language school on Bencoolen Street but, even in the middle of term, he seemed able without difficulty to leave his duties to visit a sick uncle in Bangkok and might be gone for days at a time. It was not his business to wonder at such occurrences, Raj eventually decided; he had only to learn the language. Beside him now Takeshi ate his noodles hungrily, sucking them up with relish. Yamaguchi, red in the face from an excess of beer, pushed the empty dishes to one side and leaned over towards him.

'I have already taught him some new vocabulary. He has learned *gun, military installation, naval base* and *defence*,' Yamaguchi informed him in amusement. Takeshi looked up over his chopsticks and nodded approvingly. As Mrs Yamaguchi reached to refill his glass with beer, Takeshi stopped eating and dabbed his wet mouth on a napkin in a womanly manner.

'He is a good student and will be a credit to us both,' Takeshi smiled, his Adam's apple rising in his throat like the bubble in a spirit level. Raj could not hide his pleasure at such praise, but he noticed the glance that was exchanged between the teacher and Yamaguchi. He also noted Takeshi's conspiratorial tone, and was puzzled.

When Raj returned again to Middle Road the following week for his Japanese lesson, the street lamps were being lit. He looked up at the weathered façade of Yamaguchi's office and was surprised to see it in darkness. At this time Mr Yamaguchi was usually still working, and a light shone in the window. Raj climbed the stairs to Yamaguchi's door and rapped the small brass knocker in the shape of a fox. After a while, the old Malay servant opened the door a crack and Raj saw Mrs Yamaguchi's frightened face peering at him from behind the man. Recognising Raj, she stepped forward immediately.

'Very sorry for inconvenience, we keep everything dark; better people think nobody here. I am afraid they will take the Master away. Sorry also, no Japanese lesson today. Teacher send message he is gone to Bangkok to visit sick uncle. But, please, come in, you are welcome,' she bowed, smiling.

In the small living room behind the office Raj found Yamaguchi, shirt unbuttoned, sitting morosely at the low table, a bottle of whisky before him; the room was hot and airless. Mrs Yamaguchi picked up a paper fan and kneeling beside her husband waved it vigorously about to cool him. Mr Yamaguchi offered Raj some whisky but he refused, finding the drink like fire-water. The servant appeared as always with a bottle of beer, and Mrs Yamaguchi filled a glass for Raj. In spite of the heat Yamaguchi wore a high, knitted *harumaki* wrapped about his waist, his bare chest beneath the open unbuttoned shirt glistening with sweat. Usually, Yamaguchi was unshakeably affable and it filled Raj with alarm to observe his bloodshot eyes and grim expression.

'War in Europe is now causing us Japanese in Singapore much trouble. Because Japan has become Britain's enemy we are now a suspect people here in Malaya, arrests are being made on any suspicion. They arrested Shinozaki-san after a visit to me yesterday.' Yamaguchi swilled the whisky absently about in the glass.

'Maybe tomorrow they will come for me,' he said, forcing a smile.

'Why should a war so far away affect you here?' Raj was still unable to understand the full implications.

'The world is just a large pond. When a stone is thrown in, the ripples reach everywhere.' Yamaguchi sighed and stared into his whisky glass before looking again at Raj.

'Shinozaki-san is in Outram Prison. He has sent a message to me asking for some books from his house, and foodstuffs and cigarettes to be brought to the prison. I cannot visit him but there is no danger for you,' Yamaguchi said, his voice lifting on the thought.

Raj was conscious that Yamaguchi's gaze, focused intently now upon him, contained the weight of his obligation to the man. He thought of the help Yamaguchi had given, the business pushed his way, the Japanese lessons, the meals, the beer, the waving now of Mrs Yamaguchi's fan, ordering coolness in his direction, and knew this was the moment when Yamaguchi expected a return.

Outram Prison was weathered black by age and the mould of tropical dampness. A high wall fringed with iron spikes surrounded bleak blocks of cells. As the gate swung shut behind Raj the clang of metal reverberated and he faced a bare yard with a few spindly trees. The Chief Warder, a European with muttonchop sideburns, considered Raj from across his desk as he placed the things Mrs Yamaguchi had tied in a blue silk carrying cloth, upon the table. The cloth was printed with the design of a stork in flight, and Raj stared at the delicate pattern of its wings wrapped about the bundle as the warder opened the cloth and took out a pile of books. Holding each up to the light, he examined the titles with interest.

'*Crime and Punishment*; *Old Chinese Poetry*; *Nanking Road*. I see our Mr Shinozaki likes highbrow stuff.' The warder turned the books over in his hand and then poked about amongst the packets of foodstuff Shinozaki had requested. They were mostly bags of dried fish and squid and a variety of strong-smelling bottled mixtures to eat with white rice. The warder took the tops off these bottles, peering at them closely and turning his nose up at the contents. At last he seemed satisfied and replaced everything in the carrying cloth, except the cigarettes.

'We have to ration their cigarettes,' he said as Raj tied the ends of the cloth together again.

Shinozaki was imprisoned in a smaller block where Raj was told to wait in a meeting room, bare except for some high-backed wooden chairs and a small square table. The dank smell of old brick was everywhere. At last Shinozaki entered the room with a warder, his footsteps echoing on the concrete floor as he walked towards Raj. The dark suit he still wore was badly crumpled, his unshaven face drawn and his tie off centre; he stared at Raj in surprise. The guard settled down by the door to wait, squinting at them uninterestedly from time to time.

'Do you have a cigarette?' Shinozaki enquired immediately, in an urgent voice, and Raj pulled a packet of Naval Cut from his pocket. Shinozaki fumbled for a cigarette with trembling hands as Raj struck a match, and after a few deep inhalations grew calmer. The glare of two bare bulbs hanging from the ceiling cast distorted shadows on the wall as Shinozaki leaned forward to talk.

'I am as yet just detained here. I am not yet charged with anything. I am still allowed a bath and have a reading light. I get three cigarettes and three matches each day and a small pork chop for lunch. I do not yet have to live with a toilet bucket or broken rice full of weevils, but this may change after the trial if I am found guilty of spying. They may send me to Changi Prison if I am convicted. Of course it is nonsense. I am not spying on military installations like they say,' Shinozaki said. Blowing smoke indignantly from his nostrils, he reached forward to examine the things Yamaguchi had sent, picking up the books appreciatively.

'I cannot live without my books, they are my real friends.' Shinozaki caressed the worn spines and held up the volume entitled *Nanking Road*.

'I particularly like this book. It is about a Chinese man who marries a French girl and returns with her to China after the civil war. There is a character in it that says, "A dog during peace is better off than a man during war".' Shinozaki smiled and Raj remembered Yamaguchi telling him that Shinokazi had once been in love with a German woman. Raj listened, at a loss for a reply, feeling awkward conversing alone with the diplomat who had always seemed dismissive of him.

'In the present circumstances, I suppose my arrest was to be expected but things may soon change. Japan is making great military advances in this region and soon our troops will look towards Malaya. Keep this in mind and continue to study the Japanese language; your skill may be of value soon. When that time comes I shall remember you.

We Japanese do not forget a favour,' Shinozaki confided in a low voice as the guard came towards them to lead him back to his cell.

'Is there anything else you need?' Raj asked as Shinozaki stood up.

'I need my spare glasses and some extra razors for shaving. And I need more books. You are a good boy; I shall remember you,' Shinozaki repeated over his shoulder as the warder led him away. Raj was left alone in the silent room; beyond a small grimy window rain had begun to fall.

By the time Raj returned to Middle Road from Outram Prison the street lamps were once more being lit. Looking up to Yamaguchi's office window, Raj saw that a light was now burning and hurried into the shophouse and up the stairs, his mind full of Shinozaki and all he had to tell Mr Yamaguchi.

'The Master is not here,' the old Malay servant said as he opened the door, surprising Raj. He went to call Mrs Yamaguchi and Raj sat down to wait in the small airless sitting room. Mrs Yamaguchi's dolls in their glass cases surrounded him like an aviary of exotic stuffed birds; the aroma of pickles lingered as always in the air. When Mrs Yamaguchi at last appeared Raj saw she had been crying.

'Soon after you collected the things for Shinozaki-sama, policemen came to take the Master away. I do not know where he is. Did you see him in that prison where they have Shinozaki-sama?' Mrs Yamaguchi drew a trembling breath. Raj tried to absorb this news as Mrs Yamaguchi continued to explain the situation, her face set with the effort of control.

'Just recently Shinozaki-sama brought two high-ranking Japanese military men, Colonel Tanikawa and Major Kunitake, to our house. The men wanted to travel around Singapore examining the coastline. As the Master's work takes him out to the shipping lanes, they had many questions to ask him. Afterwards, the Master became very nervous because of this visit. He felt he had endangered us by meeting them, but he could not refuse Shinozaki-sama.' Mrs Yamaguchi pulled a small folded handkerchief from her obi and dabbed her eyes.

'What kind of questions did they ask?' Raj queried, his concern rising.

'I remember Colonel Tanikawa saying "It's impossible to attack Singapore from the sea. Attack is possible only from the north." At that time I took no notice of these remarks. I was pouring tea, refilling cups at the table. The spout of the teapot was troublesome and I was trying not to spill a drop of liquid. Afterwards, the Master told me that Colonel Tanikawa is Planning Chief at Imperial Army Headquarters in Tokyo. At that time I felt flattered that such men should seek out the Master. The day after these military men left Singapore to return to Japan, Shinozaki-sama was arrested. And now the Master has also been taken away.' Mrs Yamaguchi pressed her lips together, stifling her sobs.

Raj soon left Mrs Yamaguchi and on Middle Road hailed a rickshaw to take him to Race Course Road where he was to meet Krishna at the Indian Youth League. He was filled with anxiety for old Yamaguchi but, as the rickshaw bowled along, he wondered with a pang of fear if he too was being watched because of his association with Mr Yamaguchi and Mr Shinozaki. As they neared the League the rickshaw swerved to avoid another rickshaw that had halted suddenly before them and was swaying dangerously about on a broken wheel. Raj was thrown off his seat and clung to the side of the contraption, expecting to be flung to the ground. The two runners at once began arguing heatedly, and passers-by stopped to follow events. Hurriedly Raj climbed out of the rickshaw, and turned to stare at the offending vehicle. He was amazed to see that the passenger alighting from the broken rickshaw was the Eurasian he had met at the tea stall. Striding forward he took Howard's hand, pumping it up and down in greeting; Howard greeted Raj with no less surprise and enthusiasm.

'It is destiny that you have stopped outside the Indian Youth League. My brother-in-law Krishna, who I told you about, is to speak here tonight; he is my guru, he has risked his life in the cause of Indian freedom. You must come and listen to him. Afterwards, we will all have a beer,' Raj insisted.

The accident had shaken Howard and the mention of a drink was tempting. He had not forgotten the man at the tea stall whose strange ideas had revolved in his mind, and was immediately drawn to his suggestion. Raj steered him across the road to a small bungalow before which a crowd of young Indian men were gathered.

'We're just in time,' Raj said, leading Howard up the steps and into a large room where rows of chairs were quickly filling up. Krishna was sitting at a table shuffling papers. He nodded gravely when introduced to Howard but did not smile. Unlike Raj, who was smartly dressed in a white cotton suit and exuded pragmatic energy, Krishna, with his wire-rimmed spectacles, cloud of black hair and traditional *dhoti*, appeared distant and austere.

They took seats in the first row and soon, as the room quietened, Krishna stood up and began to speak. At first Howard had difficulty understanding him, but as the audience grew attentive Krishna's voice gained strength and his eyes grew bright behind his spectacles. For the first time Howard heard the name of Mahatma Gandhi, a lawyer who wore only a loincloth, aligned himself with the poor and preached the novel concept of passive resistance to British rule. As he warmed to his subject, Krishna became more and more animated, his eyes flashed and his hands gestured freely as he told the story of the Salt March that had galvanised India.

'All salt was heavily taxed to the detriment of the poor. The Mahatma wished to break the terrible burden the colonial government had imposed upon the local people. In the broiling sun Gandhiji marched at the head of a two-mile procession, like a conqueror, refusing all gifts of food. "We are marching in the name of God, on behalf of the naked, the hungry and the unemployed. So, how can we ourselves eat so plentifully?" he said. At last he reached the sea and on the beach bent to pick up a lump of salt. The following week a storm swept across India at this symbol of defiance. Everyone began gathering salt, burning foreign cloth, boycotting everything English, acting in dis-obedience of colonial rule in any non-violent way they could.'

Howard sat forward on his chair; everything he heard was new to him and the story of Gandhi's rebellion stirred him deeply. He could imagine the small man, half naked, his *dhoti* drawn up between his spindly legs, a wooden staff in his hand, positioning himself fearlessly against the might of colonial rule.

'A nation of three hundred and fifty million does not need the sword or the bullet. It needs a will of its own.' Krishna's voice rang out. A burst of clapping interrupted him and when it died down he began to speak about a different revolutionary, a younger man, Subhas Chandra Bose. This leader of men he described as a burning rock, a leaping flame and a springing tiger. It appeared there was so much burning and springing within this man that he had quickly upset the saintly Mahatma. Subhas Chandra Bose was a man of military leanings who inspired the throwing of bombs, the assassination of British officials and the martyrdom to be acquired through this violence. He had no patience with the slow pace of passive civil disobedience adhered to by Mahatma Gandhi.

'Once more Subhas is in jail and is on a hunger strike. He drinks only a few drops of water each day. By now you must all be knowing that Europe is at war. England's fight against Germany will divide the world. Germany is aligned with Japan, and both these nations support India's struggle for freedom. Subhas Chandra Bose predicts that England will be defeated and surrender to Germany. At that time the Indian people must make an immediate demand for a Provisional National Government.' The cheers went on for some time as Krishna finished speaking.

Afterwards, as promised, Raj suggested a beer and led the way to a table in the library where the atmosphere was quieter and free of the groups of young men who still stood around, arguing about the things Krishna had said.

'Krishna has taught me everything I know,' Raj informed Howard as a Tamil waiter placed drinks in front of them. Krishna inclined his head in gentle acknowledgement, his fiery tongue now folded away like the sting of an innocuous insect.

Howard stared at him in admiration, self-conscious before someone of such radical conviction. 'We must end British rule here in Malaya as well,' Howard enthused, his imagination stirred by the notions the man had voiced. To his surprise Krishna frowned and replied primly.

'The situation here is different from India. In India our culture is an ancient one and we yearn for freedom to regain our soul. Malaya was never a country stripped and raped and imprisoned upon its own soil. Singapore was a mangrove swamp, a pirates' den, when Raffles set foot upon it. The British took nothing from Malaya; instead they created opportunity here for anyone who sought it. Singapore is a transient place; it has no ancient culture; it is nobody's homeland. People come to make money, and then return home.' Krishna picked up his beer dismissively.

Howard stared at the man in perplexity, filled with a sense of loss, struggling to crystallise his thoughts. He remembered Olive de Souza. A homeland is where your heart is, she had said. If England was the de Souzas' heartland, where then was his? He was not a transient person: he had been born in Singapore and knew no other place. He remembered Wee Jack and his communist revolution in faraway China. Looking through the doorway into the room beyond, he observed the ardent young Indian men, their faces aflame with patriotism, still discussing their fight for freedom. Indian or Chinese, he was surrounded by men who would lay down their lives for their country; a feeling of emptiness welled up in him. Howard too was convinced he could lay down his life, if only he had something to lay it down for.

14

ONCE THE CHINA RELIEF Fund meeting was over and Mei Lan had said goodbye to Wilfred, she got back into the car for the journey home. She was in a state of some excitement. All she could think of was Howard Burns and the sudden proximity to him she felt through Wilfred Patterson. Time had quietened her emotions and thoughts of Howard were now intermittent, but he remained firmly in her mind. When she reached Bougainvillaea House the sun was low and the sky flamed over the trees. Entering her room, her eyes went straight to the window and the view of Belvedere on the slope beyond the canal. For the first time in many months she opened the drawer and took out the compass with its needle still pointing in the direction of Belvedere. Sometimes she saw Howard from a distance, in the garden or entering his home. Once, she passed him in a rickshaw and he waved until she was out of sight. And always, there were the notes of his saxophone, floating to her through the bamboo fence. She threw herself restlessly down on the bed, and knew that all she felt about Howard had only waited silently for a moment like this to reassert itself.

Later, she bathed and changed and joined her father as he sipped his evening *stengah* on the downstairs veranda. Since her mother's death and JJ's departure, they were closer than before. Boon Eng now sought out his daughter each evening, sipping his first drink of the night, discussing the gossip of the day. In spite of the financial disaster he had brought upon the family with his extravagant ways, he made little effort to curb his lifestyle. He was dressed formally as always each evening, in a white dinner jacket and black bow tie, prepared for a night with his friends at one of his clubs, and later with the inevitable women.

She had never before asked her father about his mother but tonight she needed to know Chwee Gek's story. Her name, spilling so painfully from her grandfather's lips that morning had stirred the real woman to life in her mind. At first Boon Eng looked at his daughter in alarm and then stared into his whisky glass, clinking the ice against the sides.

'I have a right to know; she was my grandmother,' Mei Lan insisted. Boon Eng nodded reluctantly, but when he spoke his voice was low and hard.

'I was not allowed to see her body after she killed herself.' Boon Eng fell silent, searching memories compressed behind a locked door of pain. When he continued the words burst angrily from him.

'Why could she not accept Father's marriage to Second Mother? She had no right to take her life over so little a thing. We were not able to keep it secret and it made our family a laughing stock. Father did no more than other men. In those times no woman with a wealthy husband expected to be an only wife; poor men kept just one wife because they could afford no more.' Boon Eng's face was flooded by emotion. He put down his empty glass with such force that it rang upon the tabletop. Then, abruptly, he pulled himself out of the deep rattan chair, suddenly anxious to get on with the evening, unable to bear any more.

'At ten years old she left me alone in the world.' Boon Eng could not keep the bitterness from his voice. He strode hurriedly away towards an open French window and disappeared into the darkness of the house beyond.

After he left Mei Lan continued to sit on the veranda amidst the lengthening shadows, filled with a confusion of feelings. Soon she heard the crank of the car engine and then the crunch of gravel on the narrow drive as Boon Eng was driven away for the diversions of the evening. A wave of loneliness swept through her. Until now Chwee Gek had been an unknown face in a dim photograph and Mei Lan felt little connection to her. Now, suddenly, the woman had emerged from the mists of time, aching and grief stricken, catching hold of Mei Lan's own emotions across the divide of generations. It was as if her ghost had waited all these years to present its plight.

Later, Ah Siew squatted down to massage Mei Lan as she lay on her bed in pink silk pyjamas. The old woman's fingers, although arthritic, were still strong and she pressed her thumb hard upon each acupuncture point. Mei Lan rested her head on her arms and squinted up at Ah Siew. Nobody knew how old she was; even Ah Siew herself did not know for births and deaths were never registered in the village. A mosquito coil burned in the room, while outside bats rustled the leaves of the mango tree. Mei Lan coughed as the acrid smoke of the coil caught in her throat.

'Tell me about First Grandmother, what was she like?' Mei Lan demanded.

'She was a good mistress,' Ah Siew replied and fell silent.

'Why did she die?' Mei Lan persisted as Ah Siew pressed down on the knots of her spine.

'Because, in the end, she could not accept the Second Obeying,' Ah Siew answered grimly. 'Just like me and my sisters.'

'Why will no one talk about her?' Mei Lan demanded. Ah Siew sucked her teeth and frowned.

'Her in-laws bought her from her parents when she was four years old, for the purpose of being their daughter-in-law. When she was grown she would already know their ways, already be one of the family. Then, the chances of needing to divorce her for one of the Seven Outs would be much less: barrenness, disobeying, neglecting parents-in-law, adultery, wantonness, jealousy or gossiping, theft or diseases,' Ah Siew explained, going through the list.

'Then First Grandmother and Grandfather must have grown up together, working and playing side by side.' Mei Lan raised her head in interest.

'She was ashamed of her feet,' Ah Siew admitted, suddenly ceasing to massage Mei Lan, breathing the words out softly. 'Young Master, your father, was born late in First Mistress's life, only after she arrived in Malaya. Before that she was left alone in China for years with Ancient Master's parents and when they died she must have been nearly thirty. I entered the house at that time, to look after your father. I was here when Second Mistress, Lustrous Pearl, came into the House of Lim. She had the smallest feet and she was just fourteen years old.' Ah Siew sighed and rubbed some of the massage oil over her own arthritic knuckles as she continued.

'Once Mistress called in an old foot binder to ask if anything could be done about her large feet, if it was not too late to bind them. She said she would put up with any amount of pain. I told the foot binder to get out of the house and begged First Mistress to come to her senses.'

Mei Lan listened in horror, staring at the photograph of First Grandmother that had stood on her bookshelves beside a picture of her own mother for as long as she could remember. Her grandmother sounded half out of her mind. From the photo frame Chwee Gek faced her granddaughter with a cool gaze, sitting formally on a chair with a son of some months upon her knee. Lim Hock An, already the owner of a successful tin mine, stood beside her dressed in a dark jacket worn over a white cotton waistcoat and trousers. One hand rested casually in a trouser pocket and from a high brow his hair grew thick as a hat above the wide sensual features of his face. Chwee Gek's long, delicate earrings softened the severity of her drawn-back hair and high-necked blouse, her sensitive lips and wide clear eyes were full of stoic austerity. The son in her lap was not Mei Lan's father, her only surviving child, but an infant who had died soon after the photograph was taken. A whole life was on view in her grandmother's face and the child, destined so soon to die, would bring further pain to her eyes. Mei Lan stared at her grandfather's features in the photograph, and thought she could see the sensualist Lim Hock An had so famously been.

Ah Siew rubbed more oil into her sore knuckles and continued. 'Second Mistress said her lily feet were for a man's pleasure. They should be so small that a man could take the whole foot into his mouth, if this was what he liked. Other men liked to hold them tightly as they took their pleasure. So many shameful things she told us servants, laughing all the while; I didn't want to hear.'

Mei Lan was acutely uncomfortable at these revelations. All she could see was Chwee Gek's grave and sensitive face in the photograph before her; all she could feel was rage at both her father and her grandfather. Behind each man stood the wasted ghosts of so many women's lives.

'You are like her,' Ah Siew sighed sadly. 'Your grandmother was a proud woman, she always needed to have her way.'

Mei Lan had never been to Belvedere before but she had imagined the look and the smell of it. The steep driveway was lit for her by the moon. The door swung open at a touch and she entered into a world of candlelight; smells of candle wax and cabbage surrounded her as she stood in Belvedere's small vestibule. She heard low voices in the distance, and by the clink of china and cutlery guessed the lodgers were still at their dinner. As she looked about for a bell, Wilfred emerged from the shadows.

'I was waiting for you, you're right on time,' he smiled, extending his hand in greeting, leading her to a couple of easy chairs in the alcove behind them. Once she was seated he disappeared in the direction of the dining room to request some coffee.

When he returned she handed over the envelope of information about the China Relief Fund, and pointed out the translations she had scribbled in the margins of the pamphlets. Within a few moments Rose appeared, a houseboy following with a tray of coffee. Wilfred jumped up to make the introduction.

'She's our neighbour from across the canal,' he explained to Rose who smiled warmly, relieved Wilfred Patterson had found some female company at last and might now takes his eyes off Cynthia. At that moment Howard emerged from the dining room. Turning down the corridor towards his room he glanced casually over his shoulder and stopped in surprise.

'Mei Lan.' Her name involuntarily escaped from him and Rose frowned with sudden understanding. In the several years since the Chinese family across the canal had erected their protective fence, Howard had stayed away from the girl of the house on Rose's explicit orders. Yet, by the way the girl's eyes were now fixed upon Howard, it was clear to Rose that she still had designs upon him.

Speaking directly to Howard, Mei Lan hurriedly explained about Wilfred's interest in the China Relief Fund. It was four years since she had seen him; he was taller, his hair curlier, his eyes deeper, and there was now a prominent edge to his features. A girl of Howard's age came to stand curiously beside him and Mei Lan knew immediately this was his green-eyed and tawny-haired sister, Cynthia. Wilfred Patterson moved forward in confusion and Mei Lan sensed that something connected him to Cynthia. From his hurried explanation to her of Mei Lan's visit, it was clear he wanted no misunderstanding.

'Why didn't she just deliver the pamphlets to *The Straits Times* office? You'd better be careful, son,' Rose warned Howard when Mei Lan had gone.

Mei Lan returned to Bougainvillaea House and stood at the window in her room, looking across the black mass of the mangosteen trees to the untidy shape of Belvedere, filled by a sense of desperation; everything she had thought was disassembled within her had only hidden itself away, and she could not control the way her feelings now ignited. Soon, in the distance came the notes of a saxophone. It was worse the next day; she could settle to nothing and in the late afternoon she heard him playing the same tune again, as if to send her a message.

The following day at the first sound of the saxophone she made her way once again to the gazebo, slipping under the dividing fence unseen, into the grounds of Lim Villa as she had not done for years. The clearing waited as before, the *lallang* grass neatly clipped by gardeners, the tall encircling trees pressed together, hiding the place as always. He was already there and when she reached him he pulled her to him roughly with none of the leisurely voluptuousness she remembered. Now he was kissing her, pushing open her lips, feeling the inside of her mouth with his tongue, just as she was responding, pressing herself against him. When she pulled away to take a breath, she tasted blood on her lip. Then, as he had never done before, his hands were reaching for her body, unbuttoning her clothes, pushing them aside. She was eager to help him, easing her arms from her blouse and arching her back so that he could pull away the last of her coverings. She felt his bare flesh against her and all she wanted was to enfold him, to feel him within her. The wrought-iron seat pressed uncomfortably into her shoulders. Without taking his mouth from her lips he fitted himself against her and she felt the hardness of him and then a pain, so sharp as he entered her that she cried out.

When at last his body was still and he lay heavily upon her, she ran her hands through his hair, tears in her eyes at the strange wonder of it all. The discomfort she was left with only confirmed his possession of her and she wanted it never to ease.

They came then to the gazebo each day, without rest from the longing that consumed them, the innocence of that other time far behind them. She waited only for the moments she was with him, unthinking and unfeeling of all else. Everything in the day underlay that time: the colour of the sky and taste of breakfast porridge, the musty smell of the canal, the touch of silk against her arm – everything increased in intensity. Her body throbbed at the thought of him, wanting him within her at every moment, in anguish until he thrust into her, craving the pleasure he brought her. Together, they stepped into another dimension and beyond the gazebo the world was far away. Nothing else mattered; however many times they came together it was never enough. The protecting trees, the sound of birdsong and the rustle of leaves embraced them, condoning this ecstasy.

'Will I get pregnant?' she asked him once, not caring if she did, the need of him was so great. Her own body had revealed itself to her in all its gratuitous carnality.

'We'll marry if anything happens. We'll marry anyway,' he promised, and she knew it was true. Already they were as one.

But just as before, it could not last. Within weeks a gardener saw them, spying upon them through the trees, and told the kitchen boy in Bougainvillaea House, who then told Ah Siew.

'What have you done, Little Goose,' the old woman moaned in distress. She was beyond anger, fearing the whispering of servants and slave girls would eventually reach Second Mistress as before.

When at last this happened, Second Grandmother's explosion of anger knew no bounds. Mei Lan's impiety embodied all the wanton sensations Lustrous Pearl had always longed to experience herself. Lim Hock An, stricken not so much with anger as with fear for the reputation of his granddaughter, made a grim decision.

'Your father is in Hong Kong and is likely to stay some time. You will join him there; he is arranging for you to take a secretarial course, and later help him in the office. When you return here you must accept that it will be time for you to marry.'

'You must do as they say, you must go,' Howard told her, guilty at her unhappiness, anxious not to create more trouble for her. 'I will write to you every day.'

PART THREE

1941–1946

15

ROSE COULD BARELY CONTAIN her excitement. Mr Churchill's great battleship the *Prince of Wales,* the largest ship of its kind to be built, had arrived at the naval base and Howard was taking her to see it. Accompanied by the *Repulse*, the *Prince of Wales* had berthed just days before, on 2 December, to great celebration and everyone who could was making the journey to see it. In the face of increasing Japanese hostility, the ship had been sent to Singapore on the personal orders of Winston Churchill. It would display the might of the British Empire and defend the waters of South East Asia should the Japanese get any upstart ideas.

Rose was not interested in battleships, she was visiting the naval base because of her respect for Mr Churchill. She was sure the arrival of the ships in Singapore was Mr Churchill's way of shaking his fist at the Japanese. The naval base had only recently been finished and, if it lacked a fleet yet to fill it, these two great ships made up for any inadequacy. Rose felt sure the Japanese, with their supposedly paper planes, bad eyes and beer-bottle glasses that hampered their ability to fight, would not be foolish enough to tangle with such might. She had chosen a dress sprinkled with mauve and grey flowers for the outing, and had clipped on some rarely worn pearl earrings that Charlie had given her at the time of Howard's birth. Howard had ordered a taxi for the journey to the naval base and she scolded him for the expense; she herself still went about by rickshaw.

At last they arrived and joined a long queue of people craning their necks to observe the cliff-like hull of the *Prince of Wales* rising impressively out of the water. The sea slapped softly against the quay, but the great ship sat solidly where it was berthed, stretching above Rose to impossible heights. Against the sky a grey metal rail could be seen, and occasionally a young sailor was sighted in a white uniform, a breeze filling out the legs of his shorts. Further along the quay was the *Repulse*, which had accompanied the *Prince of Wales* to Singapore. It was an old tub of twenty-five years that had already fought many battles; nobody was interested in the *Repulse,* Howard informed his mother.

People were being taken on to the ship in small groups to tour the interior and walk on the vast plateau of the deck. The upper echelons of the European community had already been invited to dinners and dances on board the battleship; lesser ranks had been left to queue in the equatorial sun along with crowds of locals. Rose dabbed her perspiring face with a handkerchief under the shelter of her linen parasol. Although the queue was made up mostly of local people, she noticed a smattering of Europeans. Some distance behind her was a tall blonde woman in a straw hat, holding a parasol similar to her own. Catching the woman's eye Rose smiled, but in reply received a cool stare of query.

A sailor in the smart white uniform and peaked cap of an officer appeared, and walking along the length of the queue stopped to converse politely with the Europeans. As he returned to the ship, they left the queue one by one, to follow him aboard ahead of all the locals. This did not bother Rose in the way it bothered Howard, who grumbled angrily at the Europeans' preferential treatment.

'It is the way things are; it is their right as our rulers,' Rose told him impatiently. To complain seemed ungrateful to Mr Churchill and the young British sailors who, impeccable in uniforms and caps, might soon risk their lives for her. Looking up at the towering bulk of the vessel, she caught the faint odour of fried fish from the ship's kitchen, edged with the sea's oily perfume.

The European group walked forward behind the officer, amongst them the woman with the parasol, accompanied by her husband. As she came level with Rose she appeared to stumble, and her husband quickly reached out to support her. She was painfully thin, and Rose knew from the slight curve of her abdomen that she was pregnant. She remembered how ill she had felt while expecting Howard and stepped forward impulsively in concern.

'It is very hot. Perhaps she is just feeling faint,' Rose advised.

The woman's husband gave Rose a brief but appreciative smile before turning back to his wife.

Opening her handbag, Rose pulled out a clean folded handkerchief and the miniature bottle of eau de cologne she always carried with her. Wetting the cloth with the cologne, she offered it to the man. He took it gratefully and dabbed his wife's brow. Within a moment the woman steadied herself and looked at Rose askance. Shaking herself free of her husband's grasp, she moved forward after the group.

'Keep the handkerchief, she may need it again,' Rose said. The man nodded, an expression of helplessness on his face, and hurried after his wife to press the handkerchief into her hand. Beside Rose, Howard glowered unpleasantly, and she hoped he was not going to make further derogatory remarks that would be heard by the officer or other Europeans. Instead, to Rose's relief, he returned his attention to the *Prince of Wales*, refusing to involve himself.

'Battleships like these should always have air cover. They're sitting ducks without it. Apparently the aircraft carrier with the *Prince of Wales* ran aground on a sandbank somewhere on the way,' Howard said, mopping perspiration from his neck.

Unseen by Howard, the Englishwoman was now rebuking her husband angrily. 'It's a local woman's handkerchief; who knows where it has been. Why ever did you bring me to this place?' she protested, loud enough for Rose and others to hear. With a toss of the head she walked up the gangplank and, before stepping into the belly of the ship, stretched out a hand to drop the handkerchief into the water below. The incident had taken no more than a few moments, and Howard had not noticed.

'Air power is what will win a modern war,' he continued to grumble, looking up at the ship.

Rose did not reply. The Englishwoman's words repeated unpleasantly within her, filling her with resentment, and she was thankful her son had not seen the flow of events. Absorbed in trying to justify the woman's response to her own impulsive action, Rose was overcome with feelings of self-reproach. Perhaps the woman felt ill and was not used to the tropical heat Rose reasoned, but the fault was hers: she had stepped out of place and appeared too familiar. It was all because of Wilfred. His recent marriage to Cynthia had left Rose feeling socially confused. Her son-in-law's unfailing politeness and affection, and the relaxed manner in which she responded to his presence, had upset her sense of how things were done. Lost in these thoughts, she was conscious of Howard guiding her forward, and to her relief saw they were at last being hustled up the gangway on to the *Prince of Wales*.

Rose collapsed her parasol, but as she neared the ship could not stop herself from looking down over the side of the gangplank. The handkerchief floated far below, a small white square washed this way and that on the water between the ship and the quay. Rose was shocked to feel anger flooding through her.

As they stepped aboard, a young British sailor came forward to greet them. His bony knees, protruding below the stiff white shorts of his uniform, gave him an appearance of vulnerability; he looked too young to be defending the Empire, Rose thought.

'Ladies and Gentlemen, I am Ordnance Seaman John Jefferies and I am your guide to the *Prince of Wales* this afternoon. Please follow me. Hold on to the handrails, the ship's companionways are steep, and mind your heads for ceilings are low.' He turned smartly, leading the way to the top deck.

When they emerged on that high plateau, Rose was unprepared for the breeze that blew about her at this height. Before her the ocean stretched away dotted by small islands she could not name. The great space of it elated her. Ordnance Seaman Jefferies pointed out the heavy mounted guns, and explained that they could be rotated 365 degrees to take down an enemy plane from any angle.

Soon, they came into the dining room where the Captain's table was pointed out. Ordnance Seaman Jefferies read the week's menu and revealed interesting details about methods of transporting and maintaining the freshness of vegetables. He showed them the kitchens and the clamps that would keep a lidded pot strapped to the stove in an unruly sea. In the big dining room, rocking gently beneath her feet on the swell, Rose's eyes settled on a portrait of the King nailed firmly to a wall. Perhaps the King had visited the ship, touring it just as they were doing. Mr Churchill too must have walked all over it, examining its many intricacies. He might have sat at the Captain's Table on the very chair that was now before her.

They were shown the High-Angle Plotting Table in the small but important Communications Room. Here, in the event of a crisis, the officers below decks would plan the ship's response. The technical area of the vessel with its ultra-modern radar and surveillance rooms was quickly bypassed, disappointingly off limits to all but an initiated few.

'Even I am not allowed in there,' Ordnance Seaman Jefferies confided.

Eventually the tour was over and they were guided back to the gangway for the return to shore. Once on land, Howard began complaining that as well as the radar and surveillance area, they had been denied sight of the torpedoes for which the battleship was famous.

'Well, I for one shall sleep well tonight, knowing such ships are patrolling our waters,' Rose announced firmly in the taxi as she and Howard returned to Belvedere. She inhaled the leathery smell of the vehicle and the heady essence of petrol fumes. All frightening talk of a Japanese advance had been put into perspective now that she had seen Mr Churchill's great ship.

Some weeks before, in early November, Brigadier Simson, Chief Engineer, Malaya Command, had agreed to an interview with Wilfred for *The Straits Times,* over a beer at the Cricket Club. The Brigadier had been sent to Singapore four months earlier, with instructions from the War Office in London to evaluate and improve defences on the island. After the interview Simson had arranged for Wilfred to visit a military camp in Johore. Captain Jenkins, smart in his khaki uniform, had been delegated to accompany Wilfred on the drive there. A square-set man with broad shoulders, he spoke to Wilfred from the front of the army truck, staring all the while straight ahead.

'The top brass don't like journalists poking around. With all due respect, Brigadier Simson is new to things here. We don't want defeatist talk, not good for morale,' Jenkins told Wilfred in careful clipped words. They had crossed the Causeway on to mainland Malaya, and had been travelling for more than an hour. The metal seat in the truck had grown so hot Wilfred could not put a hand upon it. Above him, the canvas canopy gave only partial shade. Occasionally a plane droned over the jungle road and they both looked up. Jenkins nodded in satisfaction.

'Good to know the RAF is overhead.'

'All I ever see up there are old Brewster Buffaloes,' Wilfred replied, trying to suppress his growing resentment of Jenkins's superior manner. 'Whitehall should have sent us some modern aircraft.'

'Nonsense,' Jenkins replied curtly. 'Buffaloes are more than a match for antiquated Japanese aircraft; they have no adequate air power.'

'A Japanese Zero is far in advance of any Buffalo,' Wilfred argued in an even voice.

'If they want to attempt an invasion, they'll approach Singapore from the south, from the sea, and we're ready and waiting for them. They will never get through the jungle,' Jenkins insisted impatiently. This was not what Brigadier Simson had told Wilfred, but he chose not to argue. He remembered Simson's complaining that his proposals for strengthening Singapore's defences were being blocked by arrogant local military personnel.

The most important event the year had produced for Wilfred, was his marriage to Cynthia. The wedding in January had been small and witnessed only by Howard and Rose, Boffort with his new wife Valerie, and Collins from the office.

'Not done to get married during your first tour of duty, I waited five years to marry Valerie. Have you told them at the office?' Boffort was unable to resist the opportunity to make his disapproval known.

They had been married in the Church of Our Lady of Lourdes and Cynthia had worn her mother's white satin wedding dress and veil, altered to fit her slighter frame. Wilfred had initially suggested a no-fuss civil wedding; because of the disapproval of early marriage in most British companies, it was important to keep a low profile. Rose had been so shocked he did not pursue the suggestion. As a Catholic, she wished Cynthia to marry as she had been brought up, in the Catholic faith. Wilfred had talked through the matter of faith with both Cynthia and her mother. At one point he was tempted to say he felt Agnostic, rather than Anglican, might better describe his religious views, but thought it politic to remain silent. In the end, he was prepared to go along with any request, as long as it meant he could marry Cynthia. When at last they stood before the priest, the perfume of incense and lilies filling the air, sun falling through stained glass upon them, he knew that whatever the future held, he would not regret this moment; he had never been so happy.

'If *The Straits Times* object to my marriage, I'll join *The Malaya Tribune*,' Wilfred had answered Boffort in a jocular tone. 'Being a local paper they don't care about such piffling things.'

There had seemed no practical reason to wait to marry; Rose had offered them a large downstairs room in Belvedere free of rent, unable to hide her delight at the wedding. Wilfred had proved that his intentions were honourable and Rose was full of relief. Wilfred thought of Rose fondly; he had hardly known his own mother and was happy to let her fuss about him. As a staff nurse at the General Hospital, Cynthia was earning enough to supplement his income if necessary. From the beginning, Wilfred decided his marriage should be presented to *The Straits Times* as a fait accompli.

All Simmons said when Wilfred eventually faced him was, 'She's a local girl; you should expect problems with your social life.'

'We'll be all right,' Wilfred told him, suppressing his anger. He had already decided not to join the clubs that *mattered,* from which Cynthia would be barred entry because she was not European; he would not put her through that humiliation.

The jungle pressed forward on each side of the road; a cloud of green parrots flew low overhead. The day before a flock of raucous cockatoos had settled noisily in the trees outside the bedroom window at Belvedere as he lay on the bed with Cynthia. Their precious hours together were frequently ruptured by the harsh pattern Cynthia's work imposed upon their life. She was working full time at the hospital and could not escape her turn of night duty. My part-time wife, he jokingly called her, but could not at times eradicate his resentment at the long hours she was forced to spend away from him.

Eventually, the truck turned off the road, accelerated noisily up an incline and then descended into the camp. A wide swathe of land had been cleared in the jungle, and rows of barracks stood about a parade ground where men were drilling in neat formations. The shout of orders rang out, whistles shrilled. The number of turbans and dark skins amongst the men surprised Wilfred, and Jenkins followed his gaze.

'Those are Indian Army units who have never seen combat. It's our job to lick them into shape. Anyone with experience is already fighting in Europe or the Middle East and cannot be spared from those fronts. No need to worry – those Japs have only ever fought the Chinese. If they come up against British steel I predict they'll fall flat on their faces,' Jenkins said, as they skirted the parade ground.

In spite of blackout practices and military preparations, few people in Malaya were of pessimistic mind. Japanese belligerence as their armies marched triumphantly across South East Asia, was not viewed as a threat to peace. British Singapore was more concerned with the run-up to Christmas; Robinsons department store was crowded with shoppers, decorations were everywhere. Some 'just in case' procedures had been put in place: people were encouraged to join one of the auxiliary services and air raid practices were now humorously tolerated. People responded to these exercises according to mood, a few taking shelter beneath tables or beds when the siren sounded, but most blithely continuing their activities. In temperate Europe blackouts might be compulsory, but on the Equator heavy cloth across a window reduced a room to suffocation. Singapore had adapted procedures in a cavalier fashion, covering windows only partially and renaming blackouts, brownouts. The town was full of swagger, and the confidence of constant government bulletins made alarmist thought impossible. Japanese reconnaissance flights, seen daily over the island, were accepted as defiant enemy bravado in the face of British strength. Singapore was impregnable.

Jenkins led Wilfred to an empty administrative hut and went off to find someone to show him about the camp. Left alone, Wilfred walked over to the netted window to stare out at the drilling men. A pile of leaflets was stacked nearby and picking one up he read a Whitehall War Office instruction for non-technical methods of dealing with enemy tanks. Jenkins soon returned with a young private behind him, and nodded sadly when he saw what Wilfred was reading.

'That's the kind of nonsense they send us from Whitehall. They might need tanks in the desert, but what would we do with them here? How would a tank get through 700 miles of Malayan jungle? That jungle is our best defence; those Japs will never get through it,' Jenkins stated.

After lunch rain came down, making a muddy lake of the parade ground. An army mess meal of fish curry and rice repeated unpleasantly on Wilfred as, his tour of the camp finished, he waited about for transport back to Singapore. In the late afternoon a jeep was found, and Wilfred climbed in next to the driver. Once more the bumpy road stretched ahead and the deep rich scent of the jungle steamed under the sun. The power of this impenetrable world filled Wilfred just as it had when he was a child. The rubber plantation on which he had been born could not be far away, he guessed, and on occasions his parents had visited Singapore, taking him with them. Such shadowy memories were always creeping up on him. The jeep rattled on as the sun mellowed; shadows were everywhere now, deepening between the trees. He knew that the reason he was here, the force that had propelled him so far across the ocean, was the need to enter again that distant place of childhood, the safety he had found under the dark leaves of the old swing on the mango tree. He thought of Cynthia, her burnished skin, the dark bruise of her mouth, her pale cat's eyes, and the earthy essence of her filled him. When he took Cynthia in his arms the taste of her lips beneath his own seemed full of a world he had lost.

Soon they crossed the Causeway back on to the island but found the road ahead was flooded after the rain. The driver turned on to an alternative route that ran along the north-west coastline where beaches were gripped by the giant claws of mangroves. Coconut palms, seaside shrubs, mango and wild nutmeg grew everywhere. The tide was out and the gaunt, tangled roots of the mangroves stood in menacing shadow under the setting sun.

After some distance the driver stopped the jeep to relieve himself and Wilfred walked off down a path to the beach. Atop their stilts fishermen's huts were crowded together on one side of the sandy cove. The spindly timbers of the fishing *kelong* stretched out into the sea; small boats were already setting out for the night, lanterns swinging on poles. A cool breeze blew upon him. Across the water, a short distance away, lay the Malay Peninsula. As he surveyed the empty beach, Wilfred was filled with unease. He saw that these northern Singapore beaches lay open to attack; no pillboxes, guns or landmines, no searchlights – not even the deterrent of barbed wire stood as fortification against an enemy landing. He remembered his interview with Brigadier Simson who, to the annoyance of Jenkins's 'top brass', held an opinion contrary to all others.

'In my view the jungle is not impassable for determined infantry, even during the monsoon. Our troops are not trained for jungle warfare, nor do we possess any tanks, for they are not thought to be necessary. Any defences we have are built entirely to meet a seaward attack. If an attack were to come from the north, Singapore could by no means be called an impregnable fortress.'

Wilfred stood on the darkening beach and remembered Simson's words. Across the water the lights on the mainland already lit up the night.

A few days later, Wilfred awoke with a start at night, and was surprised to find he was sitting upright in bed. The air raid siren was wailing, and the clock on the table registered 4.30 in the morning. The sheets lay smooth and untouched on Cynthia's side of the bed; she was on night duty again at the hospital and had left the evening before. Although he had not panicked during previous air raid alerts, Wilfred jumped out of bed and crawled under the desk a few feet away. There had never been an air raid practice after dark or this early in the morning. It was 8 December and Wilfred thought the alarm might be the grand practice the government had threatened for so long; it had been forecast that this dress rehearsal for war might come in the first week of the month, leaving everyone free to enjoy the rest of the festive season. Crouched in the narrow kneehole beneath the desk and looking up at the window, Wilfred could see the half-moon against a black sky. He had thrown the shutters back the night before, pushing aside the blackout cloth. As the siren faded away, he felt the ridiculousness of being squashed beneath the desk and eased himself out. The low drone of aircraft could already be heard. Thin fingers of searchlight thrust into the sky, illuminating formations of bombers like polished studs on a dark cloth. In the sweeping lights he could make out the red sun of Japan on the bodies of the planes. Silhouetted against the pale cup of the moon, the planes flew on across the island. The drone of the engines became fainter as Wilfred waited for them to disappear into a bank of cloud over the sea. Instead, there was the distant crack of anti-aircraft fire. The planes flew beyond the reach of the guns and in reply began to drop a litter of bombs. Picked out by the search-lights, the silver flecks fell in the planes' wake, like a shower of confetti. Wilfred heard a muffled thudding and saw bursts of fiery light. The aircraft flew on and disappeared at last. The sky was now a deep pink over the area where the General Hospital was situated.

All Wilfred could think of was Cynthia. Under his hand the window frame still radiated the heat of the day, the paint flaking and uneven. In the dark garden the usual boom of bullfrogs echoed through the night, crickets continued their incessant whirr and the smell of night flowers came to him. Everything was as before, yet he sensed a line had been crossed and nothing would be the same again.

He pulled on some clothes and ran from the room. The hallway of Belvedere was in darkness but he heard a cough and sounds of breathing. A torch was switched on and he saw several of the lodgers crouched under the stairs. Wilfred strode on down the corridor towards

Rose's room. On the way he passed Boffort, who stood in the doorway of the large room he now occupied with his wife Valerie.

'What's up?' Boffort enquired, stifling a yawn as he pulled on a dressing gown. Valerie peered anxiously over his shoulder, her hair wound on metal curlers.

'The Japs have dropped bombs,' Wilfred said over his shoulder as he hurried past.

'Not possible,' Boffort shouted after him. 'It must be that big practice air raid they've threatened. Don't be taken in.'

The door to Rose's room was open and Howard was already with his mother, helping a confused Rose up from where she had hidden under the bed. She brushed dust from her pink smocked nightdress; grey hair straggled over her shoulders, and a cobweb trailed from her head. Wilfred hesitated, embarrassed to see his mother-in-law in this dishevelled state, but Rose seemed unaware, reaching for a dressing gown and wrapping it quickly about herself, picking the web from her hair.

'They've dropped bombs near the hospital; they must be aiming for the docks and Chinatown. I'm going to Cynthia,' Wilfred said from the doorway, and Rose hurried forward in concern.

'Why did the *Prince of Wales* not shoot them down?' Rose gripped Wilfred's arm, refusing to let go. She remembered the great guns she had seen just days before, and Ordnance Seaman Jefferies striding about the huge ship.

'Right now the battleships are steaming up the peninsula to get rid of Japanese transports sighted off Indo-China,' Wilfred told her impatiently as he pulled himself free.

'Practice or real raid, I'd better get to the Air Raid Precaution station,' Howard said, tucking his shirt into his trousers. Although he had volunteered for ARP duties these were only in the day: the post shut down at night as no one expected a real raid, least of all after dark.

Howard ran behind Wilfred up the corridor, buckling his belt into place. They made their way to the gardener's shed where a couple of bicycles were always kept, then pushed them hurriedly down the drive towards the gate. They parted to cycle off in opposite directions, Howard towards his Air Raid Precaution centre and Wilfred to the hospital.

As Howard passed the old rain tree on the corner and turned out on to Bukit Timah, he slowed to a halt, craning his neck for a glimpse of Bougainvillaea House between the dark shapes of the trees. Mei Lan had come back from Hong Kong the week before; Rama the gardener had told him. She had been away for more than a year, and during that time he had heard nothing from her. He had written each day but she had not replied to a single letter. When Rama gave him the news of Mei Lan's return, he had gone down to the canal and played his saxophone in the hope that she might hear. Now, looking up at the sky in fear of more bombs, Howard saw a dim light in Bougainvillaea House, and felt again the pain of Mei Lan's rejection.

The night was warm, and Wilfred pedalled furiously, head down, the breeze rushing against his ears. As he drew near the town the air was heavy with sulphurous fumes, and his panic grew. The leafy roads about Belvedere were dark and silent with only an occasional street lamp, but here he saw there was no blackout and streetlights blazed everywhere. People had come out of their houses to watch the air raid, and were running about excitedly.

As Wilfred neared the hospital the mournful shriek of the all-clear siren was heard at last. Wounded people, all poor residents of Chinatown, packed the hospital driveway, and a queue of ambulances carrying bomb victims added to the chaos. Propping the bike against a wall, Wilfred forced his way through the crowd into the Admissions Room. Almost immediately he saw Cynthia on the far side of the room, bent over an old Chinese woman with a bloodied limb, and relief flooded through him. He caught her eye but she waved him away, too busy to give him attention. Returning outside he sat down on a low wall, lighting a cigarette with trembling hands, drawing on it gratefully. Above the black silhouettes of trees the sky was alight with fiery reflection. He could not believe what was happening. Just as he had feared, just as Brigadier Simson had forecast, war had begun.

For Cynthia the unexpected sight of Wilfred across the crowded room was the comfort she needed: it meant Belvedere was safe. It was difficult to know exactly what had happened, except that Chinatown had been bombed. Even without the present emergency, it had been a bad week. The last few days she had been on the children's wards, where there was an excess of tuberculosis. Although they wheeled these children out into the gardens, it was difficult to see what good this did in the swamp-like climate of Singapore. Many of the new-born babies had contracted tetanus from unsanitary conditions while the umbilical cord was being cut, and when they died she had to accompany their bodies to the mortuary. A number of nurses had succumbed to the current wave of malaria sweeping the town, leaving the hospital short staffed, and Cynthia had been shunted from one ward to another. For a while she had been on the First Class ward to which only Europeans were admitted and where the nursing staff were predominantly British. The most difficult thing there was dealing with the lewd comments of a sick Scottish sea captain. In that elite ward, patients presented nurses with chocolates and champagne, and staff dined on extra roast pigeon and lamb chops in the ward kitchens. The Second Class Asiatic wards were clean and orderly, but it was the crowded Third Class wards that Cynthia hated. They were for the poor who lacked concepts of hygiene and, as the beds were free, there was not the same standard of cleanliness. The nursing staff on these wards were all local women, and it was here Cynthia spent most of her time.

Now blood was all around her and in the midst of hysteria she must remain calm. The badly wounded were lined up on trolleys in the corridor near the operating theatre. For the first time she saw what shrapnel could do, the terrible fractures, burns and maiming; the wounds were unlike anything she had seen before.

She turned as a young woman, screaming incomprehensibly, stepped suddenly out of the crowd thrusting a bloody parcel at her. Cynthia stared at the tiny feet protruding from the blood-soaked towel. Usually she could keep a professional distance from a patient's pain, but now she was flooded with horror and quickly looked away. The first weak light of day was growing in the open door of the Admissions Room; she had lost all track of time.

When Howard reached his local Air Raid Precaution station where they had been instructed to gather in an emergency, he was still convinced the raid was a practice. A couple of trucks were lined up outside the ARP station and a warden was issuing everyone with shovels and picks. Most of his group had already arrived and everyone appeared confused. Mr Barber, the group commander, drew up in his Austin car. Abdul, who lived in a nearby *kampong* had been first to arrive at the station, and greeted Howard excitedly.

'Sky red over Chinatown and docks. Looks like real air raid, real fire,' he announced to a clamour of disbelief.

'Cannot be,' said Wen Lit, the youngest of the group, a small, delicately boned youth with dark burning eyes.

'It's the real thing,' Mr Barber confirmed, unusually flustered as he walked briskly up to them. He was a tall grey-haired Englishman with an insignificant chin and an army bearing who, Howard thought, resembled the newspaper pictures of Lieutenant General Percival, General Officer Commanding, Malaya.

'I have our helmets at last, just in time for our baptism,' Mr Barber said, instructing several boys to bring in the boxes from the car.

As ARP auxiliaries they were supposed to have a uniform and a metal helmet with a badge, but supplies had run short. Mr Barber cut the string of the box and triumphantly pulled out a helmet. It did not resemble the helmets other ARP volunteers were wearing.

'Sir, it is German helmet,' Abdul pointed out immediately.

Mr Barber blanched and spluttered and bent to the box in desperation.

'Dear God, what have we been given?' he exploded.

'Helmet is helmet, sir,' Abdul comforted.

'Quite right Abdul,' Mr Barber replied, straightening up resignedly. 'Wherever they're from, they may save our lives. We are needed in Chinatown at the double. Our transport is already outside.'

They were ten in the group, and wearing their new German helmets they filed out to climb into the open truck. Mr Barber swung himself up beside them and the vehicle moved forward. As they neared Chinatown a strong sulphurous odour blew about and street lights illuminated the extensive damage inflicted by the Japanese bombers. Fires blazed everywhere; the Auxiliary Fire Service was already at work. Howard's group was unloaded from the truck, to join other ARP groups from different parts of the city. They marched behind Mr Barber to the wet rubble of a bombed house and were ordered to search for bodies. The AFS had just put out a nearby fire that had raged after the bombing, and moved on. Water and black ash swilled about their feet; a charred odour engulfed them. Gutted houses steamed and dripped from the AFS dousing, a distance away flames still leapt about. A great swathe of the road had collapsed and through the gap Howard could see the houses in the street beyond.

'Use those picks; use those shovels. Quickly now, there are people under this mess,' a senior ARP warden urged briskly as they began searching for casualties or signs of life. Soon, Howard's mouth was full of gritty dust and he was sweating profusely in the hot night. When he had first joined Air Raid Precaution it seemed to demand only some walking about checking that glass windows were taped, and that all premises had an adequate brownout.

He knew he would never forget the first bodies they found; he turned away to vomit. Sometimes all they unearthed were bits and pieces – a torso, a hand, some arms, three legs; limbs had to be matched to corpses and piled up beside them. The body of a young woman was found intact but without her feet.

'Her feet, you must find her feet,' sobbed an old woman who had been hovering nearby, the mother or grandmother of the dead girl. Howard began to feel faint; he had lost count of time, they seemed to have been working non-stop for hours. His head sweated beneath the helmet but he dared not take it off. The noxious odour of the blast still hung heavily everywhere, and the stink from smashed honey buckets in the bombed buildings was overpowering. Behind Howard a woman was screaming 'My baby, my baby!' over and over again.

'Why must we find her feet?' Howard asked Wen Lit savagely. The boy dug stoically beside him; the pick seemed almost as big as himself and the helmet nearly covered his eyes, the strap swinging loosely under his chin.

'She cannot be buried without her feet. She must go whole into the next life. If we cannot find her feet they will have to get some wax ones made for her,' Wen Lit told him between breaths, shovelling diligently.

At last, day broke and the sun blazed down upon the smashed road, revealing the destruction in all its grotesque detail. Howard was exhausted. His head ached and his knees were shaking.

'We need a break,' Mr Barber said at last, coming up and putting a hand on his shoulder.

He led the way to a canteen set up in a truck near the bomb site. Howard took a mug of hot sweet tea and sat with Wen Lit and Abdul on the remains of a crumbling wall. Soon Mr Barber joined them, his face puffy and smeared with dust. Across the road bodies were laid out beside the neat piles of dismembered limbs. Already, the heat and humidity were rising; the stench of death had come to overwhelm every other smell. A constant stream of people trying to find missing relatives bent to examine the corpses and stray limbs. A Red Cross van finally arrived to carry bodies away to a morgue. Mr Barber drank his tea in silence beside Howard. No one had an appetite for the buns that were offered in the canteen, but Abdul walked over to get some more tea. Within a moment he returned, hurrying towards them in excitement.

'Hong Kong also bombed by Japanese last night, just before Singapore. And a place from where they are getting pearls in America was also bombed. All American ships there were sunk. Because of this America is also now joining the war. News is on the radio just now,' Abdul announced. Mr Barber stood up in shock.

'You must mean Pearl Harbor, the American naval base in Hawaii! Is their fleet wiped out?' He strode off towards the canteen where everyone was grouped about a radio connected to a generator.

'Whole world is now at war.' Abdul smiled happily.

16

ROSE SAT AS ALWAYS on the chintz sofa in the alcove off the dining room, a large mixing bowl resting on her lap. Christmas was no more than a week away and the cake was not yet ready. She prided herself on her preparedness with regard to the festive season; the cake was always baked and regularly doused with alcohol for weeks before the great day. Beyond the roofed patio of the dining room rain emptied down, splashing from the guttering on to the shrubbery. The cook, Ah Fong, hovered disapprovingly near the sofa, a pained expression on his thin face. As Rose drove the wooden spoon through the sticky mix of Christmas cake, his mouth tightened. He was affronted, as he was each year, that he was not left to his own devices with the Christmas cooking. The recent bombing had upset everyone's routine and Rose was so late with the cake it would have no time to mature but must be eaten immediately, although the puddings had been made in September. Yet, whatever the dastardly things happening about her, Rose was determined not to be done out of Christmas. Everyone felt the same. Newspapers were full of the need to ignore the Japanese and concentrate on positive things.

Japan's posturing belligerence was brushed aside in Singapore, although their army had occupied Indo-China, Burma, Thailand and Vietnam. The Japanese were establishing bases in the Pacific like a man securing stepping stones over a river, but no one saw cause for immediate worry. The distant rumble of fighting on the peninsula disturbed life in the way a ripple disturbs a still pond. The European community continued to follow their usual hedonistic routine, daring the bombs to fall. *The Malaya Tribune* had announced in bold headlines after the first air raid, SINGAPORE TAKES IT – WITH A GRIN, thumbing their nose at the enemy. The management of Raffles Hotel had perfected a blackout technique and the dance band played on. Strawberries, fresh roses and rock oysters were flown in as usual from far and near.

Although a victim of the first air raid, Robinsons department store moved its coffee shop to the basement and was as ever filled to capacity with smart European women. Tennis continued to be played at the Tanglin Club, and cricket on the Padang. Unlimited hard liquor was freely available. The only news received by everyone with a painful jolt on 10 December was that the battleships *Repulse* and *Prince of Wales*, so recently on view at the naval base, had – unbelievably – been sunk.

On hearing the announcement Rose had sat transfixed, the blood running cold in her veins. She remembered the vulnerability of Ordnance Seaman Jefferies's knees, and his toothy smile. She remembered the High-Angle Plotting Table and wondered why it had not served its purpose on that great, unsinkable ship. Where was the picture of the King, nailed so firmly to the wall? Had the clamps on the cooking pots held them in place as the ship turned upside down? Now, as she stirred the Christmas cake mix, she imagined the great vessel lying at the bottom of the ocean like a wrecked cathedral, and her throat constricted with emotion.

A ring of the doorbell brought Rose back to herself. Outside, rain sluiced off the eves and foliage; the deluge had not let up all day. The monsoon seemed heavier than usual. Pillows and mattresses oozed a fusty smell, and in Belvedere the servants were forever putting things out to air the moment they saw the sun. Rose handed the Christmas cake to Ah Fong as she listened to Hamzah shuffling forward in response to the bell. A woman's voice was heard and soon Hamzah reappeared with a middle-aged matron, a hat of purple gauze limp from the rain, slightly askew on her head. With a start Rose recognised her cousin Mavis from Penang. Mavis gave a cry at the sight of Rose and stumbled towards her. It must be ten years since we last met, Rose thought. Mavis had always been proud of her willowy frame but now she swelled generously, an ample bosom resting on her waist. With a sob Mavis threw herself upon Rose, tears spilling down her face.

'Penang has fallen to the Japanese. They're thick on the ground in George Town and doing terrible things. I could not think of anyone but you. There is fighting everywhere and Singapore is the only place left to come to,' Cousin Mavis wailed. 'British troops have not held a single town on the peninsula. When they knew the Japanese were coming every European man, woman and child cleared out of Penang overnight and left us to our fate.' Mavis's blue flowered dress was stained and crumpled; a feral odour escaped her as if she had not had a bath for days. Rose, in shock, steered her to the chintz sofa where, still sobbing, Mavis continued with her story.

'There was a stampede to leave when we discovered what was happening. But only Europeans were allowed on the launches, and we locals were turned away. A kind English couple got me on to a train full of wounded soldiers along with the European women and children.'

It was difficult to fully comprehend Mavis's garbled talk. Even as a child, Rose remembered, Mavis had been a drama queen. Obviously, she had suffered a terrible trauma and Rose indicated to Ah Fong, who was still standing with the bowl of Christmas cake cupped under one arm and following events with interest, to return to the kitchen and bring some fresh tea. Hamzah reappeared from the direction of the front door, carrying a battered leather suitcase and a dented hatbox. Mavis drew a shuddering breath and continued with her story.

'The Japanese are coming down the peninsula on bicycles and in tanks; nothing can stop them,' Mavis said. Taking a cup of tea from Ah Fong, she put in four lumps of sugar, picking the cubes up with her fingers and ignoring the silver tongs, much to Rose's disapproval. Lifting off her hat, she placed it carefully on the sofa beside her, revealing short hair plastered damply to her head. She had been sitting tensely on the edge of the sofa, but now she settled her bulk more comfortably. The buttons of her dress strained over mountainous breasts as she turned to assess Belvedere's cavernous interior.

'You have a big place here, very comfortable, much bigger than I remember when I visited last.' Mavis looked about, her eyes taking in every detail.

Over the years, Rose observed, Mavis had swelled but changed little; there were the same round cheeks and vacant gaze, and the shadow on her upper lip was now a bristly grey. Mavis had married Raymond Dias, a senior clerk in a British paper mill, and had moved from Malacca to Penang before Rose met Charlie Burns. There had been two children, a girl who married well and went to live in England, and a boy who was killed in a traffic accident. Raymond had died of a lingering disease when the children were in their teens. Since then, Mavis had supplemented his frugal pension by working as a stenographer in a bank.

'You need a bath and a rest,' Rose comforted her, knowing room must be found in Belvedere. This would not be difficult; the house had emptied at a steady rate with young men returning to fight for England after war began in Europe.

Rose came down the stairs from settling Cousin Mavis to see Arthur Boffort and his wife Valerie struggling into Belvedere with brown paper packages and Cold Storage bags. They were almost the only lodgers left.

'Here we are, Mrs B – a bit of Christmas cheer,' Boffort puffed, placing before her a bottle of wine wrapped up in coloured paper.

'They have extra rations available at Cold Storage. Many people are taking the precaution of stocking up. What about you, Mrs B, have you stocked up?' Valerie's voice was full of suppressed anxiety. She was a slight woman with flyaway hair and round grey eyes; her collarbones protruded to such a degree they appeared to be deformed.

'The Japanese will never get to Singapore.' Rose spoke with unintended sharpness. The arrival of Cousin Mavis with her harrowing story had upset her more than she liked to admit.

'We have corned beef, tinned salmon and rice. We thought we would seal it all up in a bread tin and bury it in the garden. Would you mind if we dug ourselves a hole, Mrs B?' Boffort's anxiety was evident in the way he spat out his words. Rose felt a speck of saliva land on her cheek.

'In Penang they say the Japanese are commandeering all supplies,' Valerie burst out, fear now getting the better of her.

The days went by and, as Christmas approached, the raids accelerated and casualties soon became more than hospitals could cope with. Penang had been abandoned with almost no fight just as Mavis said, and Singapore was awash with refugees and military casualties transported back to the colony. Finally, Christmas came and went, slipping away almost before it could be grasped. The tree Rose annually ordered failed to arrive from the Cameron Highlands because of the worsening state of war on the peninsula. Rose festooned branches from a mango tree instead, covering the unripe fruit with gold paint and adding some extra baubles; nothing could alleviate the tension.

Mei Lan had stayed more than a year in Hong Kong with her father. It had been a time of both boredom and excitement. She had loved the view from her father's house, of the bay of Hong Kong with its armada of square-sailed junks. She had enjoyed the brief winter, the fresh bite in the air, and the deep fur coat of silver fox her father had bought her to keep off the evening chill.

Just as in Singapore, Boon Eng was constantly absent from home, and much of the time Mei Lan had been left to her own devices. She had taken a secretarial course, and then worked in her father's office trying to fill the empty hours. There had been efforts by her father, with the help of a great aunt and a matchmaker, to introduce her to a variety of wealthy young men. She had sabotaged these arrangements at every turn and soon gained a reputation as an unsuitable girl. She hated the constant talk of marriage, and felt nothing in common with the groups of idle young people she was pushed to join, who whiled away the days in tennis, dancing or mah-jong and social chatter over elaborate banquets of food. All she wanted was to return to Singapore and Ah Siew, who had stayed behind.

Her father had not accompanied her back to Singapore but had remained in Hong Kong, and she suspected that it was a new woman who kept him there. When Hong Kong finally fell to the Japanese it was impossible to get news of him. In Bougainvillaea House they could only wait and hope. As soon as things calmed down, as he was sure they would, Lim Hock An said optimistically, they would hear from him.

On her return to Singapore Mei Lan feared Second Grandmother would incarcerate her in the house and, like the great aunt in Hong Kong, call for the matchmaker again. In the familiar confines of her room, she both dreaded and desired the sight of Belvedere beyond the window, intimate as an old friend, forcing her thoughts back to Howard. His rejection lay within her, a constant and painful humiliation from which there was no respite. From Hong Kong she had written to him each day, and he had not replied to a single letter. Then, on her return she had opened the drawer of the dressing table and the first object she had seen was Howard's compass, its red finger pointed as ever towards Belvedere. Quickly, she had thrust it away. In the evenings, she sometimes heard the notes of his saxophone, and wondered if he knew she was back. She could focus on nothing, the knowledge that he was near underlying everything.

The only thing that heartened Mei Lan was that JJ was now living and working in Singapore. In 1939, when war threatened to begin in

England, he had abandoned his studies at Oxford, returning home on one of the last boats to leave the country safely; he had barely managed to finish his undergraduate degree. When he arrived back in Singapore, after a leisurely journey home via India where he stayed for several months, Lim Hock An had sent him to work in his Ipoh office, to manage a pineapple estate and its cannery. This provincial assignment was not to JJ's liking; he had begged to be sent to the fast moving world of Shanghai or Hong Kong, but Lim Hock An stood firm. He relented only in agreeing to JJ being employed in the Singapore office. But in the years away JJ had grown distant from Mei Lan. He no longer treated her as a confidant but assumed the stance of a man of the world. Like his father he now wore a white silk scarf with his dinner jacket, and had bought an open sports car he could ill afford in which to roar around town. He used his father's clubs and, after work at his grandfather's office, his life transferred to the tennis courts and the dance floor. Like his father, he was always to be seen with a woman on his arm.

In the house Mei Lan listened each day to Second Grandmother's throaty voice ordering her slave girls about, calling for barley water or chrysanthemum tea, bringing up wind and moaning with the pain of her twisted feet. From behind the closed door of JJ's room, if he was home, came the trumpeted rhythm of jazz from a brass-eared phonograph. Lim Hock An, now that his health had improved, often left Bougainvillaea House for the East Coast home of Little Sparrow. Before his stroke he had taken up visiting her again after a long hiatus, much to Second Grandmother's fury. A child had been born from this renewed relationship, another girl. She had been named Wen Yen, but Little Sparrow had visited the cinema to see a Greta Garbo film before her daughter's birth and, determined not to be outdone by Lustrous Pearl's naming of Bertie after an actor, had added the name Greta to Wen Yen's identity.

After the shock of the first bombing, when the people of Singapore prepared to defend the city, many joined one or another of the auxiliary services. Mei Lan wanted to do the same. At dinner one evening she announced to the family that she would join the Medical Auxiliary Service. The heroics of such a commitment appealed to her, and in extravagant moments she saw herself comforting the dying. It was also a perfect means of evading the constrictions of Bougainvillaea House.

'Girls of good family do not work in hospitals,' Lim Hock An replied, looking up from a slice of watermelon and spitting out black pips.

'Everyone who can is doing something, including women from good Chinese families,' Mei Lan protested, standing firm. Second Grandmother, who had a better idea of the essentials of nursing, lowered her spoon above a bowl of coconut sago.

'House of Lim girl cannot touch strange person's bloody bandages. Cannot wash strange person's filthy body. Cannot.' Second Grandmother shuddered at the thought.

Mei Lan could not control her anger; the old people, preoccupied with their food, condensed her life to the narrowness of a coffin. The sound of Lim Hock An spitting out another volley of seeds filled the sudden silence and she knew they were waiting, united in their expectation of her disobedience.

'I'm going to join.' She was amazed at her own determination. The old people exchanged a quick glance, but even as she spoke she knew they could do nothing against the force of her will. Her life was her own to use as she wished; the thought came to her as a revelation. The following day Mei Lan enrolled in the Medical Auxiliary Service, and was immediately sent to the General Hospital.

'What man wanting strong-willed wife? *Aiyaah*. What in-law putting up with disobedient girl?' Second Grandmother screamed when she heard, slapping her brow in exasperation. Mei Lan listened, unperturbed, knowing something bigger than herself led her on. Across the room, sunk in a rattan chair and hidden behind a newspaper, Lim Hock An sighed as he listened to his wife's angry wailing, counting the moments until he could leave for an evening with Little Sparrow. Although he could not put the thought into words, he understood his granddaughter had done no more than, as a young man, he had done himself; she had inherited his stubborn will.

With casualties overwhelming every medical facility, Cynthia seemed never to leave the hospital, much to the anxiety of Wilfred and Rose. People are dying, what can I do? she said. Wilfred had joined the St John Ambulance brigade as a volunteer ambulance driver, after taking some training in stretcher carrying and first aid. He often drove casualties to the General Hospital and was able to catch a few minutes with Cynthia. As his wife hurried down a hospital corridor looking for places to install the military casualties Wilfred had just brought in, he kept pace determinedly beside her. The hospital was overflowing with wounded soldiers, every corridor was crowded with makeshift beds. Whenever she managed to have an occasional hour or even a night alone with Wilfred, Cynthia found herself too tired to respond to the passion he seemed able to effortlessly summon. As they came out of the hospital into the fiery blast of the sun, a wave of desolation swept over her and tears filled her eyes. She could only live hour to hour.

Wilfred's ambulance stood on the driveway and, with Cynthia beside him, he walked over to direct the auxiliaries as they unloaded further wounded men. Cynthia bent to assess the new casualties, stopping a passing orderly.

'Call a volunteer nurse and more orderlies here quickly. We need to get these men inside,' she told him. The man disappeared into the building, returning almost immediately with a white-coated doctor who issued directions for the wounded men to be taken to the operating theatre. Cynthia instructed the orderlies to pick up the stretchers and then turned to the volunteer nurse, demure in her hospital uniform and square of white linen folded over her head, and felt there was something familiar about her.

'Mei Lan,' Cynthia exclaimed in surprise, remembering the girl, noting her elegance even in her volunteer's uniform. She wondered if Howard knew she had returned from Hong Kong, but decided it would be best not to mention her brother.

Mei Lan seemed embarrassed, refusing to look Cynthia in the eye, her gaze on the stretcher patients. At the hospital entrance, the doctor accompanying the patients stopped and turned back to Cynthia, waving an admittance slip he had forgotten to give her. Mei Lan immediately hurried over to collect it from him, as if grateful to get away. Cynthia shrugged her stiff shoulders wearily; she had had almost no sleep that night. There had been another heavy raid on Chinatown, and the flow of injured was never ending. As the days went by she found herself accepting violent death with a casualness that distressed her. Wilfred drew her aside, putting an arm about her.

'I'll come back tonight. We'll have a few hours together,' he said. She had been given a room of her own at the hospital and no longer had to live in the nurses' dormitory. It was as small as a cupboard but it gave her privacy, and Matron turned a blind eye to Wilfred's visits.

The first time she had seen Cynthia in Admissions a few days previously, Mei Lan had stopped in shock, flooded by emotion and images of Howard she had tried to suppress for months. She did not have the courage to approach Cynthia so backed away, finding ways to avoid her whenever she saw her in the distance. Yet Cynthia's presence in the hospital gave an edge to the day; she carried with her the aura of Howard, allowing Mei Lan to sense him again.

The hospital allowed Mei Lan to escape the confines of Bougainvillaea House. However, she was loath to admit a volunteer's work was nothing like she had expected. She was immediately taught how to cut badly burned clothing from open wounds, change dressings, give a bed bath, take temperatures and pulse rates. Nothing prepared her for the need to have contact with the odorous excretions of the human body or the sight of the full bedpans, even if an orderly took them away. From the beginning she was ordered to go round the wards and dark crowded corridors of the hospital with a torch, a pair of forceps and a kidney bowl picking maggots, hatched by swarms of odious flies, out of the oozing wounds of soldiers. When she had finished she sat down and cried. There was nothing heroic about this distasteful work; at the first bedpan she had turned away to retch. She found no dying person in need of her comfort; all they wanted was relief from pain. On the second day she would have given up, but for the thought of Second Grandmother's derision.

She had no option later but to return to Cynthia with the signed admission form. Cynthia smiled, trying to put Mei Lan at ease, even as she watched Wilfred's ambulance disappear down the hospital drive. 'Why don't you come along with me to the nurses' quarters? I've got to bring over spare blankets from the storeroom,' she said.

Mei Lin walked beside Cynthia through the grounds of the hospital listening to the singing of birds and the constant whirr of cicadas, glad to be free for a short time from work. She wanted to ask a thousand questions about Howard, but swallowed them down. What use would it be even to ask, when she knew he had lost interest in her? There could be no other reason for his silence, when she had written him letter after letter.

'Looks like giant worms have been at work in the gardens,' Mei Lan commented as they walked towards the nurses' quarters behind the hospital building. Trenches furrowed the lawns around the hospital, the mountains of soft loose earth piled up beside them acting as breeding ground for swarms of malarial mosquitoes. They had been dug for protection during air raids, but few people bothered to run to these damp shelters, preferring to take their chances in the hospital under tables or beds. The alert was now almost permanent, with deadly formations of aircraft flying over too frequently to monitor. Soon the blankets were gathered and Cynthia and Mei Lan began the short walk back to the hospital. A small plane hovered above them in the sky, and they stopped apprehensively to observe it.

'It's just a single reconnaissance plane, not a bomber,' Mei Lan decided, squinting up at it.

The blankets were piled high in their arms and it was difficult to see where they were going on the narrow path with its border of bougainvillaea, the purple flowers faded because of the continuous rain. Ahead of them a group of medical students came out of a side door of the hospital, and one of the young men waved to Mei Lan. Earlier, he had been on duty in the emergency room and she had helped him with a tourniquet on an old woman. Mei Lan was about to comment on this when the sound of shelling began without warning. The medical students scattered, some running for the hospital, others pushing through the hedge to jump into the trenches.

A sudden explosion moved the ground beneath Mei Lan, the blast ricocheting through her head. One moment the earth spurted high about her and the next she was lying deep in a trench unable to move for the weight of bodies upon her. Loose earth covered her face and hands; there was a dense scent of wet soil and the stench of brackish water collected below her in the pit. Mosquitoes swarmed about. Machine-gun fire, sounding like a bag of marbles dropped on a stone floor, followed the explosions. Bodies pressing down heavily upon her, muffled the noise. Panic overwhelmed Mei Lan: she thought she might suffocate and struggled to dislodge the heavy mass. Then there was movement, she heard voices, the load upon her lessened and people were climbing out of the trench.

'Are you all right?' She heard Cynthia's voice above her, and realised they had both jumped into the trench. One of the medical students gave her a hand, and Mei Lan scrambled up into the sunlight, weak with relief. The sky was thick with a dark cloud of twittering birds; disturbed by the blast they were now settling noisily again in the trees. Mei Lan turned to peer back into the trench. Just a short distance from where she had been thrown she saw the young man who had waved at her minutes before, staring up at her, dead and open-eyed. The blankets she had carried were strewn about, covered by clods of damp earth.

For Singapore, the New Year's Eve that saw in 1942 was a dismal affair; no one could any longer deny that the enemy were only 150 miles from the island. Troops were already retreating into the city from more northern posts on the Malayan mainland, filling Singapore's streets and dance halls. Already, preparations for a siege were under way. Amongst other premises, the Capitol and Pavilion Cinemas had been turned into food dumps. Nine thousand cattle had been imported from Bali for slaughtering; 125,000 pigs had been counted in the colony. Two large dairy herds from Johore had crossed the Causeway on to the island, and now grazed by the roadsides and on golf courses. Confusion was everywhere. On government orders trenches were forever being dug and then re-dug in a contrary design, and then filled in for unfathomable reasons, leaving the Padang and other public spaces furrowed and rough. At the docks vital military equipment could not be unloaded; coolie labourers had already fled town and all the wharfs were bombed.

January brought a change of pace in the bombing. Sporadic raids on the docks and the airfields, with occasional sorties over the town, became ever more frequent, increasing in viciousness as the days went by. The raids were almost always in daylight and carried out by massive formations of up to eighty planes. No British planes were to be seen in the skies, and Japanese bombers flew like proud birds far above the reach of anti-aircraft guns. Through it all, the monsoon kept up its steady drumming. Finally, the Japanese reached Johore and occupied the Sultan's palace: they were now fifty miles from Singapore. The European community danced on defiantly at Raffles Hotel, while swarms of restless, drunken soldiers queued for taxi girls at the barn-like dance halls of the Great Worlds. Only the Chinese community, understanding there was trouble ahead, withdrew the age-old chit system, demanding cash from every European for even the smallest purchase. Chinese were leaving the town in droves for more rural areas, and were seen every day pushing loaded carts of belongings out of the city. Tinned food and whisky were still available at Cold Storage, but fresh fruit and vegetables were hard to come by; Johore was Singapore's market garden and the Japanese now controlled it. Hundreds of corpses were trapped irretrievably beneath bombed buildings, and their decomposing perfume pervaded the city; nothing could scrub the dreadful odour away. Bodies lay unattended in the street waiting for burial squads, black with flies, just like the meat hanging on hooks in the Beach Road market.

Weeks had slipped by in growing and nightmarish confusion. The naval base, where Rose had toured the *Prince of Wales,* was deliberately fired and evacuated by its European personnel, following a scorched earth policy. A black miasma hovered over the city as oil burned day and night at the base. Abandoned cars and bomb craters littered roads, damaged water mains flooded streets, making progress about the city difficult. Finally, at their Orchard Road premises the staff of Cold Storage, in spite of continued government bravado that Singapore was in no danger, stood on the first floor balcony of the shop disposing of their liquor stores, unwilling to leave such comfort to the Japanese. Bottles of spirits, wines and champagne were tossed at a great rate into the street below. Soon, thirty thousand British troops had crossed on to the island from mainland Malaya, blowing up the bridge of the Causeway behind them. The last ninety men on to the island were pipers of the Argyll and Sutherland Highlanders, who marched over the Causeway playing 'I'll Take the High Road' on their bagpipes. Dishevelled soldiers packed the island, wandering drunk in the streets, desperate with fatigue, with no unit, no billet and no one to give them orders. Only those battalions that still had commanders were returning gunfire at the front line. Across the narrow stretch of water separating the island from peninsular Malaya, the Japanese could now be seen walking about, to everyone's indignation.

17

In December of 1941, soon after the first enemy air raid, all the Japanese in Singapore had been interned in Changi Prison, joining Mr Shinozaki who had earlier been charged with spying.

'Japanese internees may be sent to India, Singapore is too small a place to imprison so many people,' Mr Ho said, and shook his head sadly when Raj discussed the matter with him. 'I sent Yoshiko and the children out of town, to Mrs Ho's sister in Katong. Nobody there knows Yoshiko is Japanese, so she will be safe.' Mr Ho's face was furrowed by anxiety.

As the weeks went by, Raj tried to keep his mind on the good news that he was soon to be an uncle. Leila was pregnant and she was sure the baby would be a boy. It excited him to think of the things he would teach this nephew, things the boy could not learn from his unworldly father. When he was born he would buy the child a silver rattle, and gold bangles for its mother. Other than this future happy event, everything around him appeared to be deteriorating. The New Year, when it arrived, offered only a further bleak forecast.

There had been rain earlier in the evening, and it was cool up on the small terrace of Manikam's Cloth Shop where Raj sat in the evenings to smoke a quiet cigarette. He heard the drone of planes approaching, and watched them emerge from the clouds to be caught in a net of searchlights. Whenever he watched an air raid, he found himself remembering the first plane he saw long ago as a child in the village. It had sounded as if a great bee was above the schoolhouse; everyone put down their slates and rushed to the window. The plane had circled high above, a great bird in the empty sky. Then, without warning, the aircraft turned in an arc and began to descend like a faulty firework, a trail of black smoke behind it. The children ran out of the schoolroom, and raced to the nearby millet field where the plane had fallen. A great heat issued from the charred wreckage, but there were no flames. The dead pilot sat bolt upright, strapped to his seat, eyes hidden behind dark goggles, a leather hat covering his head and ears. The teacher arrived to shout at the boys, driving them back into school with a cane. Soon, the pilot had been buried and the machine dismantled and cleared by the villagers in the manner of ants disassembling an insect and carrying its parts away. Now, so many years later, Raj still remembered the plane gliding freely across the sky, and felt little sympathy for the pilot. He had learned that once airborne a man must find the currents that will lift him high and hold him aloft, like a great creature of prey.

The following day Raj made his way to Krishna's home. In the crowded tenement, the room was squashed between that of a tailor, an Ayuvedic doctor and an Indian Chettiar moneylender. The house was always full of the doctor's patients, and they pushed past Raj as he climbed the stairs. The humming of the sewing machines in the tailor's room mixed with the sound of Indian music playing on a phonograph in the road below. Raj was hungry and, as he lifted the thin curtain over the doorway, he hoped Leila would have something for him to eat.

Two middle-aged women, the wives of a milkman and a wheat grinder who also rented rooms in the house, were crouched beside Leila who lay groaning on the sleeping mat. The milkman's wife was wringing out a towel above a bowl of bloody water. Leila's sari was pushed up about her legs and the wheat grinder's wife was pressing down upon her stomach as if she was kneading dough. His sister let out a scream of pain and Raj started forward, his eyes on the bloody cloth bundle lying beside the mattress. The milkman's wife sprang up at once to bar his way, waving her slimy wet hands before him. She was a muscular woman, and quickly thrust him back into the corridor through the curtained door. Krishna had gone as usual to the schoolroom in the Ramakrishna Mission and was not to be seen anywhere.

'What has happened?' Raj shouted at the woman.

'Baby is gone, that is what has happened. It is God's will. There is nothing a man can do here.' Even as she spoke the air raid siren wailed, and almost immediately the sound of aircraft was above them. The woman turned and disappeared behind the curtain again.

Raj rushed down the stairs and forced his way through the crowd sheltering under the five-foot way, running out into the middle of the road to stand looking up at the sky. The shock of what was happening to Leila made him lose all fear of the bombing. High above him the planes roared over in perfect formation, like a flock of migrating birds. People shouted for him to take shelter, but he stood where he was, watching bombs drop with the effortless beauty of streamers taking flight in the wind. Serangoon Road had yet to be hit and it was reasoned that the Japanese, knowing India's wish to be free of British rule, avoided targeting the area. In the distance the sun glinted on the falling bombs, Raj waited for the thud of explosions. Instead, a deafening blast from behind him tossed him to the ground. A cloud of dust and a hail of debris descended upon him. From the direction of the slaughter-house came the wild screams of wounded animals. People were running about, shouting hysterically. Raj saw with surprise that he was unhurt and that the buildings still stood about him.

He raced back up the stairs to Leila. The milkman's wife had thrown open the window shutters and with the wheat grinder's wife was leaning out to converse excitedly with people in the street below. Raj crouched down beside Leila, who now lay quietly on the mat, hollow cheeked, eyes smudged with dark shadows. Her sari was tucked neatly about her and the bloodied water and bundle were gone. He knelt and took her hand. Leila clung to her brother, but turned her head away to hide her distress. She had not expected that, once again, it would end like this in blood and pain and a sodden parcel of remains that was taken away to where she did not know. It was the second time this had happened.

'My baby!' she had screamed seeing the milkman's wife clearing away the metal bowl with its bloody pile of wet newspaper.

The wheat grinder's wife shook her head, wiping her clean and pulling her sari back into place. Leila looked up at the dirty walls and the ceiling spotted with the droppings of insects and geckos, and despair washed through her. Each day the child grew within her she had felt her life more real, more whole. Immediately he heard the news of her pregnancy, Krishna had bought a small, carved wooden crib on rockers. For our son, he had said, beaming at her and she knew what the child would mean to him. What Krishna wanted most from her had been this child; his son.

'There will be another time, you are still young,' the wheat grinder's wife said briskly.

'I could not stop it. The baby is gone,' Leila sobbed to Raj as he squeezed her hand.

'There will be another time. It is God's will.' Raj searched for words of comfort.

As the days progressed and the bombing accelerated in early January, Lim Hock An became increasingly focused on the safety of his opium and jade. Mei Lan, returning home one afternoon from the General Hospital, heard her grandfather's gruff voice in the garden of Bougainvillaea House giving loud directions. Lim Hock An was seated in his wheelchair wrapped in his ancient purple dressing gown. He had lost much weight since his illness, and had the appearance now of old and delicate porcelain. Before him half the garden was dug up, the dark open wounds of wet trenches were everywhere. Boxes of jade, carried out of the storeroom of Bougainvillaea House where they had lain since the family vacated Lim Villa, were stacked about. Bougainvillaea bushes had been ripped out of the earth and lay in a pile, their roots like dark claws pointing uselessly at the sky. Metal cases containing the old man's opium, left to mature in a shallow grave beneath a tree, had already been exhumed and resettled in a small pit of their own. Coolies were busy lining the trenches with sacking and lowering in the boxes of jade.

Second Grandmother now appeared in the garden, carried upon a young *mui sai*'s back like the gold and silver so long ago. The girl was no more than fourteen years old, and was bent double under the old woman's weight. Second Grandmother rode the girl as she would a horse, kicking her with a heel whenever she slowed down. A second *mui sai* followed, dragging a suitcase of Grandmother's jewellery, her mistress's ivory-topped canes under one arm. As soon as Second Grandmother was balanced once more upon her canes, she gave angry instructions for the suitcase to be handed to Lim Hock An. Standing before him, still protesting the decision to bury her jewellery, she glowered at her husband, defiantly patting the roll of pink satin wrapped about her waist beneath her clothes and into which were now sewn her best diamonds. Lim Hock An sighed; energy leaked from him and he tried to accept his diminished state as gracefully as he could. The evening was drawing in, shadows thickening in the trees. As he stared at the distant silhouette of Lim Villa, his mind was full of what once had been, and his eyes turned wistfully to the slave girls. Second Wife met his gaze boldly, happy to flaunt their young bodies before him now that profligate ways were beyond him.

Later, Mei Lan helped her grandfather back into the house for dinner. The great round table was a relic from Lim Villa and days of previous glory when a dozen people had been easily accommodated around it. Bertie hurried in as they sat down, and Lim Hock An frowned at him. Although now adolescent, Bertie was still treated by everyone like a small child and ate excessively to fill those parts of him everyone knew were missing; as a consequence his girth was excessive. Second Grandmother spent much time crooning to him and rubbing his stomach with herbal balm to lessen his dyspepsia. He was an affectionate child, easily returning to Second Grandmother emotions she said made her life worthwhile.

JJ was late as always and when he appeared Lim Hock An said nothing, resigned to seeing the ways of his dilettante son repeated in his grandson. Ah Siew was helping to serve fish soup with noodles when at last he arrived, entering the room with his lazy smile, a tennis racquet in one hand and exuding the pungent masculine odour of sweat. Apologetically, he rushed upstairs to bathe and change. Lim Hock An did not raise his head, concentrating on the noodles as a sign of his disapproval. Nowadays, it needed continual focus to get the slippery strands successfully to his mouth. The ivory chopsticks and the small porcelain spoon knocked against the bowl in his trembling hands. Soon, JJ reappeared smelling of pomade and cologne. Lim Hock An observed him dispassionately; when he had been JJ's age he had been working as a coolie in a tin mine. He drew up the last of his noodles, his eyes on his grandson.

'Tan Kah Kee is talking to the Governor about forming a Chinese volunteer force to fight beside the British. I've told him you will join,' Lim Hock An announced. JJ looked up in alarm.

'It's going to be nothing but a group of ruffians. They're releasing communists from jail on condition they join the force.' JJ reported the rumours he had heard, resting his chopsticks on the rim of his bowl and clenching his jaw in anger. Rubbing shoulders with communists, students and rickshaw men, and whoever else might join these motley troops, was not his idea of a war.

'People like us must set an example,' Lim Hock An answered with something of his old authority, drawing himself up in his chair.

The lights were on in the room and although they heard the siren wail, no one bothered to seek shelter except Bertie. With a terrified scream he dived under the table where, with nervous giggles, he began running his fingers up everyone's legs.

'Hide and seek!' he cried out. Lim Hock An kicked out at him viciously. Mei Lan left her chair to crouch down beside Bertie in an effort to calm him, and soon Second Grandmother, with the help of a slave girl, knelt down stiffly to join her.

No one saw the rain of silver sticks that were scattered like tinsel over Lim Villa, blowing up that great mansion with a resounding explosion. The blast shook the heavy table and blew the windows out of Bougainvillaea House. JJ dived forward to shield his grandfather, but Lim Hock An was already covered with dust and bleeding from a cut on the head. Lumps of plaster and shards of glass littered the table before him. Although unhurt, JJ was trembling even more than his grandfather and his teeth began to chatter. Mei Lan climbed out from under the table followed by Bertie and Second Grandmother, who moaned in terror at the sight of her husband. Lim Hock An gave a grunt and shook himself free of debris as a dog shakes off a dousing of water.

'I am not yet dead,' he roared angrily.

As the bombardment increased, the pressure for men to enlist in the army intensified. Advertisements were everywhere for last-minute local volunteers to help defend the city: *Your Country Needs You*. After tossing and turning throughout the night, Howard decided on an early morning at the end of January to volunteer. Once the decision was made, a boundary seemed to have been crossed and he could not turn back. He had said nothing to his mother. Unlike everyone else in the queue at the registration centre, his reasons for enlisting were not patriotic. He was signing up to do something illogical but courageous; he wanted to throw his life away and he did not know why he felt this.

All he knew was that his life seemed like a never-ending tunnel from which he sought to burst free. Each day the same small details were depressingly repeated: the incurably weak water pressure in Belvedere, the bicycle ride to the Harbour Board, the ritual filling in of obsolete forms for ships that never arrived, Mr and Mrs Boffort's bright greeting each morning at breakfast in the empty Belvedere dining room, the painful view of Bougainvillaea House and his thoughts of Mei Lan. He remembered long-ago punishments in school when he must write down the same meaningless sentence a hundred times. At the Harbour Board bombing had destroyed the wharfs and slowly closed the port. Men were laid off and he was amongst them. Cooped up in Belvedere, his frustration and anger increased.

'Sign your name here,' a uniformed army man told him, pushing forward a sheet of paper. Howard signed, the decision taken from him as he watched the movement of his own hand. At last his name lay spread before him and below it the date, 29 January 1942. Even as the ink began to dry, he knew his life was irrevocably changed.

'I will go to confession; I will pray,' Rose said, horrified but proud when at last he returned to tell her the news.

The first week of February was taken up with basic training at a military camp at Ulu Pandan, and was an intensive and constant round of drilling and running and diving down holes or clambering up rope walls. They were told they must prepare for street fighting in case the enemy invaded. When the week of training was over, Howard was issued a uniform that looked as if it had come from a second-hand store; also a gun that appeared no better than an air rifle, a helmet, a metal plate and a mug. Each man was given seven rounds of ammunition and two hand grenades and Howard's unit was called for a briefing. They filed into a packed assembly hall and the commander, a large Sikh in a khaki turban, stood on a stool and addressed them.

'Yesterday the Japanese launched sustained bombing on the forward Australian positions. There have been many casualties. As a result you will now be sent to the front line, and inserted between Australian divisions as reinforcement. You will leave tonight.'

In the truck Howard sat next to a young Indian called Ravi who, while in the camp, had been full of bravado. Now, under the occasional street lamp, Howard saw one of Ravi's bare knees shaking nervously. On his other side was a Malay Muslim boy, Abbas, who constantly murmured prayers and had to kneel to face Mecca at the required time, balancing himself in the jolting truck while he bowed in obeisance. Howard remembered that it was Sunday and his mother would have prayed for him in church; it was exactly a week since he joined the army and already he was on his way into battle. Every so often the truck changed gear with a raw metallic groan; everyone was silent listening to the engine, and the rush of tyres over the road.

Here and there the sky was red with the distant flames of bombed and burning kampongs; there was the constant and now familiar hammering of shells. Howard wanted to jump off the truck but instead, like everyone else, stared up at the soft fronds of passing coconut palms silhouetted against the reddened sky. At last the truck drew to an abrupt halt, and they were ordered to climb down. By the dimmed headlights they saw a soldier in a helmet silently gesturing for them to follow him. From what he could make out, Howard thought they must be on a rubber plantation.

'You've reached the killing zone, boys.' The man spoke with an Australian accent. 'We're ready to greet the enemy with a giant burst of fire. The Japanese are bobbing over the water towards us in their little rubber dinghies. We have a battery of hidden searchlights and they'll go on as the Japs arrive. Then we'll blast the buggers out of the water. You'll be all right, don't worry. We professionals will be doing the fighting. You're just here as ballast.'

The darkness was constant. The path entered a patch of secondary jungle and Howard stumbled along with his group. The smell of the sea and the thick odour of mud enclosed them. Soon, cold water splashed unexpectedly about his ankles and Howard saw they were in mangrove swamps where they must tread carefully amongst tangled roots and debris. At last they reached a makeshift command post and were taken to their final positions to await the Japanese advance.

'Just remember, we're not far away from you. When we give the alarm, fire at every Jap you can see. When the lights come on it's show time.' The Australian laughed and disappeared into the blackness.

'Does he know we have almost no ammunition?' Abbas whispered. They were crouching down amongst the cages of the mangrove roots, the water around their ankles gradually deepening as the tide came in.

'Did you see the heavy gun that man was carrying? That's the real thing for fighting,' Ravi said and cleared his throat nervously. Howard fingered the grenade hanging from his waist and stared into the unrelenting blackness. In what circumstances would he be required to throw the thing? There was the crash of waves on the shore, and the rustle of crabs making their way through the wet debris around their feet. It was difficult to believe that hundreds of Australian soldiers were hiding hearby; no sound broke the silence and they seemed quite alone. The land behind Howard appeared to slope upwards into the rubber plantation. On the opposite shoreline a faint row of lights was visible. It was then, staring hard into the darkness, that he became aware of the shadowy armada of dinghies moving over the water and the low purr of outboard motors.

The boats were all but upon them before an order was shouted to fire. At once the crack of guns rang out in a blanket of artillery and mortar fire. It took the Japanese by surprise. There was the sound of desperate back-paddling from the boats as orders to retreat were shouted. Howard's battalion of volunteers shot wildly into the darkness.

'Where are the lights? Why have they not turned them on?' Abbas whispered desperately, for the darkness remained thick upon them. Angry shouting for light was also now heard from the Australian troops.

Soon, a second wave of boats was heard approaching but still the promised lights did not come on. Without light they were shooting blindly into the night at invisible targets. More shouting rose from the Australians, and Howard guessed something was wrong. Blackness enfolded the beach and, once the Japanese switched off the low whirr of their outboard motors, it was impossible to tell where they were. Another great eruption of firing burst upon them, followed by the sound of splashing water. Cursing and more calling for light from the Australians was now answered by rough shouts in Japanese. Gunshot was everywhere. On the water some dinghies were ablaze and this gave the scene a weak illumination; a smell of burning rubber filled the air. It was in the glow of these flames that Howard saw his first Japanese soldier. The dinghy punted in on the shallow water amongst the mangroves with four or five men preparing to disembark. Howard raised his gun and fired. Beside him Ravi and Abbas fired in unison. Two Japanese in the boat dropped with abrupt precision and then, in a blast of noise, their fire was returned. The Japanese were all around them.

From the raised ground behind the mangroves came the clash of metal as hand-to-hand skirmishes began. Howard's feet were sunk deep in cold mud; he had lost sight of Ravi, but could see Abbas backing desperately away into the wet cages of the mangroves. The mud made a soft sucking sound each time Howard pulled a foot free; his heart thumped uncomfortably. Bullets whistled past his ear. He turned, looking in terror for shelter, and stumbled over a body half submerged in the shallow water. His gun dug painfully into his chest as he fell into the cold mud. A flare was thrown up, its light revealing the chaos. Sounds of crashing and slashing and firing surrounded him. Howard staggered forward with no idea of where he was going, colliding with trees, breaking free of vines as he scrambled up on to higher ground, desperate only to get away. The land sloped unevenly and he fell once more, losing his gun, hitting brackish water, the salty liquid filling his mouth. A further flare went up and as he searched for Abbas or Ravi or any other member of his unit in its brief light, he heard a deep growl behind him. As he turned, a Japanese soldier materialised before him. The man raised his gun and fired. Howard felt a sharp pain in his shoulder, and fell forwards into the water.

18

WHEN HOWARD AWOKE, FIRST light was breaking and he heard the sound of lapping water. The equatorial dawn was all but instantaneous: one moment a ray of light cracked the dark and the next sun blazed on his face. The rabid buzzing of flies and the odour of seaweed came to him, and with it the sweet, thick stench of death, a smell he knew now too well. He opened his eyes and saw he was lying on a narrow strip of sand edged by mangroves. Burnt trees fringed the rubber estate behind, dead bodies and abandoned weapons littered the beach around him; the sea crept slowly forward to claim these spoils.

He struggled to sit up and pain shot through him. A wound on his arm was thick with congealed blood, and to move his shoulder was excruciating. For a moment he lay looking up at the sky, trying to remember events, listening to the screech of wheeling seabirds and the roll and suck of breaking waves; the sun was hot on his face. Suddenly, everything came vividly back to him. As he pulled himself to his feet, pain and nausea ricocheted through him so that his head reeled and he felt faint. Only he appeared to be alive on the silent beach. The bodies of Australian soldiers littered the sand and lay amongst the mangroves, lanky young men with golden moustaches, sunburnt faces and red knuckles. Here and there Howard saw Japanese corpses, shaven headed and still clutching their bayonets, their short legs in bound puttees. He staggered forward and almost immediately saw Ravi lying dead, staring open-eyed into the sun. A bayonet had sliced his belly and his innards were spilt out over his uniform in a dried mass of dull grey rope. A fiddler crab traversed his chest waving its one great claw. Flies settled crustily over the entrails, buzzing excitedly. Howard turned aside and vomited.

After some time, he steadied himself and with his one good arm took hold of Ravi's shirt. Bit by bit, wincing with the pain, he pulled him back up the beach to a place he hoped was above the tide. The movement caused more of Ravi's guts to spill out in a glistening slippery blue heap, beneath the already dry entrails. The flies, disturbed, buzzed in an angry cloud about him. Howard positioned Ravi's body as best he could, the pain in his shoulder bringing a cold sweat to his brow, the vile smell making him vomit up yellow bile. He found a wallet in the pocket of Ravi's shorts that contained an address and some photographs and then, seeing no alternative, left him.

Returning to the beach, he searched unsuccessfully amongst the corpses for Abbas before, holding his wounded arm to lessen its weight and the pain, he took a path leading away from the beach through secondary jungle and the rubber plantation, and knew, by the presence of yet more bodies, that the battle had raged here too. For some time he stumbled on, faint and nauseous, shivering now with fever and exhaustion. Eventually, in a clearing beyond the trees he saw an attap-roofed hut and made his way towards it, dragging himself up the steps on to a narrow veranda with the last of his strength. Then, as he heard steps approaching, blackness overcame him.

When he opened his eyes again he was lying on a firm pallet looking up at wooden beams below an attap roof.

'Feeling better?' Howard saw a Malay man in his mid-thirties staring anxiously down at him. The nostrils of his thin-bridged nose were so large that, from where Howard lay, they appeared like black tunnels running into his face. Turning his head, Howard saw that the wound on his arm was thickly bandaged and that under a thin cotton sheet he appeared to be naked but for a *sarong* about his lower body. The man noticed him taking note of this.

'We burned your uniform; it's safer,' he said. The events that had brought him to the hut flooded into Howard's mind.

'Where are the Japanese? What's happening?' He tried to sit up.

'The British army have retreated, but you're safe here.' The man pushed Howard gently back on to the bed. A woman came forward carrying a small bowl. She knelt beside them, and began spooning a warm drink that tasted strongly of ginger into Howard's mouth.

'Make you sweat, then fever come down,' she said and smiled, her plump face creased in concern. She was much younger than the man and Howard wondered if she was his sister or even his daughter.

'My wife, Ayesha,' the man explained. 'My name is Mohammad

Abdullah. Sleep now,' he suggested. A wave of fatigue swept over Howard and he closed his eyes, breathing in the warm sun-baked odour of the thatch and the lingering cooking smells in the hut.

When he awoke next, the sun was streaming down on him through a small window of bamboo bars. He did not know how long he had slept; his head was filled with the residue of weird dreams. With an effort he managed to prop himself up on an elbow, and saw a small boy sitting cross-legged on the floor staring at him. Ayesha, who was squatting on her haunches stirring something in a pot, stood up immediately.

'Fever gone? Two whole days you slept,' she told him; Abdullah seemed not to be about and the child moved nearer Howard's mat and continued to regard him curiously.

'My son, Hassan.' Ayesha smiled and began gently to untie the bandage on Howard's arm. A scent of *champaca* wafted from her; a small white flower was tucked into the coil of her hair.

'Must change,' she said as Howard winced in pain and pulled away, his shoulder stiff and sore. When the bandage was removed he saw a clean but inflamed wound.

'There is infection still, but you were lucky, bullet go in and go out again. Bone not broken.' Ayesha showed him the holes on his upper arm. Placing a fresh poultice of pounded leaves and roots on the wound, she bandaged it up again. Then she heated a bowl of rice gruel on a primus stove and fed him spoon by spoon for he could not lift his arm. Soon, he was shivering and knew the fever was rising again.

'Rest,' Ayesha ordered, clearing away the dirty poultice.

Howard lay back on the pillow, his mind full of the memory of Ravi, lying dead, staring up into the sun. And what of Abbas? Howard wondered. Exhaustion and weakness weighed him down and made him want to cry. He could not absorb the enormity of what had happened, why they had to die. He remembered the jolting truck with Abbas kneeling to pray; he remembered the dark beach where they had waited with their paltry guns, the soft chug of the Japanese outboard motors. However fearful they had been at that moment, they had not expected death to claim them so quickly. When he signed up to fight, Howard realised now, he had never thought of dying, just of breaking open his life.

'I left friends on the beach . . . dead friends . . .' His voice broke and

Ayesha, kneeling to some work on the other side of the room, sat back on her heels and observed him.

'Some the sea took and the others were buried. Men came, Red Cross volunteers, and buried those left on the beach in a big grave,' Ayesha said gently. Howard nodded and lay back on the pallet again, knowing he was helpless to change what had passed. Nothing made sense any more. He turned his face to the wall and wept silently.

Once again he passed through a long sleep of strange dreams and distorted images. He saw Abbas and then Ravi, running along the beach towards him. A monstrous wave rose up, like a great curling tongue, rolling down to claim them. 'Ravi! Abbas!' he screamed. Hot tears poured down his cheeks; in the belly of the wave, as if behind glass, he saw the boys tossed about like sticks; he tried to follow but the water pushed him back, spitting him up on to the beach, rejecting him. He awoke with a sick start, his heart pounding; he found the fever was gone and another day had passed. Ayesha brought him food and then sponged his body with tepid water and he was too grateful for the luxury to feel any shame. As she finished bathing him, Abdullah came in through the door carrying a bundle of vegetables.

'I have become a farmer,' Abdullah laughed giving the vegetables to his wife, who was sitting down on the floor beside Howard's pallet. 'We were worried about you – that wound was bad in your arm. My wife knows about old remedies. Once she was a nurse in a Singapore hospital, but she left to marry me.'

Howard observed that Abdullah did not appear to have the hands of a farmer: his slender fingers and fine-featured face of Arab ancestry appeared more that of a scholar. He wore a loose shirt over a *sarong*, on the sleeve of which was an armband with a tortoiseshell emblem embroidered on it. When he had dragged himself up the steps of Abdullah's hut, Howard now remembered, there had been a paper with the same emblem, pasted beside the door.

'I was once a civil servant in a government office in Kuala Lumpur,' Abdullah admitted when Howard asked. 'War changes everything,' he added, his face becoming stern.

'What's happened? Where are the Japanese?' Howard demanded with sudden urgency, remembering Ravi and Abbas again.

'From Kranji where you were, they advanced south along Woodlands Road. Now they are all over the island, there is fighting everywhere these last days, but you are safe here with me,' Abdullah assured Howard, seeing the effect of this news upon him. As he spoke there was the sound of a plane overhead. The hut seemed to be under the path of Japanese bombers, for the sound of aircraft was constant. Sometimes the distant thud of explosions was heard.

'There is fierce fighting today for Bukit Timah; when they capture the area they will have control of the main water supply. It cannot last long. The British have underestimated the enemy,' Abdullah elaborated.

'How long have I been here?' Howard asked; he had lost all sense of time.

'Three days,' Abdullah smiled, seeing the shock on Howard's face.

By evening Howard felt well enough to eat a meal of rice and a dish of some spicy beans. As they ate, Abdullah gave him further news, always speaking without fear of the Japanese advance.

'You didn't hide when the Japanese came through here?' Howard was puzzled.

'They will not harm us,' Abdullah assured him with such confidence that Howard fell silent, confused.

'I must go,' he worried, thinking of his mother and Belvedere now that the Japanese had arrived on the island, but his head spun when he tried to stand up.

'Another day or two and you will feel stronger,' Abdullah insisted, laying a hand on his arm.

After dinner Abdullah helped him into a chair on the narrow veranda of the hut, and Ayesha brought them sweet drinks of ginger juice and lemon grass. Moths blundered against the hot glass of the oil lamp and with a soft sizzle, died. Fireflies lit up the trees, while the moon shed its empty light on the dark jungle, illuminating the shapes of flitting bats. The night was noisy with crickets. Howard absorbed the peace with some unease, aware of how near the violent reality of war really was. As he sipped the aromatic drink his eyes fell again on the strange tortoiseshell sign pasted on the wall of the hut and he decided to ask Abdullah about it. The man was silent before he replied, as if debating how he should answer.

'It is the crest of Fujiwara Kikan, a Japanese intelligence unit run by Major Fujiwara,' Abdullah finally replied in a matter-of-fact way.

'Am I a Japanese prisoner?' Howard sat forward in alarm, for the first time feeling unsure of the man. Abdullah's eyes rested on him for a moment, then he sighed resignedly.

'No, brother, you are free to go whenever you want, as soon as you are well. You are in no danger,' he repeated, but seeing Howard's agitation continued.

'Listen, I will tell you how it is. I tell you because the British cannot prevent what is now happening. Soon, the Japanese will control the island; already as we speak it is happening, and nothing can prevent it. In Kuala Lumpur Japanese army officers approached me. I belong to a small group of people working to improve the status of our Malay race, to awaken our people to themselves and the need to fight for their independence. The Japanese support the efforts of our Kesatuan Melayu Muda because they believe in a free Asia. They wanted KMM members to accompany the Japanese army down the peninsula and liaise with our Malay people for them, helping to make good relations. I was assigned to F Kikan.'

'Were you happy to go with them?' Howard asked, trying to hide his growing anxiety as Abdullah spoke.

'When people with guns and swords *invite* you to go with them, you have no choice. For the safety of my family I have done as I was asked. The British have never helped us Malays improve our status. They see us only as tillers of the land. Our children are more likely to be taught to weave bamboo baskets than to become scientists and lawyers. The British have never wished to see us educated, fearing we might rise up against them one day. This is our chance now, the Japanese want to help us.' For a moment Abdullah's voice rose, then he fell silent.

Listening to him, Howard was overcome with a sense of familiarity and knew he had heard this story before. He could have been listening to Raj's brother-in-law Krishna. Abdullah even reminded him of the man. Both were tall and slim; both were men of ideals, as too was the aggressive Wee Jack, who also spoke of similar things. Only he, Howard, seemed to have no ideology to consume him. A feeling of desolation swept through him again, and he leaned back exhausted in the chair as Abdullah continued to speak. From within the hut came a strong smell of grilling meat and Ayesha's voice speaking to the child. Soon, she called them for the evening meal. The child slept on a mat in a corner as cooking smoke drifted above them, trapped in an aromatic cloud under the thatch of the roof.

Two more days passed before Howard felt strong enough to find his way home. He had lost a whole week and did not know what he would find when he returned to town, or where his unit might be. When it was time for Howard to go, Abdullah opened a battered tin chest and pulled out a fresh shirt and a sarong.

'Wear these. If any Japanese see you they'll think you are a Malay; they do not take much notice of us Malays.' He laughed good-naturedly as he shook out the *sarong*, holding it up for Howard to inspect.

It was many miles back to Belvedere, and Abdullah arranged for a friend with a cart and a mule, who was going in Howard's direction, to take him to Upper Bukit Timah. Abdullah and his wife and child stood at the door of their hut and waved as Howard departed, until he could see them no more.

'*Inshallah*. We shall meet again,' Abdullah's voice floated after him.

It was dusk by the time Abdullah's friend dropped Howard off near Bukit Timah. The familiar sound of guns and shelling surrounded him once more. He stood numbly on the edge of the road, weak and exhausted and still unsteady on his feet. Night was almost upon him and he knew he could not continue. A short distance off the darkening road he saw a bombed-out bungalow and made his way towards it. Little of the house remained but Howard found two rotted basket chairs and collapsed gratefully into one, putting his feet up on the other; his shoulder was stiff and painful, his head aching. As he stretched out he loosened the sarong about his waist and Ravi's wallet dropped out. He had folded it in the top of the sarong, rolling the cloth about it. In the fading light he turned it over in his hands, unable to think of the unknown world Ravi and Abbas had now passed into, and from which only he had returned.

The next morning he saw all too clearly the state of Bukit Timah. The road was pitted with craters and littered with abandoned vehicles; houses were destroyed or empty. Trying to clear his mind, counting back over the week of lost days since the night on the beach at Kranji, he realised that it must be 15 February, the morning of Chinese New Year. He wondered immediately about Mei Lan, and what kind of celebration they or anyone else could have at so grim a time. Only the hundreds of ducks and chickens that would escape slaughter for the usual celebratory feast would have reason to rejoice.

In the distance Howard heard the sound of marching feet, and hid hurriedly behind some trees. Looking up the road he saw what appeared to be a bank of moving foliage bearing down upon him. As the strange sight drew nearer he saw that it was no more than Japanese soldiers, helmets crowned with leafy antlers, a camouflage of foliage. Yet more soldiers followed, straggling into Singapore from their long, hard journey through the jungle of the Malayan Peninsula. Next, battalions of soldiers on bicycles passed him, the whirr of hundreds of revolving wheels like the rush of a powerful wind. Both the antlered soldiers and the cavalry on their wheeled mounts drew to a halt a few yards from Howard, and turned off the road abruptly. He saw then that, a short distance from the bungalow where he had spent the night, a large Japanese encampment was spread out. In sudden panic he realised that he must be behind the Japanese front line.

When at last he saw the road was clear, he began slowly to make his way down Bukit Timah, keeping as best he could behind the shield of bushes and trees. His arm throbbed and his legs felt weak but he forced himself to push on. Eventually, at the junction of Whitley Road and Stevens Road he saw troops again, holed up behind walls of sandbags. These men were not Japanese but British or Australian, and he realised with relief that he must have crossed a demarcation line. He wondered if he should ask about his unit.

'Get off the road, you bugger!' someone screamed at him from behind the sandbags as he stepped forward. A soldier appeared from nowhere and pulled him roughly out of the way of an oncoming tank.

'D'you want to get yourself killed?' the man yelled.

'What's happening?' Howard asked, looking into the man's red and sweating face.

'We're trying to stop the bloody Japanese advance, that's what's happening.' The man pushed him angrily to one side.

Still unsteady on his feet, Howard half stumbled into the bushes at the side of the road, falling painfully on his injured arm. As he picked himself up he heard shouting and saw soldiers emerging from behind the sandbags, coming forward to line the road. The tank had drawn to a halt and was overtaken by a car, in which could be seen several military men in peaked caps. The vehicle drove slowly past the tank, and then proceeded up Bukit Timah towards the British front line and the Japanese encampment beyond. It was only after the car had passed that Howard registered the white flag that flew from its roof.

'Bloody hell. We're surrendering!' a soldier shouted.

19

SOON AFTER THE SURRENDER, when General Yamashita had settled his troops and secured the city of Singapore, he sent *kempetai* officers to Changi Prison to fetch Shinozaki and bring him to Yamashita's headquarters. Since then, Shinozaki had been busy. He had cordial meetings with top military men, although General Yamashita himself, Commander of the 25th Army, had been too busy to say more than, 'Good, you have come back.' He had met up again with Major Kunitaki, one of the high-ranking officers he had shown about Singapore, a duty that had precipitated his arrest in 1940; Kunitaki was now part of the Planning Office. Shinozaki was surprised to find himself something of a hero because of his time in Changi Prison; his story had been printed in the *Asahi Shimbun* in Japan and in all the army newsletters.

Major-General Kawamura at Defence Headquarters had congratulated him on his safe return in a cultivated voice. 'You are here so long, and have good relations with the citizens of this place; you are a valuable man. As everything now is in the hands of the military, you need a military title. I will make you Adviser to Defence Headquarters.'

'What is my job?' Shinozaki asked nervously.

'To protect the good citizens of this town, and see no mistakes are made by our soldiers. You must wear the Defence Headquarters armband at all times, and you may also have one car for your use,' Kawamura replied.

It was in this car that Shinozaki came to Nanyo Kaiun in Middle Road, to visit Mr Yamaguchi again. Raj had arrived only minutes before, delighted to hear from Mr Ho about Mr and Mrs Yamaguchi's release from internment in an army barracks near Changi Prison. Due to age and infirmity they had not been sent to a camp in India with the rest of the Japanese community at the beginning of the war, when the British rounded them up. Prison life had aged the elderly couple, but

Mr Shinozaki appeared unchanged. The diplomat greeted Raj warmly; his visit to Changi with books and pickles had not been forgotten.

'I read *Nanking Road* and *Crime and Punishment* many times,' Shinozaki laughed as they sat down once again to drink beer at Yamaguchi's low Japanese table. His visit would have to be brief, Shinozaki said, as he had an appointment with some young auxiliary *kempei*. The beer and camaraderie about the table lowered his natural reticence, and he voiced some reservations about these recruits to the army's dreaded special intelligence unit.

'These men should not be used to help the regular *kempei* with law and order. The auxiliary *kempei* are very young soldiers, and not well educated because they are from the countryside. They are very strong for fighting, very brave, but do not really have much common sense. Like all villagers they are pure of heart, but ignorant. The only thing they do well is to die when ordered. They are never afraid to die. However, they know nothing of the local people; I shall have my work cut out for me.' Shinozaki lifted his glass for Mrs Yamaguchi to refill with beer. He had brought this beer with him from the store at Defence Headquarters. It was a long time since any of them had tasted beer. He had also brought tins of Naval Cut cigarettes for Yamaguchi. Both men were smoking determinedly, and the room was thick with tobacco fumes as they savoured the taste of nicotine and beer, remembering the difficulties of the past two years.

'In Changi my salary for repairing mailbags was three cigarettes and three matches a day. Later, there were no more cigarettes and that was hard,' Shinozaki said.

Mrs Yamaguchi's hair had turned white, and although she was alarmingly stooped and frail, she was as usual immaculately dressed in a kimono. Yamaguchi had lost his paunch and his cheeks hung loosely about his wide jaw. Although his eyes were rheumy and he was missing some teeth, his joviality was as before. Their home had been saved from the local looters after the surrender because it was up on the first floor. Mr Ono the barber on the ground floor had had his chairs and basins ripped out, and not a camera remained at Nemoto's Photo Studio.

'I went to Nassim Road this morning, to see the Swiss Consul-General. I had orders from Tokyo to get back the Imperial Seal, and all the documents of the Japanese Consulate that had been given to the Swiss for safe keeping when we Japanese were interned. Nassim

Road was full of looters. They were local people, stripping the big European houses, carrying off whatever they could. These looters are the only people out on the streets since we entered the city. The *kempetai* will not like this lawless behaviour.' Shinozaki exhaled smoke and then turned to Raj, observing him appraisingly.

'I need a young man to assist me, someone local I can trust to liaise with the different communities. All businesses now belong to the military; everything must now be done through the military authorities. Singapore is to be rebuilt in the Japanese way,' Shinozaki explained. Raj was taken by surprise, and was about to ask a question when there was a loud rapping on Yamaguchi's front door. A tall Japanese army officer entered the room, gold buttons agleam on his uniform, and gave a brief bow. Yamaguchi beckoned him in effusively.

'We have some good beer at last, Shinozaki-san has brought it for us,' Yamaguchi said as the man took off his peaked cap and knelt to join them at the table. It was only then, much to everyone's amusement, that Raj recognised his Japanese teacher, Takeshi Nakamura.

'Doesn't he look handsome in his uniform?' Yamaguchi chuckled.

'You've joined the army? I thought you were in Bangkok.' Raj was puzzled.

'I came from Bangkok the day after the surrender with Major Fujiwara,' Takeshi replied.

'Takeshi is with Army Intelligence Centre. He's part of Fujiwara Kikan, a vital intelligence unit,' Shinozaki said as he lit another cigarette. Takeshi leaned forward to explain.

'In Fujiwara Kikan we work to free Asia from colonial exploitation. We are also working with the different Nationalist organisations in Asia, like your Indian Independence League whom we support.'

'I thought you were a Japanese teacher,' Raj protested, feeling suddenly like a swimmer in a choppy sea. Shinozaki and Yamaguchi laughed indulgently, and Takeshi gave a condescending smile.

'You could say I was a Japanese teacher with a special purpose. F. Kikan is centred in Bangkok, and from there we spread out to prepare for the invasion,' he explained.

'You needed a teacher, he needed a student.' Yamaguchi chuckled and Takeshi nodded, amused.

'All Indian civilians should now join the Indian Independence League to fight for Indian independence with Japan's help. Singapore will be the League's headquarters; everything will happen from here. We have also established a military wing, the Indian National Army, and are now recruiting for this.' Takeshi accepted a glass of beer from Mrs Yamaguchi before continuing.

'Many Indian soldiers in the British army have already come over to the Japanese side. These Indian soldiers are now part of the new Indian National Army, and will invade and liberate India together with the Japanese army.' Takeshi's shaven head gleamed and his narrow eyes flashed in satisfaction.

Shinozaki raised his glass to drain the last of his beer and then, looking at his watch, prepared to take his leave. 'No detectives standing downstairs to trail us now,' he remarked with a chuckle to Yamaguchi. Takeshi also readied himself to leave with Shinozaki, pulling down his high-collared jacket and putting on his peaked military cap. At the door Shinozaki paused before leaving, and turned to Raj.

'Come to my office tomorrow morning,' he instructed him.

Raj left Middle Road a few minutes later and returned to Serangoon Road, anxious to pass on his news about the formation of an Indian National Army to his brother-in-law. He found Krishna in a state of high excitement; men from Fujiwara Kikan had already paid him a visit.

'They're wasting no time. Everyone in the Youth League has already been visited and told to join the Indian Independence League. After that, if they want to go on and join the Indian National Army, they will receive military training. This is the moment we have waited for. The Japanese intend to liberate India and give us Independence. Soon we'll have Home Rule and I will then be able to return home.'

As they talked, Leila spread banana leaves before them and spooned out rice and vegetables. Krishna was too excited to eat. 'I am to be part of the new organising committee of the Indian Independence League. Rash Behari Bose, the great freedom fighter living in exile in Japan, is coming here to organise Indians from all over Asia into one great movement. The Indian National Army will also train civilian volunteers like myself, and I am going to join them.' Krishna could not contain his euphoria.

In the morning Raj reported to Mr Shinozaki's office at Defence Headquarters in Fort Canning. Impressive colonial buildings, an ancient botanical garden and an old cemetery that dated back to the time of Raffles topped the slopes of shady paths and trees. The place was now awash with Japanese army men hurrying about on pressured errands. An order had come from the Emperor of Japan to rename the city Syonan, Light of the East. The town remained plagued by looting and the sky above dark with the smoke of oil that continued to burn at the Naval Base; there was little water, food, gas or electricity. Corpses still lay rotting on every corner amongst heaps of rubble, their stench pervading the town. Sitting at a small desk piled with stacks of paper, Shinozaki was full of concern at this state of affairs.

'There is much work to be done if we are to live up to the Emperor's expectations. We Japanese are freed from internment. Now it is our turn to round up British civilians and intern them in Changi. We are exchanging places. British army POWs will have the job of clearing the city of corpses.' Shinozaki looked at Raj over his spectacles, surrounded by tobacco fumes. A cigarette burned between his fingers, an ashtray of cigarette butts sat on the desk before him and his brow was furrowed with distraction as he explained his job at Defence Headquarters. As they talked, people came in and out of the room to take orders from Shinozaki. From the nature of the instructions Shinozaki gave, Raj gathered that the diplomat now commanded an army of spies gathering information in the manner of hungry bees. An orderly entered with a pot of coffee and Shinozaki welcomed the break.

'How I longed for good coffee in Changi. I expected every day to be executed. In fact I'm surprised to find myself still alive,' he sighed, lighting up another cigarette and pouring out cups of the strong brew for himself and Raj.

'Everyone will now need a Good Citizen Pass for their protection. I do not want to see ordinary citizens troubled by our military admin-istration. People must not be afraid to move about. You must help me with these passes; each must be written by hand. You must learn how to write Japanese characters in order to do this. I have given the cook at the Toyo Hotel where I am staying, a pass. He brought many of his relatives to see me. This is my cousin, this is my uncle, he said, and I gave them all passes. You had also better have one immediately.' Shinozaki reached for a piece of stiff paper, the pen scratching as he wrote, the soft whirr of the ceiling fan breaking the silence and stirring the trapped cloud of smoke. Finally, he stamped the card with his seal, and translated the Japanese characters for Raj.

'"Bearer of this card is known to us since before the war. Please look after or protect him." That is what it says. My title, Adviser to Defence Headquarters, is a powerful one. Keep this safe.' Shinozaki handed the paper to Raj.

Then, picking up his pen he began to show Raj how to form each stroke of the intricate Japanese script, amused at his pupil's first inelegant efforts. 'Soon you will be an expert, and will help me live up to my name, Shinozaki. *Shino* means China, *zaki* means cape, as in Cape of Good Hope, and my first name, *Mamoru* means protector: Chinese Cape of Protection. It is quite a responsibility to have such a name in these difficult times.' Shinozaki gave a wry smile, watching Raj laboriously forming each Japanese character with his pen, and continued.

'Last night I worked until one in the morning preparing passes, and they are already all gone. Look, it is not so difficult to copy my Japanese characters. You write, I write, and then I will stamp my seal on them all.' Shinozaki pushed a pile of paper across the desk to Raj. For the rest of the day this work absorbed them both.

When Raj reached Defence Headquarters the following morning for his second day of work, he found Shinozaki waiting impatiently for him. 'We have our first important job. Bishop Devels says Catholic people are in danger in the Geylang, Katong and Upper Thomson Road areas because soldiers there are acting roughly. He wants his people, especially the children, bussed into town to the convents for safety.'

Raj was busy all morning arranging for school buses to bring children to the Bras Basah area, into the safety of the Convent of the Holy Infant Jesus. He wore his Defence Headquarters armband like Shinozaki and kept out of the way of soldiers. Later, he went with Shinozaki to meet Bishop Devels. They had to leave the car some distance away as the road was being cleared of bomb rubble. As they walked from Queen Street towards the convent where Bishop Devels waited, they passed a row of small terraced houses from which came shouting and screaming. Two soldiers appeared in a doorway with several young Chinese men, and marched them down the steps with bayonets at their back. A woman ran after them, pleading with the soldiers. Shinozaki stopped and stiffened as he stared at the scene, Raj standing anxiously beside him. Then, abruptly, he hurried towards the woman. Seeing Shinozaki, she gave a desperate cry and ran over to him.

'Mr Shinozaki, help them,' she implored, pulling on the diplomat's arm. Shinozaki at once sprinted after the soldiers, shouting to them in Japanese. The men came to a halt and turned their bayonets on the diplomat, who pointed repeatedly to his Defence Headquarters armband as he spoke. Finally, with a show of ill grace, the soldiers released their prisoners and walked angrily away. Raj watched as the woman and her brothers bowed repeated thanks to Shinozaki before returning home.

'That woman used to work in the Japanese Embassy,' Shinozaki explained when he returned to Raj, still breathless from the altercation.

'Why were the men being taken away, had they done something wrong?' Raj asked as they continued on to the convent, unsure of what he had just witnessed.

'They're rounding up all Chinese men between the ages of fifteen and fifty for screening; everyone must gather at one of the concentration points. They are not going about this in the right way,' Shinozaki admitted, lips pursed disapprovingly beneath his small moustache.

'This is all Lieutenant-Colonel Tsuji's doing; he is in charge of planning and action,' Shinozaki confided. 'They want to search out all anti-Japanese elements, people who supported the China Relief Fund and young men who joined the Chinese volunteer forces to fight against us Japanese; it's a clean-up operation. They are also looking for communists and other undesirable people who will undermine the new Singapore. All this is being done for the people's own good, but who will understand this?' Shinozaki worried as they walked along.

The strangest thing of all since the Japanese arrived was the unexpected silence: no aircraft or bombs. Cicadas rattled in the garden and there was no need to wonder now if the sound was the distant trail of a shell. Instead, there was fear of a different kind. Mei Lan had been forbidden by Lim Hock An and Second Grandmother to continue working at the General Hospital. Japanese soldiers had brusquely entered another hospital, the Alexander Hospital, and because it was a British military hospital they had massacred patients, doctors and nurses in a vicious bloodbath.

Although not subjected to this form of aggression, the General Hospital was in chaos after the staff were ordered to remove every patient within twenty-four hours to free the facilities for wounded Japanese troops. Soldiers with bayonets at the ready stood everywhere.

'The General Hospital is not a military hospital so they've spared everyone here, but we've orders to get out. Over a thousand patients are being discharged. Those who are too ill to go are being sent to Woodbridge Mental Asylum, which is being cleared of its patients to make way for us. I will be going there with them,' Cynthia explained to Mei Lan as they worked in the Admissions Room. In the hospital people were running here and there as convoys of ambulances were loaded with the sick, ready for transfer to Woodbridge.

'Why are you staying on?' Mei Lan asked, fear rushing through her. Already, British doctors and nurses, some with stethoscopes still about their necks, were being loaded at bayonet point into open trucks to be taken for internment to Changi Prison.

'I'm a local nurse; I'm not in immediate danger. Besides, it's my job, I don't have a choice. Patients need me. Your position is different and you must do as your grandfather says,' Cynthia insisted, calm as always, showing no hesitation.

It was time for Mei Lan to go home, Cynthia thought. Whatever lay ahead would take a toughness of nerves she felt Mei Lan did not have. As a volunteer, Mei Lan had worked diligently but she came from a background of privilege and was clearly unused to the menial demands of nursing; at home Cynthia knew Mei Lan's old *amah* still fetched and carried and slept on the floor by the side of her bed. The jobs she had been required to do – the dressing of wounds – the handling of dishes of vomit or effluvium, the washing of sour perspiring bodies, picking maggots from wounds, were things that nothing in her life could have prepared her for. Yet, Cynthia observed, Mei Lan had persevered, overcome her repugnance for these tasks, and could be relied on in most situations. Cynthia called upon her often and there was an easy relationship between them now, although Howard was rarely mentioned in more than passing reference.

'Go quickly now, and take care of yourself.' Cynthia gave Mei Lan a small push.

For the first time Mei Lan was relieved to do as she was told, and gratefully fled the turmoil of the hospital. The sight of rough, squat

Japanese soldiers shouting orders and waving bayonets filled her with terror. As she drove herself home in her own small car, avoiding the usual potholes and shell craters, corpses and fallen cables, she found there were now Japanese staff cars, horns blaring, to be avoided as they roared about the city. At a roadblock a Japanese sentry came forward and peered at her through the car window. She met his eyes and held her breath but eventually, with a lewd smile and incomprehensible remark, he waved her on. As Bougainvillaea House came into view she found herself limp with relief.

'Stay inside!' Lim Hock An yelled when he saw her, knowing this time she would not disobey.

Only Ah Siew or the houseboys went out each day trying to find a piece of fish or some vegetables for them. JJ had returned to Bougainvillaea House after the surrender, limping back covered in mud and blood, but alive. Now he was lying sick and weak in bed after the terrifying experience of combat. Against all inclination, pressured by his grandfather, he had finally joined Dalforce, Tan Kah Kee's group of last-minute volunteers from the Chinese community. In terrible conditions and with little ammunition, they had fought bravely at the front line taking heavy losses. From his recruitment into Dalforce to the decimation and disbanding of the desperate group had taken all of eight tumultuous days. JJ was full of anger.

'It was madness to send us there. We were without proper guns and not trained to fight; we had only a few days of drilling.' His once carefully combed and pomaded hair was now cropped close to his head, giving him the look of a plucked chicken.

'I suppose it will be something to talk about over a drink at the club when things are back to normal again,' JJ decided as he began to rally.

Lim Hock An's old friend Tan Kah Kee, initiator of Dalforce and JJ's grim experience, driving force behind Japanese boycotts and the China Relief Fund, had hurriedly left Singapore before the surrender. Before leaving he had advised Lim Hock An to accompany him. 'We will be wanted men because of our opposition to the Japanese. Come with me to Indonesia, or go somewhere else; go anywhere. Whatever you do, get out of here,' Tan Kah Kee had urged.

'What will they do with an ancient like me?' Lim Hock An argued apathetically; he could not imagine he would be seen as a threat.

'You have China Relief Fund documents. Better burn them,' Tan ordered before he fled to Sumatra.

This much Lim Hock An thought pertinent to do. Smoke rose from a tin drum in the garden all one afternoon, black ash collecting on the windowsills of Bougainvillaea House. Even as he watched the documents burn, Lim Hock An worried not about himself, but about his jade and opium, hobbling anxiously about their burial ground, kicking extra leaves over the roots of the replanted bougainvillaea bushes.

20

THE CLEAN-UP OPERATION proceeded briskly and kept Shinozaki busy in an unexpected way; people who knew him, or knew of him, sought him out as a last desperate hope after their men were taken. As and where possible, Shinozaki did what he could to help.

'The situation is so bad I sometimes fear it might become another Nanking,' he worried as his car sped along towards River Valley Road.

'What happened in Nanking?' Raj asked from where he sat in the front seat, next to the driver.

'Many terrible things,' Shinozaki replied, refusing to elaborate. He was sitting in the back with a Chinese nurse who had once shown him much kindness in the Japanese Hospital, during a bout of jaundice. The night before she had come to the Toyo Hotel where Shinozaki was living, to desperately plead for his help. Her father and brother had been rounded up with others at bayonet point during the clean-up operation to find anyone who was anti-Japanese, and taken by soldiers to one of the screening centres from where they had not returned.

On River Valley Road the car drew to a stop beside the large playing field of a school. The ground was open to the sun and fringed only by a few tall trees. The area was filled with a huge crowd of men of all ages, who had been forced to squat in orderly rows. Those who wore shirts drew them over their heads as shade against the roasting sun. Others leaned into the slim shadow thrown by their neighbour, enduring stoically.

Raj got out of the car with Shinozaki and walked to the edge of the field where they silently surveyed the scene. As soon as they were noticed there were cries of 'Water, water' from the captives. A man at the edge of the field nearest to them stood up, waving to attract Raj's attention. He pointed to an older man collapsed beside him. 'He is sick. Please help. We have been here two days without food or water. We cannot last much longer,' he shouted.

Immediately, a guard with a bayonet came running up and slapped and kicked the man. Shielding himself against the attack, he crouched hurriedly down again on his haunches. The sick man too was viciously prodded, and made a weak effort to reposition himself. A stench of excrement blanketed the area. Clearly, there were no toilet facilities and, denied the freedom to move about, men were forced to relieve themselves where they squatted. Flies swarmed thickly. They buzzed about Raj, settling on his face even as he brushed them away. The nurse ran repeatedly up and down the road along the length of the ground searching for her family members, unable at first to recognise them in the large crowd of exhausted men. Eventually, she gave a cry and Shinozaki hurried to join her.

'Father, Elder Brother,' she shouted, pointing to where they sat. The younger man supported his father, who had wilted against him, and neither seemed to hear the nurse. She started forward, shouting frantically again, but Shinozaki put a hand on her arm to hold her back. Seeing the commotion a young *kempei* strode up.

'Who are you?' he demanded brusquely. As soon as the diplomat revealed his status the man's tone changed, and he hurried off to call an officer. The nurse stared at the crowd of weary men, biting her lips in distress as her father and brother now waved imploringly to her. Within moments the *kempei* returned with his superior officer and Shinozaki bowed, polite but determined.

'I know those men over there. This woman, their relative, is a nurse who has helped many Japanese patients and has worked in the Japanese Hospital,' Shinozaki told the man.

The officer knew of Shinozaki and the power of his position at Defence Headquarters, and the two prisoners were soon released. They stumbled forward through the rows of exhausted men and the nurse ran towards them with a cry as they reached the edge of the ground. Once outside the roped area they fled with the woman, not looking back once at Shinozaki, much to his disappointment.

'No thanks, you see. Although, of course, I do not do this for thanks,' he commented to Raj, before turning back to the officer in charge.

'Why do these men not have water or food? How long have they been here like this?' Shinozaki asked sternly, gesturing to the thousands of cowed and silent men.

He demanded to inspect the screening area and was reluctantly taken to a queue of detainees who were being questioned at a barrier point. A row of tables had been set up here to deal with the interrogation, and several large open trucks were parked beyond the area. The soldiers showed no awe of the diplomat, yet they could not ignore his status. The Chinese lined up before the tables ranged from adolescent boys to grey-haired men, the wealthier in good cotton shirts, the poor in frayed singlet vests, all exhausted by their wait in the sun. They stepped forward apprehensively as they were called, clearly in fear for their lives. Soldiers with bayonets at the ready controlled the queue with angry shouts. At the tables the men were required to write their name in a ledger. Some then received a red stamp on their bare arm and were allowed to walk free through the barrier; others were stopped and held to one side, then loaded on to the waiting trucks. Once a truck was full it moved forward with a loud growl of grinding gears. Shinozaki observed the departure of a truck with an angry frown.

'Why do these men not have water?' he repeated even more sternly to another officer.

'They may have been here since yesterday, but we have only now got orders to begin interrogation,' the officer stiffly replied, and Shinozaki's usually impassive face darkened.

'You are interrogating these Chinese men in Japanese. How will they understand Japanese? And how can you know who is anti-Japanese?' Shinozaki's thunder was barely contained.

'We have not got enough interpreters,' the officer protested, looking towards the tables. Behind the military interrogators stood hooded individuals who occasionally bent to speak in the examiner's ear. Immediately, the detainee at the table would then be herded to one side, to be held with the group waiting to board the trucks.

'Who are the hooded people?' Raj whispered to Shinozaki. Although he spoke in a low voice the officer overheard and looked at Raj so sharply that he fell silent in fear.

'Few of our *kempei* speak a local language. Those assisting us are local people who know the anti-Japanese agitators in their communities. They are hooded to shield their identity as they may face reprisals from their own people for helping us,' the officer coldly explained.

The methods of determining who was anti-Japanese and who was not appeared arbitrary to Raj. If a man wrote his name in English instead of Chinese he was not given a protective stamp on his arm but held to one side. If he had a tattoo he was asked if he was a member of a secret society, and also held to one side. If he looked down at the ground he was detained; if he looked his interrogator in the eye, he was equally marked.

Shinozaki, in spite of his position of power, was apprehensive himself of the *kempetai*, and decided to push matters no further. Bowing curtly to the officer in charge, he turned to leave, and Raj hurried behind him relieved to be free of the terrible place. As they walked back to the road, another truck filled with detainees started up its engine. The men, crowded together uncomfortably, fell against each other like skittles as the vehicle moved off.

'Are they being taken to Changi?' Raj asked in a low voice, feeling suddenly sick with anxiety. Shinozaki shrugged and did not answer, turning towards his waiting car, jaw clenched hard in anger.

'What is happening here is a terrible thing, a very terrible thing,' Shinozaki burst out as the car moved slowly off, making its way past the screening tables with their *kempetai* examiners and hooded helpers. For the rest of the ride to Defence Headquarters Shinozaki remained silent, and Raj hesitated to question the implications of all they had observed.

From behind a curtain Mei Lan stared out of an upstairs window at the continuous trail of men passing the house, tramping down Bukit Timah on the long walk to the concentration points where they would be screened. Posters about the registration were everywhere, but nobody knew exactly why they were being summoned and fear hung over the town. Fear gathered in Mei Lan too; she slept in a state of tension and awoke equally tense. Thoughts of Cynthia, braving whatever must be braved in a working life under the Japanese, filled her with shame for her own cowardice. It was also difficult to know if the order for Chinese men to assemble at various points in the city was as innocuous as it sounded. JJ, after his recent experiences at the front, had no desire to investigate.

'It may be a trap,' JJ said, and his grandfather agreed.

'Lie low. It will pass,' Lim Hock An advised and so JJ stayed in bed, pulling the sheets up over his head and smoking the last of his cigarettes.

The Japanese military had anticipated such tactics of defiance. The following day soldiers appeared, searching homes and dragging out reluctant men. They stopped before Bougainvillaea House and burst in through the door. JJ was pulled from his bed in his singlet and shorts without even an opportunity to put on his trousers, which were slung waiting over a chair. He grabbed them as he passed and, with a bayonet pricking his back, was thrust out of the front door and into the sun.

Lim Hock An, when he realised what was happening, came out of his room in a state of wrath to face the soldiers, and was knocked to the floor with a rifle butt. He lay winded; the gun had caught him in the stomach and he thought his ribs were broken. Bertie, who had a partial view of the commotion through a half-open door behind the protective back of his mother, began to jump up and down in excitement.

'Want to go too. Going with JJ.' Bertie pushed past his mother to hurry down the stairs after the soldiers.

Mei Lan opened her door when the shouting started, but was unable to discern what was happening. She thought Second Grandmother might have fallen down the stairs, but almost immediately Ah Siew was there beside her, pushing her back into the room, thrusting Mei Lan into the big wardrobe. Ah Siew's face, glimpsed in the oval mirror as she swung the cupboard door open, dried all protest on Mei Lan's tongue.

Within moments the bedroom door was flung open and a soldier entered, his bayonet needling the space before him. Through the keyhole inside the dark cupboard Mei Lan watched as Ah Siew looked up with a startled expression from where she squatted innocuously folding a pile of clothes. The man stared at the old woman from beneath his low-hanging brow, and gave a snort of disappointment. Soon his feet were heard padding away along the corridor.

The soldiers next entered Second Grandmother's room, bayonets again at the ready. Second Grandmother confronted them bravely, her face pinched in terror as she balanced unsteadily on her tiny feet, supported on either side by a slave girl. For a moment the men paused to take in the unexpected sight of Second Grandmother, regal in her embroideries, diamonds flashing in her ears, jade upon her wrists. Then, stepping forward with a loud guffaw, they tore the slave girls from her, as if ripping the wings off a chicken. The girls began to scream. Second Grandmother gave a terrified wail as she tottered and fell, her ivory-topped canes clattering to the floor. Still screaming hysterically, the girls were thrust down the stairs, bayonets at their backsides. Outside, they were loaded into a waiting van that already contained several captive women.

JJ stood with a crowd of local men who had all, like himself, been ferreted out of their homes. Bertie was beside him but was jumping around in such excitement that a burly *kempei* punched him viciously, pushing him to the ground. The soldiers went back to the house for a further search, but found only the wizened Ah Siew and Second Grandmother, sobbing hysterically. Lim Hock An, who had been lying at the bottom of the stairs, was now on his knees, trying to find some support with which to lever himself to his feet. Thoughts ran confusedly through his mind; he knew he should do something to halt the situation, but was suddenly unsure of what exactly had happened. The soldiers clattered down the stairs and, observing the feeble old man on his knees, set about him again with the rifle butt.

The truck with its cargo of women had already moved off. The group of young men, with much prodding of bayonets, were encouraged to march in the direction of the town. JJ pulled Bertie to his feet and began to explain his brother's infirmity, but the soldiers responded by slapping his face. Bertie, shocked to see blood spurting from his brother's lip, took his hand in concern as, two by two, the men began the walk into town. From an upstairs window Second Grandmother leaned out as far as she dared, and began a low desperate keening.

Two days went by and there was no news to be had of Bertie or JJ. For the first time in his life, Lim Hock An felt helpless. He could not pull a string or milk a connection as he was used to doing. Tan Kah Kee was now running for his life, and every other likely friend was lying as low as Lim Hock An. Second Grandmother moaned all day on her lacquer chair, rocking with grief and anxiety. Forbidden to step outside the house, Mei Lan was confined to her room, away from the windows. She lay on the bed and stared out at the distant roof of Belvedere and could not hold back her thoughts of Howard. There was no sound now of the saxophone, and the canal had run inexplicably dry with only a trickle of water between its rough lichen-covered sides. She remembered Howard's arms about her as she lifted the long-handled net, the grey shelly bodies of the crayfish tumbling into the lobster basket. Was he still at Belvedere, or had he been taken like JJ?

The following day Ah Siew decided to assert herself. She appeared with a pair of scissors and, in spite of Mei Lan's protests, pushed her into a chair and proceeded to chop off her hair. Next, she produced some old clothes of her own and insisted Mei Lan step into them. The pair of worn black trousers and white top did not disguise Mei Lan's youth or attractiveness as Ah Siew hoped, and she looked at her in despair. Besides Ah Siew there were now only two ancient houseboys left in the Lim residence, Ah Pang and Ah Fat. They had remained when other servants disappeared as the Japanese neared Singapore. Ah Siew now sought the help of these elderly men, sending them out to scout about town and glean some knowledge of what was happening. The few facts they returned with plunged Bougainvillaea House into further dejection.

At the concentration points Ah Pang and Ah Fat had seen thousands of exhausted men, but no sign of Bertie or JJ. The Japanese military were looking for anti-Japanese elements, communists and criminals, particularly those belonging to the secret societies and men who were volunteers in Dalforce. As they spoke the old men looked down at their feet, not daring to meet their master's eyes. Two more days went by in further agonised waiting, and still neither JJ nor Bertie came home. Ah Pang and Ah Fat went out again to reconnoitre, and returned with news that all the screening centres had now been disbanded and no one remained at these places.

'We must continue to wait. Do not give up hope,' Lim Hock An encouraged them, although he was sunk in despair.

After a few days the military cars drew up again before Bougainvillaea House. Soldiers got out, and also an officer from the *kempetai* who wore a long sword, distinguishing his rank from the others. Ah Siew had seen the car arriving and again pushed Mei Lan into the wardrobe. The soldiers were not looking for women on this visit: they had documented evidence listing all senior members of the China Relief Fund, and had come to arrest Lim Hock An.

'Where is Tan Kah Kee? Where has he fled to?' the officer demanded, pushing old Lim Hock An into a chair and standing over him with a pistol.

'I do not know where he is,' Lim Hock An replied and received several slaps about the face for this impertinence.

'You are listed as a major supporter of the China Relief Fund. You have practised subversion and insubordination to Japan. The sentence for this is death,' the officer yelled.

Lim Hock An was given no time to protest, no time to collect even a handkerchief. He was bundled out of the house and into a waiting van and the doors were slammed shut on him. Second Grandmother, roused from her sorrowful lethargy, hobbled after her husband on her canes and began to scream at the soldiers. There was laughter at her sudden appearance and some flashing of bayonets, as if she was an animal to be baited. Second Grandmother swayed about precariously and then, finding her balance, raised one of her sticks to the officer who had arrested her husband. The man stepped forward in fury, Second Grandmother was knocked to the ground and a sword was unsheathed above her. From the van Lim Hock An pressed his face to a small barred window and began to shout and rattle the door.

The officer stared down at Second Grandmother who glared defiantly up at him, her gold teeth bared in a grimace, and gave her a sudden hard kick. She groaned and curled up into a ball, trembling and sobbing. The officer laughed, strode to his car and drove off followed by the van. From the back window of the vehicle Lim Hock An kept his eyes on Bougainvillaea House, and his wife lying in the road before it, until both were lost from sight.

21

AFTER BREAKFAST COUSIN MAVIS got out Rose's wooden sewing box with an expression of determination. 'Everyone is making flags to welcome the Japanese. We need a large one over the porch and another to wave when needed. We must show them we have no hard feelings.' She was well settled in Belvedere and made herself useful where she could.

'The Japanese anger easily,' Rose agreed.

She found some old sheets from which to make flags and Mavis cut them to the appropriate sizes. For the red sphere of the rising sun Rose found a picnic cloth that she had used when the children were small. She remembered sitting upon it in a bathing suit on the beach at Katong. They spent the morning sewing quietly on the chintz sofa beside the window that looked out on to the mangosteen orchard. Soon the work was finished, and Hamzah and Ah Fong hung the large flag where Mavis directed over the portico of Belvedere. Several smaller flags were sewn on to sticks that Mavis put into a box for a time when they might be needed.

Rose went about her daily chores in a constant state of anxiety; it did not seem possible that the war was lost. Even the acquiring of twenty-four tins of sardines for $5 from the small store at the bottom of the road, gave her no pleasure. Cynthia had been transferred to Woodbridge Hospital and was working in dangerous conditions, but Rose was grateful Howard had returned. He had arrived home from some distant battleground in a dirty sarong, thin and weak with a bullet hole in his arm, and would tell her few details of his ordeal. For some days he had kept to his bed while she fussed about him. Now he was stronger, but against her wishes had gone out that morning to reconnoitre and had yet to return.

Mavis kept up a bright babble of talk, trying to ease Rose's tension. She took upon herself many of Belvedere's small chores, checking that the empty house was properly dusted, making a new inventory of linen and seeing that Hamzah regularly cleaned out the stone water filter in the dining room. Belvedere was now an echoing place; even the Bofforts had been evacuated on one of the last ships to leave the island.

In the afternoon Wilfred unexpectedly returned to Belvedere with Cynthia, who was still in her nurse's uniform. They drove up in a St John's ambulance and looked askance at the flag hanging from the portico.

'I have to get ready for internment. The British community have been ordered to collect upon the Padang by ten o'clock tomorrow morning, and from there to march to Changi,' Wilfred announced as they entered Belvedere, and Rose and Mavis hurried towards them.

'Internment?' Rose halted in alarm.

'At the moment it's the Chinese and Europeans they're interested in, but Eurasians may also be called for screening later,' Cynthia said grimly, pulling off her nurse's cap and freeing her hair. 'We've come home to pack Wilfred's internment kit. I managed to get off work until tomorrow. Woodbridge Hospital is chaos, morphine had run out and some minor operations are being done even without anaesthetic.'

'We have to bring clothes for ten days, but they say food will be provided.' Wilfred assumed a brisk manner that Rose now understood often covered disaster.

'Come and see my kit,' Wilfred invited Rose later, showing her a leather suitcase open upon the bed.

'Iodine, Dettol, Andrews Liver Salts, Elastoplast, soap, two pairs of shorts, three cotton shirts, a jacket, two pairs of socks, extra shoes . . .' Wilfred went through a lengthy list while Rose and Cynthia stood looking into the case, trying to think of further useful things to add.

'Scissors,' Cynthia remembered.

'A torch and some aspirin,' Rose suggested and hurried out to find these things, filled with a weight of dread. With his ambulance duties Wilfred had always managed to be near the hospital and Cynthia, and this had kept her worry at bay. Nothing seemed real.

'We will be in good company at Changi. The Governor and other assorted bigwigs are being interned as well.' Wilfred sounded almost jocular as he packed the scissors and the torch. Rose hurried away again in the direction of the kitchen building, and returned with two small parcels.

'Here's some bread, tinned cheese, pickled onions and some rum fruitcake.' Rose held out the packages, blinking back tears.

'Very soon the taste of rum might be much appreciated,' Wilfred predicted. Cynthia sat down suddenly on the bed and burst into tears.

They saw their first Japanese the next day, soon after Wilfred and Cynthia's departure. A group of four soldiers walked up the hill and turned into the driveway of Belvedere. They stood looking up at the elegant balconies and then put their heads around the door. Rose decided to treat the soldiers as she would a new lodger, pleasantly polite but from the first letting them know who was in charge.

'Can I help you?' she said, wishing Howard were home and not out again inspecting the lie of the land.

The men turned to stare at her and then burst out laughing, revealing large, nicotine-stained teeth and conferring together incomprehensibly; Rose prepared herself for the worst. The men were darkly weathered from weeks of fighting their way through the jungle under fierce sun and monsoon rain, and their uniforms were in tatters. They were smaller than Rose had imagined. It was then that she noticed their bayonets and that they wore strange canvas shoes that split the big toe apart from the foot, like the cloven hoof of an animal.

Ignoring Rose, the soldiers turned towards the stairs, stopping to observe the dining room stretching away in a sea of red tiles. Rose waited, listening to the pad of feet on the floor above and the knock of bayonets on the skirting board. There was a constant banging of doors as they opened and inspected each room. Shouts echoed along the corridor, and Rose could not tell if the harsh guttural voices spoke positively or negatively about Belvedere.

Eventually, they reappeared and made their way down to Rose. She noticed now that their weapons were almost as tall as the soldiers themselves; the gleam of the sun from the upstairs window fell on the thin blades of the bayonets. One of the soldiers nodded to her as he passed, before running off across the dining room and out of the open patio doors to the kitchen building. The other soldiers went through the front door and disappeared around the side of the house. Within a few minutes they all reassembled on the gravel driveway, and without a backward glance left as they had come.

The following day they were visited by a Japanese soldier of higher rank. Rose knew he was an officer because he wore a sword. He was a thin man with skin that gleamed like oiled paper stretched tautly over his face. A wide jaw above a reed-like neck made his head appear too large, but his bulging eyes were not unkind and his manner was civil.

'I Captain Tanamura,' he introduced himself in English. Several soldiers accompanied him, all anxious to show him deference.

Captain Tanamura stood looking with interest about Belvedere, almost courtly in his attitude and his few words of English. Rose felt bound to offer some tea, and he accepted agreeably. She showed him to the alcove with the chintz sofa where Mavis was waiting to be introduced. He had some difficulty manoeuvring his sword as he lowered himself on to an upright chair, and it pushed up awkwardly at his waist. Military aides stood to attention behind him. Hamzah served tea, the cups rattling slightly on the saucers in his nervous hands. The officer sipped the tea with a loud slurping that Rose took as a sign of appreciation. At last, placing his cup on the table, he leaned forward over his sword.

'You. Leave house.' He spoke suddenly in a forceful manner that reminded Rose that their meeting was not a social occasion.

'We have been told it is safer for us to stay at home until things settle down,' Rose reassured him, thinking he was enquiring if she had been out, but the officer frowned.

'You. Leave house,' he repeated in a louder voice. One of the young soldiers standing behind him stepped forward and spoke in fluent English.

'Captain Tanamura wishes you to vacate this house. It is needed as an officers' army billet. You have very nice house, it will be useful to the Japanese Imperial Army.'

Rose recoiled in shock. Beside her Mavis gave a small cry that caused Captain Tanamura to frown even harder. He said a few stern words in Japanese to the young interpreter.

'Captain Tanamura is giving you two days to vacate your house. Two days is very generous time. Everything must be left as it is, no food or linen or anything else is to be taken away. You may take only your clothes and personal items. By 5.30 day after tomorrow we will move in. You will not be expected to be here.'

As the young soldier finished this speech, Captain Tanamura gave a nod of approval. He rose from the chair and walked back to the door followed by his aides, his sword trailing the ground behind him. Soon there was the sound of car doors shutting, engines starting and a crunch of gravel beneath car wheels as they drove away.

Within a short time of the soldiers' departure Howard returned from a further reconnaissance and was told the news.

'I should have been here,' he said, distressed that his mother and Mavis had had to face rough soldiers alone for the second time.

'Better you weren't. They say they're taking young men for slave labour,' Rose answered, feeling sick at the thought.

Howard said nothing, not wanting to admit to his mother the things he had seen on his outing. It was not young men so much as young women who were at risk. He had seen a girl of no more than twelve or thirteen dragged from her home into the bushes to be raped by three soldiers, while her parents sat helpless within the house, held prisoner by a fourth man waiting his turn with the girl. The men had left, laughing. The child's screams still echoed in his ears; he knew he would hear them for ever. Trembling with horror and revulsion he had run off, shocked by his inability to do anything.

At the corner of Prinsip Street he had bought three small sweet potatoes for Rose from an old woman hawking a basket of the vegetable, and watched a group of emaciated British POWs go about the business of clearing the city of corpses. They pulled a rotting body from a pile of rubble and threw it into a handcart on top of other corpses. Japanese sentries stood everywhere, stopping people and questioning them. Then, rounding a corner, he found himself facing three decapitated heads stuck upon spikes by the roadside. The heads were so fresh they did not look properly dead; blood still oozed, congealing about their necks. The eyes of one were open and stared straight at Howard. A cigarette stub had been thrust between the blackened lips of another. Howard began to run and did not stop until he was in the vicinity of Belvedere. It was impossible to tell his mother any of these things or that the Radio Delhi news he heard each night on his short wave radio was only of Japanese victories and British retreat.

'What are we to do? Where are we to go?' Rose moaned softly, giving in to despair.

'We could go to Cousin Lionel,' Mavis suggested, getting up and pacing about to clarify her thoughts.

'I have not kept in touch with him,' Rose replied, her heart sinking, imagining the indignities that might now await her; Cousin Lionel lived in Katong in a disintegrating house on a coconut estate.

As she assessed the future, there was a knock at the entrance. Howard opened the door, peering into the dark garden. A figure stepped abruptly out of the bushes and Howard drew back in trepidation. In the porch light he saw a filthy face with a head of short matted hair and the androgynous loose clothes of a Chinese servant. He started when the woman spoke and he heard Mei Lan's voice.

'It's dangerous for women to go out. Ah Siew would not let me come until she had made me look as ugly as possible,' Mei Lan apologised, glancing nervously about her. Howard was silent with shock, his heart leaping beneath his ribs.

'Come in quickly,' he said at last. As she slid past him he caught the scent of her again and recalled the smooth skin of her cheek beneath his lips, the taste of her mouth. Mei Lan gave him a hesitant smile, trying to conceal her agitation at the sight of him and the turmoil of feelings that had brought her so desperately to his door.

The agony of waiting had overwhelmed them at Bougainvillaea House. Neither Bertie, the slave girls or JJ had returned, and there was no news to be had of Lim Hock An. Second Grandmother was half out of her mind. Mei Lan had suddenly remembered Cynthia telling her that Howard had an Indian friend who supplied Japanese ships and knew many Japanese people. The thought that such a man might have the power to help them would not leave her, however tenuous the hope. Ah Siew had insisted on rubbing boot polish into her hair and smearing mud over Mei Lan's face and blouse. Although it was only a short distance along Bukit Timah and up the slope to Belvedere, Mei Lan had kept to the shadows, stooping as if she were an old woman.

Rose looked from Howard to Mei Lan in irritation. Beneath the dirt she now recognised the headstrong girl from Bougainvillaea House who had led Howard astray. Her annoyance was so great that at first she did not listen to Mei Lan's story, or wonder why she had appeared at Belvedere in such a filthy disguise. Within a few moments the girl's words began to filter through, and Rose listened to her distressing story. After the visit of the military men to Belvedere, Rose was newly sensitive to all issues concerning the Japanese. The day had been spent in the heartbreaking business of packing for the move to Cousin Lionel. What to take, and what could not be taken had involved them all. The thought that Belvedere's beds would now be filled by rough Japanese soldiers, sleeping on Belvedere linen and eating off Belvedere plates, was more than Rose could digest. She felt too ill now to protest about the unexpected arrival of Mei Lan. Imagining the three frightened women – the young girl, the old grandmother and the ancient servant – she felt her resistance dissolve.

'You'd better sit down,' she told the girl, gesturing towards the alcove beyond the dining room where they usually sat in the evening. She called to Ah Fong to bring a lime cordial.

'I have only met the Indian a few times, at political meetings. He has a shop in Serangoon Road,' Howard explained and, seeing the disappointment in Mei Lan's face, knew he would explore any risky and unlikely hope in order to see her again.

In Serangoon Road the street lamps were either destroyed or without gas and Manikam's Cloth Shop was in deep shadow. At first Raj did not recognise Howard in the darkness; he had just returned from the Toyo Hotel where Mr Shinozaki was still staying at the invitation of Colonel Yokota of Defence Headquarters. It was a shock when two people stepped out of the gloom before him; nowadays, everyone waited to be apprehended and, like everywhere else, Serangoon Road was deserted, shops boarded up against looting. No one could do business without a licence from the military, and these licences had yet to be distributed. Raj opened up the shop, lit an oil lamp and invited Howard inside. A Chinese woman of servant class followed. Raj was annoyed that Howard did not tell her to wait outside.

'It is for her we have come,' Howard smiled as he sat down and began to explain about Mei Lan's situation. 'You know Mr Shinozaki, perhaps he can help her,' Howard urged.

Raj nodded politely, but did not want to hear of any new trouble the occupation was causing. He knew exactly the situation Mei Lan described. He had been running about all day on rescue errands of this nature for Shinozaki. Each night when the diplomat returned to the Toyo Hotel a queue of desperate people was waiting for him. Shinozaki's reputation as the man to contact to liaise with the Japanese military was now firmly established.

'There is nothing I can do tonight.' Raj rubbed his brow with the back of his hand and yawned. All he wanted to do was sleep.

'My brothers have done nothing to deserve arrest, and Grandfather is old and sick. He may not survive,' Mei Lan protested, trying to keep her voice steady. Raj sighed deeply and stood up.

'I do not know why I am doing this,' he said, picking up his keys. 'Mr Shinozaki is probably still at dinner with Colonel Yokota at the Toyo Hotel. He will not be pleased to see us at this hour. Find a rickshaw if you can while I lock up the shop,' Raj told Howard.

The Toyo Hotel employed a Hungarian orchestra. The *kempetai* did not harass the musicians because their lively music was much liked by Colonel Yokota and also by General Kawamura. Mr Shinozaki had left the room and the dinner party to go to the bathroom, when Raj came hurrying up to him in the foyer of the hotel. The diplomat listened to Raj's brief explanation, and with a nod of resignation followed him to where his friends waited.

'I have only a moment,' he informed them impatiently, looking at the woman standing before him and then turning to frown at Raj.

Of the many people who now flowed about Shinozaki like a river swirling around a lone rock, he had never been confronted by such a bedraggled figure. If it were not for Raj and the personable young Eurasian man accompanying her, he would have dismissed her outright. Shinozaki turned his head in the direction of the dining room, from where the notes of a dashing mazurka drifted, and sighed. Sitting down on a red velvet chair he took out a cigarette, interrupting Raj's long-winded description of Lim Hock An.

'*She* is the granddaughter of Lim Hock An? Of course I know who he is.' Shinozaki looked intently at the girl over his thick-framed spectacles. Lim Hock An's name was high on a list of wanted persons in connection with the China Relief Fund's anti-Japanese activities.

'Nowadays, women must find any way they can to avoid being raped by your soldiers,' Mei Lan retorted, head erect, eyes ablaze in her blackened face. Shinozaki glared at her and Howard pressed her arm in warning, wondering why Mei Lan could not control herself at a time like this.

'They are probably holding the old man at the YMCA building on Orchard Road,' Shinozaki told Howard, turning away from Mei Lan. The *kempetai* had taken over the YMCA, and after some renovations to the building to install a number of cells, had made it one of their main interrogation centres. Shinozaki thought of the graceful red-brick building he had always admired and felt sad. The door of the dining room swung open as waiters went in and out and Shinozaki caught snatches of a Viennese waltz and noisy laughter. Everyone was drinking copiously and the room was thick with cigarette smoke and the smell of beer. Shinozaki stubbed out his own cigarette, anxious to get back to the dinner.

'Grandfather is an old man,' Mei Lan repeated, holding Shinozaki's eye, her tone now one of appeasement. The diplomat had a small triangular moustache that stopped short of the ends of his mouth; thick straggly eyebrows reinforced a kindly but inscrutable expression, making it difficult to know what he was thinking. Shinozaki gave a reluctant but conciliatory nod.

'I have no information about your brothers. I am sorry, but it is better you understand that many young men who were suspected of anti-Japanese activities have already been killed. If your brother was part of Dalforce, then he is guilty of a criminal offence for which death is the sentence.' Shinozaki spoke curtly, taking no notice of Mei Lan's stricken face as he continued.

'The 25th Army have already moved on to Bangkok. Many top members of the *kempetai* who knew me are no longer stationed in Singapore. I have less influence now than before, and the new men are not so willing to give me information.' Shinozaki absently lit another cigarette, pulling on it thoughtfully. It was as he said, there had been a change of authority at the top and he felt a waning of his already small power. Many of the military men about him now were rough and arrogant individuals, who not only bullied and threatened prominent Chinese but had little respect for Shinozaki who, although Japanese, was not a military man. Sometimes now he worried about his own safety. Although he said nothing to Mei Lan, he was concerned that an old man like Lim Hock An should have been arrested, although he knew this was inevitable. All the Chinese leaders were under arrest, and as all had been supporters of the China Relief Fund and worked against Japan, retribution was severe.

'The Chinese community here is in great danger,' Shinozaki told them, remembering the intelligence reports handed to him and the things he had seen. 'I am a friend of the Chinese people and I am encouraging suggestions that an organisation be formed to allow the Chinese community to co-operate with the Japanese military. This co-operation will be a way for the Chinese people here to protect themselves. It is to be called the Overseas Chinese Association and will be headed by an ancient of the Chinese community, Dr Lim Boon Keng.' Shinozaki leaned back in his chair and blew a perfect smoke ring, watching it drift towards the ceiling.

Dr Lim had been arrested some days before and had been asked to be the leader of the newly formed Overseas Chinese Association. When he refused, citing frail health and extreme age, Shinozaki had been ordered to persuade him to accept. During the time Shinozaki was with him, Dr Lim's old wife had been made to kneel for hours in the scorching sun, subjected to brutal insults. All this Dr Lim had watched through an open window. None of it was to Shinozaki's liking, but he was unable to protest. Instead, he had reasoned with the old man, whose long white beard and kindly face gave Shinozaki the confidence to address him as 'Papa'. Finally, after listening to sounds of his wife's increasing discomfort, Lim Boon Keng had meekly agreed to lead the Overseas Chinese Association. Remembering this, Shinozaki returned his gaze to Mei Lan.

'I am about to submit a list to the *kempetai* of prominent people who should be released from prison to run this new organisation. It is being suggested that wealthy men, such as your grandfather, should make a donation in apology for their previous anti-Japanese behaviour. I will put your grandfather's name on the list. That is the best I can do.' Shinozaki pulled deeply on his cigarette, still staring at Mei Lan.

After the visit to Shinozaki, Mei Lan and Howard began the long walk back to Bougainvillaea House in awkward silence. As they hurried along in the darkness, the sound of soldiers' voices occasionally reached them and Howard drew Mei Lan into the shadows until the danger had passed. As they neared Cairnhill, they saw a long queue of drunken soldiers, waiting before a block of terraced houses for their turn with the women kept prisoner there. Howard pulled Mei Lan quickly away and they ran, seeking another route to Bukit Timah. Only when they neared Bougainvillaea House and were on familiar ground did they sit down at the side of the road, catching their breath, the tension easing at last. The moon was full and lit the road with its cool light.

'Why didn't you write when you were in Hong Kong? I wrote to you for a while each day,' Howard burst out, unable to contain the turmoil of emotions that had burned in him all evening. Mei Lan stared at him in distress.

'*I* wrote each day and *you* never answered,' she replied.

Piece by piece, they unravelled what must have happened: that Howard's letters had been intercepted by Mei Lan's father before they reached her, and her letters to Howard, which she had always given to a maid to secretly post, had been taken straight to her father. Howard would have kissed her then but the sound of a car, travelling at speed down the shrapnel-pitted surface of Bukit Timah, forced them to draw apart and begin the last short stretch of their journey. At last, as they reached Bougainvillaea House, Howard drew her to him.

'Tomorrow we're going to our cousin Lionel in Katong,' he told her as they parted, explaining the commandeering of the house by the military.

'I'll find a way to get back here, to see you,' he promised after explaining in detail where Lionel lived.

Next day Lim Hock An returned home, pushed out of a military vehicle before the gate of Bougainvillaea House. Second Grandmother gave a cry of distress as the car shot off with a screech of tyres, and tottered forward on her ivory-topped canes to where her husband lay. Mei Lan, followed by Ah Siew, ran to the half-conscious Lim Hock An. The houseboys, Ah Pang and Ah Fat carried the old man upstairs and lowered him gently on to his Blackwood bed. Bruises and burn marks covered his body and his fingers bled where his nails had been ripped out. Whatever else had been done to him they never knew for, within a few hours, Lim Hock An silently died, never regaining full consciousness

Later that evening Bertie limped home, blubbering and trembling. His soft egg of a brain had saved him from death. The soldiers, seeing his infirmity, had impatiently tossed him aside, not bothering to waste a bullet on him. Running off, he had crouched down behind a clump of tall *lallang*, shivering and shaking, to watch JJ's execution on a beach as the tide came up. The sea had run red with blood, he sobbed.

22

Rose had been only once to Cousin Lionel's house, when a relative from Malacca had stayed with him many years before. At Mavis's suggestion Howard had gone to Katong to explain their position to Lionel, and had returned with a message of welcome.

There was very little transport available. Rickshaws, trishaws and taxis had all but disappeared from the streets, and anyone going anywhere was walking. A large handcart was found and a couple of wheelbarrows into which they piled their belongings. In spite of the warning to take only personal possessions Rose packed linen and towels and as much tinned food as she dared, as well as sugar and rice. She had tied up her silver framed photographs along with other items of family silver in an old tablecloth, and hid the parcel beneath some sheets. She was worried about Cynthia, who had been transferred from Woodbridge Mental Hospital to a small hospital on Joo Chiat Road, along with some Chinese doctors. Joo Chiat Road was not far from Cousin Lionel's so at least this thought was a comfort to Rose.

Howard roped things to his bicycle and strapped his saxophone to his back, along with his short wave radio concealed in a canvas rucksack. He looked over his shoulder at the roof of Bougainvillaea House that could just be seen above the trees. They set off for Katong with Hamzah and Ah Fong harnessed like animals between the shafts of the cart to pull it along. Rose and Mavis puffed with the exertion of pushing the wheelbarrows; both women wore straw hats, and gloves to prevent them blistering their hands.

It had been a traumatic few days. The Eurasian community, like the British and Chinese, had been summoned for screening. They had all gone in trepidation to the Padang, and stood before the Singapore Recreation Club to await their fate. A Japanese officer had delivered a reproving lecture full of ugly threats. Eurasians of particularly fair skin had been separated for internment with the British, their colour taken as proof of genetic complicity. Those of duskier hue were sent home with stern warnings to mend their Anglophile ways. For the first time in her life, Rose was glad to have a dark skin.

It was late when they reached the coconut estate on which Lionel Pereira lived. Rose surveyed the beachside village of ramshackle dwellings and attap-roofed huts with a sinking heart. The estate had many fishponds from which the residents eked out a living. Lionel's home was built of wooden planks and raised some feet above the ground, and was next to the track that served as a road into the estate. Stray dogs slept beneath the veranda, chickens pecked around the house and a vegetable patch ran along one side.

Lionel was waiting for them on the steps of the veranda, strumming a guitar. A cigarette hung from his lips and his family were arranged about him. Rose observed his grubby vest, muscular biceps and worn trousers rolled up above rubber sandals, in growing apprehension. As she had dreaded, he gave her a hug and she caught the odour of alcohol as his sun-warmed flesh imprisoned her. Lionel was a lift repairman who had married relatively late in life, and now had five children under ten. His wife, Ava, who was of the same Portuguese–Malacca descent but much younger than her husband, was a slight woman with a full moon face, wavy hair and an aura of good humour. She immediately sent the older children forward to help Howard and Hamzah unload the carts.

Inside, the house was dim and untidy; its thin plank walls held stale smells of cooking, shrimp paste, garlic and rancid oil. Ava led the way to a roofed extension around the side of the house that was part of the veranda, and where they were to be accommodated.

'We usually store things out here,' she said, pointing to a conglomeration of boxes and baskets, an old sewing machine and two bicycle wheels. A chicken walked through from the house and Ava shooed it away. The bird jumped on to the balustrade with a squawk and flapped down into the yard.

The lean-to was narrow with a floor of splintered boards. Three *kapok* sleeping pallets were spread upon it with worn coverings of indeterminate design. Rose was suddenly too tired to speak. She observed the lumpy mattresses and tried not to feel ungrateful, thankful that she had with her some good Belvedere linen. At one end of the balcony was a dusty, waist-high ledge holding a few filthy paint tins and Rose decided she could put her photographs upon it. With each minute that passed she had to work harder at not feeling despairing. Howard was stacking their rice and tinned food in a corner, watched silently by the children and Lionel.

'You'll need a metal bin for that rice or the rats will be at it,' Ava remarked, going to the pile of junk in the corner and pulling out a large storage container into which Howard pushed the cloth bags of rice.

'You're not supposed to have a short wave radio. Got to send it for fixing so you'll listen to only Japanese broadcasts.' Lionel jumped forward in alarm as Howard unwrapped the radio.

'We have to know what's happening with the war. Japanese stations are all propaganda,' Howard protested. Even knowing that it carried risks, he still listened each day to Radio Delhi or the BBC.

'Put it away, boy. They'll kill my family if they see that. I've sent mine for fixing.' Lionel viewed the radio nervously and his children whispered behind their hands.

'Hide it. It's sure death now to have a radio!' Lionel ordered angrily as Howard prepared to argue. Sending a child to the kitchen for a knife, Lionel pushed aside one of the beds and levered up a floor-board, pointing determinedly to the dusty space beneath. Howard lowered the radio into it and Lionel replaced the floorboard, pulling the pallet back into place.

Later, Ava showed Mavis and Rose the lavatory, taking them out of the house and down a short path to a bog house with a warped and splintered door. This was built out over a fishpond, and waste dropped straight down into the water.

'Several other families share the bog house with us. The fish feed off the waste in the ponds; that's why they're all so fat. The bigger ones wait near the surface and jump for their food as it drops. You'll never find one of these fish on *my* table,' Ava assured them with a raw laugh. Rose nodded, sick and shocked and beyond protest. Ava's eyes, full of amusement, rested questioningly upon her. Instinctively Rose knew that, despite Ava's affability, she would be watched for superior ways.

After a dinner of chicken curry from a bird Lionel had killed that morning in anticipation of their arrival, they slept. The *kapok* poked through the Belvedere sheets with which Rose had covered their pallets, and the mosquito nets rigged up above them were so full of holes that insects entered without compunction. The scuttling of rats was everywhere. In the darkness Rose closed her eyes and wept. From the dark chambers of memory rusty images pushed into her mind. Charlie had never seen the home in Malacca where she had been born. Rose had met him in Singapore after she had been adopted; he had known only Aunty May's small but immaculate house in Queen Street, and she was thankful for this. In Malacca she remembered a similar house to Lionel's home. She remembered another lavatory with a disintegrating door reached by a path through *lallang*. Between the splintered gaps in the wood she had once, as she squatted over the toilet, watched a neighbour's boy pleasure himself while crouching in the tall grass. She tried to shut away these distant memories, and thought instead of Belvedere in which soldiers must now be preparing to sleep stretched out upon her walnut bed, a wedding gift from Charlie's family. Beside her Howard slept, exhausted, and from Mavis there came small snores. She stared up at the star-filled sky above the open balustrade of the veranda. A night bird squawked, and there was the rhythmic crash of waves on the nearby shore, the smell of the sea was about her. With a sob she pressed her palms together and began to pray.

Just at the time Rose and her family left Belvedere, Bougainvillaea House had also been visited by the military with a view to commandeering the residence. Because of Lim Hock An's death, the family were given an extra two days in which to arrange a funeral and vacate it. They had buried Lim Hock An hastily in the local cemetery. The city was full of rotting corpses in need of quick interment and no one had time to conduct a formal funeral. Lim Hock An had bought his coffin many years before, and this handsome item had waited for him in the storeroom of Bougainvillaea House along with his boxes of jade. He would have been happy to keep it on prominent display, but Second Grandmother had objected vehemently because of the space it took up in so small a home. At least, she had sighed during the funeral wake, they had not had to search out a coffin in such fraught times. Bougainvillaea House's ancient houseboys, Ah Pang and Ah Fat had been sent to a funeral shop in Sago Lane. The undertaker had refused to prepare the body for burial in the house as Second Grandmother wanted, but after much persuasion had agreed to collect the corpse, taking it back to Sago Lane for dressing. Rigor mortis had already set in by the time the undertaker arrived with an extra trishaw.

Eventually, with difficulty, Lim Hock An's body was installed inside the vehicle at an upright angle and a hat placed upon his head to disguise the fact that he was a corpse. He was then pedalled back to Sago Lane to be washed and dressed in white before being returned to his family. Later a Taoist priest held a makeshift ceremony to release Lim Hock An's soul from Purgatory, so that he might escape the places of suffering in the eighteen levels of Hell. No paper money could be found to throw in the fire, nor could effigies be made to burn of the many things he would need in the other world. No band walked before a grand hearse to frighten away bad spirits. Everything had been done with unseemly haste and it was less than a pauper's funeral. Second Grandmother moaned that Lim Hock An's spirit would wander for ever seeking revenge for such treatment. Bertie had stood about miserably, silently watching proceedings, picking at a scab on his face.

When the time came to leave Bougainvillaea House, there was no place to go but Little Sparrow's small home on East Coast Road. Trishaws could still be found in Katong and Little Sparrow had promised to send several of the vehicles from there to transport them. Although they waited, none arrived at the designated time and Mei Lan decided the only way to transfer Second Grandmother to East Coast Road was to put her in a wheelbarrow. At this prospect Second Grandmother grew angry, insisting that the lack of trishaws from Katong was Little Sparrow's way of humiliating her.

'The Year of the Snake is gone and now we have the Horse. *Aiyaah*. What kind of a Horse Year is this? Some mad kicking thing intent on killing us all?' Tears rolled down her cheeks as she screamed at Mei Lan.

Silk cushions were placed in a wheelbarrow and Second Grandmother was installed upon them to be pushed along by Ah Pang. Ah Fat handled a top-heavy cart piled with belongings. Bertie walked silently beside the wheelbarrow holding his mother's hand, lost in a world of his own. The terror of witnessing JJ's violent death had turned his soft brain even softer. Since his return he had not spoken, and they had no way of knowing what he had endured.

Second Grandmother's feet, in embroidered leather shoes laced with gold string, dangled over the edge of the barrow, her ivory-topped canes rested on her knees, tortoiseshell pins secured her hair. Although she wore a long, dark-coloured *sam* in keeping with the sad formality of the occasion, her face had the wild look of the sea tossed about on a windy day. Around her waist her jewels were hidden beneath her clothes in a roll of silk. Her favourite pipe and a supply of opium were packed beneath the cushions, and Ah Siew carried the case of unguents and bandages that must be used upon her feet. When the moment came to leave Bougainvillaea House, Second Grandmother sobbed and clung to Mei Lan with her little hands, turning her head into Mei Lan's shoulder so that she would not see. From Second Grandmother's embroidered silks Mei Lan breathed in the perfume of mothballs and beneath this the familiar scent of *Schiaparelli*, so old now it had thickened and darkened in its crystal bottle. Mei Lan realised suddenly that she was now the head of the family and that each decision must be made by her. She gave one last look at Bougainvillaea House and the roof of Belvedere beyond it, and drew a determined breath. They had already reached the main road when the trishaws sent by Little Sparrow at last arrived. Second Grandmother climbed aboard with an angry grunt and Mei Lan took the seat beside her.

At the East Coast house Little Sparrow waited, no thought in her mind but to see her son. Senior Wife was no longer a Lustrous Pearl but a cantankerous old woman without any teeth and Lim Hock An was dead; all that mattered now was Bertie. Little Sparrow had prepared for the arrival of her husband's wife as best she could. Bertie was to be given his sister Ching Ling's bed, next to his blood mother's room. The girl was moved with the baby, Greta, into Little Sparrow's own bed. Little Sparrow did not care if arrangements were not to Lustrous Pearl's liking. Even if she was Senior Wife, their husband was gone and the house on East Coast Road was now the property of Little Sparrow.

In the late afternoon the sea took on a new density, darkening so that Howard imagined the depths below the surface where sharks might circle silently. Clouds were blowing up over the horizon, later there would be rain. The sand was hot beneath his bare feet and rubbed between his toes. Each day his mind was full of Mei Lan. He had considered trying to find Little Sparrow's house on East Coast Road to seek news of her, but had yet to do so.

Cousin Lionel's home was made tolerable for Howard by the

proximity of the beach. He went there at night to play his saxophone and sometimes Lionel joined him with his guitar. There was also John James, an old friend of Lionel's from Malacca who lived nearby and played the accordion and the piano; his brother Cyril was good on the double bass. They could make a band, Lionel suggested. Each night from his pallet on Lionel's veranda Howard looked up at the star-filled sky and listened to the crash of waves. Above the house in the coconut palms Lionel kept earthenware pots for tapping liquor from the trees. Everyone bought toddy from Lionel: the house was always full of his tipsy friends drinking the potent brew. Ava worried about the *kempetai*, for it was now illegal to produce such illicit liquor.

Although the Japanese were asking staff to return to the Harbour Board to get the port working again, Howard preferred to stay out of the authorities' eye for the time being. Each day he reported to a nearby labour recruiting centre, waiting for work with other men on an open piece of ground. Usually, he was employed by the Health Department as a grass cutter or an oiler. Malaria and dengue fever were rife and the battle with mosquitoes required never-ending vigilance. Grass verges or open fields must be kept cut, every drain needed attention; old tyres or receptacles left out in the rain must be tracked down and sprayed with DDT. Every day, Howard pulled on a filthy uniform impregnated with evil-smelling insecticide, strapped a tin drum to his back and set off on patrol with a cart and a couple of other men. Besides drains, every puddle must be sprayed with a film of oil to prevent mosquitoes breeding. Work began at seven in the morning and was finished by one. He received $2.50 a day and a food ration. Howard sensed a growing feeling around him of people finding their bearings, settling down resignedly to life under the Japanese. In Katong, soldiers were less in evidence and life was relatively undisturbed.

In the afternoons, like almost everyone else, Howard became a black-marketeer. This work had begun with a Belvedere sheet that he sold to buy his mother some shoes. Next, a silver ashtray from Belvedere bought curtains to rig around their beds on Lionel's veranda. There was enough money left over to buy a typewriter and two dozen boxes of coconut oil shampoo. These things he soon sold for a profit, amazed at the ease with which deals were struck; in the evenings he was part of Lionel's new band. They played one-night stands for the Japanese that Lionel came by through a Chinese agent; what Howard received

in tips was more than he earned by day. The Ioki, a popular restaurant on Middle Road, gave them the most engagements. There were
always requests for Japanese songs and Lionel borrowed records from
which the band could learn.

He had been oiling an open drain the other side of the coconut
estate when he noticed the abandoned shack, its roof collapsed, the
floor splintering. Inside, it was dry and smelled of rotting wood. He
began to go there each day, putting in a black market mattress, a
chipped cup and a crate of black market soft drinks, savouring the
time away from the cramped chaos of Lionel's home. Mostly he read,
the books he had brought with him from Belvedere or those he could
find on the black market. Or he just lay on the mattress listening to
the distant slap of the waves, thinking of Mei Lan. The sun came
through the warped windows beneath the sagging roof and fell in
warm lozenges over the floor.

Now, standing before the darkening sea, he picked up a shell and
threw it far out and watched it pitch about without purpose. Before
him the waves crashed and receded. Three days earlier he had stood
on the damp sand with people from the estate, staring silently at a
swollen body washed up under the palms. The man's hands were tied
behind his back, sharks had savaged his torso and a bullet hole scarred
his forehead. Another day part of a leg was found, chewed off at the
knee by sharks but still wearing a rubber shoe. The body was hurriedly
buried, as was the leg, and nobody spoke of the rumoured massacres
or the bodies thrown into the sea.

In the distance someone was approaching, an androgynous figure
dressed in red shorts with bare legs and short tousled hair. As the
figure drew nearer Howard saw that it was Mei Lan and stared at her
unbelievingly, his pulse lurching as she came into focus, walking towards
Cousin Lionel's house. The breeze ruffled her shorn hair and her feet
were bare; she held her shoes in her hand.

'I was trying to find you,' Mei Lan said as she reached him. She
began to explain about the commandeering of Bougainvillaea House,
and how Little Sparrow's home was not far from Lionel's place. Her
face was drawn and he sensed the worst even before she spoke.

'Grandfather and JJ are both dead,' she whispered. He reached out
and took her hand. Behind her he saw the old nursemaid approaching,
hovering uncertainly in the road when she saw Mei Lan with Howard.

'She never leaves me now,' Mei Lan explained, seeing he had noticed Ah Siew.

From the beach he led her into the shade under the palms behind Lionel's house, and from there they walked along the beach to a breakwater where he often sat. Before them the sea was the colour of pewter and the setting sun glowed above as she told him all that had happened at Bougainvillaea House. Ah Siew crouched down to wait beneath a palm some yards away, her eyes resting anxiously upon them.

'Grandmother is half out of her mind,' Mei Lan whispered, looking down at her hands as she told him about the death of Lim Hock An.

Every time she shut her eyes brutal images of his arrest and the callous manner of his return filled her mind, and she knew they would be imprinted within her for ever. It was impossible to know what JJ had suffered and whenever she tried she saw only a darkness before her. At night she woke often, struggling to be free of nightmares; her teeth were always clenched. Second Grandmother no longer wailed in sorrow but spent her days with her opium pipe, scraping out the dross in the bowl, kneading it into new pellets to be smoked again and again, eking out her small supply. What she would do when this supply was finished, Mei Lan did not know. Ah Siew appeared suddenly shrunken and forgetful, her energy focused on Mei Lan with such vigilance that the *amah*'s unrelenting concern had become a trial for her. Little Sparrow absorbed herself with the traumatised Bertie; Second Grandmother, silent with sorrow, was glad to hand over charge of her son to his original mother. Any decisions of importance were left to Mei Lan to make, and the weight of the grieving family hung heavily upon her.

23

SHE CAME TO THE beach each day in the late afternoon, and sat with
Howard on the stones beside the breakwater. Ah Siew trailed after
Mei Lan, squatting down to wait, always under the same coconut
palm. Howard felt the old woman's eyes upon him, resigned but disapproving. He was surprised when one day Mei Lan arrived as usual,
but without Ah Siew.

'She didn't see me leave,' Mei Lan said and he knew she had waited
for an opportunity to evade the old woman.

'I've something to show you,' he said, taking her hand and pulling
her after him. They walked on the firm, wet sand, feet bare and
gleaming under the soft honeycomb of foam that edged each incoming
wave. For the first time in days the events swirling about Mei Lan
seemed distant. The weight of Howard's arm about her shoulders, the
immediacy of him walking beside her was all that mattered. The
shallow waves rolled over their toes, splashing about their ankles, and
Howard remembered how they had waded through the clear water of
the canal to catch crayfish so long ago. He observed Mei Lan's neatly
shaped toes, the high arch of her foot, the narrow heel, and knew time
stood still and there was only this moment, this walking together over
the sand. The fragility of her filled him, reminding him of a bird he
had once held in the palm of his hand, its heart beating against his
fingers. In the silence he knew the same hunger was building within
them both and that the same trepidation filled them. At last he stopped
before the old shack, and they stood looking up at it.

'It's my secret place,' he told her, pulling her up beside him to stand
on the crumbling balcony.

'Is it safe?' she asked, observing the splintering floor as he pushed
open the door and led her inside.

'You have to be careful where you walk,' he replied, knowing these
mundane words were but a bridge across the awkward moments.

Already, he was unbuttoning his shirt and she was helping him, even as he pulled at her wrappings, fumbling with buttons, impatient with the complication of it all. Then, at last he could crush her against him, feel the swell of her breast beneath his hand, the soft inner thigh. He heard her moan, her lips wet against his shoulder, dissolving like him, carried up on the crest of sensation until it broke upon them both. It was over quickly. For a while they lay unmoving, then Mei Lan struggled free and pulled herself up on her knees to look out of the window above them.

'I knew she was there. I knew she would come,' she said softly.

Howard knelt beside her and saw in the distance the small, bent figure of Ah Siew scurrying desperately up and down the track that led to the beach near the breakwater. Hurriedly, Mei Lan began to pull on her clothes. He sat on the pallet looking up at her and knew she wanted to get away from him, to erase what had just happened, and this knowledge filled him miserably.

'I can't do this to her,' Mei Lan said, almost under her breath. 'I can't come here again. It's wrong; everything has changed.' All she could see was the image of Ah Siew, bent with age and anxiety, clinging to her like a lifeline. Suddenly, things she had done so easily before, the reckless pleasures of disobedience, were gone. She had waited and planned for this time with Howard and yet everything now seemed wrong. All she could think of was Lim Hock An, his hatted corpse jolted away in the trishaw with the undertaker, and JJ, bound and shot beside a sea that ran red with blood. To seek life in the shadow of so much death seemed too great a decadence.

'What do you mean, everything has changed? I didn't force you,' Howard protested, filled now with angry humiliation. Mei Lan threw him a look of such distress that he fell silent and watched sullenly as she pulled her shirt into place.

'I should not have brought you here,' he admitted, feeling guilt as much as anger.

What she said was true: what had happened in the past between them was different from what happened now. She was changed by the trauma of the last weeks, and the world they had once entered so easily was gone. She paused, as if to say something then shook her head and was gone, the warped door creaking behind her. From the window he watched her making her way along the beach so that it would seem to old Ah Siew that she was returning alone from a walk.

He was surprised the next day when she came as usual to the break-water, the old nursemaid behind her. Howard knew this was how it would be from now on; she would stay safely in Ah Siew's view, giving the old woman no anxiety. This new obedience, he instinctively under-stood, was her way of acknowledging the weight the dead had placed upon her. To ease the tension, he suggested they go to the Joo Chiat Hospital to see Cynthia. The hospital was only a short walk from Lionel's home, and Howard went there often to visit his sister. The quickest route was along the beach and they walked silently, barefooted, carrying their shoes. Ah Siew, trailing behind them, kept to the dry sand in her worn canvas slippers. At the end of the beach they wiped their feet with Howard's handkerchief before putting on their shoes and then climbing up the slope to the road and the hospital beyond.

'It's more like a prison than a hospital,' Mei Lan decided when they reached the small, drab building hemmed in by walls scarred by shrapnel and shells. They found Cynthia almost at once, and she greeted Mei Lan with delight.

'Dr Wong was ordered to come here with a dozen of us nurses one morning. We were all loaded on to a truck and driven here to start work the same day,' Cynthia told her. 'It's a small hospital but on the road to Changi. POWs and the sick from the internment camps are sent here if medical treatment is needed.' Cynthia spoke in a level voice, but the mention of the word Changi summoned up the lost Wilfred to them all as they stood in the Emergency Room. Cynthia fell silent, unable to suppress the wave of emotion that passed over her face. Then, finding her balance again she turned briskly to Mei Lan, forcing brightness into her voice.

'You're a trained medical auxiliary after all that time at the General Hospital. We could do with extra help here; you can't waste that training,' she argued. 'I'm now in charge of the nursing staff as all the British matrons have been interned; it's taken a war to put a local person in charge.'

'When do I start?' Mei Lan asked, overcome with relief at the thought of a structured life, and a valid reason to absent herself from the East Coast Road house.

Although POWs and internees were brought in regularly to the hospital from Changi, and although she prayed day and night for a miracle, Cynthia had not expected to see Wilfred. The shock was so great when he appeared that she could barely manage to give directions to the Japanese guard who accompanied him. Wilfred was brought in on a stretcher, moaning and groaning and holding his stomach and making as much noise as possible. For a moment Cynthia thought the pain was real. She placed a hand on his shoulder and Wilfred gripped it. Relief and emotion made her weak, and she gritted her teeth, determined not to cry or give in to the impulse to bend and put her arms about him.

'We have to X-ray him. It may be an appendix,' Dr Wong told the guard sternly as he hurried to stand beside Cynthia. It was the usual procedure, to insist on X-raying the POWs. They would only get to the hospital in the first place if they were in severe pain. Although there was a steady flow of real patients from Changi, there were also many who reached the hospital on false pretences. Dr Wong had set up a lifeline for prisoners and internees at great risk to himself. Each time a Changi POW or camp internee like Wilfred was brought to Joo Chiat for medical attention Dr Wong went through the same procedure. First, the excuse of an X-ray behind closed doors and then, as soon as the door was shut, money and medicines were concealed inside his shorts in special pouches sewn in for this purpose. Dr Wong kept a stock of medicines for them and also radio parts; there was a constant demand for radio parts. Messages were smuggled in and out of the internment camps and Changi Prison in this way as well. Wilfred had managed to send Cynthia the occasional note by this route, and she was able to reply.

Two orderlies carried Wilfred into the X-ray room and departed. The guard waited as he was told to, outside the door. Japanese guards could not speak or read English, and so were slow to pick up on what was happening.

'You have only a few minutes with him,' Dr Wong told Cynthia as the door to the X-ray room shut behind them. He turned away, busying himself before the shelves of medicines, giving them what privacy he could.

'Don't cry,' Wilfred whispered. 'The guard will suspect something if he sees you've been crying.' She nodded against his shoulder as he rocked her in his arms. 'I had to come. They're sending me away,' Wilfred whispered into her ear. Cynthia drew back in alarm to look into his face.

'Some of us civilian internees have given them trouble in the camp. As punishment for insubordination, we've been sent out to work with the POWs from Changi Prison. Now it's rumoured we're all being sent as a labour force to Burma, to build a railway there.' As he spoke the guard knocked on the door impatiently with the butt of his rifle.

'You'll have to go. Keep groaning, I'll say I've given you an injection to calm you down.' Dr Wong began putting the usual money and medicines into Wilfred's pockets.

'They're building a radio in the camp; we're sending in parts bit by bit. These are today's batch,' Dr Wong told him. Wilfred nodded, pushing wires and screws into a secret double waistband in his shorts, before buckling up his belt again.

'He has to go or they'll suspect something,' Dr Wong repeated, taking Cynthia's arm and drawing her away from her husband. When Wilfred returned to his stretcher, the guards and orderlies were called in again to transport him back to the waiting truck for the return to Changi.

Cynthia stood at the hospital entrance, watching Wilfred being loaded on to a Japanese military vehicle. As the engine started she bit her lip and could not control the panic flooding through her. It was all she could do not to run after the lorry, screaming for it to stop. The truck slid out of the gate and vanished. She remained at the door until the sound of the engine was lost to her.

On those nights when Lionel's band had no engagements Howard went to the hospital to see Mei Lan, who now worked in the Emergency Clinic with Cynthia. The hospital was short staffed and since through his Air Raid Precaution duties Howard knew enough first aid to be of help, Cynthia insisted he too should do what he could. He accepted the chance to work with Mei Lan with alacrity. Often, in the late evenings, when the normal queue of patients with cuts and broken bones and fevers diminished, Howard noticed that a queue of people with entirely different ailments always formed. It was invariably made up of young men of sallow complexion with pus-filled sores on their limbs. Without exception, these patients also required treatment for malaria. Howard was expert now in mixing up a solution of quinine powder and distilled water for Cynthia to inject during the late evening influx.

After he had been working some weeks in the dispensary with Cynthia and Mei Lan, Howard was shocked one night to see Wee Jack walk in and join the late night queue. It took him a few moments to be certain he was not mistaken as he stared across the room in disbelief. Wee Jack had left the Harbour Board soon after trying to recruit Howard to his communist cell, and no more had been heard from him. Now, here he was. Always cadaverous, he had lost more weight and was of skeletal appearance, his cheeks sunken, his jaw ridged sharply above his thin neck. Wee Jack turned his head and met Howard's eyes, giving a surly nod of recognition. Eventually, once Cynthia had seen him and dressed a septic wound on his leg, he walked over to collect his medicine from Howard, who was in charge of dispensing.

As he came closer Howard was shocked again at the unhealthy jaundiced tone of his skin. One arm of Wee Jack's spectacles was held together by sticking plaster; the sparse beard he had grown on the end of his chin gave him a goatish appearance.

'I'm here with my friends,' Wee Jack said, nodding in the direction of the young men Cynthia and Mei Lan were attending to.

'Why are so many of your friends ill?' Howard frowned as he observed the ragged group across the room.

'Conditions are bad in the jungle. We've walked all day to see your sister.' Jack laughed, raising his eyebrows at Howard's uncomprehending expression.

'Don't you see, we've just exchanged one colonial master for another. The fight to be rid of imperialists continues. The jungle protects us; the Japanese cannot find us there.' Wee Jack lowered his voice, observing Howard over his lopsided spectacles.

'You're holding out in the jungle?' Howard had heard it rumoured that there were groups of communist guerrillas living in the jungle. Wee Jack nodded, amused at Howard's incredulity.

'No doctors there. We have a stock of quinine and medical supplies, but it is never enough. Your sister helps us.' He looked over at Cynthia, who was administering swabs and injections to the last of his comrades.

'*She* helps us as well,' Wee Jack whispered, gesturing to Mei Lan, having already noticed how Howard's eyes rested upon her. Howard drew back in shock.

'They're risking their lives for you,' he protested, cold at the thought of the dangers that helping Wee Jack must involve.

'We're all risking our lives.' Wee Jack gave a derisive snort of laugher.

Later, when the clinic emptied and Wee Jack and his men had disappeared into the night, Howard strode angrily across to Cynthia, who was clearing up used syringes for Mei Lan to sterilise.

'Do you know those men are communists? They're dangerous. Don't let them in here. What do you think you're doing?' Howard demanded. Cynthia turned upon him equally angry, the used syringes clattering into a metal dish.

'I just have to think of Wilfred in that camp and it's all I need to join the resistance against the Japanese. Now he's been sent to Burma. I don't know if I'll see him again.' Her face twisted with emotion as she spoke.

'How can you encourage Mei Lan in this?' he argued, watching Mei Lan opening the steriliser on the other side of the room and angry that, in spite of the hours she spent with him, she had not told him she was putting her life in danger each day.

'She feels like I do. You know her brother and grandfather were murdered by the Japanese.'

'There are informers everywhere; someone will talk.' Howard took hold of her arm, seeing the further danger.

'We're careful no one sees us,' Cynthia answered.

When Howard arrived at the hospital the following evening he found Mei Lan in Cynthia's small room secretly packing a bag with quinine. At first she was unwilling to tell him where she was going, her complicity with Cynthia made all the stronger by his alarm. He began to argue, but when he looked into her defiant face he was suddenly frightened.

'The Japanese are everywhere looking for people doing just this kind of thing. It's too dangerous, too great a risk,' Howard pleaded, pulling her towards him, his voice breaking with distress. Mei Lan did not resist but put her arms about him, leaning against him in mute appeal.

'They killed Grandfather, they killed JJ. I'll do whatever I can to help the resistance,' Mei Lan whispered fiercely, drawing away from him. 'The communists have a hideout near here. I've only taken medicine to them once before. This time one of the boys is too sick to get to the hospital. Usually, Cynthia goes but tonight she can't leave the clinic as a Japanese doctor is around.' Mei Lan turned away to add some last items to the bag.

'I'll come with you, then,' Howard said grimly when he saw she would not be deterred.

Wee Jack sent a boy of nineteen with broken teeth and a scar on his chin to lead Mei Lan to the hideout. Before the war Brokentooth told them, he had worked in a foundry as a welder. Howard took the bag of medicines from Mei Lan, furious that someone like Wee Jack had been able to persuade Mei Lan to risk her life for his men.

They came into a field of *lallang* and skirted a patch of tapioca. The moon had settled behind the clouds, and in the darkness Brokentooth occasionally shone a small torch on the path to point out a rutted area. After some time, they reached an abandoned *kampong*. Mei Lan half stumbled into a shell hole and Howard tightened his grip on her arm. Wee Jack materialised suddenly out of the darkness and they followed him silently up a few rickety steps into the remains of a wooden hut, raised on stilts above the ground. In the beam of Wee Jack's torch they saw two men crouched beside the patient who lay on the floor, moaning deliriously. Mei Lan stepped forward, putting down the rucksack.

'He's burning with fever,' she said as she knelt to the sick man. Wee Jack shone his torch and Mei Lan gasped in shock.

'You told me he had malaria but he has a septic bullet wound. I'm not a doctor; I'm not even a nurse. I can give a malaria injection but no more. Quinine is all I have in this bag. You'll have to bring him into the hospital.' She raised her voice angrily, but Wee Jack gestured for her to be silent, and stood listening intently. Soon, they heard the sound of an approaching car, then a slamming of doors and loud voices shouting in Japanese.

'Get out of here,' Wee Jack whispered hoarsely, running to escape through a back window followed by Brokentooth and his friends. In the corner the wounded man moaned loudly.

Howard pulled Mei Lan with him through a splintered gap of wall, half jumping, half falling out of the hut. They crawled under the house and by the headlights of the military truck, left on to illuminate the area, Howard made out a mound of debris from a collapsed portion of the house a few feet from where they crouched. As a volley of shots rang out, he pushed Mei Lan behind the pile of splintered planks.

Above them, inches from their heads, was the sound of running feet. The wounded man's screams grew louder and Howard drew Mei Lan close. She buried her face in the crook of his arm. The headlights of the military jeep blinded him, limiting his view of what was happening in front of the house. Another shot rang out, and the sick man's screams stopped abruptly. More footsteps thudded above them. A torch was shone down on to the debris they hid behind, and then it was gone. The soldiers ran out of the house and off into the *lallang* to search for Wee Jack and his friends, their torches spearing the darkness. More gunshots were heard, but at a distance now.

'Wait,' Howard whispered into Mei Lan's ear; the car with blazing headlights was still before the house.

After a while the soldiers returned, dragging with them one of Wee Jack's friends. The man was thrust into the back of the jeep and the vehicle drove off. Silence and darkness returned.

24

THE FOLLOWING DAY THE *kempetai* visited the house on East Coast Road and took Mei Lan away. Ah Siew could think of only one place to go for help. She appeared at the Joo Chiat Hospital before Cynthia, wringing her hands, her face drawn in fear and anxiety.

'She has no one but me. Elder brother and Grandfather are dead. Second Grandmother is going out of mind and Third Grandmother only thinking of own children. Half-brother's brain is not correct and Father is staying in Hong Kong. She is always speaking about you. Help her. Please.' Ah Siew prostrated herself before Cynthia in the Emergency Clinic in the early evening.

After calming the old woman and sending her home, Cynthia hurried to Cousin Lionel's house in search of Howard, running part of the way from the Joo Chiat Hospital before she found a free rickshaw.

'The man the soldiers caught yesterday at the hideout must have informed on her. They probably tortured him,' Howard said, seeing again the soldiers dragging the man into their car. He remembered burying his face in Mei Lan's hair, inhaling the flowery scent as he held her in his arms.

'Go to that Indian again, the one who got her grandfather out. For God's sake, go to him quickly,' Cynthia told him. Howard needed no prompting; already he was following her down the veranda steps, his heart beating fast in distress.

'Again?' Raj said irritably as Howard stood before him in Manikam's Cloth Shop. Howard was unable to find a rickshaw and had run the whole distance to Serangoon Road, slowing only when he saw soldiers or had to pass a checkpoint, bowing low before the guard.

'I cannot keep asking Shinozaki for favours,' Raj frowned as he opened the door. It had been a day of problems, and he had been dozing when the knocking woke him. For a moment Howard thought the Indian might refuse to help, but with an exasperated sigh Raj searched for his keys, shut the shop and went with Howard to the Toyo Hotel where he knew the diplomat would be. As on their last visit, Shinozaki was at dinner with Colonel Yokota. Once again, as Raj and Howard waited in the foyer, the strains of a lively mazurka from the Hungarian orchestra drifted from the dining room.

'Again? Shinozaki queried drily when at last he appeared, looking at Howard in unfeigned displeasure as he sat down on the same red plush chair as before. His cheeks were noticeably pouched, and his eyes puffy behind his heavy spectacles.

'I cannot save everyone from everything all the time,' Shinozaki announced wearily, stubbing out his cigarette before going off to make enquiries about Mei Lan. In a few minutes he returned, a grim expression on his face.

'It is a serious case of anti-Japanese activities; it seems the woman is a communist. Please understand, it is difficult for me nowadays. I am no longer in charge of the Chinese Overseas Association; Colonel Watanabe is running it now.' Shinozaki's voice trembled with anger at the thought of the many humiliations he had recently suffered at the hands of Colonel Watanabe. Sitting down again he reached for his cigarettes.

'Colonel Watanabe knows I was trying to help the Chinese people through the Chinese Overseas Association. He has told everyone I am not a suitable man to be employed during wartime. I have even been asked if I am really a Chinese instead of a Japanese, because I am so soft on the Chinese community.' Shinozaki gave a harsh laugh and blew out one of his perfect smoke rings, watching it widen and float away before continuing.

'Colonel Watanabe and his friends have come up with the idea that the Chinese community must make a donation of $50 million to Japan in apology for their anti-Japanese behaviour before the surrender. Everyone must pay, especially if they are property owners. They say this is a voluntary donation, but I can assure you there will be nothing voluntary about it. I have suffered many humiliations. My voice is no longer heard.' Shinozaki frothed with anger.

'Can you do anything for Lim Mei Lan?' Howard interrupted, unable to sit through any more of the diplomat's self-absorbed musings.

'Mayor Odate has understood the difficulty of my position at Defence

Headquarters and has asked me to leave the Military Administration Department and join him in the City Administration Department where I can better help the people of Singapore. Soon I shall move there,' Shinozaki informed them, blowing smoke through his nostrils.

'Did you find out where she is? You have to get her released.' Howard was unable to control the desperation in his voice. Shinozaki looked at him coldly.

'Tomorrow you can try going to Orchard Road, to *kempetai* head-quarters at the YMCA. They are keeping her there. Ask for Lieutenant Colonel Hirose, you can say I sent you. I can do nothing more.'

The YMCA was a prominent landmark with an imposing portico and a gabled roof. Bamboo blinds shaded its airy balconies. It was now one of the *kempetai*'s main centres and used for interrogation. It had become a building to dread. People avoided walking past it; terrible sounds were said to come from its depths and few of those who entered it emerged again in one piece. Howard went there the following morning with Raj. He had steeled himself for the worst, but saw only an innocuous buzz of bureaucracy as he entered the building. It was a busy place with uniformed men hurrying up and down a flight of stairs, carrying files or sheaves of paper.

They were shown into an office on the second floor where they met Lieutenant Colonel Hirose.

'You realise of course that you have only got to see me because of Mr Shinozaki,' he informed them immediately, his voice smooth and cool as he gestured to the chairs before his desk. He spoke good English; all the top *kempei* spoke English so that the interrogation of non-Japanese could be all the more thorough. They sat down and Howard asked the question he had come to ask.

'Ah yes. That woman.' Lieutenant Colonel Hirose nodded. 'There are several serious charges against her. From the beginning we were aware of her anti-Japanese activities with the China Relief Fund but her grandfather was of more interest to us. However, she is now known to be consorting with communists and supplying them with medicines. Her home was searched and documents of an incriminating nature were found.' Hirose reached across his desk for a small cup of Japanese tea and took a sip.

'What is your relationship with this woman?' he asked, his eyes upon Howard.

'She has no family to speak for her; that is why I have come.' Howard returned the man's gaze, holding his anger in place, sensing danger.

'You keep the company of communists? That is most interesting.' Hirose raised his eyebrows above the blue patterned teacup.

'She is not a communist and neither am I.' Howard could not control the indignation in his voice.

'Interesting,' Hirose said again, almost under his breath.

Howard had the sensation that he was sinking to the bottom of a great empty space. Then, unable any longer to control his desperation he found himself on his feet, facing Hirose behind the desk. Before he could speak Raj jumped up and stepped forward beside him, bowing to the officer in a subservient way.

'We apologise for wasting your time. The woman is not related to Mr Burns. He is a kind-hearted man and did not know properly the charges against her. Of course, he now understands your need to keep her here.' Raj bowed low again.

Observing them sourly, Lieutenant Colonel Hirose replaced his teacup on its wooden saucer and with a curt nod of dismissal turned his attention to the documents on his desk. Raj took hold of Howard's arm and hustled him from the room.

'Why don't you help find out where she is?' Howard burst out furiously as the door shut.

'Keep your voice down. He will do nothing. I have an idea. I will ask Shinozaki to request them to release her so that she can arrange to make her share of that $50 million donation Watanabe wants from the Chinese community. She cannot make arrangements for this while she is a prisoner. I have heard some prisoners have already been released for this purpose,' Raj said.

As they came down the stairs a guard was ascending with a middle-aged Chinese man, thin as an ancient in filthy clothes, who climbed the stairs painfully beside him. As they stepped back to let him pass, Howard found his mouth was dry and his heart beat rapidly with the thoughts that came to him. Somewhere in this terrible place Mei Lan was incarcerated, subjected to a force of malevolence he had yet to fully comprehend. He wanted to run from the building, but instead made himself walk without haste down the stairs.

'You have put both of us in danger by coming here,' Raj whispered angrily from behind him.

At last they reached the entrance and passed the guards with bayonets. A thick blade of sunlight thrust into the building as they pushed open the door. Outside in the road, Howard saw a stray dog cock its leg against a tree; a man on a bicycle passed, cars and rickshaws rattled by and he clung to these harmless sights. The menace he felt from the building pressed upon him: he expected at any moment to be apprehended and dragged back into the darkness. Before meeting Lieutenant Colonel Hirose he had hoped someone could be persuaded to release Mei Lan, or take him to her so that he could assure her he would soon get her out. A guard was watching and seeing Howard's hesitation stepped forward, gesturing to him to leave, his bayonet catching the light.

Howard breathed in the wholesome smell of the road again. As he turned away he heard at last the cry he had steeled himself to hear all the while he had been in the building. It came from the depths of the place and floated down upon him, a spasm of tortured sound that carried all the pain of a ravaged humanity. He began to run.

A year had passed since Singapore surrendered to the Japanese. Chinese New Year approached again. Everything was becoming scarce. A place had to be secured in the ration shop queue by 4.30 a.m., otherwise things ran out. Ingenuity was stretched to the limit. Soap, like every other commodity, was hard to come by. Ava announced she was going to make some soap, but produced only a grey pebble that refused to lather and was the consistency of pumice stone.

'They put lots of ash in it, you know,' Rose told her, turning the misshapen rock in her hand. 'You don't get soap at the ration shop unless you can give them a bag of ash.' She was aware of Ava's crestfallen expression, and was ashamed at the pleasure this gave her. All she wanted was for the war to end, so that she would be free of life with Ava and Lionel and could return to Belvedere. Even Mavis's continual effort at good spirits now annoyed her.

Singapore had become a vegetable garden: the slogan everywhere was GROW MORE FOOD. Every available patch of grass was dug up and in its place tomatoes, cucumber, tapioca, sweet potato and spinach of all varieties were planted. The vegetable of choice was tapioca because it took only three months to grow; no amount of neglect could obliterate it and nothing filled the stomach so quickly, if tastelessly. It became a wayside crop. Every road was lined with the plant, schools gave part of their playgrounds to the tuber and balconies that had once grown ornamental bamboo or bougainvillaea, now cradled the ubiquitous root.

'There may be no flour for bread but we grow tapioca. Tapioca bread cannot be hard to make,' Mavis suggested; the ration shop bread for which they queued for hours was stale and weevil ridden. Desperate recipes now circulated for adhesives, soap, hair dye, tapioca cake, tapioca bread, tapioca biscuits, tapioca noodles, tapioca ice cream and tapioca face packs.

Although Mavis's tapioca bread was a trial for bad gums and loose teeth, people still came some distance to buy it. Everyone wanted to know the secret, but Rose kept her tins of condensed milk well hidden. Nothing was allowed to go to waste. When the starchy tapioca tubers had been steamed, the discarded pink under-skin was dried and fried and the crisps sprinkled with chilli and sold in rolled newspaper cones of the *Syonan Times*, a propaganda tabloid extolling everything Japanese. Ava and Mavis began to be known for these products.

Lionel went into business in a bigger way than bread, harvesting his toddy to purpose, buying up empty bottles on the black market in which to distil the liquor. He also set up a makeshift bar beside his distillery at the back of the house. Friends who had been served freely before were now charged for a drink; the bar quickly became an evening gathering place. Lionel was now collecting toddy from other people beyond the estate, and great vats of the alcohol fermented in the house. The place smelled yeasty and Lionel was permanently high on his produce, forced to taste it frequently for professional reasons. At night the loud strumming of his guitar could be heard accompanying his friends' drunken singing. A pub-like atmosphere pervaded the house.

Howard kept clear of the place, continuing to work as a grass cutter and oiler. He volunteered at the hospital each evening. All he could think of was Mei Lan and his inability to help her. His sleep was disturbed by raw images, and that one terrible sound he had heard as he left the YMCA building. He had gone to the East Coast house but they had no news, and the old nursemaid, eyes wild with worry and imaginings, had clung to him, imploring him to find Mei Lan. Behind her he had seen the old grandmother stumbling about upon her canes, vacant eyed from opium and dementia. Of Little Sparrow there had been no sign. The misery of his powerlessness consumed him afresh.

'There is nothing more to be done. Communists are not so easily released.' Raj was irritated beyond measure by Howard's constant visits. He was also nervous for himself; Shinozaki's need to keep running around doing good had brought them both under the *kempetai*'s eye. The diplomat's own band of spies had now been set to watch their spymaster.

Howard worried about his radio. He no longer felt easy about retrieving it from the space beneath the balcony, to listen to the news on Radio Delhi; he knew he must find a new hiding place for it. Lionel, his mind in free flight on his toddy, did not know what he did half the time. The day before, just as Howard was retrieving the radio from beneath the floorboards, he had stumbled on to the veranda with Ronnie Remedios, who had worked with him before the war in lift repair.

'He's a good friend; won't tell a soul about the radio. Only wants to hear the news,' Lionel spluttered. Ronnie had nodded agreement, drawn a line across his throat and rolled his eyes to heaven.

'It's broken,' Howard replied hastily, thrusting the radio back into its hiding place. He slept fitfully that night; Ronnie Remedios, with his large soft belly and wide flat nose, loomed ominously in his dreams. However much the man laughed and joked, his eyes remained watchful in his fleshy face. *Kempetai* informers were everywhere, offering the authorities information in return for their own protection. For this reason Rose had begged him to get rid of the radio, always prowling about anxiously while he listened to the news, on the lookout for anyone suspicious.

To Howard's relief Ronnie Remedios did not appear the next evening. Later, as Howard sat on his pallet cleaning his saxophone he heard loud guttural shouting coming from the back of the house where Lionel had his bar. There were often inebriated fights about the toddy bar and Howard leaned over the veranda balustrade, trying to see what was happening. He drew back quickly in alarm. The place was surrounded by *kempei* flashing their bayonets, and Lionel's friends were fleeing in all directions. A tall thin *kempei* had got hold of Lionel and was slapping his face and shaking him. Lionel was sobbing and squealing like an abattoir animal, yelling out Howard's name and pointing into the house. Howard turned in panic, uncertain what he should do, his heart pounding in his throat, sure that Ronnie Remedios had informed the authorities about his radio. As he looked wildly about, Rose appeared before him in a pink flowered housecoat, Mavis behind her.

'Run. Go to Cynthia,' Rose hissed, pushing him down the steps.

When Howard reached the Joo Chiat Hospital, breathless from fear and exertion, the Emergency Clinic was almost empty and Cynthia was filling in charts in a far corner. As soon as he told her what had happened, she stood up, took his arm and pulled him after her out of the room.

'The only reason they didn't arrest me with Mei Lan was because that boy they tortured only knew her name and not mine. We're all being watched now in the hospital, those jungle boys can't come here any more. If your name is on their list, and they know you have a radio, then you have to get away.' Cynthia opened the door of a broom cupboard under some stairs and shoved him into the blackness inside.

'Stay here until I let you out, however long it takes,' she told him. It seemed hours before the door opened and he saw her face again.

'Quickly,' Cynthia whispered, thrusting two shoulder bags stuffed with bulky packages into Howard's hands as she led him to the door.

'It's food and medicines. You know how to use the quinine. Brokentooth will take you into the jungle, to their camp. You'll be safe there. Go quickly.' She pushed Howard out of a side door and on to a narrow path between two buildings. Brokentooth was waiting: he beckoned for Howard to follow.

They kept away from the road, taking well-worn paths through patches of secondary jungle and then crossed a large rubber plantation. The thick leaves of the rubber trees prevented the sun from penetrating, and trapped the stench of latex from the processing huts. Howard knew he would remember the sickening odour for ever as connected to this night. He stumbled behind Brokentooth. The boy was familiar with the path, only occasionally shining his torch, finding the light of the moon enough. Howard's heart beat fast and his thoughts were confused. Every few minutes he glanced over his shoulder, fearing the *kempetai* were following. Possession of a radio was punishable with death: how could he have thought he'd get away with it? Now he was running for his life, filled with remorse at having taken a risk that endangered everyone. He might have escaped – but what of his mother and Mavis? Would Cynthia now be arrested? Everything was his fault; he gave a groan of anguish. Seeing him lag behind, Brokentooth drew to a halt, waiting for Howard to catch up. They were free of the rubber estate. Now there was the smell of the sea and Howard heard the crash of waves.

'We must cross the water to mainland Malaya before it is light. The overland route is dangerous, we are safer travelling by sea.' Brokentooth led the way along the beach to a cluster of fishermen's huts built on stilts above the water.

Howard followed him up a ladder into one of the huts. He had thought Brokentooth was taking him to a hideout somewhere on the island: he had not expected a journey over the sea. Confusion and panic raced through him; he was not thinking properly but just stumbling blindly after a stranger who was a known communist. In the hut a woman crouched over a paraffin stove and heated rice porridge for them by the light of an oil lamp; two children slept in a corner, oblivious to their presence. They ate quickly, listening to the slop of water below the house as the woman's husband prepared the boat; from the beach came the stink of drying fish. Everything had happened too quickly. How deep in the Malayan jungle was the camp? How long was he to remain in it? When would it be safe to return home? All Howard had were questions, and without answers his anxiety grew. The only thing that kept him following Brokentooth was the thought of the *kempetai* if he now returned home.

Soon, they clambered into the boat, helping the fisherman to push it from the beach out into the open sea. The boatman took an oar and gave one to Howard and they rowed silently towards the dark coastline of Malaya, Brokentooth sitting in the back of the boat, waiting his turn with the oar. The moon hung low, lighting a narrow path of silver over the dark oily skin of the sea. Howard gripped the paddle, pushing it deep into the water so that a spray sprang up and stung his face and he tasted the brine on his lips. They seemed to row for hours, his body part of the endless rocking rhythm. Only the boat ploughing the water broke the silence of the vast and empty darkness, with the moon their only light. The night swallowed everything, and he felt his smallness on the limitless ocean. Here, existence and death seemed of no more consequence than the breaking of a wave upon the shore and he shivered with new terror. His mother, Mei Lan, Cynthia . . . everyone was far away now. He wondered if Mei Lan shared this feeling in whatever conditions she now lived. If there was a God, he thought bitterly, it must be like the sea, impervious to man's small trickle of emotion, immune to love or hate, moved only by the laws of its own ceaseless and measureless swell. In that moment, he knew for the first time he would never share his mother's deep faith in her god.

He had no idea how far they had travelled or for how long. Time had lost dimension. Shadowy inlets, rocky islets and sweeping bays passed, lit faintly by the moon. Then, unexpectedly, the boatman was turning towards the shore. They must be along the coast of Johore, Howard reckoned. Day was already breaking when the boatman left them on the sandy beach of a small cove, and then rowed quickly away. Howard looked back into the emptiness behind him. The first pincers of light were needling open the sky and he wondered when, if ever, he would cross this ocean again. In the course of a night his life had changed.

25

THEY BEGAN THE TREK through the jungle. At first the land was open, with patches of tapioca and sweet potato, and Howard saw butterflies of brilliant colour. Kingfishers streaked across a stream, the warbling of a bird and the constant crackle of crickets were heard. Then, abruptly, the jungle closed upon them and the way forward was dense with vegetation. He was sweating profusely and his limbs, covered by insect bites, itched unbearably. After a while Brokentooth stopped before a tall tree and pointed to markings on the trunk. Clearing damp leaves away from the roots he pulled a loaded sack out of a hole.

'Rice and salted fish for the camp,' Brokentooth said, heaving the bundle on to his shoulders along with his own load. Howard wondered how a man could carry such a weight; after the trauma of flight and a night of rowing, all he wanted to do was sleep. Instead, he felt he was floundering helplessly through a dream, enclosed inescapably in its weird universe. A wave of desperation swept through him again.

Unhooking the *parang* from his waist, Brokentooth slashed at vines and hanging branches as the jungle thickened about them. The light was suffused and gloomy; mist rose from the thick mulch of rotting leaves, fallen trees and branches that covered the jungle floor. Creeping plants wound up to the glow of light, so far above it seemed to be another world. At times the forest canopy fused above them and light almost disappeared, as if they had entered a cave. Then, the sun when glimpsed around the edge of the jungle, appeared like the distant glow of a lamp and the shrieks of birds took on a menacing edge. There were sounds all around them in this primordial forest: the crash of a broken branch, the calls of animals or birds or the knocking of a wood-pecker. Squirrel, wild boar and mouse deer were seen, and once a jungle cat; monkeys swung in the trees. Everything in the jungle lived for centuries, Brokentooth told him. The boy's resourcefulness and stamina made Howard ashamed of his own weak limbs and thimbleful of energy. The paltry packs Cynthia had given him weighed him down and Brokentooth laughed.

'Comrades who are part of the food chains bringing provisions into the camps carry forty, even sixty pounds. Everything has to be carried into the camps.'

Gradually, the gloom began to lessen and Howard saw the sun again, cutting down through the trees in thick wedges of light. They emerged into a furnace of heat and began to climb a hill of tall *lallang*. They were now on a high ridge and either side of them the jungle rolled steeply away in a vista of blue-green slopes. A fast-running stream crashed over the ridge and disappeared into a long waterfall, foaming and pounding into the lush emerald forest a great distance below.

'Drink only fast-moving water and you're safe.' Brokentooth knelt down, cupping the water in his hands, drinking thirstily. Howard sank gratefully to his knees beside him and buried his head in the fresh rush of water.

At this height it was cooler. Howard stood gazing in awe at the endless green swell of jungle-covered hills without sign of human life or habitation. Below this sunny ridge was the darkness of the forest from which they had just emerged; above was the steep climb to the top of the hill and then down again into the jungle.

'You can't go home,' Brokentooth laughed, as if reading his thoughts.

Howard nodded wearily, already certain that, without a guide, he would never find his way out of the jungle alive. Ahead was only more desolate jungle, waiting to close behind him. They walked all day, passing through boggy swamps where mist welled up eerily in ghostly apparitions and even the birds were dull in colour. Howard's legs ached and sweat ran from him. As the light faded they came upon an attap-roofed hut.

'This is one of our places,' Brokentooth announced, putting his bags down on the sleeping bench that ran along one flimsy wall. Howard sat down, grateful to have reached any destination at all. It was then that he saw the black leeches clinging to his legs, fat slugs the size of his thumb, bloated with his blood.

'It's part of jungle life; they drop upon you from the trees. See, I have them too.' Brokentooth laughed at Howard's horror and lit a cigarette. With the glowing butt he touched each swollen leech, and immediately they shrank and dropped off Howard's legs, leaving a small red mark.

'You get used to all this,' Brokentooth comforted him as he gathered twigs with which to light a fire.

Soon, he produced a rough meal, unwrapping hard biscuits, opening a can of corned beef and boiling up tea. Mosquitoes kept their distance while the fire smoked, but when it died down and they lay in the hut, the insects swarmed viciously about them. Howard covered himself with his blanket, pulling it over his head, but the whine of mosquitoes still hummed in his ears. His sleep was fitful; his dreams were strange and drowned in a green infinity. Beneath the filthy cloth he was hot and sweaty and the rungs of the bamboo bench pressed uncomfortably into his back. Each time he woke the same wave of panic swept through him. Where was he going, when would he return home? At almost this time the day before, he had been cleaning his saxophone in Cousin Lionel's house.

When at last the next day they came into the guerrilla camp, everyone had just finished eating; no food was left for them. The camp was in a clearing hacked from the encompassing vegetation. A sentry with a machine gun stopped them as they approached. Password, he shouted and Brokentooth shouted back that he did not know the password of the day. After some discussion with a hefty man wearing an Air Raid Precaution helmet who was assisting him, the guard dropped formalities and allowed them to enter the camp.

'Even known people can be spies; we have to be careful, informers are everywhere. The password changes every day,' Brokentooth explained.

The sight of the guard's familiar ARP helmet in such an incongruous place seemed only to emphasise the distortions Howard faced. The letters ARP stamped on the front filled him with nostalgia and memories of Mr Barber and the long-ago first air raid. Before them rattan huts with attap roofs stood about a rough parade ground on which combatants were drilling, a few young women amongst them.

'That's a food-carrying party getting ready to leave to bring back provisions.' Brokentooth pointed out a group assembling beneath a tree. 'We depend upon the carriers for survival. There are about seventy comrades in this camp.'

Brokentooth led the way to a solitary hut at the top of an incline. As they approached, he withdrew a peaked cotton cap from his rucksack and quickly pulled it on. Inside the hut, seated before a rough table Howard was shocked to see Wee Jack, his head bent in concentration over some papers. Howard halted in confusion: it had never occurred to him that Wee Jack would command a guerrilla camp. Brokentooth entered the hut nervously and stood to attention, giving a clenched fist salute.

'*Chinli*,' he said, head erect, peaked cap with its three metal stars pulled smartly forward. Wee Jack stood up and returned the salute before turning to Howard and beckoning him into the hut. He was dressed in a worn olive green uniform, and observed Howard's exhausted bewilderment with amusement.

'Didn't you expect to see me here? So, you've been forced to join us at last.'

At Wee Jack's invitation Howard seated himself on the sleeping bench beside the Commissar's desk. The bench was heaped untidily with papers, boxes of tea, tin mugs, propaganda leaflets, a comb, a box of pencils, a peaked cap and a bayonet. Howard hesitantly cleared a space for himself while at the other end Wee Jack searched for a bottle of Camp coffee that he said was buried beneath the mess. Unscrewing the lid, he poured some of the sticky essence into a dirty tin mug. Then, burrowing again into the mound of belongings, he unearthed a tin of condensed milk in which he punched a hole with an army pocketknife. Adding cold water to the drink, he stirred the liquid with a finger before handing it to Howard. Wee Jack had several suppurating jungle sores on his arms and legs and Howard was in no hurry to take the coffee.

'We don't think too much about hygiene here,' Wee Jack announced dismissively as he mixed himself a mug of the coffee.

'Why have you chosen to join our fight against the Japanese?' he asked, extracting a creased printed form from beneath the untidy pile on the bench. Already, Howard realised, the balance between them had changed. Wee Jack was now Commissar of the camp and he, Howard, was a dispensable refugee dependent upon his largesse.

'I have to fill in this form and you must sign it. We are strict about procedures here. This is a military camp and everything is documented; I represent the Malayan People's Anti-Japanese Army,' Wee Jack told him proudly holding a pencil poised above the sheet of paper, frowning over his spectacles, his unhealthy colouring apparent even in the gloom of the hut. As Howard seemed lost for words, he sighed resignedly.

'We'll just say you want to fight the Japanese because you hate all Imperialists and, after they have been defeated, you will continue to fight until the People's Republic of Malaya is established. In the Republic everyone – Chinese, Malay, Indians and all other minority races – will have equal rights and opportunities.' Wee Jack made a sweeping gesture towards the open entrance of the hut where a flag of the new Republic hung limply on a bamboo pole.

'As soon as it's safe I must return home,' Howard protested.

Wee Jack gave a bark of scornful laughter that turned into a deep, racking cough. After it subsided he spat into a hollowed out coconut shell that stood by his desk. 'You're safe here, remain as long as you wish, but while you are here you must obey camp rules and work like the others. We're all comrades; we allow no differences.'

'You can write that I agree with a fight against the Japanese, because I do. I have not thought beyond that,' Howard conceded begrudgingly, as Wee Jack turned his attention again to the form.

'Then it is time that you began to think,' he replied curtly, not raising his head from the paper. Beyond the hut Howard observed the thick wall of the encroaching jungle and felt his helplessness, the weight of the miles he had trekked to this spot.

There was no option but to adapt to camp life. Howard found himself regretting he had never been a Boy Scout, had never slept in a tent, built a fire or learned to tie knots, for now the life about him depended upon such resourcefulness. He slept in a hut with a dozen other men, allotted a section of the sleeping bench and a portion of shelf for his belongings. Since he had fled in what he stood up in, all he carried were Cynthia's medicine and some food. A ragged towel and a razor for shaving were given to him. Everyone shared the same couple of shaving brushes and bars of soap; teeth were cleaned with the chewed end of a twig. The food was tasteless, a thick gruel of rice and the meat of whatever animal had been caught that day, frog, deer, snake or rat, with tough inedible leaves or grasses thrown in. After a few days Howard shovelled it into his mouth like everyone else, exhausted, disgusted but too hungry to care. Brokentooth stayed near him, offering advice and encouragement; at times he wished the boy would leave him alone but here nobody respected privacy. Privacy was a bourgeois concept that pandered to an individual's ego, Brokentooth said.

Camp routine settled about him. Brokentooth had been allocated the sleeping space next to Howard. All the guerrillas slept fully dressed with weapons on them and spare clothes packed at their side. The Japanese were constantly searching for guerrilla camps and they lived in apprehension of an attack, alert to every crack of a falling branch, every rustle of a passing animal. In the morning a wake-up whistle blew at 5.30 a.m. and within five minutes Howard stumbled out on to the parade ground behind Brokentooth and the other comrades. After exercises, fifteen minutes was allowed for washing and cleaning teeth. He had soon discovered the horror of the latrine, an open pit of excrement seething with maggots over which he must crouch on two narrow planks a foot apart, sometimes in the company of several others; the stench made him retch, to everyone's amusement. Howard knew he was watched, and knew that in the camp they saw him as an outsider, as soft, indulged and decadent, and that they were waiting to deride him, to break him down. The first week or two went quickly as he braced himself and learned their ways, determined to show that, like them, he too could live at subsistence level and not complain. He did not know how long he must stay, but instinctively he knew that if he resisted the experience time would go even more slowly and painfully. The quicker he appeared to fit in, the easier it would be for him; he must adapt to their ways, however difficult that was.

Each morning the flag was raised to a clenched fist salute followed by the singing of 'The Red Flag'. Howard learned the words and sang with everyone else. There was daily training in sabotage techniques and rigorous drilling. He was relieved to relax in the hours given over to manual labour: cutting down trees, repairing huts, hunting large lizards for dinner in the diffused light of the forest. The sun filtered through the thick canopy in a dank green glow; he was told that eventually everyone's skin absorbed the green hue of the jungle. Time was also given to the winnowing of rice, which contained lime to preserve it and innumerable weevils that, like everyone else, Howard learned to consume. When the last whistle blew he took his place on the bamboo shelf to sleep fitfully, lined up head to foot with the other men on the narrow resting place. The discomfort of the knobbly bamboo rungs, the whine and bites of mosquitoes, the snores of his companions and the night sounds of the jungle were a constant distress. The proximity of Brokentooth's feet just above his head, and the head of his neighbour just below his own feet, was something he could not get used to.

Yet, in spite of Wee Jack's disapproval, there were ways in which Howard's presence at the camp was helpful. He had a rudimentary knowledge of first aid, had carried medicines into the camp and also knew how to administer them. He was immediately delegated to help in the sick bay. Already he had learned from Cynthia the ailments of the jungle: malaria, beriberi, scabies and other uncomfortable skin diseases. The sick bay was a long hut with the usual sleeping bench running around its walls. Outside a girl was seated on a log washing her ulcerated legs with Chinese tea; this improvised antiseptic was all that was available. In the hut patients were stretched out on the narrow bench, shivering and groaning, and the putrid stench of unwashed bodies and suppurating jungle lesions closed about him. Swallowing his repugnance, Howard examined everyone and saw that without exception all of them had malaria, besides a variety of other afflictions. At the end of the hut a man lay moaning loudly, and Howard was shocked to see an ugly bullet hole dark with dried blood on his calf. Flies swarmed about the wound and the leg was swollen and blue, and Howard wondered if gangrene had already set in. An image of Mei Lan bending to the wounded man in the hideout filled his mind, and a spasm of sorrow ran through him. He wondered if she was held captive still, and wondered also how long it would be before he lay sick here with malaria, septic ulcers or worse. Before that time came, he promised himself, he would find a way to escape.

Cynthia had packed a supply of permanganate of potash and he made up a solution of this to bathe everyone's sores. A sour-faced woman called Pin, who Howard soon realised knew even less about medicine than he, was the designated nurse. She made it clear by an obstinate refusal to help, that she resented Howard's intrusion into her domain. All the women in the camp had cut off their hair, but Pin still kept a long greasy plait and was always scratching a head full of lice.

'Give quinine injection now,' she told him in broken Malay.

It seemed useless in the circumstances to tell her he had never given an injection before, although he had watched Cynthia many times. Resignedly, he set up a sterilising bath and mixed up the quinine solution and then, with trepidation, set about injecting the patients. Pin, arms folded over her chest, silently watched his fumbling attempts to find a vein. With the lack of fresh fruit and vegetables, many of the camp inmates inevitably suffered from beriberi and scabies and Howard made a note to speak to Wee Jack about this. Beriberi was easily treated by eating rice bran, which could be obtained from any of the villages supplying the guerrillas with rice. It was rolled into marble-sized balls for convenient chewing, and he had made these for Cynthia in the hospital.

'And this will help?' Wee Jack asked in genuine interest when Howard spoke to him later, after reporting on the medical situation.

'There is also a man with a bullet wound. I can do nothing for him,' Howard said, making his responsibilities clear.

'He was shot running from the Japanese,' Jack told him. 'I have heard the Grass Doctor is visiting a nearby village, we will send for him.'

The Grass Doctor came at night with an assistant carrying a lantern and a bundle of roots and leaves wrapped in yellowed newspaper. Water was boiled and towels were found, and Howard waited to see what the *sinseh* would do after he had cleaned the wound with the usual solution of tea. The medicine man gave orders to his assistant to pound the roots to a powder, and chew the leaves to a paste. When the poultice was ready it was applied to the wound and bound up. Howard remembered his own bullet wound, tended so successfully with herbal remedies by Mohammad Abdullah's wife. Once his work was done the Grass Doctor left, giving instructions to Pin about changing the poultice. Howard was amazed to see that within a few days the bullet had surfaced and was easily squeezed from the wound; a few more days and the man was walking about and back into camp routine.

Howard soon realised he had entered a mirror world, where everything was the opposite of what he knew. His education had been in English-medium schools, while most of the combatants in the camp were educated in the Chinese vernacular, if they were educated at all. Their social backgrounds were far from Howard's comfortable upbringing. Here, the Chinese sons of night soil carriers, cane cutters, vegetable sellers and *nipah* palm gatherers had joined to struggle for their rights in a new republic. The deputy captain of the camp had previously been a cleaner of toilets in a big British company. Howard had no trouble with the chasm between his social position and that of the others. He admired their aspirations and was happy to champion them; in their place he knew he would feel the same. Yet, it disturbed him to find he was not accepted for himself, but was despised for his privilege and faced with constant suspicion. As much as he tried to fit in, the label of bourgeoisie was already set upon him.

Soon after he arrived he had managed to send a message to Cynthia and Rose: one of the boys in a group of food carriers had promised to get word through that he was safe. The complete lack of communication and his isolation from the world he knew weighed upon him as much as the deprivations he faced. Every night before he slept his mind went over possible ways to escape. Many villages had suffered at the hands of Japanese soldiers and were sympathetic to the guerrilla fighters. If he could find his way to one of these villages and then to the main road that ran through the narrow valley far below, he could find his way back to Singapore. Each day he gazed up through a dark lattice of trees at the patches of sky far above, listened to animals going about their daily lives and tried to conquer his resistance to yet another camp day. More and more, he realised the extant to which he was watched and distrusted. The world of the camp was a world of suspicion; everyone watched everyone else, to later report and criticise.

Time was set aside each day for these tribunals and confessionals. Individuals gave detailed accounts of their weaknesses and errors and then endured a long, haranguing criticism from their fellow comrades. In the same manner, a group evaluation of the day's work usually followed and Howard was expected to take part. When he could not see what errors he had committed or what weakness he revealed in the communist context, he was doubly harangued until his brain was battered and exhausted and in desperation he said the things they wanted to hear. Educational lectures were another daily part of camp life. After a few weeks, Wee Jack suggested Howard give talks on first aid, nutrition and hygiene and he was glad to oblige, if only to break the boredom and regimentation of camp life. Everyone was required to attend all lectures, and the muscular man in the ARP helmet always pushed his way to the front. The camp's political secretary gave daily indoctrination lectures on Marxist theory, to which Howard was required to listen. Like everyone else he was forbidden to ask questions, and was ordered to memorise the principles of communism. During breaks in camp chores this was the only diversion: study, write, memorise communist ideology and recite the Manifesto.

'Repeat. Repeat,' they urged him.

His brain grew more and more tired.

'*The modern bourgeois society that has sprouted from the ruins of feudal society has not done away with class antagonism but established new conditions of oppression.*'

'Repeat. Repeat.'

The greater the ambition of combatants, the greater the emphasis placed upon dogma. Everyone talked communism, breathed communism and ate communism; knowledge of dogma was valued above courage or a skill, and none of it made sense to Howard. The endless ideological pounding was like the constant shrilling orchestra of jungle crickets from which he was never free.

'Think of yourself as a piece of clay,' Wee Jack said one evening as they sat smoking, observing Howard through narrowed eyes, his face seeming even more angular and emaciated. As he spoke, a bout of coughing seized him. When it had finished he spat into the grass and turned again to Howard.

'You are worthless, your life is useless, but the Party will remould you. We will give you an edge of steel. The criticism is only for your own good, to make you more disciplined, a stronger member of the Party. A good communist has the strength to remake the world, just as the Party has remade him. We remake a person, we remake a country and then we will remake the world.' Wee Jack's words drummed into Howard's head. At first he had recoiled from Wee Jack's ranting, but sometimes now he found himself thinking that what he heard made sense.

'We need only a few months to turn you into a trusted agent of the revolution,' Wee Jack said softly, observing Howard intently, his mouth above his goatish beard bent into a lopsided smile.

Wee Jack established a routine of sitting with him for a cigarette in the evenings, and gradually at this time he began to drop his strutting authority. Howard suspected that for all his propaganda talk, Wee Jack looked forward to his company, to talk of the past and things other than the Manifesto.

'Communism is the only hope for the world,' Wee Jack exclaimed when Howard discreetly probed the reasons for his dedicated fanaticism. Taking the cigarette from his lips Wee Jack leaned forward, his face filled with unexpected agitation.

'Injustice. Everywhere you look, injustice.' Anger spread across his face in a way Howard had not seen before. Gone was the posturing cynicism, the fanatical arrogance, and in its place Howard had the feeling he saw for the first time Wee Jack's real emotions.

'You talk about racial inequality, but you have always had food, education, medicine, a home when you needed it. You don't know about real injustice; you don't know what it's like to live with one meal in two days, to live in a few rooms with fifty other people, sleeping in shifts just to fit into the place, watching your mother die, your father die, your brothers die, your sisters sold into prostitution. You don't know about real injustice. The Party will remake the world, raise up the workers, put an end to your bourgeois concepts, everything judged on a full stomach and a soft bed to sleep in.' Saliva collected at the corner of Wee Jack's mouth as the words spilled from his lips, one falling over another under the pressure of his feelings. Then, as quickly as he had dropped his cover he pulled it back into place, inhaling deeply on his cigarette, his eyes assuming their usual cool and impenetrable authority. Howard drew a breath and wondered what caused such a copious leak of passion, but whatever it was, it had gone. Wee Jack leaned back against a tree and assessed the effect of his words upon Howard, the usual sneer locked again to his face.

On other nights when they sat together, Howard heard further unexpected revelations. For the first time he learned, incredulously, that communist guerrillas were now working with their former enemies, the British, in a counter-offensive against their common enemy, the Japanese.

'I do not believe it,' Howard told Wee Jack. The man laughed so hard his racking, tubercular cough seized upon him.

'The British themselves sent me to India for a crash course of training in a commando camp in Poona. We were taught everything needed for guerrilla warfare,' Wee Jack spluttered when he could speak again, enjoying the amazement on Howard's face before he continued.

'The British can't mount a counter-offensive against the Japanese without the Malayan People's Anti-Japanese Army. They need us; we have a network of camps throughout the jungle. They give us training:

we provide them with manpower. The camp in Poona was an Indian army camp and Englishmen trained us. Some of those same Englishmen are now here in the jungle organising resistance and guerilla activities, and we are in touch with them,' Wee Jack boasted. Howard could not tell if the man lied or told the truth; it all sounded preposterous.

'How did you get to India after Singapore fell and how did you get back here again?' Howard asked, suspicious of such a mercurial change of loyalties.

'By submarine; British submarines come secretly into Japanese-controlled waters and bring in supplies and weapons for the commandos,' Wee Jack revealed.

'You were working against the Imperialists before the war started, now you are working *with* them?' Howard puzzled. The contradiction appeared not to bother Wee Jack.

'It is all just a means to an end. At the moment we have a common enemy and are mutually agreed we must get the Japanese out of Malaya. Once we do that, we will be back to working against the Imperialists and they will be back to trying to stamp us out,' Wee Jack gave another derisive bark of laughter as Howard shook his head in disbelief.

'I want to return home. If one of the food-carrying groups can get me to the road, I'll make my way back from there,' Howard said. Encouraged by Wee Jack's growing communication, he judged this might be the right moment to speak. The man swallowed his hilarity immediately and Howard saw the depth of his mistake.

'What do you mean, return home? Do you think you are here on holiday? You are one of us now; there's no going back.' Wee Jack stubbed out his cigarette, grinding it angrily into the ground.

Howard drew back. Once again despair spread through him as he realised to what degree in this impenetrable jungle he was a prisoner, held as securely as a fly in a spider's web. Whether he liked it or not, he was now part of the communist network. He turned away under Wee Jack's hard, penetrating gaze and fell silent.

The monotony of camp life closed about him and he began to lose track of time. Soon it was difficult to know how long he had been there – two weeks, four weeks or ten. Time was meaningless here, and its ebb and flow through the events of his life unfathomable.

In the end he gave up trying to count the days and surrendered himself to the dull rhythm. Far away in another world men were fighting to gain dominions and capture souls; nothing made sense any more.

26

IN APRIL MR SHINOZAKI was transferred, along with Raj, from MAD, the Military Administration Department to CAD, the City Administration Department. It was a relief to escape the high-handedness of Colonel Watanabe. The Colonel had taken over the running of the Overseas Chinese Association from Mr Shinozaki. He was an ambitious man intent on collecting the $50 million donation demanded of the Chinese community. To do this he had released many people from prison to arrange their finances, but he did not release Mei Lan.

Mayor Odate welcomed Shinozaki to his new office in City Hall overlooking the Padang. Shinozaki as Chief Officer of Education at once focused his attention on reopening schools. Welfare and liaison were also part of his work and he continued to issue Good Citizen passes and trace people disappeared by the *kempetai*. Shinozaki gladly left his team of spies at MAD; those working with him at CAD he regarded as genuine helpers without the same level of ulterior motive.

He did not, however, find himself entirely free of Colonel Watanabe's influence. There were brothels enough in Singapore but no high-class geisha house where top army staff could hold a party. Colonel Watanabe was a man of big appetites who enjoyed carousing with his friends. He liked the idea of such an establishment, which was to be housed in the Cricket Club overlooking the Padang, opposite City Hall. Porcelain, chopsticks, *tatami* mats, Japanese rice, soy sauce and *miso* paste were all quickly imported from Japan for Colonel Watanabe's new venture.

The high-pitched singing of geisha, the twang of *samisen* and the answering calls of drunken officers in the Cricket Club across the road were constantly heard in the offices of City Hall. This noise, which started early in the day, disturbed not only Mr Shinozaki but also Mayor Odate. The dignity of civilian administrators in the City Department was diminished by the goings-on across the road, the

Mayor fumed, affronted. Soon, he made the situation known to higher authorities and eventually the Cricket Club geisha house was closed.

In his new position Shinozaki felt free to work discreetly for Mei Lan's release. Already, the *kempetai* had held her for months. 'It may still take time but I have not forgotten her,' he told Raj with a smile one morning.

'It means nothing to me,' Raj replied, afraid to show any interest in a woman suspected of having communist connections.

'Her Eurasian boyfriend seems to have disappeared. It appears he had a radio and the penalty for this, as you know, is death,' Shinozaki added.

Much of Shinozaki's time was taken up by the reopening of schools. The Military Administration had ordered the Japanese language to be taught to every child in Singapore. This was not an easy order; there were no Japanese-language textbooks and also a shortage of school buildings as so many had been requisitioned by the military for their own purposes. Shinozaki employed an able Eurasian as Inspector of Schools and with this man Raj was busy about town, collecting chairs and desks, chalks and notebooks and the occasional piano to rebuild the looted schools. Although teachers were traced and, if still alive, persuaded to return to work, there were still no Japanese-language textbooks. Mr Shinozaki took it upon himself to personally write out lessons that were then printed in volume and distributed to all the schools.

Mr Shinozaki's department was a large one with many local staff. Raj found it easy to slip away to attend to his own work. The war had catapulted him aggressively into the black market business. People constantly needed things Raj could acquire through his Japanese contacts. He had been given licences to trade in many of the commodities he had previously supplied to Japanese ships. Loot from the first chaotic days of the occupation was also now reappearing for sale on the black market. Much of this was from abandoned European homes: furniture, lace dresses, silk cushions, refrigerators, violins, watches, sewing baskets and ice-cream makers. Raj was able to buy sought-after items and sell them advantageously, often to the Japanese themselves. There was now a continuous influx of civilian Japanese arriving from Japan to populate the new colony of Syonan. Licences to trade were given first to these new immigrants, before distribution to local people.

Arriving at City Hall one morning, Raj found Shinozaki in a heat of excitement. 'General Yamashita has ordered that for the Emperor's Birthday celebration, all Syonan schoolchildren must gather on the Padang to sing '*Aikoku Koshin Kyoku*' and then they must sing '*Kimigayo*', the Japanese National Anthem. The Emperor's Birthday is on 29 April, ten days away and schools are only just now reopening. We have no time to prepare.'

But prepare he did, personally overseeing the printing and distribution of the musical scores, just as he had the school textbooks. When, on the Emperor's Birthday General Yamashita, Tiger of Malaya, portly, chubby cheeked and gruff of voice stood before City Hall, the foreign children's unfailing rendering of Japanese songs brought tears to the strong man's eyes.

'Just like Japanese children,' he said, blinking hard to suppress emotion.

When she could free herself from Ancient Mistress's service, Ah Siew spent her time cleaning Mei Lan's room. She ironed again the clothes she had carefully ironed just a few days before, rearranged underwear in drawers and books upon shelves and re-polished the silver photo frames, staring long and hard at the photo of the four-year-old Mei Lan with her arms around her mother. Each day she spoke to the photo of First Mistress who Mei Lan so much resembled and, eyes shut, tears streaming down her face, beseeched her to bring Mei Lan home. Every day she stood at the window that looked out towards Lim Villa and remembered the long corridors she had traipsed to Ancient Mistress's rooms, Mei Lan tightly clasping her hand. Whenever she saw Mei Lan in her mind, she saw her as a child. Ah Siew could not eat and each night was spent battling fiendish thoughts that only the daylight put behind her.

Things had deteriorated between Leila and Krishna. Sometimes they barely spoke for days. When they did, they argued.

'They say not all Indians are wanting to join the Indian National Army but are forced into it by the Japanese out of fear,' Leila told Krishna, daring his disapproval as he handed her the rough notes of his latest lecture to copy out.

'I have joined because soon with Japanese help, we will liberate

India,' Krishna answered, pursing his lips, as if even to reply was a favour to her. '*Chalo Delhi*.' This was how it was now between them. Anger simmered within them both and Leila knew it was her fault; her body refused to accept his child, rejecting it roughly each time, as if to deliberately slight him.

In the few years of their marriage he had taught her to read and write and now trusted her with drafts of his Indian National Army lectures. Leila was glad to copy them out, still marvelling at her new-found literacy, carefully forming each letter with her pen. Every new word she looked up in a dictionary Raj had given her, writing it down and learning it. Now that she could read, she entered as if by magic worlds that continually astounded her and journeyed through experiences that left her expanded. Although Krishna took credit for her learning, what this gift had done to the deepest part of his wife he dismissed. All he was interested in, apart from the Indian National Army, was that she should bear him a son.

Since Krishna had joined the INA his views had sharpened fanatically. There was now a growing split between himself and Raj on matters of ideology. Like his brother-in-law, Raj too had joined the INA after the Japanese arrived, but his position with Shinozaki left him no time for soldiering duties, while Krishna had become deeply involved. Krishna now lived almost permanently at the INA Officers' Training School at Newton Circus where he was an instructor. His expertise was not in the tough areas of drilling and guns but in the arena of morale. He gave propaganda lectures, lessons in Indian history, map reading and more, extending his former role in the Indian Youth League.

Sitting on a low *charpoy*, Leila hung her head, her knees drawn up under her chin. She looked no more than a bundle of rags, Krishna thought, observing her impatiently. He had not lived at home properly for weeks and knew he was neglecting Leila at a difficult time; she had suffered yet another miscarriage. In a corner near the bed was the wooden crib that still waited for their child. Just the sight of it made Krishna angry for it seemed to encapsulate everything that was wrong with their life. If there had been a baby, Leila would be busy and happy and he would not always feel guilty. A woman needed a baby to be fulfilled, and if she could not make one she must blame only herself, he thought angrily. He leaned forward, grasping Leila's arm roughly.

'Today is an important day. Subhas Chandra Bose is in Singapore. He has come all the way from Germany on a submarine. He is addressing people on the Padang. General Tojo, who is visiting Singapore from Japan and who seems now even more powerful than the Japanese Emperor, will also be there.' Krishna's eyes shone as he spoke of Subhas Chandra Bose who now carried the title of *Netaji*, Great Leader. He had heard the man speak the day before at the Cathay Building. Flags and bunting and a huge arch had been erected to welcome *Netaji*. Thousands had packed the area.

'*Netaji* has accepted the presidency of the Indian National Army.' Krishna shook his wife again, wanting her to share these great moments.

Leila stared up at Krishna. In his INA uniform he appeared a different person. He was no longer the husband she knew in his worn sandals and *dhoti*, but a fanatical uniformed stranger. She turned and curled up on the bed, her back towards him, her eyes shut, wondering even as she turned away how she had the courage to so stubbornly disobey her husband.

'You will come with me,' he ordered harshly, furious that she should reject him. 'I want you to see him. It will do you good to get out,' he insisted, speaking more kindly.

They began the walk to Beach Road and the Padang where Subhas Chandra Bose was to speak. Leila was surprised to see that from everywhere Indian people were streaming in the same direction. When they finally reached the Padang they found the ground already packed, people squashed tightly together. On the steps of City Hall a raised platform had been erected, decorated in red and white bunting. Krishna pushed his way to where Raj, who had arrived earlier, waited in a VIP enclosure with a good view of proceedings. Leaving Leila with her brother, he marched off to join his regiment.

'It is like God himself has arrived,' Raj said. As he talked he smiled and nodded distractedly, acknowledging the greetings of passing people. He was now a person of some weight because of his Japanese connections. Leila stared over her shoulder at the waiting crowd that stretched behind her in a dense blur of faces. The INA troops, guns to their shoulders, chins thrust proudly to the sky, stood waiting for their leader. She searched for Krishna but could not see him in the great pool of khaki uniforms.

An open car flying pennants of Japan and the new Free India drew up to deposit its passengers before the dais. From one side a small man with a short moustache climbed out and from the other the powerfully built Bengali.

'That is General Tojo with *Netaji*,' Raj shouted to Leila above the cheering that had erupted on the arrival of Subhas Chandra Bose.

As the two men made their way on to the decorated dais the jubilation rose to a thunderous pitch. Men stood up and shouted; women began screaming, *Netaji! Netaji!* The word reverberated around the Padang.

The Japanese premier came forward to speak through an interpreter. He reminded Leila of a picture she had seen of the German leader, Hitler, except for his Japanese eyes. The interpreter spoke in a thick accent and his words were incomprehensible to Leila, who could understand nothing of what was said but kept her eyes upon *Netaji*. '... *India's emancipation ... the peoples of Greater East Asia will inevitably bring ... the glorious day of independence and prosperity to India.*' As the Japanese premier sat down, Subhas Chandra Bose stepped briskly forward to another eruption of cheering.

He was thickset, straight backed, balding and bespectacled, with the full-throated voice of the orator. His dark skin appeared as soft as chamois leather; his high polished boots caught the light. As he reached up to adjust the microphone Leila felt a dull leap of energy within her; she was near enough to see the determined flash of his eyes. She sat forward as he began to speak, his smooth voice rolling effortlessly to her.

'... *This must be a truly revolutionary army ... I am appealing to all the civilian youths to come forward to join the army. I am appealing also to women ... half the population of our country is women ... women ...*'

Afterwards, she could not clearly recall his features or the things he said. There was only the burning shower of him falling upon her.

'... *women must also be prepared to fight for their freedom, to fight for independence ... along with independence they will get their own emancipation ... Give me your blood and I will give you freedom.*'

Even before he finished speaking women rushed forward, breaking through the barriers, some with babies in their arms shouting, '*We will fight; we will fight for the freedom of India!*' Leila ran with them to where he stood looking down upon them with a proud smile, arms outstretched as if he would embrace them. She wanted to touch him, to tell him she would do whatever he bid. Instead, Japanese soldiers were suddenly holding them back with bayonets.

Give me your blood and I will give you freedom. His words flowed into her flesh.

She was not the only one who felt the intensity. He asked for the support of women and they came, giving jewellery to fund his cause, pushing forward sons and husbands to swell his army. Within days a women's regiment was founded, named after a legendary national heroine who rode into battle against the British army in 1857. Women of every age came forward to join the Rani of Jhansi regiment – even illiterate women from the rubber plantations; training camps were established, uniforms designed and sewn, new guns acquired for the women from the Japanese.

'I want to join too,' Leila told her husband.

Her eyes shone with the thought of it. She would train with the other women in the camp beside Krishna, she would be given a uniform and a gun. Soon, she would shoot like a man. Krishna stared at her askance and laughed nervously at her enthusiasm. Looking down into her face, he realised with a shock that the emotions he saw there were not for him.

In Mei Lan's cell the electric lights glared down twenty-four hours a day and even with an arm across her eyes, she could only sleep for minutes before waking with a start of fear, heart pounding sickeningly. The wall of the cell facing into the corridor was meshed like a cage with heavy wooden bars, and had a small opening for passing food through in one corner; guards patrolled the corridor beyond. Twice a day a scant bowl of rice with a scrap of meat or vegetable, and a bucket of tea with one filthy mug to be shared by them all, was delivered. To leave the cell for interrogation prisoners crawled through a knee-high door. Most of the area was taken up with a wooden sleeping platform and it was here they were ordered to squat, silent and uncommunicative, unmoving all day. Rats scuttled in and out of the cell; large spiders and cockroaches stalked about. Many of the inmates had been arrested unexpectedly in the early hours of the morning and some were still in pyjamas. At night the guards shouted 'Sleep!' and they lay down crushed together under the endless glare.

From the cracks of the wooden sleeping platform large ticks emerged to fasten upon them, bloating with their blood. They were ten, sometimes twelve in the cell and Mei Lan was the only woman. Most of the men were Chinese, one was Eurasian and another an elderly Englishman. At the back of the cell was a filthy latrine, encrusted with deposits of dried excrement growing a slippery carpet of moss; sometimes it clogged and overflowed. When she wanted to use the latrine the men turned their backs, making a wall before her and hiding her from the guards. The water that flowed into the latrine from a high faucet must also be used for drinking and washing. At first she waited for the mouthful of tea that was served with each meal, but eventually she learned to drink from the vile outlet, as did everyone else.

In the cell, and the other cells in the corridor, people were always coming and going, dragged out through the tiny door and later thrust back through it in varying states of collapse and injury, marks of torture and beating evident upon their bodies. Sometimes they were gone for hours; screams could be heard echoing through the building. Everyone waited, knowing their turn must come. The summons was arbitrary and unpredictable yet mechanically and inhumanly regular. The cell was imbued with the smell of this fear, rank with the leaking bowels of dysentery and the metallic effluvium of blood. At first there had been another young girl who, like Mei Lan, was said to be a communist. She came back almost unscathed from interrogations and within two days was gone.

'Make up names, say anything,' she advised. This Mei Lan would not do; the only names she could give were those of Howard and Cynthia.

'Give us the names of your communist friends.' The question was repeated endlessly.

'I know nothing,' she answered and was slapped about for such upstart determination. Captain Nakamura stood in the background at these initial sessions held in a bare, concrete-floored room with barred windows, a table and a chair and a large hook in the middle of the ceiling. Behind the roars and iron-like hands of her tormentors, Nakamura stood impassively, arms crossed, booted legs apart, watching silently. A short square man with a thick neck, protruding eyes and rough umber skin, his bandy legs forced him to walk with the roll of a drunken man.

They began to come for her every day. She was made to kneel on rough logs, unmoving for hours at a time, a block of wood between her legs to keep her knees apart. Her legs lost all feeling, pain burned through her body. Every time she toppled over she was viciously hit. Then came the beatings with a long bamboo cane, usually on those soft parts of the torso where there would be bruising but no internal injury – the calves, the buttocks, thighs, inner arms. She screamed for them to stop. Usually, there were two of them but more and more the one in charge was Nakamura. From silent detachment, he now stepped forward as her chief tormentor. He bent over her and she caught the rancid odour of him, saw his wide teeth, yellow like those of an old horse.

'Tell us the names of the communists you help. Where is their hideout, where is their camp? How many men are there? What are their names? Tell us and everything can stop in a moment.' Nakamura flexed the cane, stroking it tenderly, bending it between his fingers.

She was stripped, and the shame of her nakedness preoccupied her even when the beating began. Her hands were tied and the rope slung over the ceiling hook. Nakamura brought the cane down again and again, lashing into her flesh, and the agony of it ripped her apart. Soon she was ready to say any name, say anything, Cynthia's name, Howard's name; she held them back by screaming. Screaming brought relief, stopped the names from falling out of her. Tears streamed down her face, her nose ran, she felt her bladder open and the warmth of urine spill down her legs. Still Nakamura went on, stopping now and then to grip her by the hair and shout into her face. *Tell us.* When she collapsed in a faint they threw water on her face and started their work again.

'This is nothing,' Nakamura said when he had done with her. She was dragged into an adjoining room where the water treatments took place. He showed her the tap with the hose that would be pushed down her throat to bloat her innards before they jumped on her belly. Water ran over the floor from the leaking tap; blood stained a corner near the wall.

'Two or three treatments and your stomach will burst,' Nakamura told her.

Her body was broken; her flesh became a bloody pulp. She heard Nakamura clear his throat, saw him flex his fingers, cracking his joints for relief. She wanted to wipe her nose and the tears on her face; the discomfort of having no handkerchief filtered through as a further torture before blackness swept mercifully through her.

A middle-aged Eurasian man arrived in the cell but did not last a week. Each day he was taken away for hours, to be returned dazed and bloody and semi-conscious. The little medical knowledge she had was useless; all she could do was to hold a filthy wet rag to his brow, offer him words of comfort. When he was unable to walk, he was taken away on a rattan chair and later tipped back through the door like a lump of carrion. When the man died in the night his body was left in the hot, airless cell until the end of the following afternoon, when the stench of the corpse was unbearable even to the patrolling guards. By the time they came to remove him, rigor mortis had set in and to pull him through the tiny cell door his arms must both be broken.

She lost count of the days, and lay staring up at the small barred window near the ceiling. A patch of sky, and a branch of green leaves glowed luminously, like a light beyond the cell. At night she sometimes saw the moon through this keyhole, gliding translucent across the dark sky and knew the beauty of the world she had left. Once she heard a golden oriole sing, saw the brief flash of its molten wing. She struggled in an ocean of torment and terror, no sight of shore to guide her. In this place of nightmare she remembered the phoenix, its strong wings, its great beak, its fabulous tail, its undying resolve across time. Then, in the blackness of the cell, the moon through the window was but the luminous eye of the phoenix. Strange hallucinations carried her up until she floated freely between life and death and knew that whichever claimed her in the end was but a guardian of the same essence. Then, as one breath ran out of her and another filled her, she knew that life and death were not opposite forces but different sides of a single thought; death gave birth to life.

There was no day; there was no night. There was no past or future. She lived only in the present. The lamps glared down and even if the tiny window with its blaze of sun or dark moon sky showed her the passing of days, all that mattered was that one moment she stood poised upon, compressed by fear and pain: no yesterday, no tomorrow. No comb, no toothbrush; she rubbed her teeth with a finger, straightened her hair with her hands and then gave up as it knotted with sweat and filth; her clothes hung upon her, rank and torn, she stank of blood and pus and urine. Inside her and outside, Nakamura invaded her, lived in the deepest corner of her being, in unspeakable intimacy. She had become his object and he called for her now each day. The beatings had ceased, he was the inflictor now of a new agony. She knew the vile scent of his breath, every pore and pit on his face, the spittle on his rubbery lips, the feel of his hands and his body upon her. Dreams of the man possessed her even if she did not sleep. There was no space now between her thoughts and the looming shadow of Nakamura; he had ripped the skin of her mind away.

Then, one morning, she was released. The guards pulled her out of the cell and she shrank from them, paralysed by the sick terror of what must wait for her that day. Instead, they took her to an office on the ground floor and returned to her a purse of coins, a hand-kerchief and the watch she had worn the night of her arrest. An officer came to see her to explain the conditions of her release. The donation of $50 million to be made to the Imperial Army by the Chinese community was slowly being collected. A sum based on her grandfather's estimated wealth must be produced by her on his behalf. The figure quoted made her gasp. They left her to find her way home. The sun was hot and unreal, the world a raucous cacophony of unbearable colour and sound. It was an effort just to lift an arm to stop a rickshaw and, the words rusty now in her mouth, she gave the directions that would take her back to Little Sparrow's house. She had been away for nearly three months.

Even in his tormented dreams Wilfred seemed to be digging, or hacking his way through virgin jungle. For part of its excavation the railway ran alongside the river, Kwei Noi, and the camps with their POW labourers were on the muddy riverbank, camps were strung out through virgin jungle below the craggy granite mountain peaks. Each camp was responsible for completing its own stretch of railway that would later be linked to the others so that it would stretch eventually from Thailand to Burma, carrying troops and goods across the Japanese Empire. Here, deep cuttings must be hacked out with crude tools and the rock dynamited; often the falling debris killed men. Wilfred lay in the hut too sick to move yet knew they would come for him. The Japanese took no notice of illness; those shaking with malaria were beaten for slacking. The shivering took hold of him again, knocking his bones and teeth together, splintering through him in an unbearable ache, splitting his head apart. Consumed by the shaking and pain he did not hear the guards enter the hut. They set about him with bamboo canes so that, standing, collapsing and standing again, he was prodded like an animal out of the hut to join the waiting work gang.

They called this camp Wampo after a village some distance away, and there were almost two thousand of them here, mostly Australian and British POWs. From Singapore they had been transported to the place like cattle, in metal goods carriages that heated to boiling point under the glare of the sun. Against orders they kept the sliding door open, not only for air but also so that those with dysentery could relieve themselves by sticking their backsides out of the carriage while their arms and legs were held. No water, no food. Then the march to the transit camp, twenty miles a day with constant savage punishment for supposed insubordination. When they finally reached Wampo many of the men were already dead, left on the roadside for scavenger dogs.

Wilfred remembered the internment kit he had packed with Cynthia, the smart jacket and polished shoes and sets of underwear, and wondered at the innocence of that far off time. At Wampo everyone had been forced in the end to cut up their shirts and trousers and make Japanese style loincloths, *fundoshi*, for comfort and because the steaming heat and the acidity of sweat quickly rotted clothes or produced raw rashes that rubbed painfully under shirt seams on their undernourished, overworked bodies. Sweating also caused loss of salt that brought on agonising muscular cramps. Everyone without exception was blotched all over with septic sores. Everyone without exception had malaria.

When they arrived they were ordered to build themselves bamboo huts. Scorpions were found, fourteen inches from pinchers to tail. Hastily dug latrines with no roof quickly filled up and overflowed with the monsoon rain. A man had coughed his dentures into a latrine pit and when they were retrieved he boiled them for hours in his tin tea mug. As ever, beatings and other punishments were freely meted out. Wilfred did not know how long he had been at work on the railway: time was meaningless, daylight and darkness and exhaustion was all anyone ever registered.

The Wampo work site was below a high tree-covered ridge. All day was spent shovelling earth from the digging pits, carrying it on rice sacks stretched across bamboo poles up the embankment to where it must be dumped, then levelled. They must bring supplies up to this site on their backs, climbing the steep incline on their wasted legs. If they put the loads down to rest they were too heavy to lift on to their shoulders again. As he trudged uphill holding one end of the heavy stretcher, Wilfred thought of those other stretchers with wounded soldiers that he had carried into the General Hospital to Cynthia. He remembered her face on the pillow beside him, the scented silk of her hair. He wondered if he would be able to stay alive for however long was needed to survive this hell. Men were flogged to death, worked to death, starved to death and, if they still survived, disease waited to do its worst. Death swatted men like flies each day.

27

As the Occupation proceeded, the war began to turn against the Japanese. Oceans were heavily mined and bombed by the Allies, and supplies coming by sea to Singapore often failed to arrive. Food became so scarce that the military authorities began to think of ways to dispatch large numbers of people. A decision was made to somehow reduce the population of the island. This was a new worry for Mr Shinozaki. A similar plan had been implemented by the Japanese military government in Hong Kong; there, it was rumoured, people had been loaded on to boats that were sunk far out at sea.

'We cannot let something like that happen here,' Shinozaki confided to Raj one morning, handing him some documents to take to the Mayor's office on the floor below. Shinozaki's appearance was dishevelled by anxiety. The small room was smoky and a growing pile of cigarette stubs accumulated in the ashtray as he wrestled with the population problem. When Raj returned after ten minutes, Shinozaki's expression was miraculously changed. Greeting Raj enthusiastically, he displayed a face now creased in smiles.

'I know exactly what we must do.' Shinozaki said excitedly, pointing to a notepad on which he had been scribbling hard. The cigarette in his mouth drooped a long string of ash and his eyes were bright.

'When I was in Changi I read a book from the prison library about an Italian settlement in the Libyan desert. Apparently, Italy had a similar problem to us. They sent specialists to Libya to dig wells and build houses. When everything was ready, five huge ships transported ten thousand settlers from Naples. This is what *we* must do. We must clear the jungle, establish settlements on the peninsula and invite people from Syonan to go there.' Shinozaki's voice rose to a feverish pitch.

One of the reasons Shinozaki could dream this dream was because so many people in the Military Administration had moved on to other conquered Japanese colonies. The occupation of Singapore was now, for the larger part, steered by minds that were other than military. Mr Odake, who had first recruited Shinozaki to the Mayor's office, had returned to Japan and the new Mayor, Mr Naito, had been a university professor in Tokyo before the war. He was all for Shinozaki's idea.

'You say they will grow their own food and be entirely self-supporting? How many people do you want ordered there?' Mayor Naito enquired.

'Oh, we cannot force them,' Shinozaki hastily replied, a faraway look in his eye. 'Instead, we must give them a dream.'

Mr Shinozaki went straight to Dr Lim Boon Keng, the white-bearded elder of the Chinese community that Shinozaki called Papa, and who had helped him run the Chinese Overseas Association before Colonel Watanabe stepped in. 'It will be a Chinese settlement, run by Chinese people for Chinese people. Until the time that you are self-supporting I guarantee to send you rice. No Japanese laws or regulations will govern the settlement, and you will be safe from the reach of the *kempetai*,' Shinozaki promised the old man.

Shinozaki sent inspectors upcountry to study the soil of different Malayan states, and at last a site was chosen beside the Endau River in Johore. Two hundred young woodcutters set to work and Mr Shinozaki himself went into the jungle to direct operations, sometimes forced to find his way through the rainforest with no more than a compass.

As September 1943 approached, Shin Syonan as it was called, was finally ready for settlers. Advertisements were posted and applications quickly came in. Convoys of lorries carrying settlers began rolling back and forth between Syonan and Shin Syonan every two days. Even though they had no previous experience in farming, even though there were as yet no proper roads and rain caused mud to run in rivers, even though as city people they must now become villagers and the lawyer must bend to the paddy, none of the settlers complained. Pumpkin, cucumber, tomato and maize were all eventually proudly displayed to Mr Shinozaki. He was happy to explain to anyone who would listen the reason for such success.

'Even though their life is so hard, they can stand it because they have freedom.'

Howard could not heal the festering jungle sores on his legs. His wrists and ankles were puffy and itched; he thought he must have scurvy or beriberi, and worried which it might be. The quinine he had brought into the camp was finished and now he too had malaria and suffered the same violent shivering cycles as everyone else. When he was not ill, he was anxious and depressed. He had lost weight and lost count of how long he had been in the camp. Months had passed; the year had changed again, and still the war went on. The radio had broken down and they were waiting for spare parts; he had heard no news for weeks.

With several other men in the camp, he was digging a new latrine pit to replace the present overflowing cesspool, and had taken up a lone position at the far end of the growing hole. As much as he could, he tried nowadays to keep to himself, putting up a silent wall before the others in the camp. Wherever he turned the comrades were about him, he slept with them, ate with them, shat with them, washed with them, sang with them, worked with them, exercised with them; he was never left alone. He remembered the crumbling hut near Lionel's house where he had taken Mei Lan, where he had spent so many hours by himself and the exquisite luxury of that privacy. Now, as he worked, thrusting the spade into the mulch of soil, throwing each shovelful over his shoulder, he knew that under their breath they spoke about him, watching him as always.

'If you dig alone the pit will be uneven and the shit will touch our backsides at your end,' one of the diggers shouted and everyone laughed.

Howard ignored them, put his foot on the spade and pressed down hard; sometimes he felt he was going crazy. Morning to night they all lived by a regiment of rules, like a class of schoolchildren with Wee Jack their teacher, strutting around, aloof in his authority, gun at the ready. The green wall of the jungle, always about them, was no longer a protective fortification but closed in about Howard like a prison. Each night he fantasised about escape. He saw his return to Lionel's house, the open arms of his mother, Mei Lan's body wrapped around him, the crash of the waves on the beach. Mei Lan. She was now part of a distant dream. In the beginning it had been a constant torment not to know if she had escaped; he had lived with half his mind beside her. Now, so much time had passed, and he had submitted so completely to the rhythm of the camp, as monotonous as the chanted sacraments of the Manifesto, that he seemed to float in limbo without connection to himself. His thoughts, his opinions, his ideas, his values and ideals, all had been brutally shredded. Now he was at war, like everyone else in the camp, with that one implacable enemy, the capitalist and imperialist world. He could no longer clearly remember his previous ideas and when he did they appeared like dry, shrivelled leaves before the fresh, rabid sprouts of doctrine that overwhelmed him. In fleeting moments he had the feeling he was no more than a figment of his own imagination.

He was helping Brokentooth and the boy in the ARP helmet to stoke a fire one evening. Nearby, the two cooks were washing pots after dinner in the stream that ran through the camp. Someone was singing a propaganda song. Comrades with ulcerated legs were as ever bathing their limbs with Chinese tea. The men were relaxed at this last hour of the day; guns had been laid aside and cigarettes lit.

A fresh piece of wood was thrown on to the fire and as it flared up a shot rang out. Everyone jumped up in panic and reached for their guns. Howard waited, holding his rifle at the ready, heart pounding, eyes upon Wee Jack. For a moment Wee Jack hesitated, thinking the shot a possible misfire in the camp, for the Japanese rarely attacked at night. Beside Howard, the cooks hurriedly packed up their pots in case they must suddenly run. For a moment everyone stood frozen, waiting for a signal from Wee Jack. Then more shots sprayed into the clearing and panic whipped through the camp. Everyone scattered, combatants streaming from the barracks, the bathhouse and the latrine hut and running for cover into the jungle. Bullets whistled about, hitting the trees.

In the clearing the fire roared up, illuminating fleeing figures and several bodies sprawled on the parade ground. Howard looked back once and saw Pin, the sick bay nurse, drop to the ground as a bullet hit her. He ran with the others, Brokentooth beside him, crashing blindly through the dark wall of vegetation, falling, scrambling up, ripping aside vines and foliage. Behind them the rattle of pots and the knock of metal ladles was heard as the cooks hurried along, cauldrons swinging upon bamboo carrying poles. He could not tell how long they ran as panic propelled them forward.

Wee Jack led them deeper into the jungle until they could no longer hear firing. To Howard every direction appeared dark and equally impenetrable, but they seemed to be on paths that everyone knew. A full moon could be seen through wide gaps in the canopy as they climbed upwards. At last they emerged from the dense forest to find themselves beside a rocky hill face honeycombed with caves. There was the sound of voices and Howard saw a group of men he recognised who had recently visited the camp. They had been sent to guard a cache of weapons and ammunition hidden in one of the caves. The men had pitched a camp overlooking a grove of *nipah* palms and were preparing to settle for the night, cooking their dinner over a fire, a half-roasted monkey skewered on a spit.

'We are safe here,' Wee Jack told Howard, breathing hard. Sinking down beside the fire he began a long spasm of coughing.

They were brought water and later a fermented drink that set the blood humming in Howard's head. As the alcohol flowed through him, strength returned to his limbs. The smell of roasting monkey made him realise how hungry he was. In a bubbling cauldron of rice gruel he saw the small bulbous heads of frogs. He was now used to eating a wide variety of meat. Snake was the most usual, with a taste between chicken and lobster. There were also the plentiful monitor lizards and their tasty eggs, monkey, wild pig, jungle fowl and mouse deer. Without the spoils of hunting their diet was no more than rice, salt fish and tough edible leaves.

They slept on the dusty floor of a cave. There was a storm in the night and rain curtained the entrance beneath an overhanging crag, running into the cavern and wetting the ground. Lightning broke open the darkness and thunder crashed, vibrating through the rock. From time to time Wee Jack coughed and turned and Howard wondered at the determination that drove these men to a life of such intense deprivation. For all their ideological spouting, each man in the end stood alone upon his own personal battleground, just as Howard did. How had he arrived here, where would it end? His life lay before him obscured by uncertainty and he could see nothing of what it would be or how long he must endure this incarceration. The thunder was distant now, even as lightning flashed again. He could not stop the sobs that rose within him as he turned upon the damp ground, his head pressed into the bundle of rank-smelling clothes that had been given him as a pillow. Deep within him, smooth as a pebble, there still lay the hope of escape like something familiar recognised obliquely through a thick fog. He must believe that within the chaos was a larger plan that would finally reveal its purpose. He was shocked to discover this stubborn residue of his former self had not yet been beaten out of him. In the damp cave, as he listened to the sound of the lessening rain, he knew suddenly that he must protect this precious remnant of self, and that to survive he must keep it secret, hidden away.

It was necessary after the attack to set up a new camp straight away. It must be far enough from the last camp, yet near enough to one of the safe *kampong* from which they received supplies. Although many villages had suffered Japanese brutalities and shared the guerrillas' sentiments, and were prepared to secretly help them, it was a dangerous business as informers were everywhere.

'Someone must have informed on us. The Japanese pay the villages well for information. Locals are always snooping around in the jungle, looking for our camps. If we catch them, we kill them,' Wee Jack said savagely.

A location was soon found near a stream, and the *nipah* palms needed for thatching the huts were cut. Howard helped with building the new camp, raising frameworks of raw green bamboo, securing attap roofs and walls. It was back-breaking work, but at last it was done, and camp routine settled about them again.

Howard had gone out with his gun, promising to come back with one of the wild pigs they had heard snorting and crashing about nearby. Sometimes, he was trusted to hunt on his own around the camp clearing and valued the time alone this gave him. Because he was good with his gun and always brought back something – lizard, monkey, birds; once even a long-nosed anteater – he was free to pursue this activity without the usual watchful eyes upon him. If he planned it properly, he soon realised, a hunting expedition might give him the chance to escape. He knew roughly the route the food-carrying parties took to the nearest village. Over the months he had gleaned a knowledge of marked trees, the way along the stream, the hut midway; he thought he could find the path.

The rifle hung over his shoulder, and while hunting he always took a sack containing a long *parang* and a rope. Into this now he added a flask of water and some cooked rice he had secretly rolled up in a large leaf. He had also put in a compass and a torch he had taken from Wee Jack's hut. Food-carrying parties always left well before midday, to reach their destination before dark. It was already afternoon and Howard worried about a night in the jungle, and the danger of snakes or creatures of prey. He made his way quickly forward, slashing through the undergrowth with the *parang* as Brokentooth had done on the journey into the camp so long ago.

At first the route ran easily along the stream, but soon he came to the first marked tree and knew he must turn into thicker jungle. Although he could make out the previous path hacked out by the food carriers, the jungle had already grown back and he needed to use the *parang*. Progress was slow for he was unsure of the direction, and kept consulting the compass; once he doubled back, fearing he had made a mistake, once the way was impassable and he retraced his steps to find a new path. Soon the water in his bottle was almost finished, and he had to admit he was lost. The hoots of monkeys as they swung from branch to branch in the trees above, the strange grunts and roars of invisible animals, and the shriek of birds now made him nervous. The light was fading. He sat down on a tree stump to reassess his situation, but jumped up in terror when he heard the crack of branches underfoot and a slashing and crashing some distance away. Then, to his relief there were voices and he hurried forward, hoping to see a group of tribal people who would take him to a nearby village. Instead, he found himself face to face with Brokentooth and others from the camp.

Sweating and panting he was eventually flung down before Wee Jack. It was almost dark, fires were lit in the camp and there was the smell of the usual unappetising meal being cooked, of stale boiled rice, like the perfume of old socks.

'Traitor!' Wee Jack yelled, and gave him a vicious kick on the thigh.

'I was lost. I was hunting as usual.' Howard struggled to get to his knees.

'Hunting? With rice and a compass and a torch stolen from my office? Mad Imperialist, running dog, traitor!' Wee Jack yelled again, his frenzied shouts bringing on a bout of coughing.

'Rabid dogs who betray the party must be exterminated.' Wee Jack bent over Howard, coughing and shouting and showering him with spittle. Howard cringed, his heart beating fast.

'Vulture; living on our body, drinking our blood, hiding your claws from those who feed you. You think you'll fly away and bring those Japanese monkeys to our door? We'll show you what happens to the

Imperialist running dogs of capitalism.' Wee Jack's voice swung above him, unhinged by anger.

As Wee Jack waited, flexing a long bamboo cane, Howard's hands were tied and he braced himself for the first stinging blow on his back, biting his lips to make no sound as the cane came down upon him, again and again. At last it was over and he lay, eyes closed, on the ground before Wee Jack, his back raw. Wee Jack gave an order and an old rice sack was pulled roughly over his head. He was dragged to his feet and forced to walk forward, stumbling blindly about, falling once and hauled to his feet again. Eventually, he was shoved into a hut and his feet were bound like his hands.

The sack over his head was impregnated with rice dust that settled drily in his mouth and nose and smarted in his eyes, but he had no way to push it away. His back was fiery with pain and he lay as best he could on his side or stomach. No water or food was given to him. Night came down and his bladder was full and he shouted to be taken to the latrine. At last someone came and his feet and ankles were briefly untied, but the sack remained on his head. He was guided to balance on two planks, to crouch over the stinking pit of excrement. Afterwards he was bound again, the sack was removed, and he was thrown back for the night into the hut.

Exhausted, he dozed, the discomfort extreme, hands numb beneath the rope and his back sore and bloodied. The screech of a night bird came to him and he could not brush away the mosquitoes that settled upon him, drawn in swarms by his blood. Without water his tongue was dry and swollen; each time he shut his eyes fear pumped through him. He began to shiver and wondered if a fresh bout of malaria had caught him. The ache knifed through his head, he was sure his skull would burst and that before morning he would be dead.

This did not happen and a further day went by. As he lay in his own filth, a bowl of rice and another of water were placed beside him and he had to squirm his way towards it, hands still tied behind his back, and eat like an animal, the bowl rolling over, spilling rice and water on to the ground, leaving him still parched and starving. As the sun rose the following morning he listened to reveille and then the off-key singing of 'The Red Flag'. Later, when he judged they must have eaten breakfast, he listened for the usual activity but heard nothing. His mind drifted, time had stopped. He could not say how long he lay there before they came to loosen the rope on his ankles and drag him from the hut.

Stumbling and shivering and disorientated, he no longer cared what they did with him. The sack was over his head again and it was impossible to know which comrades pulled him along. Blind and groping, he was thrust roughly forward and then pushed up against something hard. A rope was wound around him, tying him tightly to the stake. Then the sack was torn off his head and the glare of sunlight blinded him. As his eyes focused he saw he was roped to a tree and facing the parade ground and that the whole camp was silently gathered before him. Wee Jack stood a distance away, dressed in his official uniform and high peaked cap, gold studs glinting, rifle in hand. With his henchmen beside him, Wee Jack began to speak from a prepared text.

'You have been found guilty of the sin of persistent liberalism. Liberalism is a corrosive that eats away unity, undermines cohesion, causes apathy and creates dissension. It robs the revolutionary ranks of organisation and discipline. For this sin, and the refusal to reconstruct your decadent nature, you have been sentenced to death. The sentence will be carried out immediately. Do you wish to be blindfolded?' Wee Jack spoke coldly.

'I have done nothing!' Howard shouted, his heart pumping in terror, but the protest became a weak bleat as it left his lips.

He began to shiver, and only the bindings held him steady as he listened to the knock of his chattering teeth. Brokentooth came forward with a blindfold, but Howard angrily gestured him away, fury beating through him. He wondered if he was expected now to recant and beg for mercy? Instead, he straightened up and stared at Wee Jack with whatever challenge he could project. As Wee Jack and the henchmen raised their rifles he shut his eyes, taking a breath, waiting for death to whistle through him. He settled his thoughts on his mother, Mei Lan and Cynthia, but it distressed him to find they evaded him, slipping away even as he tried to hold them down. These were his last moments and yet no meaningful thoughts appeared. Then he heard the cracking retort of the guns.

He felt nothing and wondered for a moment if this was death's way of protecting him from pain. Then, opening his eyes, he saw Wee Jack grinning and guffawing, bent double by the joke, slapping his hand up and down on his knee, while about him the comrades shouted approval. Tethered still to the tree, Howard listened to the cackles of laughter. After some moments Wee Jack abruptly straightened up, his hilarity died and, turning smartly on his heel, he marched back to the administrative hut. Brokentooth came forward and, with an apologetic smile that showed all his broken teeth, unbound him. A girl appeared with a bowl of warm tea.

Afterwards, Howard was taken back to the same hut, but his hands and feet were no longer tied, nor was the sack pulled over his head. In the evening he was led to the camp where everyone was assembled for dinner. He was given a bowl of rice gruel cooked with the usual assortment of almost inedible leaves, and a piece of salted fish. As the meal finished and the fire still burned, Wee Jack stood up. The comrades gathered around, squatting down on their haunches. Wee Jack began to speak, quoting further rhetoric.

'*A person with appendicitis is saved when the surgeon removes his appendix. So long as a person who has made mistakes does not hide his sickness for fear of treatment we should welcome him and cure his sickness so that he can become a good comrade. In treating an ideological or a political malady, one must adopt the approach of "curing the sickness to save the patient", as the only correct and effective method.*'

Howard began to sob.

'Shin Syonan in Endau has all the ingredients needed to sustain a settlement but this other place, Bahau, is not a good choice,' Shinozaki told Raj leaning back in his chair and lighting up one of his strong cigarettes. 'There is not enough water, the soil is clay and it is a hilly place unsuitable for rice planting. Without enough water how will people survive? The Eurasians are mad to go there.'

The Eurasian community had watched the Chinese exodus to the freedom of Shin Syonan with envy. Because of their British connections the Eurasians were especially watched by the *kempetai* and so felt they too deserved a settlement. As Mr Shinozaki prepared to begin a second search for suitable land, the Malay state of Negeri Sembilan unexpectedly offered the area of Bahau for settlement. The Eurasian community jumped to accept the offer, brushing aside Shinozaki's misgivings.

Lionel Pereira was not worried about clay soil or inadequate water, he was anxious to leave for Bahau with Ava and his children on the first convoy. His brief experience with the *kempetai* had shaken him through and through. On the night Howard had escaped into the jungle he had been taken away and kept some days for the crime of distilling illicit liquor. He had received a few brutal slaps, and listened to the screams of those being tortured. All his stock of toddy and distilling equipment was taken by the *kempetai* but – you have your life, said Ava.

'Wherever this place Bahau is like, we're going there,' Lionel said, digging into a fish head curry that Ava had made with coconut milk that, like tapioca, was abundantly available. It was a fish from the pond beneath the bog house, but Ava was now past all such discernment. The unending diet of tapioca had worn all of them down and the fish tasted no different from other fish despite its repugnant diet.

'And you're coming too,' Ava said, turning to Rose and Mavis as they sat together at the table for the evening meal.

'It must be better than this, whatever it's like. They'll also need nurses, so tell Cynthia to come,' Mavis suggested to Rose, pausing on a mouthful of food as she felt the prick of a fishbone.

Rose watched Mavis pick the bone from her mouth and looked down at her own plate, wondering how she could have eaten a fish fleshed from human waste, but unable to deny her enjoyment. 'If Howard comes back how will he know we're in Bahau? I will wait here in case he returns,' Rose decided. Christmas was once again almost upon them and she prayed it would bring Howard back to her.

'Well, we're going before the New Year, that's for sure. We'll begin 1944 in the place,' Lionel announced, leaning back in the chair replete, a splash of fish curry down the front of his worn sleeveless vest.

Some weeks later Lionel and his family departed for Bahau. Cynthia refused the offer to be a nurse in the new settlement, preferring to stay at Joo Chiat Hospital and, like Rose, wait for news of Wilfred and Howard.

'There's a malaria epidemic in Bahau,' she told Rose disapprovingly.

In spite of her initial enthusiasm, Mavis had also decided to decline the offer, unsure of what she would find and unwilling to be parted from Rose. They settled down to an ordered life with afternoon tea upon the rickety veranda, walks on the beach and less fear about *kempetai* visits now that Lionel was gone. They abandoned their *kapok* pallets on the back balcony and moved into their cousin's bedroom, sleeping together on the double bed. After some weeks a letter arrived from Ava, confirming for Rose the rightness of her decision to stay in Singapore.

'They did not tell us about the malaria. There have been so many deaths. We have all been down with it and are dosed with quinine. Mr Shinozaki visited here yesterday and told us about Endau, where they do not have much malaria. He says the people there are more enterprising than us Bahau people. Lionel told him Chinese want to die working but we Eurasians like music and singing and enjoying life.'

28

Raj had taken recently to wearing a tall crowned panama hat with his white cotton suit. He held this hat awkwardly in his hands as he stood in Little Sparrow's house on East Coast Road. He had been surprised to receive a message from Mei Lan asking to see him. He had heard nothing of her since her release by the *kempetai* in the middle of the previous year.

When Mei Lan at last appeared Raj was shocked at the change in her. He remembered her bright energy, and the direct assessment of her gaze. Now everything in her face was drawn inwards, as if a great weight sucked her into her core. She led him out on to a narrow veranda where there were two basket chairs and a small table. Almost immediately, an old crone appeared with glasses of water and Raj noticed Mei Lan's hands tremble involuntarily as she picked up the tumbler.

'As soon as they arrested you, Howard went to see Mr Shinozaki and I accompanied him to the YMCA to ask for your release,' Raj explained, describing the unsuccessful interview with the Japanese officer.

'I have no money to pay this donation; I have tried many ways to raise the amount,' Mei Lan said dully. She had the look of a stray creature about her and the old woman hovered anxiously in the background, darting disapproving looks at him.

'Other people have raised money by selling their homes. If you even raise part of the amount, they will be satisfied and leave you alone; you can say you will give the rest later,' Raj advised quietly.

'Where is Howard?' Mei Lan asked abruptly. She had sent Ah Siew to Cousin Lionel's house soon after she returned home, but the old woman had brought back a confused tale that made it clear he was no longer there.

'Someone told the *kempetai* he had a radio for which, as you know, the penalty is death. He has gone into hiding somewhere, but

I know nothing more. It was many months ago now,' Raj told her. 'Lots of men are hiding out in the jungle,' he added as an afterthought. Mei Lan fell silent, trying to suppress her concern. She had little trust of Raj, a man whose loyalties if put to the test were clearly with the Japanese, but his connections were useful.

'Can you find me a buyer for some jewellery?' she asked. Second Grandmother's diamonds, worn for so long in a roll of silk about the old woman's waist, might at last have their use, she thought. The time she had been given to raise the donation money was fast running out. It had taken months to regain some degree of health and Ah Siew had nursed her devotedly. She thought of the boxes of jade and opium and the suitcase of jewellery Lim Hock An had buried in the garden of Bougainvillaea House before the Japanese arrived. Once or twice she had passed her old home, which was now occupied by a civilian Japanese official, and had seen that the garden, although deteriorated, appeared to be undisturbed. One day she vowed to reclaim the place and the precious hoard beneath it.

'My grandmother died and she left me her diamonds; I can sell those. I need to produce the money soon,' she told him.

She had returned to the East Coast house to find Second Grandmother ill and ravaged by pain, a scrawny and almost unrecognisable bundle of embroidered silks. As Mei Lan had entered her room, Second Grandmother turned her head as she lay on her bed.

'Bring me the *Schiaparelli*,' she croaked impatiently, as if Mei Lan had not been away. Ah Siew ran for the vial and unscrewed the heavy glass stopper. Second Grandmother had raised a wilting hand to be anointed with the precious nectar, thick and dark as amber in its ancient crystal bottle. At once, the perfume splintered the room with shards of painful memory. Nothing in all the preceding hellish weeks had made Mei Lan break down and cry, but Second Grandmother's *Schiaparelli* cut to the very centre of her.

'My pipe,' Second Grandmother demanded, her breath rattling like marbles in her throat.

'There is no more opium, Ancient Mistress,' Ah Siew reminded her and hung her head. During the *kempetai* search on the day Mei Lan was arrested, the opium had been found and taken away by the soldiers. Second Grandmother gave a whimper, and took Mei Lan's hand as she sat down beside her. She gestured weakly to Ah Siew, who pulled back the bed sheet and gently lifted Second Grandmother's sleeping *sam* to reveal the slack flesh of her body. The rolled silk belt with what remained of her diamonds was still tied about her waist.

'Take it,' Second Grandmother whispered to Mei Lan, the words barely leaving her throat. Ah Siew untied the belt and placed the soft roll, that still held the warmth of Second Grandmother's body, into Mei Lan's hands. The hard facets of stones could be felt through the silk, and Mei Lan took Second Grandmother's hand. The old woman gave a sigh and closed her eyes and fell into a shallow sleep. As morning broke she awoke with a start, drew a few gasping breaths and died. Mei Lan, who had sat beside her through the night with Bertie and Little Sparrow, dropped her head into her hands and sobbed. Bertie began to howl, but Little Sparrow did not give the customary cries of grief, rising instead with alacrity to begin the funeral arrangements.

'Diamonds?' Raj lifted his head to meet Mei Lan's emotionless gaze.

'I want a good price. I know their value, they are of a high quality and carat,' she warned him, her gaze sharpening.

'Diamonds are good. Many men high up in the military will be interested in diamonds.' Raj nodded encouragingly. He did not add that small pieces of jewellery were easily secreted and transported back home and were much desired by Japanese military men seeking recompense for the hard years of war. He might even be interested himself.

'I will do what I can,' he said as he stood up. Seeing with discomfort how pompous and unfeeling he must appear to her, he was pricked by sudden shame. Replacing the panama hat on his head, still searching for words that would convey his sympathy, he prepared to leave. She made him feel guilty, as if in some way he had colluded in the events that had destroyed her.

'I'm sorry,' he said in a low voice and could find no other words with which to journey to her dark world. She nodded absently, but before he reached the door he heard her speak and turned to her again. She still stood on the veranda, looking out at the sun caught in the leaves of a coral tree.

'In the cell there was a tiny barred window high up; I could watch the sky and the clouds pass by. Once I heard a golden oriole sing.'

'I'm sorry,' he repeated, stiff with embarrassment, wanting to run from the room and the discomfort she made him feel. The words were a whisper, barely reaching his lips as he turned to hurry away.

Once he had gone she sat down to absorb the news about Howard, her face filled with the emotion she had refused to show Raj. Ah Siew shuffled forward, attentive and anxious.

'Go quickly to the Joo Chiat Hospital, to Cynthia, ask her for news of Howard, ask her to come,' Mei Lan said. Pulling some notepaper from the drawer of a desk, she wrote a quick note to Cynthia, something she had not found herself able to do before.

Please come. I do not yet have the strength to go out. Ah Siew looks after me, she wrote, forming the words with difficulty.

Wilfred found that any small cut turned septic and ate deep into his flesh. No one had shoes and the hard labour, the scratches from clearing bushes and trees, the knocks from breaking stones, were a continual aggravation to the suppurating lesions they all had on their bodies. Once or twice Wilfred had sat with his legs in the river and let the small fish there nibble at the sores to clean them, but this was a painful process. Then a novel treatment was found. Cement dust, if packed into an open sore, would bind with the pus and mucus there to dry into a hard protective scab. Eventually, these heavy scabs fell off and revealed new skin beneath. Every day they dug graves for those who died. No one prayed any more.

Cholera came. They were warned that when monsoon rain swelled the river, dead animals, decayed rubbish and the contents of village cesspits upstream would be carried down to them and cholera would come; it came every year without fail.

The Japanese held white squares of cloth over their faces for protection but, within hours of the first case being reported, the rotted, leaking tent set up as an isolation ward was full. The monsoon rolled down, drenching dying men who writhed in agonising spasms. Vomit and diarrhoea covered the ground in pools of slime. Few men could survive, and the growing pile of bodies must be buried quickly. Mass graves were dug and bodies were unceremoniously thrown in, layered one on another up to the top. There needed to be six feet of earth above the bodies, or maggots would crawl to the surface from rotting corpses and immediately metamorphose into cholera-carrying blowflies. All the time they dug it rained; their feet were ankle deep in mud. They were warned not to touch their mouths with their fingers, mess tins and spoons must be dipped in boiling water before a meal;

no fly must be allowed to settle on food. As flies congregated in a metallic black swarm on any morsel, this was a difficult order to fulfil. There was also no way to shift a corpse except by grasping it with bare hands and Wilfred dreaded falling into the toxic mud or that it would splash on to his mouth; there was no way to protect themselves against contamination. Each day he wrapped himself around the same silent mantra, the words repeating and reverberating through him. *I will not die. I will not die.*

PART FOUR
1946–1956

29

THE DENSE SHADOW OF the jungle broke at last and Howard found himself in the dazzle of sunlight. As the trucks careered along the narrow road a green carpet of rice fields spread out around them. People bending to the paddy straightened and waved. When the rumour that war was over and the Japanese had surrendered reached them in the jungle camp, they had not known whether to believe it; they were again without a radio. It was many weeks before they eventually set out to join the other groups of Malayan People's Anti-Japanese Army liberating the country.

Howard held his face to the sun, as if to wash away the green and cloistered years. He had grown so used to the filtered half-light of the rainforest, a dark canopy of branches always above him, that the endless vista of sky filled him with amazement. The breeze on his face, the unrelieved heat on his skin, the brightness of it all was disorientating; he wondered if, after hiding so long within the dark mansion of the jungle, his skin had absorbed its green light. He was weak with illness and lay stretched out in the back of the truck. The thought of freedom was frightening; he remembered how he had once longed to escape the camp. Now, without the cohesion of its organised life about him, the world appeared daunting.

Malaria gripped him so that even now he ached and shivered. Before they left the camp, dysentery had also taken hold of him and he had wondered if, now that the war was finally ended, he was destined to die. Instead, he had been placed on a bamboo stretcher and carried along with the guerrillas, who had orders from the Malayan Communist Party to liberate nearby towns; Howard was too weak to protest. Everywhere, as the Japanese moved out, making way for the returning British troops, the communist guerrillas moved in. Roads were clogged with the retreating Japanese army, sullen faced and with truckloads of equipment, and the loot of furniture, pianos and bicycles, with soldiers seated precariously atop these loads.

'The Shorties are going,' Wee Jack laughed, shooting about the feet of Japanese soldiers, making them dance and run.

In village after village the Communist Party's red flag with hammer and sickle emblem now flew above the Union Jack and the guerrillas' own Malayan People's Anti-Japanese Army pennant. When Wee Jack and his men entered a village, their first task was to establish a rule of terror. Any remaining Japanese police or soldiers were immediately shot. The guerrillas marched up and down the main street flashing guns, demanding enthusiasm from the populace. People's Committees were put in place, and a village jury tried those who had collaborated with the Japanese. The guilty were carried around in pigs' cages before being butchered before a cheering crowd. The punishment and dispatch of women who had been the mistresses of the Japanese was greeted with the greatest approval.

Howard was required to see little of this. Racked by illness, he was exhausted by the smallest exertion and Wee Jack finally installed him in the house of an elderly couple, ordering them to care for him.

'Get yourself better soon. We're returning to Singapore,' Wee Jack announced one day. 'The Malayan People's Anti-Japanese Army are being honoured by the British. Our leaders are getting medals.' Wee Jack gave a bark of laughter, and Howard stared at him in amazement, wondering if this meant he was free at last.

Now, the truck bumped over the trunk road taking them back to Singapore. Howard was weak, but no longer so ill after the medicine, food and kindness shown him by the elderly couple in the last town. The truck was going too fast for safety, throwing them about, the men shouting and laughing. They were one in a convoy of six Malayan People's Anti-Japanese Army trucks, and behind followed a further truck with a cargo of weapons. Similar convoys were heading to Singapore from all directions. Sitting beside Howard, Wee Jack wore his official high peaked cap with three gold stars, and a creased and unwashed uniform.

'It will do for the ceremony, I'm not one of those receiving medals from Mountbatten,' Wee Jack told Howard. 'The British want to make a pact with us. If the MPAJA gives up its weapons and disbands, they've promised to officially recognise us, to recognise the Malayan

Communist Party.' Wee Jack threw back his head in triumphant laughter. Howard leaned his aching head on the side of the bouncing truck, too weak to argue. He could not share Wee Jack's buoyancy; all he felt was apprehension at the thought of returning to Singapore. How would he take up his old life again? How would he fit back into society, mix with people like Lionel again? Even his mother now seemed unrelated to him.

At the Padang, a platform had been erected on the steps of City Hall on which sat uniformed British generals, air marshals, admirals and brigadiers, and a lone representative of the Malayan Communist Party. At their centre was Lord Louis Mountbatten, Supreme Allied Commander South East Asia, waiting to honour the communist guerrilla fighters. The music stopped as a fleet of open cars drew up carrying the guests of honour, the sixteen leaders of the newly disbanded Malayan People's Anti-Japanese Army.

There was cheering as the men climbed out of the cars, wearing olive green uniforms and peaked caps. The band struck up 'God Save the King', and as this ended paused discreetly for a moment before beginning 'The Red Flag'. As the last notes died away, Lord Louis Mountbatten stepped forward to pin medals on each MPAJA leader. Tall Lord Louis bent low to secure the Burma Star upon the smaller Chinese men, but although he smiled gravely as the occasion demanded, shaking the hand of each man, his gestures were interpreted as condescending. As the band played 'Land of Hope and Glory', the guerrilla leaders gave a sudden clenched fist salute, their arms thrusting up to the sky. Wee Jack nudged Howard who stood beside him.

'The British think they're returning to the old order of things. Instead, they'll find it's a different world. If the Japanese could get the British out, then so can we, that's what we've learned from the war: the British are not invincible.' Wee Jack laughed.

Later, the truck dropped Howard off near Lionel's house before bumping away over the rutted track and finally disappearing. For a moment he panicked, overwhelmed with loss, suppressing an urge to run after it. Illness had left him debilitated; his head spun and his legs were weak as he turned to walk along the sandy track towards the coconut estate. The familiar landscape appeared surreal, as if he saw it in a dream. Perhaps, he thought, Lionel's house might no longer be there; he did not know what he was returning to, he did not know if his mother was still alive. In the distance he heard the unchanging rhythm of the sea, and breathed in the familiar comfort of the briny air, edged by the odour of drying sardines. The sun was going down, there was the smoke of cooking fires and shadows settling for the night, just as there had always been, just as he remembered. Soon, he came to the old shack where he had spent so many hours hidden away, where he had taken Mei Lan, and stopped. The hut had collapsed inwards and now lay in a heap of splintered struts and planks and disintegrating attap leaves. He knew he should feel some emotion, but within him his feelings congealed, unyielding. Mei Lan was so distant he could not clearly recall her face; he himself was but a spectre visiting a previous life.

Lionel's house was not only standing as before, but Lionel was sitting on the steps strumming his guitar. He stood up in amazement at Howard's sudden appearance, and yelled into the house for Ava. She came running, her children behind her, all now grown and lanky. It was an emotional reunion, and Howard immediately learned his mother had returned to Belvedere. Lionel kept slapping him on the back and Ava insisted he spend the night.

'It's dangerous out there. Wait for daylight, then you'll be all right,' she advised.

'She's right, boy. It's every man for himself out there – looting and plunder and the law of the street now that the Japanese have gone. Almost as bad as when they were here, in a different sort of way,' Lionel agreed. Howard sat down on the top step of the veranda, the noisy welcome surging about him was more than he could take. He dropped his head into his hands and tears streamed down his face.

'Now the British are back, law and order will return, just you wait and see.' Ava drew her daughters into her arms and they leaned against her biting their nails, regarding Howard curiously as she gave him news of Rose.

'Your mother and Mavis hurried home to Belvedere as soon as they could. Lionel took them back. It upset them to see what had happened to the place. It's full of homeless people. Lionel said even though the place belongs to Rose, she had to battle for a few inches to call her own. Cynthia is back at the General Hospital.'

Howard left Lionel's house in the morning and as he came into town was shocked to see the number of destitute people and the unspeakable filth piled up everywhere. Eventually, he reached Belvedere and as he walked through the gate he thought for a moment he had made a mistake. The garden was a shanty town of squatters' huts. Ragged, emaciated people passed constantly in and out of the house, while two coolies squatting down to smoke outside the front door looked up at Howard with interest. As he stepped into the vestibule, the dining room opened before him and he saw not the usual sea of red Malacca tiles, but a further squatters' village. Old sheets, curtains and pieces of tarpaulin were strung up, dividing the great room into many small cubicles. Behind these flimsy walls Howard saw families, sleeping babies and bits of furniture: a box, a mattress, a chair – even the small round tables at which Belvedere's lodgers had once sat. There was a foul odour. He walked anxiously down the corridor to his old room and found the door open. A crowd of faces turned towards him as he peered in, and he drew back hastily. The door to his mother's room was firmly shut, but he forced himself to open it. For a moment he stared disbelievingly. His mother sat on a chair by the window sewing while Mavis, sitting on another chair, was reading a book. In the midst of chaos the room appeared almost as before. On the chest of drawers the usual silver-framed photographs were arranged beside a bowl of mangosteen. Rose's walnut double bed stood in its usual place. The women looked up as he entered. Rose lowered her sewing, frozen in shock; Mavis jumped up and rushed towards him.

They had set up a small spirit stove in a corner and upon it they heated whatever food they could find. They said it was better than queuing to use the gas rings in the kitchen. Some precious tea was unearthed, and boiled up in celebration of Howard's return. A valuable tin of sardines was also opened to accompany a hard heel of bread, that Mavis told him excitedly had been made with real flour and not tapioca.

'We came back as soon as we dared after the Japanese left, but Belvedere had already been occupied by squatters.' Rose held her son's hand, stroking his fingers, conscious above all that he was beside her. Mavis added a spoonful of condensed milk to the tea and poured it into cracked mugs; she had lost weight and her clothes hung pitifully upon her.

'We had to fight for this room. Three families were in here, and we bribed them to vacate it with almost everything we had. We have to queue to use our own bathroom and it's filthy beyond words.' Rose burst into tears, the shock and relief of seeing Howard opening a floodgate of feeling.

'Cynthia and Wilfred share the room with us.' Mavis pointed to a curtained-off section behind which a mattress could be seen. Over tea the women told him how, after the surrender, Wilfred had been repatriated from Burma with other POWs. Wilfred now resembled a walking skeleton, Rose whispered with a shudder.

'Cynthia knows best how to handle him. She's working part time now, so that she can nurse him back to health.' Rose stared at her son in growing concern, her throat constricting with emotion, her eyes filling again with tears. He was gaunt, his eyes sunken and, even though he was standing before her, appeared more absent than present in a way she could not explain. Although she knew nothing of his lost years in the jungle, the imprint of experience was stamped on his face.

Later, at Rose's direction, Howard went into the garden to find Wilfred sitting by the mangosteen trees. The shed Howard had used for assignations with ugly Nona so long ago still stood but now, he saw, a family lived in it. Wilfred sat unmoving, one thin leg crossed over the other, staring blankly ahead into the gnarled depths of the orchard. As Rose had said, the bones stuck out all over him, the flesh of his face was sucked away, his hair had thinned and some of his teeth were missing. He turned his head as Howard approached, and with a look of amazement stood up to embrace him tearfully.

'Both of us back from the dead,' Wilfred said, wiping his eyes on the back of his hand.

For some time they sat in silence and Howard was startled when, unprompted, Wilfred began to speak, staring ahead without emotion. 'They did terrible things. We were kept in small cages in the sun without water; you could not stand up, you could not lie down. A few days of it and your legs no longer worked. Men dug their own graves and were shot beside them. We watched and then buried them as we were ordered. Even if they were still alive, we still buried them. One man opened his eyes and said, please . . . please. We buried them all.' His voice sank into silence. Howard wished he knew what to say, what emotion to feel, but everything seemed to happen at a great distance from him; he was distant even to himself.

As the days went by Howard felt a shift within himself. Nothing yet seemed real; the abundance of light still hurt his eyes, the threadbare food his mother and Mavis produced seemed decadent after the fare in the jungle camp. He was by turn irritable and tearful, angry and depressed. He knew he should be glad to be back and yet Belvedere's ragged population, always milling around him, his mother and Mavis's effort to resurrect the polite remnants of their old life, their concern at his refusal of a mattress and his preference for sleeping on a bare floor, their constant fussing and worry, flooded him with anger. Cynthia examined him and dosed him, like Wilfred, with precious quinine and vitamin B brought from the General Hospital. Within days he felt physically stronger, but his mind was still dull and confused. Often a sense of panic ran through him; without Wee Jack to guide him, he was lost. He waited, sure the man would contact him, but Wee Jack did not come. Then, he wondered if he should search out the office in Middle Road that he knew the Malayan People's Anti-Japanese Army now occupied, but he did nothing. He did nothing but lie on the floor of Rose's room staring at the ceiling, or sit silently on the bench beside Wilfred. Hours passed, days passed in this limbo, and he was happy to float in nothingness, waiting for the lost parts of himself to return, if they ever would.

It was weeks before he finally made his way to Mei Lan, to the house on East Coast Road, propelled more by obligation than emotion, and by Cynthia's constant urging. She had told him about Mei Lan's imprisonment and her suffering at the hands of the *kempetai*. In the end he went to Little Sparrow's house to please his sister. Again, he knew he should feel some emotion at the things Cynthia told him, but whatever had once tied him and Mei Lan together, he felt sure had loosened. There was little transport about and he walked a distance before finding a rickshaw, feeling weak and dizzy, but pushing himself on. When he reached the house he found a girl of eight or nine playing outside, digging up shoots of tapioca.

'She's inside,' the girl replied to his query and led him up the steps, the muddy tuber still in her hand. Howard followed her, surprised to find himself feeling apprehensive; he wondered suddenly what changes he would find in Mei Lan. As he climbed the steps his head reeled again from the exertion of his journey.

Mei Lan appeared from an inner room, and stood unmoving before him. Unexpectedly, his heart constricted violently and the emotion locked inside him for so long, which he had thought was unreachable, flooded through him again. It was not just the pale frailty of her, her hair cropped brutally close to her head, but the dullness of her eyes that made him feel something was gone from her, just as it was gone from Wilfred. For a moment the sense of separation dropped away and he wanted to take her in his arms. Almost immediately the moment faded and he kept his distance, knowing instinctively that formality was best. The child still stood beside him, staring curiously up at them both.

'Go and ask Ah Siew to bring some water for the visitor,' Mei Lan told the child, leading Howard into a small back room where Little Sparrow sat sewing buttons on a dress. The woman withdrew to a basket chair on a narrow veranda, but kept glancing over her shoulder to where they sat, as if to guard against impropriety.

'She has been good to me,' Mei Lan told him, looking at Little Sparrow's back.

'How long did they keep you?' he asked almost below his breath, unable to stop the question but dreading to hear her answer. For a moment she was silent, her eyes lowered to her folded hands and he noticed how tightly her thin fingers were clenched.

'They told me it was sixty-five days. They only let me out to pay Grandfather's part of the $50 million donation, some of which I managed with that jewellery Second Grandmother always carried upon her. I couldn't raise the whole amount, but they didn't bother me again.' Her voice was toneless and he saw how she trembled.

'Every day I still expect them to knock on the door,' she whispered. Her life limped along, the mechanics of it propelling her forward each day, but something essential was absent. In a stream near the East Coast house she has seen the bleached skull of a dog, caught and held by weeds growing near the bank. The skull lifted and moved in the current but could not break free, the dark empty sockets of its eyes staring up at her. That was how she felt, like a heap of pared bones under water, drifting aimlessly back and forth in the swell. There was nothing left to build upon; nothing left to restore. Cynthia had given her some herbal medicine that she said would take the worst dreams away, but even in daylight Mei Lan still lived in Nakamura's shadow.

Already, Howard knew they would have to relearn each other all over again; the people they had been were vanished. Even though Mei Lan appeared connected to the everyday world, he saw she lived hidden within herself, her memories a coffin from which she could not escape. His own harsh experiences in the past three years gave him some insight into the spectres that must haunt her. Some part of himself, he realised now, must have resisted Wee Jack and the indoctrination of the camp. Something within him had remained inviolable for, compared to all he intuitively sensed about Mei Lan's ordeal, he saw that slowly he was already struggling free of those jungle years. Thoughts he recognised as his own had begun to flow through him again. Eventually, he would reclaim himself, whereas the pitiless decimation Mei Lan had endured had done its work too well, robbing her of herself.

'Where did you hide?' she asked. Even as he told her of his forced residence in the jungle she seemed preoccupied, her thoughts far away so that he felt she only waited for him to fall silent.

'War Trials have begun,' Mei Lan told him when he stopped speaking. 'I have been called as a prosecution witness. The British Government have given me a medal, but for what I do not know. For surviving when others died? They're really giving it to Grandfather, for standing up to the Japanese and always supporting the British.' Mei Lan gave a short bitter laugh.

She knew he wanted to reach out, to touch her, to reclaim her, but between them now there was the distance of strangers. She wondered how she could feel so little when before she had felt so much. Nobody knew the details of what had happened to her in those weeks at the YMCA, not even Ah Siew. Locked too deep for retrieval, the words would not spill out at her summons. The old *amah* had nursed her silently, never enquiring, massaging almond oil into the scars, feeding her ginseng scrounged from goodness knows where. At night the comfort of Ah Siew's light snoring came to Mei Lan as she slept. The old woman was there when she awoke with nightmares and screams of terror, night after night. Ah Siew boiled up the precious herbs Cynthia had given, an ancient potion for sleep, but even when Mei Lan drowsed, oblivion never pulled her completely into its bottomless void. Each night she must navigate the darkness of her mind, held hostage by unspeakable memories. For many weeks after being released from the YMCA she lived as a ghost in the East Coast Road house, seeing nothing, passing as if invisibly from room to room, from hour to hour. Nakamura stood everywhere, pulling her back into his dark arc as she tried to live again.

'They have also given me a scholarship to Oxford, to study law. My departure has been delayed so that I can give evidence at the trial; that is what the Governor wants. He himself asked me to be a witness. I will leave for England after the trial. I don't know how long I'll be away; two or three years, maybe longer.' She looked at him suddenly with the direct appraisal he knew from before, assessing his reaction to what she said. He nodded, knowing they had no control over what had happened, nor over what was now being shaped.

'I will be at the trial, they always allow spectators,' he promised.

'I'd rather you did not come,' she replied, averting her eyes.

Thoughts of the trial pressed heavily upon Mei Lan, but the day finally arrived when she must make her way to the court, to face Nakamura again. It was an effort to dress, and Ah Siew fussed anxiously about her. At last, the old *amah* left the room, and Mei Lan sat down at the dressing table and picked up the silver-backed brush that had once been her mother's. As a child she remembered watching it slide through Ei Ling's lustrous hair; now it was heavy against her own head. With imprisonment she had lost so much hair and weight and her health had been slow to return; the birthmark was even more prominent along the fragile line of her jaw.

The door opened and Greta appeared; a shy child of eight, with plaits of hair pulled up high either side of her head. Greta was Little Sparrow's youngest child, born many years after the daughter, Ching Ling, who had quickly followed Bertie, and with whom she had lived quietly in the East Coast house. Although still very young, Ching Ling had been married the previous year. The matchmaker had come forward with a suitable groom, the son of a school inspector, and Little Sparrow accepted immediately, relieved to see her eldest daughter securely settled.

Greta was technically Mei Lan's half-aunt, but it was impossible to think of her in this way. Since Mei Lan's arrival in the East Coast house the child, constantly usurped in her mother's affections by Bertie, had turned to Mei Lan for affection, slipping into her bed at night, demanding stories before sleeping and the goodnight kiss her mother so often forgot to give her since the return of her brother.

'Why can't Bertie go away now that the war is finished?' Greta asked, clambering up on to the bed.

'Your mother had to give him up when he was a baby and now she has got him back it would be difficult for her to do that,' Mei Lan explained, replacing the silver brush on the dressing table and observing herself in the full-length mirror. Ah Siew had chosen a simple white dress for her to wear, the only good dress in the cupboard. Her arms stuck out of the short sleeves like two thin sticks and the colour did not flatter her paleness. She opened the dressing table drawer to find a pin to keep the neck of the dress together, and pulled out not the tin of safety pins but the wooden case with the compass Howard had given her so long ago.

'What's that?' Greta scrambled off the bed as Mei Lan turned it over in her hands.

'It's a compass,' Mei Lan explained, opening the box and seeing once again the smooth dial of the instrument, its needle steadfast as ever, pointing in the direction of Belvedere.

'Where did you get it?' the child asked.

'Someone gave it to me years ago,' Mei Lan replied but there was no longer the quickening that would once have gripped her at the thought of Howard. The compass and all that went with it belonged to another life. She remembered Howard's visit a few days before and felt a great tiredness, and knew she did not have the strength to recover the mercurial emotions she had once known so well.

'What does a compass do?' Greta insisted.

'It points you in the right direction,' Mei Lan answered dully, staring down at the needle but seeing for herself no clear course ahead.

There was the sound of a car drawing up and Greta rushed across to the window. 'They've come for you,' she said, pulling excitedly at the curtain.

Mei Lan stood at the window behind the child, hidden by a fold of cloth, looking down on the big black car with a Union Jack pennant, in the road before the house. The driver jumped out and opened a door and a short, thickset Englishman emerged. The sky had darkened over East Coast Road and she saw the first drops of rain spotting the stone gate pillars below. She straightened her collar and made herself turn, and walked slowly towards the door.

On the back seat of the car Mei Lan sat with her hands clasped tightly together, her eyes on the small flag fluttering on the vehicle's bonnet. John Scott, a personal aide to the Governor, had been ordered to accompany her to court. As they slowed at a crossroads the rain, turning from a light shower into a sudden downpour, spat through the half-opened window, and Mei Lan felt its soft touch on her face.

'Better close the window or you'll get drenched before we get to court,' the Englishman advised.

When Government House was cleared of its decorative Japanese touches and a British Governor was once again settled in the white palace upon a green hill, Mei Lan had been summoned to meet him. The new Governor told her that the British Government was awarding her an MBE for bravery during the war. She had been classed as a 'battle casualty', and would therefore be compensated in some way by the colonial power.

'Your grandfather was an exemplary British subject. His efforts against the Japanese aggression in which he lost his grandson, who fought with Dalforce and the British Army, will not go unappreciated.' The Governor had smiled. The British Government, he told her, had noted her desire to study law in England and arranged a scholarship. A place had been reserved for her at St Hilda's, a women's college in Oxford. As the Governor spoke she had looked over his shoulder through the open windows of Government House to the fiery blossoms of a flame tree. In the car now Mr Scott cleared his throat and attempted polite conversation.

'You must be nervous. Not very nice to dig up bad memories,' he sympathised. 'However, without evidence from people like yourself we cannot convict the monsters, cannot give them their just deserts.' *Monsters. Just deserts.* The words ran easily off his tongue. Mei Lan turned her face to the window.

The courtroom was heavily panelled, the warm wood giving off a thick smell of polish. The close, hot atmosphere and the subdued hum of conversation pressed in upon her as they entered the chamber, which was packed with people. Mei Lan took her seat beneath a high ceiling with softly turning fans; Mr Scott sat beside her. The trials had started some weeks before and continued every day. People sat shoulder to shoulder, crushed in together to see the accused, marvelling repeatedly at the brutal capabilities of such insignificant looking men. There was some coughing and settling as the proceedings began, and then a hush as the defendants were called into court. They entered the room, four small unexceptional Japanese men, correct and freshly shaven, filing in quietly one behind the other to sit at a table with their defence counsel. Mei Lan began to tremble and Mr Scott leaned towards her in concern.

'That is the witness box over there. An officer will escort you to it when your name is called. Until then, I am here beside you,' he reassured her. The prosecuting counsel, Colonel Sheppard, was already rising to give his opening address.

The last man in the row of accused was Nakamura. At first glance Mei Lan was unsure if it was really he. Drained of authority he appeared shrunken, a small ugly man, insubstantial in every way. Yet, she remembered him as a coiled spring, his eyes always sparking a loathsome energy. Each time she was brought before him, he appeared to fill the room. As she stared at him now her body clenched, her pulse quickened, her mouth became dry. The prosecuting counsel was speaking and Mei Lan tried to listen.

'. . . it transpires very clearly through the course of this case that the *kempetai* followed, almost without exception, one of their normal methods of investigation. That is to say, they allotted a particular Warrant Officer or NCO the task of interrogating one particular suspect, and this WO or NCO was supposed to see the case of this particular suspect through to the end from start to finish . . .

'. . . conditions under which the witnesses were detained were rigorous in the extreme . . .' She closed her eyes and the bland flow of words ran over her.

Eventually, it was her turn to give evidence and she followed the usher to the witness box. She kept her eyes down; the cold flame was shrinking and expanding inside her until she felt sick and she feared she might vomit before the crowd. Nakamura's eyes rested on her in the same way they had always done, as if she were an inanimate object. Even at the height of his anger, when he had thrashed her until he was able no longer to bring the cane down with adequate force, when her ribs were broken, when her flesh was a bloody pulp, when he was emotionally cleansed as a man after sex, even then his eyes remained detached.

'Miss Lim, will you answer the question?' Colonel Sheppard raised his tone slightly and she looked up, startled.

'I did not hear. What was the question?' she asked, making an effort to keep her mind tethered.

'How often were you taken for interrogation?'

'Once a day, sometimes not for several days. I don't remember. It is difficult to say. I lost count of time in prison.'

'And who conducted the interrogation? Was it always the same man, Captain Nakamura?'

'Yes,' she whispered and closed her eyes. What was she doing here? What could she say, what words could she use? There was no language to describe pain.

'Speak up Miss Lim, so that the court can hear your answer. Can you describe for us the cell in which you were kept.'

'It was a filthy place, filthy.'

'Can you describe the cell, Miss Lim?' Colonel Sheppard repeated patiently.

Why were they forcing her to go back? Why must she return, why must she tell them, why should she not run from the room? She remembered the corpse whose arms had had to be broken to drag him through the door of the cell. Stop! she wanted to scream but Colonel Sheppard continued, tugging words from her, reeling them in from the hiding place where she had kept them for so long.

'What form did the interrogations take?'

'Beatings,' she whispered. 'And other things.'

'What other things?' the Colonel asked gently.

She remembered Nakamura saying, *You will not die.* And yet so many did.

'What questions were you asked during interrogation?' Colonel Sheppard demanded.

'If I knew any communists; I was always asked for names.' She remembered the questions hammering upon her and how she had screamed 'I don't know', again and again. All the time Nakamura's eyes rested impassively on her. Pain was his pleasure, destruction his goal and she had been his unwilling partner, she was linked to him now for ever; his stain was upon her soul.

'Did the accused rape you?' She heard the question but the words would not come.

'Miss Lim?'

Nakamura had tried kindness. He called for coffee and small

Japanese cakes but when she repeated that she knew no communists he became angry again, twisting her lips hard between his fingers before returning her to the cell. The next time she was taken to a different room, an office with filing cabinets and a desk that Nakamura sat down behind. As she climbed the stairs to this room with the guard they had passed a window. She looked out at the road below, at cyclists and cars and carts, a woman with a child strapped to her back, and was filled by amazement that such a world continued to revolve in the strong blaze of the sun, oblivious to the dimension she lived in. Even the depth of natural light after the continuous glare of electric bulbs was dazzling, magical. Then she was pushed through the door to face Nakamura; he had been alone.

'Just tell me what you know and you can go free. I can send you to places much worse than that cell, where you will be used day and night as a woman.' She sat on a long, hard-backed seat against the wall and he stood before her, hands behind his back, booted legs apart.

He placed a hand upon her bare knee then moved it roughly along her thigh until he found the place he sought, pushing back her skirt, thrusting her over the hard arm of the bench as he pressed himself upon her. He took no notice of her screams as he unbuckled his heavy belt; he was used to such sounds in his ears every day. He was used to a struggling body and pleas for release.

'Miss Lim.' Colonel Sheppard sounded a note of impatience.

'Yes, he raped me.' She lifted her eyes to look directly at Nakamura.

'More than once?' Colonel Sheppard asked.

'Yes, many times,' Mei Lan replied, her voice a whisper.

Soon, she returned to her seat and as she sat down such exhaustion overcame her that she felt she might slide into sleep as she sat on the chair. Nothing was real; she was walking through a dream. Other witnesses were called, and so repetitious were the abominable things they said that it all began to sound routine. At last it was over and Colonel Sheppard stood to begin the day's summing up. She closed her eyes as his voice droned on, describing the dense hedge of evidence erected about the accused men. None of it made sense any more; her mind was like torn linen and her thoughts were full of holes.

30

MR HO TURNED HIS head and from his bed raised a weak hand in greeting. His bony knees were drawn up under the cotton sheet in a mountainous shape. Raj remembered the asthmatic portliness of the man when they had first met on the trolleybus at Kreta Ayer. The effort of welcome set off a new bout of coughing, Mr Ho turned to spit into an enamel bowl then leaned back on his pillows, exhausted. A window beyond the bed looked on to a straggly papaya tree in which Myna birds squawked and quarrelled.

'Do not talk,' Raj ordered and Mrs Ho, hovering nearby, nodded agreement; she too had shrunk to bird-like proportions and her eyes were opaque and rheumy. Neither of the old people could come to terms with their son Luke's murder in the war time massacre of young Chinese men. A friend of Luke's, who had also been apprehended by the Japanese, had come to the house to tell them. Luke and fifty others had been taken in a lorry to the seventh milestone on Siglap Road. Luke's friend had managed to loose his bindings and made a run for the nearby jungle. From there he had watched Luke gunned down with everyone else by Japanese soldiers.

As Raj pulled up a chair beside the old man's bed, the blood-curdling cries of Ho's grandsons playing in the yard outside floated through the window, but the mouth-watering smell of biscuits no longer filled the air. Since the return of the British the factory had been closed; flour was unavailable to Mr Ho because of his collaboration with the enemy.

'History repeats itself,' Mr Ho sighed, remembering the buckets of tar and the dead cats on his veranda at the time of the boycott of Japanese goods by the China Relief Fund. He had done well out of the occupation, awarded a licence to bake in bulk for the military. At Mr Yamaguchi's insistence, a Japanese general had sampled a Ho biscuit and liked it. Raj observed Mr Ho's decline with distress, for the old man had been like a father to him.

'The closure of the factory can only be temporary. Soon you will be allowed to reopen; food is needed, everyone is hungry and Ho Biscuits are known as the best,' Raj tried to comfort Mr Ho. The old man placed a bird-like hand upon Raj's arm, looking anxiously at him from old eyes clouded by cataracts.

'Now that the British have returned we're in for another round of internments. It's getting to feel like a merry-go-round. All the Japanese civilians here are to be interned once again, just like they were before the surrender. They've already taken Yoshiko along with her parents, Mr and Mrs Yamaguchi, to a camp at Jurong. Yoshiko is still a Japanese citizen, but the boys are Chinese like their father. Because of this they were not interned, and are allowed to remain here with us.' Mr Ho drew a trembling breath before continuing.

'Once all Japanese civilians are rounded up, they are to be repatriated to Japan. They will send Yoshiko away from her children; already the poor boys are fatherless. Speak to Mr Shinozaki. I believe he is the only Japanese who has not been interned. Perhaps even now he can do something to help us.' Mr Ho began to cough again. Raj thought of Yoshiko, the fullness of her soft upper lip, the creamy skin of her cheeks, the light flowery scent that lifted from her and felt a stab of anxiety.

'Mr Shinozaki was not interned because so many people pleaded on his behalf after the good things he did for everyone. I hear he is now working with the British Army Field Security Service. I will go to him at once,' Raj reassured the old man.

Mr Ho nodded in relief as Mrs Ho returned to the room, followed by a houseboy carrying a tray with glasses of barley water and tapioca chips. The Myna birds set up a new squabble in the branches of the tree outside the window, and Mr Ho beckoned Raj nearer, speaking above the din of the birds.

'I want you to take over Ho Biscuits,' he rasped in a shaky voice. Raj straightened up in shock, thinking he might have misheard Mr Ho.

'I do not have long; we all know that. I have left everything to the boys and Yoshiko. She has helped me run the factory since Luke was killed, and managed it herself since I became sick. After me it will be difficult for her alone. You must take a partnership and help Yoshiko when I'm gone. She will do the day-to-day running of the place but she needs someone like you beside her. There is no one I can trust, but you are like a son to me. It is all written down in my will.' Mr Ho leaned back on the pillow, exhausted by this long speech. Raj tried to control the emotion that flooded through him at Mr Ho's extraordinary words.

Within a moment Mr Ho, now at peace with himself, fell asleep and began to snore, his mouth open upon toothless gums. Raj left the room and took his leave of Mrs Ho who was supervising the preparation of food in the kitchen. The veranda steps were splintered, a plank near the bottom was missing and to steady himself Raj put a hand on the wooden rail. The old house had come to feel like home and he looked about proprietorially; he had only to step inside the gate to feel a sense of security. When he took over Ho Biscuits, Raj decided, he would immediately repair the broken steps and leaking roof and then renovate the factory sheds; he might import machinery from England. Even as the idea took shape, Raj was ashamed that his mind could run ahead of events so rabidly. Mr Ho's grandsons were still playing in the yard with wooden swords. As soon as they saw Raj they ran to him.

'Uncle, Uncle,' they yelled, dancing about him. He dug into his pocket with a broad smile and pulled out a handful of coins that he divided between them. The boys ran off, shouting their thanks. It was the usual procedure; whenever he visited he made sure he had a good supply of coins. He did not think Leila would ever give him a nephew now, and it was hard to tell when he would marry and have children of his own. Until that time he was happy to treat Yoshiko's sons as his own.

It did not take long for Raj to find Shinozaki at the British Army Field Security Service headquarters. He had lost his puckish grin, but otherwise appeared as always, dressed in a dark suit and tie. Raj was allowed to meet him in a busy reception room with rickety rattan chairs, a ceiling fan and a couple of desks. The room was constantly astir as people walked in and out on various missions. British army personnel were everywhere and it was strange to see again tall thin men in khaki shorts, instead of small men in high boots or puttees. Unexpectedly, a bowl of orange heliconia sat vividly on a table, lifting the threadbare room.

'I picked them this morning. They grow beside the entrance,' Shinozaki explained as he came forward to greet Raj, seeing his approving gaze.

'You have to pick them as soon as they bloom, otherwise they become full of insects,' Shinozaki said over his shoulder, as he led Raj to some basket chairs with worn cushions.

'What do they do in this place?' Raj asked, looking about him.

'It is an investigative unit,' Shinozaki explained importantly. 'Now the war is over, the British want to understand our Japanese battle strategy and how we administered Singapore. They also want information the *kempetai* gained about communists during interrogations. With this information the British will know later how to control things. They feel I can be of help to them, as a translator and liaison officer. I translate the *kempetai* interrogation reports that were handed to the Field Security Service at the transfer of power. Some *kempei* ran away at the time of surrender, but they have since been caught and brought back here and it is my job to question them. All these British Field Security Service men are very intelligent people.' There was a note of pride in Shinozaki's voice at being associated with such men, even if they were former enemies.

As they sat down, two Gurkhas entered the room with a tall, dignified Malay wearing handcuffs. He was released to a waiting British officer and led away up a corridor as Raj and Shinozaki watched.

'That man, Mohammad Abdullah, is also helping the British to understand Japanese operations with regard to the Malays. I have spoken with him. I believe he knows your friend Howard,' Shinozaki said and Raj looked with interest at the Malay. The diplomat shook his head ruefully.

'I'm lucky not to be handcuffed like him but to live in comfort here at Field Security Headquarters. Every day that poor man is taken back to Outram Prison. He was a member of a group working for Malayan independence, the KMM, and associated with Major Fujiwara's intelligence outfit, just like the Indian National Army people. However, I am told he raised his gun to a Japanese officer who he says insulted the Malay race. All we Japanese wanted was to form these KMM men into a military force like the Indian National Army, but Malays are too peaceable; no one wants to fight.'

'How is Takeshi?' Raj asked. The mention of Major Fujiwara had reminded him of his Japanese teacher.

'Takeshi is dead. He died the day after the surrender. Along with many others, he killed himself in shame.' Shinozaki shook his head sadly. Raj sat forward in shock, the image of Takeshi's prominent winged ears suddenly before him. The room was uncomfortably hot; there were no fans and a shaft of sun fell upon Raj, forcing him to move his chair nearer to Shinozaki.

When at last Raj explained about Yoshiko, Mr Shinozaki nodded. 'I too was interned at first. I walked with Yoshiko and her parents to the camp in Jurong. It was a long walk and a great ordeal for Mr and Mrs Yamaguchi. On the way Chinese children threw stones at us, and this angered many of our people. I told them, we forced the British to walk to Changi and now they are making us walk to Jurong. We cannot complain. This is how things are in war. I carried old Mrs Yamaguchi on my back for the last few miles. I will ask if something can be done for Yoshiko,' Shinozaki promised as Raj stood up to take his leave.

Raj now had his own car. It was a second-hand vehicle and he had acquired it just before the surrender with the help of Shinozaki, but nowadays he used a rickshaw or a trishaw to get around and left the car at home. The special licences Raj had had from the Japanese military, to trade in cloth and other commodities, had made him a wealthy man. Yet, it was now dangerous to be seen as having prospered under the Japanese. Raj had not ventured far beyond Manikam's Cloth Shop for days. Gangs of locals still roamed the streets, meting out vigilante justice to those they viewed as collaborator 'dogs'. At the height of the fear, Raj had heard of people being killed on the spot, or tied to lamp posts and having their ears and noses hacked off. It was impossible to hide his association with Shinozaki, but the man's largely benevolent reputation had overflowed advantageously onto Raj. The British were slowly picking up the pieces, and this terrifying anarchy of the streets, encouraged by the communists in the Malayan Peoples Anti-Japanese Army, had all but ceased. In spite of this, Raj still kept a low profile. He was thankful that, before the surrender, he had invested his money with Shinozaki's help in a terrace house on Waterloo Street with a narrow front but a roomy interior.

Leila and Krishna had moved with him into the place, and lived in the upper part of the house, while Raj had his home on the ground floor. It was a spacious residence compared to the cramped rooms above Manikam's Cloth Shop or the tenement room Krishna had rented. Krishna had resumed his job at the Ramakrishna Mission

School and Raj, his once illiterate student, was now his landlord, although no rent was ever taken. Krishna's meagre salary was barely enough to keep himself and Leila. All his dreams were now painfully threadbare. India was not yet free of colonial rule and Subhas Chandra Bose was dead, killed in Taiwan at the end of the war, in a mysterious plane crash.

On reaching Waterloo Street, Raj paid off the trishaw and approached his house, gazing up as always with a sense of proud bewilderment. The pungent aroma of cooking hit him even before a servant opened the door. He sniffed and thought he detected the smell of mutton curry and wondered where Leila could have found goat meat; food was so scarce people fought over scraps, and the ration shop queues were even longer than those under the Japanese.

'Your nose is playing tricks on you; still only tapioca. You're just smelling our black market spices,' Leila said as Raj greeted her.

Leila had taken over the management of the house. They no longer ate from banana leaves on the floor, but from banana leaves on a table sitting on upright chairs. The main room was furnished with a narrow wooden bench and a rattan sofa, a standing bookshelf and a sideboard, in which Leila kept a Japanese tea set hand painted with scenes of Mount Fuji. A large cupboard was built into one wall and a metal *almirah* with a lock and key in which they kept their valuables, stood beside the window. There was also more than enough room in the house for a wife, should Raj decide to marry.

As a servant appeared with the food, Krishna entered the room, his hair dishevelled, the smell of alcohol about him. Leila looked at him coldly. A large framed photograph of Subhas Chandra Bose hung on the wall behind the table, draped with a garland of everlasting flowers. With a respectful glance at the picture, Krishna pressed his hands together in obedience to *Netaji*. Taking his place at the table, he sat silently hunched over his food, his face thin and morose. Two deep frown lines were now etched between Krishna's brows like antennae sprouting from the bridge of his spectacles. *Netaji's* violent death in Taiwan had engulfed him in such desolation it seemed he might never recover.

Everything had collapsed for Krishna with the disbanding of the Indian National Army. The Indian soldiers, who had crossed from the British Indian Army to the Indian National Army, had all been arrested by the returning British authority and shipped to India to be tried as traitors in Delhi. To save their lives, civilian soldiers like Krishna had quickly discarded their uniforms and melted back into everyday life. Every time he shut his eyes, Krishna remembered it all anew. They had trekked up the Malay Peninsula and into Thailand, the women of the Rani of Jhansi Regiment in trucks, the men walking, and then on through Burma to the border town of Imphal. At last they were almost in sight of Delhi. From the slopes of the hills and from the encroaching jungle there were calls of *Inquilab Zindabad* and *Azad Hind Zindabad* from the different INA regiments. Shots rang out. Someone fell beside him as they ran, rolling ahead of him down the slope, blood pouring from his head, but Krishna could not stop to help. They had fought for sixteen hours. They had waited for this fight and the great distance they travelled had been fuelled every mile by hope and then at Imphal after the terrible battle, came the news that they must retreat. *Netaji* spoke to them, giving them strength.

'Our retreat is a temporary retreat. We are not going to stop until India is liberated.' Krishna heard *Netaji*'s voice in his mind once again, and then suddenly, rudely, there was Raj's voice, bringing him back to reality.

'So you have decided to come home,' Raj remarked to Krishna, as he joined them at the table. He exchanged a glance with Leila. Krishna had not been seen for the last two days, and Leila had been sick with worry about him.

'Why are you spending your time with left wing rabble, and worrying your sister?' Raj was unable to keep the anger out of his voice. Krishna frowned but did not reply. Taking hungry mouthfuls of food, he kept his thoughts upon *Netaji*. Krishna's regiment had suffered appalling casualties, both in the battle and on the retreat from Imphal. It took nearly two weeks to reach Bangkok. Krishna arrived alive but half-starved and in a terrible condition; he had marched for one thousand miles. Now he tried to shut out the voices of his sister and his brother-in-law, but they would not let him be.

'Nowadays, he is keeping the company of communists and mad radicals, and not fighting any longer for a pure cause. *Netaji* kept him straight,' Leila commented bitterly. Krishna stirred and emotion flooded his face.

'The Japanese murdered him because he was seeking Russian help to liberate India. When Russia declared war on Japan they killed him; his plane was sabotaged,' Krishna raged.

'Go back properly to your school teaching. How will the Ramakrishna Mission School keep you if you run around with communists?' Leila reproved him.

'The British are promising India independence next year. You should be happy such a great dream is at last coming true,' Raj said. Both brother and sister looked sternly at Krishna over the table.

'Communism is the same as socialism, only stronger. I am always for left-hand thinking,' Krishna growled.

'If workers rise up against employers, how will commerce function? Who will make the world go round in a sensible way, if only left-hand rabble are ruling? No one will be able to make any money,' Raj raised his eyebrows.

After school finished at the Ramakrishna Mission Krishna wandered the streets, getting drunk or debating politics with one or another group of left-wing rabble. *Netaji*'s death had destabilised him. He came home late at night, throwing himself down on the old string bed, his breath foul with home-brewed liquor. He refused to sleep on the new Western-style beds Raj had acquired for his house, and always woke late with a hangover so that Leila must make excuses to the school to explain why he did not appear.

'Too much education has made your brain mad in old age.' Leila sighed, thinking of the idealistic man she had married, and how many things had changed between them.

'You have become a fanatic,' Raj announced in a critical voice. 'And you are an Imperialist. Only interested in money and in consorting with that Japanese Imperialist Ho Ho woman,' Krishna shouted. Leila stared at him in alarm, and Raj looked as if he had been slapped.

The subject of Yoshiko Ho was a sensitive one for them all. Leila had met the woman several times over the years, but since Mr Ho's decline she had become uncomfortably aware of her brother's interest in Yoshiko. She could not understand it. Yoshiko was unfailingly polite and affable when they met, but Leila found her so self-contained, so neat and precise, so different from anyone she had ever met; it was difficult to fathom the woman.

Several times over the years she had gone to a matchmaker or tried to engineer a suitable match for Raj. Nothing had materialised because

Raj himself refused to take any prospective bride seriously. Now, Leila realised, his negative attitude towards an arranged marriage sprang from his interest in Yoshiko Ho. Perhaps, she thought, he may only recently have stumbled upon his real sentiments, now that Mr Ho was so feeble and Yoshiko was in such ascendancy at Ho Biscuits. Their working relationship had allowed an intimacy to blossom, Leila thought, hot with a jealousy that surprised her.

She too was now a businesswoman. Every day she spent some hours helping in Manikam's Cloth Shop at her brother's request. Krishna did not like this. Although, at the time of their marriage, he said he wanted a modern woman, Leila found his ideas of what was modern differed from her own. The war had changed them both. At Manikam's, business had picked up, not for cloth which was still largely unavailable, but for all the cheap sundry items Leila suggested the shop should sell, such as needles and thread, scissors and buttons, paper and ink, boot polish, tape measures and shoulder pads. She had persuaded Raj to drop the words Cloth Shop and call the place simply, Manikam's. A new sign had gone up above the shop.

After lunch was finished and Raj had returned to his rooms downstairs, Leila lay down upon the old string *charpoy*; like her husband she too rejected her brother's purchase of the hard new Western-style bed. Krishna had stormed out of the house and might not return until the early hours; she had not confided to her brother the extent of her worry about him. Across the room the wooden crib on rockers that Krishna had found before her first miscarriage was now used as a receptacle for all manner of oddments, its homely status representing her acceptance that she would never now bear a child. Yoshiko Ho had two sons who Leila knew looked upon Raj as an honorary uncle, if not an honorary father. It was more than she could bear. There was so much she wanted to do, so much that might have been.

Within a week Mr Ho died and was given a Christian burial. Raj stood at the graveside with the family. As the coffin was lowered into the grave Mrs Ho slumped forward as if in grief. Yoshiko and Raj bent to her in concern, but saw with horror that she too was dead. The grave was left open and quickly widened to take two coffins instead of one. Within a day Raj stood at a further funeral beside Yoshiko Ho and her sons.

'Uncle, we have no one now but you,' the elder of Mr Ho's grandsons said tearfully as they left the cemetery. Yoshiko nodded agreement, dabbing her eyes with a handkerchief. Thanks to Mr Shinozaki she had soon returned home, but her old parents were still interned at Jurong. Raj put a fatherly hand on the boy's shoulder, looking over his head at Yoshiko's tearful face, and knew he would do whatever he could to help them.

Howard sat wedged behind a small round table, a remnant from Belvedere's heyday of lodgers and that Rose had salvaged from the house. Mavis cooked him breakfast on a primus stove; the hot room was full of the smell of frying egg.

'Soon the British will have things back to normal; at least now we live without fear.' Rose looked up from darning Howard's socks, to stare hopefully out of the window at the huddle of makeshift dwellings that still filled her garden.

Howard frowned and finished in one mouthful the tiny Bantam egg that Mavis had bartered for a spoonful of sugar from a squatter who kept a hen. Their shabby life, crowded into one room of Belvedere amongst an army of malnourished strangers, and queuing all day at the ration shops, did not give him hope.

'The British may be back but unemployment is phenomenally high and the cost of living is just, well, unliveable,' Howard remarked, wiping his mouth on the back of his hand.

'Restoring life to a broken city is a daunting task,' Rose replied reprovingly, continuing with her darning. Howard felt a moment of fury as he stared at his mother's bent grey head.

'Nothing will ever be the same again, and the British know it. When they knew they were losing the war the Japanese gave Indonesia, the Philippines and Vietnam their independence, handing over to nationalist movements. If the Japanese surrender had been just a little later, Malaya too might have been independent by now. We have a right to rule ourselves; that's the one thing we've learned from the war.' Howard could not control his impatience and his voice rose angrily. He remembered the gangs of starving British prisoners of war forced by the Japanese to clear the town of corpses. That sight alone had altered everyone's perspective of British invincibility.

Howard still woke with bad dreams and experienced bizarre flash-backs, but the sores on his limbs had healed, his hair had thickened and his gums no longer itched. Although the dank green chamber of the jungle with its grim secret life still held him, its grip had lessened in the months since his return to Belvedere. Small things no longer upset him so quickly, and at every turn the familiar reasserted its hold on him. Slowly, he reclaimed himself.

'No one here wants independence.' Rose put down her darning heel, observing him anxiously. She viewed Howard's extreme political views as a further residue of his unspeakable ordeal in the jungle and hoped that like his gums and his hair, this too would respond to loving care. Although it had taken some months, there was flesh on Howard's bones again and his defensive expression had eased; he looked much more himself, Rose thought with relief.

Howard decided not to pursue the subject of change that always irritated his mother. Life in the jungle with Wee Jack, for all its fear and hardship, had forced upon him a political awareness from which there was no turning back. Through the comrades in the camp, he had gained painful insight into lives of grinding poverty and the struggle to live without education or privilege. He had begun to think about things as he had not before.

After many months, Howard had returned to the Harbour Board, one of a lucky few to get a job. He found everything much as he had left it and yet, like everywhere else, irrevocably changed. He had returned resignedly, in need of money, depressed by the place as it closed around him again. Working from the same office, he once more overlooked the dock and the sea, but what remained of the quay was just a pile of bomb rubble. The arrival of ships was still infrequent, and even these could not dock easily in port because of wrecked vessels in the water. The port was awash like everywhere else with gamblers and prostitutes and opium dens, all of which had been legalised by the Japanese. Secret societies proliferated and strikes were to be expected each week. The only thing that heartened Howard was meeting Teddy de Souza again. It had shocked him to see the man no longer sitting at a desk, but doing the lowly work of a messenger boy, stooped and emaciated. When he had first seen Teddy's bent figure hurrying along a corridor, he had not believed it.

'The days of Calthrop were halcyon ones,' Teddy de Souza sighed.

He had been just a month in England with his daughter before war broke out and trapped him there. They sat outside in the shade of the building, and shared some tapioca chips Rose had packed for Howard's lunch.

'Took the first boat I could find back here when it all ended. We didn't see the best of England,' Teddy sighed sadly again.

'Olive died in the Blitz, you know, buried beneath our daughter Elizabeth's home. When peace came Elizabeth and her husband Jim decided to emigrate to Australia. They told me to go with them, but I'm too old to make a fresh start. Besides, there's no place like home. Couldn't wait to get back here,' Teddy said, chewing contemplatively on a tapioca chip. His hair was now no more than a few sparse grey strands stretched over an oily scalp, and his sad eyes were deeply pouched behind a pair of cheap glasses. He had come back to live in a crowded rooming house, and shared a bed with another man.

'He does a night shift and I do a day shift. Works out just fine; he has the bed by day and its mine each night,' Teddy gave a weak chuckle.

'How can you come back here and do a *peon*'s work?' Howard asked, distressed at Teddy's plight.

'Didn't think a bright boy like you would still be at the Harbour Board,' Teddy retorted defensively.

'What else can I do?' Howard replied, seeing again the powerlessness of his life. His mother talked about making his way up the ladder, but when he looked up there was always the inevitable European backside above him.

'You're just a young sapling, boy. You've still got a chance to do what you want with your life. No doubt the British will get it back together again, but the calibre of the men they're sending out now leaves something to be desired.'

Howard knew what Teddy meant. These days he worked under someone much younger than Calthrop. Mr Lambeth, with his narrow jaw, wide forehead and deep-set watchful eyes had fought in the war and killed Germans. The effect of such deeds had undermined him; he was a man in search of opportunity and the lining of his pockets. He was not averse to petty black market trading or even weightier work, and Teddy de Souza knew all about it.

'I've heard it said he's pilfering large quantities of goods from the harbour warehouse, commodities that are meant for the ration shops and selling it on the black market. Also buys watches and jewellery from anyone here, small things to put in his pocket and sell again in England. Making a packet on it all – many of these new men are doing it. Whatever his faults, our Mr Calthrop would not have stooped to that; shows how times have changed.'

Howard had been given a supervisory position as a section manager, but like everyone else worked hard for low wages. As Calthrop had done before, he now took his own boarding parties to the ships, checking cargo and tonnage, and found himself responsible for his team of men and involved in the training of harbour labour. The problems of his men concerned him, as did the living conditions of the workers and the sight of gangs of emaciated coolies hauling unthinkable weights. The war and life in the jungle had changed him; he had accepted such sights before.

IT WAS THE END of the day and he had left the office, pushing his way past the beggars and agitators at the gate. As Howard walked towards the trolley stop he noticed that the crowds of workers who filled the street were all hurrying in one direction. In the distance he heard shouting and cheering. He wondered if another strike was brewing. Following the crowd he turned a corner into a cul-de-sac, and was faced with the unexpected sight of Wee Jack standing on a table haranguing a mass of men. Howard halted in shock. Already, excited workers were pushing up behind him and he found he was trapped in the crowd. Wee Jack was his usual bony self, and Howard knew by the familiar rasp in his voice that he was waiting to cough up a globule of phlegm. Wee Jack punched the air with his fist, shouting out well-worn slogans.

'Our Imperialist masters have not seen the hovels their workers live in, in which our children must die for want of food and medicine. They know nothing of the wretchedness of their workers' lives and yet they suck your blood, grind out your lives. Without us to carry their loads, dig their fields, build their mansions, they could not reap their harvests of gold. And for this, what do they pay you? What do they care if tomorrow you die leaving fatherless children?' Fury erupted in the showers of caustic words and the crowd responded in angry agreement, raising their fists with Wee Jack. Behind Howard the assembly had increased uncomfortably, and he was wedged against a wall. The ragged, malnourished men about him, their faces aflame with emotion, filled him with apprehension even though he understood their need to strike; without work or food he might do the same. When at last it was over and the men began to disperse, he knew he could no longer put off the need to face Wee Jack.

'You saw the crowd?' Wee Jack laughed, effusive after his oratory, the blood still high in his face. He had changed only in a sharpening of features, a more concentrated gaze, a receding hairline and a healthier tone to his skin. Howard stared into the same emotionless eyes and was thrown back into a bog of fear from which he thought he had struggled free.

'There's a place down here that serves good toddy,' Wee Jack suggested affably, and Howard followed, unable to protest.

Night was already upon them and the alley full of dark shadows. In a cul-de-sac the liquor stall, stacked with earthenware toddy jars, released the raw smell of spirit. The cart was surrounded by labourers, who turned to observe Howard as he walked up with Wee Jack. When at last they were sitting on a low wall with the toddy, Howard sniffed at the cup apprehensively. The stuff had a strong and foul aroma; it smelled nothing like the toddy Lionel had brewed.

'Whatever it is, it's alcohol,' Wee Jack said impatiently, seeing Howard's hesitation and tipping up his own glass. 'There's to be a general strike; everyone is coming out – firemen, bus drivers, hospital workers, food hawkers, cabaret girls, trishaw riders; every union has given notice to their management. There's no work, no food, the cost of living is rising and the rice ration has been reduced to three *kati* a week. How can the people live?' Wee Jack demanded. He sat now in the office of the General Labour Union, organising its growing following of workers and expanding union power.

'I'm a member of the Singapore City Committee,' he told Howard proudly. Any organisation Wee Jack was involved in, Howard was sure, must have communist sympathies.

'Drink up. We're going to force constitutional change, bring about a world in which the workers have power,' Wee Jack picked up his cup and threw back the toddy. Howard too raised the thick glass to his lips and drank down the foul brew, aware of how obediently he followed Wee Jack's bidding, and he knew he must get away. As he stood up, the alcohol burned through him and his head began to spin.

'We'll meet again soon.' Wee Jack laughed, as Howard took his leave.

The alley was full of potholes and for a while Howard stumbled forward, his head rolling and his innards on fire. Then his knees buckled beneath him and he fell, hitting his head on a stone. Vomit rose on his tongue and spewed out of him as he lay in the gutter unable to move. He heard voices and the passing of feet near his head. Once or twice someone stopped, prodded him with a foot, turning him over, feeling in his pockets, and he knew he was being robbed. These wretched lanes were home to gangsters, hired killers and violent secret societies, besides prostitutes and thieves. He wondered lethargically if he would soon be murdered and, if he was, how long it would take for the news to reach Mei Lan. She had left the week before for England. He had gone to the dock to see her off on a ship that had seen better days. He thought of her now steaming over the ocean, and wondered when, if ever, he would see her again. He closed his eyes and knew nothing more. When he awoke again first light was breaking, and his face lay in a stinking pool of his own stale vomit. He stood up with difficulty, wiped his face with a handkerchief and stumbled on, eventually finding a rickshaw to take him home to Belvedere.

Howard lay half conscious on a mattress beside his mother's bed. A few yards away beyond a dividing curtain he could see Wilfred who, still physically weak and emotionally fragile, spent many hours of the day asleep. Rose had wanted to call a doctor when Howard returned, but Cynthia had pronounced that he would live.

'He drank country liquor; it's poison. It's not toddy like Lionel made, but raw methylated spirit with any rotting matter thrown in. Sometimes they add dead rats; he's lucky to be alive.' She advised he be left to sleep it off.

Although their electricity was still sporadic, Howard sometimes felt the breeze of the ceiling fan on his face as he drifted in and out of sleep. His mother spooned food into his mouth that he sometimes kept down and sometimes not; he was washed and the functions of his body managed with bedpans and bottles. He was only vaguely aware of these things. In strange dreams he journeyed again through thick jungle. Sometimes through the muted light he saw Wee Jack and turned and fled, or he glimpsed Mei Lan, her back to him, disappearing into the forest, lost to him even as he found her. Yet, when at last the fever broke and he awoke to the soft hum of the turning fan, he knew something he could not name had refocused within him. Through the window he stared at the sun on the leaves of a mango tree and the heavy weight of the green fruit. When he next opened his eyes it was raining and water beat softly on the same green fruit.

Food was scarce and they still lived largely on sweet potatoes and tapioca, and from the ration shop broken rice and dirty sugar, often yellow with insecticide. People's Kitchens were set up everywhere to feed the starving population, and the Singapore Co-operative Store opened above the Liberty Cabaret on North Bridge Road to provide other necessities. The Co-operative bought cheap goods in bulk from Europe and sold them cheaply to those in need: clothes, household items, shoes, soap, underwear – it could not be predicted what might be on sale at the store. Sometimes Howard went there after work to see what he could find. Once, he bought Polish-made sandals for himself and Wilfred, and at other times a teapot, flannelette knickers for Rose, hairpins, scissors and a saucepan.

Below the Singapore Co-operative Store, the Liberty Cabaret was a cavernous, dingy place on a dark stretch of North Bridge Road where all the street lights had been smashed. Sometimes, if he was early, members of a newly formed political party, the Malayan Democratic Union, were to be found sitting on the dance floor of the cabaret drinking warm Tiger beer. When the girls arrived the men repaired to an office upstairs, a room with a few desks, a variety of worn chairs and a telephone.

Howard had been back at work after his liquor poisoning for more than a week when Rose asked him to go to the Co-operative, to enquire about a promised consignment of soap. The Co-operative was open until late in the evening and when Howard arrived loud music already blared from the dance hall downstairs. During the war, when the Japanese used the cabaret for entertainment, he and Lionel with their band had occasionally played at the Liberty. Curious, he pushed the door open and peered inside, remembering his glimpses of the cabaret at Great World when he visited there with his father. The gloom inside was partially lifted by a few red lights but these could not erase the dispirited atmosphere. In the dimness the bodies of dancing couples glided past, like fish in an aqueous world. A strong smell of beer permeated the place, just as it had when he had played his saxophone there.

Shutting the door, he took the stairs to the upper floor and the Co-operative, its rooms crowded with piles of cardboard boxes and samples of merchandise. The long-promised soap had arrived and after buying some bars, he also took a pair of stout court shoes for his mother on condition they could be changed. There was nothing else he could afford that week and he soon left, making his way back along the corridor towards the stairs. Music from the cabaret drifted up to him.

Outside the office of the Malayan Democratic Union the corridor narrowed uncomfortably around a table tennis table by the door. A coffee stall had been set up a short distance away and this, together with the table tennis, gave the MDU premises the atmosphere of a clubhouse. One of the reasons Howard looked forward to visiting the Singapore Co-operative Store was its proximity to the MDU. The new political party had been formed by a multicultural group of English-speaking intellectuals who were vehemently opposed to the continuation of colonial rule.

As he drew level with the MDU office, the door swung open and ten or twelve men spilt out into the corridor. Howard stepped aside to let them pass, happy for a chance to observe first hand these curious political animals. As he waited for the corridor to clear, he was taken aback to see Raj Sherma's brother-in-law, the schoolteacher Krishna, emerge from the room with other MDU members. The sight of Krishna was so unexpected that Howard thought at first he might have made a mistake, but Krishna stepped forward to greet him in equal surprise.

'The Liberty Cabaret is having very much diverse activity,' Krishna agreed as Howard explained his visit to the Co-operative. 'Some of the trade unions also have their offices up here; Singapore Teachers' Union and the Army Civil Service besides some others.' Krishna pointed down the corridor to a row of closed doors.

'Have a coffee,' he offered, leading Howard towards the knot of MDU men crowding about the refreshment table.

'India is to get her independence soon,' Krishna told him as they found a corner to drink their coffee, his voice full of pride. Howard remembered the schoolteacher's impassioned lecture at the Indian Youth League, and wondered at the distance of that time. Krishna had not aged well, Howard observed; his thick halo of hair had receded dramatically and his face was stern, with deep lines about his mouth and brow.

'Stay for a meeting; always interesting debate to hear,' Krishna suggested, having observed the way Howard was trying surreptitiously to listen to the discussion of the men standing nearby.

'I have only recently joined the MDU,' Krishna admitted. 'Now with India's independence soon coming, I am finding new ways to direct my energy.' He did not explain the personal sense of looming irrelevance the news of India's imminent independence had brought him.

The MDU had been formed some months after the Japanese left Singapore, and was whispered by some to be an open front for the Malayan Communist Party, a hotbed of communist sympathisers. This was disputed by MDU leaders, all well-educated, English-speaking men of assorted multiracial origin, some of whom had even been to university in London, Oxford or Cambridge. They were socialists, they insisted, united by their impatient desire to be rid of colonial rule. These sentiments suited Krishna admirably, one set of convictions melting seamlessly into another.

When the meeting started again, Howard took a seat beside Krishna. Full of anticipation, he had the feeling it was not pure coincidence that he had stumbled into this. Looking about the room, absorbing not only the sight of the faces around him but the charged atmosphere of debate, he knew he had waited for such a moment, waited to be amazed; to be politically awakened. Wee Jack's haranguing dogma, coupled with the fear it produced in him, had constricted Howard's ability to find his own political direction.

Before the coffee break there had been discussion about a proposed Malayan Union, a British idea to give the Malayan states self-rule, and the argument continued as the meeting was called to order. 'It's a bungled scheme hatched by the British to produce a mirage of independence,' a stocky Indian with heavy spectacles exploded.

'Also, Singapore is to be excluded from the Union and will remain a colony under British rule. It's unacceptable. Singapore must be merged with the peninsula, and independence given to a united Malaya,' a lanky Chinese protested.

'The Malay States won't agree to that because immigrants would have equal status and Chinese would then outnumber Malays. And in this plan the Malay sultans will no longer hold power,' the Indian pointed out.

As the debate raged, the floorboards trembled beneath their feet with the thump of the music below. Howard had listened to Krishna's angry rhetoric at the Indian Youth League as well as to Wee Jack, but the high stepping debate that now unfolded was new to him. What excited him most was that the issues discussed all centred on Singapore; a place he had given little thought to before. Why think of the freedom of the world, of China or India, he suddenly thought, when he was imprisoned in his own home?

'British rule is over. Now we must fight for self-government. Our future lies under a different sky,' the lanky Chinese shouted.

'The Malayan Democratic Union is the first real political party here, and what we want is Independence, freedom from colonial rule and a socialist state,' the bespectacled Indian said, turning to speak directly to Howard. With a start, Howard realised he had already been taken as a new recruit.

As Krishna walked with Howard to the trolley stop they discussed the meeting. 'They're men who want to change the past; they are not people like you and me. We are small time socialists, they are big time men; highly educated men – men who can make a difference.' Krishna spoke admiringly, enthusing through a cloud of cigarette smoke as they waited for the trolley to arrive.

'A socialist party such as the Malayan Democratic Union could not have been formed before the war; then it would have been seen as treason to speak out like this against British rule and we would all have been put in jail.' Krishna continued to ruminate as the trolley arrived. Howard climbed aboard and Krishna turned to find his own way home.

As the trolley moved forward Howard took a seat and through the window watched Krishna walk away. His pulse beat fast and his mind churned with the new ideas he had heard. He thought of the men of the MDU, lawyers and teachers and intellectuals, all men with special skills. *They are men who can make a difference, men who want to change the past; they are not like you and me.* Krishna's words echoed in his head and, as the euphoria left him, he began to feel depressed. He looked down at the string bag on his lap with the shoes for his mother and the bars of soap from the Co-operative Store. *The future lies under a different sky*, one of the MDU men had said. More than anything he wanted to be part of what lay ahead. The talk he had heard was exciting, and the men he had met inspiring, but one clear, cold strand of reasoning stood out in his fevered thoughts. What difference could he make to the world without higher education, without a special skill?

He mentioned something of this to Teddy de Souza, who listened with sympathy as they shared a plate of shaved ice and strawberry syrup bought from a hawker on the wharf. 'Skills are only things you acquire. Where would those men be if they didn't have their university education? They'd be just the same as you and me. You could easily get yourself skills, boy. Get yourself a degree in something; you're still a young man. This war has delayed many people's education and they are all going off to do it now,' Teddy said.

'I didn't get a Queen's Scholarship, and I don't have the money to go privately to England,' Howard replied in a low voice.

'Australia is right there in our own backyard. The education is cheaper, not quite the prestige of England of course, but you come out with the same degrees, and in the end that's all that matters.' Teddy crunched the crimson ice between his dentures, his tongue stained shockingly pink.

'There is still the question of money,' Howard replied, staring beyond the wharf to the limitless expanse of the sea. Teddy sighed, unable to offer a solution to a problem that plagued them all.

As the weeks went by the idea that he must seek a shift in his life grew stronger. Howard stared morosely at the restless labourers assembling each day in the cul-de-sac to listen to Wee Jack and other union leaders. Strikes came and went to a regular rhythm, work was sabotaged and life interrupted in ways never known before. Communists, backed up by vicious gangs from the secret societies, controlled the picket lines at the dockyard gates, and men could not work if they wanted to. Everything was changing.

Some months later Howard was walking to the trolley stop with Krishna after an MDU meeting when Raj, passing the Liberty Cabaret by chance in his chauffeur-driven car, stopped at the crossroads beside them. Raj was effusive in his greeting, but Howard could see by Krishna's surly expression that he was not pleased to see his brother-in-law. Raj insisted on giving Howard a lift home, accepting no excuse.

'Only one condition: you must first see my new place which is nearby, then the driver will drop you back to Belvedere,' Raj insisted affably.

The Waterloo Street home had cool tiled floors and high airy ceilings with electric fans speeding around in each room. Except for the rushing of fans, the house lay empty and silent. Howard learned that Krishna and his wife lived on the upper floor, while Raj was the sole occupant of the ground floor. After Belvedere's many squatters, and the homeless who thronged every available space in the city, there was something obscene in the vacant essence of the house. A smell of Indian spices permeated everything, and gave the impression that food was plentiful here.

Raj offered a choice of whisky or beer, and his sister Leila appeared with snacks of things Howard had not tasted for years. The hardship they experienced at Belvedere did not seem to exist in this house, and Howard realised with a shock how extensive Raj's black market dealings must be, and also how much he had profited by his association with the Japanese.

'That Lim woman has gone to England. It was in the newspaper,' Raj said, pouring himself another whisky. 'Very terrible, all the things she suffered. Is the man who tortured her hanged yet?' He threw a mouthful of cashew nuts into his mouth and offered the bowl to Howard. It was so long since he had eaten a cashew that Howard had difficulty adjusting to the unexpected taste. Raj's lack of interest was understandable, but his casual reference to the brutality Mei Lan had endured resonated painfully with Howard. As they talked Krishna hovered uneasily in the background, ignored by both his wife and brother-in-law. Unlike his loquaciousness at the MDU, at home Krishna sank into silence and Howard began to feel uncomfortable.

'I hope Krishna is not pulling you into his mad politics?' Raj warned as he sipped his whisky, turning suddenly upon his brother-in-law.

'All he is wanting is to get back to some studies,' Krishna retorted, the sharpness of his tone revealing the antagonism between himself and Raj.

'Study? Why do you want to go back to studies? You have a good job at the Harbour Board,' Raj replied testily, staring at Howard over the raised rim of his glass. The subject of education made him nervous; he was always afraid it would be found that he had none.

'I'm not a businessman. It's difficult to get far in the world without qualifications.' Howard defended himself before the intensity of Raj's gaze.

'You seem educated enough. You have more education than me, so why are you now wanting more?' Raj spoke fiercely, and Howard felt bound to explain himself.

'If I could get to a university, perhaps in Australia . . . but of course there's no money just now . . . men who have education can make a difference in the world . . .' Howard broke off, embarrassed, prepared to be ridiculed by the worldly, wealthy Raj who continued to stare at him intently, saying not a word. Then, with a shrug of his heavy shoulders, Raj took another mouthful of whisky and spoke almost angrily.

'Education. You want education? You have developed ambition, that's why you want education.' He gave a sceptical snort and fell silent again, peering down into his glass. He understood only too well Howard's sudden interest in further education. The man was bright, very bright. He might easily have been a Queen's Scholar and done what he wished with his life many years before, but luck had been against him. If he, Raj, had had even half Howard's education, he too would be looking at more. Raj remembered Manikam, and the investment the man had made in his own education, meagre as that had been; he remembered his early admiration for Krishna, who had taught him all he knew. He remembered crouching down beside his brother-in-law, dictating those long-ago letters to Leila, and for a moment the smell of jasmine from the garland shop came to him over the years. He sighed and began to speak again.

'What little education I have, I owe to Krishna. Even now, it takes me so long to read a newspaper, and many words I still do not yet know. I am like a child in that way, but I can read, and that is the important thing. I too had much ambition, but instead of education God gave me good wits and I used them. And there were men who helped me from the goodness of their hearts, like Krishna.' Raj threw his brother-in-law a look of sudden, grudging gratitude. He remembered his other mentors, Mr Ho and Mr Yamaguchi and Mr Shinozaki, whose assistance had brought him to this Waterloo Street house.

'Such education as helps men fly high is not my destiny. Indians with that kind of education are few and far between here; mostly here in Singapore we Indians are lowly merchants. Long ago I decided my ambition would be always to have money, and this I have achieved. Money can be made with no education.' Raj gave a smile, and for a moment his face lost its shrewd, impenetrable guard. His voice was filled with new depth when he spoke again to Howard.

'Perhaps, at last, through you I can repay a debt to the men who helped me. Tell me what it is you are needing, and perhaps I can help you.' He held a hand up to silence Howard, who had started in surprise.

'This is just a further investment for me, but as on all my investments, I expect a good return.' Raj raised his whisky glass in a toast to Howard, but his eyes rested on Krishna, who at last gave a slow smile and a nod of approval.

32

WILFRED DROVE SLOWLY, CONCENTRATING hard. Although his physical health had recovered in the years since the war, his nerves were still bad and he found driving a strain. In the chaotic traffic conditions of the rutted Singapore roads, he was always afraid of killing someone. The car was third hand, but in good condition and served his purpose. Some mornings he dropped Cynthia at the General Hospital and then, if it was necessary, drove to the Reuters office in Cecil Street.

He had not returned to *The Straits Times* when his health improved but had instead joined Reuters on a freelance basis. He had also agreed to be the Malaya correspondent for the *Observer* in London, writing a weekly column for the newspaper. He was working mostly from home where he could break off and rest as the doctor insisted. His back and legs never stopped troubling him after the experiences in the Japanese camp. There were also headaches, and frequent shivering fits that were the remains of malaria. He still could not sleep without a pill; but generally he was better, and refused to complain.

Although the city was still battered in appearance, life in Singapore had returned to normal, and food was once more available. Except for a remaining couple of families living in makeshift huts in the garden, the squatters were long gone from Belvedere; the house looked much as before, if shabbier. They had reclaimed their old room and Cynthia had somehow managed to buy new curtains and a spring mattress for their bed. Now that Wilfred was stronger and earning money again, he and Cynthia had decided to move out of Belvedere and look for a home of their own, much to Rose's distress. They had also decided to try for a child; they were full of plans and Cynthia had agreed to give up work if they had a family. She held a responsible position at the General Hospital, involved with the training of young nurses at a newly established nursing school. Although this absorbed her, it was disheartening to find that on their return the British had brought back all the old structures; senior nursing staff were again European and Cynthia, as a local, was once more second-rung personnel. Once Wilfred's health had improved, he encouraged her to return to full-time work, knowing she missed it. It was impossible also for Wilfred to tell Cynthia how much he wanted to be alone; sometimes he did nothing but lie on the bed all day, staring up at the whirling fan.

That morning he had dropped Cynthia not at the General Hospital, but at Joo Chiat Hospital where she had a matter to discuss with Dr Wong. From there he planned to drive to the Reuters office. The Joo Chiat area was less familiar to him than the central roads in town, and trying to take a short cut he was soon lost. By the many road-side stalls and *kampong*-style houses and the preponderance of Malay faces, he knew he was in Geylang Serai. On the narrow street the traffic was unusually thick and he wondered if there was an accident ahead. The strong rotting smell of durian from the many fruit stalls along the road drifted to him through the open car window.

Soon he was forced to draw to a halt behind a thick mass of stationary traffic; in the distance he heard shouting. Although he pressed the car horn, nothing moved and the driver of the bullock cart ahead glanced over his shoulder and gesticulated angrily. Already, exhausted by the stress of driving on a strange road, Wilfred's hands were trembling on the steering wheel. He could not move backwards or forwards for the press of carts and trishaws now piling up around him. A group of Malay youths rushed by waving their arms and yelling aggressively. Usually, it was the Chinese communists who ran around shouting and agitating; the Malays were a peaceful people and Wilfred stared out of the open window in surprise, noticing in alarm that several of the young men were carrying lethal looking *parangs*. He decided to make an attempt to turn the car around and drive back in the direction he had come to find an alternative route.

Slowly, after much tooting of the horn, room was reluctantly made for him to edge the car out into the opposite lane. Another group of excited Malays appeared, shaking their fists. At the sound of Wilfred's impatient honking the youths halted, staring angrily at him as he peered anxiously out of the window. With a shout of fury, one of them stepped into the traffic as if he would approach the car, but then decided other-wise and ran on behind his friends. Wilfred saw with further alarm that all the young men carried an assortment of knives, as if prepared for violence. Everyone had now turned to observe him, and he realised with a throb of panic that he was the only white man in the vicinity.

With difficulty, he completed the turn and felt relieved as he began to drive back along the road. After a short distance an acrid smell of burning rubber came to him, and he saw that a car ahead of him had been overturned and set on fire. Flames shot up as the petrol ignited. The young men who had passed him earlier were running around the burning car, shouting wildly. Wilfred's heart leapt in fear. Quickly, he turned into a narrow unpaved road to his right, hoping his car had not been seen. His head thumped painfully, and his hands now trembled so violently he was afraid he would lose control of the vehicle. The narrow dirt track was deserted; filled with relief, he stopped the car beside some *kampong* houses, mopping his brow and bending to retrieve the water flask that had rolled off the seat on to the floor. Before he could straighten and take a drink, shouting welled up around him. Out of the back window he saw a crowd of men racing towards him. In panic he reached for the ignition, fumbling with the key.

Before he could start the engine, they were around him. The door was tugged open and he was pulled out. All he could see was a mass of dark angry faces, wet mouths, white teeth. He was thrown to the ground and kicked. Other blows followed, hurled down viciously at him. Beyond the pain and shock of attack was the knowledge that these men were prepared to kill him. He saw the flash of *kris* and *parang* and prayed he would not feel the sharp blades.

A man in the camp had been beheaded because he was too sick to lift a stone and, no longer caring, spat at the Japanese guard. He was pushed to his knees and the guard's long sword came down upon the man, severing his head in a single stroke. It rolled down the slope like a football, while blood fountained out of the fallen body. Wilfred remembered the rushing sound of the blade as it cut through the air before slicing into the man. Now, holding up his arms to fend off blows, he did not see the iron bar coming down until it cracked sickeningly upon his head. His mind floated over the black edge of consciousness, just as it had many times before in the camp.

When Wilfred opened his eyes the first thing he saw were the blades of a fan turning lazily above him. Everything was white and light.

There was silence, and the louvres of a half-shuttered window threw slatted shadows on to the wall. A smell of flowers came to him, and when he turned his head in the direction of this perfume he saw Cynthia sitting on a chair a short distance away, a vase of flowers beside her. She came to him immediately, and put a cool hand on his head.

'The police found you. Luckily you had identification on you and they called us,' she told him. He saw she wore her nurse's uniform, and that he was in a hospital ward.

'I cannot feel my legs,' he said, trying not to sound desperate.

'You have been in and out of consciousness for three weeks.' Cynthia pulled a chair up beside the bed and wiped tears from her eyes with the back of her hand; she had requested Matron to take her off her usual duties so that she could nurse Wilfred privately.

'I cannot feel my legs,' he repeated, trying to remember what had happened and seeing only confused images.

'You're lucky to be alive,' Cynthia admitted in a low voice. He realised then that his head was heavily bandaged and his limbs were weighted down with plaster. Cynthia's voice was calm and professional but he saw tears spring again to her eyes. Both his legs were broken and the doctors said he might have difficulty walking again, the blow to his head had fractured his skull, Cynthia told him. All their plans must be put on hold.

'There was Muslim rioting; it was that custody case,' she told him later, mentioning the court case everyone had been following in the paper, of a Dutch girl, adopted by a Muslim woman when the Japanese had interned her parents during the war. The girl had been brought up as a Muslim but the Dutch mother now wanted her back and returned to the Catholic faith. The Muslim community had gone mad, massing in front of the court, indiscriminately attacking white people and property.

It took many months for Wilfred to recover from the vicious attack but slowly he regained some use of his limbs; his head wound healed without the predicted dire consequences. Eventually, he was discharged from hospital and returned to Belvedere. Then, every day with Cynthia's help he hauled himself out of the wheelchair and, supported on each side, attempted to walk, his legs buckling painfully beneath him. Although his body responded to rest and care, he had fallen again into depression, speaking little and erupting often into uncontrollable anger.

Cynthia was distraught. It had taken so long for him to return to physical and mental health after his experiences as a POW. When he joined Reuters she had been happy to see him interested again in life. Now, in a stray moment of violence, everything was wiped out and the struggle back to health must begin again.

Yet, once he was free of the plaster casts and his wounds had healed, she sensed the difference in him. She caught not sorrow, but the hard fist of his anger. He railed at her continuously, and even when he apologised began almost immediately shouting again over things she thought were trifling. She knew he could not help himself, and that his anger must be taken as a positive sign.

'I do not want to sit with your mother,' he told her sharply one morning, as she pushed the wheelchair across the red Malacca tiles of Belvedere's dining room to where Rose sat crocheting on the old chintz sofa.

'Two invalids keeping each other company. You know she misses Mavis.' Cynthia laughed to humour him. Mavis had returned to Penang some time before, and Rose was surprised to find how lonely she felt without her. She had aged suddenly and now suffered from angina that required her to rest.

'I'm a wreck,' Wilfred admitted to Rose, as Cynthia settled the wheelchair beside the sofa and drew up a chair for herself. Ah Fong brought coffee and they sat together before the open windows facing the orchard. In the war a shell had landed in the middle of the mangosteens and many charred and leafless trees still clustered lifelessly about the crater.

'You should clear them away,' Wilfred advised, staring critically at the trees as he picked up a copy of *The Straits Times* that lay folded across his knees.

'They're not yet dead,' Rose insisted calmly. Wilfred shook the newspaper open with an angry flourish.

'Sometimes it's hard to die. Nothing seems to finishes you off – it only leaves you half alive.' Wilfred spoke so fiercely that Rose fell silent and returned her attention to her crocheting. Cynthia looked down at her hands and for once had no words of comfort to offer. It pained Rose to see her daughter suffer, always caring for others, her own life not yet begun; now, tied to the routine of nursing an invalid husband again. And Rose herself was now added to Cynthia's burden.

Because of her angina Rose was forced for a good part of the day to rest on the old sofa, her feet propped up on a cushion. When they eventually got rid of the squatters, the sofa had been discovered in a far corner of Belvedere, its springs broken, its stuffing regurgitated but with its frame intact; she had it reupholstered in the usual pink chintz. Its condition was similar to her own she thought; the war had taken its toll on them all.

Beside her in his wheelchair, Wilfred was locked into a world of silent misery. She stared at his angry profile, the uneven bridge of his nose, the gaunt cheeks and the sensitive lips, clearly revealed now that he had shaven off his moustache, and felt for him. She observed his hand on the arm of the chair, permanently callused from forced labour on that terrible railway, and now crookedly healed after the riot when his fingers had been smashed.

'Why don't you write about that time in the camp?' Impulsively, she voiced an idea that had occurred to her earlier, but then regretted her words. The subject of Wilfred's ordeal as a prisoner of war was taboo. She saw his jaw tighten immediately and lowered her eyes to the crochet hook, working it in and out of the lacy threads of a growing tablemat. Cynthia looked at her mother in surprise, struck by the idea, and dared to say what Rose could not.

'That's what you must do. You need to tell the world about it. People need to hear. And the dead would be happy if you spoke for them; how else can their story be known? If you can do this, then all those poor men will not have died in vain.'

There was a gruff intake of breath from Wilfred and then a noisy folding up of *The Straits Times*. In fury he placed his hands on the wheels of the chair and propelled himself back to his room. Cynthia sighed deeply, staring down at her hands, while Rose looked after Wilfred in sad perplexity as he slammed shut the door of his room.

'Perhaps everything here is too old or broken to recover,' Cynthia remarked, looking up at the cavernous Belvedere ceiling. Once the squatters had gone the true state of the place had been revealed. There was no money to repair the damage but they had patched it up as best they could over the years since the Japanese departed.

'We'll advertise again for lodgers,' Rose said in false brightness.

'You know that's useless. Who will want to lodge in a place like this?' Cynthia replied, observing the peeling paint and splintered, lopsided blinds. A three-legged planter was propped up with a stone; on the dirty wall was a pale square where a picture had once hung.

Although the British had returned to the island, Rose soon discovered that young men with fresh faces and a spring in their step ignored Belvedere's run-down accommodation. Only two ancient Eurasian widowers, and an old British major who could afford no better, had been installed as lodgers. And worst of all, Howard had gone to Australia.

Against her advice he had got himself a place at the University of Sydney to study politics and economics. It was pure madness, she thought, throwing up a good job at the Harbour Board for an unknown future, but he had refused to listen. He had even put himself in debt to a wealthy Indian who Rose was sure would squeeze every penny of interest from him. It was after he left that the angina started and, although he wrote regularly, Rose had not told him the pain she suffered or her loneliness without him.

It was some weeks later, when he could hobble by himself upon a stick, that Wilfred asked Cynthia to set up his typewriter in their room. For the next few months, when he got up each morning he went to his desk and was seen thereafter only at mealtimes. He wanted nobody near him, not even Cynthia. She tiptoed about as quietly as she could, observing Wilfred in a frenzy of anguish as he ripped half-written pages out of the typewriter, throwing them in the waste paper basket at such a rate that she wished she had never suggested he write about his experiences.

'I can't find a way in,' he shouted at Cynthia, dropping his head in his hands, his memories, although so vivid within him, seeming inaccessible. He had tried first to write down his experiences in the form of non-fiction, then as autobiography, then in diary form but nothing worked; he could not find the voice that would lead him to himself. Then, one night in the early hours he shook Cynthia awake.

'Help me to the desk,' he said urgently. After settling him there, she returned to bed.

In the morning she was surprised to find he was still at the typewriter, the sound of his fingers hitting the keys competing with the morning chorus of birds. He tried to explain that he had been woken by a sentence pacing about in his head. When he had written it down another appeared, followed by yet another, one sentence piling up behind the last. By morning he knew a book was being painfully forced from him, twisting his gut inside out. To his surprise he found he was writing a novel, something he had not thought of doing. Yet, he knew he must follow the invisible thread now offered him and go wherever it led.

From then on, day after day, he refused to move from the desk as he journeyed again through an underworld, falling deeper and deeper into its darkness. Once he could transpose emotion on to another person, even if that other was a creature of fiction, he found he could enter experience. The release this brought him made him ill in a different way, as he fought to transcend and examine the evil that had trapped them all in its hellish world. The fibres of his being were worn thinner and thinner by the effort of reliving, but as the pages piled up he knew in some way he was regaining himself.

Sometimes, he stared at the innocuous words on the page and wondered at the dark universe compressed into those small black letters. If he stared at them hard enough they lost all meaning, appearing an incomprehensible mumbo-jumbo of ciphers. Yet, still he wrote and wrote and could not stop. Lunch, and sometimes also dinner, was taken in swift bites at his desk. Then, suddenly, it was finished, as unexpectedly as it had started. He put a full stop at the end of a line and knew it was done, that there was nothing more to say. For days then, he was drained and listless and sad, and free. He cried unashamedly.

Cynthia went through the manuscript, packed it up and sent it to a publisher in London, for Wilfred was unable to look at it again. Now that it was done, he did not know where the words had come from and immediately recoiled from them. Reading the book, Cynthia was deeply shaken, for until then she had not known the details of his time as a prisoner of war. He had said nothing, and she had not dared to question. Now, she was haunted by what she knew.

The few years in England had passed quickly for Mei Lan and she had stayed longer than intended, passing her law examinations with honours. When, after she had given evidence at the war crimes tribunal, she finally left Singapore for Oxford, she found St Hilda's College already primed for her arrival. Her tutor persuaded her to see a psychiatrist, an eminent Oxford man who was an expert in the treatment of traumatised minds. She could not say how much he helped her, but she tried to believe that a process of healing had begun; if she believed, then it might happen. At first study had been almost impossible, but slowly she learned to concentrate again, her memory improved, the dynamics of everyday living fell into familiar places; life caught her once more. She managed to form tepid friendships with a few of the other women students, but took such care to seal her past from examination that it was said she was aloof. Men gossiped about how she rejected even flippant advances, drawing back into herself like a threatened animal. The general opinion was that she was academically brilliant but a social misfit; a Chinese oddball, they called her.

During this time letters arrived regularly from Howard, telling her of his life in Australia, the university in Sydney, the work, the beaches, the kangaroos and arid hinterland. Each one reiterated in different words the sentiments he held for her. Once or twice she had replied, but his letters lay like stones in her hands. The effort of correspondence grew too heavy to support, and she turned away in silence, reading but not answering, unsure of her feelings for him, unsure of anything in her life. In one letter he even raised the subject of marriage, suggesting that once they both finished their studies, they consider becoming engaged. She found the idea of marriage confusing. She no longer knew who she was: how could she bind herself to another? Howard's letters grew less frequent, as if responding to her silence.

Now, she sat at a desk in the office of the law firm Able Long & Swynburne in London. The job at Gray's Inn had come to her through a contact of JJ's. Norbert Swynburne, an elderly and benevolent lawyer, had originally been introduced to JJ by Mr Cheong of Bayley McDonald & Cheong, the law firm Lim Hock An used in Singapore. A widower with grown-up children, with a grey beard and ample girth, he had been guardian to JJ when he was studying in England. Norbert was the senior partner in Able Long & Swynburne, and he suggested Mei Lan work for some time with the practice.

'You're the only woman here besides Miss Wakefield,' Norbert had said on her first day, pointing out a thick-waisted spinster with a bolster-breast and spetacles. 'If the war hadn't happened, JJ would have worked with us too,' he added. Her throat constricted and tears pricked her eyes.

She liked living in London, liked the graceful buildings, the sedate introspection of the place; the greyness of it all suited her emotions. The city struggled, as did everywhere else in Europe, with post-war austerity. Memories of the Blitz were everywhere still, in the sudden empty spaces between crowded houses or the occasional mound of bomb rubble sprouting weeds. These scars only pulled her closer to the city, for she knew it shared with her a common trauma. She had rented a small flat in Kensington, just off the High Street, and travelled each day to work by the Underground. The sun was seldom seen and she had not missed it and would have run from its joyful flamboyance had it stayed in the sky for too long. She felt no desire to return to Singapore.

Her desk in Able Long & Swynburne was beside a narrow window in a panelled room of warped beams and creaking, thinly carpeted floor. There was a smell of dampness. Norbert told her the building was of eighteenth-century construction, all its parts huddled excessively together; door frames were crooked, staircases narrow and sewage pipes often blocked. From the window she could see the great dome of St Paul's Cathedral, and the grey clouds blowing about in the sky, the light changing by the hour.

Norbert spoke Mandarin and some Cantonese and had been born in China, living there until he was seven. 'My parents were missionaries although, as you can see, I didn't follow in their footsteps and disappointed them terribly,' he told her.

He invited her frequently to dinner at a small family run Italian restaurant near the office, with candles stuck into the necks of wine bottles and red checked tablecloths. He liked to talk about China, its history and art, for which he had a great fondness. Singapore was a place he knew well, having lived there when his parents moved from China. Unlike with the students at Oxford or the other bowler-hatted men in the office, there seemed nothing to explain to Norbert and talk flowed easily between them. Mei Lan had never tasted wine before meeting Norbert, who always consumed copious amounts. Although she drank only a glass or two, the charge of release it gave her began to be addictive. Inside, she softened unmanageably, but she liked the feeling; a weight was eased. Norbert was the first person to whom she told anything of her imprisonment by the *kempetai*. Yet, even to him, she was ashamed to admit how much the shadow of Nakamura still underpinned her life. She could not show him the scars on her back or tell him how, in the red-brick streets of Kensington, on a bus or in the green oasis of Hyde Park, Nakamura might appear, rising up suddenly like an evil genie in an oddly shaped tree trunk, a shadow, or in the image of an innocent man walking briskly towards her. Once, in Oxford, on the calm stretch of St Giles he had stood squarely before her, booted legs apart, and she had stopped, poleaxed, and sunk down on the pavement, hands covering her head. People had rushed to help; an ambulance had been called.

Norbert asked nothing, understanding that the worst was still locked deep inside her. He waited for her to tell him, or not to tell him, as she wished. In the office of Able Long & Swynburne everyone thought they were having an affair. He took her home, to a tall gloomy house in Putney with a garden of ancient rhododendrons dappled in sunlight and shadow. The place had a bachelor smell about it of whisky dregs, old furniture and cold, closed-up rooms.

'I only use a bedroom and kitchen and this one room downstairs since Diana died,' he admitted. Their companionship was peaceable. They sat in separate chairs and talked, on either side of a gas fire that resembled blazing logs.

'We could get married,' he said wistfully one day across the space between them. It seemed outlandish and she told him so, and in reply he sighed and nodded.

Once, when the opportunity arose, he pulled her to him and she felt the soft, bearish bulk of him and the wiry brush of his beard enfolding her. He kissed her wetly, and she let him. In the second year, on his birthday, she gave him the only gift he wanted. She had not thought it out, had not intended it. The wine they had drunk slowed her impulses, and that night he had been persistent, leading her gently step by step towards the place she dreaded to go. When his hands at last travelled over her body she struggled to pull away, the old terror surging through her, but it was too late. Already the cushioning of his soft body overpowered her, and she closed her eyes and bit her lip as he rocked above her, unresponsive and dead to his touch, enduring. It happened several times again, when wine had got the better of them both. Their relationship was a stately dance of minimal contact and, once the rules were established, it remained that way.

'Marry me,' he had mumbled into her neck, still lying upon her, the weight of him pressing the breath from her body before he rolled awkwardly off her and she could breathe again. He had asked her several times before and she made no reply, but now she was tempted to agree. His kindness and strength were becoming addictive, like the wine she looked forward to drinking with him each night. It might be a means of escape, she recognised, but escape was all she wanted.

'Marry me,' Norbert pleaded again, lying flat on his back beside her. She turned her head away, her eyes settling on his clothes folded over the back of a chair – the worn, long-sleeved woollen vest, the baggy underpants, the looped braces of his pinstriped trousers – and inhaled the medicinal smell of his hair oil and knew in that moment that there was no escape, and that she would return to Singapore.

'I must go back,' she told him. 'I cannot go forwards unless I go back. I'm just living in limbo here.' As the words fell from her she knew something inside her must work independently, shaped by a will of its own.

33

THE LAND DREW AWAY, the water cutting about the boat in foamy streaks of quartz. The sound of the engine vibrated in Raj's ears and a breeze blew on his face. Ahead, the small island of St John's was a green blur, and the weight of memory shifted within him. He remembered the long-ago day of his arrival in Singapore. He remembered standing on the deck of a ship as, wrapped in mist and mystery, this same shoreline approached and at last Singapore was before him. In those times all deck passengers were quarantined at St John's before entering the town. Now, since the government had declared a State of Emergency, St John's, although still a quarantine area and a medical facility for opium addicts, was also a detention centre for political subversives. Surrounded by water, cut off from contaminating contacts, it was hoped that in isolation radicals might mend their seditious ways. Nowadays, there were too many of these men about for comfort, and the colonial government was hard pressed to keep track of them. It was here that Krishna had spent the last few years, detained without trial under the government's Emergency Regulations.

A gust of wind lifted Raj's thinning hair as he sat in the prow of the small boat. Looking across the water, he sighed as memories passed through him. To take in that first view of Singapore so long ago, he had wrapped himself in a filthy blanket against the early morning breeze, a blanket he had slept on every day of the voyage. As he left the village his grandmother had given him the cloth, rolled up and tied tightly with string. He had it still in an old tin trunk, for he was unable to throw it away. As the launch bucked and dipped over the waves, Raj looked down at the panama hat in his hand and the gold watch on his wrist and felt giddy, not with the movement of the craft but at the thought of how far he had travelled.

The boat neared the shore and a rope was thrown out. Raj disembarked, but a rush of resentment filled him at the thought of Krishna's return to the Waterloo Street house. While his brother-in-law had been shut away on St John's, Raj had felt only guilty relief to be free of his brooding presence. Head held high, Krishna had walked out of the house on Waterloo Street to be imprisoned with the cream of Singapore's radical core, as if arrest were a badge of honour. The ensuing shame and notoriety had not been easy for Raj or Leila to face.

'He'll be out of trouble for a while,' Raj had told Leila at the time of the arrest, guessing she was no less relieved than he.

Leila shook her head. 'All prisoners on St John's belong to the Anti-British League; they are all people like him; all communist sympathisers. They will have a lot of time to talk together about their mad ideas, so how will anything change?'

The Malayan Democratic Union had been forced to dissolve five years before. Heavily infiltrated by communists, it was seen by the colonial government as an open front for the Malayan Communist Party whose post-war honeymoon with the British Government had not lasted long. MDU members, faced with arrest on these grounds, quickly and prudently disbanded. Soon afterwards the Anti-British League was born and paraded many of the Malayan Democratic Union's familiar faces. It met, like the MDU before it, at the Liberty Cabaret, although now in a highly furtive manner, and Krishna attended meetings as before.

The two years Raj and Leila had spent alone together had been a peaceful interlude; Leila was now running Manikam's on her own, leaving Raj free to concentrate on Ho Biscuits. The Emergency Regulations that had resulted in Krishna's arrest had not affected Raj's life in any way. Law-abiding people lived as before grateful that, by declaring a State of Emergency, the colonial government had put the lid on communist-backed subversion. Communists had undermined the colony since the end of the war, penetrating every walk of life, instigating strikes and violence and terror.

It was a steep climb up the hill and there was no transport. Raj huffed and puffed and sweated resentfully as he walked. Soon he stopped to catch his breath and looked up at the buildings above him on the top of the hill, buildings full of communists who, to his mind, were like an infestation of cockroaches; nothing stamped them out. Raj and Leila had expected Krishna to be kept on St John's indefinitely, but now he was suddenly free. They heard he had recanted his seditious ways, although Raj found this hard to believe. He took out a handkerchief and wiped his perspiring neck and his anger overflowed; he must now take a suspected communist back into his home and what this would do to his reputation he did not know.

The road continued up the slope to low, whitewashed buildings enclosed by a thick metal fence. His anger hardening by the moment, Raj pulled the panama hat well down on his head for the sun burned hot on his back. Singapore had been an orderly town when he first arrived, he thought grimly. Now, Ho Biscuits was beset each month by escalating agitation and union demands. Workers seemed to be on a permanent go-slow, always threatening a strike. Fanatical communists had caught the imagination of the mob and men like Krishna were to blame. At least, thought Raj, the Emergency had forced most of the communists back into the jungle from where they had so audaciously emerged after the war. On mainland Malaya they now waged an armed insurrection against the British, identical to the one previously waged against the Japanese. Communist guerrillas were murdering British rubber planters at such a steady rate that even in faraway Singapore men like Krishna were detained without trial. Raj had lost all patience. While he worked hard at Ho Biscuits to maintain them all, his brother-in-law lived the idle life of a political dilettante.

At last, breathless and dripping with sweat, he reached the top of the hill, mopped his face once again with a handkerchief, stated his business at the guardhouse, and sat down on a bench before the barbed wire fence to wait for Krishna. In a few minutes his brother-in-law appeared with a prison guard, and the gate in the fence was opened. Raj nodded a silent greeting, feeling both unable and unwilling to speak, rose to his feet and turned back to the road with Krishna following him. Soon, they climbed mutely into the waiting boat for the journey back to Singapore.

From compulsory exercise as a political prisoner Krishna had acquired new physical fitness. His face was relaxed, his biceps developed, the harried look had gone from his face, but he had aged. His thick hair was now almost grey, although his eyebrows remained as black as ever. A rush of euphoria filled him as he turned to look back at the whitewashed buildings where he had spent the last few years.

There was no one to wave goodbye. His exit from St John's was considered paramount to treason by his fellow prisoners. Krishna had not yet served out his detention but bargained his release with a British Special Branch officer who occasionally visited the inmates of St John's.

'If you admit you are a member of the Anti-British League and renounce it, we can consider releasing you,' the officer had told him. Two other detainees had already left the island in this way and Krishna began to think more deeply about his incarceration. Martyrdom on St John's served no useful purpose he decided; his work lay back in the world, undercover. Now, as the motor launch pushed off from the shore he looked out at the boundless space of the sea and knew he had made the right decision.

'The feeling of being cut off is the worst thing about St John's. Prisoners are allowed to mix freely; we even cook our own meals and play cards. Sometimes, it seemed like a seaside holiday, but it was still detention,' Krishna said conversationally to Raj, turning again to observe the retreating island as the boat gathered speed.

His time on St John's had passed slowly in a state of seamless monotony. His fellow detainees on the island were all card-carrying communists, fully-fledged members of the Malayan Communist Party. They were men who had been in and out of the trade union offices above the Liberty Cabaret, and Krishna's network of subversive contacts had widened considerably during his stay on the island. Every day at the detainment camp, there had been secret indoctrination sessions to deepen and strengthen their communist spirit, as well as heated discussion and the surreptitious reading of subversive books smuggled on to the island by a guard they bribed.

'Prison is not a hotel. You should have thought about life there before you got yourself arrested,' Raj replied angrily. Nowadays, he was no longer ashamed to admit that his mind shut down at any discussion of abstract ideals, unless they led to trade.

'I'm warning you now, before you reach the mainland, do not get involved again with that communist group, or their filthy newspaper, *Freedom News*. You have put us through too much; think of Leila.' Raj glowered at his brother-in-law.

Krishna shrugged and stared silently at the sea. On St John's, like everyone else, he had secretly continued to write inflammatory articles for *Freedom News*, which were smuggled to the mainland by the guard who brought in their books. The boat pushed against the swell, a fine spray hit his face, and Krishna licked the salt from his lips. After two years of monotonous incarceration, the risky nature of a life spent courting arrest was something he looked forward to. The Anti-British League had gone underground, and *Freedom News* was still in business, its printing equipment and editorial staff forced to move constantly from one safe house to another. To allow for easy concealment the publication was now printed on thin translucent paper. If for any reason printing had to cease, militant students in the Chinese Middle Schools, who were the staple fodder of Anti-British League cells, devotedly copied out the newspaper by hand many hundreds of times.

As the boat pulled against the incoming tide its frail body shuddered against the waves. Krishna stared at his brother-in-law's fleshy neck and well-greased hair as he sat before him in the prow of the boat. Raj's belly protruded substantially, and there was a capable, consolidated aura about him. He used pomade from England and cologne from France and changed his shirt twice if not three times a day. He had acquired a large wardrobe of Western-style suits and refused to be seen in Indian clothes, only wearing a *dhoti* now to bed. Krishna realised with a start that his former illiterate pupil was already forty-two, and that he himself was fifty.

The launch neared a busy wharf crowded with sampans and other small boats, and a rope was thrown out to them. On the quay Raj's car, a large new Rover, stood waiting. As they disembarked, the driver eased the car forward and scrambled out to open the door for Raj. As both the driver and Raj ignored him, Krishna walked around the car and climbed in from the other side, eyeing his brother-in-law sourly. When the car drew up before the house in Waterloo Street Krishna got out, but Raj sat on in the car and spoke to him through the open window.

'Leila is still at Manikam's; I don't know what time she will be home. I am returning to Ho Biscuits,' he said, then left Krishna to the ministrations of a servant who hurried out of the house.

Raj's car crossed Anderson Bridge but drew to a halt in a mass of traffic about the General Post Office in Fullerton Building. Horns honked, bicycle bells rang and irate tradesmen trapped in the bottleneck with loaded carts, shouted their annoyance. Raj looked out of the window in vexation. The postmen were striking, and people were forced to collect their own mail. The strike had been in progress for more than a week, postmen picketing peacefully outside the building. The area before the monumental structure was crowded, with everyone intent on pushing inside to retrieve letters and parcels. Gurkhas stood about with guns at the ready to prevent any violence. Beside placards demanding pay revisions, Raj saw one apologising to the public for the strike. He gave the group of picketing postmen a look of fury as he drove past.

This was the first strike since the Emergency, and local newspapers like *The Malayan Tribune* were making the most of it; screaming headlines on behalf of the postmen pushed out all other news. A young lawyer called Lee, determined to pit himself against the government, was legal counsel for the striking postmen. His high-handed rhetoric was reported in the press every day, in special coverage of the strike by a young Indian journalist by the name of Rajaratnam, newly returned from England. Special meetings had been called in the Legislative Council to debate what should be done. Local opinion was largely behind the postmen, who were aflame with defiance in previously unthinkable ways. After the stress and exertion of the visit to St John's, the crowd queuing to retrieve their mail spiked Raj's anger anew. He had recently developed high blood pressure, and reached into his pocket for one of the pills he always carried with him.

When Raj drew up before Ho Biscuits the usual smell of baking poured through the car's open windows. Even after all these years the vanilla-edged perfume never failed to melt him. He left the car and walked through the gate, feeling as always a sense of homecoming; Mr Ho's spirit seemed to remain in the house. On the altar shelf inside, his Ancestor Tablet stood between that of his murdered son Luke and his wife, and Yoshiko tended them devotedly, putting out fresh offerings and making obeisance each day. Raj too made it a habit to press his hands together before the altar, remembering Mr Ho with gratitude.

The bungalow had recently been modernised at Raj's insistence, to the delight of Yoshiko. They had also rebuilt the factory; the sheds were now solid brick and concrete constructions, with modern ovens and fans and the latest machinery. A new biscuit cutting machine was on its way from Germany. Mr Ho would not know the place, all he would recognise was the shape of some biscuits: the strawberry or pineapple jam centres, chocolate fingers and vanilla rabbits for children.

As Raj left the car, Yoshiko was returning to the house from the factory and they climbed the steps together. She had remained slim and bright and her hair had not greyed. The boys were grown and now helped with the running of the factory, and looked upon Raj as a surrogate father. He sat with them often in the evenings and it was rewarding to dispense advice and have it appreciatively received; he no longer missed not having a nephew.

'See, Uncle is right again. He always knows what he is talking about,' Yoshiko frequently told the boys, and it pleased him to hear her say this and to know the family depended upon him.

He was now a man of property. Beside the Waterloo Street home he had bought houses in exclusive areas of town for rent to Europeans. Ho Biscuits had given him the dignity of industry, always more weighty than trade.

'They're still picketing at the post office. Gurkhas with guns are everywhere,' he told Yoshiko as they climbed the steps.

'Our workers held a meeting today, so tomorrow you can be sure they'll have fresh demands. Maybe we should offer more; we don't want trouble,' Yoshiko suggested with a sigh.

'Management means strength. If you give workers an inch they'll demand a yard because they think you're frightened,' Raj replied firmly.

Ho Biscuits continued to have labour problems. Yoshiko bargained ferociously whenever the factory went on a go-slow and threatened to strike. Raj had not noticed this hard-nosed facet of her personality when she was married to Luke Ho. He had come to admire her, and also to desire her. Her face was still wet with the heat in the factory and the scent of vanilla and cinnamon rose from her. Raj walked slightly behind Yoshiko as they climbed the steps to the veranda. He had a fine view of her neatly shaped buttocks in the fashionable slacks she had recently taken to wearing beneath her Japanese apron. Lust, he suspected, did not have a place in Yoshiko's orderly mind, but marriage might be acceptable. The thought had been with him for some time. It would be a far more physically substantial arrangement than his weekly visits to an establishment on Lavender Road. In return, he would officially assume the position that he had unofficially held for so long: that of head of the Ho household.

On the top step Yoshiko stumbled and he reached out to support her and prevent a fall. He found himself with his arms about her, her small breast cupped in his hand, his mouth against her hair, its lingering vanilla perfume filling his nose. With his free hand he reached beneath her apron and slid his hand between her thighs. Yoshiko did not move, but he heard her breath quicken and her heart fluttered beneath his hand.

'After the cutting machine arrives from Germany, perhaps we should get married,' he suggested into her ear, and moved his hand to cover her crotch. Yoshiko pulled away and continued into the house as if nothing had happened.

'The machine will take many months to come. It is better we marry before,' she replied over her shoulder, as the darkness of the house enveloped her.

As often happened, Raj did not return from the factory in time for dinner but ate with Yoshiko and her sons at Ho Biscuits. Krishna sat sullenly before his wife at the table while a servant served them their meal. Leila had hurried home early from Manikam's, but had not been in the house to greet Krishna as he'd expected, on his return from St John's. Her absence had shocked him deeply; it was not right for a wife to ignore a husband's homecoming after an absence of two years. Observing her across the table, he noted the authority with which she ordered the servants, and the briskness with which she ate. He was surprised to find she had evolved into a different person in the time he had been away; she had learned to live without him.

'You cannot live by ideals alone,' she told Krishna in the new commanding voice she used. 'Those striking post office workers are only encouraged by people like you. You must find proper work and not waste your time any more with politics.' Leila gestured to the waiting servant to spoon more rice on to her banana leaf. The Ramakrishna Mission School wanted nothing more to do with Krishna, considering him an unsuitable person to mould young minds.

Some weeks later, when Leila had returned to Manikam's after lunch, Krishna left the house on his own and made his way into Chinatown, to a noodle stall where he was to meet a cell member known to him only as BK. The boy appeared no more than eighteen, with hair that stood up all over his head and two smouldering slashes for eyes. Krishna had received a message to meet BK concealed in a bun of steamed rice, secretly passed to him by a food hawker as he left the house on Waterloo Street. These were the slippery ways by which communist cell members communicated. After ordering some noodles, Krishna sat down at a rusty table in the filthy alley, and waited. When the boy at last appeared he circumnavigated the stall several times looking for undercover spies, before ordering noodles and then joining Krishna. The table rocked on the uneven cobbles and rats ran boldly about in the evil-smelling effluent that overflowed the shallow gutter. BK was dressed in the disguise of a common labourer, in a dirty singlet, torn shorts and wooden clogs, although in reality he taught calligraphy in one of the Chinese Middle Schools, and was usually decently dressed. To Krishna, he appeared no more than a political upstart, full of smart-alecky ways. BK slurped up the hot noodles and began the meeting by listing untrustworthy people who had all recently been assassinated, accused of treason by the Party.

'Traitors must be exterminated, that is the rule. However, you have a chance now to prove your loyalty to the Party.' BK did not look up from his chopsticks as he continued.

'Party discipline is so strict that once a termination job is done, comrades must surrender their guns. Then, at the next assassination order, they are handed the guns to use again. Between assassinations the weapons must be hidden. Only people the Party trusts completely are given the task of hiding weapons. We have selected you for this task.' For a moment BK stopped eating and glanced furtively about to be sure no one had heard him. Krishna started in alarm on hearing the nature of his task. His hands trembled so badly as he lifted his chopsticks that the noodles sipped back into the soup.

Krishna found he had returned from St John's to a different world; during his years in detention everything had changed. Boldness was now in style. Daylight assassinations on crowded streets were happening every day. The Malayan Communist Party, in the secrecy of numerous political cells, decided who was an enemy of the people and killer squads were activated to liquidate offenders. This sudden change of tactics shocked Krishna deeply; not only the new lawlessness and brutality, but also the youthfulness of Party members. It was clear the age of gentlemanly subversion was over. *Freedom News* still operated deep underground, and were glad to accept his articles through the many devious routes of delivery they devised. Yet, the front line Krishna had stood at all his life had now moved so far forward he did not know where it was. The old rules no longer applied.

'I'm an old man, this is young men's work,' Krishna protested, knowing the test he had waited for since joining the cell was upon him; he had not yet been passed for full membership of the Party. BK nodded agreement.

'But an old man can still be useful, and show his loyalty to the Party. Young or old, loyalty is the same. Selection for a task like this is an honour.' BK leaned forward to suck up a hank of noodles.

'Young men take risks more easily than old men. I have proved my loyalty,' Krishna argued. He could imagine BK with the other cell members gleefully hatching this test for him.

'Then you should have no problem with the order,' BK frowned. His noodles finished, he sat back and searched for a cigarette in the pocket of his shorts.

'You live in a big house. Your brother-in-law is a respected man, a rich man. No one would expect to find guns in the house of such a man. There is also a garage that opens into a storeroom with a large padlocked cupboard,' he added.

Krishna struggled with the panic of knowing he was watched. His home had been reconnoitred in minute detail, and he had known nothing about it. A sudden spurt of anger gushed through him. Such tactics were nothing but an alternative form of oppression, and he had always stood up to oppression.

'I cannot do this,' he said firmly, looking BK in the eye.

'Cannot or will not? Comrades happily give their lives for the Party, if they are true believers. Are you saying you cannot be trusted?' BK replied coldly, shaking his head as he pushed back his stool.

Krishna watched as he disappeared into the crowd. His own noodles remained untouched on the table, the fat congealing in an oily ring around the sides of the bowl. The stench of sewage rose up about him from the road and he watched a large rat scuttle along the side of the alley. He had never been frightened before.

34

MEI LAN FOUND A stool and carried it out into the garden. On her return from England some months before, she had found Bougainvillaea House in a derelict state, still scarred by bomb damage, squatters inhabiting its decrepit shell. She had immediately set about reclaiming the place. For a time then she had lived with Little Sparrow in the East Coast home while Bougainvillaea House was being repaired and the vagrants moved out. Ah Siew was still hobbling around serving Little Sparrow, weathered skin loose on her bones and eyes blue with cataracts; during her time in England Mei Lan had missed the old woman more than she liked to admit. Ah Siew was now a great age, although no one knew exactly how old she was. She squatted down on her haunches beside Mei Lan in the garden of Bougainvillaea House, breath rattling in her stringy chest, chewing on toothless gums. A lack of teeth now limited her choice of food, her joints needed rubbing with medicated liniment and her mind was developing holes, but she was still around. The old woman placed her sleeping pallet at the foot of Mei Lan's bed once more, and each night the sound of her snoring reassured Mei Lan, as it had when she was a child.

When the decision to return to Singapore was made she wrote to Mr Cheong of Bayley McDonald & Cheong who had always handled Lim Hock An's legal business. Mr Cheong agreed to take her into the firm, although he made it clear that he was setting a precedent by employing a woman.

The garden of Bougainvillaea House was once again furrowed with open runnels, and bare-backed coolies threw up spade after spade of damp soil just as they had when Lim Hock An buried his precious jade and opium and Second Grandmother's jewellery. Now, at Mei Lan's order the treasure was being exhumed. The remaining sickly bushes of bougainvillaea had been ripped up and lay in a pile, black-clawed roots exposed. Mei Lan was filled with a sense of déjà vu and fought to control her tears. One by one, the stout wooden boxes of Lim Hock An's jade were hauled up into the light, dark and damp from long burial, clods of earth dropping from them. Although neglect and shelling had destroyed the garden and few of the original bougainvillaea bushes remained, Mei Lan knew exactly where to find her grandfather's priceless cache. His ghost seemed to sit beside her, wrapped like old porcelain in his ancient purple dressing gown, Second Grandmother beside him. As each box was unearthed her throat tightened with emotion for all that had befallen the great House of Lim; apart from soft-brained Bertie, there was no male line of descent. Her father, Boon Eng, had died in Hong Kong in an air raid, but this news had not come to them until the war was over.

Once Lim Hock An's treasure was unearthed she vowed to restore the garden, planting fresh bougainvillaea. Already she had taken down the fence her grandfather had erected so long ago along the canal, to stop her meeting Howard. During the war the Japanese had built a narrow walkway across the storm drain and the two lots of land were now firmly linked. Bougainvillaea House, its dark corners filled with memories, even if painful, comforted her. She had made a bedroom habitable and also part of the sitting room with a desk and a sofa and a small dining table. For the moment she needed little more, and the other rooms of the house lay empty. Mei Lan had been away almost seven years. As the boxes of Lim Hock An's valuables emerged from their damp grave, they were carried into the house and temporarily stacked in the old dining room.

'Belvedere boy coming home,' Ah Siew croaked out the news suddenly, chewing her gums, squinting up at Mei Lan with unusual lucidity. Mei Lan looked at the old woman, her grey hair now so thin the scalp could be seen beneath, the tight knot of once luxuriant hair no bigger than a walnut, and felt the shock ripple through her.

Whenever Mr Cheong had a case concerning a difficult female, Mei Lan was called in to participate; she was the only woman in the office of Bayley McDonald & Cheong. Otherwise, most of her work centred upon the bread and butter issue of conveyancing, and was not what she had imagined herself doing on her return to Singapore. As Mei Lan entered the office after the trying weekend with Lim

Hock An's treasure, she was told that Mr Cheong wanted to see her urgently.

'The woman is in prison for attempted murder of her husband. It would be useful to interview her; the husband has enough means to take legal action and has approached me. I am undecided whether or not I should take the case.' Mr Cheong sighed, and Mei Lan recognised the bored note in his voice at the thought of yet another neurotic woman.

'He wants her committed to a mental asylum. He says she is mad. You had better go and hear her story before I consider the case,' Mr Cheong added. Most of the cases Mei Lan worked on with Mr Cheong involved women living in polygamous marriages and Mr Cheong could never hide his lack of interest; it was rumoured that he himself kept a concubine.

There was no way she could refuse to go to the prison. Mei Lan had steeled herself for the visit, and knew it would be a test. As the outer door of the prison shut behind her, Mei Lan found herself facing an inner door, with a disembodied eye staring at her through a spyhole. At last a bolt was drawn and the door swung open. Already, she was trembling and forced herself forward, hearing the heavy slam of metal behind her and the bolting of a lock. A stout Tamil woman in a uniformed khaki jacket buttoned over a green cotton sari, led her through two further doors and down a dingy corridor to the Matron's office.

All the cells opened on to the corridor and through the bars she could see the women prisoners, three or four to a cell, sewing pieces of thick canvas. Other women were making brooms, collecting straw into bundles of even length; they observed her passively as she passed. Her mouth was dry and she drew a deep breath to steady herself. In the YMCA on her way to interrogation, she had walked down the corridor between the cells and other prisoners had shouted encouragement, braving the guards' recriminations. A clergyman in the end cell always chanted the Lord's Prayer as she passed. Now, as she walked behind the warder, her heart pulsed in her throat, it was difficult to breathe. Unable to look at the barred cages to either side of her, she stared at her feet, fear darting through her. At any moment, she was afraid, her body would refuse to move forward, she would turn and run to beat hysterically on the closed door, pleading to be freed. If for a moment she raised her eyes, she knew she would see Nakamura at the end of the corridor, the faint light skating on his polished boots, hands behind his back, waiting.

The Tamil warder stopped before an open door. Inside, at a desk sat the Matron, a large-boned Eurasian woman with circles of dark pigmentation under her eyes. The room was surprisingly bright and sunny with a patterned rug and a shelf of files, and Mei Lan took the chair the woman offered.

'Would you like a cold drink or a cup of coffee?' The woman stared at her appraisingly. Mei Lan struggled to control her emotions, knowing fear lay open on her face.

'Just some breathlessness I sometimes suffer from,' she replied, feeling an excuse was needed, and the Matron nodded sympathetically.

'The prisoner is in the workroom; I will have her called. The women start making postbags or brooms in their cells, then later go to the workroom for finishing,' Matron explained, after ordering the warder to bring a bottled drink for Mei Lan.

'What crimes are these women imprisoned for?' Mei Lan asked conversationally while they waited for the prisoner. A bottle of orangeade arrived, and she drew the juice up gratefully through a waxed straw; her breath was flowing more easily now.

'The usual women's crimes of petty stealing, hawking wares in the wrong area and, of course, prostitution. They're usually illiterate women, abandoned by their husbands and with children to support. Your prisoner however is not illiterate; she has had some basic education and her husband is a relatively rich man. She's not the kind of prisoner we usually get, even if she is accused of attempted murder,' the Matron explained.

Soon, the warder returned escorting a slightly built woman with pale lips and anxious eyes. When the Matron left them alone, Mei Lan drew up a chair opposite her own, and told the girl to sit down.

'What is your name?' Mei Lan asked. Even in her grey prison uniform of loose trousers and shirt, the woman had a neat appearance and an intelligent face, the drawn back hair exposing fine boning.

'My name is Fang Ei Ling,' the girl replied and Mei Lan felt a stab of shock at hearing the name that had been her mother's.

'Your husband accuses you of attempted murder. If he succeeds, you could get years in prison or a mental asylum,' Mei Lan told her.

'He's taken my children,' Ei Ling sat forward in desperate appeal. A single strand of shorter hair tucked behind her ear fell over her face and she pushed it distractedly back into place.

'How many children do you have?' Mei Lan asked.

'Four. Now that I am in here, Husband's First Wife and Second Wife throw my children out of the house each morning without food or proper clothes to wear, barefoot. They only care for their own children. I am Husband's Third Wife and he keeps us all in the same house. He is an old man; I did not want to marry him but my step-mother tricked me into it. He's a rich man and paid her a good bride price for me. My father is dead and could not protect me; I was not even fifteen when Husband married me. Now he has divorced me and I knew nothing of it until it was done. He has taken my children and also married again, another young girl of fifteen who he has brought into the house in place of me. Can he do so much without me knowing?' The girl was distraught but spoke clearly, making an effort at control.

'You stuck a knife into him,' Mei Lan reminded her.

'He beat me, and he beat my children. He punched me in the stomach so hard that two times babies came out dead. One was already seven months.' Ei Ling pressed her lips together at the memory.

'Was it after this that you tried to kill him?'

'Yes,' the girl answered, and shivered.

'How old are you?' Mei Lan asked. Women like Ei Ling had no way to respond to a husband's dismissal. Always ending up in dire situations, many were forced to turn to prostitution to survive or keep their children. Custody of children was always given to the husband. Women could rarely turn to their own family for help, because of the shame they had incurred for everyone by not pleasing a husband or their in-laws.

'I am twenty-three,' Ei Ling answered. The grey prison clothes drained all colour from her face.

Since the woman had entered the room and begun her story, Mei Lan had had the feeling of something familiar closing over her. The rotting odour of Second Grandmother's broken feet as the bandages were removed came strongly to her over the years, as did the memory of First Grandmother Chwee Gek, discarded by her husband for Second Grandmother Lustrous Pearl, a fifteen-year-old sing-song girl. She remembered Ah Siew's *kongsi fong*, where she had learned that women could be sold for a bag of rice or a few silver pieces, just as Little Sparrow had been sold to Lim Hock An. Even her own mother, the other Ei Ling, in spite of beauty and education, had been dismissed and devalued by her husband. Now, another Ei Ling sat before her, too proud to sob, with little in life to nourish her and raising for Mei Lan many disturbing questions.

Later, Mei Lan gave Mr Cheong her evaluation. 'It is the usual marriage thing. She has been discarded for another woman, divorced without her knowledge and her children taken from her. It made her angry; nothing more, nothing less.' Mei Lan spoke savagely.

'The husband is quite a well-to-do man. She stuck a knife into him, he nearly died,' Mr Cheong replied, unmoved.

'If he brings a case, I will defend her.' The words sprang away from Mei Lan, as if it was her life that was being threatened.

'No need to get so worked up. Illiterate women are conditioned to expect such lives. Her husband, by contrast, is an educated middle-class man and has done relatively well in his printing business. She should be glad she has such security; what more would such a woman want? I doubt she will have money for a legal defence,' Mr Cheong said and raised his eyebrows humorously over tortoiseshell spectacles. Mei Lan felt emotion billowing up and struggled to hold it down.

'That is the trouble; she will be easy to lock away. As you know, she is not illiterate and no woman ever expects such a life – they just cannot hope for anything better. She deserves some kind of legal aid. Women like her have nowhere to turn,' Mei Lan replied grimly, holding Mr Cheong's gaze, her thoughts taking shape as she spoke.

'Yes, it is a fact, they have nowhere to turn, but that is the world we live in and we must bow to its inadequacies. There is nothing you can do about it,' Mr Cheong reminded her, his voice frayed by impatience.

'I will defend her even if she cannot pay,' Mei Lan announced determinedly, turning to the door, hearing Mr Cheong's exasperated sigh behind her.

That night Mei Lan slept fitfully. In her dreams she stood again in her room in Lim Villa. From the photograph on the tallboy, Grandmother Chwee Gek, still sitting erect with the soon-to-die child on her lap, stepped out before her, elegant in a high-necked blouse, long dark skirt and hanging jade earrings. Her sorrow echoed painfully through Mei Lan.

'See my large ugly feet,' Chwee Gek said, raising her skirt to reveal the dainty toe of a beaded shoe, tears filling her eyes. 'Too big for *him*.' She shook her head sadly. When Mei Lan looked again at the tallboy she saw that the phoenix now sat upon it, its feathers iridescent with light, its proud head erect upon its slender neck. As the great bird shifted on its perch, something turned within her. When she looked again, Grandmother Chwee Gek had shrunk back into the silver frame and the child sat once again on her lap. Mei Lan woke to the hammering of her own emotions and the first weak light of the day.

Lim Hock An's exhumed treasure was stacked in the empty dining room of Bougainvillaea House. Mei Lan ached with memory as she stood before the mountain of damp stained boxes, remembering that day with JJ in Lim Villa's jade museum as the pieces were packed away for the move to Bougainvillaea House. The treasure had never seen the light of day again, first lying boxed and in store, and then buried before the Japanese arrived. Closing her eyes and breathing in the earthy scent of damp wood, Mei Lan knew now what she would do with it. The opium must be relinquished to the government, but the jade belonged to her, as did the suitcase of Second Grandmother's jewellery. The best jade she would give to the Raffles Museum, but lesser pieces could be sold to good profit as could the jewellery, and the money once invested would give her additional income. This solution filled her with relief and, as she began to think of the details such a transaction would involve, a commotion was heard outside the house, followed by a thumping on the front door.

'Mei Lan!' Little Sparrow's voice screamed hysterically.

'Come quickly, they will arrest her,' Little Sparrow shouted, bursting into the room and pulling Mei Lan out of the house towards a waiting taxi.

'Who will be arrested?' Mei Lan asked; she had never seen Little Sparrow in such a wild state. Her usually immaculate hair was dishevelled, her face twisted with emotion.

'Greta will be arrested; the schoolchildren are demonstrating against the government.' Little Sparrow's voice splintered into sobs. Mei Lan dismissed the taxi and ran to her own car, pushing Little Sparrow inside.

'The students are against the government calling up young boys for National Service. I cannot control her. She has become a communist. Those communists have got into all the Chinese Middle Schools and led innocent children astray,' Little Sparrow explained between sobs.

In the few years Mei Lan had been away in England, Greta had left childhood behind. Pigtails still thumped about her shoulders, but in the demure school uniform there was now the body of a woman, and Little Sparrow was involved in a continuous mother and daughter battle.

When they arrived at Clemenceau Avenue, the road was a mess of broken glass. Bottles had been thrown, there was a sulphurous smell in the air, but no students were to be seen. Whatever battle had taken place, it had already moved on. A few anxious parents stood about in the road asking for information and conferring fearfully. Little Sparrow leaned out of the car window to stop a passing policeman.

'Where is my child?' she screamed.

'The riot squads are at King George V Park, so they must be there,' the man replied, hurrying off as Mei Lan parked the car.

On the road before them empty trucks were lined up, first aid was being given to injured policemen and schoolchildren in the back of ambulances. Some handcuffed students were being pushed into police vans. Little Sparrow ran up to the knot of worried parents with Mei Lan following her.

'My son registered for the National Service Ordinance before the deadline expired; he didn't want to, but he saw no other way,' a man told Little Sparrow.

'We Chinese are given no rights in the colony; why should we do National Service? Chinese High School and Chung Cheng High School both sent petitions to the Governor demanding total exemption from National Service, and they received no reply,' another man said.

'The police will kill our children; they have guns and batons,' a mother shouted, turning to run in the direction of Fort Canning and King George V Park. Little Sparrow gasped and ran after her; again Mei Lan followed. As they neared the park Mei Lan heard the rousing rhythm of 'John Brown's Body' being sung.

The park lay along the Fort Canning incline and was bordered by railings the length of the road. Against these white railings, in their white uniforms, the students were lined up several deep. Although they sang loudly to the tune of 'John Brown's Body', they yelled out different words:

'Unity is strength, Strength is iron, Strength is steel. Harder than iron, Stronger than steel, March towards the glorious ideal. Eliminate all corrupt systems – On freedom and on New China the brilliant light shines.'

Mei Lan craned her neck to see over the dark mass of heads, in the hope of recognising Greta. It was a shock to find that some of the students appeared no more than twelve years old although others, whose schooling had been interrupted by the war, seemed well above average age. Rows of riot police behind wicker shields were lined up ready to charge.

'We must find her.' Little Sparrow tried to push through the crowd, while angry policemen forced everyone back. Mei Lan found herself against a low wall and managed to scramble up on to it.

'Get up here,' she said, pulling Little Sparrow up beside her so that they had a view over the heads of the crowd. Confused policemen were alternately tying students to the railings and trying to prise them away. The children met each tactic with wild responses, kicking, struggling and hitting out at the frustrated policemen, who could find no humane way to subdue them. Older children screamed encouragement to younger children; police brought their batons down hard upon the boys but backed away from the girls. Then, as the riot squads prepared to charge, the girls crouched down in a protective cordon behind which the boys showered the police with a hail of stones and bottles. The advancing riot squad held wicker shields over their heads and the girls shouted and jeered ecstatically.

'She's there. I saw her,' Little Sparrow screamed, preparing to jump down from the wall.

'You can't get to her – and look: something new is happening,' Mei Lan said. She held on to Little Sparrow.

Things had suddenly quietened: a boy was now talking to the police. Soon, the empty trucks they had seen in Clemenceau Avenue appeared and drew to a noisy halt behind the crowd of onlookers. The students were filing away from the railings in an orderly manner, the girls no longer yelling harridans and the boys defiant but subdued. The crowd parted to make way for them and police helped them into the trucks.

'Where is she?' Little Sparrow shouted. Jumping off the wall, she battled through the crowd trying to reach the trucks but eventually came up against a cordon of police who refused to let her pass.

'Where are you taking them?' Little Sparrow screamed as the lorries started up and began driving off with their cargo of uniformed school-children. A Sikh officer appeared and asked Little Sparrow to control her violent behaviour.

'The students have requested to return to the Chung Cheng High School in the same trucks that brought them here. You can collect your child from the school. They are going peacefully of their own accord.' The policeman gave instructions in a loud voice to a crowd of anxious parents.

Mei Lan and Little Sparrow returned to their car and began the drive to Chung Cheng High School. When they arrived the trucks had already deposited the students. The school gate was shut and locked, and a group of schoolboys stood guard outside before a growing crowd of parents waiting to see what would happen next. Little Sparrow peered through the loose weave of a fence and saw a large playground filled with white-uniformed students.

'We have orders not to open the gate,' the boy guards answered stubbornly.

'I must see my daughter. She may be hurt,' Little Sparrow shouted, joining other parents in protest. One of the boys stood on a box to make an announcement.

'The police have arrested forty-four of us. Twenty-six students have needed first aid, but there is nothing serious. Everyone else is all right.' The boy stared apprehensively at the hundreds of parents pressing about him.

'How many of you have locked yourselves in the school?' a father shouted.

'We are two thousand,' the boy replied.

'What are you going to do?' another parent asked.

'We are camping here until the National Service Ordinance is abolished,' a different boy answered.

'That is nonsense. You might wait for ever!' someone shouted.

'The service is only a few days a year. Just do it and get it over with. Why make all this fuss for just a few days?' a woman suggested.

'The colonial power calls us "aliens". They give Chinese educated in English-medium schools their citizenship, but we Chinese educated in the Chinese vernacular schools are shunned; we cannot claim citizenship, political rights or get jobs. We cannot practise law or medicine or qualify for any post in government service. We are forced to live in a separate world, a lower-class world; we are not included in the life of the colony. Why should we do their National Service even for one day?' The boy spoke angrily and his fellow guards at the gate shouted agreement.

'We will fight only for China,' the boy yelled, raising a clenched fist to the crowd.

'How will you eat in there?' Little Sparrow demanded fiercely, more interested in practicalities.

'We're agreed that parents can bring us food, but it must be deposited here with us at the gate,' the boy replied in a more conciliatory tone.

35

WHEN MEI LAN CAME out of the courtroom reporters were waiting
for her. The trial had caught the interest of the press. She had taken
the case to prove a point: to bring about public awareness of the plight
of women like Ei Ling; to her surprise she had won. The verdict set
a precedent and was life changing, for both herself and for Ei Ling.

'What made you take the case, Miss Lim?' A young Indian reporter
shouted. Courthouse smells of old wood and insect repellent pressed
upon her; she was faint with relief that the trial was over.

'The law that allows polygamous marriages needs to be changed;
it is outrageous,' she replied, trying to walk forward as reporters
surrounded her. The flash of photo bulbs was blinding, and she shielded
her face with her hand.

'What do you propose in the way of change, Miss Lim?' another
reporter shouted.

'A charter for women which will require marriages to be monoga-
mous and provide for divorce, safeguard the rights of women and
protect the family. A minimum age for marriage must also be set. Our
Civil Marriage Act allows many marriages to take place outside its
statutes, and so fails numerous women.' Mei Lan paused to speak to
the reporters, seeing a chance to reiterate her views.

'A lot of men will not like such a law. Do you think it can ever be
passed?' someone called from the back of the crowd.

'How many wives did your own grandfather have, Miss Lim?' the
Indian shouted again.

'Is it true you have taken no payment for defending the accused?'
another voice asked.

'My client is no longer accused of anything, she has been acquitted,'
Mei Lan answered. Suddenly, Mr Cheong was at her side, fending off
reporters and steering her into the judge's chambers.

'Better wait here until they go away. Don't say too much; they just want sensationalist news.' Mr Cheong shut the door firmly on the newsmen.

'What is sensationalist about a woman wanting to escape abuse, and a mother wanting custody of her children?' Mei Lan snapped, and saw Mr Cheong frown.

'You must be satisfied with making your mark with this case. Social change moves slowly. Things don't happen overnight.' Mr Cheong peered at her sternly from under bushy eyebrows. 'You're making quite a name for yourself, you know. You are always in the newspapers.'

She had been called to the Bar in her barrister's robes and it had been an important occasion. Few women in Singapore had been called to the Bar, so newspapers covered the occasion. All this, with the added ingredient of her war experiences and family name, made her a person of public interest.

'I didn't take the case to make my mark, I didn't expect to win,' Mei Lan replied. The helplessness of the prisoner, Ei Ling had incensed her enough to take any risk. Although Mr Cheong had not taken the husband's case, the man had found another lawyer to press charges of attempted murder against his wife. It had been a drawn-out case with unreliable bribed witnesses and much circumstantial evidence. In the end the judge had unexpectedly ruled in Ei Ling's favour, throwing out the case. He had also ordered the husband to return the two youngest children to her, providing she could prove she had the means to keep them.

'You must never expect *not* to win. So much depends upon the judge and you were lucky enough to have a progressive minded man sitting for this case.' Mr Cheong poured a glass of water from a flask on the table and placed it before Mei Lan. She nodded and lifted it to her lips; she had not realised how thirsty she was, how much the last hours had taken out of her.

'If I may give some further advice, it would be best not to offer your services again for free. It will be difficult to make much of a living if you are too altruistic. It is besides not a professional attitude,' Mr Cheong added.

'There should be some sort of legal aid for people like Ei Ling,' Mei Lan replied defiantly. She had shocked everyone in the office by defending Ei Ling without charge.

'Probably in time there will be such aid, but for now you cannot go against the tide; you are a woman, not a man,' Mr Cheong answered with a warning frown.

'I am aware of that; I should also be fighting for equal pay,' Mei Lan answered bitterly. Her daily workload was no less than that of the male lawyers at Bayley McDonald & Cheong, she was as well qualified as anyone, and yet her pay was half that of a man. Mr Cheong did not reply.

When the reporters had gone and Mei Lan left the room she was surprised to see Ei Ling sitting alone on a bench outside the court. Each day Ei Ling had been taken back to the prison, and Mei Lan was so wrapped up in presenting her defence that she had not thought beyond it.

'You're free, you know. Do you have somewhere to go?' she asked. Ei Ling shook her head as Mei Lan sat down beside her. Mei Lan's life had been in stasis for so long, but by defending Ei Ling she had been forced into action, forced to summon up parts of herself she had almost forgotten. Ei Ling was drained of colour, thin as a waif.

'My parents are dead. I have no family except my stepmother who is the one who married me to my husband.' Ei Ling spoke in a whisper, never raising her eyes from her hands. For a brief moment Mei Lan was filled with emotion and knew that, just as Nakamura's destructive force had dismantled her, Ei Ling too had been destroyed. Although so many years had passed, nightmares still woke her; she still took something to sleep each night, to bring blackness upon her. So much time had gone by. Nakamura was dead, hanged by the neck, and she had helped to condemn him with her evidence; she should be free of him.

Mei Lan's mind ran over the few places that might offer help to Ei Ling. She wondered if she should contact the Salvation Army or even the Po Leung Kuk, a government refuge for prostitutes, but quickly decided against this. Wherever Ei Ling went she would have to work, and would have no one to look after her children; they could end up in an orphanage and Ei Ling might yet be forced into prostitution. Mei Lan realised with a pang of guilt that if she had been standing on a precipice before a bottomless drop, the woman could not have appeared more terrified. Mei Lan had been so wrapped up in her own role in the case that its implications for Ei Ling had bypassed her.

'Whatever he did to me, I had a home. Even prison is somewhere to live,' Ei Ling whispered. Mei Lan heard the slight resentment in her tone and realised in further distress that freedom placed the woman on a confusing trajectory. She thought again of how easily Ei Ling might be forced into prostitution and abandonment of her children.

'You had better come home with me until I can find a place for you,' Mei Lan said reluctantly, regretting the words even as she spoke but seeing no other way, feeling her responsibility.

Ah Siew was not pleased at the appearance of Ei Ling. The woman trailed behind Mei Lan, wan and undernourished, and stood awkwardly inside the door.

'What are we to do with her? 'Ah Siew asked loudly, making sure Ei Ling could hear.

'We shall see,' Mei Lan answered, not wishing Ah Siew to know how much she already regretted her action. Ei Ling, thin as a stray cat, stared at her appealingly, dependent now upon her.

That night Mei Lan lay staring up at the turning fan, listening to its protesting creak and thinking about Ei Ling. How could she support the weight of someone else's needs when already it was too much to carry her own? She tossed about in agitation, her emotions in turmoil. That evening Ah Siew relayed some gossip picked up from across the canal: Howard had at last returned from Australia. The thought of him settled in Belvedere once again filled Mei Lan with alarm.

Greta came home eventually after the school sit-in with her head cocked defiantly, her long plaits gone.

'Who has cut off your hair?' Little Sparrow screamed.

'Lots of girls cut their hair. Short hair is the fashion in the Party,' Greta replied, observing her mother from beneath a fringe hacked off too short with a knife. With her new helmet of hair and eyes that glittered rebelliously, she was transformed into a formidable warrior. Little Sparrow stepped back in confusion.

'We disbanded only because the Chinese Chamber of Commerce promised to take up our case with the government,' Greta growled.

'Why are you so worried about National Service? You're not a boy; you will only get married.' Little Sparrow was unable to make any sense of it.

'It's a new age, a new world order. I will never get married, and women are now equal to men,' Greta informed her mother.

Over the next weeks the fight with the students went on. In schools, committees were formed to agitate for the release of arrested comrades and for the unconditional right *not* to serve Queen and Country. Three thousand students from the eight Chinese Middle Schools once again barricaded themselves into Chung Cheng High School and refused to leave until exemption from National Service was granted. When this did not work, other long camp-ins took place, one lasting twenty-three days, supported by thousands of Middle School students who organised their own lessons and sports.

'You have been shut up with boys overnight. Who will marry you now?' Little Sparrow wailed after yet another sit-in.

'We do not indulge in corrupt bourgeois behaviour,' Greta replied scathingly. From outside there was the honking of a car horn. Greta looked up and rushed immediately to the window.

'Where are you going?' Little Sparrow ran uselessly after her daughter, who dashed out of the front door towards a waiting car filled with young people.

'We are going to see Mr Lee the lawyer; he will represent us, get our friends out of jail,' Greta replied over her shoulder as she disappeared through the door. Little Sparrow at once took a taxi to Bougainvillaea House.

'Who is this Mr Lee?' Little Sparrow yelled at Mei Lan when she returned from work.

'He is legal adviser to a number of trade unions,' Mei Lan replied.

'What are trade unions?' Little Sparrow asked, with a loud sob of distress.

Little Sparrow sat in the darkening room, her feet stretched out in front of her. Once again Greta had not returned and Little Sparrow wondered resignedly if there had been another sit-in at school. This seemed to be all pupils did in school nowadays: protest, run wild, sit in. One sit-in seemed to end as another took shape. A perplexed government had already backed down and postponed National Service, caving in to the students' demand for the release of those arrested. Parents were helpless and without control. The government retaliated by closing all schools.

Upstairs, Little Sparrow heard Bertie moving about. She longed for him to come down and crouch by her chair, putting his head on her lap as if he understood the years they had lost. This happened rarely now that she had arranged for him to go once a week to a brothel on Lavender Road; his mind was filled by thoughts of women other than his mother. In the depths of the house the servants quarrelled, the knock of pans and the hiss of running water from the kitchen heralding the preparation of dinner. The earthy smell of onions came to her through the open window and gave her a feeling of consolation. She had got used to having a small vegetable garden during the war, and continued to keep one; it reminded her of home. As a child, the smell of onions and the family's own ordure was always around her. Every day they had spread their own night soil over the earth, beneath the puffball heads of the onions her mother sold in the market. They all helped with the job, ladling out the stinking mess from a wooden bucket.

Lim Hock An had ridden past her home on a tall horse and stopped for a drink of water, ordering it boiled and cooled before he would touch a drop. While he refreshed himself she had sat outside the hut with a bowl of green beans her mother had given her, stringing them for dinner. She remembered the sound of her mother's soft sobbing coming from inside. When Lim Hock An strode out and mounted his horse, her father had lifted her up to sit behind him. At first the ride was a novelty, but soon the animal's sweating back and the smell of the man she clung to filled her nose unpleasantly. As it grew dark they reached an inn and he lifted her down in his arms.

'I want to go home,' she had said.

'Your home is now with me,' he answered, and showed her a rough sleeping pallet in the corner of his room. All night she remembered she had lain awake listening to the sound of him turning and snoring, her body numb with terror. Little Sparrow sighed sadly as these memories washed through her.

Now, at last there were sounds of arrival and the gate swung open with a metallic ring. Greta entered the house in a rush and made straight for the stairs, taking them two at a time. Little Sparrow jumped out of her chair.

'Where have you been?' she shouted, following her daughter into the bedroom. Greta did not turn. Busily she pulled out clothes from drawers and the cupboard and stuffed them into her schoolbag.

'Where have you been again? Do you want to kill me with worry?' Little Sparrow clenched her fists and shook them at her daughter.

'Why should I tell you? You don't understand my life,' Greta yelled in reply, the hacked-off fringe of hair a hard jagged line above her angry eyes.

'This time we're going to hold out for as long as it takes at Chinese High; we'll organise our own lessons, cook our own food. We'll force the government to listen to us,' Greta shouted.

'I am your mother!' Little Sparrow screamed, afraid she might cry, the frustration was so big inside her.

'You are bourgeois. The Party is my family now,' Greta replied, and returned to her packing. Little Sparrow could not comprehend the strange words her daughter used, but she understood that she was disowned.

'What about your duty to me?' Little Sparrow thought she might choke on the words.

'Duty to parents is from the old life. Our duty is to uplift the masses who break their backs in the fields for people like you.' Greta spat the words out scornfully.

Little Sparrow drew a breath of pain. For the first time she realised that her daughter knew nothing of her past, had accepted only that she was the wife of a rich man, born to ease and comfort. Suddenly she needed to sit down, but there was no chair.

'The Party is my mother,' Greta yelled, swinging the bulging schoolbag over her shoulder.

'I'm leaving. I will go to China and give my life for the revolution.' Greta turned and ran down the stairs and out of the door. Once again Little Sparrow heard a car engine start up. A door slammed as the vehicle drove away. She stood transfixed at the top of the stairs, looking down at the open front door and the dark vegetable garden beyond. She bent to pick up a white cotton sock that had fallen from Greta's schoolbag. The faint perfume of onions came to her from the garden.

During the months that followed Ei Ling's arrival at Bougainvillaea House, Mei Lan found that the things she had worried about were decided for her. The wide press coverage of Ei Ling's court case had spread Mei Lan's name amongst a deprived community. No sooner was Ei Ling settled in a small room with two of her children, than the sister of a woman trapped in a similar marriage appeared to beg Mei Lan's help. A young prostitute fled a brothel, and arrived on her doorstep having heard of her through a sympathetic client. A mother brought her teenage daughter, beaten and molested by her stepfather, to Bougainvillaea House. Another prostitute, half dead from a botched abortion appeared, as did two sisters who had escaped from the hold of a ship during abduction to a brothel in Penang. A girl covered in burns and cuts from torture by her stepmother collapsed at the gate one night, and was found almost dead the next morning. A First Wife, poisoned by a Second Wife and their common husband, was brought to Mei Lan by a housemaid. Unmarried mothers, raped women, battered wives: soon Bougainvillaea House was filled to capacity by this needy population and Mei Lan was hard pressed to cope, finding it impossible to turn any woman away.

Almost every day she was in touch with the Salvation Army or the Poh Leung Kuk, and moved some girls to their care. Both institutions were themselves stretched to the limit and reluctant to offer help. Ah Siew, and the houseboy and two young housemaids she had been forced to hire, were worn out and struggled with the cleaning, feeding and organisation of the growing crowd. Every few days a fresh arrival appeared as, by word of mouth, Mei Lan's reputation grew. She took extended leave from Bayley McDonald & Cheong to deal with developments at home, and Mr Cheong was not approving. Ei Ling then surprised Mei Lan by a sudden show of assertiveness, ordering servants about like a martinet, standing no nonsense from anyone, running the house in a capable way. Her face brightened, she began to take care of her appearance and became almost stylish, her hair drawn up and secured with a long ornamental pin. Mei Lan had managed to get custody for her of her remaining two children, standing guarantor for them herself. All were now settled in Bougainvillaea House with Ei Ling, a rowdy crowd of small boys and girls who were packed off each day to school and kept busy with chores when home. The children, who had been scrawny rascals, filled out almost instantly on the plentiful food and responded to care and attention.

At the first medical emergency Mei Lan had called upon Cynthia for help. She had been grateful to find Cynthia at Belvedere when she returned from England, acknowledging against her will that this link again with Howard stirred emotions she would rather not face. Cynthia began to go each day after work to Bougainvillaea House to check on the sick women, setting up a makeshift clinic in the kitchen. In the worst cases she contacted Dr Wong who, still at Joo Chiat Hospital, was prepared to take some patients as charity.

Bougainvillaea House was small and already crowded to over-flowing. It was Cynthia who suggested they ask Rose for use of the Belvedere kitchen with its huge gas rings and cooking pots. Rose was hesitant at first to oblige someone she had previously viewed with such suspicion, but frail with angina and bored with the sparse events of her day, Rose found herself suggesting menus and imparting domestic advice, even lending Belvedere linen and mattresses to Mei Lan. Once or twice when Bougainvillaea House could take no more inmates, she had accommodated Mei Lan's bedraggled women in Belvedere's empty rooms.

On Howard's return to Belvedere from Sydney, it had begun to rain and Ah Fong had hobbled from the house under a large black umbrella to help with his suitcases. Howard saw with a shock that all the old man's teeth were gone. In the rain Belvedere stood sadly, weeds sprouting from guttering, paintwork worn, metal rusting, shutters crooked or missing. His mother had thrown herself upon him, sobbing to such an extent that he suddenly felt responsible for the decay about him, just because he had escaped it. He was upset to find she suffered from angina and had told him nothing about it. She now spent much of her day resting on the old chintz sofa that he saw had been re-covered in the usual pink design. The squatters had gone in his years away, and Rose had refurnished his old room with salvaged bits and pieces. Nothing in it was familiar except his saxophone, which stood in a corner in need of a polish. The rain had pelted down all day, drying up only in the evening. Within a few days he was to start work in the Social Welfare Department of the civil service.

That first night Howard heard the scuffling and squeaking of rats, the clank and wheeze of ancient pipes, sniffed the odour of decay and knew he was back in Belvedere. He was no longer afraid of the lurking presence he had sensed as a child in the dark heart of the house, yet, as he lay in bed, he felt the weight of the pace creep over him. He pushed aside the mosquito net, got out of bed and went to the window. The empty white light of the moon spilt over Bougainvillaea House.

The fence was gone from the canal and a bridge now stretched across it linking the two plots of land, but in the years he had been away, nothing else appeared to have changed. He had heard from Cynthia that Mei Lan had returned from England some time before and was involved in a prominent court case reported in all the newspapers. In the distance there was the rumble of thunder; lightning shot across the sky. The restlessness he had felt all day took hold of him again. It had begun even before he disembarked from the ship and the clamour, intense odour and heat of the city closed about him again. Anticipation had quickened his pulse as, from the deck of the ship, he watched the green shoreline of Singapore approach.

Howard asked Cynthia about Mei Lan the next evening, when he sat alone with her in the dining room after dinner. Cynthia looked at him sharply but Howard's face gave nothing away. She told him then about the interlocking arrangements between Belvedere and Bougainvillaea House and the history of Mei Lan's shelter.

'She's changed many women's lives for the better, and for her it's a way of healing; by helping the damaged she's helping herself. It's like Wilfred writing his book,' she said, listening to the shuffling feet of Belvedere's three old lodgers as they left the dining room.

Howard said nothing as Cynthia spoke, knowing she was waiting for a reaction from him but refusing to show how any talk of Mei Lan still affected him. His sister had aged, he noticed. The stress of long hours of work at the hospital and her committed care of the invalided Wilfred had taken its toll. Wilfred was walking again, although with a limp and the aid of a stick, grim faced and speaking little; his preferred communication with the world was now through the written word. Wilfred's book, *Lost Paradise*, had been published in London to great acclaim the year before. He had made some welcome money and his reputation as a writer was sealed; he and Cynthia were leaving for England within a few weeks. A lecture tour of the country had been arranged, and also a big reunion with other men who had survived the camps along the Thai–Burma railway. Cynthia worried about leaving Rose.

'You've come back just in time. I didn't want to go with Mummy in this condition, although I know Mei Lan would have kept an eye on her. Wilfred needs me and this is such a chance for him. He's talking of settling in Wiltshire where he was born; but we'll see how we feel when we get there.'

Howard nodded absently as Cynthia talked, absorbing her news of Mei Lan. Over the years while they lived at opposite ends of the world Mei Lan's unbridgeable distance, both physically and emotionally, had shrunk everything there had been between them. In anger he had turned to other women. He was older than most at the university and knew he was attractive to women; he had the looks and manner they liked. Gossip returned to him; he'd heard it said he was suave and worldly and was considered a catch. It was said he was destined for a brilliant career; he had taken a good degree in Politics and Economics and not found the study too arduous. He had relationships with many of the women around him, sometimes balancing several at a time; one or two he had even considered seriously. There had been one called Jacky and another called Sandra and both had been small, dark haired and determined. He wondered even then if he chose them because they reminded him of Mei Lan.

Marilyn had been different, tall and blonde with a face that was in constant motion, talking, laughing, thinking; never still. Individually her features were not attractive, but put together they had a striking effect. People said she was beautiful and then wondered why they said so; her hazel eyes were too close together, her nose was long, her mouth too generous and her strawberry blonde hair hung limply. She was aware of herself, and this gave her the confidence to take what she wanted from life; she was never without a boyfriend. Marilyn worked as a journalist on the paper where Howard had a part-time job; a colleague had introduced them. Those who did not like her said she had slept with everyone in the office. When his turn came, Howard saw no reason to resist. Her sun-warmed body, always soft and scented from the tanning oil she used, and the invitation offered in her eyes, demolished him quickly. In bed she was far more experienced than he, and taught him things he thought no woman should know. On the small balcony of her studio apartment she liked to sunbathe naked and once, at a party in the midst of a crowd, she drew him into a corner and slid his hand beneath her skirt, and he found she wore no underwear. It had driven him mad. Marilyn wanted him to marry her, and the affair had drifted on for months on the promise that they would announce their engagement. Howard always found excuses to delay, and in the end they parted. Now he was back in Belvedere, he knew the reason he could not marry Marilyn was because of Mei Lan.

'Come and see Mei Lan with me, I'm going over now to Bougainvillaea House,' Cynthia suggested. Howard started at the suggestion, his heart constricting. At first he hesitated but then he allowed himself to be carried along, and stood up to follow Cynthia. Events were already shaping themselves, and he would not prevent them.

He could see the shock in Mei Lan's face when he stepped into Bougainvillaea House, but she recovered and moved towards him. There was flesh on her bones once more, and she smiled; the direct look had returned to her eyes. He saw in relief that the business of living involved her again. The house was full of noisy bustle and crammed with women wherever he turned. A baby screamed, then a child ran by and was quickly followed by another. The old crone, Ah Siew, hobbled past at a sprightly pace but stopped when she saw Howard, to give a toothless smirk.

'She's still alive?' he asked Mei Lan wonderingly.

They faced each other like strangers and talk was formal. As Cynthia went into the kitchen with her medicine case to attend to a queue of waiting women, Mei Lan offered to show him around and Howard realised that he had never been inside Bougainvillaea House before, only imagined its interior from the windows of Belvedere. When Mei Lan had last resided here, her grandparents had been alive and the fence along the canal divided them from each other.

'I thought you were a lawyer – how have you got yourself into all this?' he asked, hearing an accusatory note in his voice as two small children bouncing a rubber ball pushed past him.

'I heard you were getting engaged,' Mei Lan replied, ignoring the question, preferring to verify what Cynthia had told her. He had changed, filled out and had an aura of sureness; he was a handsome man, with a feeling of quiet substance about him. In Australia, she was suddenly aware, experiences of which she knew nothing had claimed him. Would he have thought of other women if she had replied to his letters? she wondered with a stab of regret.

'It didn't work out,' Howard replied, wishing to place things quickly in perspective. Mei Lan nodded silently, absorbing the information as she turned to the stairs, hiding her confusion in the task of showing Howard Bougainvillaea House.

'The place is too small and we've had to utilise every corner. I'm thinking of building an extension,' Mei Lan told him as she walked slightly ahead of him up the stairs and along the corridor. Through every door she opened he saw the same scene: a room full of mattresses or trestle beds, chatting women and some children. There was an atmosphere of cheerfulness and he remarked on it to Mei Lan.

'They've found shelter; they're no longer living in fear,' she said shortly, opening the door to Lim Hock An's old room. The great Blackwood bed with its inlay of mother-of-pearl, reared up like an island in the small space. A baby slept at its centre, and the now familiar sea of mattresses were laid out around it, filled by Mei Lan's stray women. She shut the door and opened the next.

'This was Second Grandmother's room. I sleep here. That is her phoenix bed,' Mei Lan said pointing to the ornate throne of worn red and gold lacquer that, like Lim Hock An's bed, had survived the Japanese only because its size and weight prevented removal or sale. When Mei Lan returned from England and reclaimed the house, the sight of these two indestructible monuments still standing in the filthy, empty rooms, holding a world of memory in their old wood, made her break down and cry. Now, each night she slept in Second Grandmother's bed, staring up at the phoenix in its carved bower and asking for its protection.

Howard's mind was already querying the practical obstacles to Mei Lan's enterprise. 'How are you going to keep this afloat? Have you worked things out properly; is it going to be a permanent thing?' he dared to ask, suspecting that Mei Lan probably ran the house as she would an extended family, stretching her own means to cover the outgoings. He could see by her expression that this was a sensitive point.

Mei Lan was forced to admit that Howard's words held resonance. She had moved forward willy-nilly and knew she could not continue as she did, her direction confused and the money scrounged from here or there, leaching quickly away. Mr Cheong at Bayley McDonald & Cheong had been scathing of the shelter, explaining that goodwill was not enough, that soon things could topple about her, but Mei Lan saw no way to draw back.

'A foundation with interest generated on a good investment is the way a charity is run,' Howard told her, and was rewarded by the sudden appeal in her questioning glance. For a moment he sensed an unspoken shift of emotion between them and then it was gone, as Mei Lan retreated into herself again.

'Until now I have been selling off bits and pieces of Second Grandmother's jewellery and the money from the sale of Grandfather's jade will soon come in,' Mei Lan replied, reluctant to admit that the shelter had materialised so suddenly in her life, and involved her so completely, that a basic financial structure was missing. As she stood beside Howard, she was uncomfortable with the unexpected stir of emotion she had felt. In confusion she hurried to tell Howard her news.

'Grandfather's jade collection has been sold at auction in New York. It's gone to an American investor for an enormous sum of money. All those erotic jade curiosities are to go on display at the Metropolitan Museum of Art.' As she spoke, she considered this powerful new resource of cash for the first time.

They stood in a recess where she had opened another door, showing him a storeroom she was converting into a further bedroom. A small high window looked out on to the trees in the grounds of Lim Villa next door. Mei Lan stood close to him, her hair falling straight and thick along her cheek, hiding the birthmark on her jaw. The need for her ached abruptly in him, but he could say nothing. Beyond the window, buried within the trees was the gazebo that had sheltered them so long ago. He remembered the kisses with which he devoured her, sliding his lips down her body, lifting her clothes, unbuttoning and she unresisting, offering herself without restraint as they clung to each other as if they were drowning until it was over and he lay still upon her. 'I love you,' she had said. 'I love you,' he had replied, and knew it was not a lie. He remembered the trees that had closed to enfold them. In the undergrowth a lizard had stirred. An oriole's sweet warble had filled the clearing.

The emotions he had always struggled to hold in place would no longer obey him and he reached out for her, gripping her hard by the shoulders and drawing her brusquely towards him to kiss her savagely. A familiar panic filled Mei Lan and she pulled away, pressing herself against the wall, trapped in the tiny alcove as he blocked her escape.

'Get on with your life; forget me,' she whispered, edging past him. The constriction she had felt when Norbert embraced her seemed to paralyse her again. When Norbert had persuaded her to go to bed with him there had been wine to dull her senses, and she had come to the moment slowly, led there step by step like a frightened animal, relaxing slowly until he had her in his grasp. Norbert had shown urgency, but no passion, and she was required to do little but spread herself beneath him. Now her life lay wide open between darkness and light, and she did not know yet how to cross the chasm before her.

Howard stepped back, and she moved past him into the corridor again. He had thought the time in England, the doctors and medicines, the achievement of her professional dream would heal her fractured life. His mind filled with memories of his mock execution: the excruciating hours of imprisonment, the fear, the constant rhetorical haranguing. It was only later, when he had returned to a normal life, that he knew the true effect on him of long incarceration and indoctrination. It had taken months to slowly reclaim himself, but now flashbacks were rare, the nightmares had faded. If his journey back to wholeness had been so long and troubled, what of she who had suffered so much more: how would she reclaim an identity so thoroughly demolished? He reached out to catch Mei Lan's hand as she turned away and she looked at him miserably, waiting for release. Her sadness filled him. They were different people living different lives, and what had been, he realised at last, could not now be returned to.

Rose leaned back on the sofa and stared up at the ceiling of Belvedere. It was ingrained with dirt and cobwebs, home to geckos and spiders and birds nesting filthily in corners. Bits and pieces of straw were forever floating down upon them. All she could see of the future was decay. It was there in herself with the degeneration of her health and the narrowing space of old age. It was there in the sight of Wilfred limping about on a stick, and Cynthia's struggle to support him. In warped window frames, splintering wood and crumbling stucco, in the overgrown garden, and broken flowerpots, Belvedere too had succumbed inescapably to old age. Even the elderly Eurasian widowers grew more doddering by the day. Rose had shut off the upper floor of the house except for the occasions when Mei Lan had use for it, and at night, listening to the scampering of rodents and the knocking of pipes, she gave in to despair.

From where she sat Rose stared out of the window at the familiar view of the mangosteens. The trees had never recovered from the pounding they had taken during the war, and had decayed with the same stoicism that now engulfed Belvedere. It could not go on, Rose decided; Belvedere must be sold. As the thought appeared she wondered why she had not considered it before. A terraced house, like the one she had inherited from Aunty May in Queen Street, would be more than adequate for her needs. She thought of the day she had first seen Belvedere with a house agent and recalled, in spite of its dilapidated state, her feeling of hope. She remembered her delight in identifying with a road, the thrill it had given her to be Rose of Mount Rosie. She leaned back weak and sad, but seeing at last a way to arrest the downward curve of her life.

36

HOWARD FOUND HE HAD returned to a place of shifting landscapes, regroupings, realignments and new beginnings. Singapore was now a place of strikes, mass meetings and general unrest, stirred up by communist activists and socialist-minded nationalists. Assassinations were commonplace, as was the sight of rioting school children proficient in mayhem as much as in study. Communist rhetoric was everywhere, *The British imperialists' bloody rule of Malaya has squeezed us to the marrow,* was written on a wall in fresh red paint near the building that housed the Social Welfare Department as Howard arrived for work the first day. It shocked him to see such bold defiance. He wondered if Wee Jack was still in the thick of things, gleefully directing this vicious unrest.

Within a few days of his arrival home, Howard had begun his new job. He had written to Raj telling him about his plans to return to Singapore, and his need to find suitable work now that he had earned his degree. It had not taken long for Raj to reply, saying he had spoken to a contact in the Social Welfare Department and that someone with Howard's qualifications would be welcome there. Raj had contacts everywhere and was, Howard learned, involved with more than just business now; politics had claimed him through a back door. He had made large donations of money to the Progressive Party. The British Government was at last allowing the initial steps towards self-government to be taken. In a few months Singapore would hold its first election, which the Progressive Party was expected to win.

Amongst the people Howard now came into contact with, politics was impossible to ignore. Within the Social Welfare Department Howard found a growing breed of politicised civil servants who saw it as their duty to work for the underdog and for a struggling local society. Malayanisation was the call heard everywhere now; the transfer of senior government posts from British expatriates to local civil servants could not come quickly enough for these men. The Council of Joint Action had been formed with representatives from twenty-one government unions and, as well as squeezing better pay out of their European masters, it forced the process towards self-government to become political. No longer, they vowed, should British expatriate officials be allowed to sit comfortably on their backsides. Some days Howard felt he had walked into a maelstrom: half the office was out demonstrating on the street instead of working. While civil servants were fighting to raise local pay to equal that of British expatriate civil servants, government unions and staff associations organised mass walkouts and rallies. The atmosphere, in this outwardly dull administrative backwater, was charged with hope and anger.

A study of the poverty line, the *Survey on Urban Incomes and Housing* had been published just before Howard joined the department and had involved many researchers investigating hundreds of case studies. Some follow-up material was still being researched and Howard was immediately thrown into this, drawing graphs, editing material, writing numerous reports; even re-checking interviews, which necessitated visits to some of the poorest areas of Chinatown. He walked the crumbling, filthy streets remembering the look on Wee Jack's face all those years ago when, sharing cigarettes in the jungle, the man had tried to explain why he was a communist. Injustice, everywhere injustice, Wee Jack had said, his face filled with emotion. Now, observing the grinding poverty around him Howard felt helpless to make a difference in any way. He knew Wee Jack had real reason to fight, real reason to choose the communist path as the only one that might bring results.

As he walked towards the main road to hail a trishaw to take him back to the office, he looked up at the sky and remembered the Liberty Cabaret and the Malayan Democratic Union. Although the MDU had been forced to disband, the commitment to Independence was now even stronger. *The future lies under a different sky*, a bespectacled Chinese had told him on that first MDU meeting Krishna had taken him to. Perhaps, Howard thought, behind the thin clouds drifting above him, that unknown sky already lay waiting. Perhaps, at last, the crossroads of time before which he now stood, would give him the opportunity to make that difference.

Now that he was back from Australia, Howard was conscious of the need to visit Raj. He was grateful to the man, and had written to him regularly about his progress, wanting him to know his investment was sound. Raj was a busy man, but at last an appointment was made. Howard set out for the Waterloo Street house, but when he arrived found only Krishna there with Leila.

'He will come soon, you will have to wait,' Krishna told him, leading him up flights of steep narrow stairs to the upper part of the house, where he said he had his own space.

'Soon we will occupy the whole house. Our landlord is moving out,' Krishna informed him sarcastically, explaining about Raj's forthcoming marriage to Yoshiko Ho.

'He is building a fine home on Cluny Road near the Botanic Gardens for himself and that Ho Ho woman. How can a rich man live in a humble house like this?' Krishna said bitterly. 'He is forgetting how we once all lived on Sarangoon Road, how he was sleeping on Manikam's counter top. To forget where you come from is no good.'

'He has done well, you should be proud of him,' Leila admonished him after greeting Howard. 'He has no good word to say for anyone nowadays. My brother keeps us here, rent-free, and with my earnings from Manikam's, I am keeping my husband.' Leila's tone was long-suffering.

As Raj prepared to move out of the house, Leila was taking over her brother's old ground floor rooms and turning them into an administrative office for Manikam's. Under her organisation Manikam's was now a busy place. As well as the original Manikam's they had expanded into different premises further up the road. Leila had a staff of ten young men, five to each shop, and to them her word was law. She had developed ideas to attract new customers, new lines to sell, new advertising. If you could not get something in other shops, you could always get it in Manikam's. *We have what others do not,* became Manikam's slogan after Leila took over. In contrast to her lofty-minded husband, Leila found she was shrewd and thrifty and could run a business as well as a man.

While she worked in Manikam's, Krishna secluded himself in the upper areas of the house, reading old newspapers. The house was now furnished with shiny carved furniture upholstered in red velvet. Upstairs, in the area that was his domain, Krishna spurned such luxury. His old Indian style desk, low near the floor, was battered but he still sat cross-legged before it, writing secret inflammatory missives for *Freedom News*. Since Leila would have little to do with him, he slept by himself on his old string bed while his wife, in a separate room, now had a spring mattress on a mahogany bed. Krishna had the look of a mangy dog, Howard thought, his grey hair uncut, a wild look in his eye and his beard several days gone; his politics were ever more radical. He had also aged, the lines on his face now deepened to sculptural depth. He was obsessed with Raj's backing of the Progressive Party.

'That party is just a government puppet, its members collaborating with colonials to line their own pockets.' He gave a snort of harsh laughter as he lay on his *charpoy*. 'This upcoming election is getting everyone excited. New political parties are being born every minute. But people will find, whatever happens, whoever gets in, the British will still keep control.'

'It is a first step; it's hopeful,' Howard said from where he sat on the floor, leaning back on the bolsters of an old *kapok* pallet. The room was hot but dim, fierce sunlight entering the place in bright bars through louvred shutters. A small electric fan beside Krishna's bed twisted about, stirring sheaves of paper stacked on the floor by the desk. Leila had sent a servant up with glasses of sherbet and a plate of freshly fried banana chips. Howard was hungry, and took a handful. The room had a stale, mouldering smell because Krishna never opened the window, and never let the servants in to clean unless he was present to oversee them.

'I do not want them looking into my business,' he told Howard.

'They cannot read,' Howard retorted, impatient with Krishna's logic.

'Nowadays spies are everywhere,' Krishna snapped as they heard sounds of Raj's arrival downstairs, and then his step on the stairs.

Krishna got off the bed and went over to put a record on an ancient gramophone with a large brass horn. A blast of Indian music filled the room as Raj entered and greeted Howard effusively. Raj's girth had expanded and he had acquired a portly appearance; there was grey at the temples of his pomaded hair. He assessed Howard affably, asking questions about his life in Australia. His investment in Howard had been worthwhile, Raj decided, scrutinising his protégé intently. There had been a big change in Howard: physically he was leaner, his face sharper; his eyes had added judgement. The war and his time in the jungle had deepened him with realisations nothing but experience could bring, while education and the few years abroad had added polish and insight. Raj found him an impressive man who had more than fulfilled his promise; the kind of person the country would need when it came into its own. Howard might be without the businessman's hard-edged guile but he had the commitment and moral clear-mindedness people sought in their leaders. He would do well, Raj decided, and was filled with a sense of proud ownership, such as when he bought a new car.

'I am backing the Progressive Party in the election, I am funding them with a lot of money,' Raj said proudly, sitting down on a rickety folding chair to tell Howard his news.

'Ask him why he is wasting his money like this,' Krishna interrupted, lying back on the *charpoy*.

'I may be a lowly merchant, but everyone wants my money. So, by the back door of funding, I have entered politics. If this party gets in, then many favours will be owed to me.' Raj chuckled, pleased with himself. Howard smiled; he had developed a fondness for the man, seeing beneath the pomposity, a generous heart. Krishna raised his head to regard him sourly.

'All he wants is power,' he commented.

'A first class election campaign is needed.' Raj continued, taking no notice of Krishna but looking pointedly at Howard. 'Votes must be canvassed and people prepared. The Progressive Party must win. You are the right man for such a campaign.' Raj reached out for a handful of banana chips, unaware of Howard's sudden change of expression.

'I have only just started the job at Social Welfare,' Howard reminded Raj unhappily.

'This is a part-time job; you can choose your time. And it is a well-paid job, no free volunteer nonsense.' Raj laughed, wagging a finger, knowing Howard could not refuse him.

Howard listened resignedly, his heart sinking. He was not interested in any furthering of the Progressive Party, a party still happy to leave the better part of governance in colonial hands, but he knew he was in no position to protest. Although he had paid back a substantial amount of Raj's interest-free loan, something still remained.

'Tomorrow, that new People Action Party is having its inauguration at Victoria Memorial Hall,' Raj said. 'They are hot-headed radicals but I shall go and see what they have to say. Everyone is going. I do not expect they will be any challenge to the Progressives,' Raj remarked, standing up. Krishna jumped up in fury at Raj's observation and began to wind up the phonograph, turning to shout at him over his shoulder.

'The People's Action Party intend to get us Independence!'

'Then perhaps they should ask *you* to fund them. I hear they are all as poor as temple mice,' Raj responded with a laugh, turning to the door.

'Come with me tomorrow,' Krishna urged Howard, once Raj had gone. 'Let us see what this new party has to say.'

The warbling sounds from the gramophone now grated on Howard's nerves. He soon found an excuse to leave, after agreeing resignedly to accompany Krishna the following day. As he stepped out of the house on Waterloo Street, despondency settled upon him. Raj had trapped him in happenings with which he wanted no involvement.

The next morning Howard stood with Krishna beneath the clock tower of Victoria Memorial Hall waiting for Raj to arrive for the new People's Action Party inaugural meeting. The sky was cloudy, the rain that earlier flooded the streets had petered out. Large puddles reflected slices of sky, as if the world had turned upside down. Krishna's eyes were bloodshot; he had not slept all night and his energy had a rabid edge as he spoke excitedly.

'That trade union lawyer, Lee, and his friends have formed this new party. That radical union leader Lim Chin Siong is also with them,' Krishna said, shifting from foot to foot as he stood beside Howard under some dripping trees. He was clearly excited by the essence of the new party, and Howard began to feel wary. It was a fine line he now walked, he realised, wanting change as so many people did, yet wanting also to steer clear of fanaticism.

'He's here,' Krishna commented sourly, as Raj's car drew up a few feet away from them. A knot of waiting men hurried to meet Raj as he emerged from the car. Raj greeted Howard warmly, but did no more than nod to Krishna before turning away into the hall, guided by his friends. Howard and Krishna trailed behind him. As they entered the crowded auditorium, a wall of stale air hit them. An electrical failure had stopped the fans and a strong human smell pervaded the place. An emergency generator now powered the lights while microphones were being tested, releasing the occasional hollow tapping sound or word, over the excited buzz of conversation. Men stood chatting in the aisles and the rows of chairs were quickly filling up.

Howard and Krishna found seats near the back. Raj sat apart in an area reserved for VIPs, much to Krishna's relief. He looked about disapprovingly, observing the large imposing portraits of past colonial governors on the walls. Eagle-eyed and patriarchal, as removed in their frames as they had been in the flesh, they looked down disapprovingly upon a meeting that proposed to end their legacy. Krishna began inspecting the audience in the auditorium and was affronted to find that, although many union people were present, powerful Lim Chin Siong was not on the platform with the other conveners of the new party, but sitting on a chair in the stalls.

'They are not wanting to put him in the spotlight because of his radical views. They are saying that once Lim Chin Siong has full control of all the trade unions, he will kick that Lee Kwan Yew out of the party,' Krishna announced with satisfaction, craning his neck for a sight of the union leader.

'It is time all those old portraits in the hall were replaced with Sun Yat-sen, Mao Tse-tung, Lenin and others,' Krishna continued, glaring again at the august portraits staring down at him.

'There must be more than a thousand people here,' Howard commented, turning in his seat to assess the crowded hall. Looking up at the cavernous space above him, he saw a beam of light, thick with drifting dust motes. In Victoria Memorial Hall anticipation was ripe.

On the stage the last man was now seated and the lawyer Lee Kuan Yew, as Secretary of the People's Action Party, took the podium to begin the meeting. Behind him the conveners of the new party were dressed in white to symbolise their political purity and the sleeves of their open-necked shirts were rolled up in a workmanlike way, to confirm their wish to serve. Like Lee, the core members of the party had studied in London and had belonged to the Malayan Students' Union there. Their political passions were fanned in the intellectually liberated environment of European academia, and influenced by the views of a socialist society under a British Labour government. When these students returned to Singapore, they returned with a political mission that had finally come to fruition on this wet morning in Victoria Memorial Hall.

Lee Kuan Yew stood waiting for the auditorium to still. As silence settled in the hall he began to speak, his voice resonant with conviction. Howard sensed the flaming ambition, the impatience and intolerance in the shrewd chiselled face, tense and focused as he spoke. The theme of Independence was immediately confronted.

'There can be no compromise on this issue . . . No constitution which curtails the sovereignty of the people can be acceptable to us,' Lee said, not mincing his words.

'. . . to abolish inequalities of wealth and opportunity inherent in the present system . . . to give all citizens the right to work, and ensure a decent living and social security to all those who through sickness, infirmity or old age can no longer work . . . to create a prosperous, stable and just society.'

When at last he finished speaking, cries of *Merdeka* erupted around the hall. *Merdeka!* Freedom. The word echoed in Howard's ears.

Eventually, the meeting ended somewhat abruptly because the hall was booked for a concert in the afternoon, and the organisers were waiting to get in. The last speech of the meeting was given by an elderly man known for his long-windedness. In comparing the new party to the more pro-government Progressive Party, he gave the analogy of a thin dog that was free and a fat dog that was chained before time ran out and he was signalled to stop. Soon people were streaming out of Victoria Memorial Hall, grateful for fresh air after the stale auditorium. The sun had emerged full blast and had already almost dried the wet ground.

'This party's views are like those of our old Malayan Democratic Union,' Krishna said, as they stood waiting for Raj. He was in a good mood; in the People's Action Party he already saw enough revolutionary ideas and suspected communists to keep him happy.

Raj emerged from the hall surrounded by a crowd of admirers. Smart as always in his cotton suit and panama hat, he pulled a monogrammed handkerchief from his breast pocket and mopped his perspiring face with a flourish. As he stepped into the sunlight he was spotted by his waiting driver and the car slid forward to meet him. Seeing Howard and Krishna, Raj waved them towards him, signalling them to get into the car. He was relieved by the opinion he had formed of the new party.

'It's a party of unionists, for the unions; its members are riff-raff, and its leaders are rabble-rousers,' said Raj, dismissing the inauguration once they were settled in the car. 'They'll be no threat to our Progressive Party in the election.'

Howard leaned back on the soft leather as the car moved slowly through the dispersing crowd. People's Action Party men in their white shirts and white trousers still stood about conferring, the lawyer Lee amongst them. The man's intent face and razor sharp expression remained with Howard, as did the spontaneous cries of *Merdeka*. He heard the word shouted again as the car drew away from Victoria Memorial Hall. *Merdeka!*

Yet already, in spite of its appeal, he knew he would not join the People's Action Party. Although sympathetic to its aims, he saw it as divided by dangerous elements, courting a mass vote through the communist-backed trade unions. As the car gathered speed the cry of *Merdeka* came to him again, and he knew that on it would turn the future.

Howard was busy the following week in the office. Preparations were made for a new survey by the Social Welfare Department on incomes and savings. Information was needed on the Central Provident Fund, a compulsory savings venture. The fund was the brainchild of David Marshall, a legendary lion of the courtroom, famous for sensational trials. He had championed the fund into reality some years before when he was still part of the Progressive Party. On his way to Marshall's office to interview him about the CPF, Howard had to walk past the Cricket Club, and was surprised to see the man himself addressing a crowd of people in the shade of a tall tembusu tree. Marshall, a flamboyant Sephardic Jew, was now a colourful part of the political scene as leader of yet another new party, the coalition Labour Front, a multiracial party also bent upon quick independence like the People's Action Party, but with a more velvet-gloved approach. It was lunchtime and clerks from nearby offices were out eating their lunch beside a coffee stall. A small van with a loudspeaker stood behind Marshall, and his deeply eloquent voice carried across the Padang to the Cricket Club. As he spoke he made sweeping gestures towards the building. Howard noticed that club members were leaning out of the windows to listen to the man and shout occasional jeers. On the Padang a cricket match was, as ever, in progress.

'We cannot wait another eight years for Independence as the

Progressive Party solemn-facedly advises us after conferring with their colonial friends in the colonial government. There, right before us is the very temple of Britishness, the Cricket Club, and on its veranda sit our so-called masters, the *tuans,* sipping beer and eating their *tiffin.* Let them hear what we have to say, let them know we can no longer be yoked to their Empire, driven to plough their fields and fertilise their wealth with our sweat. Just look at them over there at the Cricket Club, craning their necks to see me, rushing their lunch to hear me . . . Why should so many be enslaved for the benefit of so few . . .'

The voice had such melodic resonance, rose and fell in such smooth undulations that the crowd of locals gathered before the tembusu tree, stood as if mesmerised. Marshall's large penetrating eyes beneath bushy eyebrows stared fiercely. Howard took his place at the edge of the crowd, listening with the same attention as everyone else, caught by the spellbinding effect. Marshall had already made his anti-communist stance clear and his vehement denial of communism was nothing but reassuring to Howard. The meeting soon ended and Howard introduced himself, and was invited immediately by Marshall to drive back in the loudspeaker van with him to his office; the man talked all the way.

'The press attacks me but I welcome it; they are getting my name known all over the island and I am getting the Brits used to brutal criticism and debate. By taking my campaign to the roadside under "the old apple tree" so to speak, I am awakening the people. The most immediate and urgent task facing any serious political party in Malaya is to end colonialism as swiftly as possible. There is a near volcano of impatient youth thirsting for Independence. It is our duty to give it to them.' Marshall rattled on as he led Howard into his office, talking all the time over his shoulder.

'I am not interested in just getting a seat. I am interested in putting before the people of Singapore what they are facing. You can vote for the Progressive Party if you like, but they are capitalist colonial stooges who, in order to maintain their leisured way of life, will never push for Independence. Or you can vote for me, I am a socialist and I am a Singaporean and I will push for Independence immediately. That is the choice.'

David Marshall sat down behind his desk and gesturing Howard into a seat before him. His mobile features of large nose, sad eyes, generous mouth and brow were crammed with difficulty into his narrow face under a shock of unruly hair. It was a face of reckless emotion and reckless courage, and Howard was strongly drawn to the man. He seemed everything a liberal socialist should be, and Howard knew he could support him wholeheartedly. Even as this thought took root in his mind, the weight of his commitment to Raj pressed down upon him, and his heart sank.

Krishna had fallen into one of his depressions again. His moods changed quickly from bouts of excitable energy to troughs of darkness; what seemed full of affirmation one day appeared like a punctured balloon the next. The depression could last for days. Then, instead of being absent and untraceable most of the day, he seldom went out of the house. He sat in his room playing Indian songs full of warble and lilt on his ancient wind-up gramophone, a relic of the black market during the Japanese occupation. There was now a modern radiogram in the house that combined a radio and a record turntable, but Krishna was not interested in this contraption and continued to play his records on the old machine, much to Leila's annoyance. The sound of the music with its background crackle of age filled the house at all hours of the day. In the kitchen, directing a new cook in the proper combination of spices for a vegetable curry, Leila felt ready to scream. The songs were mournful with sorrowful themes, and one in particular Krishna played again and again. The kitchen was hot and she sweated, the aromatic smoke of frying onions full in her face. Her patience was wearing thin, and after a long day at Manikam's she was tired.

Death's happy release. Death's happy release. The needle was stuck, but Krishna lay on his *charpoy* content to listen to the repeating wail. The sound hammered in Leila's head and with an abusive shout at the servant, she ran up the stairs and into her husband's room to snatch up the arm of gramophone.

'What's the matter with you?' she shouted.

'I'm old and useless,' he replied, prone upon the string bed. She was tempted to agree but held her tongue; the fuller her life became at Manikam's, the more the sight of him annoyed her. It was not the way a wife should feel, but he had failed her as a husband, she thought angrily.

'What about the new political party? You were full of enthusiasm not long ago,' Leila reminded him. She was secretly relieved that the People's Action Party, although apparently riddled with communists, appeared to offer her husband a welcome alternative to the Malayan Communist Party. She had recently discovered writings of such an inflammable nature in his desk that she had openly gasped. The article was rolled up in a copy of the notorious *Freedom News* and destined, she knew, for publication in the underground paper. If he were not careful, she feared he would soon be back on St John's.

'You said with this new People's Action Party, Singapore had a future,' Leila repeated.

'Well, now I'm not so sure,' Krishna replied aggressively. He did not feel he could give his allegiance to any party. Everyone was young and gung-ho, filled with ideals and energy, undeterred by the prospect of ploughing a minefield of impossible obstacles to achieve political goals. He thought sadly of Subhas Chandra Bose and knew, even more sadly, that he had once felt the same. Once, as an INA soldier he had held a gun easily, killed men at Imphal without thought in the cause of Indian Independence, and even seen his dream of Independence achieved. He did not know why he was depressed instead of fulfilled and elated. Now, he was afraid even to hide a cache of weapons for the Malayan Communist Party, did not like the thought of its vicious cadres in his house, and abhorred the way he was ordered about by arrogant youths half his age. BK had tried again to persuade him to shelter a cache of weapons, even threatening expulsion from the Party if he did not obey.

'I'm too old,' he had told BK firmly once again as they sat at the same noodle shop.

'I'm old,' he repeated now to Leila, who sighed in exasperation.

'See here, the needle is broken,' Leila said, examining the arm of the phonograph. 'Why can't you use the new radiogram downstairs instead of this old thing?' Krishna did not reply.

The sound of loud knocking at the front door came to them from downstairs. A servant boy soon appeared at the top of the stairs to announce that two Chinese men were asking for the Master.

'All the riff-raff in Chinatown expect you to be at their beck and call,' Leila admonished as Krishna heaved himself off the *charpoy* and stood up. She wished she could speak more patiently.

Leaving Leila searching in a drawer for a new needle, and grateful of an excuse to be free of his wife, Krishna went downstairs to attend to the visitors. He found two young men he did not recognise waiting by the half-open front door. At first he took them to be students; they were neatly dressed and smiled at him politely. The taller boy, whose hair was shaved above his ears in a pudding bowl cut, stepped forward and apologised for disturbing him. He said he came from the Town Committee with an urgent message.

'What is the message?' Krishna asked. The other boy, whose face was pitted with acne, moved to stand in front of his friend. Krishna grew suspicious and frowned disapprovingly, wondering what he should do if a cache of weapons was now to be thrust upon him. He was sure this was why they had come, and that perhaps already guns were installed in the garage and protest would be helpless.

Still fumbling to insert a new needle into the gramophone, Leila heard a sudden loud crack, like the backfiring of a car in the road. A moment later the servant boy came running up the stairs for her, and one glance at his face made Leila follow. Krishna was lying on the floor, blood pouring from his chest. The front door stood open to the view of cars and carts trundling past in the street. With a moan Leila dropped to her knees beside her husband. The servant boy ran outside, shouting for help. Food hawkers stopped to turn and gawp.

'Fetch the police, fetch a doctor!' Leila screamed at the motley crowd gathering curiously about her door. Within a moment a large car drew up and Raj got out, accompanied by Yoshiko Ho. Alarmed, he hurried forward but stopped in shock at the sight of the wounded Krishna. Yoshiko put a hand to her mouth in horror.

'Fetch a doctor, fetch the police,' Raj yelled at the onlookers, his heart racing in panic.

Leila gazed down at her husband's face as she cradled his head in her lap. Everything seemed like a dream. Krishna opened his eyes and moved his lips, but no words took shape. Leila gave a sob, stricken by guilt at the way she had earlier spoken to him. Transfixed by horror, she held his hands as blood trickled from his mouth. Krishna looked up, fixing his eyes upon her face, and even when they stilled and the light was gone from his gaze, he continued to stare urgently up at her.

37

THE FIRST DAY OF April, the day before the election, was one of frenzied activity. Howard spent the day in the constituency, going from door to door in streets that still might be persuaded to vote Progressive. In this mixed Chinese area of prosperous shopkeepers and well-to-do residents, a Progressive win was expected. In the weeks leading up to the election Howard and his team of volunteers had been out canvassing every spare moment, but he knew he gave up too easily, did not have the needed evangelical belief in the party he worked for. The new People's Action Party, for all their bluster, had only fielded four candidates, preferring to await political maturity and to strengthen their muscle in opposition. Both the volatile lawyer Lee Kwan Yew and his radical colleague Lim Chin Siong were standing as candidates in working-class Chinese areas where unionists, poor factory labourers and disenfranchised youths were a supportive electorate.

Howard had lost count of the number of doors he had knocked upon, shaking hands and distributing pamphlets. He had organised loudspeaker vans and driven around, his own voice echoing in his ears, promoting a candidate he barely knew and who was rarely seen in the constituency. As he himself was frequently to be seen there, people came to him with their grievances. Residents from a street called Lorong Sakai wanted permission to change its name, as the Japanese echo was distasteful to them. A poor area of one ward wanted electricity. People showed him their homes, which they complained were worse than stables, and he could not but agree. Other residents requested the removal of a hawker area or complained of a preponderance of rats. In these wards, much to Howard's chagrin, his face became known as the face of the Progressive Party.

Momentum had built all over the island as the election loomed. Under the tall tembusu tree, David Marshall continued with his lunchtime forum but as much as the issue of Independence, he was now pressed to discuss the question of whether he would or would not wear the required formal robes if elected to the Legislative Assembly.

'I hope to walk in dressed as I am,' he said firmly, standing his ground in his perennial belted safari jacket and trousers. 'Will you at least wear a necktie?' someone shouted.

'In this lovely climate, the necktie is not only not required, it is a constriction,' he responded.

The polling booths opened at 8 a.m. and from an early hour there was a reasonable turnout, although much less brisk than expected. Police were on standby, ready for incidents. Chinese Middle School students had promised not to march as intended on Government House with a new protest and the weather was forecast to be no hazard to voters. Howard was busy all day urging people to vote, driving those in need to the polling station at a local school in one of the cars Raj had hired. The ballot boxes were closed at 8 p.m. and when it was done he was exhausted.

A strong smell of the river drifted on the night. Howard was late arriving at Victoria Memorial Hall from the campaign headquarters and found Boy Scouts carrying in the last ballot boxes. Already a crowd had gathered outside the hall in anticipation of the results. As far as Howard could see, most of those waiting appeared to be the usual young trade unionists. Empress Place was filling up, cordons were erected to hold people back. Police vans and riot police were in evidence; an atmosphere of expectation was tight upon them all.

Arc lights blazed on graceful colonial buildings, and Howard thought of the Englishmen who for over a century had ruled the colony, showing no chink in their armour. Now it was possible the radical lawyer Lee Kuan Yew and Lim Chin Siong, a man of communist sympathies, as well as the anti-establishment David Marshall, would enter those portals of power, intent on razing the past. Howard was pushed uncomfortably about in the crush, and over the heads before him saw Raj entering Victoria Memorial Hall, with Yoshiko beside him. Light from the great lamps set up outside reflected lustrously on Raj's pomaded hair. With his usual authoritative manner, he was demanding that people step back to allow him to move forward. From the river came the hoot of a boat's horn.

Inside, the counting of votes had started and the long wait for results begun. As the hours stretched out the crowd outside continued to grow, and by midnight many thousands overflowed the area around the hall, spilling back to the Cricket Club and the Padang. Never before had the country been stirred in this way and the crowd was restless, impatient for news. Inside the hall the mounting tension was almost unbearable as everyone waited; already a clear, unexpected and shocking swing to the left was emerging.

When at last the results were announced at two in the morning, the Progressive Party had taken only four seats out of twenty-five, and David Marshall's Labour Front had a landslide majority. Flushed with victory, Labour Front supporters ran riot in the hall. The People's Action Party candidates, Lee Kuan Yew and Lim Chin Siong had, as expected, taken their constituencies with unprecedented numbers of votes. As this news was announced to the waiting crowd, cheering students and trade unionists broke through police barriers to lift the successful candidates on to their shoulders, jubilantly carrying them forward, their shouts and cheers echoing into the night. *Merdeka! Merdeka!* Howard heard the cry all around him. The great arc lights picked out Lee Kuan Yew as he was jolted and pitched about on the shoulders of his supporters. Howard feared the man might slip from his precarious perch. Instead, he kept his balance, raising his arms in triumph.

Until the end, Raj had been sure the Progressive Party would win. His face wet with excitement, dark patches of sweat staining his shirt under his armpits, he had walked about confidently during the counting. The Labour Front victory was a shock for which he was unprepared. Crushed and perplexed, he grew petulant then furious, especially at the success of the two People's Action Party candidates.

'How will they allow such radicals into the Legislative Chamber? That Lim doesn't even speak much English, only Chinese. What's the matter with people?' Raj asked Howard accusingly, his fleshy face creased with disappointment, still baffled by the distressing vote.

'I invested so much money in this. I have never before made a bad deal,' Raj raged as they stood watching the triumphant, cheering crowd as it was announced that David Marshall would become Chief Minister of Singapore. It was a warm, close night and a bloated moon, spongy as a piece of bean curd, hung low in the sky. Above them the clock tower of Victoria Memorial Hall rose darkly into the night.

'The electorate has changed,' Howard said quietly, observing the scene before him, feeling guilty at failing Raj yet secretly jubilant that the Labour Front had won. 'Anyone who wants to stand in politics here today can't afford to ignore the Chinese masses, or the people's desire for self-government.'

'The Governor will not like working with such raggle-taggle people'. Raj was unable to contain his anger; his lips bunched together threateningly.

Soon David Marshall, the ebullient new Chief Minister, responding to the ecstatic crowd, appeared on an upper balcony, waving excitedly to the throng. A man of great gestures and blazing eyes, used to promoting courtroom drama, his voice boomed out through the public address system, filled with crusading zeal. Raising his arms in victory before the crowd, he threw his head back and roared into the night.

'It is the people's victory. Today victory is yours.'

Howard walked over from Belvedere to Bougainvillaea House each evening to be with Mei Lan after he returned from work; it was now a regular routine. Often, he ate dinner with her squashed around the large table with more than a dozen women and several children. He was not sure what the status of his relationship with Mei Lan was, and feared to ask, but he seemed to have a definite if undefined role to play. A habit had built up and he knew this was all she wanted and he must be content. Although he kept a formal distance, she did allow the occasional brief touch to pass between them but he felt this was in kindness to him. Now, sitting beside her on a bench outside the back door of Bougainvillaea House, facing the canal that had once been such a source of contention, he resolved to tell her about the sale of Belvedere. Light from the house lit the patch of grass and the bougainvillaea bushes about them. A smell of brackish water came to them from the dark trench of the canal, and the ragged fringe of trees behind which the old gazebo of Lim Villa still lay, could just be seen.

'Agents have already been to see it and some potential buyers as well but Belvedere is not easy to sell. No one wants such a run-down place. The agents say we must look for someone who wants the land to build upon after pulling down the old house.' Even as he spoke, he saw shock gather in her face as she tried to digest the news.

Now that the election was over Howard had returned to a calm routine at the Social Welfare Department; he was even asked to lecture on economics to students at the University of Malaya. At Social Welfare he was well liked, yet restlessness filled him. His brush with the excitement of politics had unsettled him, had left him wanting to be part of the exhilarating rush for freedom. When unexpectedly, after only a month in office, David Marshall offered him this chance Howard did not hesitate to take it. He was invited to lunch at a small restaurant and had hardly sat down when the Chief Minister fixed his large sad eyes upon him.

'I need a young man like you in the Chief Minister's office,' he said, taking out a box of tobacco and pressing some into the bowl of his pipe.

'You hardly know me.' Howard could not hide his shock.

'I have done my homework and besides, I know the worth of a man immediately I look at him.' Marshall lit up his pipe, releasing the heady perfume of tobacco. He had not forgotten Howard, and had noted his quiet confidence and insight as exceptional; just the qualities he needed to have in the men around him now.

'I intend to ask for immediate independence for the country. No more stalling or delays from all those old government farts – we'll push the thing through. Until now I've had undefined functions as Chief Minister, but not any more. After the election it was assumed by the Governor that I would regard the title of Chief Minister as an honorific one. They did not even have an office for Chief Minister at Government House, and didn't intend to give me one either. When I threatened to set up office under "the old apple tree" where I had held my lunchtime public talks, they cleared a space under the stairs, quite literally. A small room, no more than a broom cupboard with a table and a telephone; the Governor tried to humiliate me. So, when I entered the August Presence I wore a bush shirt; I thought that would be insult enough.' Marshall was gleeful, puffing fiercely at his pipe. Then his face became serious as he leaned back in his chair, staring at Howard over the table.

'At some point there will be another election. Times are changing, and a few months ago who would have thought we'd get this far?

The future will be nothing like our past. The country will need young men like you. Working with me will give you political insight and experience. You should think of standing as a Labour Front candidate in a future election. Until then, if you stay by my side, I'll teach you the tricks of the trade.' Marshall flashed an impish grin.

Over the following days and weeks Howard thought about what Marshall had said. He remembered the men he had met at the Malayan Democratic Union, men who could make a difference, and knew a seed was planted in him then that had only now begun to germinate. He was grateful to Marshall for pointing the way ahead. The next day he gave in his notice at the Social Welfare Department, and Marshall whisked him away within the week.

From then on Howard was at Marshall's beck and call, in and out of the small office in Government House, and the larger premises in town. When he entered the colonial depths of Government House he felt both awed by his own audaciousness and anger at the inflexible pomposity of the place, impatient for the changes Marshall promised would come. He grew used to the sight of the colonial immortals: the Governor, the Chief Secretary and all the others at Government House that Marshall required him to meet. Marshall was tireless and full of verve but, from the day he was elected Chief Minister, trouble loomed and dangerous strikes appeared imminent.

Across the canal, Belvedere's garden was entered through a gate in the fence. From here the land sloped upwards past the tennis court and the mangosteen orchard with its ancient, half-dead trees. The land was overgrown and Mei Lan walked carefully, always looking for snakes in the long grass. She had thought hard about what she was doing, and had decided it was the only way. The French doors were open to the dining room, and she could see Rose at rest on the old sofa; she had lost weight and did not look well. Mei Lan was full of apprehension as she approached Belvedere, realising how much she now depended on Rose's agreement to her plan.

Rose looked up as she came through the door, and immediately brightened. She had grown fond of Mei Lan and now secretly hoped she would one day be her daughter-in-law, even though Howard made her understand that this might never be. From Belvedere's great kitchen came the smell of frying onions and the preparation of lunch. Each day now meals were wheeled on a large metal trolley down the bumpy slope of Belvedere's garden and across the bridge to Bougainvillaea House. Already, Rose felt guilty that her need to sell Belvedere would complicate life for Mei Lan and her expanding shelter.

'I'm going to have to sell. I have no other means of stopping the place from falling down around us,' Rose tried to explain, smoothing down the antimacassar on the arm of the sofa, not wanting to meet Mei Lan's eyes.

Mei Lan looked out of the window at the decaying mangosteen trees and wondered why Rose had not cleared them away. A musty smell of grime and old cooking impregnated the crumbling house. From above came the cooing of a pigeon, and a single wisp of straw floated down from a nest perched on a beam under the ceiling.

'Where will you go?' Mei Lan asked, and listened as Rose explained about the Queen Street house inherited from Aunty May and how it would be so much more comfortable.

'Why don't you stay on here, just as you are, and let me buy Belvedere from you? You know how badly I need the rooms,' Mei Lan burst out, unable to contain herself any longer. She saw Rose's eyes widen in shock and broke off in sudden apology, sure she had blundered.

At the back of her mind, although she did not want to admit it, Mei Lan knew she needed to keep Howard across the canal. The news of Belvedere's imminent sale had forced her to acknowledge that the thought of him moving away was untenable. It was difficult to imagine him not sitting down at dinner with her each night, squashed around the crowded dining table of Bougainvillaea House, along with abandoned mothers jiggling crying babies on their knees. This arrangement was not what Howard wanted, she knew, but each time she considered anything more, something closed within her.

'You're used to running Belvedere as a boarding house and already we're using your kitchen, your linen, your pots and pans. You have even accommodated some of the women and Cynthia runs the clinic; nothing needs to change. It will be like before when you had lodgers, but you will not have to spend a single cent.' Excitement rushed through her and for the first time Mei Lan felt she was looking squarely at the future, and not turning away from all it might hold. Recently, at last, she'd had the feeling she was beginning to heal.

The day before, for the first time, she had forced herself to walk past the YMCA. Against all probability the building still stood, renovated and restored to its old function as a student hostel. After the war the specially built prison cells were bricked up, the termite-infested woodwork ripped out and burned, but the place had not been pulled down as expected. There was talk of demolishing the building and leaving the open ground as a memorial to the suffering of so many. For a while the place lay as a dilapidated ruin in an overgrown wilderness of trees, but within a year it had been spruced up and opened its doors as a hostel again. For ten years now the building had lived a regenerated life: laughter was heard in its corridors, mah-jong was played in its games room, the original billiard table and record player had been located and reinstalled. It seemed almost obscene. Yet, the tortured building had somehow managed to shrug the past away.

'I will restore Belvedere and you can help me by supervising the running of things here again. I have set up a foundation, the Bougainvillaea Trust. I was able to do it with the money I got from the sale of Grandfather's jade; Howard has helped me set it up. I have enough money to buy Belvedere and to run both homes as a shelter.' Mei Lan grew animated as she explained, then broke off again before Rose's silence. For a moment they observed each other apprehensively. Rose pressed a hand to her chest as if to control another flutter of palpitations.

'It's the answer to a prayer,' she whispered at last, tears of relief filling her eyes.

David Marshall's problems with the Governor continued. Discussions concerning the formation of a government were fraught and complicated. As the Governor was delighted to remind him, Marshall did not have an overall majority in the Assembly. Besides the elected members and the handful of colonial officials who still sat in the Assembly, Marshall had to rely upon the Governor's extra British nominees to shore up support for the Labour Front. Beside this, the new Assembly had to deal with the pugnacity of the newly elected People's Action Party members, Lee Kuan Yew and union chief, Lim Chin Siong. Although Lim might struggle with his English, Lee was a man of fluent and razor-sharp words. In his maiden speech he lost no time in pouring scorn on the archaic proceedings of the Assembly and the 'phoney constitution' it stood for.

Yet, adhering to his election promises, Marshall was already chipping determinedly away at the colonial administration's Emergency Regulations that, even after so long, remained in place. But just as he had the first tentative agreement to some minor dismantling of these regulations, such as the curfew that inconvenienced so many, a darker cloud was blowing up on the horizon. The management of the Hock Lee Amalgamated Bus Company in Alexander Road were on a collision course with Lim Chin Siong whose powerful Singapore Factory and Shop Workers' Union had attempted to take over the Hock Lee Employers' Union with its two hundred bus drivers and force a strike. At Hock Lee troubles escalated quickly, much to Chief Minister Marshall's distress.

'Two suspected reds in the People's Action Party who are now honourable Assemblymen have the power to stop this if they wish,' Marshall fumed, seeing the storm ahead.

Since the early morning, pickets had manned the gates of the Hock Lee Bus depot shouting defiance with clenched fists. Hundreds of agitated Middle School students lined Alexander Road in support of the striking bus drivers at the depot. Eventually, police with water jets cleared a way past the pickets and militant schoolchildren and some buses, whose drivers were loyal to the company and wanted to work, left the depot. As they turned out into Alexander Road, they were pelted with stones by jeering students. The battle had raged all day between police, strikers and schoolchildren, and although it was evening it still showed no sign of abating.

Marshall's office had been in an uproar all day with the Chief of Police on the phone to the Chief Minister, the Governor on the phone to the Chief Minister, members of the Legislative Assembly making enquiries of the Chief Minister. Howard was on the phone to the Police Commissioner's secretary when Mei Lan telephoned him at his desk, a thing she had never done before.

'It's Greta. I told you she refuses to come home and has been living with a school friend. Now, we've heard she's at Alexander Road and there's rioting there. I have to find her.' He could hear the desperation in her voice, and the sound of Little Sparrow sobbing beside her.

'Cynthia was here just now, and she says your mother has not come home either. She went to visit your Cousin Lionel who has moved to a new house somewhere near Alexander Road. Can you come with me? I'm going there.' Mei Lan 's voice sounded far away.

'You cannot go alone,' Howard replied in alarm, already putting the top on his fountain pen and moving papers to one side on his desk. She had never asked anything of him before.

38

THE AFTERNOON SUN TURNED the reservoir to burnished bronze. A small boat had pushed out from a jetty and a child with a dog ran along the water's edge. The dog's sharp bark was drowned in the rumble of engines as the trucks started up one after another. Moon, whose plump face generated this nickname, pulled Greta down beside him, but she landed instead on Snakehead's lap and laughed. The lorry moved off with a sudden jerk, and Greta was finally thrown upon Moon. She lay against him inhaling his masculine smell, all the deeper for the hour of dancing with which the picnic had ended. Games had been played and rousing songs sung, leaving them buoyed up with emotion. She could hear his heart beating against her ear, and knew by the tenseness of his muscles the effect she had upon him. The other girls in the crowded lorry had linked arms and were singing again, unwilling to surrender the afternoon. Boys and girls sat easily together, and although they were aware that Love was the Enemy of the People and romantic involvement was frowned on, it was impossible for eyes not to meet or hands not to touch.

Moon was on the committee of the Middle School Students' Union, and had helped to arrange the picnic. Snakehead was older than the others, already at the university, but he always returned to school to accompany them on excursions. Both Greta and Moon took their orders from him for he was cell leader, and had recruited them. The week before she had been assigned her first courier job, delivering a communication to the manageress of a hairdressers'. This directive had been concealed in the tissue wrappings of a box of perfumed soap and she had given it to the woman as she sat under a hairdryer. Another directive had been packed in a roll of fruit drops and this she had delivered to a man waiting at a bus stop with a small child. Party communications were often written in an invisible ink made of sago powder that was later developed with a solution of iodine.

The sun was still hot, and the wooden planks on which they sat had absorbed the heat of the truck engine. Greta shifted and Moon pulled himself up, daring to put his arms loosely about her. She did not move as he bent forward to rest his chin on her shoulder. The ragged heads of coconut palms swept by, a flock of green parrots rose from the trees in an emerald cloud as the truck sped along. She noticed that Snakehead was watching them. He was nicknamed Snakehead because of his bullet-shaped skull and glittery eyes. Even when he smiled his eyes were assessing; without Moon she was frightened of him. Later, Greta was sure he would lecture them on dissolute behaviour, but for the moment she did not care. Shutting her eyes she relaxed against Moon, feeling the growing intensity between them.

The truck had stopped and she opened her eyes to see Snakehead standing up, towering above them. In the distance there was a confusion of noise; a crowd of angry men could be seen, shouting and gesticulating. She sat up in surprise: she had thought they were returning to school. Snakehead began to shout instructions.

'We are needed here at Alexander Road. You know all about the bus strike and the troubles here; I don't have to explain. Students have been here in shifts since last night, fighting with the police. Now the strikers need your encouragement. Raise their spirits with your dancing and singing.' As Snakehead spoke there were cheers. The back flap of the truck was let down and they jumped out, a short distance from the bus depot. Greta looked nervously over the side of the truck at the crowd of angry men at the top of the road. There had been trouble at the Hock Lee bus depot since early in the year, and it was now mid-May. She had already been to several strikes in support of the workers and participated enthusiastically, but now she was apprehensive. Other trucks were drawing up to deposit further loads of students. Greta stood up but hesitated to jump down. Further along the road, strikers could be seen before the depot; a man was standing on a table shouting propaganda before the closed grilles of the bus sheds. Inside the sheds, Greta could see several stationary Number Eight buses. Then Moon was helping her down, almost lifting her so that he had a chance to draw her body close to him; his warm breath filled her ear. Once he had touched her breasts lightly, as if brushing against her; once he had reached out boldly to cup them in his hands and she had stood before him, unmoving. Then he had leaned forward and taken her lower lip between his own, pushing the tip of his tongue into her mouth. Snakehead knew nothing of this. She caught a further look of disapproval from Snakehead before he turned away, lifting up a megaphone, shouting instructions to the students.

'You know the drill. If you are caught in the middle of anything, whether it's police batons or tear gas, cover your eyes and your ears, put your head in your hands. Do not split up. If you're forced to spread out, regroup quickly – the pickets will do their best to hold you together.'

In an area beside the bus depot, wives of the striking men had set out food and were serving tea and noodle soup with the help of a continuous shift of Middle School students. The girls from the trucks trooped into the refreshment area, while the boys turned as one into the street, already shouting excitedly, waving clenched fists in the air. Snakehead continued yelling into the megaphone, his voice blaring out in a hollow way. *Keep left. Move into the centre. Back up behind the group ahead.* Greta tried to keep track of Moon but he had vanished into the mass of workers and hooligans, all intent on mayhem. Once, she had a brief glimpse of him, his face transfigured by a strange exultant expression before she lost sight of him again.

Men were picketing around the clock. Momentum had built up, from the first band of strikers squatting outside the bus depot's gates defying the gangsters hired to move them, to the thousands who were now inflamed. Agitators yelled through loudspeakers day after day while mobs of fist-shaking workers were supported by fist-shaking students. The mood had grown progressively ugly.

In the open space before the food tables, the Middle School girls took up positions for dancing. The striking busmen, sucking at bowls of noodles or drinking tea, looked up expectantly. A few Middle School boys, not physically up to the rough atmosphere on the street, had remained with the contingent of girls and they now whipped out harmonicas. As the first tinny wheeze of notes was heard the dancers began, tripping one behind the other, waving thin red handkerchiefs in the rhythm of the *yangko*, the dance of the new People's Republic of China. As they danced they sang to the resting strikers, some of whom knew their catchy songs and attempted to join in.

'The years of the Japanese took its toll! But now we suffer more! After the Japanese dogs have gone, the Imperialist monkeys returned.'

As each verse of the song ended, the audience cheered and clapped. The harmonicas rose and fell along the peaks and valleys of gusty melody. Greta held on to the waist of the girl in front, angled her head and kicked out her heels as they twirled about, waving their red scarves.

At the end of the dance they were panting and laughing, sweat streaming off their faces. Finishing their tea and noodles, the strikers returned to the more pressing business of the road. The afternoon was fading fast, darkness already casting its net over the sky. Now that the music had stopped, the sound of the strike grew louder. Shouts and yelled orders from megaphones and the rush of police water hoses upon the rioters were more clearly heard. Greta could think only of Moon, and the exultant look she had seen on his face as he turned away from her.

It was nearly dark and the lights of the bus depot were on, shining into the road. Greta left the other students who were busy taking refreshments themselves and, keeping close to the wall, made her way towards the depot. Climbing on to a low plinth and clinging to a drain-pipe for support, she had a better view of the road beyond. In the dying light the mass of agitating men packed into the narrow street appeared like an army of ants swarming about an anthill. A crescendo of renewed shouting was heard and then the abrasive odour of tear gas drifted to her, her eyes began to water. Unable to hold on to the drainpipe, coughing and gasping with the fumes of gas, she half fell, half jumped back into the road. Behind her at the refreshment stalls, she heard the harmonicas begin again in a rush of hoarse notes as the dancing re-started. In the distance there was the baying of men's voices, the wail of police cars and the thud of hurled rocks and stones.

The odour of gas still stung in her nose and in the growing darkness she could see nothing of Moon or Snakehead or any of the boys from the picnic. The lights shone out, revealing passing groups of rioters, their faces distorted by anger and the same transcendent expression she had seen on Moon's face, as if he were freed into an unknown part of himself. Besides the strikers and the students, there were Secret Society gangsters elbowing in on the action, gangs of rough men carrying shovels and hoes and iron piping. There was a sudden great flare in the darkness as a car was set on fire, and she caught a glimpse of water jets arching over the flames and the crowd. Riot police, lined up in battalions, basket shields before them, were pushing forward into the jeering throng; a group of Gurkhas rushed past her with guns. Soon, above the noise, she heard the crack of shots ring out.

It seemed she waited for ever before, at last, she saw him. He came towards her borne aloft on the shoulders of others, slipping and sliding on a bed of hands. At first she thought there was some cause for jubilation, that he was carried victoriously, just as she had seen pictures of politicians riding aloft upon the shoulders of supporters, their faces split by a smile. But Moon was stretched out unmoving as if asleep on the bed of hands and she caught her breath, knowing suddenly that something was wrong. A long procession of excited strikers followed Moon. She grew desperate then and ran out into the crowd, trying to force her way through to him. The men jogged on ignoring her, chanting hackneyed slogans, moving like a many-legged centipede carrying Moon on its back, triumphantly parading him through the streets, as if he was a hero. Greta began to cry, fighting her way into the mass of men, reaching up to grip Moon's hand as it hung limply down over the shoulders of his pall-bearers, screaming his name. He turned his head weakly and she sobbed with relief that he was not dead. Then, as he passed under a street light, she saw blood leaking from his chest.

Clinging to Moon's dangling arm, she was pulled along beside him. She saw then that, from everywhere, men stepped forward as Moon passed to join the cortège, all chanting the same refrain. *Victory. Victory. Death to Imperialists.* The words drummed in her ears, and still she held on, feeling the pull of his fingers intertwined with her own as he was jolted forward. At last, even that slight pressure was gone. His hand became limp and his fingers slipped from her, and she was forced to step back. The procession continued up the road until Moon was lost from sight, his dying already of greater use to the mob than his life.

Rose Burns had chosen the day of the Hock Lee bus riots to visit Cousin Lionel's new home off Alexander Road. He had had to move from the sandy estate by the sea as a wealthy man had purchased it, and was building new houses upon it. The strike had been in place for weeks, causing buses to be infrequent and frazzling nerves; people returned home late for dinner and were late the next morning for work. The strikers themselves elicited little sympathy from the public. Taxis were hard pressed to cope with the need for transport and old trishaws, discarded and rusting for years in garages, were resurrected again for service.

It was in one of these battered trishaws that Rose was attempting to locate Cousin Lionel's new home. She had been unable to find a proper taxi; time had been getting on and the decrepit trishaw had come pedalling past Belvedere, moving at no more than five miles an hour. Stuffing protruded from a rip in the passenger seat and the driver gave off a strong acrid odour that only faded as they drove along and a breeze blew across the vehicle.

The man was an Indian in a blue checked shirt over a worn striped *dhoti*. He bent forward, pedalling hard and breathing hard, staring fixedly ahead. He had advised Rose to take a wide detour around the Hock Lee bus depot, but as they progressed she began to fear he was taking an unnecessarily roundabout route and would charge an exorbitant fare. She was already an hour late, and there was still some distance to go.

'That road looks quiet enough. It will lead us in the right direction, clear of the bus depot and save us precious time.' She pointed out a road she was sure would take them directly to Lionel's new address.

The man seemed about to argue, but then nodded and turned the trishaw as Rose directed. A few tumbledown houses stood on small allotments growing *bok choi*, Chinese cabbage and aubergine. There was a strong smell of human manure. A mangy bitch with a brood of puppies lay in the middle of the road, and rose lazily as the trishaw driver tooted his ancient horn. The sun shone its last mellow rays and darkness was hovering at the edge of the sky; the sound of the rioters' shouting was far away. A fish farm bordered the road, and Rose saw a carp jump clear of the water, a mercurial flash in the setting sun. Then, unexpectedly, a small car appeared around a bend, with a band of angry men running behind it. The car was forced to slow down to avoid colliding with the trishaw and the men, who were stragglers cut off from the main crowd of rioters at Hock Lee, surged forward with a shout. Rose's heart flew into her throat and thudded in her ears.

'Turn back!' she shouted to the trishaw driver.

The whites of the driver's eyes grew so round they reminded her of boiled eggs, his breath came quickly, and he released a loud sulphurous trumpet of air from beneath his soiled *dhoti*. He began pedalling backwards as fast as he could, pulling into the side of the road to allow the car to pass. The vehicle sped by at breakneck speed. In alarm, the trishaw driver pedalled further on to the verge, wedging his contraption precariously over a ditch of filthy water. The car swerved dangerously and with a screech of brakes veered off the bumpy road into a bank of weeds and came to a sudden stop.

The strikers, rough men who looked more like hooligans than bus drivers, although what the difference might be Rose was not sure, ran past the trishaw in pursuit of the car. Swinging sharp-edged hoes and spades, they filled the road. The trishaw rider gave a terrified scream and jumped off his vehicle, his *dhoti* pulled loose from his waist to reveal a pair of green boxer shorts. Clutching the yards of unravelling cloth, he vaulted over a fence bordering the fish farm, and ran off beside a pond.

The stalled car had now been overpowered and two struggling men were pulled out. One managed to escape his attackers, jumped into the ditch and sprinted towards the trishaw. The other went down, lost beneath the mob. Rose saw the picks and hoes rise and fall upon the victim, who was mercifully hidden from her sight. She sat frozen with fear in the trishaw, clutching her handbag to her breast. The man in the ditch laboured towards her, a well-dressed Chinese in his early forties, wearing an open-necked shirt and a trilby hat in a pale shade of grey. A brown snakeskin belt encircled his waist, a gold watch moved loosely on his wrist. Rose glimpsed his desperate eyes and crooked teeth. He came level with the trishaw and it rocked dangerously as, reaching up, he tried to grip the handlebar and pull himself out of the ditch. She had time only to notice the mud on his trousers and the fearful roll of his eyes beneath the brim of his hat before the strikers were upon him. A crowd of angry men now splashed about in the muddy dyke below her, their yells beating the air like a gong.

Stop, she wanted to scream. *Stop!* Instead, as she watched, the man was pushed into the filthy water and the hat was knocked off his head. The picks and hoes with which the men were armed flailed savagely about. Rose looked down helplessly from her precarious perch at the violence being done below her. One of the hoes came down on the man's head and slipped to slice off his face. Rose stared in horror as his wild eyes pleaded with her for help. Then a hatchet was lifted to finish the job, and the victim fell to his knees. The strikers drew back and suddenly quietened, seeing their work was done. In the lull a small splash was heard as a fish jumped again in the pond. A dog barked and a *koel* called with sudden urgency, over and over again.

Mumbling sociably now amongst themselves, the strikers climbed out of the ditch. One peered into the trishaw at Rose, and nodded apologetically. Then they were gone; the distant rioting at the Hock Lee depot claiming them once again.

Rose began to shiver, her teeth chattering unstoppably. She stared at the dead man lying face down in the water that was now red with his blood. Trapped in the weeds beside him was the dove grey trilby hat. Rose remembered the long-ago riot at Kreta Ayer. She remembered the Chief Inspector's bloodied sun helmet, rolling in the road. She gave a loud sob as the crushing pain of angina swept through her, and bent forward on the seat. The trishaw, unsettled by the movement, tipped slowly forward, rolling over the edge of the bank into the ditch and throwing Rose into the mud beside the dead Chinese.

Howard left the car some distance away and walked towards the sound of shouting. The odour of tear gas floated to him and his eyes begun to sting. He had told Mei Lan to stay in the car, but found she was beside him, as she gripped his arm.

'This is no place for a woman,' he told her savagely, wishing he had never agreed to her accompanying him.

'It's just as dangerous to leave me alone there,' she answered, cupping her hand over her mouth against the fumes of gas as he steered her along beside him.

The dark road was potholed and uneven, street lamps were infrequent. A stray dog slunk past as they emerged from the alley and saw the crowd. Flames spurted up ahead of them, illuminating the confusion.

'A car has been set on fire,' Howard said, gripping Mei Lan as they approached the scene. The vehicle lay on its side, wheels in the air, acrid black smoke belching from it. A driver struggled out and was set upon by the rioters. In the light of the fire students were seen running wildly about, identifiable by their white uniforms, throwing stones or bottles at the police. The road was wet, full of muddy puddles; hoses trained on the flaming car could not control the conflagration. Choking fumes blew everywhere, and the road was strewn with glass.

Following the directions of a policeman, they eventually found the bus depot where they were told some girl students had earlier been seen. It was quieter here; ambulances were parked in this area and wounded police were being attended to.

'There are no girls here now, they've all gone home,' an ambulance man told them as he bandaged the arm of an exhausted policeman.

They made their way back in the direction of their car keeping to the shadows, skirting the fiery mayhem. Mei Lan clung silently to Howard's hand, her fingers stiff with fear. They drove for what seemed hours searching for Lionel's new address, but at last they found it.

'We waited for Rose but she did not come,' Lionel said, annoyed at having been woken from sleep just after he had gone to bed. Beside him, Ava anxiously clutched a faded housecoat about her breast.

On the way back they stopped at a police station. There a Malay officer, half asleep, was disinclined to take down details.

'Everyone here has been drafted to Alexander Road. Even though it is midnight, the rioters are still going strong. Maybe your mother and the young girl are already at home.'

When at last Howard stopped the car before Bougainvillaea House, Mei Lan was half asleep on the seat beside him, her head thrown back, her eyes shut, her hands linked together in her lap. He stared at her for some time, wondering at her struggle in the black ocean of sleep. He wondered about the world she found there, the secret rooms she entered filled with hungry ghosts. She had told him little of her experiences, and he asked no questions even after all this time. He woke her gently and watched her surface to see his face above her, before he took her in his arms. For some time she lay quietly against him and he brushed the taut skin of her cheek with his lips and cursed the violence that seemed to circumscribe their lives without end. He remembered the crumbling shack near Lionel's house, the heavy voluptuousness of it all, and in the distance the sound of the waves folding and unfolding. It seemed to him now that the expectation of love might hold only sorrow for them both.

Only afterwards, as he parked the car and entered Belvedere's garden, did he realise with a pang of horror that in those few moments he had forgotten about his mother. The lights were on in Belvedere and he found Rose in bed, her hair damp, her face flushed and pinched, with Cynthia hovering beside her.

'She may have had a mild heart attack. She saw a man killed right in front of her. The police brought her home. The doctor has been to see her.'

'Will she be all right?' Howard asked, stricken with guilt.

'She needs to sleep now. It has been a terrible shock,' Cynthia replied as calmly as she could, although he saw the anxiety in her face.

Alerted by the fleeing trishaw driver, the owners of the fish farm had found Rose in the ditch pinned beneath the fallen vehicle, with a dead man beside her. She had been carried to the farmer's shack and eventually the police had come and driven her home.

39

WORK WITH MARSHALL WAS never dull. From the first day in office the problems of government were overwhelming for a man without political experience, but Marshall was full of determined resolution. Almost at once, Howard was involved in conducting a survey on education in preparation for a White Paper. As Chief Minister, Marshall was immediately forced to examine the situation in the Chinese-medium schools and to produce a new education policy; rioting schoolchildren in gymslips and shorts was an indigestible phenomenon.

'Chinese education is of the utmost importance. Any government in the future aspiring to rule this country must integrate the Chinese-medium education system into mainstream English vernacular education. We are a multiracial society, and cannot think of Independence without also thinking of building a multicultural, multiracial nation. This can only be done through a common education system,' Marshall prophesied, wiping his brow as, hard and fast, the problems of government showered upon him. His sincerity fell on deaf ears, and the continuing strikes and riots wrought havoc upon his best efforts.

'We must find the middle road between communism and colonialism,' Marshall insisted, but however heartfelt his honesty, he was unable to read the mood of the predominantly Chinese community upon whom the future rode.

The riots at the Hock Lee bus depot ended in a triumph for the Singapore Bus Workers' Union and Lim Chin Siong's Singapore Factory and Shop Workers' Union who had backed the strike, but it had repercussions for the students. Arrests were made and schools were threatened with closure unless the ringleaders were expelled and discipline restored. In their usual manner of protest, two thousand students then barricaded themselves yet again into Chung Cheng High School demanding the release of those arrested, and the Singapore Factory and Shop Workers' Union prepared to call a general strike in support of the students. Soon, Marshall backed down, schools reopened and the students paraded about in victory.

All these events, falling one upon another in quick succession, were a constant anxiety to the parents of politically active students. Little Sparrow wished she had not opposed Greta so vehemently in the first school protests, for she might now know where she was. Day after day she sat slackly in a chair, and even the clack of mah-jong tiles could not distract her for long as she waited for Greta to return. Weeks had now gone by, and Little Sparrow could neither eat nor sleep.

'You know so many union people. Can't you ask if anyone knows anything?' Mei Lan begged Howard. Greta had been missing so long she had begun to share Little Sparrow's fear that the girl might be dead; she had disappeared the night of the Hock Lee bus riot and had not made contact with them since.

'I am her mother. If she is alive she would contact me.' Little Sparrow sat forward in her chair as Mei Lan spoke to Howard, and the words became a sob.

'She might have gone underground with someone; nowadays communists live underground,' Howard suggested, noting the purple shadows beneath Little Sparrow's eyes, as she looked up at him in new desperation. The very word 'underground' caused Little Sparrow to panic; she imagined her child wedged into a deep, dark burrow.

Howard pitched forward, stumbling on the rutted surface of Middle Road. He steadied himself and walked on, looking up at the mass of signboards plastering the filthy peeling arches of the five-foot way. A beggar and two half-naked children poked about for food in a pile of rubbish, yellow-legged Myna birds rummaging beside them.

With the Japanese gone, Middle Road was now the enclave of trade unions, the subversive heartland of the town. A few brothels, photographers and ten-cent stores now under Chinese ownership remained, but the many small restaurants and food stalls serviced the union offices of Middle Road. At last Howard saw a sign for the Singapore Factory and Shop Workers' Union, and climbed the stairs to the second floor of the narrow building. In a room with dirty plaster walls and warped floorboards he found uniformed schoolboys, some sitting around a table, heads bent industriously to paperwork, others clearing cobwebs from the ceiling with long-handled brooms. A stack of blankets in a corner gave Howard the impression that some of these young men might be living there. At the back of the room, behind a desk, sat Wee Jack. Howard's heart lurched uncomfortably at the sight of him.

Wee Jack crossed the room to greet Howard and called for one of the schoolboys to bring them drinks from a crate of bottles by the window. Although there were several older men in the room, Howard was surprised to see so many schoolchildren, and thought of the reason he had come to Middle Road with renewed concern.

'They come after school of their own accord to help.' Wee Jack followed Howard's gaze and seemed to read his thoughts.

'You catch them young,' Howard replied.

Wee Jack gave a derisive smile. Years of deprivation had emaciated him and his cough now sounded even more tubercular. His sunken eyes stared fixedly at Howard from beneath a receded hairline. Wee Jack was now a paid official of the Singapore Bus Workers' Union and was prominently linked to Lim Chin Siong and other radicals amongst the agitators. His name was often mentioned in the newspapers in connection with unsavoury goings-on. Howard was thirsty, and quickly finished the orangeade. Even as he sat before Wee Jack he struggled to feel free of him, returning the man's assessing gaze as determinedly as he could. Finally, Wee Jack shrugged in apparent defeat, and reluctantly divulged the information for which Howard had journeyed to Middle Road.

'I could find out very little about the girl,' Wee Jack told him casually, sipping at the fiercely coloured orange juice, his Adam's apple bobbing up and down.

'All I know is that she may be with a man they call Snakehead. It is difficult to keep track of young people once they have gone underground.' Wee Jack pulled a packet of cigarettes from his pocket, clicking his fingers to one of the schoolboys, who ran forward with a match.

'Her mother is worried,' Howard said, irritated by Wee Jack's superior manner.

'Nowadays, many mothers are worried about their children,' Wee Jack replied, looking coldly at Howard.

Underground for Greta was not a dark burrow but a vermicelli factory on Coronation Road. Snakehead moved frequently to avoid detection and arrest. Before the vermicelli factory they had hidden in a rattan shop on the outskirts of the shanty town, Holland Village, in a crumbling *kampong* hut, and later in the servants' quarters of a large colonial style bungalow. The Hock Lee bus riot had thrown Greta abruptly from a world of teenage rebellion into a world of professional revolutionaries. If Snakehead had not taken her hand and pulled her after him in the chaos that followed Moon's shooting, she would have been arrested. For the first time she began to understand the single-mindedness of the committed.

Wherever they went, Snakehead's typewriter soon appeared, smuggled to him in the dead of night so that, in each safe house, he could continue to manufacture inflammatory articles for *Freedom News*. In each place different comrades joined them, sometimes a 'mother', sometimes a 'brother' or a 'sister', so that to the outside world they appeared always an innocuous 'family'. In return for safety in the community, the comrades gave classes in Chinese culture. They visited the sick, distributed food and medicine and mediated in domestic disputes, and spread communist propaganda wherever they went. Comrades also helped Snakehead relay his articles back to *Freedom News*'s secret underground printing press. Greta was unused to the filth that was common to all the wretched hiding places they were forced to use. She thought of her room in the East Coast house with nostalgia. The pungent stench of toilet shacks, the eating bowls encrusted with the remnants of previous meals, and the filthy sleeping mats filled with armies of bedbugs, distressed her. Snakehead, who had grown up in a hovel with twelve siblings and only one meal every other day, was used to such things and chastised her.

'This is the truth behind the revolution, this is what it is about, not picnics and shouting and *yenko* dancing,' he told her scornfully.

However often they moved about the insalubrious hiding places, her role was always the same: she was Snakehead's wife, washing and cleaning and cooking for him. If she had to be anyone's wife she would have preferred to be Moon's wife, but he was dead. Greta had lost count of the number of days she had been on the run with Snakehead. Although he was her 'husband' by Party orders, he did not lay a hand upon her. Instead, he stared at her with as much dislike as she had come to feel for him. Neither of them had been free to go to Moon's funeral: as a martyr of the riot, he had been carried to his grave on a decorated truck with hundreds of students and trade unionists streaming behind. In all the safe houses Snakehead had regular visitors, undercover contacts from the Middle School Action Committee who passed Party information between a network of hideouts and message drops. These contacts were usually dressed as fruit or vegetable sellers.

Greta had arrived at the vermicelli factory the night before with Snakehead, trudging the country road in the dark to avoid detection. The danger of arrest was ever present, and Snakehead was vigilant in watching for the spies with which he said the countryside was riddled. The vermicelli factory had been reached after midnight, and in the darkness all Greta could make out were a few crumbling attap-roofed shacks. On their arrival, a mangy dog sleeping in the yard set up a fierce wall of barking. Inside, she was shown a heap of foul rags to sleep upon, and was too tired to complain.

As light cracked open the sky Snakehead prodded her awake. As 'daughter-in-law' of the vermicelli factory she must prepare breakfast for the family. Her 'mother-in-law' looked her up and down and laughed. Children seemed to be everywhere; the woman bellowed constantly at them. The two oldest girls, no more than eight or nine, had younger children strapped to their backs with winding cloths, and continued to skip about their games despite their cumbersome burdens. After a meal, Snakehead went out and Greta was glad to be free of him. The woman set her to wash clothes in a yard surrounded by straggly trees and a thick fence of dwarf banana. Snakehead assured her that if she did not obey instructions it was no great matter to dispose of her, and she believed him.

She squatted down by the pump with a tin tub and a bar of hard soap. The wooden clogs she had been given were uncomfortable, the clothes in the tub were of hard thick fabric and the soap did not lather easily. Chickens pecked about her, the sun burned down on her back. She remembered her mother screaming that the sun would darken her skin and make her so ugly no one would marry her. At the thought of her mother she wanted to cry; it was possible she might never see her again. Behind the vermicelli shed was a pigsty from which came much grunting and squealing; beside it was a large covered pit of animal and human deposits. The smell from this slurry was overpowering, making her retch as she set about washing the clothes.

Under a lean-to beside the pump, large wooden vats of water mirrored her face; beneath the surface long skeins of vermicelli floated limply, like dead worms. In the shed men were already at work, kneading glutinous dough for the noodles. As she squatted down before the washtub, she watched her 'father-in-law' swing the dough with expert abandon. Long strands were formed, which grew thinner and thinner the more he twirled them about. Immersed in scrubbing clothes, trying to work up lather from the rock-like soap, she did not hear Snakehead calling as he came in at the gate. He walked straight up to Greta with a determined expression; in his arms he carried a baby.

'This is your child,' Snakehead said, thrusting the child at her. The infant, who was about six months old, drew back to look at her with startled eyes before beginning to scream. The weight of its small body of tightly packed bones rested in the crook of her arm.

'It is better that we have children,' Snakehead announced. Greta wanted to speak, but no words came. The baby flailed about and she jiggled it up and down as she had seen mothers do to quieten an infant.

'It's a girl,' Snakehead clarified. The child was indeterminately dressed in a loose top and trousers and its hair had been shaved close to its head in an effort to rid it of lice.

'I don't know what to do with a baby,' she answered with new desperation. The child squirmed in her arms. If she dropped it, she thought, its head would break open like a cracked egg and all its brains would pour out.

'You will learn, like all new mothers. It cost $200 of Party funds,' he replied as he turned away. The baby continued to scream, filling her ears until she felt they would burst. Behind her the piglets in the sty set up a new round of squealing.

The child was soon sodden and stinking. Greta sat in a corner of the hut with her head on her drawn-up knees and the child on a mat beside her, still screaming. She had no idea what to do with it, but marvelled that so much energy could be released from so small a bundle.

'Probably it is hungry,' the wife of the vermicelli manufacturer said, arms on her hips, sighing in exasperation. 'Probably it is not yet weaned and is expecting a breast to feed from,' she observed with a further sigh.

'What am I to do about that?' Greta shouted angrily, her eyes filling with tears.

'We will give it some diluted condensed milk and hope it will take it. You should always buy a baby weaned. It also needs a new cloth about its bottom. You will have to wash the cloths every day,' the woman replied. She was a gaunt and poker-faced woman, but had softened a little before the baby.

From the next day the baby was tied to Greta's back with long knitted strings. Its weight was forever upon her as she washed the clothes and cut up the vegetables, and picked insects from raw rice. The child snuffled in her ear all day, its tears wetting the back of her neck. Worst of all were the stinking cloths about its small hips filled with warm, squashed excrement that she must change and wash. Condensed milk, either diluted or undiluted, was not to the baby's taste and it protested ceaselessly. After three days it began to look sickly. It cried less, and its face acquired a translucent sheen.

'If it's put back on the breast it will be all right,' Greta's 'mother-in-law' decided and approached Snakehead determinedly.

'It's starving to death. You will have to give it back. Buy another, one year older and weaned,' she told him.

'I have paid $200 for it, and I will have to pay the mother all over again to give it back,' he grumbled.

'It is Party funds and the Party has plenty. Look at how many they have bought for me,' the woman argued, gesturing to the children playing about her. Snakehead snatched the baby roughly from Greta, and with a fierce expression marched out of the yard towards the road.

He had covered no more than a few yards when he came face to face with a group of men walking towards him down the lane. Snakehead stopped and ran back to Greta, thrusting the screaming child into her arms before disappearing around the side of the house followed by her 'mother-in-law'. Only the children continued to skip about, absorbed in their play, small siblings bumping about on their backs, some sound asleep through it all.

The men hurried into the yard. One approached Greta and took her arm so roughly she almost dropped the screaming baby, whose open mouth now seemed to consume its whole face. She could see its soft, toothless gums and the tunnel of its small red throat. The strange men were running about everywhere, and soon dragged Greta's 'mother-in-law' and 'father-in-law' and all the vermicelli workers into the yard. The children had ceased to play, and stood about nervously waiting to see what would happen. A van appeared and the back doors were opened. They were all encouraged to climb inside, including the waiting children.

'What is happening?' Greta whispered to her 'mother-in-law'. She clung in fear to the baby who, as if understanding the seriousness of the occasion, had stopped screaming and was looking with interest at the faces about her.

'We're being arrested,' Greta's 'mother-in-law' replied, climbing into the van behind her 'husband'. The excited children struggled to climb in after her, agog at their first car ride.

There was no sign of Snakehead. Greta looked desperately about, not knowing what she should do; there seemed no choice but to follow the others into the van. From the pigsty there was a continuous loud squealing; looking over her shoulder Greta noticed the pigs were running about in agitation. The slurry was partially covered, but in the gap beneath its slatted wooden lid and the top of the pit she could just make out Snakehead's anxious face. He stared at her in mute appeal, hidden up to his chin in excrement. It was all she could do not to laugh.

Little Sparrow waited with Mei Lan in the Police Inspector's office. Her hands were shaking and her face hollowed out by worry. Soon the inspector, an Englishman with a hearty voice and a few sparse grey hairs combed over his balding head, accompanied Greta into the room.

'Since she has obviously been badly misled and then threatened with her life, we have found her to be of no great danger to the world. I have decided to release her. However, let this be a warning. Should anything similar happen again we will not overlook it. It is not possible to arrest every Chinese Middle School child in town, but if need be we shall try,' the inspector sighed.

Greta was pale and subdued and looked down at her feet, not raising her eyes to her mother or Mei Lan. Little Sparrow jumped up with a cry as she came into the room, and ran forward to embrace her daughter, who burst into tears and sobbed.

'Take her home. A good meal, a nice bath and early to bed,' the Police Inspector advised.

'What will happen to the baby?' Greta asked, looking up at the inspector as Mei Lan steered her to the door. The child had been taken away from her on arrival at the police station and she had seen nothing of it since. The echo of its pathetic screams now haunted her, as did the knowledge that the many children of the vermicelli maker had all been purchased for convenience by the Party.

'All the children, including the baby, are already in the care of a good Christian orphanage,' the inspector smiled.

Each morning Rose settled for the day on the chintz sofa beside the open windows in the dining room. The shock of the accident during the afternoon of the Hock Lee bus riot had brought on a heart attack. Although it was a mild attack, the doctor said she should be thankful people from the fish farm had found her so quickly. Now, it was rest and more rest and she was too tired to protest; wherever she turned it was to be confronted by the imprisoning bars of disability. The only thing that lightened her mood was the regeneration of life in Belvedere and Cynthia's delay, however temporary it might be, in leaving for England. Wilfred had gone ahead to take up the post of senior editor on the *Observer* newspaper. He had also become something of a celebrity after the sensational publication of his book, *Lost Paradise*. Observing her daughter over a cup of Horlicks, Rose could not deny that Cynthia looked brighter and happier at the prospect of life in England. She spoke with animation of the things that now lay ahead.

'We've found a house to move into near Wilfred's old uncle in Surrey, and I've been promised a job as senior staff nurse at the local hospital; they say I could even be promoted.' Cynthia effervesced with news; it had surprised her to find that in Britain merit and experience was given more acknowledgement than in colonial Singapore.

'Wilfred's novel has been such a success we can almost live on the royalties; he's now writing a book about the psychology of war crimes,' Cynthia informed her mother.

Rose no longer felt anxiety when she observed her daughter, she had a feeling things would now be all right. Maybe at last she could look forward to being a grandmother. About Howard she was not so sure. She worried when, if ever, he and Mei Lan would marry. Even at church, people discreetly enquired about the situation, politely refraining from pointed remarks. Rose found herself uncomfortable with the strangeness of it. Howard and Mei Lan were together all the time, yet things seemed to go neither forwards nor backwards.

Whenever she broached the subject with Howard, he shrugged and said, 'I'm waiting for the right moment.' When that moment would come, Rose had given up asking, although she continued to pray each night for God's positive interference in the matter. Mei Lan herself was in Belvedere most days.

All the necessary papers had been quickly signed, and the sale of Belvedere to Mei Lan had gone through easily. Immediately it was done Rose was filled with relief, realising only then the anxiety the place had become to her. Just as Mei Lan had promised, nothing changed in her life except that she was no longer responsible for Belvedere's upkeep. In every way she lived as before, and Mei Lan was grateful for her help in supervising the place. Many of the women from Bougainvillaea House had already moved in and Ei Ling, who was now capably running everything the other side of the canal, had overseen the opening up and cleaning of Belvedere's mouldering, long-shuttered rooms. As Rose rested on the chintz sofa she was conscious of the hustle and bustle about her all day; voices from the kitchen outhouses, the cry of a child, the running of water, the clank of obstinate pipes, and a constant step on the stairs. To hear the old house shake with life once more brought a lump to her throat. New tables and chairs had been purchased for the dining room, and professional polishing returned the red Malacca tiles to their former mellow glory. The roof was retiled and ceilings replastered. The kitchens gave out the constant smell of cooking, the garden was orderly, the bathrooms refurbished, and Mei Lan had insisted on covering once again Rose's old chintz sofa. Rose had worked around the doctor's orders of enforced rest by making her day bed a centre of operations, drawing a desk up beside it and planning menus and shopping lists and doing Belvedere's accounts, as she had always done. Sometimes, looking up from a ledger, she stared across the dining room to Belvedere's vestibule, and remembered the day long ago when she had first seen Wilfred standing there, wiping his sweating neck with a red spotted handkerchief, suitcases beside him, solar topi in hand, and wondered at the passing of the years.

Mei Lan came in each day to visit Rose and inspect operations in Belvedere, always followed by her ancient nursemaid. The old woman now suffered from dementia and often did not know where she was, clinging like a child to Mei Lan's hand. From the sofa Rose stared out of the window at the decrepit mangosteen trees that Mei Lan had at last persuaded her must be cleared. Nests of cobras had been found under the roots of two of the trees, and Mei Lan had set about Rose immediately.

'You know the trees will have to go; they have been half dead with a blight for years. The cobras will return; they always do.'

Rose reluctantly agreed; the house belonged to Mei Lan now and she knew she clung foolishly to the wasting trees that had become a danger to them all. The gardeners were coming the following week to clear the orchard and she could hardly bear to think about it. It would be the end of something for her when the trees came down.

40

MEI LAN HURRIED AFTER Ah Siew as they walked beside the canal. The old woman's mind wandered easily, rooted in a previous time. Nothing else mattered to her but to find Ah Pat, Ah Ooi, Yong Gui and all the other sisters who had shared her *kongsi fong*. As often now happened, Mei Lan had seen Ah Siew open the door of Bougainvillaea House and let herself out and had followed her, fearful the old woman might tumble into the canal; nowadays someone must watch her all day. Ah Siew stopped and looked about anxiously as Mei Lan caught up with her.

'The sisters were here a moment ago. They're trying to hide from me because I said we must take Ah Pat to the Vegetarian House. She is so far gone the place may already refuse to take her, and send her straight to the Death House. In the Vegetarian House the nuns will look after her and prepare her for death,' Ah Siew worried.

Mei Lan remembered the growth on Ah Pat's neck and her bare feet sticking off the end of the sleeping shelf. She remembered the riot at Kreta Ayer and the bodies of men in the road. She remembered a day of growing up that had never ended. The old woman shuffled along in thick-soled cloth shoes, bent heavily over her stick. It had rained excessively the last few days and the canal had a flow of water. The smell of lichen came to them, and looking into the stream Mei Lan saw a crayfish and thought of Howard.

'What do you want for your birthday?' Mei Lan asked to distract Ah Siew, steering her away from the edge of the canal; the old woman's birthday was not far away. Nobody knew Ah Siew's real age, nobody knew her birthday, but one had long ago been decided for her and Mei Lan remembered it faithfully. Every year Ah Siew gave the same answer to Mei Lan's question, that she desired nothing but a peaceful death, but now a thought came to her.

'Before I die I want to sail the great sea again,' Ah Siew unexpectedly replied, a faraway look in her cloudy eyes as she remembered the long-ago voyage from China when the power of the ocean took her breath away.

Mei Lan turned in surprise. The old woman was panting from the exertion of walking, her mouth open upon toothless gums, the black *samphoo* tunic and trousers voluminous on her scrawny limbs; what remained of her hair was scraped into a tiny knot. She had shrunk to birdlike proportions, her hand a little claw on the knob of the stick, her skin slack and creased and as soft as old chiffon, blotched with the spots of age. Mei Lan was frightened by Ah Siew's talk of death; she had never known a time without the old woman.

'I watched from the rail of the ship each day; they could not drag me away. The sea was so wondrous and without end. I was never seasick.' Ah Siew turned to Mei Lan, her cloudy eyes alive with memory. Ah Siew's wish must be fulfilled for indeed, Mei Lan thought sadly, it might be her last.

'There is a large junk, an ornate Chinese tourist boat, that sails out from the island into the bay,' Howard suggested when Mei Lan told him about Ah Siew's wish.

'The trip only takes a couple of hours. I will come with you,' he decided. Seeing the concern on her face, he wanted to pull her towards him, but did no more than reach for her hand. He no longer expected anything perfect, was too aware of the haphazard process of growth. What he wanted was to regenerate her, to bring back the wild soul she had lost. Use my heart to live, he wished to tell her, until you are whole again. He loved her now without illusion and knew he must trust where love would take him. Mei Lan nodded, glad that he would accompany her and Ah Siew on the birthday outing.

The birthday fell on a Sunday and from early morning Ah Siew was excited. She took out a worn white *samfoo* blouse with elaborate frogging; her old black trousers had been washed and ironed the night before. She wore a jade bangle, Mei Lan's birthday present to her, as protection on the ocean, and a pair of black embroidered shoes that was Howard's gift.

The junk was a massive vermilion affair with gold-painted railings running around its several decks. Small gilded guardian lions, ferociously carved, were perched here and there on balustrades. The highest deck was topped by a small pavilion room of red lacquer pillars crowned with a fluted green-tiled roof. Looking up in awe, through failing eyes, Ah Siew saw this great sea monster only cloudily, but she saw enough.

'It is not a boat, it's a palace. I did not come here on a ship like this.' From the quay Ah Siew gazed at the vessel. For a moment Mei Lan feared the ship might not be to her liking, but a smile broke across the old woman's face.

'I'm going home in style,' Ah Siew croaked, as Howard and Mei Lan helped her up the gangway.

Part of the first deck was glassed in for passengers' comfort with some seating of tables and chairs, and here they settled with Ah Siew. They ordered coffee from an attentive waiter and orangeade for the old woman, while watching people stepping from the gangway on to the deck of the boat. It was a popular trip on a Sunday afternoon and families with excited children predominated. Small boys and girls ran irrepressibly about, chased by anxious parents screaming caution. The deck moved gently below their feet on the swell of the waves.

The pickled odour of the sea mingled with leaking oil from the junk, the aroma of delicacies steaming or frying in the galley below, drifted up to them. The smell of the sea returned Mei Lan to the coconut estate and the wooden shack near Lionel's house, and the palpitating hours so long ago that she had spent there with Howard. She remembered her body dissolved and weak with pleasure, and the roll of the waves on the beach where light and water ran together. She looked at Howard across the table as he inserted a straw for Ah Siew into a bottle of orangeade, bending attentively to the old woman, and knew how much she tried him. Even now she could not overcome the distance that separated them even in love, and that left her always detached. Her faith in the transformative had been lost, and experience had wasted her. She watched Howard helping Ah Siew, his hands as kind and patient in gesture as he was himself, and wished for an end to the isolation that laid her bare so painfully. He believed in her, and hoped this belief would work deep within her. Lifting his eyes, Howard caught her observing him and smiled across the old woman's head, his gaze intent upon her, shutting out all else but what they shared together. She saw the query in his eyes and sadness moved through her as she held out her hand to him; Ah Siew put her lips to the straw and sucked orangeade greedily with a gusty noise. Howard laughed and Mei Lan was glad to join him, to toss aside the darkness that gathered so quickly and easily in her.

The junk was drawing away from the quay and pushing out into open water. 'See, land is already far away,' Mei Lan told Ah Siew as the green coast slid slowly by, but with her poor eyesight and a wall of thick glass before her Ah Siew could see nothing.

'Let's take her out on deck,' Howard suggested and Mei Lan nodded, helping the old woman up.

'There must be a fine view from that top deck,' Howard said as they emerged into the sun, squinting up at the pavilion with its vermilion pillars and green fluted roof.

'Go up and have a look, I will stay here with Ah Siew,' Mei Lan suggested, knowing how much he wanted to do this.

As Howard began to climb the stairs to the upper decks, Mei Lan steered Ah Siew towards the rail, where passengers were wedged shoulder to shoulder, to observe the passing scenery. People were reluctant to make a place for the old woman, but near the bow there was more space. Mei Lan guided Ah Siew along the deck, which was now rolling beneath them, and soon found places for them further down. A cool breeze lifted off the sea, blowing the hair across Mei Lan's eyes.

'There is the island of St John's, and see the waves on those rocks over there. There are many small tugs passing by and the men on them are waving to us.' Mei Lan pointed things out to Ah Siew, knowing these sights were no more than a blur to the old woman's faded eyes.

Ah Siew nodded and smiled her toothless smile, trying to imagine the scene Mei Lan described. She gripped the rail, feeling the smooth wood under her hands, smelling the abrasive sea air. She could hear the water rushing by far below as the ship gathered speed. The wind blew on her face and tunnelled into her ears, just as it had when she stood on that ship long ago. The deck had been crowded with ragged immigrants, without protection from the elements. At that time, looking out at the endless burnished sea and looking down at the churning foam in the wake of the ship, Ah Siew could forget the miserable conditions in which she travelled. She had spent many hours marvelling at the great space of the world and the immeasurable distances that could be journeyed. As they drifted towards the horizon she had wondered what lay waiting beyond it for her. Now her story was told, and nothing more waited ahead but that final great journey that was hidden from them all. When Ah Siew looked back over her life, she saw many things to be thankful for; nothing really bad had happened and there had always been her 'sisters' and Mei Lan; there was nothing she found to regret. This, in her judgement, was a great thing to say at the end of a life. There was no one she knew in the House of Lim who could say they had no regrets.

Ah Siew could feel a familiar roll beneath her feet. So much was coming back to her. Even in a bad swell, she remembered, she had become adept at remaining on her feet and had not vomited up precious rice and noodles. Now again there was the rushing of the sea as it swished by beneath her. She looked down over the rail, straining to see the foamy white wake of the ship. Mei Lan put an arm about the old woman's shoulders and Ah Siew looked up and smiled, happiness clear on her face.

'It is just like I remember. We sailed over the horizon not knowing what we would find.' Ah Siew's memory once awakened could not be staunched, and she grew more and more excited. Mei Lan listened and stared into the distance, and felt the great ocean trying to heal her. She had lived too long in a halfway place; it was time now to take back her life, find a way to return from the past. Howard's fierce belief that he could remake her had begun the convoluted process of renewal. It was he who was willing her up through a labyrinth of dark passages towards, not the crack of light she had always feared would vanish as she reached it, but a whole open sky. And she realised now she loved him for this, for the faith in her that would not die, and would make her whole again.

As she thought these thoughts she became aware of a small sobbing noise and turning, saw a child of three or four standing alone nearby on the deck. Clearly, the child was lost and Mei Lan stepped forward to help her. Almost immediately, she spotted the mother hurrying forward, and led the girl by the hand towards her.

As Mei Lan turned away from her, Ah Siew gave a cry of excitement for, looking down from the rail of the junk, she saw a small boat coming towards her. It sailed forward with purpose and through her dim eyes she discovered, just as Mei Lan had said, that people were waving to her. It seemed beyond belief but, as the boat approached, she saw that Yong Gui, Ah Tim and Ah Pat stood there and behind them she spotted Ah Thye and Ah Ooi. They were waving wildly now and calling out her name.

'Ah Siew! Ah Siew!'

'I'm here. I'm here,' Ah Siew answered, tears of joy spilling down her cheeks as the tug approached.

'Come and join us,' they called, reaching out towards her.

'I'm coming,' she shouted, stretching out as far as she could, further and further, so that they could grasp her hands and pull her to safety amongst them.

Mei Lan handed the child to its mother and turned back to Ah Siew. She saw there was a commotion at the rail, people crowding excitedly several deep before it. There was much shouting, and some of the white-uniformed crew were running about the deck, holding red lifebelts. Mei Lan looked about wildly but could not see Ah Siew. With a cry, she pushed into the throng before the rail, but oblivious to her frantic shouts no one would let her through. A short distance away a flight of steps led to a higher level of the deck where the rail was bare of passengers. It seemed she ran for ever, but at last Mei Lan reached the steps and could see over the side of the junk. Far below the water foamed in runnels of crushed quartz as the ship cut through the waves, its great propeller beneath the red bow churning up a marble sea.

Ah Siew could be seen, her small monkey head sometimes rising and then falling beneath the foaming water. Her arms flailed about like a windmill as the boat moved forward, each moment drawing her nearer the thrashing propeller.

'Ah Siew!' Mei Lan screamed.

'Ah Siew!' The words were pulled from her like a rope she threw down to the desperate woman, but nothing now could reach Ah Siew. Once again the old woman sank under the waves. The lifebelts, thrown down to her from the boat, floated uselessly on the water, too far away for the old woman to reach. Lifeguards stood peering over the rail with the rest of the passengers. Nobody jumped to save Ah Siew.

'Ah Siew.' There was never a time when Ah Siew had failed her, had not been mother and father, confessor and friend. Mei Lan did not hesitate, but jumped as the old woman surfaced again far below. Only she could reclaim Ah Siew from the depths of the sea and give her the breath of life again.

The salty wind blew against her face, her hair streamed out about her. Mei Lan spread her arms as if they were wings and knew with a surge of joy what it felt for a bird to fly. Both death and life flew in the wind beside her, and she knew in that instant that love itself was but a series of deaths and rebirths. She had run from life as she had run from death, ignoring the transformative power of each. Now, as she flew towards Ah Siew she knew at last that death had released her; life claimed her again with all its palpitating power. Pain was gone and she embraced emotion freely, living and dying with each breath she took, letting go of one to enter the other, a continuous cycle, as ancient as time. She remembered the phoenix with its great wings, and knew it too flew beside her. The joy was too much and she wanted him to know, and screamed out his name. The wind ripped it from her like a ragged streamer and blew it away behind her.

'Howard!'

The water hit her like a board, harder than concrete, foaming and frothing. Nearby, Ah Siew was tossed about in the lather churned up by the noisy propeller. Mei Lan struggled forward to close her arms about the limp woman, feeling again the tiny birdlike body, seeing once more the blue rheumy eyes that perhaps already could watch her no more. She reached out for the red lifebelt bobbing on the water, to pull it over Ah Siew's head, but before she could grasp it a great hand seemed to take hold of them both, pulling them forcibly down into the bottomless depths of the ocean.

In the eagle's nest pavilion beneath a green fluted roof Howard became aware of a disturbance below and peered over the head of a small gilded lion on to the lower deck. People milled about the rail where he had left Mei Lan; he heard a confusion of screaming and shouting. Although he was unsure of what was happening, a sick dread already filled him. The vessel had slowed now and almost stopped. As he watched, two crewmen jumped into the sea where red lifebelts bobbed about on the swell. As the ship slowed, the water no longer bubbled in feverish ferment but quietened like an animal that had suddenly lost its roar. Quiescent now, it offered up meekly in a bloody halo the smashed bodies it had so voraciously claimed. Howard looked down in horror.

'Mei Lan!' he screamed, starting down the steep companionway.

When at last they pulled Mei Lan aboard the junk, he clasped her wet body to him, letting no one touch her. He was sure there was still a pulse. He pressed down on her ribs as he had been taught so long ago in first aid lessons at Air Raid Precaution, willing life into her, willing his breath to awaken her. Suddenly, he felt the quiver of energy returning. She gave a sob and the briny ocean spewed up from inside her, letting her free.

Mei Lan had escaped the blades of the vicious propeller, but Ah Siew's mangled body was quickly covered with a sheet of canvas. Howard cradled Mei Lan in his arms as she sobbed. All that could be seen of Ah Siew was an arm flung out clear of the canvas; her wrist, encircled by the jade bangle, lay on the smooth wooden deck. People stood around in a silent circle. Howard's shirt was soaked from Mei Lan's dripping body. Her hair hung over his arm, running with water like the weeds he remembered in the canal so long ago when they had stalked crayfish.

FROM THE MORNING IT had been overcast and the weather was on the rise, a hood of dark cloud advancing across the sky. It was hoped by everyone that it would not rain at the rally. Walking along the side of Kallang airfield Howard saw that already an enormous crowd had gathered, although it was not yet three o'clock. There was a holiday atmosphere, a few women and even some children could be seen, as if the occasion was a family outing; people carried umbrellas and looked anxiously at the sky. Ice-cream vendors pedalled about on bicycles calling out their wares, lifting the lid of iceboxes to produce mounded strawberry cones. Hawkers of noodles, tea and glutinous rice cakes were everywhere. A large audience surrounded a man with a troupe of performing monkeys in blue jackets with gold epaulettes. A van selling soft drinks and shaved ice frappé did a brisk business, as did a seller of home-made lemonade with a pushcart of earthenware jars. Mei Lan had insisted she would meet him at the rally, but surveying the growing crowd Howard was uncertain that this was the right decision, but he had no way now of getting in touch with her.

As he stepped on to the field the excitement of the crowd surrounded him. Lightning flashed suddenly across the sky, followed by a distant roll of thunder. He looked up at the darkening clouds and then towards the stage, where sound engineers were busy setting up microphones, and was surprised to see that a flimsy *wayang* platform had been erected for the meeting. He had expected a more substantial construction since Marshall was so intent on impressing the visiting British MPs who had been invited to witness the rally. None of the arrangements were Howard's responsibility but he thought it a pity not to have a structure with more panache, or at least the pomp of bunting.

Howard made his way to the lemonade cart and bought a heavily sugared drink. Near the cart, a group of young men were unfurling a massive banner, having carried the long supporting poles to the field on their shoulders. He stood beside them, sipping his drink, watching with interest as the banner was unrolled to reveal a crude drawing of a barbed wire fence and a hand uprooting a withered tree. *Kami Mahu Merdeka. We Want Merdeka* was written across it in both English and Malay. Nearby, another huge banner had been unfurled depicting men of the three Singapore races, Indian, Chinese and Malay, in a clenched-fist salute beneath the logo of the People's Action Party. Written upon it was that one word: *Merdeka. Merdeka* read another banner being launched into the air on a phalanx of bright balloons. *Merdeka. Merdeka.* Everywhere Howard looked the word was scrawled again and again. Marshall would be pleased, he thought.

The rally was the culmination of what Marshall called *Merdeka* Week. Since his first day in office the Chief Minister had hammered away at the things he considered important; a new constitution to give the colony immediate independence and the long-desired merger with the Federation of Malaya without which, economically and politically, Singapore could not survive. Soon after the rally, Marshall planned to take an all-party delegation to London to pressure the British Government to consider the issue of Singapore's independence.

'It must be an all-party delegation because this is no longer the game of politics so much as the business of birthing a nation,' Marshall insisted.

As a preliminary to this visit, an ebullient Chief Minister had invited a parliamentary delegation of six British Members of Parliament to witness first hand the Singapore people's wish for freedom. The *Merdeka* rally had been arranged to showcase the nation's feelings. Howard made his way through the thickening crowd towards the airport building and the stage beyond it, from where the rally would be addressed. Flags of the Federation of Malaya and various political parties hung limply from rickety poles, with no breeze to give them life. Police were in evidence everywhere, their black berets and khaki uniforms dotted amongst the crowd. The days leading up to this meeting had been fuelled by building emotion. During a hectic week, a petition of 167,259 signatures had been obtained demanding Independence. The petition was leather bound, for presentation to the British parliament, and Marshall hoped to return from England with the writ of freedom in his hand.

A cordon of police held back the excited crowd as Howard climbed the steps on to the stage. There appeared to be trouble with the sound system. 'It will soon be fixed,' the engineer promised as Howard strode forward to investigate. One of the organising team hurried to tell him it was estimated that a crowd of twenty thousand already covered the great expanse of the airfield.

The rows of chairs on the stage were filling up as VIPs began to arrive. As their cars drew up one after another, the waiting spectators surged forward against the barricade to see who was alighting from the vehicles. Howard searched anxiously amongst the arrivals for Mei Lan. Raj arrived in his new car and looked apprehensively at the rowdy spectators as he made his way up the few rickety steps to the stage. Seeing Howard, he gave a wave and walked towards him. He wore his usual white cotton suit and panama hat.

'I was not expecting so many people. This is a typical Marshall idea, always wanting drama and attention.' Raj frowned disapprovingly. Then Mei Lan's car drew up and Howard hurried forward to help her out. She looked anxiously at the platform rearing above her. They found chairs together at one side of the stage beside Raj.

'Lots of troublemakers here today; communists and gangsters and the unions are out in full force,' Raj observed, fiddling with the strap of his new gold watch, which had been a wedding present from Yoshiko. After Krishna's assassination he had not waited the customary length of time required following a family death, before marrying Yoshiko. He had scaled down the wedding to a simple civil ceremony and a small reception afterwards at a hotel, but Leila had not been pleased and for a while refused to speak to Yoshiko. Raj, with his bride, had moved into the newly built Cluny Road house but Leila stayed on at Waterloo Street, drowning both her grief at Krishna's death, and her grief at her brother's marriage, in a further expansion of Manikam's.

Another deep crack of thunder rumbled through the sky. The crowd, dense and restless, was beginning to feed off its own energy. Already it was nearly four o'clock and so far the rain had held off. Mei Lan wished she had not insisted on coming; women were few and far between. All she saw was a sea of restless men. The constant chant of slogans blew on the wind across the field. Howard had tried to discourage her, but since Ah Siew's death she found herself seeking ways to demonstrate commitment to him.

'Too much tension now rising. More delays are no good,' Raj commented, looking again at his watch.

'Mr Marshall is late because the police have tightened security. He did not get clearance to set off for the rally, but just now he is arriving at the edge of the field,' Howard was told when he enquired about the delay.

David Marshall had chosen an open-roofed car to arrive in, and as police cleared a way for it through the crush of people he stood up triumphantly to acknowledge the constant shouts of *Merdeka,* jubilant at the turnout.

'Where are the British MPs? Everything is running so late,' Raj grumbled again, watching Marshall's slow progress. He had bought machinery for his new factory extension from a British businessman who was one of the MPs' delegation, and was pleased at the unexpected opportunity to personally consolidate the connection.

The stage was full of local dignitaries. Behind a cordon of police the crowd below swarmed about the structure, threatening at moments to break through. Perched above the multitude, the flimsy platform trembled with every vibration and Mei Lan had the feeling she was floating on a raft in the midst of a wild sea. The field was lost beneath the throng for as far as she could see. A few drops of rain spat down upon them and the black hoods of umbrellas appeared, and then shut again as the rain did not materialise. Carried aloft on a bank of red balloons a streamer with the one word, *Merdeka,* floated against the thunderous sky, tethered to earth by a slender thread. White banners stuck up everywhere, draped like bunting over the crowd, all proclaiming *Merdeka. Death to colonialism. End colonialism NOW.*

The lawyer, Lee Kuan Yew, and the union leader, Lim Chin Siong, stood in the back of a loudspeaker truck with the banner of the People's Action Party, shouting PAP rhetoric to the crowd through a megaphone. Some distance away another huge banner picturing Picasso's Peace Dove, now an emblem of the communist party, was hoisted above the crowd. Near the stage a large group of Chinese Middle School children were assembling to sing their communist songs and dance the *yenko.* As they started off, tripping and turning to the wheeze of accordions and harmonicas, people rushed to watch. The dancers' red scarves waved against a sky that frowned ever more blackly upon them. The lively music, mixed with the PAP's loud haranguing, was buffeted about the field. In the midst of this cacophony sound technicians conferred anxiously on the stage, tapping the silent, faulty microphones for a reaction and twiddling the knobs on equipment, trying to coax the machines into life. At last an echo of sound was heard, and the engineers fell back in relief.

Finally the Chief Minister's car arrived and he alighted, clasping his hands yet again in victory, his face ablaze with triumph. Police escorted him as he climbed briskly up the steps and on to the stage, striding towards the microphone to greet the waiting crowd. Head thrown back, his famous eyebrows, so thick they seemed almost to precede him, arched up as his voice boomed out.

'*Merdeka.*' The word left his lips in a trumpet of sound, projected to the far corners of the field. He raised his arm to punch the air. *Merdeka*, the crowd replied, the roar bursting from them like the release of a pent-up river.

The Chief Minister began his speech: his lips moved but no sound carried to the waiting crowd. The microphone refused to function again, and technicians darted forward. Below the stage the crowd, effervescing with excitement, saw the hitch as an open door. No longer willing to be contained, they charged suddenly forward, overwhelming the police and surging on to the flimsy platform. They flooded up the steps to surround the Chief Minister, raising jubilant fists, shouting *Merdeka* in his face.

The Chief Minister's smile died as the stage trembled and swayed beneath the deluge. He tottered unsteadily and reached out for support. With a shudder and a loud creak of breaking wood, the dais collapsed, its supports buckling beneath the impossible weight, tipping everyone forward. Those watching from afar saw the stage disappear, like a great ship sinking from view beneath the ocean. The Chief Minister too vanished from sight, as the stage folded upon itself. VIPs, pressmen and volunteer ushers slid helplessly across the platform and came to rest one upon another in an undignified muddle. Howard was thrown to the ground with Mei Lan, Raj tumbling beside them.

'I'm all right,' Mei Lan told Howard as he scrambled up and turned to pull her to her feet. No one seemed to be hurt, although the stage was dangerously lopsided. The Chief Minister was also getting to his feet, reaching again for a microphone to calm the crowd. The machine still refused to work, and all that could be seen by spectators was Marshall once more soundlessly mouthing his words. Instead, in the distance, from the People's Action Party loud-speaker, came the voice of the lawyer Lee, calling for order. His voice rang out authoritatively and the crowd drew back, obedient. Then, once more, shouts of *Merdeka* were heard.

Eventually, it was decided to move everyone from the collapsed rostrum to the main airport terminal. Escorted by police, Marshall led the way, walking the short distance to the new location with all the occupants of the stage trailing behind him. Thousands followed in their wake, the excited crowd shifting its focus from the wrecked stage to the airport building. The Chief Minister and his party entered and proceeded upstairs to the first floor, and then out on to a large balcony where Marshall stood high above the crowd, his arms raised in triumph again. Holding Mei Lan by the hand, Howard accompanied the rest of the evacuees from the beleaguered stage. He wished there was a way to send Mei Lan home, but they were swept along by events and the massive crowd.

The terminal building had the streamlined appearance of a ship, with long balconies running around each floor. Above the main entrance, a semicircular gallery protruded from the building like the prow of a boat. Howard and Mei Lan followed Raj to the rail, and together they looked down on the multitude of white shirts, white banners and dark heads stretching endlessly out below them. Mei Lan stepped back in fear. It seemed she stood again upon the deck of that gaudy junk and the sea below her, although now of a vastly different kind, appeared just as voracious as the one that had taken Ah Siew. It seethed restlessly, and in her mind she saw again the churning marble in the wake of the ship and Ah Siew tossed about within it. The roar of the crowd rose up, restive and impatient. Beside her Howard stared at the mob.

'Where did such a sudden swell of political consciousness come from? How did they tuck so much passion away for so long?' he wondered, pulling Mei Lan back to a less exposed vantage point.

At last the British parliamentary delegation arrived, and was escorted up through the terminal building to where Marshall waited for them on the open balcony. At this elevation the frightening density of the assemblage below was clear. The British visitors peered down, assessing the crowd with visible apprehension. Earlier Marshall had assured the politicians there was no need to fear but now, like everyone else, he too was filled with uncertainty.

Over a now impeccable sound system, the Chief Minister introduced the British parliamentarians to the waiting crowd. One by one, they stepped forward to the edge of the balcony to be acknowledged by the cheering mob. After exactly fifteen minutes, anxious that there be no incidents, the Chief Minister suggested discreetly to the visitors that they now leave, and this they did with alacrity. Escorted back to their cars, they departed as they had come and Marshall saw them go with visible relief.

The Chief Minister then stepped up to the microphone to give at last the great speech he had prepared for the rally, about a car with two steering wheels. Mr Boss was as ever driving the colony with a master switch, Marshall said, while the junior driver, the local people of Singapore, sat obediently at his side.

'What kind of a crazy future can this crazy contraption lead to? We want control of our own government,' Marshall shouted into a microphone as he leaned against the balcony railing, his words now undulating over the field in just the manner he had anticipated. The crowd responded with further cries of *Merdeka*, drunk now upon the word. A streak of lightning lit the sky and in a moment thunder crashed, sharp as the crack of a gun.

Howard and Mei Lan stood to one side of the congested balcony. They had only a partial view of Marshall, whose voice rose powerfully with operatic control, accompanied by sweeping gestures and blazing eyes. This prima donna performance no longer impressed Howard in quite the way it had previously done. In office, Marshall appeared to him to have become histrionic and displayed political naivety, even if his courtroom tactics and rabid eye for opportunity sometimes carried the day. Howard could not put his finger on what was wrong, but he was disillusioned. For all Marshall's love of the limelight he was not adept at treading the corridors of power. Disdaining compromise, wearing his heart on his sleeve, he was impetuous, impatient and quick tempered. Thunder cracked loudly again, drowning Marshall's words for a moment before the rain began to drizzle.

'People are already saying that the collapse of stage and failure of the microphones is the dirty work of communists in the People's Action Party, intent on disrupting the rally.' Raj leaned forward behind Howard to murmur into his ear.

'It is going to rain heavily – they should end the meeting,' Howard said, looking down on the overheated crowd. Here and there he could see that scuffles had already broken out with police.

There was only one entrance on to the balcony and they moved forward, ready to follow Marshall from the building. Before the Chief Minister could leave, a group of People's Action Party members spilt through it, amongst them Lee and Lim Chin Siong. Lee pushed his way straight to Marshall and demanded to address the crowd. Marshall frowned, his shaggy eyebrows drawing together in a thick and dis-approving line.

'The meeting is over. Everyone is now going home. You have already said your piece earlier over the loudspeakers on your truck,' Marshall told Lee curtly. Even as he spoke police were clearing a way. They ushered the Chief Minister through the door, down the stairs and out of the building, where he was driven away in his car. At Marshall's exit a further large group of People's Action Party members crowded out on to the balcony, preventing Mei Lan, Howard and Raj from following Marshall. From the field below loud roars were continuously heard. In spite of the rain now coming down, the crowd appeared in no mood to go home.

Lee Kuan Yew had now taken the microphone and was angrily chas-tising the crowd, anxious to refute the rumours circulating about the broken stage. 'There are devils here today who have tried to spoil this rally. They are the ones who put the microphone out of order and collapsed the stage,' Lee shouted, furious at the accusations that were being flung at his party. Cheers and shouts erupted from the crowd as he spoke.

After a few minutes Lim Chin Siong, waiting impatiently beside the lawyer, began to argue with Lee who at last, reluctantly, gave him the microphone. The pulse of the crowd seemed to quicken as Lim stepped forward. Wild cheers were heard as the union leader's voice flowed out across the field. Lim was a small man, but his personality grew large with oratory and his rhetoric soon had the crowd dangerously effer-vescent. As he finished speaking, he held up his hand in a gesture of forbearance and his tone dropped to that of a stern schoolteacher.

'It is time to go home. When you leave this place, keep calm. Don't beat up the police,' Lim ordered, stepping back from the balcony rail. The crowd, now aroused, were unwilling to disband as advised; banners were tossed into the air and *Merdeka* was yelled with increasing abandon. The wildness was growing, infectious.

'I have to stop this meeting turning into a bloody riot,' Lee said, suddenly sounding anxious.

'They always like singing patriotic songs; if they sing they'll calm down,' someone suggested.

Soon, a honey-throated volunteer was found who began to sing, 'We love Malaya', and then 'Unity is Strength' over a loudspeaker. The shouting lessened and with a low growl the crowd joined in, the sound gathering in momentum for some moments before a loud retort of thunder brought the rain pouring down. Abruptly, the singing stopped and on the open balcony everyone rushed for the stairs. Howard took hold of Mei Lan's hand and pulled her along beside him. On the field, umbrellas went up in the crowd, and those without them sheltered beneath bedraggled banners or stoically stood their ground drenched, but still loudly demanding more speeches from their leaders.

It took some time for the many occupants of the balcony to negotiate their way to the ground floor. Outside, angry shouts were heard as the crowd, in spite of the downpour, still called out raucously. Crammed together in the stairwell, the occupants of the balcony were forced to move slowly, shuffling one behind the other, sweating in the close atmosphere. Rain drummed on the many windows about them as shouts from outside reverberated with a new level of anger. Howard turned to look through a window, and saw with alarm that police cordons had been broken. Instinctively he drew Mei Lan closer. The mob was now pressing in on the terminal building. Groups of police were trying to control the riot without success, and under a vicious barrage of missiles were forced helplessly back. The locked and metal-barred doors of the terminal were rattled and kicked from outside. The first of the balcony's occupants had reached the ground floor. Confronted with the mob waiting outside, faces pressed up against the glass, they were hesitant to proceed any further.

Unexpectedly, a brick was hurled at a ground floor window. It crashed through: splintering glass flew everywhere. There were startled shouts as another brick followed the first, and then another. On the stairs everyone turned and began to push their way back to the second floor against the flow of people descending from above. The mob outside watched their terror with accompanying jeers. Howard, with Mei Lan and Raj, was pushed against the metal banisters by the weight of people trying to return upstairs.

'Don't look out of the windows. If they see you looking there'll be more trouble,' someone shouted.

'Clear the building!' An order was yelled as a side door was opened and ringed with police.

To the baying of demonstrators and in danger of further flying missiles, the captives began to make their way down the stairs, arms over their heads for protection. One by one they reached the ground floor and disappeared along a corridor towards where police were successfully holding off the rioters. At the main entrance the mob were now making efforts to force the bolts with a crowbar. To protect Mei Lan, Howard had hung back but found they were amongst the last people descending the stairs.

The chaos outside was frighteningly clear, the mob out of control and locked viciously with police. A truck with crates of aerated water had been stopped, and the bottles commandeered as missiles. A St John's ambulance was stoned while the injured were being treated inside. Glass was everywhere. The lemonade man had been attacked and his earthenware jars lay smashed, pools of yellow liquid spilling over the ground. Police tried uselessly to shield themselves from the constant pitching of bottles with their waterproof capes. The rain had begun again and pelted down on the muddy pitch. People slipped and fell. The man with the monkeys in blue jackets ran for his life, the creatures screaming and chattering, pulling on their chains.

As Howard and Mei Lan reached the ground floor Raj, breathing heavily behind them, suddenly stumbled and clung to the stair rail. At that moment another brick was hurled in through the smashed windows. Hitting Raj on the temple, it knocked him sideways. Howard turned in alarm to see blood gushing from Raj's head. Outside, the police had withdrawn again, giving up all attempts to control the mob. As Howard pulled a handkerchief from his pocket and gave it to Raj to staunch his wound, the locked doors below were suddenly forced and the rioters swarmed into the building.

Pulling the wounded Raj to his feet, Howard pushed him back up the stairs with Mei Lan. At the top they sprinted along the upstairs corridor, Raj huffing and puffing behind. At the end was a fire exit and beyond it a stair that led to a flat roof below the control tower. The sound of shouts and running feet could already be heard behind them.

'Here,' Howard ordered, pulling first Mei Lan and then Raj with him through the door, bolting it shut behind him. On the open terrace, the rain spat down upon them. Unused to such exertion, Raj panted heavily, sinking down against a water tank. The handkerchief he held to his head was wet with blood, the collar of his white suit stained a frightening crimson. They heard shouts and then a pounding on the door for some moments before the rioters lost interest and ran on.

'Keep down low,' Howard instructed as he crawled to the edge of the parapet to view the field below. The mayhem continued as the rain eased again.

'What do we do now?' Mei Lan asked nervously.

'We wait. Eventually it will be over, even if it takes until morning,' Howard surmised, trying unsuccessfully to find shelter from the drizzle for Mei Lan. His wet clothes stuck to him uncomfortably.

'How did you get through the war, trapped in the jungle with those vicious communists?' Raj mumbled in a low, aggrieved voice, listening to the wild shouts still coming up from below.

'They tried to execute me once. When you come back from death, life looks different. Things change you,' said Howard, and Raj nodded agreement.

'Krishna's death changed me. He saved my life in a different way and I repaid him poorly.' Raj spoke quietly without his usual bombast, pressing the bloody handkerchief to his head, his plump face solemn. He remembered the dying Krishna staring up at him as he lay on Raj's doorstep, and knew he must live for ever with the knowledge that he had cruelly dismissed the one man he could call a brother. In that moment he had seen the full gamut of his own arrogance, and was chastened and ashamed. He found it was like this all the time now: images from the past kept returning to him to be viewed from discomforting angles. He remembered again the scent of the garland maker's jasmine where Krishna used to sit with his writing board and it seemed to encompass an innocent time, before learning gave him opportunity and changed the direction of his life. So many doors had opened to him and always, as he passed through one, another appeared. Yet he wondered if his determination to prosper had robbed him of sensitivities others understood more easily.

'Death is death, but sometimes it allows those of us that are left behind to make a new beginning,' Raj murmured almost to himself, continuing to press the bloody handkerchief to his temple.

Howard put an arm about Mei Lan and drew her close, feeling the warmth of their wet bodies pressed together. Mei Lan was silent, staring at the suffering Raj, whose strange mumbled words resonated with her. She remembered the gaudy Chinese junk that had taken Ah Siew home in style, and how she had flown like a bird above the water. Time and time again in her life, she saw that death had released her for existence to claim her.

Howard's arm grew tighter about her. 'Marry me,' he whispered in her ear, too low for Raj to hear.

'We're not the people we were,' she replied, her head against his shoulder.

'Burned forests regenerate,' he told her quietly. In answer she nodded and he gripped her tighter.

At last it grew quieter on the field below; the shouting lessened. Crawling to the edge of the roof once more Howard saw that additional ambulances were arriving, and that police reinforcements had already chased the crowd away from the terminal building, back on to the muddy airport field. The rain had stopped. Howard stood up and for a moment felt he balanced on a mountaintop, the panorama of the field stretching away beneath him in a vast plain. After a day of rain the grey sky was suddenly cracking open in runnels of molten light. A cool breeze brushed his face, and was gone. At last the field was reluctantly clearing and the mob near the airport building, deterred by the increase of riot police, had begun to disperse.

In exactly a month Howard would accompany Marshall's All-Party delegation to London to make a plea to the British parliament for independence. After the chaotic fiasco of the day, unfortunately witnessed by the British MPs, it seemed unlikely such a wish would now be granted. As he looked out over the field of dispersing men he thought of Marshall's genial, impetuous face, his reluctance to take stern measures of control, his passionate belief in the rights of the individual and the underdog, and knew his fire was not the caustic flame needed to burn a way to freedom. The twenty thousand who had earlier filled the field had not come there for David Marshall; they were there to support the union leader Lim Chin Siong and Lee, the union's astute and calculating lawyer, men whose life centred ruthlessly only on politics. Marshall had stood at the failing microphone, his mouth had moved but no words were heard across the field, then the stage had collapsed beneath him. As he sank from sight it was Lee Kuan Yew who had taken the megaphone, called firmly for order and been obeyed. The image was there in Howard's mind and would not go away. He wondered if perhaps the mayhem at this riot, and that of so many others behind it, was not the mindless chaos it appeared but the early stages of a long and painful labour that would give birth to a world no one could as yet foresee.

At last the sun was thrusting out fingers of brilliance through the grey clouds. Howard raised his eyes and saw, high above, a bank of red balloons drifting against the endless arc of the sky. The huge banner they carried still hung intact beneath, still carrying that one solitary word for all to see: *Merdeka*. The balloons had broken free of the thread that held them tethered to the ground, and now floated independently, soaring higher and higher on currents of air. Howard saw that below him police were entering the building and soon voices were heard on the second floor.

'Up here,' Howard shouted, unbolting the door and helping the injured Raj to his feet as police burst on to the roof.

Keeping an arm about Mei Lan, he guided her back into the building and down the stairs. As they came out of the terminal, Raj was directed to an ambulance where a nurse waited with first aid. The field was emptying fast. Howard stopped, his arm still about Mei Lan, and looked up again at the sky. The huge bunch of balloons was now at a great height, the word *Merdeka* on its white banner still clearly discernible as it drifted away into a different sky.

ACKNOWLEDGEMENTS

I WOULD PARTICULARLY LIKE to thank President S. R. Nathan of Singapore for planting the seeds of this book in my mind, and for his continuous support and interest during its writing and his reading of the manuscript.

The research for this book was long and varied and I wish to acknowledge my appreciation of the many people who helped me along the way, sharing their memories, lending or directing me to a book, searching out papers and documents for me. I am particularly grateful to Chew Gek Khim for the generous loan of books from the library of her grandfather, Tan Chin Tuan. I am also much indebted to the staff and research assistants of the National Library and the Oral History Department of the National Archives, especially Lily Tan, for their unstinting assistance in my research.

I would also like to thank Professor Edwin Thumboo for reading the manuscript and making some important suggestions.

My thanks go also to Gretchen Liu. Her unfailing encouragement throughout the writing of the book, her patient and repeated reading of a long and complicated manuscript, and her critical comments, have all been invaluable.

I would like to express my gratitude to James Gurbutt who first championed this book at Harvill Secker, and to David Parrish at Random House who has stood by it. My thanks also go to Georgina Capel at Capel and Land for never giving up. And lastly, my deep appreciation to Rebecca Carter at Harvill Secker.

AUTHOR'S NOTE

I WISH TO CLARIFY that although *A Different Sky* is a work of fiction, the backdrop of events that the characters live through is based upon hard historical fact. The Singapore of the time covered by this novel was, to a good degree, lawless, dangerous and poverty stricken. The first communist-inspired riot at Kreta Ayer in 1927 with which the book begins is a documented event, as are the happenings of the *Merdeka* Rally with which the book ends. In between, young men did run off into the jungle to become guerrilla fighters, people did risk their lives to oppose the brutal Japanese occupation, schoolchildren did riot with striking workers, and the activities of the Anti-British League and the Malayan Communist Party did result in numerous casual assassinations. Although I have attempted to bring to life an important swathe of Singapore history, the interpretation of events and the patterns of importance they form in the novel are my own understanding of that time, and it is an outsider's overview.

I would also like to say that, in writing historical fiction, I in no way presume to share the ground of academics and historians. Academic record and scholarly investigation construct the shape of the past as accurately as it can be done. Historical fiction attempts to create a sense of experience of that past, to bring it alive in the present and show its enduring relevance.

Most of the characters in *A Different Sky* are fictional, composite creations and bear no relation to living people. However, the character of Mamoru Shinozaki is based upon the real man of that name. The transcript of his interview, *My Wartime Experience*, for the Institute of Southeast Asian Studies Oral History Programme, was of great help to me. The characters of David Marshall, Lim Chin Siong and Lee Kuan Yew are also based upon the real people of this name. I wish to state that I have been careful to ensure that, like those of Mamoru Shinozaki, their actions and dialogue in *A Different Sky* are taken only from recorded or documented sources.

Besides listening to many hours of recorded interviews in the Oral History Department of the National Archives, I read an extensive range of books. Three particular books were a constant reference for me: *Singapore: Struggle for Success* by John Drysdale (1996, Times Books International: Singapore), *The Tiger and the Trojan Horse* by Dennis Bloodworth (1986, Times International Books: Singapore) and *A History of Singapore 1819–1988* by C.M. Turnbull (1989, Oxford University Press: Singapore).